LIFE AFTER Z-DAY

written by

Jody Slyman

"Life After Z-Day," by Jody Slyman. ISBN 978-1-62137-324-7 (Softcover).

Library of Congress Control Number: 2013911268

Published 2013 by Virtualbookworm.com Publishing Inc., P.O. Box 9949, College Station, TX 77842, US. ©2013, Jody Slyman. All rights reserved. No part of this publication may be reproduced, stored in a retrieval system, or transmitted in any form or by any means, electronic, mechanical, recording or otherwise, without the prior written permission of Jody Slyman.

Manufactured in the United States of America.

DEDICATION

This book is dedicated to the wonderful people who allowed me to make them a part of this story:

To my dad, you are the greatest man I've ever known and my only hero in this world. You've always been there with love and support. One day I hope to be as good a man as you are. I love you.

To my brother, I could not have asked for a better brother in life. You've always been there when I needed someone and I can never thank you enough. I am blessed and honored to call you my brother. I love you bro.

To Shana, words cannot express the happiness I feel with you in my life. After so many years, to be able to re-unite is truly wonderful. I cherish our friendship. I love you and I wish all the best for you, Cory, Zach and Tyler.

To Lisa, I am so honored and blessed to have you in my life. Even though we are separated by miles now, our friendship remains. I cherish whatever time we get to talk and see each other. You are a wonderful woman and a great friend. I love you and wish you and Rochelle all the best in life.

To Lindsey, I'm truly blessed to have met you. You're such a wonderful and close friend. I hope you and Michael have a long and happy life together and I wish you, Michael and Daniel all the best in life. Love you.

To Janet, I still care about you and the kids and I wish you all the best in life and hope things work out for you.

To Ryan and Codi, I'm so happy to have met both of you and honored to call you my friends. I wish both of you the best in life.

To Ashley, I'm honored to call you a friend and so happy you are a part of my life. I wish you all the best.

To Marissa, you've been one of the best friends I've ever had. Love you.

To Grace, your friendship has been a blessing in my life and I wish you all the best.

To Ken, you've been a good friend and I wish you all the best in life.

INTRODUCTION

May 25th, 2012
Miami, Oklahoma

It's a warm Friday night in the small Oklahoma town as Mike, a nice looking 63 year old Caucasian man who looks younger than he is and who stands around 5'9" tall and weighs a decently in shape 170 pounds with straight, short light brown hair with some gray showing, a mustache of the same colors and hazel eyes, is sitting in his recliner in the front room of his nice brick, three bedroom house with attached garage. Mike is wearing a maroon and blue collared shirt, blue jeans and gray Velcro tennis shoes. The air conditioner in the wall of the family room is running to keep the house nice and cool. He is watching the late night news.

Mike's oldest son, Michael, a nice looking 40 year old Caucasian man who stands 6' tall and weighs a somewhat out of shape 215 pounds with short, wavy black hair with some gray showing and hazel eyes, is laying on the couch. Michael is wearing a t-shirt with an ACU digital camouflage pattern and black sweatpants. A family friend from Texas, Marissa, a pretty 44 year old Caucasian woman who stands 5'6" tall and weighs a nice 155 pounds with short, straight red hair that hangs to the middle of her neck and brown eyes, is sitting in the other recliner in the room. Marissa is wearing a black t-shirt, black windbreaker pants and her prescription glasses.

Laying on the floor by Mike's feet is the family dog, Shadow. Shadow is a 7 year old blue heeler with the distinctive black hair patch over his right eye and he has a bobbed tail. Shadow is about 1'6" tall and 2'6" long and weighs a stout 75 pounds from being well fed and a little spoiled. The main news story starts. It has been the top story for the last month and a half.

The TV news anchor speaks, "Now we turn to our top story for this evening. It seems that for the fifth straight day the epidemic that struck across this country a mere 6 weeks ago has claimed more lives. The CDC and local doctors everywhere are still at a loss as to what kind of virus they are dealing with. As it struck so quickly and so widespread from our major cities like New York and Los Angeles to small rural towns of less than one thousand people all over the country, many people are starting to compare this outbreak to the famous Black Plague of Europe centuries ago."

Marissa speaks, "This has been crazy. When Lisa, her daughter, Rochelle, and I drove in this afternoon it wasn't the same or didn't have the same feel. It was just like, well, not as many people out and about. Cars abandoned on the road and stuff. It was just weird."

Mike nods his head, "It was the same way when I drove in from Ponca City. The towns I went through were just different. You could see some people just wandering around and cars abandoned on the roads and in parking lots. Not what you'd expect for a Friday."

The TV news anchor continues with the story, "The exact number is unknown as far as how many have been infected with the unknown virus and how many have died from it so far. The numbers are being kept very quiet from the CDC. Some people are estimating the number of infected to be in the thousands to some saying, even in the hundreds of thousands." The news anchor pauses, "Some of the more extremists are saying that this could be the starting of the apocalypse that will end the world on December 21st of this year. We are going to take a break now, but we will continue the story when we return."

Michael shakes his head, "This is just too wild. This weekend's barbeque and camp over is going to be just what we all need to get time away from everything going on. Jody had a great idea in getting everyone together this weekend."

At that time, the front door unlocks and opens. Mike's youngest son, Jody, an attractive 38 year old Caucasian man who stands 5'7" tall and weighs a fit 145 pounds with light brown hair buzzed to 3/8" and blue green eyes walks in the door. Jody is wearing a white t-shirt, blue jeans with a brown belt, brown hiking shoes and his black rimmed prescription glasses. Right behind him is his friend from Texas, Lisa, an unbelievably beautiful 40 year old Caucasian woman who stands 5'2" tall and weighs an incredibly attractive 115 pounds with straight, auburn colored hair with black highlights that is hanging down to her lower shoulder blades and stunning blue eyes. Lisa is wearing blue jeans, blue lace trimmed short sleeve top, a lightweight white zip-up jacket and tennis shoes. Last through the door is Lisa's daughter, Rochelle, an attractive 21 year old woman with darker complexion who stands 5'5" tall and weighs a good looking 155 pounds with straight, dark brown hair that hangs to her lower shoulder blades and brown eyes. Rochelle is wearing a red short-sleeve top, blue jeans and tennis shoes. Once everyone walks in, Jody turns, shuts the door and locks it.

Mike looks over from his chair, "So, how'd you all do tonight?"

Jody nods slightly, "I lost about forty dollars, but Lisa and Rochelle both won."

Marissa smiles, "Sweet!"

Lisa chuckles some, "It was so much fun."

Rochelle smiles, "I had a blast."

Jody smiles, "It was fun."

Mike questions, "So, did you come back through town?"

Jody nods, "Yeah, it was weird for a Friday night. Very few people out, cars were just parked randomly around town and you could hear sirens running in the distance. Ever since this outbreak, things have been different."

Michael shakes his head, "That's why this weekend plan you made is going to be great. Get everyone's mind off what's been going on."

Marissa smiles, "I'm looking forward to it, especially going and shooting some tomorrow before the barbeque."

Mike nods, "Yeah, it's going to be relaxing for sure." He looks at Jody, "When is everyone suppose to start showing up?"

Jody replies, "Around 9am." He pauses, "When are you picking up Nancy?"

Mike replies, "Around eleven." He looks down at Shadow, "I guess we better go outside one more time before we lay down."

Shadow's head pops up along with his ears as the little dog stares at Mike in excitement. Everyone gets a good chuckle at Shadow's excitement. As Mike takes Shadow out in the front yard, everyone else starts getting ready for bed.

CHAPTER 1

Its nearly 9:00 am the following morning. It's a warm, sunny morning with a few clouds in the sky and a soft breeze blowing. Mike is in the back yard cleaning the grill. Mike has on a white t-shirt, blue jeans with brown belt and his Velcro tennis shoes. Marissa is sitting in one of the deck chairs petting Shadow. Marissa has on a black t-shirt, faded black jeans with a black belt and tennis shoes. Marissa also is wearing a black, belt slide holster and a black, belt slide double magazine holder. Marissa has a Glock 31 loaded with a 15 round magazine in the holster and two loaded 15 round magazines in the magazine holder.

Michael is sitting at his computer in his room. Michael has on his ACU t-shirt, black sweatpants, house shoes and a red and white OU baseball cap. Rochelle is sitting on the couch watching television. Rochelle is wearing a white t-shirt, blue jeans and tennis shoes. Lisa is sitting in one of the recliners watching television. Lisa has on a black long sleeve t-shirt, khaki tactical pants with a black belt, black tactical boots and a black baseball cap. Lisa is also wearing a black clip on holster on her left hip and a black clip on double magazine holder on her right hip. In the holster is a Sig Sauer P226 with a loaded 12 round magazine. In the double magazine holder are two more loaded 12 round

1

magazines. She has a Tac Force Baron Assisted Opening Rescue Knife clipped in her front, left pocket.

Jody is sitting in the other recliner watching television and glancing out the window waiting for people to start showing up. Jody has on a gray t-shirt, light colored blue jeans with a brown belt, brown hiking shoes and he has a SOG trident tanto pocket knife clipped in his right back pocket. Jody glances out the window and sees an older model Toyota Pickup Truck, built for off road, pull up behind Lisa's Jeep Liberty which is parked on the downhill side of the driveway. Jody's friend from work, Ken, gets out of the truck. Ken is a nice looking 49 year old Caucasian man that stands around 6'4" tall and weighs a healthy 265 pounds with gray and brown hair that is buzzed down even shorter than Jody's, plus a goatee of the same colors and blue, goggled eyes. Ken is wearing a blue t-shirt, blue jeans with a black belt, black tactical boots and a woodland camouflage baseball cap. Ken has on a black belt slide holster on his right hip, a black belt slide double magazine holder on his left hip and a pocket knife clipped in his right front pocket. In the holster is a very nice Springfield 1911 A1 pistol with a loaded 7 round magazine. In the double magazine holder are two more loaded 7 round magazines.

Jody walks out the front door to greet Ken, "Hey man, how's it going? I see you're ready to do some shooting."

Ken smiles, "Hell yes. I've got my shotgun in the truck too."

Jody shakes Ken's hand, "It's good to see you. Come on in and I'll introduce you to who's here so far."

Jody and Ken walk into the house.

A few minutes later, a brand new Kia Optima pulls up and parks on the uphill side of the driveway which is already full from Michael's mid 90's Monte Carlo, Jody's early 90's Ford Explorer and Mike's early 90's Ford F150 Flareside Truck and late 90's Ford Windstar Van.

Another one of Jody's friends, Grace, is driving the Optima. Grace is a very pretty 23 year old woman who's complexion shows her Spanish and Native American heritage, but is a little lighter than most others of her heritage. Grace stands 5'8" tall and weighs an attractive 150 pounds with curly brown hair that shows a tint of red in the sunlight and normally hangs down to her lower shoulder blades, but is put up right now and she has sunglasses on covering her beautiful light brown eyes. Grace is wearing a multicolored tank top, faded blue jeans and tennis shoes.

In the passenger's seat is Grace's son, Ayden. Ayden is a cute and active 4 year old boy who's Caucasian complexion doesn't really show his mom's heritage. Ayden is tall and skinny for his age, weighing about 40 pounds, with short, straight blonde hair and blue eyes. Ayden is wearing a gray t-shirt, blue jeans, tennis shoes and a black and white baseball cap. Sitting in a car seat in the back is Grace's daughter, Ariel. Ariel is an absolutely adorable 2 year old who's complexion also doesn't really show her mom's heritage. Ariel is about average height for her age and weighs around 30 pounds with curly brown hair that hangs to her shoulders and is a little lighter than her mom's hair and she has pretty blue eyes. Ariel has on a blue t-shirt, blue jean overalls, tennis shoes and a pink bow in her hair.

As Grace gets the kids out of the car, she sees Jody walking out the front door to meet her. Grace smiles big when she sees her friend.

Grace gives Jody a big hug, "Hey FIT B!"

Jody smiles as he hugs Grace, "Hey honey-beelicious."

Grace steps back, "These are my monsters, Ayden and Ariel."

Jody looks down at the kids and smiles, "Hi there." Both kids just smile and Jody looks back at Grace, "Too bad your husband couldn't make it."

Grace nods, "Yeah, they are still working in Texas."

Jody nods, "So, you ready for the weekend?"

Grace smiles, "Oh yeah! I've got everything in the car."

Jody smiles, "Cool! Well, come on inside and I'll introduce you to everyone that is here already."

Grace replies, "Sounds good."

Grace grabs a baby bag from the car and her and the kids follow Jody into the house.

About five minutes later a fairly newer model Chevy Malibu pulls up and parks in front of Grace's car. Driving the car is longtime family friend, Shana. Shana is a very beautiful 37 year old Caucasian woman who stands 5'4" tall and weighs a very attractive 130 pounds with short, straight dark blonde hair that hangs to the middle of her neck and captivating blue eyes. Shana is wearing a gray t-shirt, light colored blue jeans and tennis shoes. Shana's oldest son, Cory, is in the passenger's seat. Cory is a nice looking 18 year old Caucasian man that stands 5'11" tall and weighs a trim 140 pounds with straight light brown hair that hangs to just above his shoulders and blue eyes. Cory is wearing a white t-shirt, faded blue jeans and tennis shoes.

In the back behind the driver's seat is Shana's middle son, Zach. Zach is a good looking 15 year old Caucasian boy that stands 5'6" tall and weighs a thin yet healthy 98 pounds with straight light brown hair that hangs to his shoulders and blue eyes. Zach is wearing a red t-shirt, blue jeans and tennis shoes. In the back behind the passenger's seat is Shana's youngest son, Tyler. Tyler is a cute and very active 10 year old Caucasian boy who stands 4'8" tall and weighs around 60 pounds with short, straight light brown hair and blue eyes like his mom. Tyler is wearing a brown t-shirt, faded blue jeans and tennis shoes.

As Shana and the boys get out of the car, Jody walks out the front door to meet them. Jody has a big smile on his face as he walks up to the car.

Jody gives Shana a big hug, "It's good to see you."

Shana smiles, "It's good to see you too."

Jody and Shana step back and look at each other for a moment.

Jody smiles and looks at the boys, "So, you guys ready for some camping, swimming and great barbeque?"

Tyler throws his arms up, "You bet!"

Zach and Cory just smile as Jody and Shana share a nice chuckle.

Shana lets out a sigh, "I know I am. I got everything in the back of the car and I'm not even going to think about work."

Jody smiles, "Yeah, you needed a break for sure. Well, come on inside and I'll introduce you to everyone that's here so far." He pauses, "If you don't mind getting with dad and make a list of stuff, I need to run to the store before a bunch of us go target shooting."

Shana nods, "No problem."

Jody, Shana and the boys head off for the house.

A few minutes later a 2002 Gold Chevy Trailblazer pulls up and parks behind Ken's truck. In the passenger's seat is one of Jody's friends from work, Lindsey. Lindsey is a most stunningly beautiful 28 year old Caucasian woman who stands 5'6" tall and weighs a petite and incredibly attractive 130 pounds with naturally curly, light brown hair that hangs down to the top of her shoulders and is straight right now and mesmerizing light hunter green eyes that had a tendency to change colors with different moods. Lindsey is wearing a dark and light pink checkered tank top, faded blue jeans, tennis shoes and sunglasses.

Sitting in one of the middle seats is Lindsey's son, Daniel. Daniel is a cute and energetic 5 year old Caucasian boy who is right around 40" tall and weighs about 36 pounds with short, dark dirty blonde hair that is darkening to natural brown and curly when long and light blue eyes. Daniel is wearing a green t-shirt, blue jeans and tennis shoes. In the driver's seat is Lindsey's husband, Michael. Michael, Lindsey's husband, is a good looking 29 year old Caucasian man who stands 5'10" tall and weighs a stout 210 pounds with dark brown hair that is buzzed very short and balding on top and he has light blue eyes. Michael, Lindsey's husband, is wearing a black t-shirt, blue jeans, tennis shoes, black baseball cap and sunglasses.

As Lindsey and the others get out of the vehicle, Jody walks out the front door to greet them.

Lindsey smiles as Jody walks up, "Hey Jody."

Jody smiles back, "Hello Lindsey."

Jody and Lindsey give each other a hug, then step back.

Lindsey motions to Michael, her husband, and Daniel, "This is my husband, Michael, and my son, Daniel."

Jody shakes Michael's, Lindsey's husband, hand, "It's nice to meet you. I've heard so much about you two."

Michael, Lindsey's husband, replies, "Nice to meet you."

Jody glances at Daniel, then back to Lindsey, "So, you all ready for a fun weekend?"

Lindsey smiles, "Definitely! We've got all our stuff in the back of the Trailblazer."

Jody nods, "Sweet. Why don't you come on inside and I'll introduce you to the others that are here."

Lindsey nods as she, Michael, and Daniel follow Jody into the house.

A few minutes later, a newer model Lincoln SUV pulls up and parks on the opposite side of the street. In the passenger's seat is one of Jody's friends from work, Codi. Codi is an incredibly beautiful 24 year old Caucasian woman who stands 5'1" tall and holds a petite yet attractive 100 pound figure with straight brown hair that hangs to her shoulder blades and brown eyes. Codi is wearing a white t-shirt, light colored blue jeans and white tennis shoes.

Sitting in the driver's seat is Codi's husband, Ryan. Ryan is a very good looking 29 year old Caucasian man who stands 6'2" tall and weighs a trim yet fit 150 pounds with medium length, curly dark brown hair and brown eyes. Ryan is wearing a black t-shirt, blue jeans, black tennis shoes and a blue baseball cap. As Ryan and Codi get out of the vehicle, Jody walks out the front door to greet them.

Jody smiles and waves, "Good to see you two. I guess the directions were good."

Ryan walks up and shakes Jody's hand, "Yeah, no problem at all."

Codi walks up and gives Jody a hug, "It's really not that hard to find, just seems like it. Good to see you."

Jody hugs Codi, "Good to see you too."

Codi steps back, "So, I brought Lucky with me. Do you think Shadow will mind?"

Jody smiles and shakes his head, "Oh no, he doesn't mind smaller dogs at all."

Codi smiles, "Cool."

Codi walks back over to the vehicle and opens the back door. She picks up Lucky which is a black and white Pomeranian that weighs about 22 pounds. Codi walks back over to Ryan and Jody.

Jody smiles and scratches Lucky, "Hey there."

Codi and Ryan smile.

Jody looks at Codi and Ryan, "Are you two ready for a weekend of barbeque, swimming and shooting guns?"

Ryan nods, "Oh yes."

Codi smiles, "I sure am."

Jody motions to the house, "Well, come on in and I'll introduce you to everyone that's already here."

Codi and Ryan follow Jody back into the house.

A few minutes later, a light blue 2005 Chrysler Town & Country mini-van pulls up and parks behind Lindsey's Trailblazer. Driving the van is a friend of Jody's from work, Janet. Janet is an amazingly beautiful 27 year old Caucasian woman who stands 5'4" tall and holds an unbelievably attractive 125 pound figure with straight, strawberry blonde hair that hangs to her shoulders and blue eyes you could get lost in. Janet has a lighter and freckled complexion that is just as cute as can be. Janet is wearing a yellow tank top with pink butterflies on it, blue jean Capri pants, black flip flops with flowers on the top of them and a pair of sunglasses.

Sitting in the passenger's seat is Ashley, another friend of Jody's from work. Ashley is a very beautiful 23 year old Caucasian woman who stands right at 5' tall and weighs a stunningly attractive 100 pounds with straight blonde hair with dark red highlights that hangs to the top of her neck and pretty blue eyes. Ashley is wearing a yellow tank top, black shorts, brown sandals and sunglasses. Janet and Ashley get out of the vehicle as Jody walks up. The two ladies see Jody and smile.

Jody smiles back, "Hey ladies. Good to see you."

Janet gives Jody a hug, "It's good to see you too."

Jody hugs back with a little bit of nervousness like he likes Janet but hasn't said anything, "Glad you could make it."

Janet and Jody step back.

Ashley steps up and gives Jody a hug, "Good to see you."

Jody hugs Ashley, then steps back and looks at her, "Happy birthday by the way. Where is your girlfriend?"

Ashley shrugs and smiles, "Thanks. She will be down this afternoon. She said I should go ahead and catch a ride so I wouldn't be sitting around bored."

Jody nods, "Good. I can't wait to meet her." Jody looks at Janet, "Where are the kids?"

Janet sighs, "They are with their dad this week." She pauses, "I'm just happy that the divorce is final now."

Jody nods, "I can understand that. Well, come on inside and I'll introduce you to everyone."

Janet and Ashley follow Jody into the house.

CHAPTER 2

About 30 minutes have passed since everyone has shown up at Mike's house. Jody has introduced everyone and now everyone is just standing around and visiting. Shadow and Lucky have taken right to each other and both are on attention overload from all the petting they are receiving. Jody is standing with Lisa and Ken.

Shana walks up to Jody, "Hey Jo, I've got the list of stuff to pick up from the store."

Jody smiles, "Okay. I guess I should get going so we can go shooting when I get back."

Shana smiles, "If you don't mind, Ty and I will go with you."

Jody chuckles slightly, "Of course I don't mind." He pauses, "I'm going to let dad know we're leaving."

Shana nods, "I'll get Ty and meet you out front."

Jody nods, "Okay." He looks at Lisa, "We shouldn't be too long."

Lisa smiles, "We'll be ready."

Shana walks off to go get Tyler. Jody pats Lisa on the back, then walks over to his dad.

Jody speaks, "Shana, Tyler and I are headed to the store. We'll be back soon. Call if there is anything else we need to pick up."

Mike nods, "Okay. Once you all get back, I'll run and get Nancy."

Jody walks off and heads for his Explorer in the driveway. Shana and Tyler are already waiting at Jody's vehicle. Jody walks up, unlocks the passenger's door and opens it. Jody presses the automatic unlock to unlock the rest of the doors. Tyler opens the back passenger door and climbs in the backseat.

Shana climbs in the passenger's seat, "Thank you."

Jody smiles and shuts the passenger's door as Tyler pulls his door closed. Jody walks around and gets in the driver's seat. Jody starts the vehicle, backs out of the driveway and starts off down the road. The first few blocks is quiet, but once Jody passes through the four way stop at the Veterinary Clinic, the talking starts.

Shana questions, "So, how long are you all going to be shooting?"

Jody replies while keeping his eyes on the road, "We'll be gone about an hour so we should be back around one o'clock."

Shana nods, "That's not bad. I'm sure the boys will be nice and waterlogged by then. It wouldn't surprise me if Zach and Cory are already in the pool." She pauses, "Which, by the way, you guys have a nice, in ground swimming pool."

Tyler smiles, "I'm ready to swim."

Jody smiles and chuckles, "So am I big man." He glances at Shana, "Having that pool is nice."

As they cross over the bridge at the park, Jody notices something weird in the park, "Look over there."

Shana looks to her right and sees what Jody is talking about. There are numerous people just wandering around the park area almost as if they are lost. As they continue on and over the railroad tracks, they notice there are even more abandoned cars on the side of the road than there have been in the past. They don't see anyone out and about.

Jody speaks as they pass through the stoplight that leads into Main Street, "This is weird. I don't see anyone else out."

Shana nods as she glances around, "I've seen a few people walking on the side roads, but only one other car. That doesn't seem normal for a Saturday morning."

Jody sighs, "No, it's not."

As they stop at the first stop sign, they glance around. The two of them see a couple of other cars, but most of the cars are parked along the sides of the streets, actually more like they were hastily stopped and abandoned there as the cars are not parked like normal cars would be. As they continue on and stop at the next stop sign, Jody sees something very unusual.

Jody motions to his right with his head, "Look at that."

Shana looks over and sees what Jody pointed out. Two cars are abandoned in the middle of the road about half a block down the street. Jody and Shana doesn't see anyone around the cars.

Shana shakes her head, "That's just plain odd. Surely the police have been called on that."

Jody nods, "I'm sure they have been." He pauses, "Let's just get to the store."

Jody continues to drive on down the road. As they pass side street after side street, it is the same thing, abandoned and parked cars. Jody and Shana see a few people in the distance along some of the side streets but they just appear to be wandering around.

As they pass the truck road turn, they see a few other cars driving on the road with them, but still not as many as they would have figured for a Saturday morning. Jody and Shana try to put it out of their minds as they continue on to the store.

Finally reaching the store, Jody pulls into the left turn lane at the stoplight in front of the store and stops. Jody looks over and sees about fifty cars in the parking lot and he sees a few people walking around the parking lot. Shana also looks over and sees the same thing.

Shana sighs, "I don't like this at all."

Jody nods slowly, "Let's just get in, get our stuff and get home."

Shana nods in agreement, "I like that idea."

The light turns green and Jody turns into the parking lot. He drives down the main isle, passing an average sized man that appears to be wandering around possibly looking for his car. Neither Jody nor Shana took a look at the man closely because if they had they would have noticed something different about him. Jody pulls around to the next isle and parks about ten spots down from the front. As Jody puts the car in park and turns it off, neither of them notice that the man is approaching the passenger's side of the vehicle.

Jody opens his door, "Ty's door doesn't open from the inside so you'll have to let him out."

Shana gets out of the vehicle and closes her door. As Shana reaches for the door handle of Ty's door, she hears something behind her.

Tyler yells, "Mom!"

Shana turns around and sees the strange man just a few feet away. The man's eyes are covered in a white milky film and he has coagulated blood around his mouth. The man reaches out for Shana. Shana instinctively puts her hands out and press on the front of the man's shoulders to keep him away. The man grabs Shana's arms and starts making some groaning noises, then tries to push his head forward and starts biting at Shana.

Shana yells in a panic, "Jody! Help!"

Jody is shocked as he hurries around the front of the vehicle to help Shana. Jody grabs the man's shoulders from behind and starts trying to pull the man away. Jody tugs his hardest, but he can't seem to pull the man back. Shana continues to hold the man back as the man is feverishly trying to get close enough to bite Shana. Jody let's go and punches the man as hard as he can in the kidney area about four times. Jody, a highly trained fighter, is shocked that his blows seem to have no affect on the man who is still trying to bite Shana.

Tyler is nearly in tears, "Mom!"

Jody finally decides that it is time to use deadly force, something his Marine Corps training has prepared him for and to use in this kind of situation. Jody reaches into his back pocket and pulls out his pocket knife. Jody flips the blade open and without hesitation, jams the knife into the man's right kidney area.

Shana continues to scream, "Stop, please! Jody, help!"

To Jody's surprise, the man seems completely un-phased by the knife. Jody also quickly notices that there is no blood coming out of the man's back. Jody's training takes over. Jody removes the knife. Jody reaches up and grabs the man's forehead with his left hand. Jody pulls the man's head backward as he brings his knife upward. There is no way Jody is going to let this man harm Shana, one of his best friends.

While holding the man's head back with his left hand, Jody rams the knife upward into the man's brain from under the back of his skull. Again, no blood runs out but this time it seems to have an instant affect. The man's arms let go of Shana and the man collapses to the pavement. Both Jody and Shana just stand there in shock as to what has just happened.

Jody looks at his knife and sees that it has coagulated blood on it. Jody gets a puzzled look on his face. Shana steps over and throws her arms around Jody.

Shana hugs Jody tight, "Oh my God! Thank you!"

Jody replies, still a little stunned, "Are you okay?"

Shana nods as she steps back, "Yes, I think so."

At that moment, Jody and Shana hear some commotion from the main doors of the store. The two of them look over and see a woman come running out the front doors looking back over her shoulder. However, there is another woman standing there in front of the doors. The running woman runs right into her and they both fall to the ground.

The second woman crawls on top of the running woman and bites the woman in the neck. The running woman screams as blood flies everywhere. Jody and Shana are completely shocked by what they see. Jody, hearing movement off to his left, looks over and sees a group of three men and two women headed towards him and Shana.

Jody wipes his knife off and puts it away, "Shana, get back in the car. We have to get out of here."

Shana looks over and sees what Jody sees. Shana quickly gets back in the Explorer and shuts the door.

Shana looks at Tyler who has tears in his eyes, "Its okay baby, mom's okay."

Jody climbs in and shuts the door, then locks the doors. Jody starts the vehicle as the group reaches the hood of his Explorer. Jody quickly backs out of the parking space, throws the Explorer in drive and races off. The group of people continue to slowly walk after the Explorer.

CHAPTER 3

Mike is finishing up cleaning the grill and getting things ready for the barbeque. Shadow and Lucky are making the rounds and getting plenty of attention from everyone. Everyone else is just sitting around or standing and visiting with each other. The talk is about work and things going on in everyday life. The talk is also about the strange virus and how weird things have gotten lately.

Mike wipes off his hands as Shadow walks up next to him. Shadow sits down and looks up at Mike with the "when is the food going to be ready" look. Mike reaches down and starts petting Shadow when his phone starts ringing.

Mike pulls his phone out of his pocket and answers it, "Hello."

Jody's voice in a panic, "Dad, something bad is going on. I don't have time to explain. Get everyone inside, fast and make sure all the blinds are closed and doors locked."

Mike replies in an unsure voice, "Whoa, slow down. What are you talking about?"

Jody's voice again, "Shana was attacked at the store. I killed the man, but there was something strange about him. We're headed home and there is chaos in the streets. Just get everyone inside, please. I'll explain more when I get there. Got to go."

Mike starts to reply when the line goes dead. Mike turns around where most everyone is at. Marissa can tell something is wrong.

Marissa questions, "What is it?"

Mike shakes his head for a second like he's trying to gather his thoughts, "It was Jody. Something very bad has happened."

Hearing what Mike said, Ken, Lisa, Lindsey, Janet and Ashley walk over closer to Mike and Marissa.

Mike looks at them, "Shana was attacked at the store and Jody said he killed the person." He pauses as everyone's face gets a shocked look, "He said something bad is happening in town, that there is chaos in the streets. He wants us all to go inside, lock the doors and shut the blinds until he gets here."

Ken replies, "Maybe he was just messing with us. He is quite the prankster."

Mike shakes his head, "My son, with everything he's been through and with his training, doesn't panic, but I could hear it in his voice. Something is very wrong for him to sound that way. I think we should go inside like he said."

Marissa nods, "I trust Jody completely."

Mike nods in agreement, "Okay, let's get everyone inside. He should be here in a few minutes."

Lisa, Lindsey, Ashley, Janet, Marissa and Ken start to round up the others while Mike works on getting Shadow back into the house.

Jody's Explorer is racing down Main Street approaching the truck route turn off. Jody slows the vehicle down as the light turns red. Jody pulls the vehicle to a stop at the intersection. Jody and Shana both try to catch their breath and Shana turns around in her seat to try and keep

Tyler calm. Suddenly, they hear screaming. Jody starts looking around and sees a woman running across the parking lot of the restaurant that is caddie corner of where they are stopped. Jody sees a group of four men chasing the woman. The four men are moving at a fairly fast walking pace, but are not running. The woman is about forty feet ahead of the men.

Jody just stares and speaks, "Look at that."

Shana looks over and sees what Jody is talking about. Both of them are stunned by what all has happened that they fail to see the car speeding towards the intersection from the truck route. The running woman also fails to see the speeding car. The woman runs out into the street and the car hits her without even slowing down. The woman's body flips over the hood of the car, breaks the windshield and flies over the roof and lands on the pavement. The woman doesn't move after she hits the ground. The car continues right on thru the intersection and appears to even speed up.

Shana's expression is that of shock, "Oh my God!"

Jody shakes his head, "What is going on?!"

The four men that were chasing the woman slow down, then stop at the corner of the street. Jody and Shana both watch the four men carefully. Then, the four men turn and look directly at Jody and Shana.

Shana speaks with panic in her voice, "Go Jody!"

The four men start to head straight for the Explorer as if they are driven by some unknown force.

Shana speaks more franticly, "Get us out of here!"

Jody breaks his stare, takes his foot off the brake and steps on the gas even though the light is still red. The Explorer takes off thru the intersection and picks up speed. Jody looks in his mirror and sees the four men start down the street after them.

Jody shakes his head and repeats himself from moments ago, "What is going on?!"

Shana tries to calm her breathing, "I don't know. Its like everyone is going crazy."

Jody keeps the vehicle at 35 miles per hour as they head towards the downtown section of Main Street. They approach another stoplight at the intersection that leads to the Civic Center.

Jody speaks, "Keep a look out, I'm not stopping if the light turns red."

Shana nods and watches the side street to make sure no other cars are coming. Shana doesn't see any other cars, other than the ones that appear abandoned, but she does see a few more people running and some more people chasing them in a fast walk. The light changes to red as they approach. Jody looks left and right quickly, then speeds thru the intersection.

Even in the midst of chaos, Jody's humor is automatic, "I don't think the cops will mind. They have bigger problems to worry about."

Shana just looks at Jody and shakes her head, yet, she manages to crack a smile. The Explorer flies over the railroad tracks and approaches another stoplight by the movie theatre. Jody slows down to 30 miles per hour as they approach the intersection. The light stays green and they drive thru the intersection keeping a close eye on the side street for traffic.

Jody starts to slow the vehicle down some as the road changes from four lane to two lane, "I'm going to take it slower thru downtown. The last thing we need to do is wreck and end up having to walk."

Shana nods, "I agree completely."

Jody looks in his mirror at Tyler, "How you doing big man?"

Tyler has a scared look on his face and is unable to reply.

Jody sighs, "Don't you worry. I promise you that I won't let anything happen to you or your mom."

19

Jody looks back at the road as they approach the first stop sign. Jody slows the car down and stops at the intersection. Shana looks to her left and the two cars that were abandoned in the middle of the road are still there. However, a police car is also stopped by the two cars. Shana can see the police officer laying on the ground with a man and a woman on top of him. The man and woman appear to be eating the police officer.

Shana just stares, "Jo, look at that."

Jody glances over and sees what Shana is talking about, "What the …"

Jody leaves the sentence unfinished as he removes his foot from the brake and presses down on the gas pedal. As he looks back at the road ahead, Jody sees a car stopped in the lane ahead of him. Jody slows down and moves over into the opposite lane. As they get up next to the car, a man steps over and tries to grab the hood of the Explorer. Jody and Shana both look at the man. He appears to be alive other than he has coagulated blood all around his mouth and his eyes have the same milky white glaze like the man at the store. The man grabs at the passenger's window as they drive by. Jody pushes down on the accelerator and speeds away as he doesn't even stop at the next stop sign.

Jody glances at Shana, "Keep a look out. I'm not stopping again."

Shana nods as Jody continues the Explorer down Main Street at a steady 35 miles per hour.

Mike and the others are anxiously waiting in the house for Jody, Shana and Tyler to get back. Everyone is packed into the living room. There is an eerie silence hanging over the house. Its like everyone wants to say something, but nobody knows exactly what to say. With none of the local channels having the news on at this time, Mike has the television turned on to one of the national news stations in hopes of hearing anything that might explain the "chaos" that Jody said was going on.

The television news anchor comes on, "We now continue with our breaking news coverage. It appears that we are getting reports from all of our affiliates around the country that strange things have starting happening. From the sketchy reports we have been getting, it appears that the people that have been infected with the strange virus have starting turning violent and attacking non-infected people." The news anchor pauses, "Again, we can't confirm these reports as of yet, but the other reports we have been getting are even stranger. We have received unconfirmed reports that the people that have died from the virus have started coming back to life."

Mike and the others are completely stunned by what they are hearing. No one in the room is able to speak as they continue to watch the news reporter try to explain what is going on.

The news anchor continues, "Okay. We are starting to get some more information in. It appears that a quick message was released from the White House declaring a national state of emergency. We have received a fax from the White House spokesperson and as soon as I get it in my hands, I'll read it to all the viewers."

Mike finally breaks the silence, "This must be bad." He pauses, "If they faxed something to the news stations instead of holding a conference of their own. Something very terrible is going on."

The television news anchor comes back on, "Okay, I have the fax. It is from the President. It says: As of 10 am Eastern Standard Time, upon the advice of the CDC, I have declared a national state of emergency. All citizens are to return to their homes or the nearest safe place and await further reports. Everyone is to remain inside with doors and windows locked. Above all, do not have any contact with anyone that has been infected by the unknown virus. As I get more information from the CDC, I will pass it on to all the national news stations. Thank you." The news anchor pauses, "That's all the fax says for now. So I will reiterate what the President has said. Get inside someplace safe and do not have any contact with anyone that has been infected with the virus. At the end of the fax it says that the White House will try to make hourly updates if it can." The news anchor pauses again, "Okay. We are going to take a short commercial break, then we will continue with this story when we return."

As the first commercial comes on, everyone is just staring at the television with a stunned look, not really sure what to make of what they have just heard.

Ken finally speaks up, " I don't know what to make of this. You don't think they are pulling a modern day 'War Of The Worlds' on everyone do you?"

Mike shakes his head, "I would almost believe that if I hadn't heard Jody's voice on the phone. No, something is terribly wrong."

Lisa looks at Mike, "So, what do we do?"

Mike replies, "I think its best if we just hang tight until Jody gets back. He'll be able to shed some light on what's going on out there."

Everyone turns their attention back to the television and anxiously wait for Jody, Shana and Tyler to get home.

CHAPTER 4

Jody brings the Explorer around the corner of the street where the house is, "When we get there, we need to get out and inside quick so nobody or anything sees us."

Shana nods as Jody speeds the Explorer down the street. Jody slows the vehicle up and whips into the driveway, bringing the Explorer to a sudden stop. Jody quickly puts the car in park and shuts it off. Shana hops out and opens Tyler's door. Jody quickly gets out of the vehicle and glances around. Jody pushes the power locks to make sure the vehicle is locked. Shana slams her door and Tyler's door. Jody slams his door shut and the three of them rush for the front door of the house.

Jody quickly unlocks the door and opens it. Shana and Tyler walk inside. Jody takes one last look around and doesn't see anyone, then Jody goes inside and locks the door behind him. Everyone in the living room looks over at Jody, Shana and Tyler.

Mike looks at his youngest son, "Jody, what's going on?"

Jody just stands at the door, trying to catch his breath for a second. Shana and Tyler are just standing there in shock at what they just went through. Everyone in the room is waiting with anticipation at hearing what Jody has to say. Jody finally lets out a sigh and turns to the living room.

Jody blinks a few times, "Everything's gone crazy out there." He pauses, "Maybe we should have the younger kids go into the other room first so we can talk openly and you can explain it to them later if you think it's okay."

Lisa looks at Rochelle, "Why don't you watch the kids while we talk. I'll fill you in later."

Rochelle nods, "Okay mom."

Rochelle gets up and starts for the family room. Shana takes Zach and Tyler into the family room, explains that it won't be long and it'll be okay, then returns to the living room. Lindsey takes Daniel into the family room, tells him to wait for her, then returns to the living room. Grace takes Ayden and Ariel into the family room, then returns to the living room.

Once everyone is back in the living room, Jody closes the door to the family room and the door to the kitchen. Jody can tell by the look on everyone's face that he needs to start explaining what is going on.

Jody takes a deep breath, "The entire drive to the store was weird. Like all the other days, cars parked all over or abandoned. People out wandering around. You know what I mean. When we got to the store, there were a few people walking around the parking lot and there were very few cars. I pulled in and parked." He pauses, "We didn't see the guy approach the car, but when Shana got out and closed her door, this man attacked her. He was grabbing at her and he was trying to lean in and appeared like he was trying to bite her."

Jody can see the look on everyone's face change to that of being startled and puzzled as if they don't know what to make of what they just heard.

Jody continues, "I ran around and grabbed the guy from behind. I pulled as hard as I could, but I couldn't seem to pull him away. He wasn't much bigger than me so I was fairly surprised. I punched him as hard as I could about four times in his lower back, but he just kept trying to bite

24

Shana like my punches didn't even phase him." He pauses, "Folks, I can hit pretty hard. I've trained a long time in hand-to-hand. So, I decided to pull out my knife. I stabbed the man in the right kidney area. Again though, it didn't even phase him."

Ken questions, "Do you think he could've been on drugs?"

Jody nods, "That's what I thought at first, but then I realized he wasn't bleeding. When I pulled my knife out, there was coagulated blood on it, not regular blood like you'd think."

Grace spontaneously interjects, "That's weird!"

Jody nods and continues, "I knew that I had to do something drastic, so I grabbed the man's head and stabbed him upward, under the base of his skull and into his brain. Again, no blood, but as soon as I removed my knife, he dropped like a sack of potatoes and didn't move at all and he wasn't bleeding at all, just more coagulated blood."

Shana finally speaks up, "It was scary and weird. The man's eyes were a solid milky white and he had either dried blood or coagulated blood around his mouth."

Jody nods, "Then, we saw a woman run out of the store and get knocked down by another woman. The one woman climbed on the other and appeared to start eating her. That's when I noticed a group of people heading for us. We got back in the car and headed back here."

Marissa speaks up, "That's just insane."

Jody nods, "You're telling me. On the way home, it was even crazier than going to the store. We saw a woman running from a group of people. She ran in front of a car and the car never even slowed down, even after it ran her over. Then we saw a police officer on the ground with two people on top of him and it looked like they were eating him."

Ken shakes his head, "Are you serious?"

Jody nods, "One hundred percent."

Grace questions, "And you're sure it was coagulated blood on your knife?"

Jody nods again and replies in a more somber tone, "One hundred percent. I've seen enough blood in my days to know what it's supposed to look like."

Ashley questions, "What's the deal about the blood?"

Shana explains from her years of experience as a nurse, "Blood coagulates when it's exposed to the open air, not inside the body. For blood to coagulate inside the body, that would mean …"

Grace chimes in, "The person has been dead for a little while."

Shana nods, "Exactly."

Lindsey questions with a puzzled look, "So, you're saying Shana was attacked by a dead man?"

Jody nods, "That is exactly how it would appear to be."

Michael, Lindsey's husband, speaks up, "Well, the news story makes more sense now."

Jody looks puzzled, "What news story?"

Mike looks at his son, "We turned on the news while we were waiting for you. A news station received a fax from the White House declaring a national state of emergency. It said to say indoors and do not have any contact with anyone who is infected. They are going to try and have hourly updates. The next update should be coming soon."

Jody shakes his head, "The White House faxed it to them? That's bad."

Lisa questions, "What makes you say that?"

Jody replies, "With today's technology, I would think that they would have released their own statement, held their own press conference or at the very least, called or emailed the news stations. Maybe some sort of national emergency broadcast on the emergency broadcast system."

Ken nods his head, "That's exactly what I was thinking."

Ashley finally asks the big question, "So, what do we do now?"

Jody sighs, "I was thinking about that some while we were coming back here. First thing that comes to mind is that we stay inside and do not attempt to travel anywhere."

Mike nods at his son's suggestion, "I would definitely agree with that."

Jody nods and continues, "I think everyone should bring anything from their cars inside like clothes, bags, sleeping bags, anything you might need. We can put it all in the garage for now." He pauses, "Once we get that done, I think we need to figure out sleeping arrangements cause it's going to be crowded in here and we need to start trying to contact people to see how things are with them."

Everyone around the room nods at Jody's suggestion. Shana starts to move towards the front door.

Jody speaks up as everyone else stands up, "Wait a second."

Jody walks to his bedroom and returns to the living room in a few seconds. Jody is carrying his Glock 17, that has a loaded 17 round magazine in it, in his right hand.

Jody speaks, "Let's go in and out the garage. I'll watch out while everyone gets their things. Let's make it quick, then meet back in the living room."

Everyone heads for the door to the garage in the kitchen.

In a couple of minutes, the garage is filled with everyone's things. The kids and Rochelle are back in the family room and everyone else is back in the living room. Shadow is sitting next to Mike in the recliner and Lucky is on Codi's lap.

Ken, who now has his Franchi SPAS-12 12 gauge shotgun loaded with 9 shells, sits down on the end of the couch and leans the shotgun against the couch next to him. Everyone gets settled back in.

Michael, Jody's brother, speaks up, "Now that we got that done, what's next?"

Jody nods, "While we go over sleeping arrangements, everyone should start trying to get a hold of people in other areas, family or friends, to see if things are as crazy there. I figure we are all spending at least one night inside the house together though."

Everyone grabs their phones and the text messaging begins.

Ashley questions, "What do you suggest about the sleeping arrangements?"

Jody takes a breath, "Shana and her boys are the largest group so if dad doesn't mind, they can take his room."

Mike shakes his head, "Not a problem. I can sleep right here in the recliner just fine."

Jody nods, "Boy we know that's true." Jody gives a slight smile, then continues, "Lindsey, the hide-a-bed in the living room is big enough for you, Michael and Daniel."

Lindsey nods, "Okay. That'll work."

Jody looks at Lisa, "Lisa, you and Rochelle can take my room."

Lisa nods, "Okay."

Jody looks over at his brother, then Marissa, "I was thinking if the two of you don't mind sharing that Marissa, you and my brother could stay in his room."

Marissa shakes her head, "I don't mind."

Michael, Jody's brother, nods, "I don't mind either."

Jody continues, "Okay then. Dad will sleep in one recliner. Ken, do you mind sleeping in the other recliner?"

Ken shakes his head, "Nope. I can make it work."

Jody nods, "Good. We have a spare airbed that we can inflate and put in here after we move the coffee table out. Its big enough for Grace and her kids."

Grace nods, "Sounds good to me."

Jody continues, "That leaves just Ashley, Janet, Ryan, Codi and myself." He pauses, "I think the couch is big enough for Ryan and Codi. We can try that and if not, we can figure something else out."

Codi nods, "Sounds okay to me."

Ryan nods also, "It will be plenty big enough."

Shana looks at Jody, "Where are you, Janet and Ashley going to sleep because that's all the places in the house except maybe the floor somewhere?"

Jody replies ever so nonchalant, "I'll pop up my little tent in the garage. The three of us can sleep in there with our sleeping bags."

Janet looks at Jody, "That will be okay with me."

Ashley nods, "Won't be the most comfortable, but it'll work for now."

Jody sighs, "Well, that takes care of the sleeping arrangements. Now I guess we move our stuff to our rooms, wait for the next news update and keep trying to contact people."

Everyone nods, gets up and heads for the garage to get their things and take them to their designated places. It is obvious by the looks on everyone's face that they are worried about their family and friends.

CHAPTER 5

After a few minutes, everyone has gathered their personal belongings and moved them into the rooms where they are sleeping except for those in the living room. Ryan and Codi have their things in the family room with Lindsey, Michael, Lindsey's husband, and Daniel. Grace has her and the kid's things in the laundry room area.

Jody and his dad have moved the coffee table out of the living room and placed it out on the deck in the backyard. Jody inflated the full sized air bed for Grace and the kids and put it in the middle of the living room floor. As everyone gets situated, the televisions in the living room, Michael's room, Jody's room and Mike's room are all on a national news station.

Jody has his tent put up in the middle of the garage. Jody retrieves his large OD green alice pack with attached frame from his room which is full of survival gear and places it in the garage, then he retrieves a clear plastic backpack with stuff in it and places it in his tent. Jody then retrieves his OD green h-harness with attached OD green cartridge belt which also has a lot of survival gear on it and places it in the garage with his alice pack. Jody lastly retrieves a black rifle/shotgun case from his room and places it in his tent. Jody has put down a couple blankets under Janet's, Ashley's and his sleeping bags to make it more comfortable. As Jody gets his things situated inside the tent, he waits for any reply from the people he has tried to contact.

Jody decides to inventory his gear while he waits for any responses. Jody starts with the clear plastic backpack. Inside the backpack is two mechanical pencils, one all weather pocket notepad, a tan riggers belt, pair of underwear, pair of black boot socks, pair of boot blouses, pair of tan nomex gloves, pair of ACU digital camouflage combat pants, an ACU digital camouflage short sleeve t-shirt, an ACU digital camouflage combat top, an ACU digital camouflage boonie cover, his pair of brown combat boots from the Marine Corps and a shotgun shell holder belt with 20 double ought 12 gauge buckshot shells in it.

Jody inventories his alice pack next. Attached to the outside of the pack is a SOG Jungle Primitive knife. In the pack is a full gun cleaning kit, complete hygiene kit, a 205 piece first aid kit, 5 green chemical light sticks, a military field survival manual, a roll of toilet paper, a package of sanitation wipes, an e-tool shovel, a desert camouflage pack cover, an ACU digital camouflage poncho, an ACU digital camouflage poncho liner, a camp towel, a washcloth, a mini LED lantern, 8 AA batteries, a sewing kit, pair of tan bootlaces, pair of black bootlaces, pair of boot blouses, 25 double ought 12 gauge buckshot shells in a zip lock bag, 300 9mm rounds in a zip lock bag and his pair of brown jungle boots from the Marine Corps.

Also in the pack is a waterproof bag with a pair of ACU digital camouflage combat pants, 3 ACU digital camouflage short sleeve t-shirts, an ACU digital camouflage combat top, an ACU digital camouflage boonie cover, 3 pair of black boot socks, 3 pair of underwear, a polypropylene top and polypropylene bottoms in it. Jody remembers what else he wants to put in the pack so he goes back to his bedroom and retrieves an OD green USMC sweat top and sweat pants, then stops by the laundry room and grabs his black zip-up hooded jacket and returns to his tent. Jody places everything back in the pack.

Jody grabs his h-harness with attached cartridge belt next. Attached to the cartridge belt, starting on the front left as it's being worn, is a pair of small binoculars in a small black pouch. To the left of that is a lenstatic compass in an OD green pouch. To the left of that, on the left hip, is a small first aid kit with QuikClot sponge in an OD green pouch. Also in the first aid pouch is a magnesium firestarter. To the left of that is a desert tan, one quart canteen cover with small pouch and in the small pouch is a small bottle of iodine tablets. Inside the canteen cover is an OD green, one quart canteen full of water. To the left of that, centered on the back of the cartridge belt, is a desert camouflage butt pack. On the other side of the butt pack is another desert tan, one quart canteen cover with a small pouch and in the small pouch is a black rescue whistle. Inside the canteen cover is another OD green, one quart canteen full of water and a canteen cup. Next to that, on the back of the right hip, is a SOG Combat Knife in a hard, black knife sheath. Next to that, on the right hip, is a desert tan, tactical drop leg holster with pouch. In the holster is Jody's Glock 17 with loaded 17 round magazine and in the pouch is a multipurpose tool. Lastly, on the front right of the cartridge belt is a coyote tan, double magazine holder with 2 fully loaded 17 round magazines.

Jody looks in the butt pack which has the following: a signal mirror, a small emergency radio, a pair of black cold weather shooting gloves, a roll of duct tape, 5 green chemical light sticks, an emergency sleeping bag, 8 AA batteries, 2 pair of spare glasses, 10 waterproof matches in a case, a camouflage face paint kit, a 300 foot roll of tan paracord, a pack of sanitation wipes, a firefly signal strobe and flashlight, a tan neck gator, an ACU digital camouflage beanie, an ACU digital camouflage Neoprene face mask and a 3 day pack of survival rations.

Once Jody is done putting everything back where it belongs, he grabs his bottle of water and takes a drink. Suddenly, Jody's phone rings with an incoming text message.

Lisa and Rochelle are in Jody's room. Rochelle has brought in a suitcase with all her additional clothes and hygiene stuff. Lisa has brought in a suitcase with all her additional clothes and hygiene stuff and a black law enforcement duty bag full of her emergency stuff. Lisa is still wearing her pistol and spare magazines, but now she is also wearing a black clip on handcuff case with a pair of handcuffs in it.

Lisa has explained to Rochelle what is going on. Rochelle is completely shocked by what she has heard. Both ladies are now quiet as they wait to her anything back from the people they have tried to contact.

Shana, Cory, Zach and Tyler are in the master bedroom. Shana brought in her backpack with all her spare clothes and hygiene stuff in it, her sleeping bag and her beach towel. Cory, Zach and Tyler have brought in their backpacks with all their spare clothes and hygiene stuff in them, their sleeping bags and beach towels. Shana and the boys have put all their things in the walk-in closet that is in the room.

Shana and Cory explain to Zach and Tyler everything that was said in the living room. Tyler is still obviously shaken up by what happened on the trip to the store. Shana does her best to try and comfort Tyler as they all wait for any responses from the people they have tried to contact.

Michael, Jody's brother, and Marissa are in Michael's room. Michael, Jody's brother, has organized his things so that Marissa has room for her stuff. Marissa has brought in her suitcase with all her spare clothes and hygiene stuff in it, her sleeping bag and beach towel. Marissa is still wearing her pistol and spare magazines.

Michael, Jody's brother, and Marissa sit quietly as Marissa waits for a response from the people she has tried to contact. Michael, Jody's brother, is on his computer messaging some of his online friends to see how things are where they are at.

Mike is sitting in his recliner in the living room and Ken is sitting in the other recliner in the living room. Mike is petting Shadow while he is flipping around through the different news stations. Ken, who didn't bring anything except his guns and ammunition because he wasn't planning on spending the night, is still wearing his pistol and spare magazines. Ken has his shotgun and spare ammunition sitting next to his chair. Both of them are waiting to hear back from the people they have tried to contact.

Grace, Ayden and Ariel are also in the living room. Grace has placed her and the kid's backpacks with all their extra clothes and hygiene stuff in the laundry room along with her and the kid's sleeping bags, beach towels and her four person tent. Grace and the kids are sitting on the air bed in the middle of the floor.

Grace has been trying to explain what is going on to her kids in a way that they will understand. It hasn't been easy for her, but she has made them understand why they have to stay inside for right now. While Grace has been explaining things to her kids, she is also waiting for a reply from the people she has tried to contact.

Ryan, Codi and Janet are sitting on the couch in the living room. Janet has already placed her things in the garage and set up her sleeping bag in Jody's tent. Janet appears quite worried as she waits for her phone to get a response from the people she has tried to contact. Ryan and Codi have put all their belongings up. Ryan is now wearing a black, clip on holster on his right hip and in the holster is a Glock 19 9mm pistol with a fully loaded 15 round magazine. Codi is wearing a black, clip on holster and in the holster is a Smith and Wesson Bodyguard that fires 380 ammunition with a built in laser site and has a fully loaded 7 round magazine in it. Ryan and Codi are waiting to hear back from the people they have tried to contact. Lucky is laying next to Codi's feet.

Ashley is sitting in the family room with Lindsey, Daniel and Michael, Lindsey's husband. Ashley has gotten all her things set up in the garage. Lindsey brought in her and Daniel's backpacks with their spare clothes and hygiene stuff, their sleeping bags and their towels. Michael, Lindsey's husband, brought in his backpack with his spare clothes and hygiene stuff, his sleeping bag, towel and their four person tent.

Lindsey has been trying to explain what is going on to Daniel. It hasn't been easy, but Lindsey has made Daniel understand why they have to stay inside for now. As the four of them sit in the family room, Lindsey, Michael, Lindsey's husband, and Ashley wait to hear anything back from the people they have tried to contact.

CHAPTER 6

The talking around the house has quieted for a bit and now all that really is going on is text messaging with others to see how things are going outside of the house. No one actually realizes how long it has been since they started getting situated and contacting people.

Mike hollers to everyone, "The news is fixing to give an update!"

Ashley, Lindsey, Michael, Lindsey's husband, and Daniel walk into the living room. Lindsey, Daniel and Michael, Lindsey's husband, sit on the couch with Janet, Codi and Ryan. Ashley sits on the air bed with Grace and her kids. Marissa and Michael, Jody's brother, stay in his room and flip over to the national news station. Shana, Cory, Zach and Tyler stay in the master bedroom and watch the news intently. Jody walks in from the garage and walks to his room where Lisa and Rochelle are watching the news. Everyone sits quietly and waits for the news report, hoping for some good news.

The television news reporter comes on, "As we promised, we would give an update as soon as we had one and we have received another fax from the White House." The news reporter pauses, "There have been major changes since we last spoke on the air. The White House has announced that the original numbers reported by the CDC about how many people were infected was off by quite a bit. Basically what they are saying is that nobody is really sure how many infected people there are. Second and perhaps the most incredible announcement, the White House has declared Marshall Law for the entire country. The President has tasked the military and National Guard units with setting up safe places for people to go and has directed them to go out and deal with the infected people."

Everyone in the house sits in complete, stunned silence. None of them are quite sure what to make of the announcements.

The news reporter continues, "Well, I'm sure all of you out there are as shocked as we are about these announcements. Keep tuned in and as soon as we have another update, we will pass the information on to our viewers. Thank you."

The station goes to a commercial. Jody sits in his chair for a few seconds, then stands up.

Jody looks at Lisa, "Let's all go to the living room and talk about some things."

Lisa and Rochelle head for the living room.

Jody looks into the master bedroom at Shana, "Let's head to the living room and talk some things over."

Shana, Cory, Zach and Tyler all head for the living room.

Jody looks in Michael's room, "Let's head to the living room and talk about some stuff."

Marissa and Michael, Jody's brother, head for the living room. Everyone makes room for each other in the living room. Jody is standing in the doorway to the living room from the foyer area at the front door.

Jody speaks once everyone is settled in, "Okay. We all heard what the news had to say and I'm sure you all are just as surprised as I am." He pauses, "I think what we should do now is just go around the room one at a time and update everyone on who you have tried to get in touch with and what you have found out."

Everyone in the room nods in agreement.

Jody looks at his dad, "Well dad, you want to start?"

Mike nods his head, "Well, first I tried to get in touch with my friend, Nancy. She lives here in town, but I never did get an answer when I called or sent a text message. The other person I tried to contact was Sandra in Joplin. I did get the chance to speak with her briefly. She said that she is trapped in her house and things have been crazy around there. She said she has seen some people wandering around the neighborhood."

Jody nods, "Okay. Ken, how about you?"

Ken replies, "I tried to get in touch with my girlfriend, but I couldn't reach her at all. I got in touch with a friend of mine in Joplin and he said things are really crazy around there and he's trapped inside his workplace."

Jody takes a breath, "Okay. Marissa, what about you?"

Marissa replies, "First, I tried to get in touch with my mom, but couldn't get a response. I did get in touch with my sister in Fort Worth. She said that they are trapped in their house and things are very crazy around there. People are wandering around everywhere. I also reached a friend in Lubbock. He said that things around there are really crazy too."

Jody sighs, "Alright." He looks at his brother, "How about you?"

Michael, Jody's brother, responds, "I got in touch with a friend in Texas. She said that things are all crazy around there. I got a response from a friend in Florida and it was the same thing. He said that he's trapped in his house and there are people wandering everywhere."

Jody nods, "Okay. Grace, what about you?"

Grace replies, "I was able to get in touch with my husband. He said that they are trapped inside where they are working in Texas and things have been crazy around there, but they are all okay. I tried to get in touch with my mom, but didn't get a response. I reached a friend in Galena and she is stuck inside her house and she said there are people out wandering around."

Jody takes a breath, "Okay. How about you Ashley?"

Ashley replies with a sad look, "I tried to get in touch with my mom, but I didn't get any response. I tried to get in touch with other family like my brother and some others, but no response from them either." She pauses, "I was able to get in touch with my girlfriend. She said that she was outside with the dogs and they got attacked by some people. She said that she was able to get back inside, but the dogs didn't make it. She also said that she was bitten on the arm."

Jody nods slightly, "I'm sorry." He pauses, "How about you Lindsey?"

Lindsey also has a sad look, "I tried to get in touch with my parents because they have my dogs. I didn't get a response from them. Michael also wasn't able to get a response from anyone in his family. We both got in touch with a couple of friends and they said that things are kind of crazy around where they are at."

Jody takes a breath, "Okay. How about you Janet?"

Janet replies in a very worried tone, "I've tried getting a hold of my ex to find out about my kids, but he won't respond. I managed to reach my brother, Jessie. He was at the house and says that they are trapped inside and people are wandering around everywhere. I haven't been able to reach anyone else so far."

Jody gazes at Janet, "I'm so sorry." He pauses, "How about you Lisa?"

Lisa replies, "I wasn't able to get in touch with any of my family. I got in touch with a friend in Dallas. She said that things are very crazy around there. I got in touch with Bryan in California. He said that he was attacked by a couple of infected people and bitten on his arm. He said that he's inside now, but things are still really crazy there too. Rochelle talked to a couple friends in Lubbock and like Marissa said, it's pretty much the same there."

Jody sighs, "How about you Codi?"

Codi sounds really down, "I tried getting in touch with my family, but I didn't get a response. I did get in touch with one of my friends and she says that she is trapped in her house and like the others, there are people out wandering around." She pauses, "Ryan managed to get a hold of his family and they said pretty much the same thing."

Jody nods slightly, "Okay. Shana, how about you?"

Shana looks a little sad as well, "I tried to reach my sister, but wasn't able to get in touch with her. I did get in touch with my mom in Baxter Springs. From what she said, it sounds the same there as everywhere else. She's trapped in her house. I got in touch with a friend in Pittsburg and it was the same thing there."

Jody sighs, "Alright."

Cory speaks up somewhat panicked, "My girlfriend is trapped in her house alone. She hasn't been able to reach her parents at all and I wasn't able to get in touch with my dad." He pauses, "Corie is scared and all alone."

Shana looks at her son, "I know Cory, but you have to try and stay calm until we can figure out what to do."

Cory replies, "But she is all alone."

Jody speaks up, "Its terrible, but your mom is right. We have to think things through before we do anything."

Lisa looks at Jody, "What about you?"

Jody replies calmly, "I tried getting in touch with the two guys from work that was going to go shoot with us today, but I never got a response. I also tried to reach family in Texas, but got no response from any of them. I got in touch with a friend in Tucson and its pretty much the same there as everywhere else." He pauses, "But the one that concerns me the most is when I talked with my friend in Washington State."

Ken questions, "What's going on there?"

Jody sighs, "The town is pretty much the same as everywhere else, however, her husband is in the Navy. According to him, their naval station has been overrun by infected people too."

Mike shakes his head, "That's not good."

Ashley questions, "Why is that?"

Jody replies, "Because, if it's happening at one military installation, its most likely happening at all of them. Which means, the help that the President is promising everyone with by declaring Marshall Law, is not coming."

Silence falls across the room. It's not exactly what any of them was hoping to hear. Each one held out in their own way that things would get better and help would be on its way, but now everyone is starting to realize that they are most likely on their own now.

Jody breaks the silence, "For now, let's just keep talking to people and we will keep the news on in case there are anymore updates. We have plenty of food and water for numerous days. Let's just keep inside and keep as quiet as possible." He pauses, "I would suggest going through your things to see if there is anything essential you might need that you don't have. I went through and inventoried all my things already." He pauses again, "I would also suggest trying to get some rest. I know it won't be easy, but we all must try."

Jody walks out of the living room and heads for his tent in the garage. Lisa and Rochelle head for Jody's room. Marissa and Michael, Jody's brother, head for his room. Shana, Cory, Zach and Tyler head for the master bedroom. Lindsey, Michael, Lindsey's husband, and Daniel head into the family room. Grace and her kids, Ashley, Janet, Codi, Ryan, Mike and Ken all stay in the living room.

Shadow and Lucky watches as everyone is moving, but they stay in the living room.

The rest of the day has been fairly quiet around the house. The news has continued to run the old updates, but nothing new has been announced. Each person is trying to deal with things in their own way. Most of them have continued to contact people, hoping for good news, but knowing that all they are going to hear is a grim reminder of how life is now outside of the house they are in.

As the sun starts to get lower in the sky, everyone finds their way back into the living room area. Cory continues to text with his girlfriend and he is obviously distraught about her being home all alone this whole day.

Jody speaks to everyone, "Well, I think we need to start looking at getting some dinner. Also, if anyone has anything new or positive news, please share."

The room stays silent as they all know that there is no positive news coming.

Mike speaks up, "Shadow is going to need to go outside. How do we want to handle that?"

Codi nods, "Lucky also needs to go out."

Jody thinks for a second, then replies, "I say we take them out at dusk. Lucky can stay in the yard." Jody looks at his dad, "If you want to get Shadow's harness and leash on him, I'll walk with you and I'll take my pistol with me. That way, if there is trouble, we can get him back to the house and I can deal with any infected people that might come around."

Mike nods in agreement, "Sounds good."

Codi nods, "That works."

Jody sighs, "Okay, let's all get something to eat, then we'll take the dogs out."

Shana, Lindsey, Ashley, Janet, Codi, Grace, Marissa and Jody head into the kitchen. Jody gets Shadow's food while the others start looking for stuff to make for dinner. After putting down Shadow's food, Jody walks back into the kitchen. Jody notices the real worried look on Janet's face. Jody walks over to Janet and puts his hand on her shoulder, knowing that it isn't much, but hoping that it gives her some reassurance.

CHAPTER 7

Its nearly 10 pm as everyone gathers in the living room to watch the final news update for the night. Everyone makes room as they hope for the best, but know that the chance of good news is about the same chance any of them have of winning the lottery now.

The television news reporter comes on, "I wish we had better news to report or at least something positive to update our viewers on, but we have received no new information from the White House. It has been several hours now since we received the last update which wasn't much at that time. We will be going off the air for the night, but we will start broadcasting again at 7 am. Our thoughts are with all of you out there. Be safe and good night."

The screen goes blank. Mike picks up the remote and turns the television off.

Jody sighs, "Well, I guess we should do our best to try and get some sleep. I know it won't be easy, but we've got to try."

Nobody says much as everyone other than Ryan, Codi, Mike, Ken and Grace and her kids get up and head for their sleeping locations.

Mike reclines back in his recliner and sets his phone on the table next to his chair. Shadow lays down in the corner behind Mike's recliner. Ken sets his phone and pistol on the table next to the recliner he's in and leans his shotgun against the table. Ken reclines back the recliner and tries to get as comfortable as he can.

Grace and her kids lay down on the air bed in the middle of the living room. Grace let's Ayden and Ariel talk on the phone real quick to say goodnight to their dad, then Grace gets back on the phone and says goodnight. Grace hangs up the phone, then places it on the same table as Ken's stuff. Grace tries her best to get situated in bed with her kids, but finds sleep very hard to come by.

Ryan and Codi lay down on the couch. They both take their pistols off and place them on the end table next to the couch along with their cell phones. They discover that finding sleep is hard to come by even though the couch is more comfortable than they thought it would be. Lucky is laying next to the couch.

Lindsey, Michael, her husband, and Daniel climb into the hide-a-bed in the family room. They wait for Daniel to fall asleep, then Michael, Lindsey's husband, and Lindsey talk quietly.

Michael, Lindsey's husband, whispers, "I can't believe this is happening."

Lindsey replies in a whisper, "I know. Me either."

Michael, Lindsey's husband, continues, "I'm just wondering if we should try to get home."

Lindsey replies, "I don't know. I would like too, but with as much trouble as Jody had just getting home from across town, I don't know if we could make it." She pauses, "I'd hate to try, then get stuck somewhere."

Michael, Lindsey's husband, agrees, "I was thinking that too. As much as I hate not knowing how everyone is or being there, it's too big a risk to try to drive all the way back home. Especially not knowing how bad it really is."

Lindsey agrees with her husband, "I know. Being in here, all we have is the news updates. We really have no idea how bad it is outside."

Michael, Lindsey's husband, sighs, "Yeah, we are eventually going to have to see for ourselves." He pauses, "But that's for another time. I guess we should try and get some rest."

Lindsey sighs, "Yeah, you're right."

Lindsey and Michael, her husband, do their best, but they too like everyone in the living room, find rest hard to come by.

Michael, Jody's brother, and Marissa walk into Michael's bedroom. The two of them set their phones on Michael's computer desk, then they lay down in Michael's bed.

As they get situated, Marissa whispers to Michael, Jody's brother, "Can you believe this is happening?"

Michael, Jody's brother, whispers back, "No, not really."

Marissa sighs, "I hate not knowing how my mom is doing or anyone for that matter."

Michael, Jody's brother, agrees, "I know. Being able to message with them isn't much comfort."

Marissa replies, "Yeah. What's even worse is that we have no idea how bad things are outside."

Michael, Jody's brother, sighs, "Yeah, I know. We are eventually going to have to see for ourselves because the news updates are not really helping anymore."

Marissa agrees, "Ain't that the truth."

Michael, Jody's brother, whispers, "Well, I guess we should try and get some rest. Tomorrow will be here before we know it."

Marissa nods and rolls over. The two of them try their best to fall asleep, but find like everyone else, its not very easy.

Lisa and Rochelle walk into Jody's room. Lisa takes her pistol, magazines and handcuffs off and sets them on the table next to the bed. Lisa messages Bryan one more time, then puts her phone on the table too. Rochelle sets her phone on the table as well. Lisa and Rochelle climb into bed.

Rochelle whispers, "Mom, how is Bryan doing?"

Lisa sighs, "Not good. He said he has a fever now and his whole body is aching. It started after he got bitten by that infected person."

Rochelle replies, "I can't believe all this is happening."

Lisa agrees, "Me either. Its like a living nightmare."

Rochelle questions, looking for some reassurance from her mom, "What do you think will happen tomorrow?"

Lisa replies, "I don't know. The news hasn't been very helpful lately and we have no idea how bad things are outside." She pauses, "I'm sure Jody will have a plan of some kind."

Rochelle sighs, "Yeah, he seems to know what he's talking about."

Lisa agrees, "Yeah he does. Well, let's try to get some sleep."

Rochelle sighs, "Okay mom."

Lisa and Rochelle try to get comfortable, but like all the others, they find sleep very hard to come by.

Ashley sends one last text message to her girlfriend for the night, then puts her phone down next to her head on the sleeping bag. Ashley tries to get comfortable, but her mind can't help but think about her girlfriend and how she has been telling her that she has been feeling worse and worse since getting bitten by the infected person.

Janet is laying on her sleeping bag which is next to Jody's in the tent. Janet sets her phone next to her head on the sleeping bag. Janet is still worried sick about her kids even though she did receive a brief message from her ex earlier saying that they were okay, just trapped in a store.

Jody is laying down on his sleeping bag in his tent in the garage. Jody puts his phone down after receiving his last text messages from his two friends. Jody looks over and sees that Ashley and Janet have fallen asleep. At that moment, Jody hears someone or something approaching the tent. Jody slowly reaches for his pistol. Jody stops when he sees Shana look into the tent.

Shana smiles, "Hey Jo, can I talk to you?"

Jody smiles, " Of course."

Jody gets up and steps outside of the tent.

Shana looks at Jody, "With everything that has been going on, I never got to properly thank you for saving my life and Tyler's today at the store."

Jody shakes his head, "You don't have to thank me. You know there is no way I'd let you or the boys get hurt."

Shana nods, "I know." She pauses, "The world has completely changed now, hasn't it?"

Jody nods slightly, "Yeah, it has." He pauses, "But I'm going to do everything I can to keep us all safe."

Shana smiles, "I know. I'm lucky to have you in my life."

Jody smiles, "Thanks."

Shana smiles, "Thank you Jo, for everything."

Jody nods, "No problem."

Shana sighs, "I guess I better get back to the bedroom and see how the boys are doing."

Jody sighs, "Okay."

Shana leans in and hugs Jody. Shana leans back just a bit, looks at Jody and gets a smile on her face. Jody smiles as Shana turns and walks off. As Shana makes her way through the house, Jody goes back into the tent and lays back down. Jody tries his best to get some rest, but like all the others, he finds rest very hard to come by.

Shana walks into the master bedroom where Cory, Zach and Tyler are at. Tyler is already laying down in bed. Zach finishes reading his last text message and puts his phone on the computer desk. Cory is laying on the floor next to the bed. Zach climbs into bed as Shana puts her phone on the computer desk. Shana lays down in bed with Zach and Tyler. Shana is laying on the edge of the bed near where Cory is laying.

Shana whispers to Cory, "You doing okay?"

Cory shakes his head as he finishes the text message, "Corie is still all alone."

Shana replies, "I know you're worried, but she will be okay."

Cory replies, "I should be there with her."

Shana sighs, "I know you want to be, but that's just not possible right now."

Cory looks at his mom, "We don't even know how bad it is outside anymore because we've been locked inside all day."

Shana replies, "I know we don't, but things were very bad this morning and I can't imagine they've gotten better."

Cory sighs, "Well, we need to check because it might not be too bad out."

Shana sighs, "We can't think about that tonight." She pauses, "I'm sure Jody has thought about that. We just have to be patient. It's too dangerous to just go running off, especially at night."

Cory replies in a not so nice tone, "All he's done is keep us locked up inside. He …"

Shana interrupts, "Jody saved Tyler's life and mine today. If it wasn't for him, some of the others might have gotten hurt too. He's doing his best so I don't want to hear that."

Cory looks at his phone as a text message appears on the screen, "Whatever."

Shana sighs more harshly, "I think we just need to get some sleep now. Don't stay up too late."

Cory doesn't reply as he starts to type his text message. Shana rolls over. Shana, Zach and Tyler try their best to get some sleep as Cory continues to message with his girlfriend.

CHAPTER 8

The sun breaks the eastern horizon as a new day is about to begin in the ever changing world. It's a warm morning, but is more overcast with clouds. Jody wakes at the sound of his alarm on his cell phone. Jody shuts the alarm off and sits up. Jody glances around as if hoping it was all a dream, but knowing that it's not. Jody sees Ashley and Janet still asleep. Jody gets out of his tent, realizing that he fell asleep in his clothes that he wore yesterday.

Jody makes his way into the living room. Jody is greeted at the doorway of the living room and kitchen by Shadow. Jody pets Shadow for a minute.

Jody rubs Shadow's head, "Are you hungry big man?"

Shadow wags his stub tail and butt in excitement. Jody grabs Shadow's food pan and walks into the kitchen. Jody grabs a can of dog food and opens it. Jody grabs a spoon and starts to scoop the food into the pan. Jody scoops about half the can into the pan, then taps the spoon on the edge of the pan. Shadow starts to get more excited. The sound of the spoon on the pan wakes the others up that are in the garage, living room and family room.

Jody walks into the living room, finds a place on the floor and sets the pan down. Shadow quickly starts to devour the food. Jody looks around and sees Ryan, Codi,

Ken, Mike, Grace and her kids beginning to wake up. Jody notices that everyone in the living room also slept in their regular clothes.

Jody looks at Mike, "Hey dad, I'm going to get the others up if you want to turn on the news."

Jody walks back into the garage and over to the tent. Ashley and Janet are both sitting up trying to stretch out some of the stiffness. Jody notices that they too slept in their clothes from yesterday.

Jody whispers to Ashley and Janet, "We are going to check out the news if you want to come to the living room."

Ashley and Janet both nod and Janet looks at Jody and smiles. Jody smiles back, then walks off to the family room. Jody carefully approaches Lindsey and Michael, Lindsey's husband.

Jody whispers to Lindsey, "Hey, we are going to check out the news if you want to come into the living room."

Lindsey and Michael, her husband, both nod. Jody makes his way down the hallway to his brother's room. Jody goes into his brother's room and carefully wakes up Michael, his brother, and Marissa.

Jody whispers to them, "Hey, its morning and we are going to check the news."

Michael, Jody's brother, and Marissa both nod. Jody makes his way to his room next. Jody walks in and carefully wakes up Lisa and Rochelle.

Jody whispers to them, "Hey, its morning and we are going to check the news."

Lisa and Rochelle both nod. Jody makes his way over to the master bedroom. Jody carefully wakes up Shana.

Jody whispers to Shana, "Hey girl, its morning and we are going to check the news."

Shana nods. As everyone starts to get up and move around, Jody makes his way back to the living room. Jody smiles as he noticed everyone in the house slept in their regular clothes. Everyone starts making their way into the living room except for Daniel and Tyler.

Shana walks up next to Jody, "I'm going to let Ty sleep more."

Lindsey nods, "Yeah, I'm letting Daniel sleep more too."

Jody nods, "Okay then, let's see what the news has to say."

Mike picks up the remote from the table by his recliner and turns the television on. All that comes up is a blank screen.

Mike gets a puzzled look, "Huh, let me try another station."

Mike flips the television over to another news station, but the screen remains blank.

Jody speaks up, "This isn't good."

Grace replies, "Maybe the cable is out."

Mike nods and flips the channel to a station that would have re-run programming on. The music video channel comes on the television.

Ken shakes his head, "I'd have to agree, this doesn't look good."

Jody looks at his brother, "Hey man, check your TV."

Michael, Jody's brother, walks off to his room. Everyone just sits and watches as Mike flips to the different local and national news station channels only to find them all blank.

Michael, Jody's brother, walks back in, "My room is the same."

Jody sighs, "Great. It looks like we've lost all the news stations."

Ashley questions, "So, what do we do now?"

Jody is quiet for a minute.

Lindsey looks at Jody, "Well, what now?"

Jody realizes everyone is looking at him and waiting for him to tell them what to do next.

Jody sighs, "Everyone get in touch with whoever you can and find out if they have any news." He pauses, "We'll meet back in here in about 30 minutes, okay."

Everyone nods and starts to either reach for their phones or head to their sleeping room to get their phones. Jody heads for the kitchen to get some food for Lucky.

After about thirty minutes has passed, everyone starts making their way back into the living room. Daniel and Tyler are both still in bed. Jody is the last to walk in.

Jody speaks, "I'll start and we'll just go around the room." He pauses, "My friends in Arizona and Washington State say it's the same there. The news is out and there are still people wandering around. I couldn't reach anyone else."

Shana goes next, "I was only able to reach one person and she said the same thing, no news and people wandering around."

Ken nods, "I was able to get in touch with a friend and he said the same thing."

Lisa speaks up, "I wasn't able to get in touch with Bryan again. He was bitten yesterday and was feeling bad all day. My friend in Texas said the same thing, no news."

Marissa nods in agreement, "The friend I talked to said the same thing, all the news is out and people are wandering everywhere."

Michael, Jody's brother, speaks up, "My friend in Florida and Texas both said the same thing."

Mike sighs, "Sandra said it's the same in Joplin where she's at. I couldn't reach Nancy."

Grace is next, "I got in touch with someone in Galena and it's the same there too."

Codi speaks up while petting Lucky, "Same with the people Ryan and I talked to. No news and people wandering around the streets."

Janet speaks next with worry in her voice, "I was talking with my ex when all of a sudden he must have dropped the phone. All I heard was screaming and yelling, then gunshots. After that the phone went dead."

Lindsey speaks up, "The people Michael and I got in touch with all said the same thing, no news at all."

Ashley finally speaks, "I couldn't get in touch with my girlfriend anymore. She was also bitten yesterday and wasn't feeling very well. The friend I did reach said the same as everyone else."

Jody looks around and can see the look of sadness on everyone's face, not to mention a little bit of fear in some of their eyes.

Cory speaks up, "Corie is still trapped in her house all alone."

Shana looks at her oldest son, "I know it's hard, but at least she is okay at the moment."

Cory sighs, "She's scared and hasn't heard from her parents."

Jody speaks up, "I'm sorry, but nothing has changed. We still have to take our time and figure out what to do."

Cory steps away as his phone goes off again. Jody looks back to the living room.

Lisa questions, "So, what now?"

Jody thinks for a second, "First, we just keep talking to people out there."

Michael, Lindsey's husband, speaks up, "We have to do more than that. We have no news and no way of knowing what is going on out there."

Jody nods, "I know. We will turn on a radio and see if we can find a station still broadcasting. Also, we need to think about eating breakfast." He pauses and looks at his dad, "We need to take Shadow outside so he can use the bathroom." Jody glances over to Codi, "And I'm sure Lucky will need to go out too."

Codi nods, "Yeah."

Mike nods, "Definitely. I'm sure he has to go."

Ken speaks up, "Even if we find a radio station, we still won't know exactly what its like outside unless we see for ourselves."

Jody nods in agreement, "I know, but I'm going to save that as a last case scenario." He pauses, "Also, seeing that all of you are still in your clothes from yesterday like I am, I think we need to start a bathing schedule."

Lindsey nods, "Yes! That would be wonderful."

Jody smiles, " Yes it will be. We will start with the kids first, then the women and finally the men." Jody looks at Grace, "Can Ayden and Ariel bathe together?"

Grace nods, "They may not like it, but they will if I tell them to."

Jody smiles, "Okay. The two of them can go first in the main bathroom." Jody looks at Shana, "Ty can shower first in the bathroom in the master bedroom. Once he's done, Zach can shower next."

Jody looks over to Lindsey, "As soon as Grace's kids are done, Daniel can get a bath in the master bathroom."

Lindsey nods, "Okay."

Jody sighs, "Well, while the kids are getting cleaned up, the rest of us will keep talking to people. On the showers and baths, we need to keep them as short as possible, okay."

Everyone nods in agreement.

Jody speaks again, "Okay, let's get going."

Jody walks off for the kitchen. Shana heads for the master bedroom and Grace starts to get her kids ready. Everyone else heads off to where they were sleeping.

As soon as all the kids are finished getting cleaned up, everyone makes their way back to the living room. Zach is wearing a white t-shirt, faded blue jeans and tennis shoes. Tyler is wearing a gray t-shirt, faded blue jeans and tennis shoes now. Ayden is now wearing a blue t-shirt, blue jeans and tennis shoes. Ariel is dressed in a cute pink outfit and pink sandals. Daniel is now wearing a gray t-shirt, blue jeans and his tennis shoes.

Jody walks in and notices everyone is there, "Okay, does anyone have anything new to report?"

Nobody speaks up as everyone is glancing around the room at each other in hopes of someone speaking up.

Jody nods, "I wish I could say the radio was better, but I've been unable to find any stations broadcasting. I'm going to keep at it though." He pauses, "Okay, dad and I are going to take Shadow outside."

Marissa questions, "What's next on the showers?"

Jody nods, "All the kids are done so now the women will go next. I'd give it a little bit before starting so the water heater can keep the water warm." He pauses, "How about Ashley and Rochelle start, then Grace and Lindsey next. After them, Janet and Codi, then Lisa and Shana." He pauses again, "Then Marissa will go and that will be all the females. Cory can start for the guys. I'm sure we'll be back inside before Grace and Lindsey are done. Sound good to everyone?"

Everyone in the room nods in agreement.

Jody looks at his dad and Codi, "Well, let's get Shadow and Lucky outside and the rest of you can get to it."

Jody, Codi and Mike head for the kitchen with Shadow and Lucky hot on their tail as everyone else breaks up again to their respective rooms.

CHAPTER 9

Jody, Mike and Shadow are out in the field behind the fenced in back yard of the house. Codi and Lucky have stayed in the back yard. Shadow is wearing his harness and leash. Mike is walking with Shadow holding the leash and Jody is walking next to Mike. Jody is carrying his Glock 17 pistol in his right hand. Shadow seems oblivious to everything going on as he sniffs the ground.

Mike looks at Jody, "Do you see anything?"

Jody continues to look around, "Nothing." He pauses, "What puzzles me is that if there were other people in the houses around here you'd think they would see us and maybe try to make contact."

Mike replies, "Maybe we are the only ones left out here. With where our neighborhood is at, we are away from town and being this started on a Saturday, people may have been out and about."

Jody nods while continuing to look around, "True. Being on the outskirts of town, we are lucky yet not so lucky at the same time."

Mike looks at Jody a little puzzled, "What do you mean?"

Jody replies staying ever vigilant, "Being away from town, we don't have to worry as much about infected people finding us, at least not for awhile." He pauses,

"However, being this far from town we can't see how things are going and how bad its gotten."

Mike nods his head, "You know, the time is coming when a trip to town is going to be needed."

Jody nods slightly, "I know. The trip to town will be dangerous, but I'm more concerned with what we'll find out and what we will eventually have to do."

Mike looks at Jody, "What do you mean?"

Jody sighs, "If everything is shut down because the infected people are everywhere, that means certain things are eventually going to happen."

Mike questions, "Like what?"

Jody continues to glance around, "Like the electricity and water will eventually stop because nobody is at the stations to keep them running. Our food is going to run out and so will the sources near us." He pauses, "And no doubt the infected people will eventually make it out here and we will be trapped inside the house."

Mike looks at Jody puzzled, "What are you saying?"

Jody looks at his dad for the first time, "That soon we are going to have to abandon the house and start moving elsewhere."

Mike doesn't really know what to say in response to what his son just said. Mike, Jody and Shadow continue to walk as the conversation dies down.

Grace and Lindsey have just finished their showers when Mike, Jody and Shadow come in from their walk. Lisa and Shana start to gather their things for their shower. Mike grabs a dog treat and walks into the living room with Shadow right behind him. Jody walks into the living room a few seconds later after putting up his pistol.

Ashley is sitting on the couch with the radio trying to find any station that might be broadcasting. She is wearing a blue, short sleeve v-neck top, khaki shorts and brown sandals. Rochelle is sitting next to Ashley keeping an eye on Ayden and Ariel while Grace was in the shower. Rochelle now has on a blue short-sleeved top, faded blue jeans and tennis shoes. Ken is sitting in his recliner eating a sandwich. Grace walks into the living room now wearing a yellow t-shirt, gray shorts and black sandals. Lindsey is right behind Grace and she is now wearing a gray t-shirt, black shorts and black sandals.

Michael, Lindsey's husband, and Daniel make their way into the living room as does Michael, Jody's brother, and Marissa. Mike sets the treat on the floor and Shadow quickly starts to eat it. Lisa and Shana walk into the living room with their change of clothes in their hands.

Janet is sitting on the couch still in the same clothes from the day before, awaiting her turn to get cleaned up and changed. Janet is sending messages on her phone, but everyone can tell by the look on her face, none of those messages are getting a response.

Jody looks at Ashley, "Anything new?"

Ashley shakes her head and replies with a sad tone, "No. Still nothing on the radio."

Ken looks at Jody, "Anything outside?"

Jody sighs, "Nothing. No people, no animals and no noises."

Michael, Lindsey's husband, questions, "So, what do we do now?"

Jody replies, "We continue talking to people and rotating the showers."

Janet and Codi head off to get their showers done as everyone else heads off to their respective rooms.

The rest of the morning has been fairly quiet around the house. After Shana and Lisa finished their showers, Marissa and Cory waited an hour, then took their showers. Everyone has been trying to stay in touch with people and keeping their cell phones charged. The kids have passed the time playing with Shadow and Lucky or playing video games. Cory has remained distant, in a constant worry about his girlfriend.

Its around 1 pm now and Jody calls everyone to the living room. Shana walks in now wearing a white t-shirt, faded blue jeans and tennis shoes. Cory is right behind her in his black t-shirt, blue jeans and tennis shoes. Marissa walks in next wearing a green t-shirt, faded black jeans and tennis shoes. Lisa walks in now wearing a red, short sleeve top, faded blue jeans and tennis shoes, and she is followed by Rochelle.

Codi is sitting on the couch petting Lucky. Codi is now wearing a red t-shirt, blue jeans and tennis shoes. Janet is sitting on the couch again, messaging on her phone and still hoping for a reply. Janet is now wearing a black and gray thin strapped tank top, black cloth Capri pants and her sandals. Janet's face grows even more concerned.

After a few more seconds, the rest of the group makes it into the living room. Everyone finds a place to either sit or stand. Its crowded, but they have all started to get accustomed to that feeling.

Jody questions, "So, anyone heard anything new from anybody?"

As before, there is silence in the room. At this point, they all know that no more news is coming.

Lisa looks at Jody, "Anything on the radio?"

Jody shakes his head, "Nope."

Cory speaks up, "So what are we going to do? Just sit here and do nothing? We don't even know if there is anything going on outside."

Jody looks at Cory, "I know it's hard, but this is the crucial time in survival. Where people always fail in these situations is at the beginning because everything is new to them and potentially dangerous." He pauses, "That's when people make irrational decisions and that is when people get killed."

Cory is silent. Jody looks around the room at everyone's face as he can tell his words were somewhat of a shock to most everyone except Ken and his dad.

Mike can see the look on everyone's face and decides to say something, "Look everyone, I know this is a difficult time and just sitting around seems like we are doing nothing, but that's not the case. We have to take time to plan our moves carefully." He pauses, "We all know that we are cutoff from the outside world right now, but we have everything we need to survive here in this house right now." He pauses again, "Jody and I talked outside and we both know that there is going to come a time that a trip into town is going to be needed. However, today is not that time. We are all still overwhelmed by what is going on and none of us are completely rational right now. Not to mention, every single one of us is already tired and its just now afternoon."

Ken nods his head, "He's right. I don't like sitting here any more than any of you, but none of us are ready to go out there and face what we most likely will have to face with a trip to town." He pauses and looks at Jody, "You've done good so far little buddy. So, let us know what is next."

Jody nods and gives a slight smile, "Thanks. For now we just continue with the showers. All that is left is us guys. Ken and Ryan, you go first, then the two Michaels will go. After them, dad and I will go."

Jody looks around the room and can see that everyone is a little more at ease, but still very apprehensive.

Jody sighs, "I'm thinking about a trip into town tomorrow."

Everyone in the room looks at Jody, not expecting what they heard.

Jody continues, "However, there is a lot of planning to be done before that can happen. I'm not going to make any promises, but that is a tentative idea for now." He pauses, "As for now, let's get back to what we've been doing, okay."

Everyone in the room nods in agreement. Jody heads for his tent in the garage as everyone else makes their way to wherever they plan on spending their afternoon.

The afternoon grinds by as everyone does what they can to pass the time and try to keep their minds off what might be going on with their loved ones. Even though everyone is obviously tired, no one sleeps. Jody has been in his tent thinking about a plan for a trip to town. Ken, Ryan, Mike and both Michaels have finished their showers. Jody is the last person needing to clean up. Seeing that it is nearly 6 pm, Jody gets up and makes his way for the living room.

Jody walks into the living room as Shadow and Lucky are finishing their dinner. Ashley, Grace and her kids are sitting on their airbed. Janet, Codi, Ryan, Lindsey, Daniel and Michael, Lindsey's husband, who is now wearing a blue t-shirt, faded blue jeans and tennis shoes, are all sitting on the couch. Ryan is now wearing a white t-shirt, light colored blue jeans, tennis shoes and his baseball cap. Ken, having cleaned up but is still in the same clothes since he doesn't have any spares, is sitting in his recliner. Mike, now wearing a gray t-shirt, blue jeans and tennis shoes, is sitting in his recliner.

Jody walks to the edge of the hallway, "Hey everyone, let's talk in the living room."

Lisa and Rochelle walk out of Jody's bedroom. Shana and Cory walk out of the master bedroom while Zach and Tyler walk over to Jody's bedroom to play some video games. Marissa and Michael, Jody's brother, who is now wearing a maroon t-shirt, camouflage pajama pants and house shoes, walks out of Michael's room.

Everyone finds a place in the living room and tries to get as comfortable as they can. They each know that this meeting is most likely going to be like the others.

Jody starts, "I know this sounds like a broken record, but if anyone has anything new, let's hear it."

As usual, the room is silent.

Jody nods, "I've been going over some ideas for the trip to town, but nothing is solid yet." He pauses, "I'll work on it some more after dad and I take Shadow out and I get cleaned up."

Lindsey questions, "Since the backyard is fenced in, do you think we could step outside and get some fresh air while Codi has Lucky outside, if we stay quiet?"

Grace speaks up, "What if one of those people are out there and they spot us?"

Jody replies, "Dad and I are already going to be in the field. I don't see why not, as long as everyone is quiet while they're outside. Once we come in from the walk, then everyone can come back inside." He pauses, "If you don't want to step outside, obviously you don't have to."

Ken nods, "I think some fresh air would be nice."

Jody nods, "Ken, why don't you take your pistol outside too. Just in case." He pauses, "The others that have guns can take them outside too if you want. I just wanted to make sure at least one person had a gun other than me."

Mike leans forward in his recliner, "Well, let's get that big boy outside for his walk then."

Shadow's ears perk up when he hears the word walk. Everyone smiles as Shadow starts wagging his stub tail and butt in excitement.

Its nearly 11 pm now as Jody is laying in his tent, still going over ideas for the trip to town. Jody is wearing his OD green USMC sweat shirt and sweat pants. Janet and Ashley are both asleep. Just about everyone else has finally passed out from sheer exhaustion, except this time they have all changed into their sleeping attire except for Ken.

Jody sighs as he contemplates what to do, then he hears someone walk into the garage. Jody looks over as Shana looks into his tent. Shana is wearing a black tank top and black sweat shorts.

Shana smiles, "Can I come in Jo?"

Jody smiles, "Of course."

Shana walks into the tent as Jody sits up. Shana sits down next to him. The two of them are as quiet as they can be so they don't wake up Janet and Ashley.

Jody questions, "Is everything okay?"

Shana nods, "Yeah, the boys are all asleep." She pauses, "How are you doing?"

Jody is kind of puzzled by the question, "I'm okay."

Shana sighs, "I know this has been stressful for you. You feel like you're responsible for everyone and I have to admit, we all have kind of thrust that responsibility on you."

Jody smiles, "I'm okay, really." He pauses, "But yes, I'm worried about everyone here."

Shana smiles, "I know you are, but that's just you. I really appreciate everything you've done for us."

Jody puts his hand on Shana's back, "Of course. I wouldn't let anything happen to any of you."

Shana smiles her beautiful smile again, "I know you wouldn't. As much as it hurts not knowing about my family, I'm thankful that we have you."

Jody smiles, "Thank you."

Shana sighs, "Well, I just wanted to check on you. I better get some rest. I'm exhausted."

Jody nods, "Me too."

Shana turns to Jody and wraps her arms around him in a hug. Jody hugs Shana back. Shana gets up and they smile at each other again.

Shana whispers, "Goodnight Jo."

Jody whispers back, "Goodnight Shana."

Shana makes her way through the house as quietly as possible. Shana walks into the master bedroom to find all the boys sleeping away. Shana carefully maneuvers around Cory and climbs into bed. Shana is nearly asleep by the time her head rests on the pillow. However, Cory opens his eyes, slowly grabs his cell phone and checks the time.

CHAPTER 10

Cory has been laying quietly, pretending to be asleep. Cory continues to look at his cell phone to check the time. Once his cell phone shows that the time is 2am, Cory decides to make his move feeling everyone in the house should be good and asleep. Cory slides out of his sleeping bag as quietly as he can and reveals that he has been fully dressed the whole time.

Cory makes his way over to the walk-in closet and picks up his backpack without a sound. Cory comes back into the bedroom with a small piece of paper in his hand and his backpack slung over his shoulder. Cory looks around the desk until he spots the keys to his mom's car. Cory gently picks up the keys, holding them all together so they won't make any noise.

Cory looks around and finds his mom's cell phone. Cory places the small piece of paper on Shana's cell phone, then looks at his mom and two brothers laying in bed. Cory feels saddened by leaving them, but he can't take the thought of his girlfriend being alone anymore. Cory turns and ever so quietly, makes his way out of the bedroom and down the hallway.

Every step to Cory sounds like it is echoing through the entire house, but he has managed to stay completely quiet. Cory reaches the front door and looks around to make sure no one is up. Cory gently and as quietly as he can, unlocks the front door. Cory carefully turns the handle and opens the door. He carefully opens the screen door as to not make any noise. Cory steps out of the house and quietly shuts the front door and screen door behind him.

Cory looks around to make sure there is no one around outside, then he quickly makes his way over to Shana's car. Cory gently unlocks and opens the driver's door. Cory quickly stops and glances around as he swore he heard something. Cory leans in and sets his backpack in the passenger's seat. Cory pulls his head back out of the car and glances around again, thinking he heard something.

Once Cory is sure everything is okay, he climbs into the car behind the wheel. Cory carefully pulls the door closed, just hard enough for it to latch and shut the inside light off. Cory buckles his seatbelt and places the key in the ignition. Cory takes a deep breath as he knows there is no turning back now. Cory turns the ignition and starts the car.

Cory quickly puts the car in drive, flips the headlights on and pulls away from the curb. Cory speeds up some and heads over the hill, leaving the house and his family behind him.

Its just after 7am as Shana wakes up from her first night of real sleep in a long time. Shana knows that she was exhausted, but didn't realize how much. Shana looks over and sees Tyler and Zach still sleeping. Shana carefully gets out of bed so she won't wake them. Shana notices that Cory is not sleeping next to the bed. Shana thinks nothing of it at the moment, figuring he already got up and is somewhere in the house.

Shana goes to the bathroom, then washes her face. Shana walks back into the bedroom and looks at her boys again. Shana wonders what is going to happen and can only hope that nothing will happen to them. Shana walks over to the desk to get her cell phone. Shana sees a piece of paper on top of her cell phone and she picks it up. Shana reads the small note. It says, "I'm sorry mom. I had to go after Corie.".

Shana stands there in shock for a moment, not believing what she just read. That is when Shana notices her keys are not on the desk next to her phone. Shana starts to get a panicked look as she rushes out of the bedroom with the note in her hand.

Shana rushes down the hallway and stops at the front door. Shana sees that the front door is unlocked and her heart sinks. Without thinking, Shana opens the front door and hurries outside into the front yard. It is a little cooler this morning with clouds covering most of the sky and a good, steady blowing breeze.

Shana notices her car is gone, "Cory!"

Jody springs awake from hearing Shana's voice and knows that she is outside from where her voice projected from. Jody grabs his pistol and hurries for the front door. Everyone else in the house also hears Shana and they start to stir awake.

Shana looks around frantically, "Cory!"

Jody bursts out the front door, "Shana! What are you doing?!"

Jody runs up to Shana and grabs her arm. Shana is startled by Jody.

Shana looks at Jody and speaks frantically, "He's gone!"

Jody glances around to make sure no one is around, "Who's gone? What are you talking about?"

Shana's breathing is rapid, "Cory. He left."

Shana holds the note out to Jody. Jody takes the note and reads it.

Jody speaks under his breath, "Damn it." He looks at Shana, "Come on, we have to get back inside before we are seen."

Jody pulls on Shana's arm and she reluctantly follows him back into the house. As Jody and Shana come back inside, Jody sees Ken standing there with his pistol in his hand. Jody shuts and locks the front door.

Ken questions, "What's going on?"

Jody lets out a breath, "Cory took off last night. He went after his girlfriend." He looks at Shana, "Try to calm down some. Get your phone and see if you can reach him."

Shana swallows hard and nods. Shana heads for the bedroom. Everyone else in the house, having heard all the commotion is making their way to the living room.

Lindsey questions, "What's going on Jody?"

Jody glances around and notices Lisa, Rochelle, Michael, Jody's brother, and Marissa coming down the hallway. Michael, Lindsey's husband, walks up next to Lindsey. Grace sits up and so does Ryan and Codi. Ashley and Janet walk in from the kitchen.

Jody glances at everyone, "Cory took off last night after we all went to bed. He went after his girlfriend."

Janet responds automatically, "Oh my God."

Jody sighs, "Everybody just relax. Shana is going to try and get a hold of him."

Jody walks towards the garage to put his pistol away. Everyone else heads back towards their rooms to get their phones. Shana comes walking down the hallway with a very sad look on her face. Shana walks by everyone, looking for Jody. When she doesn't see him in the living room, Shana heads for the kitchen next.

Shana walks into the kitchen and sees Jody at the kitchen table, "Jody."

Jody looks over to Shana, "Yeah. Were you able to reach him?"

Shana walks over next to Jody, "No."

Shana starts to get tears in her eyes. Jody stands up and gives Shana a hug.

Jody whispers, "I'm sorry." He pauses, "I wish I could do something."

Shana replies with sadness, "He's gone. I've lost him."

Jody doesn't know what to say. All Jody can do is stand there and keep hugging Shana.

Everyone has made their way into the living room except for Daniel, Tyler and Zach. Everyone has been talking amongst themselves, waiting for Jody and Shana. After a short while, Jody and Shana come walking in from the kitchen.

Jody whispers to Shana, "Why don't you go check on Ty and Zach, ok."

Shana nods and heads for the master bedroom. Jody sighs and shakes his head as he watches Shana walk off.

Michael, Lindsey's husband, questions, "What are we going to do?"

Jody looks over at him, "What do you mean?"

Michael, Lindsey's husband, replies, "Are you going to try and find him?"

Jody shakes his head, "No."

Everyone kind of looks a little shocked by Jody's answer.

Jody continues, "Look, she can't get in touch with him. We don't know when he left or which direction he went." He pauses, "If he left just a few hours ago, he could be all the way to Kansas City by now. Its too dangerous to go looking for him with no information."

Mike looks at his son, "So, what are we going to do then?"

Grace speaks up, "Yeah, we can't just sit here. We have no idea what's going on."

Ashley nods, "We have to see what's going on outside. I can't even get in touch with anyone now."

Lindsey nods, "Me either."

Michael, Lindsey's husband, chimes in, "Like it or not, we need to see for ourselves. We are going to have to make a trip outside."

Janet chimes in with a worried voice, "I just know something bad has happened to my kids."

Codi nods as well, "We can't reach anyone either."

Everyone starts nodding.

Lisa speaks up, looking at Jody, "They have a good point."

Ken sighs and looks at Jody, "As dangerous as it is, I don't see another choice little buddy."

Jody nods, "I know." He pauses, "And after this morning, now more than ever, we need to see what's going on."

Michael, Jody's brother, looks at Jody, "What do you have in mind?"

Jody sighs, "I've thought about it a lot. Everyone grab something to drink, use the bathroom or whatever. Meet back here in thirty minutes and we'll go over everything. Okay?"

Everyone nods and Jody walks off towards his bedroom. Everyone starts breaking up to go get cleaned up, use the bathroom and get something to eat or drink.

After half an hour, everyone is back in the living room, still dressed in their sleeping clothes. Jody walks in. Jody is wearing a gray t-shirt, faded blue jeans, brown belt and brown hiking shoes. On his right hip is his fully loaded

Glock 17 in a black, clip on paddle holster and on his left hip is a black, clip on double magazine holder with his two spare magazines, fully loaded. Jody has his pocket knife clipped to his back pocket. Everyone sees how Jody is dressed and each one of them knows that its starting to get serious now.

Jody speaks, "First, I think the kids should go into the other room." He looks at Rochelle, "Can you watch them for us?"

Rochelle nods, "Of course."

Grace takes Ayden and Ariel into the family room, then returns. Lindsey takes Daniel into the family room, then returns. Zach and Tyler decide to go back to the master bedroom.

Once everyone is back, Jody speaks, "Okay. First thing is, we have to set a few ground rules. Some of this may come as a shock, but we are talking about survival now."

Everyone in the room nods and waits to hear what Jody has to say.

Jody continues, "We all have certain skills that will come in handy. I would say that when it comes to survival situations and guns, Ken and I are probably the most knowledgeable and trained, having done it before." He pauses, "Anyone disagree?"

No one in the room says anything.

Jody continues, "Having said that, first rule will be that those with the top skills in a certain area will not travel out together unless the whole group is going." He pauses, "For example, Ken and I will not go out together unless the whole group is going. Understand?"

Everyone in the room nods.

Jody takes a breath, "Also, if anyone goes outside and gets infected, they are not allowed to return to the group. That is not negotiable. Understand what that means?"

Ken nods, "Yeah. If you become infected, you are on your own. I agree totally."

Everyone in the room is still quiet.

Jody nods at Ken and continues, "We can go over some more rules after the trip to town. However, for this first trip, I don't think everyone should go. Its too dangerous because we will be walking into a completely unknown situation."

Lisa questions, "What did you have in mind?"

Jody replies, "I think it will be best if I take three people with me."

Marissa looks at Jody, "Only four. That's not very many if you run into trouble."

Jody nods, "I know. My main concern is being able to move quickly and quietly. A small group will accomplish that best."

Mike nods at his son, "I see your point."

Jody sighs, "Since I'm going, that means three of you will go with me and one of them can't be Ken."

Grace questions, "So, how are we going to decide who goes?"

Jody replies, "I've thought about that quite a bit. For the first trip, there are a few people I'd like to exclude for certain reasons." He pauses, "Dad is best with Shadow so I want him to stay here. Same with Codi because of Lucky. Grace will stay because she is the only parent for Ayden and Ariel and they are not completely use to the rest of us yet. Lindsey will stay because of Daniel and given the recent incident, Shana will stay with Zach and Ty." He pauses again, "Finally, Rochelle will stay so the kids can get more familiar with her because I want her to help take care of the kids. For those I didn't name, well, that means you're eligible to go. Any questions?"

Michael, Jody's brother, looks at Jody, "Makes sense to me."

Ashley sighs, "So, how do we decide who's going with you?"

Jody pulls a notepad and pen out of his back pocket, "Everyone left will write their name on a piece of paper and we'll draw three names out of a hat. Unless anyone has a better idea."

Michael, Lindsey's husband, nods, "That sounds fair to me."

Jody passes around the notepad and pen. Ryan, Janet, Ashley, Marissa, Lisa and both Michaels write their names on a piece of paper and fold them up. Michael, Jody's brother, goes to his room and returns with a baseball cap. Jody drops the pieces of paper in the cap. Michael, Jody's brother, shakes the cap for a few seconds, then holds the cap out to his brother. Jody reaches in and grabs the first piece of paper.

Jody unfolds the paper and reads the name, "Lisa."

Lisa nods. Jody hands Lisa the piece of paper with her name on it. Jody reaches back into the cap and takes out another folded piece of paper.

Jody unfolds the paper and reads the name, "Ashley."

Ashley sighs and gets a shocked look, "Okay."

Jody walks over and hands Ashley the piece of paper with her name on it, "It'll be okay, don't worry."

Ashley smiles at Jody.

Jody reaches in the cap and pulls out the last name.

Jody unfolds the piece of paper, "Janet."

Janet gets a surprised look and sounds worried, "Okay."

Jody smiles at Janet, "It'll be okay babe."

Something in Jody's voice just reassures Janet to the point that all she can do is smile back at Jody.

Jody turns back to the room, "Okay. As Ashley, Janet and Lisa are getting ready, the rest of you make up a quick list of things you need other than food and water. We'll try to get what we can. If you use tobacco products, I'd suggest quitting, but put them down and if we can make it by one of the smoke shops, we will." He pauses and looks at his watch, "We will meet back in here at 9 am, okay?"

Everyone in the room nods.

Jody speaks again, "One more thing." He looks at Lisa, "Definitely take your gun." He looks over to Ashley and Janet, "If you two want a gun to take, I can get you one."

Ashley shakes her head, "No thanks, I'm okay with the two of you having guns."

Janet sighs, "I'm not that good with them so I'm okay with it just being the two of you."

Jody smiles and nods, "Okay. Back here at 9 am everyone."

Jody turns and walks off towards the kitchen as everyone heads their separate ways to get their lists made up. Lisa, Janet and Ashley head off to grab some clothes to change into as well.

CHAPTER 11

As everyone is finishing up eating and getting ready, Jody is in the living room talking to Ken and his dad. They are keeping their voices down so others don't really hear them.

Jody looks at Ken, "While I'm gone, there is a 20 gauge shotgun in the master bedroom closet. Will you get it cleaned up. I have a feeling we are going to need it."

Ken nods, "Sure thing."

Jody glances around, "My cleaning gear is in the bottom drawer of my plastic storage unit in my bedroom."

Ken replies, "I'll get it done."

Jody looks at his dad, "If you want to, start thinking of someplace locally that we can head to and camp at until we can come up with a more permanent plan on where to go." He pauses, "If my feeling is right, we won't be able to stay here much longer."

Mike nods his head, "Okay."

About that time, everyone starts making their way back to the living room. Everyone except for Ashley, Janet and Lisa are still in their sleeping attire. Janet is wearing blue jeans, a tight fitting white t-shirt that shows off her amazing body and her black and white tennis shoes. Ashley is now wearing a white tank top underneath a black tank top, blue jeans and tennis shoes. Lisa is wearing her black long sleeve t-shirt, khaki tactical pants with black belt and black tactical boots. Lisa has her pistol on her left hip, two extra pistol magazines on her right hip and her Tac Force Rescue Knife clipped in her front, left pocket.

Once everyone is in the room, Jody speaks, "Ashley and Janet, if each of you want to collect half the lists and hang onto those for us, that would be great."

Ashley nods, "Sure."

Janet nods as well, "No problem."

Ashley and Janet go around the room and gather all the lists.

Jody speaks again, "While we're gone, just sit tight and keep trying to reach people if you want. I'm hoping we'll only be gone a few hours."

Michael, Jody's brother, questions, "Where are you planning to go?"

Jody replies, "I figure on heading out to the highway and taking it around to the road that runs back into the fairgrounds. That way if we are spotted they won't know exactly where we came from." He pauses, "From there, I hope to make it to the small grocery store by the railroad tracks and the smoke shop by the casino. That way we can get as many supplies as possible." He pauses again, "After that, play it by ear. Look around some if we don't encounter any problems."

Marissa questions, "What if you do encounter problems?"

Jody sighs, "We'll deal with them and try to get back here as fast as we can. Our phones will be on silent, but we'll keep you all updated as much as possible." He looks at Ashley, "I'll have you taking care of that."

Ashley nods, "Okay."

Jody lets out a deep breath, "Well, I guess it's that time. Ready to go ladies?"

Lisa and Ashley both nod.

Janet sighs, "Not really, but I guess the time has come."

Jody smiles at Janet, "Don't worry too much."

Jody unlocks and opens the front door. Jody, Lisa, Janet and Ashley walk outside and Mike shuts the door behind them and locks it. The four of them walk over to Jody's Explorer. Jody gets in behind the wheel. Lisa gets in the passenger's seat. Janet gets in the back seat behind Jody and Ashley gets in the back seat behind Lisa. Jody starts up his Explorer and backs out of the driveway, puts it in drive and slowly heads off over the hill.

Jody, Janet, Ashley and Lisa are looking around carefully as they have made it out to the highway and are about to the turn to head back towards the softball fields and fairgrounds. So far, they have passed some abandoned vehicles in the little bit of neighborhood they passed through and along the highway, but they have yet to see any people. A fact which has each of them wondering what they will find when they finally reach town.

Jody slows the Explorer down and makes a right turn onto a narrow, two lane road. Jody accelerates up to 30 mph, but keeps the vehicle at that speed. The four of them continue to look around, but once again, they fail to see any other people.

Jody speaks to the Lisa, Janet and Ashley, "When we get to the end of this road, we are going to stop for a moment and look around. I want to make absolutely sure there are no infected people around before we continue on."

Lisa nods, "Okay."

Ashley speaks up, "I wonder, if there are other people hiding out like us, will they try to flag us down if they see us."

Janet nods, "I was thinking that too."

Jody replies, "I would think so, but we still have to be real careful, even with other survivors."

Ashley questions, "Why is that?"

Jody keeps glancing around, "First, we don't want them mistaking us for being infected and shoot us if they have guns." He pauses, "Second, people act differently in these kind of situations. They may look to steal from us or kidnap us for what they think we have or possibly want to do things worse than that."

Janet questions, "Like what?"

Jody sighs, "I'm not going to get explicit, but if some men see attractive women like the three of you and assume they might not find any others, well, I think you get the picture as to what I'm saying."

Ashley questions, "Do you really think they would do that?"

Lisa nods, "I hadn't really thought about that, but now that you mention it, I wouldn't put it pass people to do any of what you said, including taking advantage of a woman."

Jody starts to slow the vehicle down as they near the softball fields on their right and they see the fairgrounds ahead of them, "Let's just be extra careful out here."

Lisa, Janet and Ashley continue to look around as they get nearly up next to the softball fields. They all see numerous cars parked at the softball fields.

Jody glances around, "Do you see anyone at the softball parks?"

Lisa looks closely, "All I see are cars, no people."

Ashley concurs, "Yeah, I don't see anyone."

Janet agrees, "Nope. Nothing except cars."

Jody slows the vehicle down as the road is about to end at a two way intersection where they can only turn left into town or right to head back towards the house. Jody stops the Explorer at the intersection and puts it in park.

Jody glances in the mirrors, "Well, this is it. Once we turn left, we'll be headed into town. First thing we'll run into is the park and the bridge over the river. I'll want to take it slow there before we cross the bridge, just to make sure there are no infected people walking around the park."

Lisa, Janet and Ashley all nod and reply roughly at the same time, "Okay."

After making sure there is no one around, Jody puts the Explorer back in drive, turns left and accelerates up to 25 mph. Jody has decided to go real slow, just in case they spot someone or something. They continue down the road and pass the large buildings outside the fairgrounds on their right and gas station on their left. Jody, Janet, Lisa and Ashley continue to look around. They see some abandoned cars, but no people. As they slowly move forward towards the bridge over the river, the park appears on the right.

Jody swerves to the middle of the road to go around an abandoned car on the shoulder of the road. The four of them can see a few more abandoned vehicles in the park. As they near the bridge, Jody slows to a stop and puts the Explorer in park. The four of them see a couple of vehicles on the bridge.

Jody speaks to Ashley, Janet and Lisa, "Since this bridge is a choke point, I'm going to cross it on foot first to make sure we can get around those cars. Janet, you get behind the wheel." He pauses, "Once I get to the other side, I'll look around and make sure it's clear of people. If so, I'll motion for you to drive on across. Okay?"

Janet nods her head, "Okay."

Jody speaks again, "I also want to tell you all. The door where Ashley is sitting can only be opened from the outside."

Jody gets out of the Explorer. Janet gets out of the back seat, shuts the door and gets in the driver's seat and shuts the door behind her. Jody starts to walk across the bridge. Jody scans around as he walks down the middle of the bridge. Janet, Ashley and Lisa watch intently from the Explorer.

As Jody nears the first vehicle that is in the opposite lane of traffic, his hand slowly lowers to his pistol. Jody carefully approaches the car as his right hand grips his pistol. Jody cautiously walks up to the driver's door and looks in the car. Jody finds the car to be empty and the driver's window is down.

Jody glances around quickly to make sure no one came up on the bridge while his focus was on the car. After a few seconds, Jody continues on towards the next car that is facing away from him in their lane of traffic. As Jody starts to get near the back of the car, he notices the driver's door is slightly open. Jody lowers his hand to his pistol again as he reaches the trunk of the car.

Jody lowers his body into a crouch by the trunk of the car. Janet, Ashley and Lisa all hold their breath as they think Jody has spotted something. Jody slowly makes his way towards the driver's door. As he gets closer, Jody notices blood smeared along the rear driver's side door. Jody stops at the rear driver's side door and slowly raises up so he can look into the backseat.

Jody finds the backseat to be empty so he raises up some more until he is almost completely standing. Jody looks into the front seats. Jody sees a purse in the passenger's floor board. Jody reaches out and slowly pulls the driver's door open some more, being sure not to touch any of the blood around the door handle. Jody moves forward and looks in the car. Jody sees more blood in the driver's seat and on the steering wheel.

Jody gently puts the car door back to where it was and glances back at the Explorer. Janet, Ashley and Lisa look at each other, wondering if Jody found something. Jody continues on towards the end of the bridge which is about twenty more feet. Jody continues to look around to make sure he doesn't spot anyone. Once he reaches the far side of the bridge, Jody kneels down on his right knee.

Using the skills he was taught in the Marine Corps, Jody scans the park to his right. Jody looks for anything that might give away movement. As he scans, Jody listens intently. Jody sees some cars around the park area, but no people. Jody sees what looks like it could be a person laying next to a car, but it is way too far into the park for him to be certain. Once he is certain the park is clear, Jody turns his attention back to the road and buildings ahead. Jody looks around with the same scan, trying to spot anyone or anything that could be a problem.

What seems like an eternity to Janet, Ashley and Lisa, they finally see Jody stand up at the far end of the bridge. Jody waves for them to come on across with his left hand. Janet puts the Explorer in drive and slowly accelerates. Lisa and Ashley continue to look around as they pass the first car. Janet moves the Explorer over into the oncoming traffic lane so she can get around the second car. As they pass the second car, Lisa and Ashley look at the side of the vehicle and see the blood smeared down it.

Janet slows the Explorer to a stop when they reach where Jody is standing. Janet puts the vehicle in park and opens the driver's door. Janet starts to get out.

Jody holds up his hand, "Just slide over. All we have to do is go down this slight downward bending curve to the left and the grocery store is just on the other side of that fire station. Just a few hundred feet or so."

Janet slides over to the middle and Jody climbs in behind the wheel. It's a little crowded in the front seat, but not uncomfortable as Janet feels Jody's pistol against her left hip. Jody shuts the door, puts the vehicle in drive and starts to accelerate. Ashley, Janet, Lisa and Jody glance around as they pass the building and first street to their right.

Jody looks over at the parking lot of the grocery store about half a block up on the left. They continue on and Jody slows the Explorer down and stops as they pass the fire station and get to the parking lot entrance of the small grocery store. They see two cars parked in the parking lot, but neither one is parked in the spots in front of the doors. Jody pulls the Explorer into the parking lot.

Jody speaks to the others, "I'm going to back into the parking spot in front of the door. Ashley, go ahead and text the others to let them know we made it this far."

Ashley nods and pulls out her cell phone. As Ashley sends the text message, Jody backs the Explorer into the parking spot directly in front of the front doors.

CHAPTER 12

Ken is sitting at the kitchen table. He has the 20 gauge pump shotgun taken apart and is meticulously cleaning it, making sure every piece is good. Mike is also in the kitchen with a map of Oklahoma. He is going over the map and thinking of the best options for where they can go when they decide to leave the house. Ryan, Codi, Rochelle, Lindsey, Michael, Lindsey's husband, Daniel, Grace and her kids are in the living room. They are passing the time playing with Shadow and Lucky and the dogs are enjoying the attention.

Michael, Jody's brother, and Marissa are in Michael's room. They are talking some about everything that has been going on. Michael, Jody's brother, is on his computer searching the internet, which still happens to be running for the time being, for any information about what is going on outside their little world right now. Shana, Zach and Tyler are in Jody's room. Shana is watching the boys play video games, hoping that it will take their mind off what has been going on and that Cory has left. Shana continues to try and reach Cory, but doesn't get a response from him.

Lindsey is sitting on the couch watching Daniel petting Shadow when her phone receives an incoming text message. Lindsey picks up her phone and reads the text message.

Grace questions, "What is it?"

Lindsey replies, "It's from Ashley. They've made it to the grocery store. She says that they haven't seen another person yet."

Michael, Lindsey's husband, replies to what his wife just said, "Well, I guess that is a good thing."

Grace doesn't sound so optimistic, "I don't know. Is it?" She pauses, "I mean, good that they haven't seen any infected people, but then not so good cause they haven't seen any other people either. What if we're the only ones left?"

Lindsey sighs, "I don't know. I guess we'll figure that out when they get back." She gets up, "I'm going to go tell the others."

Lindsey walks into the kitchen and shares the news with Mike and Ken, then she starts towards the bedrooms. Lindsey stops at Michael's room and tells Michael, Jody's brother, and Marissa, then walks to Jody's room and tells Shana, Zach and Tyler. As Lindsey walks back to the living room, everyone else is thinking what Grace had mentioned. What if they are the only ones left?

Jody, Janet, Lisa and Ashley are sitting in the Explorer which is backed into the parking space directly in front of the front door of the small grocery store. Jody has put the vehicle in park, but has left the engine running.

Jody speaks while glancing around, "I'll leave the car running for now. Ashley and Janet, you two stay in the vehicle for now. Lisa, you'll come with me and stay at the front doors of the store to help keep a watch outside, but be close enough to help me inside if I need it."

Ashley questions, "What are you going to do?"

Jody replies, "I'm going to go through the store and make sure no one is inside." He pauses, "Once I'm sure its okay, Ashley, you and Janet will come inside and load supplies while Lisa stands watch up front and I'll keep watch inside the store. Okay?"

Ashley and Janet both nod and reply, "Okay."

Lisa speaks up, "You're going to clear the building by yourself?"

Jody nods, "Yeah. It's not very big inside. You'll be able to see me almost anywhere in the store from the door."

Lisa nods, "Okay."

Jody and Lisa get out of the Explorer and close the doors behind them. Janet slides over behind the wheel. Jody and Lisa glance around as they slowly walk over to the doors of the grocery store. Lisa stands to the left of the doors as Jody stands to the right of them. Jody leans over and peeks inside through the glass door. Once he is sure he doesn't see anyone, Jody opens the door and steps inside. Lisa quickly steps inside too before the door closes.

Lisa can see what Jody is talking about now. The cash register counter is right in front of them. To the left of the register are two isles. Directly to their right is a fountain drink station. There is one isle behind the square shaped register area, then the next isle back are the coolers full of drinks and stuff which is the back of the store. There are a few isles running parallel to the main doors on the right side of the register area. On the right side of the store is the butcher meat area. In the back right corner looks to be how to get to the back area of the store where the office and storage area is.

Jody whispers to Lisa, "Okay, wait here. I won't be long."

Lisa nods and whispers back, "Okay."

Jody walks to the left hand side of the store first. He has his hand on his pistol, but leaves it in the holster. Lisa watches Jody as he walks down the two isles on the left of the register. Lisa can see the entire inside of the store except behind the meat counter on the right. Jody walks down the aisle behind the register, then back up the isle on the right of the register, looking down each isle as he passes them, which brings him back to where Lisa is standing.

Jody whispers, "That's pretty much the main floor. Now I'm going to check behind the meat counter and the back storage area."

Lisa nods and whispers back, "Be careful, I can't see back there from here."

Jody nods as he glances out the front doors real quick. Janet is sitting in the driver's seat, looking around very intently to make sure she doesn't spot anyone that might be headed their way. Ashley continues to watch out from the backseat too. Jody sighs and starts over to the meat section. Jody looks through the glass counter first, then walks around the side of the counter. Jody doesn't see anyone or anything behind the meat counter. Jody looks inside the little storage area behind the meat counter, but no one is in there.

Jody comes back out from behind the meat counter and walks towards the back, right of the store. There is a doorway there which leads into the back of the store where there is an office and a storage room. Jody stands off to the left of the doorway. Jody can smell something coming from the back of the store now that he didn't smell when they walked in.

Jody quickly peeks around the corner first. Once he is certain he didn't see anything, Jody slides around the corner which puts him in the storage room. It's a small room with the open door to the office on the right side of the room and something else Jody quickly notices in the back of the room. The back door of the storage room which leads outside is standing open. The odor is a little stronger now. Jody figures it is coming from the office to his right.

Jody moves along the wall to the office door. The odor is much stronger now. Jody knows in his gut what he is about to find. Jody looks around the corner of the doorway and sees the body of a man laying on the floor. Blood is all over the room and the body is laying against the door, holding it open. Jody now spots a small, dried blood trail from the office to the back door.

Jody takes a closer look at the body. From the best Jody can tell, it appears something has been eating on the body. There is missing flesh on both arms and the neck area. From the best Jody can tell, it appears that the stomach area has been ripped open and the internal organs pulled out. Jody instinctively covers his nose and mouth with his left hand to try and block some of the odor. Jody stares at the body for a moment because he has seen dead bodies before, but nothing like this.

Not wanting to touch the body in case it is infected, Jody leaves it laying where it's at. Jody slowly walks over to the open back door. Jody listens for a few seconds and when he's sure he doesn't hear anything, Jody looks out the door. Jody glances around and sees the blood trail lead off towards the railroad tracks which is about a hundred feet from the store. Jody pulls the back door closed and locks it.

Jody is confident that the store is empty of any possible infected people or anyone else for that matter. Jody starts to walk back towards the front of the store.

Ken starts putting the shotgun back together while Mike is still looking over the different possibilities on the map and making notes on paper.

Ken looks at Mike, "Have you come up with anything yet?"

Mike nods while writing, "Yeah, a few options. Just writing down the different options and routes to take so we can talk about them when Jody gets back."

Ken nods, "Nice."

Ken finishes putting the shotgun together and pumps it a couple times to listen to the action.

Mike looks at Ken, "Is it good?"

Ken nods and smiles, "Like new. It'll get the job done for sure."

Mike smiles, "It sure will."

Ken stands up with the shotgun, "I just hope things are going as well for Jody and the others out there."

Mike nods and returns to his notes, "Me too."

Ken heads off to put the shotgun back in the closet and Mike continues working on his plans.

Jody makes it back to the front doors where Lisa is standing watch.

Lisa looks at Jody, "Everything good?"

Jody nods, "Yep."

Jody steps outside and walks over to the driver's door of the Explorer. Jody motions for Janet and Ashley to get out of the vehicle. Janet opens the door and climbs out. Ashley slides across to the other rear door and gets out.

Janet looks at Jody, "What's up?"

Jody reaches in the vehicle, shuts the engine off and pulls the key slightly out of the ignition so the alarm stops going off, "The store is clear. So, its time to get the supplies."

Jody presses the unlock button to unlock the rest of the doors. Janet and Ashley walk over to the front doors of the store while Jody opens the back hatch of the Explorer, then Jody walks over to Lisa, Janet and Ashley.

Jody speaks, "Okay. Lisa, you keep watch while Ashley, Janet and I go inside and get the supplies."

Lisa nods, "Okay."

Jody, Janet and Ashley walk into the store and look around.

Jody speaks, "We'll start with the general stuff like water, dry and canned food, then we'll get the lists out and get the individual stuff if they have it here."

Ashley and Janet nod and reply at the same time, "Sounds good to me."

Janet and Ashley head for the bottled water first while Jody keeps an eye on them. Ashley and Janet each grab as much as they can carry and head for the door. Lisa holds the door open with her body while keeping watch outside. Janet and Ashley make several trips back and forth with the water until they have emptied all the cases out of the store. The back of the Explorer is about a third of the way full with just water.

Jody waits for a minute while Janet and Ashley catch their breath, "Okay, let's grab the sacks from behind the counter and load them up with food."

Ashley replies while catching her breath, "Okay."

Janet nods while catching her breath, "Sounds good."

Jody walks behind the counter and sets all the sacks up on the counter. Janet and Ashley each grab a sack and head for the canned goods. Jody continues to watch the inside of the store. The two ladies load up the sacks and carry them to the car, then head back to do it all over again. It takes a little time, but Ashley and Janet fill nearly every sack with canned goods, dry food and non-perishable foods. Once finished loading the food, the back of the Explorer is nearly two thirds full now.

Jody walks over by Lisa, "Have you seen anything yet?"

Lisa shakes her head, "Nothing."

Ashley walks up and starts to catch her breath, "Whew, I wish I was in better shape."

Janet smiles, "Me too."

Jody smiles, "You two are doing a great job."

Ashley smiles, "Thanks."

Janet gazes at Jody, "Thank you."

Jody takes a deep breath, "Okay, let's get the lists out and get what we can from the lists here."

Ashley pulls out her half of the lists, "Let's do it."

Janet pulls out her half of the lists, "I'm ready."

Jody, Janet and Ashley head back in the store. Janet and Ashley each look at their first list. Janet and Ashley start wandering around look for the items while Jody keeps a watch inside the store. Janet and Ashley each find a few items and take them to the Explorer, then return to the store. While Lisa remains on watch, Ashley and Janet make their way through the lists until they are each on their last one. Ashley wanders around looking for something, but is unable to find it.

Ashley walks up to Janet, "I'm having trouble finding this."

Janet looks at the list and glances around.

Janet notices the doorway in the back of the store leading into the storage area, "Maybe back there."

Janet and Ashley start walking that way. Jody doesn't see Ashley and Janet heading into the back of the store.

Ashley steps into the storage room and sniffs the air, "What is that?"

Janet gets a sick look on her face, "I don't know, but it smells terrible."

Janet and Ashley walk further into the room looking for the item on the list. Janet and Ashley are standing with their backs to the office door. Ashley sniffs the air again, then turns around. Ashley sees the half eaten body laying on the floor just inside the office.

Ashley screams, "Oh my God!"

Janet spins around and sees the body and screams. Jody and Lisa both hear Ashley and Janet scream. Jody and Lisa glance around and not seeing Ashley and Janet in the store, they both run for the back of the store. Jody and Lisa rush into the storage room and see Ashley and Janet over by the far wall, obviously shaken up. Jody starts over to Ashley and Janet. Lisa looks around the room and spots the body laying on the office floor.

Lisa's eyes open wide in shock, "What the hell!?"

Jody looks back over to Lisa as he stops next to Ashley and Janet, "Don't touch the body."

Jody turns back and puts his left arm around Ashley and his right arm around Janet, "Its okay." He pauses, "I'm so sorry. I should have told you two not to come back here."

Janet just buries her face in Jody's shoulder. Jody runs his hand up and down Janet's back.

Ashley is shaking still, "What in the world is going on?"

Jody rubs his hand up and down on Ashley's back, "I wish I knew."

Lisa speaks up, "It looks like he was eaten by something."

Jody looks at Lisa, then back to Ashley and Janet, "We've got enough here. Let's go."

Lisa starts walking towards the front door, still disturbed by what she just saw. Jody walks with Janet and Ashley. The four of them get back to the front of the store. Lisa walks out first and looks around to make sure nothing was alerted to them. Jody, Janet and Ashley walk out a few seconds later. Lisa and Ashley head around to the passenger's side and Janet heads around to the driver's side while Jody shuts the back of the Explorer. The back end of the Explorer is nearly full now.

Ashley hops in the back passenger's seat and shuts the door. Lisa gets in the passenger's seat and shuts the door.

Janet gets in the seat behind the driver's seat and closes the door. Jody climbs in the driver's seat with two bottles of water in his hands.

Jody hands a bottle of water to Ashley, "Here, you and Janet drink some of this." He hands the other bottle to Lisa, "Here you go."

Ashley opens the bottle with her hands still a little shaky and drinks some of the water. After a few drinks, Ashley hands the bottle to Janet. Janet starts to drink some water. Lisa opens her bottle and starts to drink some water.

Jody looks at the three ladies, "You all okay?"

Lisa puts the cap back on the bottle and hands it to Jody, "Yeah, I'm fine."

Ashley replies still a little shaken, "I'll be okay."

Janet is quiet for a minute, "Yeah."

Jody can tell that something is wrong in Janet's voice.

Jody finishes taking a drink, "Okay then. Ashley, if you want to get your phone and text them to let them know we are done at the store and headed to the smoke shop, we'll get headed that way."

Ashley nods and pulls out her phone. Jody hands the bottle back to Lisa. Jody starts the Explorer and glances around.

CHAPTER 13

Ken and Mike are in the kitchen. The two of them are looking over the map of Oklahoma and the different notes Mike made earlier. Ken and Mike are weighing the pros and cons of each possible location and the course which they must take to travel there.

Michael, Jody's brother, and Marissa are in Michael's room. The two of them are talking and playing a game on Michael's computer to try and pass the time. Michael, Jody's brother, and Marissa each are waiting on their turn to clean up for the day.

Grace, Ayden and Ariel are in the main bathroom. Grace is giving Ayden and Ariel a bath. Codi, Ryan, Rochelle, Lindsey, Daniel and Michael, Lindsey's husband, are in the living room with Shadow and Lucky. Lindsey and Michael, her husband, are talking while Daniel is playing tug of war with Shadow and one of his squeaker toys. Rochelle is sending text messages on her phone in hopes of hearing something back.

Shana and Tyler are in Jody's room playing a video game. Tyler has already taken his shower and Zach is now in the spare bathroom taking his shower. Shana seems a little distant while playing the game with Tyler. Shana's mind wonders about Cory and what has happened to him.

Shana's mind also wonders about Jody and if she will get to see him again.

About that time, Lindsey's phone receives a text message. Lindsey picks up her phone and reads the message. A smile comes to Lindsey's face.

Michael, Lindsey's husband, questions, "What is it?"

Lindsey replies, "They are finished at the grocery store and they are headed to the smoke shop now."

Rochelle looks over, "Thank goodness."

Lindsey stands up, "I'm going to go tell the others."

Lindsey heads for the kitchen first to start informing everyone of the update.

Jody puts the Explorer in drive and turns left out of the grocery store parking lot. He drives about a hundred feet then turns right on the street that heads to the casino and smoke shop. Jody accelerates to 25 mph as they pass the small car dealership. Once they pass the car lot, they enter a residential area.

Ashley, Janet, Lisa and Jody all scan the houses and yards to see if they spot any infected people or other survivors. The four of them look down the first side street they pass, but do not see anyone. One other thing the four of them notice is that there are no animals either. The Explorer passes the next side street and it is the same as the others the four of them have seen so far.

Ashley shakes her head, "Its like everyone just disappeared."

Lisa nods in agreement, "I know. Its strange that not only have we not seen any people, but no dogs or cats either."

Jody glances around as they pass the next side street, "I know and that worries me. A part of me was hoping that we would at least see other people."

Janet questions, "What do you think has happened to them?"

Jody replies as they pass another empty side street, "I don't know, but I don't have a good feeling about this."

Lisa sighs, "Me either."

As the four of them continue on, they see the parking lot of the casino a couple blocks ahead. Jody continues to look around as they pass the last side street before the casino. Jody slows the Explorer to a stop when they reach the next street. If they go straight, they will cross the street and pull into the casino parking lot. If they turn right, they can go a block before the street dead ends and they will have to turn left or right again.

Jody looks left, "See that building at the four way stop there. That's the smoke shop."

Lisa, Janet and Ashley look left and see the building Jody is talking about at the end of the block on the right hand side. Jody turns the Explorer left onto the new street and starts for the smoke shop. As the Explorer passes the backside of the casino, the four of them see the parking lot on their right. The four of them notice about fifteen cars on the parking lot.

Jody pulls the Explorer to a stop at the intersection. The smoke shop is directly to their right. It is a long, narrow building that is raised up about six feet or so. The narrow end facing them has a set of stairs that leads up to the employee entrance door. Jody turns the Explorer right around the corner and the four of them see a long ramp walkway and another set of stairs on the front of the smoke shop. At the top of the stairs is the front door and its closed.

Jody stops as he nears the stairs. Jody glances around, then backs the Explorer into a parking spot next to the stairs. Jody puts the Explorer in park, but leaves it running.

Ashley, Janet and Lisa glance around again to make sure no one is around.

Jody speaks, "Just like the store. Ashley, you and Janet stay in the vehicle. Lisa, you'll stay at the front door. I'll go in and check the building out. Once its clear, Ashley and Janet will come in and get the stuff while Lisa stands guard." He pauses, "Sound good?"

Lisa, Janet and Ashley all nod.

Jody opens the driver's door, "Ashley, go ahead and let them know we made it here."

Ashley nods as Jody and Lisa get out of the Explorer, "Okay."

Ashley pulls out her phone and starts typing the text message.

Ken and Mike are still in the kitchen looking over the plans for when they might have to leave the house. Marissa and Michael, Jody's brother, are still in Michael's room playing on the computer. Grace, Ayden and Ariel are back in the living room now with Codi, Ryan, Lindsey, Michael, Lindsey's husband, and Daniel. Shadow has made his way into the kitchen and is laying down under the kitchen table while Lucky is still in the living room.

Tyler and Zach are in Jody's room. Tyler is still playing a video game on the play station and Zach is on Jody's computer. Rochelle is in the main bathroom getting cleaned up and Shana is finishing getting cleaned up in the bathroom in the master bedroom.

Shana gets out of the shower and dries herself off. Shana steps over to the sink area and gets dressed. Shana looks at her phone as if she is expecting a message. Shana looks in the mirror and sees the sad look upon her face.

Shana reaches down and picks up her phone. Shana pulls up Cory's name and sends another message to him.

Shana puts her phone down, "I hope you're okay son."

About that time, Shana hears Lindsey's voice from the doorway of the bedroom, "Shana, they made it to the smoke shop okay."

Shana looks back in the mirror and allows a slight smile to come to her face as she continues to hope for Jody, Janet, Ashley and Lisa's safe return.

Jody and Lisa are standing next to the front door of the smoke shop.

Jody looks at Lisa, "I hope its unlocked."

Lisa continues to look around as Jody reaches for the handle. Jody grabs the handle and tries to turn the knob. The knob completes its turn and the door clicks open. Jody pushes the door open, but quickly pulls his hand back. The door swings half open and stays there.

Jody looks at Lisa, "Okay, keep an eye out. This shouldn't take me long."

Lisa nods and scans the area. Jody glances inside quickly, puts his hand on his pistol and glides around the corner of the doorway and into the smoke shop.

Right in front of Jody is the glass counter area. Behind the counter on the right is a doorway into an office. The store extends about 25 feet to his right and about 50 feet to his left. It is one big open shop and Jody doesn't see anyone inside. Jody carefully makes his way over to the office door and opens it. Jody steps into the office and doesn't see anyone. He notices the small storage area beyond the office where they keep extra supplies. Jody makes his way to the storage area and looks inside. It too is empty. Jody walks through the storage area to the side door that leads to the outside. Jody makes sure that the door is locked. Once he is sure the building is clear, Jody walks back out and over to the front door where Lisa is waiting.

Jody speaks, "The shop is clear. I'm going to get Janet and Ashley so we can get the supplies."

Lisa nods, "Okay. I'll keep making sure no one is around."

Jody walks halfway down the steps so Janet and Ashley can see him. Jody motions to Janet and Ashley to come on over to him. Janet reaches up and turns the Explorer off and pulls the key out just far enough so the alarm doesn't sound when she opens the door. Janet and Ashley get out of the vehicle and head up the stairs to where Jody and Lisa are at by the front door.

Jody looks at Janet and Ashley, "If you two want to get the lists out, we'll get as much as we can."

Janet and Ashley pull the lists out of their pockets. Janet and Ashley follow Jody into the store while Lisa remains at the doorway. Jody grabs the sacks from behind the counter and Ashley reads off the first product. The three of them search the store until they find what they are looking for. Once they are done with Ashley's lists, they start on Janet's lists. Jody, Janet and Ashley load up everything on the lists into a few sacks. Once they are done, Jody, Janet and Ashley walk over to the front door.

Jody speaks to Lisa, "Anything?"

Lisa shakes her head, "Nope."

Jody nods, "Okay. Ashley and Janet, let's get this stuff in the backseat."

Jody, Janet and Ashley grab all the sacks and walk down the stairs to the Explorer. Jody opens the rear passenger's side door and sets his sacks inside. Ashley places her sacks in the backseat, then Janet does the same. Jody shuts the door, looks up at Lisa and motions for her to come back down to the vehicle.

Jody looks at the back seat, "It is getting filled up some back there. Janet, why don't you sit up front in the middle. Ashley, you can sit behind the driver's seat.

Ashley goes around to the driver's side, climbs in the back seat and closes the door. Janet goes around to the driver's side and gets in the front seat. Janet slides over to the middle as Lisa gets in the passenger's seat and shuts the door. Jody gets in the driver's seat and shuts the door.

Ashley questions, "What now?"

Jody sighs, "I've been thinking about that. We have a couple of options."

Janet questions, "What are they?"

Jody replies, "We got nearly everything except a few items and the one thing that we need to get which is some spare clothes for Ken."

Lisa questions, "Is there any place close for that?"

Jody shakes his head, "Not really. The closest place is on Main Street in the middle of the old downtown area." He pauses, "Trying to get there could be dangerous."

Ashley speaks up, "Part of the reason we came into town is to find out what has been going on. I'd like to avoid danger as much as anyone, but we really haven't learned much more than we already knew."

Lisa nods, "She's got a point. All we've seen is the edge of town. Going into town might give us a better idea of what has happened."

Jody sighs, "Are you three sure? No telling what we might run into."

Lisa nods, "Yeah. I'm sure."

Janet nods too, "As much as I don't want to, I think we need to."

Jody nods, "Okay then, Ashley, send them a message to let them know what we're doing." He pauses, "We need to stay extra sharp because we might have to get out of there in a hurry."

Lisa, Janet and Ashley all nod. Jody starts up the Explorer as Ashley pulls out her phone. Ashley types the text message as Jody takes a deep breath and puts the Explorer in drive.

CHAPTER 14

Ken and Mike are still in the kitchen going over the plans and waiting for their turn to clean up. Shadow is laying under the kitchen table at Mike's feet. Marissa is finishing getting cleaned up in the bathroom in the master bedroom. Michael, Jody's brother, is finishing cleaning up in the master bathroom. Shana, Tyler and Zach are in Jody's bedroom. Zach is on Jody's computer while Shana and Tyler are playing a video game.

Codi, Ryan, Grace, Ayden, Ariel, Rochelle, Lindsey, Daniel and Michael, Lindsey's husband, are all in the living room talking. Everyone in the house is wondering how much longer before they get their next update from Ashley.

Codi looks up at Lindsey while petting Lucky, "I would think that we should be getting an update soon."

Rochelle sighs, "I hope so."

Michael, Lindsey's husband, speaks up, "I'm sure they're okay. With as quiet as its been, we'd hear if something has happened."

Rochelle looks at Michael, Lindsey's husband, "How?"

Michael, Lindsey's husband, replies, "We would hear the distant gunshots from them."

Grace nods, "True."

Lindsey adds, "Let's just hope then that we don't hear that."

Rochelle questions, "Do you think they'll head back after the smoke shop?"

Lindsey sighs, "Who knows. I guess it depends on if they got everything or not and if they have found out enough about what has been going on."

Grace sighs, "I doubt they will since they've only been to a grocery store and smoke shop because I know they are trying to get some clothes for Ken also."

About that time, Lindsey's phone goes off. Lindsey picks up her phone and reads the message. Lindsey smiles for a moment, then loses the smile as she reads the last of the message.

Rochelle questions, "What is it?"

Lindsey replies, "They're done at the smoke shop."

Michael, Lindsey's husband, quickly interjects, "What are they doing now?"

Lindsey sighs, "They are heading into the historical downtown section of Main Street to a clothing store."

Grace shakes her head, "Wow, that's going to be kind of dangerous heading into downtown."

Rochelle just sits quietly at the news.

Lindsey looks at Rochelle, "Don't worry, I'm sure they'll be fine. Jody wouldn't have decided on that if he wasn't sure it was safe to try."

Rochelle sighs and nods.

Lindsey stands up, "I'm going to go tell everyone else."

Lindsey heads for the kitchen first to start passing the news.

Jody turns the Explorer left out of the smoke shop parking spot and onto the street. Jody stops at the four way stop, then turns right onto the street and starts to accelerate. The Explorer passes a large storage building surrounded by a fence topped with barbwire on the right and on the left is an open lot, then a building about the same length but twice as wide as the smoke shop.

Jody, Janet, Ashley and Lisa keep glancing around, but they don't see anyone. They pass through the next intersection and they can see the main road another block in front of them. It is one of the main roads that runs east and west thru town and leads out to the toll booth at the interstate. Jody starts to slow the Explorer down as they near the main road. As the Explorer pulls to a stop, there is a small office building on the left and a local fast food place on the right.

Jody, Janet, Ashley and Lisa look left and right. They see numerous abandoned vehicles spread out along the main road and in some of the parking lots, but they don't see any people. Jody sighs, then turns the Explorer left onto the road and accelerates up to 25 mph. They pass a gas station and a Lube-N-Go, then they pass a donut shop and a store that sells alcohol. Jody weaves around a couple of abandoned cars as they near the train tracks.

Jody slows down a little as they cross over the train tracks. The stoplight just on the other side of the train tracks is red and Jody stops the Explorer. Jody glances right which is the truck route that trucks have to use in order to go around the downtown area. Janet, Ashley and Lisa continue to glance around, but again, all they see are some abandoned vehicles.

The light turns green and Jody pushes down on the accelerator. They pass a drive thru pizza place and a storage unit place, then they reach the first street after the truck route. Jody weaves around a car as Janet, Ashley and Lisa continue to look around. They continue straight and pass a real estate place on their left and an office building on their right. Jody weaves around another vehicle as they pass thru the next intersection.

Jody, Janet, Ashley and Lisa see a couple of stoplights coming up. Jody starts to slow down some as they approach the first stoplight which is a one way street. The light stays green as they drive thru the intersection and continue on towards the next stoplight. The stoplight ahead of them turns red as there are a couple cars in the intersection that looks like they collided with each other. Jody stops the Explorer at the intersection.

Jody sighs, "This is Main Street." He pauses, "Have any of you seen anything yet?"

Ashley shakes her head, "Not me."

Lisa sighs, "Me neither."

Janet sighs obviously with her mind thinking of other things as well, "Nope."

Jody glances around, "Neither have I."

Jody turns the Explorer right onto Main Street, "Its about four blocks."

The four of them continue to look around as they make their way slowly north on Main Street. They pass different businesses. There are some abandoned vehicles parked along the road and a few in the road. Jody swerves around a car as they near the first intersection. Jody glances left and right as they pass thru the intersection.

Janet, Ashley and Lisa continue to look around, but they still see nothing. They continue on and near the next intersection as they pass the Friendship House. They pass thru the next intersection where there is a large bank on their left and the American Legion Hall on their right. Jody weaves around two cars in the road, having to slow down some to do so.

Jody speeds the Explorer back up to 25 mph as they are nearing the next intersection which is a four way stop. Jody pulls the Explorer to a stop when they reach the intersection. The four of them look around, but once again, all they see are vehicles. Jody accelerates thru the intersection, but stays at about 20 mph.

Jody speaks, "It's about two thirds the way up on the left."

Jody weaves around another car and slows to a stop. Janet, Ashley and Lisa look to the left and they see the clothing store. It has an all glass front. Jody pulls forward some, then backs the Explorer up to the sidewalk in front of the store.

Jody puts the Explorer in park, "We'll do things a little different here. I don't want to take too much time in having to try and clear the whole store being that we are in the downtown area." He pauses, "Ashley, Janet and I will all go in and get the clothes. Lisa, just hang out here on the sidewalk between the vehicle and the front doors."

Lisa nods, "Okay."

Jody turns the Explorer off and pulls the keys out of the ignition just enough to keep the alarm from going off. Jody, Janet, Ashley and Lisa get out and of the Explorer. The four of them make their way over to the sidewalk and look around.

Ashley sighs, "It's so eerily quiet."

Jody nods, "Yes it is."

Lisa shakes her head, "It's like a ghost town. Like everyone just disappeared."

Janet shakes her head, "I don't like this at all."

Jody nods, "Let's just get the clothes and get out of here. Ashley go ahead and let them know we are here."

Ashley pulls out her phone as Jody, Janet and Lisa glance around one more time.

Ken is in the main bathroom getting cleaned up. Mike is getting cleaned up in the bathroom in the master bedroom. Michael, Jody's brother, and Marissa are in Michael's bedroom. Shana, Tyler and Zach are in Jody's bedroom. Rochelle, Grace, Ayden and Ariel are in the kitchen now getting some food for lunch. Codi, Ryan, Lindsey, Daniel and Michael, Lindsey's husband, are in the living room having already made their lunch. Shadow is sitting and staring at Lindsey while she is eating. From his size, its obvious that Shadow likes food. Lucky is sitting by Codi.

Michael, Lindsey's husband, looks at his wife, "Its been a little bit since they left the smoke shop. I hope nothing has happened to them or the car."

Lindsey swallows her bite of food, "I'm sure they're okay. I bet they are just going slower than usual to stay safe."

Michael, Lindsey's husband, nods, "Yeah, I'm sure your right."

Lindsey, Michael, her husband, and Daniel continue to eat.

Shana and Tyler finish the game they are playing.

Shana sets the controller down, "Are you boys getting hungry?"

Zach turns around, "I am."

Tyler nods and replies with a little sadder tone, "Yeah."

Shana looks at Tyler, "Are you okay Ty?"

Tyler looks at Shana, "Mom, when is Jody going to get back?"

Shana pauses for a second having not expected that question, then she answers, "I don't know. I'm sure it will be soon."

Tyler replies, "I hope so."

Shana gets a little sadder sounding, "Me too."

About that time, everyone hears Lindsey's phone go off and they know it must be the next update. Michael, Jody's brother, and Marissa make their way towards the living room as do Shana, Tyler and Zach. About the time they all walk into the living room, Lindsey puts her phone down.

Lindsey looks up at everyone, "They made it to the clothing store okay. They said that all they've seen so far are abandoned vehicles, but no people or animals."

Marissa sighs, "That's just weird."

Shana, Tyler and Zach start towards the kitchen as Marissa and Michael, Jody's brother, head back to his bedroom.

CHAPTER 15

Jody, Janet and Ashley start towards the front door. Lisa is standing on the sidewalk between the front door to the store and the Explorer.

Jody glances over to Lisa, "If you see anything, come get us as quick as you can."

Lisa nods, "Okay."

Jody walks over to the door, "Just stay with me you two. We'll get the stuff as fast as we can."

Ashley and Janet both nod and reply, "Okay."

Jody grabs the handle of the door and pulls on it, hoping it is unlocked so they don't have to break the glass and create a bunch of noise. The door slides open and Jody steps inside. Janet and Ashley step in right behind Jody and the door shuts behind them. Jody, Janet and Ashley glance around until they see the counter.

Jody, Janet and Ashley make their way over to the counter, keeping their eyes and ears open, just in case they are not alone in the store. Once the three of them reach the counter, Ashley goes around behind it and grabs a few bags. Jody, Janet and Ashley glance around until they spot the men's section. The three of them make their way over and start looking for the clothes they need.

Lisa is looking around, keeping a watchful eye out for anything or anyone. Lisa quickly glances across the street up by the corner north of the store like she heard something. Lisa slowly makes her way over to the back of the Explorer, keeping an eye on the corner. Suddenly, a cat comes out from under the Explorer right at Lisa's feet. Lisa hops back being taken by surprise, but she manages to stay quiet.

The small tabby cat walks over to Lisa and looks up at her. Lisa smiles at the cat, knowing it's the first living thing they have seen since they came to town. Lisa bends down and pets the cat on the head a couple times. The cat seems to be liking the attention. Suddenly, the cat glances over its shoulder at the corner Lisa looked at earlier, then the cat takes off running south down the sidewalk.

Lisa watches the cat for a second, then realizes that something must have spooked it. Lisa looks back up and over to the corner and her eyes widen in surprise. A group of five people, four men and one woman, are making their way slowly towards her. They appear to be walking, but not like normal people, it's more of a staggering walk. The five people seem to be heading straight for Lisa.

Lisa turns and runs for the front door of the store as the group of people start across the street towards the store. Lisa opens the front door and rushes inside.

Lisa hollers out, "Jody, some people are coming!"

Jody, Janet and Ashley, having filled two sacks full of clothes, hear Lisa and start towards the front door. As they get near the front, Jody sees the group of people almost to the sidewalk in front of the store.

Jody hollers to Lisa, "Quick, lock the door!"

Lisa turns around and locks the front door of the store. Lisa starts to back away as Jody, Janet and Ashley walk up next to her. The group of people walk up to the front door and windows of the store. Jody, Janet, Lisa and Ashley can now see that all the people have blood on their hands and around their mouths and their eyes have a milky white film over them. The group starts grabbing at the glass on the

111

door and windows like they are trying to get in, but are not sure how to do so.

Ashley just stares, "What in the world?"

Janet shakes her head, "What is going on?"

Lisa shakes her head while staring, "They must be infected."

Jody nods, "No doubt they are infected." He pauses, "In fact, I don't even think they're alive."

Lisa looks at Jody, "What?"

The group of people start hitting the glass harder, trying to break into the store to get at Jody, Janet, Lisa and Ashley. Jody, Janet, Lisa and Ashley take a couple steps back from the windows.

Jody replies, "I think the virus kills them, then brings them back to life like this."

Ashley continues to stare, "What do we do now? We're trapped."

Jody looks at Ashley, "Do we have all the clothes?"

Ashley nods not taking her eyes away from the five people that are trying their hardest to get to them, "Yes."

Jody sighs, "Okay. I say we sneak out the back door into the alley. Then we can make our way around the end of the block and sneak behind them. They don't seem to be too intelligent. I'm sure we can get to the car before they can get to us."

Lisa questions, "And if we can't?"

Jody taps his pistol, "That's why we brought these."

Janet nods, "Sounds good to me. The sooner the better."

Jody, Janet, Lisa and Ashley make their way towards the back of the store as the five people continue to bang on the glass, trying to get into the store. Jody, Janet, Lisa and Ashley reach the back of the store and the back door. They can still hear the banging on the front windows and they can hear the people moaning. Jody unlocks the back door and slowly opens it. Jody steps out followed by Janet, Lisa and Ashley.

Jody, Janet, Lisa and Ashley stop dead in their tracks as they are completely shocked by what they see. To their left at the end of the alley is another group of people about twenty or so and they are walking in the same manner as the others were. One of the people in the group sees Jody, Janet, Lisa and Ashley. The person turns and starts up the alley towards them. The rest of the group turns and starts up the alley.

Lisa turns and looks the other way up the alley, "Oh shit!"

Jody, Janet and Ashley turn and look the other direction. They see another group of people even larger than the first group and they are headed straight for them. Jody looks around and sees another group, fifty or more, coming across the back parking lot towards them.

Jody speaks quickly, "Get back inside, now!"

Lisa, Janet and Ashley hurry back into the store. Jody steps back inside, shuts the door and locks it.

Lisa sighs, "We're trapped."

Ashley speaks with some concern, "What do we do now?"

Jody is quiet for a second, "Let's go see if there are still only five of them out front."

As the four of them make their way towards the front of the store, they hear some banging now on the back door as well as the front of the store. The four of them get back to the front and see that there are still just the five from before and they are trying their hardest to get inside.

Lisa looks at Jody, "What now?"

Jody quickly replies, "We have to get out of here before that large group makes its way around the front."

Janet questions, "How are we going to do that?"

Jody pulls his pistol from his holster, "We shoot these five and run for the car."

Lisa looks at Jody, "What?"

Jody looks at Lisa, "If we quickly shoot these five, we can get to the car and get out of here before the rest of them trap us."

Lisa draws her pistol, "Okay."

Jody looks at Ashley and Janet, "Just be ready to run once the last one falls and be careful for the glass." He looks at Lisa, "You start on the left and I'll start on the right. We'll work to the middle. Aim for the head, that's the only thing that stopped the one at the store."

Lisa nods, "Okay."

Jody raises his pistol, "I'm going to count to three, then we start shooting."

Lisa raises her pistol and takes aim at the man on the far left.

Jody aims at the man on the far right, "One, two, three."

Jody and Lisa both fire their pistols at the same time. The glass shatters from the bullets and the bullets find their mark. Both men's head snap back and they fall to the ground. Jody moves to his next target which is the woman and Lisa moves to her next target which is a man. With the glass now broken, the three remaining people start to step inside the store. Jody and Lisa both fire again. Being only fifteen feet away, the shots are dead on and the woman and man fall to the ground. The last man steps into the store and starts towards them.

Lisa moves her pistol quickly and takes aim at the man. Jody realizes Lisa has her aim so he lowers his pistol. Lisa squeezes the trigger and the last man falls to the ground about eight feet in front of them.

Jody holsters his pistol, "Let's go!"

Lisa holsters her pistol. Jody, Janet, Lisa and Ashley run for the Explorer. They hop over the small part of the front window that held the window in place and land on the sidewalk. The four of them get to the Explorer fast. Lisa opens the passenger's door. Ashley hops in the back seat with all the clothing bags. Jody opens the driver's door and looks to his left. Jody sees some of the people coming around the corner. Janet hops in the front and slides over to the middle of the seat.

Jody yells, "Here they come!"

Jody and Lisa hop in and slam their doors shut. Jody starts the Explorer, puts it in drive and turns right onto Main Street heading back the direction they came. Jody speeds to the four way stop intersection and slows down so he can get around the cars in the road.

Lisa, Janet and Ashley glance right and see even more people now making their way towards Main Street.

Ashley just stares, "Oh my God! Look at all of them."

Jody glances over and sees the large group of people.

Lisa shakes her head, "I guess we know what happened to everyone now." She pauses, "There must be hundreds of them."

Jody looks in his rearview mirror and sees more and more people coming out onto Main Street.

Jody sighs, "We got to get back to the house."

Jody mashes down the accelerator and the Explorer speeds up. Jody negotiates his way around the cars in the road until they are back to the main intersection from earlier where the two cars are wrecked. Jody pulls the Explorer to a stop.

Lisa questions, "What's wrong?"

Jody shakes his head, "Nothing." He pauses and glances around, "I'm going to take the highway out and around to the back way to the house. That way if they manage to follow us this far, we'll lose them long before we get back to the neighborhood."

Lisa, Janet and Ashley nod. Jody accelerates and turns right onto the main road that heads out of town and becomes Highway 69. Jody pushes down the accelerator and speeds up to 45 mph to put as much distance between them and the people in town, yet still maintain a safe speed.

Ken and Mike are back in the kitchen looking over the plans again. Shadow and Lucky are laying in the laundry room resting from a full morning of playing and attention. Zach and Tyler are back in Jody's bedroom playing a game again. Codi, Ryan, Rochelle, Grace, Ayden, Ariel and Michael, Lindsey's husband, are in the living room. Michael, Lindsey's husband, Rochelle and Grace are reading. Ayden and Ariel are laying down, taking a nap.

Marissa and Michael, Jody's brother, are in his bedroom. Marissa is laying in bed and reading while Michael, Jody's brother, is playing on his computer. Lindsey and Daniel are in the family room. They both are laying down, but Lindsey is still awake while Daniel is napping. Shana is in the master bedroom. Shana is laying down in bed and reading, trying to keep her mind off Cory.

All of a sudden, Shana hears a very faint sound coming from outside the house, almost like the sound of firecrackers. Shana can tell it's a long ways away, but she can swear it was gunshots. Shana gets out of bed and starts walking towards the hallway.

Marissa and Michael, Jody's brother, also hear the faint noise and look at each other. The two of them get up and start for the living room. Lindsey sits up in bed when she hears the five faint popping sounds. Lindsey gets out of bed and starts for the living room. Codi, Ryan, Rochelle, Grace and Michael, Lindsey's husband, all hear the faint sounds and look at each other as Marissa and Michael, Jody's brother, come walking into the living room. A couple seconds later, Lindsey and Shana both come walking into the living room.

Everyone is looking at each other with the same look of "did you hear that". About that time, Ken and Mike walk into the living room.

Rochelle looks at Mike, "We're those what I think they were?"

Mike sighs, "I don't know. We can't be for certain what it was."

Shana shakes her head, "I swear they were gunshots."

Lindsey nods in agreement, "I think that's what they were too."

Ken speaks up, "Let's not get panicked. We don't know for sure what it was."

Michael, Lindsey's husband, speaks up, "Come on. We all know what it was. It definitely wasn't fireworks."

Marissa nods, "I have to agree, it sounded like a gun to me too."

Ryan speaks up, "Those were definitely gunshots."

Codi agrees with Ryan, "Absolutely. I'm not an expert, but I know what gunshots sound like."

Michael, Jody's brother, tries to help calm the mood, "It did sound like gunshots, but like Ken said, let's not panic. We don't even know if it was them."

Grace nods, "That's true. It could've been someone else."

Mike speaks again, "Exactly. There is no reason to get ourselves all worried until we know more about what it was."

Ken looks at Lindsey, "Why don't you send Ashley a message and ask her what's going on."

Lindsey nods and pulls out her phone. Lindsey types the quick message and sends it.

Mike speaks to the room, "Okay. Let's just try and stay calm until we hear back from them."

Rochelle asks the serious question, "What if we don't hear from them?"

Ken sighs, "We will deal with that situation if and when it arises. Until then, let's just try and stay positive."

Everyone in the living room waits with apprehensive patience in hopes that Lindsey's phone will ring soon.

CHAPTER 16

Everyone is sitting around the house, still waiting apprehensively to see if Lindsey gets a return message. It has been ten minutes and nothing yet which is causing the anxiety level to increase. Each person wonders what is going to happen if they don't hear back from Jody, Janet, Lisa and Ashley. As time continues, each second feels like a minute as they just sit quietly and stare at each other.

Then, everyone hears what they think is a car getting closer to the house. Ken and Mike walk over to the front door. Mike looks at Ken and Ken pulls his pistol from his holster. Ken nods at Mike and Mike opens the front door. Ken steps out the front door and steps off the small porch step onto the sidewalk. Ken quickly glances around to make sure no one is there. Ken's head turns right towards the top of the hill as he knows he hears a car approaching.

A few seconds later, the familiar Explorer with Jody, Janet, Lisa and Ashley comes over the top of the hill and starts to slow down. Ken gets a smile on his face.

Ken turns back to the house, "Its them!"

Everyone in the house breathes a sigh of relief as Jody pulls the Explorer into the driveway. Jody puts the Explorer in park and turns it off. Jody quickly hops out of the driver's seat as Janet and Lisa get out of the passenger's side and Ashley gets out of the back. Jody locks the doors.

119

Jody shuts the driver's door, Lisa shuts the passenger's door and Ashley shuts her door. Jody, Janet, Lisa and Ashley quickly head for the front door.

Jody looks at Ken, "Back inside, quick."

Ken can tell something is wrong by Jody's actions. Ken walks back into the house followed by Lisa, Janet and Ashley. Jody stops at the front door and glances around. Once he's sure it's clear, Jody walks into the house and locks the front door behind him. Everyone inside is happy to see Jody, Janet, Lisa and Ashley return, including Shadow who is right in the middle of the room wagging his stub tail.

Mike hugs Jody at the front door as Rochelle gets up and hurries over to Lisa and gives her a big hug. Lindsey gives Ashley and Janet a welcome back and good to see you again hug. Shana walks up and gives Jody a hug.

Jody hugs Shana back, "It's okay. We're okay."

After a few seconds, Jody and Shana make their way over to the living room. Everyone tries to catch their breath and calm themselves down.

Mike finally questions, "Did you get the supplies?"

Jody nods, "Yeah, we got them."

Michael, Lindsey's husband, speaks up, "We thought we heard gunshots."

Jody lets out a sigh, "You did."

Ken can tell something is wrong, "What's going on? What did you run into out there?"

Jody replies, "It's going to take some time to explain. Let's get the supplies out of the heat and into the garage first, then we can talk about it."

Mike nods, "Okay, how do you want to do it?"

Jody sighs again, "We will raise the garage door. You, Ken, Lisa and I will stand guard while everyone else unloads the supplies. With that many people, it shouldn't take long at all."

Everyone nods and gets up. The kids stay in the house as all the adults head for the garage. Jody, Ken, Mike and Lisa all walk over to the overhead garage door and draw their pistols. Michael, Jody's brother, presses the button on the wall and the garage door begins to raise up. Once the door is all the way up, Jody hurries out to the Explorer and unlocks the vehicle. Ken and Mike take up positions on the left side of the driveway while Lisa and Jody take up positions on the right side of the driveway. Jody knows its a risk unloading during the daytime, but after what they saw in town, he knows it is a risk they must take.

Everyone else hurries out to the Explorer. Ashley opens the back hatch door and everyone starts grabbing stuff and quickly taking it into the garage. Jody, Lisa, Ken and Mike diligently stand guard while the others unload the supplies.

After about ten minutes, the Explorer is empty and locked up. The garage is all closed up and the supplies are stacked in the garage. Everyone is back in the house. Everyone starts finding room for each other in the living room. Its crowded, but everyone finds a spot, including Shadow who is sitting at Mike's feet and Lucky who is sitting in Codi's lap.

Jody looks at everyone, "Maybe we should have the kids wait in the other room."

Mike speaks up, "I don't know, maybe they should hear it if they want too. The younger ones won't understand anyway and the older ones might end up having to help out and need to know what's going on."

Jody nods, "Point well taken. We'll leave it up to the parents."

Lindsey speaks up, "Daniel can stay cause he won't really know what we're talking about."

Grace nods in agreement, "The same with Ayden and Ariel."

Jody looks at Shana, "What about Zach and Ty?"

Shana sighs, "They can stay if they want."

Tyler speaks first, "I want to stay with you mom."

Zach nods, "I want to hear what's going on."

Shana nods, "Okay then."

Jody sighs, "Okay, I guess it's time to let you all know what happened and what we found out."

Everyone sits quietly waiting for Jody, Janet, Lisa and Ashley to tell them how things were in town.

Jody starts, "Well, the trip to the grocery store was uneventful, just the same thing, no people, but just abandoned cars along the roads. Once we got to the grocery store, not much was different."

Ashley speaks up, "Tell them what we found at the grocery store."

Jody sighs, "Okay. We found the body of the owner in the back. It looked like his insides had been torn out and he had been chewed on."

Lindsey blurts out, "What?"

Jody nods, "We couldn't believe it either."

Marissa speaks up, "Maybe some animals got a hold of him."

Lisa shakes her head, "I don't think so."

Grace speaks up, "Why do you say that?"

Jody sighs again, "I'm no expert, but the bite marks were definitely human teeth and the way his body was torn open, it looked like it had to be done with hands."

Everyone in the room is quiet.

Jody continues, "After we got the supplies from there, we went to the smoke shop. The whole trip there was the same, no people or animals, just abandoned vehicles."

Lisa speaks up, "The smoke shop went easy. We didn't find anything there."

Jody nods, "So we decided what to do next."

Janet chimes in, "That's when we decided to go to the clothing store on Main Street."

Jody nods, "The whole way there was the same. No people at all. Vehicles were just abandoned in the middle of the streets. It was crazy." He pauses, "Once we got to the clothing store is when things changed."

Michael, Lindsey's husband, questions, "What happened?"

Jody glances at Janet, Ashley and Lisa, "While Janet, Ashley and I were getting the clothes for Ken, Lisa was standing guard."

Lisa speaks up, "First I thought I heard something, then a cat came up to me. It ran off scared and that's when I saw them."

Ken questions, "Who?"

Lisa continues, "It was a group of five people. They were staggering straight towards me."

Rochelle speaks up, "Staggering?"

Jody nods, "It wasn't a normal walk. It's like they were not able to really walk normal for some reason." He pauses, "Anyway, Lisa came into the store and locked the door. Once they reached the door and windows is when we noticed something."

Mike questions, "What was it?"

Ashley speaks up, "They had blood all over their face and mouth as well as their hands."

Janet interjects, "And their eyes had a milky white look to them."

Everyone in the room is quiet.

Jody sighs, "So, we figured on sneaking out the back and around behind them to get to the car. That's when we found out what has happened."

Jody gets quiet for a moment.

Shana questions, "What was it you saw?"

Jody sighs again, "When we opened the back and stepped into the alley, we saw a whole bunch of people just like the five at the front of the store."

Michael, Jody's brother, questions, "A whole bunch?"

Lisa nods, "Yeah, we couldn't even count them all there were so many."

Ashley chimes in, "It had to be at least a hundred or more."

Jody nods, "So I decided we had to shoot our way out the front before the rest of them trapped us in the store." He pauses, "That is the gunshots you heard. We shot the five of them, got in the car and took off."

Lindsey just stares at Jody, "Oh my God."

Jody nods, "That's not all."

Lisa speaks up, "As we drove off, we saw even more people coming out on Main Street. I couldn't even guess at how many." She looks at Ashley, "How many would you say Ashley?"

Ashley sighs, "Hundreds at least." She looks at Janet, "Is that what you'd say?"

Janet nods in agreement, "Yeah, hundreds."

Ken shakes his head, "What the hell?"

Jody speaks again, "So, we came straight back here."

Codi speaks up, "This is insane."

Marissa questions, "What do we do now?"

Jody sighs, "Let's take a moment to soak in what has happened. Let the four of us grab a bite to eat, then we'll talk about what to do next. Okay?"

Everyone in the room nods. As Jody, Janet, Lisa and Ashley head for the kitchen, the others just look at each other not knowing what to say or think about what they just heard.

After about twenty minutes, Jody, Janet, Lisa and Ashley are finished eating and make their way back to the living room. The living room has been completely quiet since hearing the news about what happened on the trip to town.

Jody looks around at everyone, "So, I'm guessing everyone is trying to think about what to do next."

Shana looks at Jody, "What do you think Jo?"

Jody sighs, "Well, I think we all now realize what has happened and I'm sure in the back of our minds we already knew." He pauses, "Society, life as we once knew it, is over. It's all about staying alive now, any way possible."

Ken nods, "After what you guys described, that's the only way I see it."

Marissa questions, "So, what do we do now?"

Jody takes a breath, "First, I want to create partners. No one goes anywhere out of this house alone, even to the fenced in back yard. Plus, that way we can also keep any doubters from maybe sneaking away in the middle of the night. I should have seen that coming from Cory." He pauses, "Second, I think we need to distribute weapons to everyone. Just in case something goes down, everyone will have a chance to defend themselves."

Mike nods, "That sounds like a good idea."

Michael, Lindsey's husband, speaks up, "That still doesn't answer the question of what do we do next."

Jody sighs, "Let's try to focus on one thing at a time before we start discussing anything major." He pauses, "You all wait here. Lisa, Janet and Ashley, come help me gather up the weapons I was talking about. We will get those distributed and set up partners, then talk about what to do next."

Lisa nods, "Okay."

Janet is just staring off into space.

Jody looks at Janet, "You okay Janet?"

Janet blinks a couple times, "Sure. Yeah, let's go."

Ashley and Janet get up from the couch. Jody, Janet Lisa and Ashley walk out of the living room. They head for Jody's bedroom first where they grab a Ruger LC9 9mm pistol with laser sight and a loaded 7 round magazine in a black clip on holster and a spare, loaded 7 round magazine in a black clip on single magazine holder. They grab a single shot 20 gauge shotgun with an 18 inch, sawed off barrel and a four round shell holder on the buttstock. The last thing they grab is Jody's SOG Seal Pup Elite knife and Lisa's SOG Seal Pup Elite knife .

After Jody, Janet, Lisa and Ashley leave there, they go to the master bedroom and get the 20 gauge pump shotgun out of the closet that Ken had cleaned. The four of them leave the master bedroom and head for the garage.

CHAPTER 17

Jody, Janet, Ashley and Lisa spend about ten minutes in the garage. When they are done, the four of them have added two wooden baseball bats, one aluminum baseball bat, the SOG Jungle Primitive knife off of Jody's alice pack and Jody's Stoeger 12 gauge tactical shotgun loaded with five shells to the other weapons they are already carrying. Jody, Janet, Lisa and Ashley return to the living room where everyone is waiting.

Jody looks at everyone, "Okay, first let's distribute the weapons and cover what everyone has, including knives." Jody looks at Ken, "What weapons do you have?"

Ken replies, "I have my shotgun, pistol and a pocket knife."

Jody nods, "Okay." He looks at Mike, "What do you got dad?"

Mike replies, "I just got my pistol."

Jody nods and sighs, "Okay." He looks at Codi, "What do you have?"

Codi replies, "I have just my pistol."

Jody nods, "Okay." Jody looks at Ryan, "How about you Ryan?"

Ryan replies, "I have just my pistol."

Jody nods, "Okay." He looks at his brother, "What do you got bro?"

Michael, Jody's brother, replies, "Just a pocket knife right now."

Jody nods and picks up the 20 gauge pump shotgun. Jody hands the shotgun to his brother.

Jody speaks, "Take this shotgun. I'll give you a box of twenty-five shells later."

Michael, Jody's brother, nods, "Okay."

Jody looks at Lisa, "What do you got Lisa?"

Lisa replies, "I've got my pistol, a pocket knife and my SOG knife right now."

Jody nods, "Okay. We'll give the SOG knife to one of the others here in a minute."

Jody looks at Marissa, "What do you have?"

Marissa replies, "I've just got my pistol."

Jody nods, "Okay." He pauses, "I have my shotgun, pistol and four SOG knives which I'll pass out three of them. Now, does anyone else have any weapons that I don't know about?"

The room is quiet.

Jody continues, "Okay."

Jody picks up his Stoeger shotgun and his SOG Jungle Primitive knife.

Jody looks at Michael, Lindsey's husband, "Here, you take these two. The shotgun has five shells with it already and I'll get you the rest later."

Michael, Lindsey's husband, takes the two weapons, "Okay."

Jody grabs a wooden baseball bat and his SOG Seal Pup Elite knife.

Jody looks at Lindsey, "Lindsey, take these two for now."

Lindsey takes the two weapons, "Okay. Thanks."

Jody grabs the single shot 20 gauge shotgun and Lisa's SOG Seal Pup Elite knife.

Jody looks at Grace, "Here Grace, take these two for now. There are five shells with the shotgun and I'll get you the other twenty later."

Grace takes the two weapons, "Sure thing FIT B."

Jody smiles and grabs the aluminum baseball bat. Jody pulls his SOG Trident pocket knife out of his back pocket.

Jody looks at Ashley, "Here girl, take these two."

Ashley nods and takes the weapons, "Okay, but don't you need a knife?"

Jody replies, "I still have my SOG combat knife in my tent."

Jody grabs the other wooden baseball bat, "Here Janet, take this for now."

Janet takes the bat, "Thanks."

Jody grabs the Ruger LC9 pistol and it's spare magazine.

Jody looks at Shana, "These are going to be yours. The holster and mag holder just clip on. I'll get you a couple boxes of ammo later."

Shana takes the pistol and spare magazine, "Thanks. I've shot pistols before, but not one of these. You'll have to give me a quick overview of this gun later."

Jody smiles, "No problem." He pauses, "Okay, now that we got the weapons distributed, next thing to cover is creating partners. I have an idea of who I want to match up with who already. Plus, I want to make sure each team has at least one gun for now."

Ken speaks up, "Well, let's hear it little buddy."

Jody takes a drink of water.

Jody speaks, "First, a couple of people will have additional responsibilities. Dad will be in charge of inventorying the supplies and I want Rochelle to help with that. Rochelle will not be in a team. Along with helping count inventory, I want Rochelle to help with the younger kids so they can get more familiar with her, in case she might need to take care of them. Also, dad will be the primary on taking care of Shadow, but I want us all to pitch in on that as well. Same goes with Codi and Lucky. Sound good so far?"

Mike nods, "I'm good with that."

Rochelle replies, "Me too."

Jody nods, "Okay. The teams will be responsible for the safety and security as well as acquirement of things." Jody looks at Lindsey, "Lindsey, you and your husband will be one team."

Lindsey nods, "Okay."

Jody looks over at his brother, "Michael, you and Marissa will be a team."

Michael, Jody's brother, and Marissa both nod.

Jody looks over at Ken, "Ken, you and Grace will be a team."

Ken nods, "Sounds good."

Jody looks over at Ryan, "Ryan, you and Codi will be a team."

Ryan nods, "Okay."

Jody sighs, "Now, the last six of us." Jody looks at Lisa, "Lisa, you and Ashley have worked together already so I figure you two can be a team. Dad and Shana will be a team." He pauses, "And that will make Janet and I the last team. Does that sound good to everyone? If not, say something now."

Everyone looks around at each other and nods.

Jody smiles, "Good."

Michael, Lindsey's husband, questions, "Okay. What now?"

Jody sighs, "I think now we need to setup some rules or guidelines for the group. Things we all agree upon to help keep the group safe." He pauses, "Given what we know now is going on, none of us will make it on our own very long so we must protect the group."

Ken nods in agreement, "Absolutely."

Jody continues, "Everyone take about ten minutes to get something to drink and think about things that you might want to bring up, then we'll talk about them."

Everyone nods as a few of them head for the kitchen.

After a short break, everyone makes their way back into the living room. Jody has a small pocket notebook and ink pen in his hands. Jody flips open the notebook.

Jody speaks, "Okay, let's start talking about different ideas for rules or guidelines on protecting the group." He pauses, "I think first we should bring up the obvious, the infection. Anyone got anything to say on that topic?"

Ken speaks up first, "I think its simple. Anyone that gets infected is out of the group, one way or another."

Marissa questions, "What do you mean by one way or another?"

Ken replies, "If someone gets infected, they can choose to leave on their own or end their own life. If they won't do either one, they are forced to leave or killed."

Rochelle replies a little shocked, "Wow, that seems harsh."

Ashley speaks up, "Ken's right. We can't have anyone infected around."

For those that know Ashley, they are kind of taken by surprise by her response.

Ashley notices the looks, "I normally wouldn't say that, but after seeing infected people up close, it's the safest way possible."

Jody nods his head, "I would have to agree with them. If anyone in the group becomes infected, they have their choices, but no matter what, they are out of the group." He pauses, "Anyone else have anything to say on that subject?"

The room is quiet as everyone glances around at each other. Everyone knows how bad it sounds, but everyone understands that it must be that way. After a few seconds, Jody scribbles it down in the notebook.

Jody looks back up, "Okay, let's move onto the next topic."

Lisa speaks next, "What if we come across someone who's infected, but not like one of those we saw in town?"

Jody looks at Lisa, "What do you think?"

Lisa replies, "I think that we should leave them. Just because they haven't become one of those things, they are still dangerous because they are infected."

Ryan nods, "I agree. Even if there is a group of people. If any of them are infected, those people can't come with us. The others will have the choice to."

Jody nods, "That sounds good to me. How about everyone else?"

Everyone in the room glances around at each other and everyone is nodding in agreement.

Jody scribbles it down, "Okay, I think that pretty much covers infected people. Anyone in the group is out and anyone outside the group is not let in." He pauses, "Next topic."

Janet speaks up, "While we were in town, you mentioned something about other survivors and having to be careful for them."

Jody nods, "Yeah."

Shana looks at Jody, "What do you mean Jo?"

Jody replies, "If we encounter other survivors, they will react in one of three ways. They will either want to get together and be helpful, be left alone or the worse, want to do us harm."

Michael, Lindsey's husband, questions, "Why would they want to do us harm if we're not infected?"

Jody replies, "For multiple reasons. The first is that they will want to take our supplies and weapons away from us and the second is worse."

Lindsey questions, "What's the second?"

Jody sighs, "To some of you this may sound ridiculous, but I assure you it's a very real threat. People will act differently in this kind of world and if they see their chance to have something that isn't readily available, they might just take it and I don't mean supplies."

Codi looks puzzled, "What?"

Mike speaks up, "He's mainly referring to you women getting attacked by men and Jody is right about that. If they see women, especially attractive women, they may decide it's their last chance."

Jody nods, "It's more possible to happen to the women, but even us guys must be careful. We all know some of the things that have happened in prisons in the past due to the fact that there are no women available or even the possibility that a woman survivor may try something like that."

Lisa nods, "I understand what you're saying and I agree with it completely."

Michael, Jody's brother, questions, "So, what do we do to avoid it?"

Jody replies, "If we are going to make contact with another group or person, not everyone will do so. We will determine at that time which of us will make contact with them. If a group or person stumbles upon us, we maintain a decisive stance that they go away or put away any weapons that they have." He pauses, "What do you all think?"

Lindsey nods, "After hearing all that, I agree totally. You're right, we can't just trust people anymore."

Jody looks around and sees everyone else nodding to each other. Jody scribbles that topic down in the notebook.

Jody looks back up, "So, what's next?"

The room is quiet for a minute.

Shana questions, "What if anyone in the group tries to hurt someone else in the group?"

Jody nods, "Good question. What do you all think?"

Lindsey speaks first, "I think it would depend on what it is."

Jody replies, "True. If it's an argument or the kids just being kids, then we will just calm the situation down. However, if its someone that is trying to physically harm someone else, then that needs to be dealt with decisively."

Ken speaks up, "I think its rather easy. If anyone in the group becomes a danger to anyone else or the whole group, then they are out of the group and if they get too dangerous, then they are dealt with."

Shana nods, "That's what I was thinking."

Jody nods, "I would have to agree with Ken. If you become hostile outside of the usual disagreement stage, you will be asked to leave. If you don't, you will be forced to leave or even worse." He pauses, "As much as I'd hate to see that one used, I think it's very important. Any other comments on it?"

Grace shakes her head, "I think it's a great idea. We have enough danger with the infected people and other survivors, we don't need it in our own group."

Jody looks around the room and sees everyone nodding in agreement. Jody writes it down in the notebook.

Jody looks back up, "Anything else right now?"

The room is quiet again. No one speaks up with anything.

Jody sighs, "I'll bring one more thing up, leaving the group voluntarily."

Marissa questions, "What about it?"

Jody continues, "Anyone can choose to leave on their own at any time. If someone chooses to leave, I think they have a right to not only take their personal belongings, but their weapons and share of the supplies too."

Marissa nods, "I think that's fair."

Mike questions, "What if they leave because they are infected, tried to hurt someone or are forced to leave?"

Jody sighs, "What do you all think?"

Michael, Jody's brother, speaks up, "I say tough luck for those people. They get nothing except their personal belongings."

Michael, Lindsey's husband, nods, "Absolutely. I don't think you deserve anything at that point."

Jody nods, "I would have to agree with the two of you. Anyone else want to say anything on the topic?"

The room is quiet again, but everyone is nodding in agreement. Jody writes it down in the notepad.

Jody looks back up, "Why don't we take a break for now and we can get back together later if need be. That will give us time to think of more things." He pauses, "Has everyone already cleaned up for the day?"

Marissa nods, "Yeah."

Jody replies, "Good. Janet and Ashley, why don't you two get cleaned up next and Lisa and I will clean up after you two are done."

Ashley nods, "Sounds good to me. I need a shower."

Lisa chimes in, "Me too."

Janet manages a smile, but is obviously distracted. Jody closes the notepad as everyone starts to get up and Ashley and Janet head off to get their stuff to clean up.

CHAPTER 18

The rest of the afternoon is fairly quiet. The clouds have cleared and the temperature has risen some as the breeze has died down. Most everyone has gone to their separate places and each person has been thinking about what they all talked about earlier. Each person wonders in their own way what is going to happen next. Everyone has noticed Jody, Mike and Ken looking over a map and making notes. Each one wonders what Jody, Ken and Mike are doing, but they figure Jody will tell them when the time comes.

No one has realized how much time has passed until they start filtering back towards the kitchen, ready for dinner. Jody, Ken and Mike are sitting at the kitchen table looking over a map of Oklahoma and the notes Mike made earlier. Shadow is laying on the floor under the table. Lindsey and Daniel are the first two in the kitchen.

Jody looks up at Lindsey, "Hey girl."

Lindsey smiles, "Hey Jody. What are you guys up to?"

Jody sighs, "Covering possibilities that we may have to face."

Daniel looks up at Lindsey and speaks in his dramatic voice, "Momma, I'm hungry."

Jody smiles, "Come to think of it big man, so am I." He pauses, "Let's take a break."

Lindsey smiles at Daniel, "Okay. Let's get you something to eat."

Jody looks at his dad, "Hey dad, after dinner do you think you and Rochelle can start inventorying everything. I'll take one of the groups and take Shadow out."

Mike nods, "Sure thing."

Michael, Lindsey's husband, walks into the kitchen followed by Lisa and Rochelle.

Jody looks at Rochelle, "Hey Roe?"

Rochelle looks over at Jody, "Yeah?"

Jody questions, "After dinner, can you help my dad with inventorying the supplies?"

Rochelle nods, "Sure."

Ryan, Codi, Grace, Ayden, Ariel, Janet and Ashley walk into the kitchen next. A few seconds later, Marissa and Michael, Jody's brother, walk in.

Michael, Jody's brother, speaks up, "Looks like we all had the same idea."

Grace chuckles, "Yep. It's getting crowded in here fast."

Shana, Tyler and Zach walk up to the entrance to the kitchen by the dining table.

Jody smiles at Shana, "Hey."

Shana smiles back, "Hey Jo. I see the gang is all here."

Jody smiles again, "Yeah." He pauses, "Okay, let's get the kids first, then the ladies. After that, us guys and Shadow and Lucky will get our food."

Everyone nods and starts making room in the kitchen so the kids can get their food first.

Jody speaks up, "Since we are all here, I need something. After we all eat, I need one team to go with me to walk Shadow while my dad and Rochelle inventory the supplies. Any volunteers?"

The kitchen is quiet for a moment.

Marissa speaks up, "Michael and I can go."

Michael, Jody's brother, nods, "Sure we can."

Jody nods, "Cool. After dinner, the inventory and taking care of Shadow and Lucky, let's meet back in the living room about 9:30. Okay?"

Everyone in the room nods and gets back to the business at hand, which is food. It doesn't take long for everyone to get their dinner and find a spot to sit and eat. They only one with a dilemma is Shadow, because he's not sure who to go and beg from first. Lucky sits at Codi's feet watching her eat.

Its been about thirty minutes since everyone has finished eating. Mike and Rochelle are in the garage starting the inventory of the supplies. Codi and Ryan are in the back yard with Lucky. Jody, Marissa and Michael, Jody's brother, are out in the field with Shadow. Jody has his pistol with him. Marissa has her pistol with her and Michael has his shotgun with him.

Jody looks around some, "So, how are you doing Marissa?"

Marissa glances around, "I'm okay. Why?"

Jody looks over at her, "I noticed you're walking is not quite normal."

Marissa nods, "Yeah, my knees have been acting up some. I'm going to have to put the brace back on. I think its mainly from not really getting to move around much lately."

Michael, Jody's brother, chimes in, "Ain't that the truth."

Jody watches Shadow, "Well don't worry. That could change soon enough."

Marissa looks over at Jody, "What do you mean?"

Jody replies, "Don't worry about it right now. We'll be talking about it soon enough." He pauses, "Just take care of your knees. Those things don't run, but they can get up to a good, fast walk."

Marissa nods, "I'll be okay."

Jody returns his focus to Shadow as Shadow continues to sniff everything he can. Michael, Jody's brother, and Marissa keep a constant watch out. The two of them haven't dealt with any of the infected people yet, but from what they heard from Jody, Janet, Lisa and Ashley, they know they must be ready in case they have to.

Its about 9:30 now and the house has been fairly quiet during the evening. Everyone is trying to pass the time the best way they can. Noticing the time, everyone starts to make their way into the living room area. Jody walks into the living room to see everyone there waiting.

Jody nods, "Good, we're all here. I'll make this as brief as possible so everyone can start getting some rest."

Jody holds up his right hand which is curled into a loose fist and has small pieces of paper folded up in it. Everyone wonders what is going on.

Jody speaks again, "Each piece of paper in my hand has the names of the teams we set up on them. We will draw them one at a time and that will be the order of watch that is stood." He pauses, "From now on, we will have one team standing watch at all times."

Mike questions, "How long are the shifts going to be?"

Jody replies, "Unless someone else has a better idea, I was thinking two hours at a time. That way you will have a full twelve hours between your shifts."

Michael, Lindsey's husband, nods, "That sounds good to me."

Shana nods, "Me too."

Jody smiles, "Good." He holds out his hand to Shana, "You want to draw the first one?"

Shana grabs a piece of paper and opens it, "First team is Grace and Ken."

Jody nods, "Okay. You two will have the ten to midnight shift."

Shana grabs another piece of paper and opens it, "Next is Lisa and Ashley."

Lisa and Ashley nod.

Shana grabs the next piece of paper, "Third will be Marissa and Michael."

Marissa and Michael, Jody's brother, both nod.

Shana grabs the next piece of paper, "Next will be myself and Mike."

Mike nods.

Shana grabs another piece of paper, "Next is Codi and Ryan."

Codi and Ryan both nod.

Shana grabs one of the last two pieces, "Next is Lindsey and Michael."

Lindsey and Michael, her husband, nod.

Jody speaks, "And that would make the last team Janet and myself."

Jody pauses for a minute.

Jody looks over at his dad, "Did you and Rochelle finish the inventory?"

Mike nods, "It's done. We're sitting okay right now."

Jody replies, "That's good." He pauses, "About ten minutes before the end of your shift, wake the next team up so they can get ready. I'll be up for awhile if anyone needs me for anything."

Everyone nods.

Jody speaks again, "That's all I got. Does anyone have anything they want to bring up before we turn in for the night?"

Michael, Lindsey's husband, questions, "You've been looking at a map. What's that all about?"

Jody replies, "Nothing right now. Just making plans in case of an emergency. We can talk about it more tomorrow."

The room goes quiet.

Jody speaks, "Okay. Well, I hope everyone can get some rest tonight. I know it will be difficult and different, but I know everyone will do just fine. I trust you all."

Jody turns and heads off for the garage. Everyone else starts to get up and get ready for bed as Ken and Grace get ready for the first watch.

Shana, Tyler and Zach are back in the master bedroom. It doesn't take long for the three of them to fall asleep. Lisa and Rochelle are back in Jody's bedroom. Rochelle falls asleep quickly, but Lisa lays in bed awake. Marissa and Michael, Jody's brother, are back in his bedroom. Marissa has laid down and Michael, Jody's brother, is sitting at his computer.

Lindsey, Daniel and Michael, Lindsey's husband, are laying down in the family room. None of them have fallen asleep yet. Ayden and Ariel are laying on the airbed in the living room and they both are now asleep. Mike is stretched out in his recliner and starting to doze off. Jody, Janet and Ashley are laying in the tent in the garage. Ashley has dozed off. Janet is having trouble sleeping as she thinks about her kids. Janet can't help but feel like she let them down. Jody is looking over a map of Oklahoma as well as a map of the United States. Jody has a couple of ideas on places he's researched.

Codi and Ryan are laying on the couch in the living room. Codi is staring up at the ceiling and finding it hard to doze off. Codi can't help but think about her family and friends that she knows she will never see again. The thought makes her sad. Lucky is laying on the floor next to the couch. Ryan has managed to doze off.

Shadow has wandered around the house and has found his way into the garage. Sensing something is wrong, Shadow walks into the tent and over next to Janet. Shadow sits next to Janet and Janet starts petting him. Shadow licks Janet on the forearm a couple times, then lays down next to Janet. Janet smiles at how simple things mean so much for a dog and how Shadow could just tell she needed someone there for her.

Janet continues petting Shadow, "Thanks big boy."

Janet closes her eyes and tries to doze off as she lays her hand on Shadow. Jody smiles as he watches Shadow and Janet.

Ken and Grace are sitting at the dining table. Ken is wearing his pistol and Grace has her baseball bat and knife on her.

Grace looks at Ken, "So, where do you think we should keep watch from?"

Ken replies, "I'd say from right here. We can look out these windows and see the backyard and field and we can walk over to the window in the laundry room and see the front yard." He pauses, "That way we can keep watch and not disturb everyone trying to sleep."

Grace nods, "That sounds good to me." She pauses, "So, what if we do see something?"

Ken pauses for a second, then replies, "Unless it figures out we're in here, I say nothing. Just keep an eye on it until it goes away. If it does know we're here or doesn't go away, then we'll talk it over with Jody about how to take care of it."

Grace asks a question she hopes they don't have to deal with, "What if there's a lot of them?"

Ken sighs, "We wake everyone up and figure out what to do."

Grace decides to change the subject, "So, what's the deal with the map you guys were looking at and making notes on?"

Ken looks thru the kitchen blinds, "Nothing for right now. Just going over possibilities that might come up."

Grace walks over and checks out the front, then returns to the table, "You're not telling me everything are you?"

Ken gives a slight smile, "Nope, but no reason to worry about it right now."

Grace just smiles and grabs a deck of cards that is sitting on the table, "Want to play some to pass the time?"

Ken replies, "Deal girl."

Grace shuffles the cards as quietly as she can, then starts to deal the first hand.

Lindsey, Daniel and Michael, Lindsey's husband, are laying on the hide-a-bed in the family room. Daniel is laying in between them. All three of them are tired, but haven't managed to fall asleep yet.

Daniel looks at Lindsey, "Momma, when are we going home?"

Lindsey is not quite sure what to say, "I don't know Daniel. We have to stay here a little longer."

Daniel yawns and questions, "Why momma?"

Lindsey sighs, "Because there are some dangerous people outside and we have to try and hide from them until its okay."

Lindsey looks over at Michael, her husband, and gives a little shrug of her shoulders.

Daniel yawns again, "Okay."

Daniel closes his eyes and finally falls asleep.

Michael, Lindsey's husband, looks at Lindsey, "I don't like this waiting game. Maybe we should try to get home and see for ourselves what its like out there."

Lindsey whispers back, "I really hate just sitting here too, but what other choice do we have. Shana's boy left and he hasn't been heard from. Not to mention what Jody, Janet, Lisa and Ashley said happened in town." She pauses, "We'd never make it. Not with a shotgun, bat and a couple knives."

Michael, Lindsey's husband, sighs, "Maybe, but he knows something that he's not telling us."

Lindsey questions, "Who? Jody?"

Michael, Lindsey's husband, whispers back, "Yes. He's been looking at that map and checking out notes. Almost like he knows something. If he does, he should tell us."

Lindsey replies, "I'm sure he'll tell us when the time is right. Jody won't keep us in the dark if its something important."

Michael, Lindsey's husband, replies, "How do you know that?"

Lindsey whispers back in a firmer tone, "Cause I know him and he's not like that. He hasn't yet. I trust him."

Michael, Lindsey's husband, sighs and rolls over, "I hope you're right."

Lindsey puts her hand on Daniel, "I am."

The two of them try again to go to sleep.

With only an hour until her time for watch and not able to sleep, Lisa walks out of the bedroom and starts towards the garage. Lisa makes her way quietly through the house and when she walks into the kitchen, Lisa nods at Ken and Grace. Ken and Grace nod back as Lisa walks into the garage where she hopes Jody is still awake so she can talk to him.

Jody is laying on his sleeping bag inside his tent when he hears someone walk into the garage. Lisa walks over to the opening of the tent and sees Jody looking over the map of Oklahoma. Jody looks up and sees Lisa.

Jody smiles, "What's up Lisa? Everything okay?"

Lisa smiles, "Yeah. I was just wondering if we could talk."

Jody slides the map out of the way and sits up, "Sure. Come in and pull up a piece of sleeping bag."

Lisa steps inside the tent and sits down next to Jody being as quiet as she can so she doesn't wake up Janet and Ashley.

Jody can tell something isn't quite right, "So, what's wrong?"

Lisa sighs, "I've been thinking a lot about what happened today in town."

Jody nods, "You did great Lisa."

Lisa replies, "Thanks." She pauses, "Obviously, that's the first time I've ever shot at a living person. I can't help but think about having killed them." She pauses again, "How do you deal with that?"

Jody is quiet for a moment, "You don't deal with it. You have to learn how to accept it, that it was something that had to be done in order for you to live."

Lisa sighs, "I know they would've hurt us, but it's still hard to get a grip on."

Jody puts his hand on Lisa's back, "First, they were not living people. They were already dead, so you didn't kill them." He pauses, "You did what you had to do. I know that might not be much comfort now, but if you remember that you did it to help save us and so you could return to Rochelle, then you can start to understand and accept what happened."

Lisa nods slightly, "I guess you're right." She pauses, "Does it get easier?"

Jody glances down, then back to Lisa, "Yes and no. You'll think about it some afterwards, but once you've gotten passed this first incident, the next won't be so hard."

Lisa looks at Jody and smiles, "Thanks."

Jody smiles back, "No problem girl. You know I'm here for you."

Jody leans over and puts his arms around Lisa and gives her a supportive hug. Lisa puts her arms around Jody and hugs him back. After about a minute, Lisa and Jody lean back again.

Lisa looks at Jody, "So, are you and Shana together again?"

Jody sighs and shakes his head slightly, "No. We decided that we're just going to be friends. I still care about her and the boys, but that's how it is." He pauses, "I'm just happy that we've managed to remain such good friends after breaking up at the end of last year."

Lisa smiles, "Yeah, She seems really nice."

Jody smiles, "Yes she is."

Lisa gets a slight smile and can tell that Jody is kind of hiding something, "There is someone else you like, isn't there?"

Jody can't help but smile, "Yeah, there is."

Lisa pushes Jody's arm, "Well, who is it?"

Jody lowers his voice and glances around, "Its Janet."

Lisa smiles again, "That so cool. She seems like a really nice girl."

Jody nods, "She is, but we've just been friends. I don't even know if she likes me in that way."

Lisa replies, "Well, she'd be crazy not too. You're a wonderful man."

Jody smiles again, "Thank you."

Lisa glances over at the map, then looks back at Jody and questions, "So, what's the deal with the map?"

Jody sighs, "Making plans. Since I plan on telling everyone in the morning, I guess I'll go ahead and let you know."

Jody motions with his head for Lisa to move closer. Lisa slides over against Jody so they can just whisper to each other and still hear what is being said. Jody starts to explain what his plan is.

CHAPTER 19

Its about 9am the following morning. It is a clear morning and a warm breeze is blowing as the temperature is in the high 60's. Lindsey and Michael, her husband, are sitting at the kitchen table for their watch shift which is about halfway done now. Shadow wanders into the kitchen and sits down next to Lindsey. Shadow looks at Lindsey with his typical smile. Lindsey scratches Shadow behind his ears as Jody walks into the kitchen from the garage.

Lindsey looks over at Jody, "Good morning."

Jody nods, "Morning."

Lindsey replies, "You don't look like you slept much."

Jody chuckles slightly, "No I didn't. Maybe four hours."

Lindsey sighs, "That sucks."

Jody smiles, "Yes it does, but I've gotten use to it." He looks at Shadow, "You ready to eat big boy?"

Shadow's ears perk up at the sound of food and from his size, it's obvious that he likes food.

Jody walks into the living room where he notices everyone is starting to wake up except for Ayden and Ariel. Jody grabs Shadow's pan and returns to the kitchen. Jody grabs a can of dog food and puts half of it in the pan. Jody let's Shadow lick the spoon, then walks into the living room. Shadow is right behind Jody with that, I'm so happy bounce in his step.

Jody looks up and sees Lisa, Rochelle and Shana making their way down the hallway. Jody walks back into the kitchen and sees Janet and Ashley walk in from the garage. Jody is soon joined by Lisa, Rochelle, Shana, Mike, Ryan, Codi and Ken. Lucky is right behind Codi, ready to eat.

Ken looks at Jody, "So, do you have anything for this morning?"

Jody nods, "Yeah, but let's get everyone fed and get Shadow and Lucky out. After that we can meet in the living room and talk."

Ken nods, "Sounds good to me."

Jody looks at Shana, "How about you, dad and me take Shadow out?"

Shana nods, "Okay."

Jody looks at Mike, "Sound good?"

Mike nods, "Yep."

Jody replies, "Okay. Let's grab our pistols and get Shadow outside."

Jody, Shana and Mike head off to get dressed and get their weapons while the rest of the house starts waking up and getting ready to eat breakfast.

About forty-five minutes have passed and Mike, Jody and Shana are back inside with Shadow. Ryan and Codi are also back inside with Lucky. Everyone is finished eating and has made their way into the living room, including Daniel, Tyler, Zach, Ayden and Ariel. Jody walks into the living room with the map in his hand. Shadow follows Jody into the living room, walks over by Ashley and sits down at her feet.

Jody speaks, "Okay. I know you all have been wondering what has been going on with us looking at this map. Well, it's simple really." He pauses for a moment, "We are going to have to leave the house, soon."

The room is quiet as everyone other than Ken, Mike and Lisa have a look of confusion on their faces.

Once the news settles in, Michael, Lindsey's husband, speaks up, "Why would we have to leave the house and risk going out there when all this time we've done everything we can to stay inside and not draw attention to ourselves?"

Jody replies calmly, "Because, soon this house will become a tomb."

Michael, Lindsey's husband, replies, "That's crazy."

Shana interjects, "What makes you say that Jo?"

Jody takes a breath, "Because in order to survive we are going to need food, water and shelter. Shelter being the least important of the three." He pauses, "And in this house, we have no natural food or water source. Plus, we can be easily trapped inside here."

Ashley speaks up, "Even if we run out of bottled water, we still have the tap water."

Jody shakes his head, "Not for much longer." He pauses, "Listen folks, there is no one out there to keep things running. Before long, we will be without running water and electricity. Once that happens, we have no choice but to look elsewhere for water and running into town will soon be useless and already is dangerous." He pauses again, "Not to mention, those zombies will eventually make their way out here and when they do, we will get trapped in this house because there are way more of them than we can fight off."

Ken speaks up, "And we don't want to get stuck in this house without access to natural resources. We'd either starve or dehydrate to death."

The room goes quiet as everyone tries to grasp what Jody and Ken have said. Everyone also realizes that the truth can no longer be avoided as they all think of the word Jody used, zombie.

Grace speaks up, "Ok, say you're right. Where could we go? I'm sure that there are zombies everywhere."

Jody nods, "Yes, I'm sure they are. That's why we have to be careful and think it through properly. We have to take careful steps to avoid running into any zombies."

Lindsey speaks up, "You've been thinking about this a lot, haven't you?"

Jody nods, "Ever since the day Shana, Tyler and I encountered them at the store."

Ryan questions, "So, what would you suggest we do?"

Jody sighs, "First, we just get our things together and get someplace close by. We can setup camp and figure out our next move."

Codi questions, "You mentioned taking careful steps. Like what?"

Ken replies, "Like avoiding populated areas. Keeping a twenty-four hour watch going. Acquiring more weapons, ammo and supplies so we can travel."

Mike chimes in, "And thinking of a final destination where we can setup a place to be safe and self sufficient. Where we would have a natural food and water source that we could protect from as many zombies that might find us."

Michael, Jody's brother, speaks up, "Do you have any place in mind?"

Jody nods, "We've come up with a place nearby to setup a campsite and discuss what to do and where to go next."

Lisa questions, "How soon are you talking about leaving?"

Jody glances around at everyone, knowing his reply will most likely shock them, "Within the next twenty-four hours. The sooner the better."

The room goes quiet again.

Ken speaks up, "The longer we wait, the more dangerous it gets for us here."

Michael, Lindsey's husband, sighs, "I don't know. That sounds awfully dangerous to go traveling the countryside."

Jody nods, "I know it does, but there is no other way." He pauses, "Remember the rules we set up?"

Janet questions, "Yeah, but what do you mean by that?"

Mike speaks up, "Anyone can leave the group anytime they want. If any of you don't want to go with us, you're free to stay here or do your own thing. You will get to keep your weapons and get your share of the supplies."

Ashley speaks up, "So, you're saying that come tomorrow morning, you are packing up your stuff and leaving."

Jody nods, "Yep."

Ken chimes in, "So am I."

Mike quickly follows, "Me too. Shadow too."

Jody sighs, "Look. I know this has been quite overwhelming to take in all at once. Let's keep on our scheduled watch rotation and everyone can take time to think about it. When we meet tonight, that's when we'll see what everyone decides."

Ken nods, "Think about it hard folks. This is going to be the biggest decision of your lives."

Everyone is quiet. Jody heads off to the garage to get ready for his watch. Janet notices that its nearly time for watch so she starts gathering her things. Everyone else starts heading their own way.

Jody and Janet are sitting at the kitchen table for their watch. Jody has noticed that Janet has been distant. Jody has really grown to like Janet for more than just a friend and hates seeing her this way. Jody knows what it is that is bothering Janet.

Jody looks at Janet, "How are you holding up?"

Janet replies in a depressed tone, "Okay I guess."

Jody leans closer, "I know you're missing your kids and that you feel you let them down."

Janet looks up at Jody, "They should have been with me. I was nice enough to let my ex take them for the holiday weekend."

Jody slides his hand over and takes Janet's hand, "Look sweetheart, there is no way you could've foreseen this happening. No one was prepared for it."

Janet sighs as she squeezes Jody's hand, "You seem to be okay."

Jody smiles, "It appears that way, but that is just me putting on my game face so to speak. Since everyone is looking to me, I can't let them see what's going on inside."

Janet looks into Jody's eyes, "Are you scared?"

Jody smiles again, "Not of the zombies. What scares me is that I won't be able to keep everyone safe. The people I've lost already, I miss dearly. I don't want to have to feel that way about anyone here." He pauses, "Especially you."

Janet gets a somewhat surprised look, "What?"

Jody gazes into Janet's eyes, "I know we're just friends, but I really like you in a more than friends way. I don't want to see anything happen to you."

Janet gazes back at Jody, "Thank you." She pauses, "I like you too, in the more than friends way."

About that time, Grace walks into the kitchen to get something to drink for Ayden and Ariel. Jody and Janet slide their hands apart. Jody looks at Janet with the, I hope I helped you a little bit look. Janet looks back at Jody with the, thank you look.

The day has been fairly quiet for the most part. Each small group mainly staying to themselves. Jody returned to his tent once his watch was over and has been going over the maps some more and making notes. Mike is sitting in the kitchen calculating up the inventory to see how far they can get on what they have and also figuring out each person's share in case someone decides not to go with them.

Marissa and Michael, Jody's brother, are sitting in Michael's bedroom. It's their turn for watch and between the times of checking the windows, they have returned to Michael's bedroom. Both of them have been thinking about what they are going to do.

Michael, Jody's brother, looks at Marissa, "So, what are you thinking?"

Marissa sighs, "I'm leaning towards going with them. I know its going to be dangerous and a little harder on me because of my knees, but there is no way I can make it on my own."

Michael, Jody's brother, nods, "I hear you. I'm going with them. They are right, it's too dangerous to stay here and going on my own is out of the question. Not to mention, I'm not in the best of shape or know how my heart will hold up after having problems last year with it."

Marissa agrees, "Yeah, it would be way too hard on us not to stick with the group. Plus, I know they could use our help too. The more the better."

Michael, Jody's brother, chimes in, "And safer." He pauses, "Well, I guess we should start organizing our things if we are going to leave tomorrow morning."

Marissa nods, "Good idea."

Michael, Jody's brother, and Marissa start looking around and gathering up their things.

Lisa and Rochelle are sitting in Jody's bedroom. Lisa has been thinking about what to do ever since Jody told her his plan the night before.

Rochelle finally breaks the silence, "What are we going to do mom?"

Lisa sighs, "Well, we have a couple of choices. We can go with Jody and the others or we can try to make it back home." She pauses, "Either way will be dangerous."

Rochelle questions, "Even if we make it back home, what would we do then?"

Lisa nods, "That I don't know and that's why I think our best option is to stick with the group. We'll be safer with them than on our own." She looks at Rochelle, "What do you think?"

Rochelle nods, "I think you're right. As much as I miss everyone, I think staying with them is better."

Lisa sighs, "Well then, let's start getting our things together so we'll be ready to leave tomorrow morning."

Rochelle responds, "Okay mom."

Lisa and Rochelle start to gather their things.

Grace is sitting on the airbed in the living room with Ayden and Ariel. Grace has been trying to figure out what to do that would be best for her and the kids. After thinking about it for awhile, Grace decides to talk to her kids.

Grace looks at Ayden and Ariel, "Hey, so I'm thinking that we should go with the others tomorrow morning."

Grace can see the sad look on Ariel's face and knows what the little girl is thinking.

Grace speaks calmly, "I know you want to find dad and so do I, but I don't think we can do it by ourselves. Okay sweetheart?"

Ariel looks at Grace with those adorable eyes, "Okay mom."

Grace looks at Ayden, "I just think it's too dangerous for us to be on our own."

Ayden replies in his typical style, "Don't worry mom. If any zombies try to get us, I'll chop them in the neck or smash them like the Hulk."

Grace smiles and slightly chuckles, "I know you would big man. That's why I'm counting on you to help take care of and protect your sister."

Ayden hops up and pretends to chop the air, "Yeah. Just like this!"

Grace smiles again, "Those zombies better watch out." She pauses, "Okay. I'm going to get our things together so you kids behave yourselves."

Ayden bounces around some more and Ariel smiles at Grace. Grace chuckles as she gets up.

Shana is in the master bedroom with Tyler and Zach. Shana has been thinking a lot about what to do since getting the news this morning about Jody's plan.

Shana looks at the boys, "So, I want to know what you two think we should do. I've already thought about it and I think we should go with Jody."

Tyler nods, "So do I. I like him. I miss everyone, but I think we should go with him."

Zach sighs, "I really miss my girlfriend, Cory and dad, but I know that we can't go off on our own and make it. I think its best if we go with them."

Shana nods, "I miss people too, especially Cory. Right now though, this is the safest thing to do." She pauses, "I'll be counting on the two of you to help out a lot."

Zach nods, "Sure thing mom."

Tyler agrees, "Okay mom."

Shana glances around, "Let's go ahead and start getting our stuff together so we'll be ready for the morning."

Shana, Tyler and Zach get up and start to gather their things.

Janet, Ashley, Lindsey, Daniel and Michael, Lindsey's husband, are sitting in the family room. Janet, Ashley, Lindsey and Michael, Lindsey's husband, have been thinking a lot about what they are going to do. Daniel is just laying in the bed, looking like he is ready for a nap.

Ashley speaks first, "So, what do you two think?"

Michael, Lindsey's husband, shakes his head, "I'm not completely convinced that leaving here is the right step. Their information makes it sound like it, but after spending all this time trying to stay inside and quiet, now they want to go traveling across the country to who knows where." He pauses, "I don't see how that is the best option."

Ashley nods, "I know what you're saying, but Jody and Ken are right. We will run out of stuff real soon if we stay here, then we'll have to get out anyway."

Michael, Lindsey's husband, shakes his head, "They just haven't made a believer out of me. I mean, this house is pretty out of the way. I don't think those things will find us

here. I just don't think that rushing out now is the best plan."
He pauses and looks at Lindsey, "What do you think?"

Lindsey sighs, "I agree, it's very dangerous and I've got to do what I think is best for Daniel."

Michael, Lindsey's husband, smiles at what Lindsey has said.

Lindsey continues, "Which is why I think we need to go with them." She pauses and Michael, her husband, loses his smile, "There is no way we are going to make it if we stay here without them or go off on our own. Not to mention, I'm guessing everyone else is planning to leave with them so it'll just be us."

Ashley nods slightly, "That's true. If it was just Jody, Ken and Mike, the rest of us might be able to make it. If it's just the four of us, I don't see how we'll make it." She pauses, "As much as I miss and want to know about my family, I think I'm going to go with them."

Ashley, Lindsey and Michael, Lindsey's husband, notice that Janet has been quiet the whole time.

Ashley looks at Janet, "What about you Janet?"

Janet sighs, "I've considered numerous times leaving to see if I could find my kids. As much as I love them and hope they are okay, I realize the truth. I understand that they are gone and that thought has killed me." She pauses, "But I also believe in God and I know that he has a plan for us all and I feel that the thing for me to do is to continue on." Janet pauses again, "I'm going with them."

Ashley smiles and nods.

Michael, Lindsey's husband, looks at Lindsey, "And you want to go with them too?"

Lindsey nods, "Yes. I think it's the best move right now."

Michael, Lindsey's husband, asks a serious question, "What if I don't want to go?"

Lindsey sighs, "I love you Michael more than any man ever, but I have to think about Daniel. We can't keep him safe without the others." She pauses, "I'm sorry, but Daniel and I will be leaving with them tomorrow."

Ashley can feel the tension, "So Michael, what about you?"

Michael, Lindsey's husband, just shrugs, "I don't know." He gets up and starts to walk off, "I guess I'll think about it."

Ashley looks at Lindsey and Lindsey gets a sad look on her face. Daniel slides over by Lindsey.

Daniel looks up at his mom, "What's wrong momma?"

Lindsey smiles at Daniel, "Its nothing Daniel. Michael and I are just trying to figure things out. It will be okay."

Daniel rolls over, "Okay momma."

Ashley puts her hand on Lindsey's shoulder, "Don't worry, he'll come around."

Janet tries to be reassuring, "Ashley's right. Just give him some time and he'll see that it's the right thing to do." She pauses, "We should get our stuff ready."

Lindsey sighs, "I hope so."

Ashley and Janet get up and head off to the living room. Lindsey lays down next to Daniel and puts her arm around him.

Codi and Ryan are sitting on the couch in the living room. Both of them have been thinking about what Jody said earlier.

Codi is petting Lucky, "So Ryan, what do you think?"

Ryan sighs, "It seems pretty dangerous, but I'd have to agree that staying here is not a good choice." He pauses, "I'm just thinking about something else."

Codi questions, "What's that?"

Ryan replies, "I'm just wondering if we should take off to try and make it back home and see if our families are okay."

Codi sighs, "As much as I'd like to, doesn't that seem pretty dangerous. Especially being just the two of us."

Ryan nods, "Yeah, that's what I'm struggling with."

Codi sets Lucky down on the floor, "I think for right now its best if we stick with the rest of the group. I hate to leave everyone behind without knowing what has happened to them, but we have to think about survival now."

Ryan nods and sighs, "You're right. Let's go with them tomorrow."

Codi smiles, "Okay."

Ryan and Codi share a loving hug as Janet and Ashley walk into the living room.

CHAPTER 20

The rest of the day has been fairly quiet around the house. Everyone has kept pretty much to themselves. After dinner that evening, everyone goes back to doing what they were doing. Janet and Ashley have stayed out of the tent feeling Jody is needing time to himself to figure things out. Jody is sitting in his tent in the garage. Jody is still looking over the maps and thinks he has the options narrowed down. Jody hears someone walk into the garage. Jody looks over at the opening to his tent and he sees Ashley walk up.

Jody smiles, "Hey Ashley, what's up?"

Ashley smiles back, "Not much. I was just wondering if I could talk to you for a minute."

Jody nods, "Of course, have a seat."

Ashley steps inside the tent and sits next to Jody, "I have never properly thanked you for everything you've done for me since this all began." She leans over and hugs Jody, "Thank you Jody, for everything."

Jody hugs Ashley back, "Its my pleasure. You're my friend and I won't let anything happen to you."

Ashley squeezes a little tighter, "I know."

Jody and Ashley finish hugging and lean back.

Jody looks at his watch, "Looks like its getting near time to meet in the living room."

Ashley stands up, "I'll let everyone know."

Jody smiles, "Thanks. I'll be there in a few minutes."

Ashley walks out of the tent and heads off to tell everyone about meeting in the living room.

Everyone is gathered in the living room as it nears 9 pm. Shadow is laying by the front door and Lucky is laying by the couch. Jody walks in the living room. The small nightlights keep the room somewhat lit up, but not too much to draw attention to the house. Jody looks around at everyone and wonders what their answers will be.

Jody speaks, "Okay. Let's just go around the room and get everyone's answer."

At that moment, the nightlights go out and the air conditioner shuts off. Everyone glances around at each other in the dark, wondering what happened.

Ayden looks at Grace, "Momma, what happened?"

Grace replies a little confused, "I don't know Ayden."

Mike speaks up, "Looks like we lost power."

Ken sighs, "It was bound to happen with no one left to monitor the power plants."

Jody speaks, "I'll be right back."

Jody makes his way back to the garage. Jody gets into his alice pack and pulls out his small, LED battery powered lantern. Jody turns it on and makes his way back to the living room.

Jody hands the lantern to Mike, "Here, put this on the end table. We'll use it for light tonight."

Mike takes the lantern and sets it down.

Jody looks around the room, "Okay, let's try this again." He pauses, "Who is going and who is not? I know myself, my dad and Ken are going, along with Shadow."

Michael, Jody's brother, speaks up, "I'm going."

Marissa quickly follows, "Me too."

Shana speaks up next, "The boys and I are going."

Lisa nods, "So is Rochelle and I."

Grace is next to speak, "The kids and I are going."

Ryan speaks up, "Codi and I are going too."

There is silence in the room for a moment.

Ashley nods, "I'm going."

Janet speaks up, "I'm going too."

Suddenly, Shadow's head perks up and looks at the door. Shadow starts to growl at the door. Everyone looks over at the front door.

Jody whispers, "Shadow."

Mike reaches over and shuts off the lantern.

Ken whispers, "Everyone quiet."

Dead silence falls over the room. The tension in the room grows with every second. Then, everyone hears the sound of crunching acorns just outside the living room window. Everyone holds their breath, wondering what it is in the front yard.

Jody whispers to Ken, "We need to find out what's out there."

Ken nods, "Okay."

Jody looks over to Mike and whispers, "Keep a hold of Shadow. Ken and I are going to go out the back and around through the side gate."

Mike nods, "Okay."

Jody whispers to everyone, "Just stay here and keep quiet. Janet, let me have your bat. Ken, grab Lindsey's bat. If there is only one or two, we can use these to be quiet. If there is a lot more, we may have to use our guns."

Janet quietly gives Jody her bat. Lindsey hands Ken her bat. Jody and Ken make their way out of the living room and to the back patio door in the family room. Jody quietly opens the blinds. Jody looks out the patio door to see if he can spot any motion in the back field or back yard.

163

Jody doesn't see anything so he gently opens the door, trying to make as little noise as possible. Jody and Ken step outside and Jody pulls the door shut behind them. Jody and Ken make their way over to the gate that is on the garage side of the house. Jody cautiously opens the gate as Ken keeps glancing around to make sure nothing walks up on them. As Jody closes the gate behind them, they both hear the sound of something banging on the front door of the house. Jody and Ken sneak over behind one of the vehicles in the driveway.

Jody looks around and doesn't see anything in the front yard or in the neighborhood, but he can kind of make out a figure at the front door of the house and knows it is a person.

Jody whispers to Ken, "Do you see anything?"

Ken whispers back, "Just the person at the front door. I don't see anything else."

Jody nods, "Me either." He pauses, "I want to get him away from the front door before we deal with him."

Ken whispers, "How do you want to play it?"

Jody whispers back, "I'll make my way to the end to the driveway and draw his attention. When he comes for me, you come up behind him and take him out."

Ken nods, "Sounds good."

Jody works his way to the end of the driveway and steps out into the street. Jody taps the baseball bat on the asphalt. The figure at the door turns around and sees Jody standing in the street. It's a male zombie with blood all over his face and hands. The zombie starts moving towards Jody in a fairly quick staggering walk.

The zombie gets about halfway through the front yard when Ken starts up behind it. The zombie, being completely fixed on Jody, never sees Ken. Ken glances over at Jody and Jody nods his head. Ken steps up behind the zombie and swings the baseball bat with all his strength. The baseball bat strikes the zombie in the back of the head. There is a crunching sound of the skull when the baseball bat makes contact.

The zombie falls to the ground from the force of the impact. Ken stands over the zombie as Jody walks up. The zombie weakly reaches out for Jody with its left hand. Ken raises the bat and delivers two more crushing blows to the zombie's head. The zombie stops moving.

Jody glances around, "Okay, I don't see anything else. Let's get back inside."

Ken glances around and nods, "Okay little buddy."

Jody and Ken make their way back around to the gate. The two of them quietly make their way into the backyard and back over to the patio door. Jody and Ken walk into the family room. Jody shuts the door behind them and locks it. Jody closes the blinds again and the two of them make their way back to the living room.

Ashley whispers, "What was it?"

Jody hands the baseball bat back to Janet, "It was a zombie. We took care of it, or rather, Ken did."

Ken sets the baseball bat in the corner of the room, "I'll give you your bat back Lindsey after I clean it off."

Lindsey nods, "Okay."

Jody whispers, "So, where were we?"

Ashley speaks up, "Lindsey and Michael are all that's left to answer. Everyone else is going."

Jody looks over to Lindsey, "So, what's it going to be?"

Lindsey whispers back, "Daniel and I are going with you."

Jody nods, "What about you Michael?"

Michael, Lindsey's husband, sighs because he was on the fence about it, but now that he's had time to think it over and given the recent loss of power and zombie at the door, he has made up his mind.

Michael, Lindsey's husband, whispers, "I'm going."

Jody nods, "Okay. So, we all are leaving in the morning. If everyone wants to grab something to drink, I'm going to go get the map and I'll explain where we are heading."

Everyone in the room nods. Jody makes his way for the garage as a few others head for the kitchen.

In a few minutes everyone returns to the living room. Mike turns the lantern back on, but sets it over by the wall opposite of the window. Everyone waits to hear what Jody has come up with.

Jody speaks to everyone, "Okay, this is what I have come up with for tomorrow. We will leave here and head south towards Afton. There is a gun shop just south of Afton that we will stop at and get more weapons, ammo and whatever gun supplies we need like holsters and stuff."

Mike questions, "Do you think it's a good idea to go through a town, even one as small as Afton?"

Jody shakes his head, "Oh no, I have the roads we will take around the town."

Ken nods, "Good. So we can get everyone equipped with guns and knives. I think we should still take the baseball bats with us just in case we need to be quiet about taking care of those things."

Jody nods, "That's a good idea. I agree."

Lisa questions, "So, what will we do after we get more weapons?"

Jody continues, "We will head south towards the lake. There is a small jut out on some back roads that we can find a good place to set up a campsite and figure out what to do next. I have a few options that I want us to discuss, but we will take things one step at a time. Let's just get the guns and get to the campsite first."

Ken nods, "Yeah, we don't want to get too far ahead of ourselves."

Michael, Jody's brother, questions, "So, what time in the morning are you looking at leaving?"

Jody pauses for a second, "Since we have a lot of gear and supplies to load up, I want to start at sunrise."

Ken nods, "So, whoever is on watch at 5am needs to wake everyone up so we can clean up and eat before we get started."

Jody nods, "That sounds good to me."

Grace questions, "So, what vehicles are we taking?"

Jody sighs, "I've been thinking about that. We will have to take a few vehicles. Mine is nearly out of gas so I won't be taking it. First, I want dad to take his van. We can remove the seats and load all the supplies in it and Shadow can ride with him. Second, I want Michael and Marissa to take our truck. We can put supplies or gear in the back of it."

Shana nods, "That sounds good. Since Cory took my car, the boys and I will have to ride with someone."

Jody nods, "Yeah, I figured Lisa and Rochelle could take their vehicle and the three of you ride with them. It might be a little crowded, but we can load all your gear in another vehicle. Lindsey, you, Michael, Daniel and Ashley can ride in your vehicle with all your stuff and some supplies. Ryan, Codi, Lucky and I will ride with Janet in her van with our stuff and supplies." He pauses, "That just leaves Ken, Grace and her kids. I'll leave it up to you Ken. You can ride with Grace in her car or take your truck."

Ken pauses for a moment, "I like my truck, but I think it would be best if I rode with Grace. With too many vehicles we could get strung out and create more noise."

Jody nods, "Good point."

Mike speaks up, "I think that about covers it, don't you."

Jody nods, "Yeah, that's everything we needed to get covered for now."

Ken speaks up, "Then I say we need to get some rest because it's going to be an early and long day tomorrow."

Lisa nods, "I agree."

Jody speaks up, "Okay, let's stop there. Whoever is on watch at 5 am, wake everyone up. Other than that, let's get some rest."

Everyone nods and starts to head their different ways. Each one wondering what the morning will hold for them and how it will be when they venture from the place that has kept them safe since this all began.

CHAPTER 21

It has been a couple hours since everyone has laid down for the night. Jody, Janet and Ashley are laying in his tent in the garage. Jody is looking over the map of the United States when Janet rolls over and looks at him.

Jody smiles, "Hey Janet, I thought you were asleep."

Janet gives a slight smile back, "I can't sleep."

Jody can tell something is wrong, "Everything ok girl?"

Janet sighs, "Can we talk some?"

Jody sits up, "Sure."

Janet sits up and moves over by Jody as Jody slides the map out of the way.

Jody looks at Janet, "How are you holding up?"

Janet looks at Jody, "It's still so hard to deal with losing my kids. My heart is shattered. I don't know what to do anymore. They were my life."

Jody slides his hand over and takes Janet's hand, "I'm so sorry sweetheart. I can't even imagine the pain that you are feeling and I know there is nothing I can say to make it better. Just know that you are not alone and don't have to face this by yourself. I'm here for you, always."

Janet gets tears in her eyes, "Thank you Jody." She pauses, "The hurt is so bad."

Jody slides over next to Janet and puts his arm around her, "I know it is. I wish I could make the pain go away." He pauses, "But I'm here and if you ever need anything, just come to me."

A few tears roll down Janet's face. Jody gently wipes the tears away.

Jody squeezes Janet tight, "I know you believe in God and I know that they are with him and he will watch over them." He pauses, "And I know your kids will be looking down at you. I know that they would want you to go on living for them."

A few more tears roll down Janet's cheek. Janet still feels unbearable pain at the loss of her kids, but Jody has made her feel a little better, even for just a moment.

Janet sniffles, "Thank you Jody."

Jody sighs and holds Janet close, "Anytime sweetheart."

Janet looks up and into Jody's eyes, "I wouldn't be able to make it without you." She pauses, "Do you think the others would say anything if I slept in your sleeping bag with you tonight? If you don't mind?"

Jody gazes at Janet so lovingly, "It doesn't matter what they think. If it would make you feel better, you can sleep here with me."

Janet manages a smile, "Thank you Jody."

Jody just smiles back. Jody slides around and lays down on his left side. Janet lays down and slides back against Jody. Jody wraps his arm around Janet. It doesn't take Jody and Janet long before they fall asleep.

Its early morning and Lindsey and Michael, her husband, are sitting at the kitchen table. It is an overcast morning as a cool breeze makes the temperature feel in the high 60's. Everyone else is still asleep, but its getting closer to time to wake everyone up.

Lindsey looks at Michael, her husband, "You okay about all this?"

Michael, Lindsey's husband, looks at Lindsey, "We don't have a choice, do we?"

Lindsey sighs, "No." She pauses, "Are we okay?"

Michael, Lindsey's husband, gives a reassuring smile, "Yes, of course we are." He pauses, "I just don't like being in a situation where I can't do more for you than someone else. I'm no expert at this stuff."

Lindsey gives her beautiful smile, "Don't worry, I know you will do everything you can for me and Daniel." She pauses, "And don't ever think I don't need you. I want you more than anyone else, ever."

Michael, Lindsey's husband, takes Lindsey's hand, "Thank you. I love you."

Lindsey smiles again, "I love you too."

About that time, the alarm on Lindsey's phone goes off.

Lindsey sighs, "It's time to start waking everyone up."

Michael, Lindsey's husband, nods and stands up, "I'll get the bedrooms in the back if you want to get the garage and the living room."

Lindsey stands up, "Okay."

Lindsey and Michael, her husband, share a brief, but very nice kiss then head off to wake everyone up.

Its nearly 5am now and everyone is awake. Jody starts packing up his stuff as everyone else washes up and gets something to eat. The kids are not too happy to be up so early, but are being surprisingly good given the circumstances. Once Jody has his stuff all packed up, he makes his way into the kitchen. Lindsey and Michael, her husband, are sitting at the kitchen table. Daniel is also at the table eating his breakfast.

Jody nods, "Let's meet in the living room."

Lindsey nods back, "Ok."

While the kids eat, Jody rounds up everyone and has them all meet in the living room. In a couple of minutes, all the adults are in the living room. Jody walks in and he is wearing his faded blue jeans, gray t-shirt, hiking shoes, his pistol and spare magazines,

Jody looks at everyone, "Is everyone packed up for the most part?"

Everyone in the room nods as they finish eating their breakfast.

Jody smiles, "Okay. First I want to load the supplies up. We will load up dad's van and the truck Michael will be driving. If there are still supplies, we will divide them between the other vehicles the best we can." He pauses, "Once the supplies are loaded, we will load up our personal things."

Ken questions, "Are we going to have anyone standing guard while we load everything?"

Jody nods, "Yeah, Michael and Marissa."

Jody knows that the physical exertion of loading everything will be hard on Marissa's knees and he doesn't want to take a chance with his brother's previous heart problems.

Michael, Jody's brother, nods, "Okay."

Jody looks at everyone again, "We start in ten minutes. Let's load quickly, but not too much so that someone hurts themselves or we make too much noise."

Everyone in the room nods and Jody walks out and heads for the garage. Once everyone finishes eating, they all get changed real quick and gather up their things.

The first into the garage is Janet. Janet is wearing her yellow tank top with pink butterflies, blue jean Capri pants and black and white tennis shoes. Janet has all of her things with her including the baseball bat. Janet looks at Jody and smiles. Janet sets down her things and waits.

Jody looks at Janet, "Hey babe."

Janet smiles at Jody, "Hey sweetie."

At that time, Michael, Jody's brother, and Marissa walk in with all their things. Michael, Jody's brother, is wearing his OU baseball hat, faded blue jeans, blue t-shirt and tennis shoes. Michael, Jody's brother, is carrying his shotgun and has his pocket knife on him. Marissa is wearing a black USMC baseball cap she got from Jody, blue jeans, green t-shirt and tennis shoes. Marissa is wearing her pistol and spare magazines.

Next to walk in is Ken. Ken is wearing a camouflage baseball cap, blue jeans and black boots. Ken is wearing his pistol and spare magazines and carrying his shotgun. Ashley walks into the garage. Ashley is wearing a green tank top, light colored jean shorts, tennis shoes and her prescription glasses. Ashley also has her baseball bat and Jody's pocket knife with her. Ashley puts her things down and waits.

Lisa and Rochelle walk in next. Rochelle is wearing a red top, faded blue jeans and tennis shoes. Lisa is wearing her black baseball cap, a green top, faded blue jeans and tennis shoes. Lisa is wearing her pistol and spare magazines and has her pocket knife on her. The two of them set their things down and wait.

Lindsey, Michael, her husband, and Daniel walk in the garage next. Lindsey is wearing a white baseball cap she got from Jody, a yellow t-shirt, faded blue jeans and tennis shoes. Lindsey is carrying the baseball bat and knife she was given. Michael, Lindsey's husband, is wearing his black baseball cap, blue t-shirt, blue jeans, tennis shoes and his prescription glasses. Michael, Lindsey's husband, is carrying the shotgun Jody gave him and is wearing the large knife. Daniel is wearing a red t-shirt, blue jeans and tennis shoes. The three of them set down all their stuff and wait for the rest of the group to show up.

Grace, Ayden and Ariel walk in the garage next. Grace is wearing a faded blue USA baseball cap that she got from Jody, a white tank top, faded blue jeans, tennis shoes and her prescription glasses. Grace is carrying the single shot shotgun and the knife she was given. Ayden is wearing his black and white baseball cap, brown t-shirt, camouflage pants and tennis shoes. Ariel is wearing a cute green outfit. Grace and the kids put their things down and wait.

Shana, Zach and Tyler walk in next. Shana is wearing a black Iraqi Freedom baseball cap Jody gave her, a black low cut short sleeve top, faded blue jeans and tennis shoes. Shana is wearing the pistol and spare magazine Jody gave her and showed her how to use. Zach is wearing a desert digital boonie cover he got from Jody, a black t-shirt, faded jean shorts and tennis shoes. Tyler is wearing a woodland digital boonie cover he got from Jody, a camouflage t-shirt, camouflage pants and tennis shoes. The three of them put their things down.

Codi and Ryan walk in next. Codi is wearing a gray t-shirt, light colored blue jeans, and tennis shoes. Codi is also wearing her pistol and spare magazines. Lucky is walking right behind her. Ryan is wearing a black t-shirt, blue jeans, tennis shoes and blue baseball cap. Ryan is also wearing his pistol and spare magazines. Ryan and Codi put their things down. Everyone is in the garage just waiting on Mike.

Mike walks into the master bedroom. Mike is wearing a maroon USMC baseball cap, a gray USMC collared shirt, faded blue jeans and tennis shoes. Mike has on his pistol and spare magazines. This place has been his home for many years. Mike looks at the table along the wall and stares at his wife's urn. The thought of leaving her behind is too much so Mike goes over and grabs the urn from the table. Mike places it gently in his bag.

In a few minutes, Mike walks into the garage with all of his things that he is taking. Jody looks around to make sure everyone is there.

Once he is certain, Jody speaks, "Okay. Once we open the garage, Marissa and Michael, you two take up watch positions on each side of the driveway." He looks at Mike, "Dad, if you will unlock your van, we will load it first with as many supplies as we can along with your personal belongings and Shadow's things, ok."

Mike nods, "Sounds good."

Everyone that has a shotgun or baseball bat sets them down with their things. Jody pulls the manual release on the garage door since the power is out and Mike and Jody raise the garage door. As soon as the door is completely up, Michael, Jody's brother, and Marissa hurry outside to take up watch positions. Marissa is on the right side of the driveway and Michael, Jody's brother, is on the left side.

Mike rushes over to his van and unlocks it. Mike sets his personal things inside and hurries back to get Shadow's things. Everyone else starts grabbing supplies and hurrying to the van.

Jody looks at his dad, "Once you get Shadow's things in the van, stay there and organize it as we bring the stuff to you."

Mike nods, "Okay."

Michael, Jody's brother, and Marissa keep a watchful scan of the area. Everyone is hurrying as fast as they can, but making sure they don't drop anything or hurt themselves. As each person takes something to the van, they look around in heightened anticipation, wondering if there are zombies around. It doesn't take long and the back half of the van is filled.

Jody looks around once the van is done, "Okay. Not a whole lot left. Dad, you and Shana take over watch."

Mike and Shana nod and head over to replace Michael, Jody's brother, and Marissa.

Jody looks at Michael, his brother, and Marissa as they walk up, "Grab your things and put them in the back of the truck. The rest of us will load the last of the supplies."

Everyone nods. Michael, Jody's brother, and Marissa head off to grab their things. Everyone else starts grabbing supplies and putting them in the back of the truck.

Jody looks at Ken, "Why don't you stay with the truck and keep it organized."

Ken nods, "Okay."

Jody looks at everyone else, "Keep one package of bottled water out for each vehicle and everyone will take one ration of food with them."

Everyone nods at the instructions. Before long, the truck is full and all the supplies are out of the garage.

Jody looks around as he catches his breath, "Okay, everyone get their personal belongings into their assigned vehicles along with the water and food." Jody looks over to Shana, "Shana, go ahead and get your things too."

Shana hurries over to get her stuff as everyone else grabs their things and head for their assigned vehicles. In a couple more minutes, everything is loaded in all the vehicles that are going. Jody motions for everyone to join him back at the garage. Everyone walks back into the garage and starts working on catching their breath.

Jody speaks, "Okay. We need to watch our gas levels. I know we have three gas cans with us and there are plenty of abandoned vehicles so if you start to get low, flash your lights and we'll stop." He pauses, "Other than that, just keep a watch out for any zombies or survivors. We don't want to stumble into anything."

Ken questions, "So, what order are we going to travel in?"

Jody sighs, "Janet's van with Ryan, Codi and I will be up front, then Lisa and her crew in her vehicle. Behind her will be dad's van, then the truck. I want to keep the supplies in the middle." He pauses, "Then Lindsey's vehicle will be next. Grace, you will bring up the rear. I want Ken in the back to guard our six."

Ken nods, "Sounds good to me."

Jody sighs, "Okay. We are going to be going pretty slow because we don't know what is out there and we don't want an accident." He pauses, "Dad and Codi, let's have the dogs walk around once more, then get them loaded up. Once that's done, we'll head out."

Everyone nods and Mike and Codi head back into the house to get Shadow and Lucky. As Mike and Codi brings Shadow and Lucky outside, Jody and Ken pull the garage door closed. Shadow and Lucky walk around the front yard for a minute. Jody and Ken stand watch as everyone else gets in their assigned vehicles. After a couple of minutes, Shadow is done and jumps in the van and Codi picks up Lucky and gets in Janet's van. Mike closes the door and walks around and gets in the driver's seat. Shadow hops up in the passenger's seat.

Jody looks at Ken, "You ready man."

Ken smiles, "Let's do this little buddy."

Ken heads off and gets in Grace's car in the passenger's seat. Jody walks over to Janet's van and gets in the passenger's seat. Everyone starts their vehicles. Janet pulls her van away from the curb and starts to drive away. Everyone takes one last look at the house that kept them alive over the last few days as each vehicle pulls away in their assigned order.

CHAPTER 22

Janet brings her van to a stop at Highway 69/59. Janet remembers this intersection from the trip into town. Janet knows that if she turns right, it will take them back into town.

Jody glances around, "We will turn left. Just take it slow, about 35 mph at the most for now."

Janet nods, "Okay."

Janet pushes down on the accelerator and turns left onto the highway. Everyone else in the convoy falls in behind her. Janet accelerates up to 35 mph and holds her speed there. It only takes a mile before they see some vehicles in the road ahead.

Jody looks at Janet, "Slow down some so we can maneuver around them."

Janet slows the van down. Jody draws his pistol from his holster just in case the vehicles are not completely abandoned. Janet weaves her way around the three cars, then gets back in her lane and accelerates up to 35 mph again. The rest of the vehicles weave their way through the three cars and quickly catch back up to Janet.

Everyone is glancing around trying to see if they can spot any zombies or other survivors. So far after about five miles, they have seen neither one.

Codi speaks, "I can't believe that we haven't seen a single survivor."

Jody nods while glancing around, "I'm sure there are plenty of others out there."

Janet questions while keeping her eyes on the road, "What if there isn't?"

Jody looks over at Janet, "The same thing as if there were, we'll do our best to survive."

Janet continues to watch the highway as they reach the halfway point to Afton.

Lisa keeps her Jeep Liberty about twenty feet from the back of Janet's van. Shana is sitting in the passenger's seat while Rochelle, Tyler and Zach are in the back seat.

Shana sighs, "I haven't seen any signs of anyone else."

Lisa continues to watch the back of Janet's van, "I know. It's not looking good."

Rochelle questions, "Are we really going to camp outside knowing that there are zombies around?"

Lisa glances at Rochelle in the mirror, "Yes we are. Jody knows what he's doing."

Shana nods, "Yeah, he does. This does seem risky, but I know he has his reasons."

Zach speaks up, "Don't worry mom, we won't let anything happen to any of you. Will we Tyler?"

Tyler shakes his head, "Nope!"

Shana, Lisa and Rochelle can't help but smile as they continue on towards Afton.

Mike is keeping his van pretty close to Lisa's Jeep Liberty. Shadow is sitting in the passenger's seat, staring at the windshield wipers.

Mike reaches over and scratches Shadow behind his ears, "I know you want to bark at the windshield wipers big boy, but we have to keep quiet right now."

Shadow looks at Mike as if to say, why haven't the wipers come on yet, I'm waiting patiently. Mike looks back at the road and concentrates on keeping close to Lisa's vehicle. Mike can tell that they are getting close to the interstate exchange.

Michael, Jody's brother, keeps the pickup truck pretty close to his dad's van. Marissa keeps looking around to see if she can spot any zombies or signs of other survivors. So far, Marissa has spotted neither. Michael, Jody's brother, knows the highway well and knows they are nearing the interstate exchange.

Michael, Jody's brother, speaks, "The interstate is just ahead. Just beyond that we will have to make a decision as to which highway to take at Buffalo Ranch."

Marissa continues to glance around, "Jody said we were going to avoid going into Afton so we must be getting off the highway soon."

Michael, Jody's brother, nods, "Yeah, I'm sure we will be taking a couple county roads around Afton."

Michael, Jody's brother, continues to focus on the road as the interstate comes into view.

Michael, Lindsey's husband, is keeping their Trailblazer about thirty feet behind the pickup truck. Lindsey is sitting in the passenger's seat, keeping a lookout and Ashley is sitting in the seat next to Daniel, also keeping a lookout. Lindsey sees the interstate ahead.

Lindsey speaks, "That looks like the interstate."

Michael, Lindsey's husband, looks up ahead, "It sure does. I know he doesn't plan on getting us on an interstate highway."

Ashley sighs, "Surely not."

Daniel looks at Lindsey, "Momma?"

Lindsey looks back at Daniel, "What is it Daniel?"

Daniel replies in a kind of sad tone, "Are we going home now?"

Lindsey sighs, "No. We are going camping. That's fun, isn't it?"

Daniel shrugs, "Sure. Are we going home soon?"

Lindsey tries not to show her emotions, "I don't think so baby."

Daniel puts his head down. Lindsey turns back around and looks out the windshield.

Michael, Lindsey's husband, lowers his voice and whispers to Lindsey, "We are going to have to tell him soon."

Lindsey sighs, "I know, just not right now."

Michael, Lindsey's husband, returns his focus to the truck in front of them and Lindsey stares out the window.

Grace is keeping her car about thirty feet from the back of Lindsey's Trailblazer. Ken is sitting in the passenger's seat. Ayden and Ariel are sitting in the back seat. Ken is continuing to look around for any signs of zombies or other survivors. Being the last car in the convoy, Ken is also looking behind them to make sure no one comes up behind them.

Ken speaks as he sees the interstate just ahead, "We are about to pass I-44."

Grace nods, "Yep. We are getting pretty close to Buffalo Ranch and Afton."

Ken sighs as he continues to look around, "Yeah, we should be getting off the highway soon."

Grace nods, "I bet we do at Buffalo Ranch where the highway splits into Highway 59 and 69."

Ken nods, "You're probably right. Although, I'm not too sure about going right by Buffalo Ranch. It's bound to have had people there when all this happened."

Grace nods, "I'm sure it did."

Ayden speaks up, "Don't be scared mom. I'll chop them in the neck if they try to hurt you."

Grace looks in the mirror at Ayden, "Thank you. Promise me you'll take care of sissy too."

Ayden smiles, "I promise!"

Grace returns her focus to the road and Ken starts looking around again as they begin to cross the interstate exchange.

Janet drives the van under the interstate exchange and she sees Buffalo Ranch up ahead. Jody glances around and sees a few abandoned cars, but nothing else. Jody sees Buffalo Ranch up ahead. Jody knows there is a chance that they might see something there. Jody draws his pistol from his holster as they cross over the new bridge just before Buffalo Ranch.

Jody glances around, "Just ahead is an intersection where the highway splits. I want you to turn left onto Highway 59."

Janet nods, "Okay."

Ryan starts looking over at Buffalo Ranch too. Ryan sees about ten vehicles in the parking lot.

Ryan looks at Jody, "I wonder if there are any survivors in there?"

Jody continues to keep a close eye on the store, "Who knows? We're not going to find out though."

As Janet approaches the highway exchange, she notices a sign for Afton pointing to the right.

Janet slows the van down, "You said left, but Afton is to the right."

Jody nods, "Yeah, we are going to turn left, then real quickly we'll get off Highway 59 onto South 530 Road. If we go right, we will have to go through the middle of Afton."

Janet nods, "Okay."

Ryan and Codi continue to watch the store as they pass by it and Janet turns the van onto Highway 59. Lucky sits between Ryan and Codi, wondering what is going on. Everyone else in the convoy slows down and turns onto Highway 59 as well, keeping about their same gaps.

As everyone makes the turn onto Highway 59, they all notice the sign for Afton pointing the other direction. Each one is puzzled about where they are going since Jody told them the gun shop is just south of Afton.

Michael, Lindsey's husband, looks at Lindsey, "Where in the world are we going? The town is the other way."

Lindsey shakes her head, "I don't know. I'm sure he has a reason for going this way."

Michael, Lindsey's husband, sighs, "Yeah right."

Lindsey sighs and changes her tone to an I don't want to get into it right now sound, "Let's just see where this goes."

Michael, Lindsey's husband, shrugs, "Whatever."

Michael, Lindsey's husband, looks back at the road as Lindsey continues to look around.

Jody continues to look around as he knows the road they need is coming up fast after the turn.

Jody glances at Janet, "Start slowing down, I think this is it."

Janet slows the van down as she sees a road coming up off to their right. Jody looks closely and nods as he sees the road sign.

Jody looks at Janet, "Okay, turn here."

Janet slows the van down and turns onto South 530 Road as Highway 59 bends off to the left. Everyone in the convoy behind them slows down and turns onto the road as well. Each one is starting to understand now why they went this way. They know that Jody is taking them around the town.

Being a county road, Janet slows down to 30 mph just to keep safe. Everyone else adjusts their speed to maintain their gap with the vehicle in front of them. Everyone continues to look around, but they each figure that on a back road, they have very little chance of running into anyone.

CHAPTER 23

Jody keeps a watchful eye out just in case they run into anything. Being on a back road, they won't have much space to maneuver. Jody sees an intersection ahead. Ryan and Codi also continue to look around. Ryan and Codi don't like not knowing where they are at, but they feel safer about it with Jody there.

Janet sees the intersection ahead, "Which way do I go?"

Jody continues to glance around, "Keep going straight. That is East 230 Road. We want the next one."

Janet replies, "Okay."

Janet slows down as they near the intersection of the two county roads. Jody and Codi are looking right and Ryan is looking left.

Ryan speaks, "Hey, there is a car down that way!"

Jody quickly looks left and sees a car stopped about a quarter mile down the road to their left, "It looks abandoned."

They pass through the intersection and continue straight. Everyone continues to follow them, wondering how far they are going to go because they each know that they have to head towards Afton at some point in time.

Jody looks around at the open fields and the trees. Jody wonders about what they will run into at the gun shop.

Jody knows there is a good chance that people will have tried to get to the gun shop when all of this started. As he continues to think, Jody sees another intersection up ahead.

Jody looks over at Janet, "Hey baby, you will turn right at this next intersection."

Janet nods, "Okay."

Janet slows the van down and puts on her right turn signal so Lisa will know she is turning. Lisa sees the turn signal and puts on her turn signal as well. Each car in line does the same to alert the vehicle behind them. Janet slows almost to a stop and turns right onto East 240 Road. She slowly speeds up to 30 mph again. Each car in the convoy turns and quickly catches back up to maintain their gap with the vehicle in front of them.

Michael, Jody's brother, is keeping his distance with his dad's van while Marissa is keeping watch. Michael, Jody's brother, has a good idea of where they are going now.

Michael, Jody's brother, glances at Marissa, "How are you doing?"

Marissa looks over at Michael, Jody's brother, "I'm okay. Why do you ask?"

Michael, Jody's brother, replies, "I've noticed you've been limping some."

Marissa nods, "Yeah, both my knees had surgery on them and they act up at times. As long as I don't have to do much running I should be okay." She pauses, "How about you? I know you've had heart related problems in the past."

Michael, Jody's brother, sighs, "I've been doing okay. I don't think I'll have any trouble as long as I don't have to do any prolonged periods of physical activity."

Marissa sighs and looks back out the window, "Aren't we a pair?" She chuckles slightly, "In this new world, we might have problems."

Michael, Jody's brother, just remains silent as they continue to follow the convoy.

Jody watches the area closely along with Ryan and Codi while Janet continues to drive down the county road. Janet sees an intersection coming up.

Janet questions, "What do we do?"

Jody looks and sees the intersection, "Go straight. Once we pass this road, it will be the next one."

Janet nods, "Okay."

Janet continues on through the intersection. Janet feels good that they are nearly to the first stop and they haven't seen any zombies yet. Ryan, Codi and Jody continue to look around. Jody hopes that the lack of seeing any vehicles or zombies means that the gun shop will be clear when they get there.

The convoy of cars continue on down East 240 Road when they see the next intersection. As they get closer to the intersection, everyone can see a large building off on the left. It looks more like a warehouse building than a shop.

Jody looks at Janet, "Okay. Turn left at the next intersection. There will be a gate and long driveway just after we turn. Park just beyond the gate on the main road."

Janet nods, "Okay."

Janet slows down and puts on her turn signal. Everyone else does the same. Janet slowly makes the turn and she sees the gate just ahead that Jody was talking about. Janet drives far enough pass the gate so everyone can make the turn, then she stops the van and puts it in park. Everyone else pulls to a stop, puts their vehicles in park, but leaves them running. Everyone looks to the left at the large gun shop building and wonders what waits for them.

Jody sits and looks at the gun shop for a minute, thinking about his plan of attack. The sun has broken thru the clouds and the day is starting to warm up now.

Jody looks at Janet, "Go ahead and shut the car off."

Janet turns the car off as Jody gets out. Everybody else sees Jody getting out and they shut their vehicles off and start getting out. The kids and dogs remain in the vehicles. Jody motions for everyone to join him at the open gate that leads to the long gravel driveway of the shop. Everyone walks over to Jody, but continues to look around in case they spot any zombies in the area.

Jody speaks to the others, "Okay, three groups will go and clear out the building. The others will stay here and keep a watch out." Jody looks at his dad, "You might let Shadow out since it will be a little while before we stop again." He looks at Codi, "Same thing with Lucky."

Ken glances around, "Where is the entrance at?"

Jody replies, "Its around on the back side of the building."

Grace questions, "So, who's going and who's staying?"

Jody pauses for a moment, "Well, I'm going since I know the layout of the shop, which means Janet is going with me. That also means, Ken and Grace are out since we all agreed that him and I will stay separate on things like this. Dad is going to take care of Shadow, so him and Shana are out. Codi is going to take care of Lucky so her and Ryan are out." He pauses, "I'll take Lindsey and her husband as well as Lisa and Ashley. Marissa and my brother will stay here and keep watch."

Ken nods, "Okay."

Jody glances around, "Everyone get their weapons and meet back here." Jody looks at Ken, "If you guys have any problems, just yell if you have to but get our attention somehow. Be ready, because if we come running that probably means the place is full of zombies."

Ken smiles, "Will do little buddy."

Jody and Lisa wait by the gate while Ashley, Janet, Lindsey and Michael, Lindsey's husband, get their weapons. Ashley and Janet walk back up with their baseball bats. Lindsey walks up with her baseball bat and knife. Michael, Lindsey's husband, walks up with his knife and the tactical shotgun he was given, plus he is wearing the 20 shell shotgun belt Jody gave him with the spare shells in it. Ken and the others set up watch around the vehicles while Mike and Codi get Shadow and Lucky out for a little walk.

Jody looks at the others, "Okay, I'll take the lead. Everyone stay close and keep their eyes and ears open. Once we get to the side of the building closest to us, Janet and I will go around to the left while the rest of you stay on the driveway to the right. We will link up again on the far side by the door. Okay?"

Everyone nods at Jody. Jody can tell by the look on their faces that they are starting to get scared of what might happen. Lisa seems to be staying fairly calm, but the others are getting really anxious.

Jody speaks, "Don't worry. Stay calm and nothing bad will happen. If you encounter a zombie, make sure you attack it's head."

Everyone nods again and Jody starts walking down the gravel driveway towards the building. The others fall in behind him. Everyone is looking around to see if they spot anything. Janet, Lindsey and Michael, her husband, are wondering if this is going to be their time where they will finally have to face the zombies.

It seems like Jody and the others have walked for an hour and they still haven't reached the building yet. The anxiety and tension grows with each step until Jody and the others finally reach the back of the building. Jody looks at Janet and motions for her to follow him. Jody motions for the others to keep going down the driveway.

Jody and Janet make their way to the corner of the building. Jody raises his pistol and does a quick peek around the corner. Sure that he didn't see anything, Jody slides around the corner with his pistol ready. Janet stays right behind him with her baseball bat ready. Jody and Janet continue down the side of the building and they continue to look around for any zombies or survivors.

Lisa and the others continue towards the far end of the building. Each one looking around to make sure there are no zombies coming their way. Before long, Lisa and the others reach the corner of the building. Lisa quickly peeks around the corner to see if anything is there. Once she is sure, Lisa moves around the corner of the building and the other three quickly follow. Lisa and the others see a couple of vehicles parked in the gravel lot. Lisa and the others each think the same thing, someone or something is going to be inside.

Jody and Janet reach the end of the building and stop at the corner. Jody quickly peeks around the corner and spots Lisa and the others heading towards the door. Jody and Janet move around the corner. Lisa brings her pistol up when she first sees Jody come around the corner, but lowers her pistol once she realizes it is Jody and Janet. Jody and Janet continue towards the door where Lisa and the others are waiting.

Jody looks at Lisa, "Did y'all see anything?"

Lisa shakes her head, "No."

Jody glances around, "I'm sure y'all are thinking the same thing that I am. With the two vehicles here, that there is a chance someone is inside. Let's just stay alert."

Jody reaches out and grabs the handle to the door. Jody pulls on it and the door comes open. Jody steps inside which is a small foyer type area with another door to his right which leads into the shop. Jody steps over to that door as Janet holds the first door open. Jody opens the second door and quickly peeks inside. Jody is sure that he didn't see anything so Jody steps inside the shop with his pistol ready.

Janet quickly follows Jody into the shop and in a couple seconds, the rest of the group also steps inside the shop. The counter with the register is to their right. There is a closed door directly across the room from them. To the left of the closed door is the pistol display counter and the rack with the rifles and shotguns. Along the wall next to them are all the accessories like holsters and things. To their left at the back of the store area are a couple of glass doors which lead back into the shop. Everyone notices one thing, there is no one in the store area.

Jody looks at the others, "Okay. Michael and Lindsey will stay here. Lisa, Ashley and Janet will come with me and we'll clear out the back area. That's where the ammo is along with other stuff. Okay?"

Lindsey and Michael, Lindsey's husband, nod as Jody, Janet, Lisa and Ashley head for the doors in the back. Jody and Janet move to the left of the doors as Lisa and Ashley move to the right of the doors. Jody looks through the doors from his side and Lisa looks from her side. Jody looks over at Lisa and nods. Lisa nods back and the two of them quickly go through the glass doors with Janet and Ashley right behind them. Jody glances around and sees the two bathroom doors in front of them about twenty feet and the rest of the shop is off to their right. Janet, Lisa and

Ashley look around at all the stuff piled up and they each think the same thing, lots of places to hide.

Jody whispers to Lisa, "You two head to the right and start clearing that way. We will check the bathrooms first, then help with the storage room."

Lisa and Ashley nod. The two of them start off down the wall to their right. Jody and Janet start walking towards the bathrooms. Everyone is wondering the same thing, where are the two people who own the vehicles out front.

Lindsey and Michael, her husband, are looking around the store area, waiting for the others to get back. As they look around, they don't see the door that appeared to be closed, start to open slowly. Lindsey and Michael, her husband, are looking at the different holsters and things with their backs to the door that is opening.

Lindsey whispers to Michael, her husband, "Let's check out the guns."

Michael, Lindsey's husband, nods and turns around. Suddenly Michael, Lindsey's husband, sees a zombie reaching for him just a couple feet away. It has blood all over it's face and hands.

Michael, Lindsey's husband, is startled, "Oh shit!"

Michael, Lindsey's husband, quickly brings his shotgun up in front of him. The zombie grabs the shotgun as it is reaching for Michael, Lindsey's husband. Lindsey spins around and sees the zombie attacking her husband. The zombie pushes forward. Even though Michael, Lindsey's husband, is a big man, the zombie pushes him back into the wall and starts biting at him. Michael, Lindsey's husband, pushes with all his strength and is able to hold the zombie at bay with the shotgun.

Lindsey looks to the back and yells, "Help!"

Lindsey looks back and sees the zombie getting it's mouth closer to Michael, her husband. Michael, Lindsey's husband, is holding on with all his strength, but the zombie is slowly getting closer. Lindsey knows she has to do something so she pulls her baseball bat back and swings it as hard as she can. The baseball bat slams into the back of the zombie's head. The blow from the baseball bat stuns the zombie and Michael, Lindsey's husband, pushes the zombie away with a strong shove. Lindsey swings the bat again and it strikes the zombie in the base of the skull. The zombie falls to the ground. Michael, Lindsey's husband, aims the shotgun at the zombie's head as it starts to move again. Michael, Lindsey's husband, pulls the trigger and the zombie's head explodes.

Jody and Janet are standing in front of the men's bathroom when they hear Michael, Lindsey's husband, fire his shotgun. Jody spins around to the glass doors. Suddenly, a male zombie bursts out from the bathroom. Jody spins back around as the zombie reaches for him. The zombie grabs Jody's right arm as Jody grabs the zombie's right shoulder. Jody struggles with the zombie, but he is unable to get his pistol on target. The zombie pushes forward and Jody trips and falls to the ground with the zombie on top of him. The zombie keeps trying to bite Jody, but Jody is able to hold the zombie away, Jody slides his knees up and uses them to help hold the zombie off, but he is still unable to get his pistol on target.

Suddenly, Janet steps over and swings her baseball bat as hard as she can. The baseball bat strikes the zombie in the right side of the head with a crunching sound. Jody feels the zombie go weak and he uses his legs to flip the zombie off of him. Once the zombie lands on the concrete floor, Janet, in a rage driven by the thought of her kids, swings the baseball bat down and smashes in the zombie's face.

Jody quickly gets to his feet as Janet raises the baseball bat again. Jody quickly holsters his pistol and grabs Janet.

Jody pulls Janet back from the zombie and close to him, "Baby, it's okay. Its dead."

Janet continues to stare at the zombie as she lowers the baseball bat. The feelings finally overwhelm her and Janet turns, puts her head on Jody's shoulder and starts to cry a little.

Jody hugs Janet, "It's okay baby. I know. It's okay."

Lisa and Ashley come running up and they see the zombie on the floor. Lisa and Ashley see Jody and Janet standing there.

Lisa quickly questions, "You two okay?"

Jody nods, "Yeah, go check on the others."

Lisa and Ashley hurry back into the store area where Michael, Lindsey's husband, and Lindsey are at. Jody continues to hug Janet as he knows she is letting out all of her emotions about her kids.

Jody whispers to Janet, "It'll be okay."

Janet sniffles, "I'm sorry."

Jody shakes his head, "Its okay baby. I more than understand." He leans back, "Hey, thank you."

Janet leans back, "What?"

Jody smiles, "You saved my life baby. Thank you."

Janet just smiles. Jody leans forward and the two of them share a nice, brief kiss.

Jody glances around, "Let's go check on the others."

Janet nods, "Okay."

Jody and Janet head back into the store area to see what happened.

CHAPTER 24

Ken and the others are waiting out by the vehicles when they hear the shotgun blast from the gun shop. Ken draws his pistol and hurries over by the gate. Marissa and Michael, Jody's brother, also rush over to the gate with their weapons. Grace and Rochelle were watching the kids and quickly go to check in on them when they hear the shotgun blast. Shana and Mike are walking Shadow and Codi and Ryan are walking Lucky when they hear the shotgun blast.

Mike looks at Shana, Ryan and Codi, "Quick, let's get the dogs back into the vehicles. We may need to get out of here in a hurry."

Shana and Mike start working on getting Shadow back to the van while Codi picks Lucky up and puts him back in Janet's van. Ken, Marissa and Michael, Jody's brother, are watching the gun shop closely.

Ken questions, "Do you see anything?"

Michael, Jody's brother, shakes his head, "No."

Marissa replies quickly, "Nope."

Ken looks at Marissa, "Michael and I will watch the shop. Go ahead and keep an eye out on the road in case someone heard it and starts coming this way."

Marissa nods, "Okay."

Marissa walks back over to the road and starts looking around in case any zombies start walking towards them.

Michael, Jody's brother, looks at Ken, "I wonder what's going on?"

Ken replies while gazing around, "I don't know. It was only one shot so I don't think anything bad happened to them or we probably would have heard more shots."

Michael, Jody's brother, nods, "You're probably right."

Mike and Shana get Shadow back into the van. Ryan and Codi walk over to Ken, Michael, Jody's brother, and Marissa. Ken, Michael, Jody's brother, Marissa, Ryan and Codi keep a close lookout for zombies and other survivors while they wait to find out what the shotgun blast was all about. Grace and Rochelle get Ayden, Ariel and Daniel calmed back down, but they too are wondering what is going on.

Jody, Janet, Lisa and Ashley are back in the store area with Lindsey and Michael, her husband. The six of them are trying to catch their breath from the recent zombie attacks.

Jody looks around, "Okay, here's what I want to do. Four of you will go back and get the others. Have everyone drive down here. We need to get things loaded quickly and it will take too long if we walk everything back and forth to the road."

Lisa nods, "Okay. Who stays and waits and who goes?"

Jody replies, "Lisa, you and Michael have the guns so you will go along with Janet and Ashley. Lindsey and I will wait here."

Michael, Lindsey's husband, looks at Jody, "Wait a minute. Why are we switching partners now?"

Lindsey looks at Michael, her husband, "This is no time for questioning things. Just do it!"

Lisa, Ashley and Janet head for the door. Michael, Lindsey's husband, sighs and quickly catches up to them. Jody and Lindsey look around the shop.

Jody looks at Lindsey, "Let's keep an eye on the front door and the glass doors in the back, just in case."

Lindsey nods, "Okay."

Jody and Lindsey move over to where they can watch both doors.

Ken, Ryan and Michael, Jody's brother, are keeping a close eye on the gun shop while Marissa and Codi are watching the road, mainly the direction that leads towards town. Mike and Shana have gotten Shadow back in the van. Grace, Rochelle, Mike and Shana start walking over towards the gate where Ken and Michael, Jody's brother, are at. The kids are in the vehicles.

About that time, Ken and the others see Lisa, Ashley, Janet and Michael, Lindsey's husband, come around the corner of the building and start running up the driveway towards them.

Ken shakes his head, "That doesn't look good."

In just a matter of a couple minutes, Lisa and the others are at the gate with the rest of the group that stayed behind. Marissa walks up to all of them to find out what happened.

Ken looks at Lisa, "What happened? Where's Jody and Lindsey?"

Lisa tries to catch her breath, "We encountered two zombies. They are okay. Jody wants us to bring all the vehicles to the shop so it will be quicker to load up everything."

Ken nods, "Okay everyone. Let's get moving. We have to hurry because we want to get in and out fast because this fence and gate could trap us if there is a large group of them."

Everyone hurries off to their vehicles. In a matter of a minute or two, the convoy is driving down the long driveway to the shop.

Jody and Lindsey are waiting in the gun shop for the others to return. Jody feels pretty confident that there are no more zombies or they would have shown up by now with all the noise.

Jody looks at Lindsey, "Let's go ahead and start pulling stuff out of the cases and off the racks so it'll go faster when they get here."

Lindsey nods, "Okay."

Jody pulls a piece of paper from his pocket, "I made up a list of what we need. First, let's get seven pocket knives out."

Lindsey walks over to the case where the knives are held. She finds the keys and opens the case. She pulls out seven folding pocket knives and sets them on the counter.

Jody nods, "Good. Now, we need six pistols. I would prefer all of them be 9mm since it's the most common ammo we will be able to find."

Lindsey and Jody walk over to the pistol cases. Lindsey unlocks the cases and the two of them start looking through the different pistols. Jody and Lindsey are able to find one full sized Glock 9mm, one full sized Ruger 9mm and a full sized Taurus 9mm. They also find a compact Ruger 9mm and a compact Glock 9mm.

Lindsey looks around, "All I see are these five."

Jody thinks for a second, "Well, let's grab the 357 Sig model of the Glock for my brother since his partner, Marissa, carries the same pistol."

Lindsey nods and looks back into the case. Once she locates it, Lindsey pulls the full sized Glock 357 Sig pistol out and places in on the counter. Each pistol has two magazines with them.

Jody looks at Lindsey, "See how many 20 gauge shotguns they have and how many 12 gauge. We need eleven total if they have that many. I'm going to grab a third magazine for each pistol."

Lindsey starts looking along the rack on the wall behind the pistol cases. Jody goes over to the wall where all the accessories are and starts getting the extra magazines. Jody walks back over to the counter and starts putting the extra magazines with each pistol. Lindsey walks up and they both hear the vehicles coming down the driveway.

Lindsey speaks, "They have one 12 gauge shotgun and eight 20 gauge shotguns."

Jody sighs and nods, "Okay. Well, let's grab the shotguns. I'll grab me the AR-15 rifle there with the scope on it. I'm very familiar with that kind of rifle and we will grab the 22 rifle."

Lindsey nods and the two of them walk back over to the wall rack. Jody and Lindsey grab the shotguns first and set them over by the pistols and pocket knives. Jody returns to the wall rack and grabs the AR-15 rifle. Jody looks around and finds three magazines for the rifle and a double magazine carrier. Lindsey grabs the 22 caliber rifle and sets it with the shotguns.

Lindsey walks over to Jody, "What now?"

Jody glances around, "They should be coming in any time now so let's just wait on them. All that is left is holsters and magazine holders for the pistols and ammo for all the guns."

Lindsey nods, "Sounds good."

Jody and Lindsey watch the two doorways again as they wait for the others to arrive.

In just a couple minutes, all the vehicles are parked in front of the shop. Everyone gets out and starts for the shop. All the kids are walking together and Rochelle and Zach are keeping an eye on them.

Jody and Lindsey look over to the doorway when they hear it open. They see Ken walk in first followed by everyone else. The first thing everyone notices is the zombie on the floor that Lindsey and Michael, Lindsey's husband, killed.

Jody speaks, "I didn't want to move this because I felt that everyone needed to see just what we are up against now and how real this is."

Everyone is quiet for a moment. Each one letting it sink in that they are truly in a life and death survival civilization now.

Jody finally speaks again, "Okay, let's get the weapons, ammo and accessories handed out so we can get out of here." He pauses, "Dad, Shana, Marissa, Janet, Ryan, Codi and Rochelle, I have a pocket knife for each of you laying on that counter if you want to go grab you one."

Mike, Shana, Marissa, Janet, Ryan, Codi and Rochelle all walk over to the counter and they each grab one of the pocket knives.

Jody nods, "Okay, now for the pistols. Janet and Ashley, we have a compact 9mm for each of you. Lindsey, you and your husband will each get a full sized 9mm along with Grace." Jody looks at his brother, "Michael, you will have the full sized 357 Sig pistol since that is what Marissa carries."

Jody walks over to the pistols. Ashley walks up and Jody hands her the compact Ruger 9mm. Janet walks up and Jody hands her the compact Glock 9mm. Grace walks up and Jody hands her the full size Glock 9mm. Lindsey walks up and grabs the full size Ruger 9mm. Michael, Lindsey's husband, walks up and Jody hands him the full size Taurus 9mm. Last, Michael, Jody's brother, walks up and Jody hands him the full size Glock 357 Sig pistol. Each of them grab their spare magazines too.

Jody motions to the wall with the accessories on it, "Each of you find a holster and double magazine carrier real quick, then we will hand out the shotguns."

The six of them walk over to the accessories wall and start going through the different holsters and magazine carriers. It only takes them a couple minutes to each find one and put them on. Once they all have their pistols and magazines on, everyone returns to the counter where Jody is at with the shotguns.

Jody glances around, "Okay, we have eight 20 gauge shotguns, one 12 gauge shotgun and a 22 rifle. I'll be carrying an AR-15. Grace, go ahead and give the single shot shotgun you have to Rochelle for now."

Grace hands the shotgun she is carrying to Rochelle.

Jody nods, "Each one of you that need a shotgun, step up one at a time and grab one. Ryan, why don't you take the 12 gauge and Codi can take the 22 rifle."

Ryan steps up and grabs the 12 gauge shotgun. Codi steps up next and grabs the 22 rifle. Lisa steps next and she spots the one tactical 20 gauge shotgun and grabs it. Mike steps up next and grabs a shotgun, then Shana steps up and grabs a shotgun. Marissa steps up next and grabs one followed by Grace who grabs her a new shotgun. Next is Lindsey and Ashley steps up after her. Janet steps up to the counter last and picks up the final shotgun.

Jody glances around again, "Okay, now that we have all the weapons, let's start gathering up all the ammo we can and get it loaded up in our vehicles. Everyone keep their ammo in their own vehicles, ok." Jody pauses, "Hang on a second." He looks at Shana, "What do you think about Zach and Tyler having guns?"

Shana looks over at her sons, then back to Jody, "Tyler is really good with a shotgun and Zach is good with handguns. It wouldn't hurt if they each had one."

Jody nods, "Okay. Rochelle, go ahead and hand the shotgun to Tyler."

Rochelle sighs in relief as she hands the single shot 20 gauge to Tyler. Jody walks over to the pistol case. Jody sees a couple of 38 revolvers left in the case. Jody walks around behind the counter and grabs both the revolvers.

Jody looks over to Zach and Rochelle, "Each one of you take one. Then go ahead and find you a holster for them."

Zach and Rochelle each grab a pistol and walk over to the wall where the holsters are at. It doesn't take Zach and Rochelle long and they each find a holster, then walk back over to the group.

Jody nods, "Okay, now let's get to the ammo."

Everyone nods. Jody starts walking towards the back double glass doors where the other zombie is laying that Janet killed in order to save him. The group walks into the back of the gun shop and they see the crates of ammo laying in the room.

Jody sighs, "All of you start with shotgun ammo first and Codi and I will grab our rifle ammo. Let's get that divided up into even stacks, then do the same with the pistol ammo." He pauses, "After Codi and I get our rifle ammo, we'll go watch the front while you all get the ammo sorted."

Everyone nods and starts over to the ammunition crates. Jody and Codi wander around until they find the ammo for their rifles. Jody and Codi each grab 100 rounds and start for the front of the shop while everyone else starts sorting the shotgun and pistol ammunition.

CHAPTER 25

Jody has loaded his three 20 round magazines. Codi has loaded her 3 magazines for the 22 rifle. Jody and Codi have the rest of the ammunition for the rifles sitting next to them at the front door. Jody watches out the front using his eyes and ears to try and spot if anyone or anything is headed their way. Jody thinks about the route they will be taking to where he plans on them camping for the night. Jody also knows that they don't have enough sleeping bags and tent space for everyone.

About that time, Jody hears someone heading for the front door. Jody looks back and sees Ken and Mike approaching first.

Jody looks at Ken, "How is the ammo situation?"

Ken nods, "Good. The three of us with 12 gauge shotguns will have 100 shells each. Everyone with a 20 gauge will also have 100 shells each."

Mike chimes in, "The pistol ammo is just as good. With what I already had, I'll have a total of 200 rounds. Marissa and your brother will each have 200 rounds of their ammo. Lisa has the only 40 cal and she will have 200 rounds. Codi has the only 380 auto so she will have 200 rounds. Ken has the only 45 ACP so he has 200 rounds. Rochelle and Zach will each have 150 rounds and everyone with a 9mm will have 150 rounds each."

Jody nods, "Sounds good. I'll stand lookout. Get the others to start bringing out their ammo."

Ken nods, "Okay."

Mike and Ken head back to the others to have them start bringing out their ammunition and weapons. While, Ken and Mike was talking with Jody, everyone else loaded their weapons.

Jody steps outside and walks about halfway into the parking lot area so he can get a good look around. Jody hears everyone heading for the front door from inside. Ken is the first one out of the shop and everyone else is right behind him. Rochelle is walking with the kids. With the help of the kids, the group was able to bring all the pistol ammunition out first. Everyone places their ammunition in their assigned vehicles, then returns to the shop. A minute later, everyone returns to the vehicles with all the shotgun and rifle ammunition. Once everything is loaded up in the proper vehicles, Jody motions for everyone to come over to him.

Once everyone walks up, Jody speaks, "Okay. We will get headed out to the campsite. We will go in the same order as before. Everyone stay sharp."

Ken speaks up, "For those of you who are not sure how to use your weapons, once we get camped, we will show you how to properly use them."

Everyone nods.

Jody glances around, "Okay. Let's get out of here."

Everyone heads back to their assigned vehicles. Once everyone is loaded up, Janet pulls out first and everyone falls in line like before. The convoy rounds the side of the building and they don't see anyone at the gate or on the road. Everyone breathes a sigh of relief.

Jody looks at Janet, "Turn left out of the gate."

Janet nods and slows down. Janet makes the turn back onto the county road. Everyone falls in behind Janet and they start on their trip to their home for the night.

Janet keeps the van at a steady 30 mph. The rest of the vehicles are keeping their close gaps. No one is sure how long it has been since they left the gun shop, but they each wonder how far until they reach the campsite Jody had talked about. Jody, Codi and Ryan continue to look around as Janet focuses on the county road.

Janet finally breaks the silence, "How far do you figure?"

Jody looks over at Janet, "Not too much longer and we will run into Highway 85. From there we will stay on the highway until it runs into the next county road we need."

Codi questions, "So, we are just going to camp out in the open?"

Jody nods, "That's all we can do."

Ryan interjects, "That seems a little dangerous given the fact that there are zombies everywhere."

Jody nods, "It is dangerous, but if we keep on our toes and everyone does what they're supposed to do, we will be okay."

Jody sees the junction to the highway coming up, "Janet, that's the highway. Just pull on the highway and keep going straight."

Janet nods, "Okay."

At that moment, the four of them hear a beep. Jody gets a puzzled look and he pulls out his cell phone.

Jody chuckles slightly, "Huh, I got a signal on my phone."

Codi gets a smile, "So, that means not every place is out of power."

Jody nods, "Yeah, at least not yet."

The talking dies back down as Janet focuses on the highway and dodging any abandoned vehicles while Codi, Ryan and Jody continue to watch for zombies.

As the time passes and the convoy of vehicles continue down the highway, everyone wonders if they will find other survivors or if they are the last ones alive. Grace looks into her rearview mirror and sees Ayden and Ariel sleeping.

Grace looks over at Ken, "I feel so bad for them."

Ken nods his head as he keeps his eyes scanning the area, "Yeah, me too."

Grace sighs as she watches the road, "They are not even old enough to really understand what's happening. They won't even get the chance to have a real childhood now."

Ken replies as his gaze over the area continues, "At least they are alive and they have you."

At that moment, Grace feels her phone vibrate in her pocket. Grace pulls her cell phone out of her pocket, surprised that it is even working. Grace can't believe her eyes when she reads the message she had just received.

Ken glances over and sees the look on Grace's face, "What is it?"

Grace can barely speak, "Its from my husband."

Ken questions, "Is everything okay?"

Grace feels the car drifting and she looks back to the highway and pulls the car back into line behind the others.

Grace barely manages a response, "Yeah, he is heading this way with a couple of his work friends. They are on Highway 69 right now."

Ken gets a somewhat surprised look, "Wow, I can't believe they tried to get back here."

Grace quickly types a text back, then puts her phone down so she can concentrate on the road. Grace gets a smile on her face, but it is also obvious that she didn't tell Ken everything as her facial expression turns to that of deep thought. Grace looks into her rearview mirror at her kids again.

Michael, Jody's brother, keeps the truck close to the back of his dad's van. Marissa is looking around, but she hasn't spotted any zombies or other survivors. Michael, Jody's brother, slows the truck down and follows his dad's van off the highway and onto another county road.

Michael, Jody's brother, shakes his head, "I have no idea where he is taking us."

Marissa continues to look around, "I'm sure wherever it is, Jody has given it a lot of thought."

Michael, Jody's brother, nods and smiles, "Yeah, he is quite the little planner."

Marissa smiles, "Yes he is."

Michael, Jody's brother, keeps pace with his dad's van as Marissa continues to keep an eye out.

Lindsey keeps her Trailblazer close to the truck in front of her. Michael, Lindsey's husband, and Ashley are looking around to see if they spot any zombies or other survivors, but they haven't seen a thing at all.

Ashley speaks, "Well, wherever he is taking us, it sure seems like it will be an out of the way place."

Michael, Lindsey's husband, nods, "Yeah, we seem to be getting back in the woods a good ways."

Lindsey smiles, "I think that's a good thing. I mean, we shouldn't run into too many people, alive or dead, if we are in the middle of nowhere."

Michael, Lindsey's husband, sighs, "True, but I'm still not feeling real good about camping out in the open with everything that has been going on."

Ashley nods, "I know. Its kind of dangerous."

Lindsey glances at the two of them, then back to the road, "It is, but I'm sure Jody has thought it out. He's not the type to do something like this without having planned it out."

Michael, Lindsey's husband, looks over at Lindsey, "I hope so."

Michael, Lindsey's husband, and Ashley return to looking out for zombies and other survivors as Lindsey stays focused on the truck in front of her and the road.

Lisa keeps her Jeep Liberty close to Janet's van. Shana is in the passenger's seat keeping a close watch of the area as they travel. Rochelle, Zach and Tyler are in the backseat. Rochelle and Zach are keeping watch out the windows while Tyler sits in the middle. Lisa sees Janet's brake lights come on so she starts slowing down. Lisa comes to a stop behind Janet's van. Lisa watches as Janet's van turns right and Lisa quickly makes the right turn and catches back up to Janet's van.

Tyler is the first to speak, "I hope we are close. I'm getting hungry."

Rochelle nods, "Me too."

Lisa looks at her watch, "Wow, I've been so focused on driving I didn't even realize its after twelve."

Shana nods as she continues to look around, "Yeah, it has been a long day already and we still have to set up camp once we get to wherever we're going."

Zach continues to look around, "I bet we are getting close. We have been off the highway for awhile now and all we've seen are more and more woods."

Shana looks left and thru the trees she sees something else, "Hey look, water."

Zach and Rochelle look left and they see the lake thru the woods. Tyler does his best to look out the window so he can see it too.

Lisa nods, "We have to be getting close if we can see the lake. Now it makes sense why Jody came this way."

Lisa returns her look to Janet's van while the others continue to look around.

Mike keeps an eye on Lisa's Jeep in front of him. Shadow is sitting in the passenger's seat, staring at the windshield, hoping that the windshield wipers will come on. Mike sees Lisa's brake lights come on. Mike slows his van to a stop behind Lisa's jeep. Mike watches as Janet's van turns left followed by Lisa's Jeep. Mike turns left onto the new county road. Mike knows the back roads around the area pretty well and knows that they are getting close.

Mike reaches over and scratches Shadow behind the ears, "We are almost there big boy."

Shadow gets his typical big smile on his face. Mike returns his look to the road.

Janet keeps the van at a steady 30 mph. Jody continues to look around. Ryan and Codi have noticed some small, dirt roads off on the left of the county road.

Jody speaks, "We should be coming to a sharp curve. As soon as we reach the curve, take the first dirt road to the left. It should take us right down to the lake."

Janet nods, "Okay."

Jody, Ryan and Codi continue to look around. Lucky looks up at Codi from in front of the seat. Codi picks Lucky up and starts petting him.

Codi speaks, "I'm glad we're almost there, Lucky is getting restless."

Jody nods, "Yeah, I'm sure Shadow is too. Not to mention its after lunch."

Ryan nods, "Yeah, my stomach has been reminding me."

Janet smiles, "There is the curve."

Jody looks forward and sees the curve coming up. Janet slows down as she takes the van thru the sharp, right curve. As soon as they come around the curve, Jody looks ahead and to the left.

Jody points, "Take that turn off there."

Janet nods, "Okay."

Janet slows the van to a stop, then gently turns left onto the rough trail that leads towards the lake. Jody looks in the mirror and sees everyone turning in behind them. Janet keeps the van at about 15 to 20 mph due to the rough trail. The trail goes about 500 feet, then it opens up. Janet slows down as the opening appears in front of them.

It's a huge open area by the lake. Ideal for camping. Janet stops the van and looks at Jody. Ryan and Codi both see what Janet sees and also looks at Jody. Jody looks towards the lake and he sees a large tent, about the size that can house 10 to 12 people. Jody looks the area over and doesn't see a vehicle anywhere.

Janet questions, "What now?"

Jody glances around, "I'm going to get out and walk. Follow me with the van. Once we get close, I'll direct where I want everyone to park."

Ryan nods, "Why don't I get out with you, just in case."

Jody nods, "Sounds good to me."

Janet looks at Jody with love in her eyes, "Be careful, please."

Jody gazes back at Janet, "I will."

Codi looks at Ryan, "Be careful."

Ryan smiles, "I'll be fine, I've got Jody with me."

Codi smiles. Jody grabs his AR-15 and Ryan grabs his shotgun. Jody and Ryan both get out and walk in front of the van. Jody and Ryan adjust their pistols on their hips from sitting.

Jody looks at Ryan, "Ready?"

Ryan nods his head, "Let's do this."

Jody and Ryan slowly start walking towards the large tent.

CHAPTER 26

Jody and Ryan start to slowly walk towards the large tent. Jody has his AR-15 at the ready, with his pistol on his right hip, spare magazines on his left hip and his combat knife attached horizontally on the back of his waist. Ryan has his shotgun at the ready with his pistol on his right hip, spare magazines on his left hip and his pocket knife in his front, right pocket.

Janet slowly lets the van idle forward as she watches Jody and Ryan closely. Codi keeps looking left and right to make sure nothing comes at them from the sides. The rest of the vehicles slowly idle forward as well, wondering what is going on.

Jody and Ryan continue towards the large tent, but both of them scan the entire open area as they slowly move forward. Jody and Ryan know that they might have to get out of there in a hurry. Jody and Ryan are about a hundred feet from the tent now. Jody stops and Ryan stops noticing that Jody did. Jody turns towards Janet's van. Jody holds his hand up and motions for Janet to stop and stay where she is at. Janet nods, acknowledging that she understands.

Jody turns back around, looks at Ryan and whispers, "Let's make sure nothing is in the tent."

Ryan nods, "Okay."

Jody and Ryan slowly make their way towards the tent which is about fifty feet from the lake. Jody and Ryan continue to look around as they get closer to the tent. Jody listens intently, trying to see if he might be able to hear anyone or anything that might be inside the tent. Ryan continues to scan the area.

Jody and Ryan are about ten feet from the front of the tent which is zipped closed. Jody and Ryan look over the area and they do not see any other belongings except the tent. Jody sniffs the air, remembering what it smelled like in the store, but he doesn't smell anything bad. Jody and Ryan finally stop at the front of the tent.

Jody looks at Ryan, "Cover me while I open the tent and check inside."

Ryan nods, "Okay."

Jody reaches out with his left hand while holding the AR-15 with his right. Jody grabs the zipper as the tension in the air is so thick you could cut it with a knife. Ryan holds his shotgun at the front of the tent as Jody slowly unzips the tent door. Once the doorway is halfway open, Jody steps to the side so he can get a look inside. Ryan continues to hold the shotgun ready.

Jody looks into the tent and he is sure that he doesn't see anyone. Jody glances over at Ryan and nods. Jody quickly steps inside the tent and brings his AR-15 up and ready. Jody looks around the inside of the tent. All Jody sees is four sleeping bags that are still rolled up and look brand new. Jody doesn't see anything else.

Jody steps back outside the tent and looks at Ryan, "Its clear." He pauses and glances around, "Keep an eye out. I'm going to bring them in and have them park."

Ryan nods, "Okay."

Ryan starts to slowly walk around the campsite as Jody makes his way back over to the vehicles.

After about ten minutes, all the vehicles are parked next to each other in a line facing the trail that leads back out to the county road. Jody has them arranged as kind of a barrier on the wooded side of the campsite while the lake provides a barrier on the opposite side of the campsite. Everyone is out of the vehicles, except for the dogs, and they have joined Jody and Ryan in front of the large tent. Everyone has their weapons with them.

Jody looks at the group, "This will make a good campsite for the time being."

Lindsey questions, "What about the people who left the tent?"

Jody shakes his head, "I haven't seen a sign anywhere. My guess is they just started setting up, then left for whatever reason."

Ken glances around, "We'll definitely need to stay sharp. This open area will give us a good chance to see anyone coming, but we can't get complacent."

Jody nods, "Exactly. We will continue the watch rotation from the house, same partners and everything."

Janet questions, "So, what next?"

Jody glances around, "First, let's get the dogs out and get them walked around. While Dad, Shana, Codi and Ryan take care of that, Janet and I will stand watch. Everyone else work on getting the kids some food and once they are done eating, the rest of us will eat." He pauses, "After that, we will get camp set up."

Everyone nods.

Ken speaks up, "I have a suggestion."

Jody looks at Ken, "What is it?"

Ken sighs, "I say we leave the keys to each vehicle in the vehicles on the dash by the steering wheel. That way if we have to leave in a hurry or the person with the keys gets separated or infected, anyone else can get in and drive."

Jody nods, "That's an excellent idea. I didn't even think about that." He pauses, "Okay, everyone who has keys to the vehicles, place them on the dashboard and of course we will leave the vehicles unlocked."

Everyone nods again. Jody starts to walk off towards the vehicles. Everyone with keys heads for the vehicles as well.

The dogs have been taken care of and everyone has eaten, while Jody and Janet are over by the vehicles standing watch. Shadow and Lucky are in Mike's van while everyone waits for what to do next.

Ken walks up to Jody and Janet, "Everyone is ready."

Jody finishes the last bite of his food, "Okay. Have my brother and Marissa come take over watch."

Ken nods and walks off. In a few seconds, Marissa and Michael, Jody's brother, walk up to Jody and Janet.

Jody looks at them, "Since neither of you has a tent to set up, you two will stand watch while we get the campsite ready."

Marissa nods, "Okay."

Michael, Jody's brother, nods, "No problem."

Jody and Janet walk over to the rest of the group. Everyone is standing in front of the large tent.

Lisa looks at Jody, "So, what now?"

Jody looks around, "First, we get our tents set up. Everyone that brought a tent, grab them along with your sleeping bags. Everyone else, just grab your sleeping bags for now."

Everyone walks off to the vehicles. In a minute or two, everyone returns with their sleeping bags. Jody, Lindsey,

Ryan and Grace also walk up, each one carrying a small, four person tent. Everyone sets their things down in front of the large tent. Mike, Ken, Lisa and Rochelle do not even have a sleeping bag.

Jody looks around, "Okay, so we have four tents we can use and this large one we found." He pauses, "Who doesn't have a sleeping bag?"

Mike replies, "I don't."

Ken nods, "I don't either."

Lisa speaks up, "Rochelle and I don't."

Jody nods, "And I know my brother doesn't." He pauses, "There are four new sleeping bags in the large tent, but that still leaves us one short."

Janet quickly speaks up, "I can loan mine to one of them and I can share with you, since we are watch partners."

Jody looks at Janet and sees her smiling, "Okay. How about Ken, Lisa, Rochelle and my brother take the bags in the tent and Janet can loan her bag to my dad." He pauses, "Now, let's set up our tents. We will set one of our tents off each corner of the large tent. Once we get that done, we'll meet back here."

Everyone nods and breaks up into groups to help setup the tents while Marissa and Michael, Jody's brother, continue to keep watch.

It doesn't take long and all four tents are setup. Everyone walks back over to in front of the large tent. Michael, Jody's brother, and Marissa have kept a constant watch, but they haven't seen or heard a thing. Jody looks at his watch and likes that they have gotten here and got camp set up with plenty of time left in the day.

Grace looks at Jody, "Okay. What now?"

Jody sighs and looks around, "Now we decide who will sleep where."

Ashley questions, "How do you want to do that?"

Ken speaks up, "Well, first we should make sure partners are in the same tent."

Jody nods, "Agreed. In my tent it will be Janet and I along with my dad and Shana."

Lindsey speaks up, "Michael and I can take Ashley and Lisa in our tent."

Michael, Lindsey's husband, questions, "That'll get crowded with Daniel too."

Jody speaks up, "I would like for the kids to be in the large tent in the middle of all of us or at least most of the kids and the dogs." He pauses, "I'd like Rochelle, Zach and Tyler along with Shadow and Lucky in the large tent."

Lindsey nods, "Daniel can stay in there with them. He'll be okay, he's a big boy."

Daniel looks up at Lindsey, "Yea!"

Jody smiles, "Okay, that takes care of our two tents."

Ryan speaks up, "Your brother and Marissa can stay with me and Codi."

Jody nods, "Okay. That's everyone except Ken, Grace, Ayden and Ariel. I guess you four can take Grace's tent."

Grace nods, "Sounds good to me." She pauses, "I think there is something I should tell all of you."

Jody looks at Grace, "What is it?"

Grace replies, "On the way here my phone started working and I got a text from my husband."

Ashley smiles, "That's great!"

Grace nods, "Yeah. Him and a couple of his work buddies are heading this way. Actually, to Fort Leonard Wood in Missouri and he asked me where I was and if I could meet him. Obviously that's if I got the text which I did." She pauses, "He said they would be passing through Vinita in the morning and heading towards Afton."

Everyone gets quiet.

Ken questions, "What are you going to do?"

Grace sighs, "I've decided to take Ayden and Ariel and leave in the morning to head back towards Highway 69 to meet up with them."

Codi shakes her head, "That's crazy. Its pure luck they made it this far, but trying to travel all that way is dangerous."

Ken nods, "Especially to a place that is probably already overran by zombies and if it isn't, can be easily surrounded by them."

Grace nods, "I know, but it's my husband and we should be with him."

Jody speaks up, "As much as I think it's a big mistake to go there, we did make up the rules." He pauses, "If Grace wants to take her kids and leave, that is her choice. She can take her weapons and her share of the supplies."

Grace smiles at Jody, "Thanks FIT B."

Jody sighs, "I would just ask you to think on it tonight and if you still want to leave in the morning, we'll get you your things."

Grace nods, "Okay."

Jody looks back at everyone, "Okay, for now let's get our personal belongings into our tents. Keep everything together in case we have to pick up and run."

Everyone picks up their things and heads for their tents.

CHAPTER 27

Once everyone's belongings are put in their assigned tents, they all meet back in front of the large tent. Michael, Jody's brother, and Marissa are still on lookout.

Jody looks at everyone, "Okay. Now I want to talk about where we are going to go." He pauses, "Zach, I would like for you and Tyler to stand watch for Michael and Marissa while we talk about things. You okay with that?"

Zach nods, "Sure."

Tyler smiles, "You bet."

Codi looks at Jody, "You're going to have them stand watch?"

Jody nods, "Sure. I trust them and they both know how to use guns if needed."

Shana speaks up, "They'll do fine."

Zach and Tyler grab their guns and head over to where Michael, Jody's brother, and Marissa are at. Michael, Jody's brother, and Marissa join the rest of the group in front of the large tent. Everyone gets as comfortable as they can.

Jody speaks up, "Okay. I already have my suggestion in mind, but I'd like to hear any suggestions about where we should travel to in order to settle down and try to survive."

Everyone gets quiet for a few minutes.

Ken finally speaks, "Well, wherever it is, it has to be a place where we can survive by our own food and water source, and a place we can fortify."

Shana speaks up, "I would think someplace out in the middle of nowhere. Someplace where there isn't people." She pauses, "Maybe Alaska."

Ashley replies, "Wow, that would be a long trip."

Janet concurs, "Yeah, that is a long ways, but Shana is right, there wouldn't be hardly any people to deal with."

Ken nods, "It sounds good, but besides the trip, we would have to survive the harsh winters. Plus, its still landlocked so those things could eventually find us."

Jody speaks up, "I had thought about Alaska." He pauses, "Any other suggestions?"

Ashley speaks up, "Maybe we should go checkout Fort Leonard Wood. It might be a safe place and its close."

Mike shakes his head, "Military installations would be an obvious choice, but it's in the middle of the country. It would eventually be surrounded by millions of those things. We'd be trapped with no possible way to escape."

Lisa chimes in, "Yeah, I'd have to agree. It's really dangerous, especially if it has already been overrun."

Lindsey finally speaks up, "I would think the best place to go would be an island."

Everyone is quiet for a minute.

Ryan finally speaks up, "That makes sense to me."

Codi nods in agreement, "Yeah."

Marissa questions, "But where is an island that we could go to?"

Michael, Lindsey's husband, speaks up, "There are some islands in the lakes around here."

Michael, Jody's brother, chimes in, "Yeah, but most of them are not very big nor would they provide us much shelter or natural food sources."

Janet looks at Jody, "What do you think babe?"

Jody finally speaks, "I did a lot of research into this and I have to agree that those are some good suggestions. However, I agree that the island is the best place, but it has to be an island where we can be self sufficient."

Ken questions, "You have a certain place in mind, don't you?"

Jody nods, "Yes I do." He pauses, "It is a long trip, not as long as Alaska, but a long trip."

Lisa questions, "Where is it?"

Jody replies, "Its called Fort Pulaski, Georgia."

Mike looks at his son, "That is a long trip, every bit of a thousand miles."

Ken nods, "Not to mention there is a lot of populated areas between here and there."

Jody nods, "You both are right."

Michael, Lindsey's husband, speaks up, "That's crazy. You expect us to take that kind of risk?" He pauses, "What about hurricanes and stuff?"

Janet speaks up, "I'm sure Jody wouldn't suggest it without having thought it out. He's gotten us this far, we should hear him out."

Lindsey nods, "I agree."

Jody takes a breath, "It's a decent sized island. The fort itself is an old civil war fort that was completely rebuilt. It is two stories high and the walls are brick and eleven feet thick. It has a moat around it as well. Its very close to the mainland and it has only one bridge leading to it. It also has a Coast Guard station there." He pauses, "We can distill the water and grow food. Not to mention, we collapse or block the bridge and those things can't get to us. However, we can have boats setup for a getaway and use to make runs over to the mainland if need be." He pauses again, "If we can get there, collapse or block the bridge and clear the island. We could setup our own place to live and survive. It's the best option I could think of. As far as the weather, we'll have to deal with bad weather no matter where we go and we'll just have to do our best when that time comes."

Everyone is quiet for a couple minutes.

Janet nods, "I like it. I'm with you."

Mike speaks up, "I'm with you too."

Ken sighs, "No matter where we go, its going to be dangerous. I have to agree with you. It sounds like a good place. I'm in."

Shana nods, "Yeah, me and the boys are in."

Michael, Jody's brother, speaks up, "I'm in too."

Marissa concurs, "Me too."

Ryan looks at Codi, "What do you think?"

Codi sighs, "I don't really know, but Jody has done good so far. I trust him. I think we should go."

Ryan nods, "Me too."

Ashley looks at everyone, "I hate leaving the area without knowing what has happened to everyone, but there is no way I could make it on my own and of all the suggestions, that sounds the best. I'm in."

Jody looks at Lisa, "What about you girl?"

Lisa smiles, "Oh, Rochelle and I are definitely going with you."

Jody smiles back at Lisa. Everyone looks over at Lindsey and her husband.

Michael, Lindsey's husband, looks at his wife, "What do you think?"

Lindsey sighs, "I know it's dangerous, but it sounds like the right move."

Michael, Lindsey's husband, replies, "As much as the trip worries me, I think we should go."

Lindsey is kind of surprised by her husband's response, "Really?"

Michael, Lindsey's husband, smiles, "Yeah, I say we're in too."

Lindsey smiles, "Okay, we are going."

Jody looks over at Grace, "Well, you know where we've decided to go. All I ask is think about it tonight and if you are still certain you want to leave in the morning, we will get you your share of everything." He pauses, "If for some reason, it doesn't work out, you'll know where we are heading."

Grace nods, "Okay."

Ken speaks up, "Well, I say that about wraps it up. Its about that time to get some food again and getting some rest."

Jody nods, "I agree. Marissa, you and my brother can grab your things and set them in Ryan's tent."

Marissa and Michael, Jody's brother, nod.

Ken speaks again, "Grace and I are the first watch group so why don't we take watch and we can just go on with the same rotation from there."

Jody looks around, "Sounds good to me."

Ken looks at Grace, "Well, let's go relieve the boys and we can eat after our watch is over."

Grace gets up, "Okay."

Ken and Grace head off to relieve Zach and Tyler while everyone else starts getting ready for dinner.

The sun has set and everyone has made their way to their assigned tents for the night except for Michael, Jody's brother, and Marissa who are finishing up their watch. Mike, Shana, Jody and Janet are laying in their tent. Mike and Shana are getting their regular clothes on since they have the next watch in a few minutes. Jody and Janet are in their sleeping clothes. Jody and Janet are sharing Jody's sleeping bag, but they haven't fallen asleep yet. In fact, most everyone is still awake as they are uneasy about their first night of being outside. Mike and Shana finish getting ready and grab their weapons.

Mike and Shana leave the tent and head over by the vehicles to where Marissa and Michael, Jody's brother, are at. Mike and Shana take their positions and Michael, Jody's brother, and Marissa head off to get changed and get some rest.

Janet is laying on her left side and Jody is laying on his left side behind Janet. Jody has his right arm around Janet. Janet nestles back against Jody.

Jody whispers in Janet's ear, "Sweet dreams."

Janet rolls over to her back and turns her head to look at Jody. No words are needed as Jody moves closer and kisses Janet. It is a passionate kiss, not like any before. Jody and Janet continue to kiss as Jody slides his hand up under Janet's shirt. Janet starts to kiss Jody more passionately.

Jody whispers to Janet, "Are you okay with this?"

Janet whispers back, "I don't want to go all the way yet, but touching is fine."

A minute of passionate kissing continues, when Janet slides her hand down under Jody's sweatpants and underwear. Jody responds by moving his hand down from Janet's chest to under her pajama pants and panties. Jody and Janet continue to kiss and touch each other and for the next few minutes, they forget about the world outside and lose themselves in each other.

Some hours have passed and the moonlight has shed some light over the campsite as the clear night has dipped down into the upper 60's. Lindsey and Michael, her husband, are now standing watch. The two of them keep a very watchful eye on the trees that are on three sides of the campsite. Lindsey and Michael, her husband, are not too worried about the lake behind them.

Lindsey listens intently also to see if she might be able to hear something moving, but she doesn't hear a thing. Michael, Lindsey's husband, slowly walks to the end of the vehicles and back to where Lindsey is standing.

Michael, Lindsey's husband, whispers to Lindsey, "How are you doing?"

Lindsey looks at Michael, her husband, and whispers back, "I'm doing okay."

Michael, Lindsey's husband, whispers again, "Come on, I can tell something has been on your mind."

Lindsey continues to glance around and whispers, "I've just been trying to figure out how to explain this all to Daniel because he's going to want to know why we are not going home." She pauses, "I'm also wondering why you didn't seem to have a problem with going all the way to Georgia."

Michael, Lindsey's husband, glances around and whispers back, "Well, I thought about things the whole drive here and I realize that it is like Jody said, the world is a different place now and its all about survival. We can't survive without the group and we have a lot to contribute to them as well."

Lindsey smiles at Michael, her husband.

Michael, Lindsey's husband, continues in a whisper, "As far as Daniel, we will just do our best to make him understand."

Lindsey looks at Michael, her husband, and whispers with a smile, "Thank you so much. I don't know what I'd do if you were not here."

Lindsey leans over and gives Michael, her husband, a passionate kiss. The kind of kiss they haven't got the chance to share since this all began.

Lindsey finally leans back and whispers, "I love you."

Michael, Lindsey's husband, smiles and whispers back, "I love you too."

Lindsey glances around, gives a sly smile and whispers again, "Next time Lisa and Ashley are standing watch, I'll show you just how much I love you."

Michael, Lindsey's husband, smiles back and whispers, "I like the sound of that."

Lindsey and Michael, her husband, kiss again, then the two of them walk around the vehicles again, then return to their watch point.

CHAPTER 28

It is morning time as the sun has began to rise over the campsite. The breeze is blowing across the lake as the temperature has warmed to the low 70's. Ken and Grace are close to the end of their watch as everyone starts waking up. Jody makes his way out of his tent as Ken is waking up Lisa and Ashley for their turn to stand watch.

Jody walks over to Grace, "How are you doing this morning?"

Grace nods slightly, "Not bad FIT B."

Jody glances around and sees some of the others making their way over to the front of the large tent.

Jody looks back at Grace, "So, you still planning on leaving?"

Grace nods again, "Yeah. The kids and I need to get to my husband if we can."

Jody nods, "I understand. When are you planning on leaving?"

Grace looks around, "Whenever we are relieved from watch, I'm going to start packing up my car."

Jody nods, "Okay. I'll get with dad and we will get your share of the supplies."

Grace smiles, "Thanks."

Jody walks off as Ken walks back up. Jody goes over to his dad.

Mike looks at his son, "So, is she still leaving?"

Jody nods, "Yep. So let's get her share of the supplies for her."

Mike and Jody walk over to Mike's van where the majority of the food and water is located. Mike opens the back of the van.

Mike speaks, "I figured it out last night and went ahead and set her share of the supplies aside."

Jody nods, "Okay. Let's pull the supplies out and get them over to her car."

Mike and Jody gather up the supplies for Grace and start walking for Grace's car. Lisa and Ashley walk up to Ken and Grace and relieve them for watch. Grace sees Mike and Jody and walks over to her car. Grace opens the trunk. Mike and Jody set the supplies in the trunk.

Grace smiles, "Thanks. I'm going to get my tent and stuff before I get the kids."

Ken walks up.

Jody nods, "Okay." He looks at Ken, "Why don't you just move into the large tent for now."

Ken nods and replies, "Okay."

Ken and Grace head off for Grace's tent. Everyone that is awake which is all the adults plus Rochelle, Zach and Tyler are watching what is going on while they eat breakfast. Ken gathers his belongings and places them in the large tent. Grace takes her tent down and packs it up, then places it in the trunk of her car. Grace walks over to everyone else who is sitting around in front of the large tent.

Grace speaks to everyone in general, "I better get the kids."

Grace walks into the large tent and wakes up Ayden and Ariel. It takes a few minutes for the two kids to wake up. Once they are up though, Grace helps them get dressed and their things gathered up. Once they have everything, Grace walks out of the large tent with Ayden and Ariel's things.

Everyone watches as Grace walks over to her car and places the things in the trunk, then closes it. Ayden and Ariel step out of the large tent as Grace walks back over to where everyone is at.

Grace sighs and nods, "It's time to go. Let's keep this short and not too emotional."

Jody watches as each person makes their way over and gives Grace a hug goodbye. Once everyone is done, Jody walks over to Grace.

Jody hugs Grace, "You be careful."

Grace hugs Jody tight, "I will."

Jody runs his hand up and down Grace's back, "You know where we're going if you all change your mind."

Grace runs her hand up and down Jody's back, "I know."

Grace and Jody step back.

Grace looks at Jody, "I can never thank you enough for everything you have done for me and the kids."

Jody smiles, "Its my pleasure."

Grace looks over to Ayden and Ariel, "Let's go kids."

Ayden and Ariel walk over to Grace.

Grace looks at Jody again, "Thanks again FIT B. I love you."

Jody smiles, "I love you too."

Grace turns and walks off to her car with Ayden and Ariel right behind her. Grace gets Ayden and Ariel in their car seats, then walks around to the driver's door. Grace opens the door.

Grace looks back at everyone, "Goodbye. You all take care of yourselves."

Everyone waves back and each responds with a goodbye. Grace climbs into her car and closes the door. Grace starts the car up and slowly starts to drive off. Everyone in the group watches as Grace's car disappears into the trees.

Lisa and Ashley are nearing the end of their watch. Michael, Jody's brother, and Marissa are getting ready to take over watch. Everyone has been pretty quiet since Grace left. Jody has been going over the map in his tent, plotting out their travel route around the lake. All of a sudden, everyone hears the distinct sound of a vehicle, maybe even two, heading down the trail towards their campsite.

Ken looks at everyone in front of the large tent, "Kids, get inside the tent. Everyone else, grab your weapons and get over to the vehicles, now."

Everyone is wearing their pistols. Everyone grabs their shotguns and Codi grabs her rifle. The group follows Ken over to the vehicles. Lisa and Ashley back up to Ken and the others. No one has noticed that Jody isn't with the group.

Ken speaks, "Everyone spread out behind their assigned vehicles and use them for cover. Nobody come out or do anything until Jody or I make contact."

Everyone spreads out to where they are suppose to be. Janet, Ryan and Codi get over to Janet's van and they finally notice Jody is not there.

Janet looks around, "Do you see Jody?"

Ryan glances around, "No."

Codi replies, "He was in his tent working on travel plans. That's the last I saw him."

About that time, a late 90's model Chevy Pickup and a newer model Chevy Tahoe emerge from the trees on the trail from the county road. The two vehicles creep towards the campsite. Ken glances around and sees everyone in place, but finally notices Jody isn't with them. Ken knows what Jody must be doing because its what he would do.

Ken knows that he is going to have to be the one to make contact with whoever this is.

The two vehicles inch closer and finally stop about fifty feet from the vehicles in front of the campsite. A decent looking 23 year old Caucasian man who stands 6'1" tall and looks to weigh about 250 pounds with black hair cut in a military high and tight style and brown eyes, gets out of the pickup truck. He is wearing a black t-shirt, black tactical pants, black boots and a black baseball cap. He has a SOG pocket knife in his right pocket, a double magazine holder on his left hip with two fully loaded 7 round magazines, a black belt slide holster on his right hip and he is holding a 45 caliber Springfield 1911 in his right hand.

An average looking 35 year old Caucasian man gets out of the driver's seat of the Tahoe. He stands 6'2" tall and weighs a massive 295 pounds. He is bald with brown eyes. The man is wearing a brown t-shirt, blue jeans, brown boots, brown belt and a navy baseball cap. He has a hunting knife on his left hip, a rifle shell holder with 10 rounds in it wrapped around his waist and is holding a 308 caliber hunting rifle in his hands. A pretty 33 year old Caucasian woman get out of the passenger's seat. She stands 5'9" tall and weighs a nice 155 pounds with short blonde hair and hazel eyes. She is wearing a yellow tank top, blue jeans, brown belt and tennis shoes. She has a brown belt slide holster on her right hip, a brown double magazine holder on her left hip with 2 fully loaded 17 round magazines and she is holding a GLOCK 17 in her right hand.

A fairly good looking 25 year old Caucasian man gets out of the back, driver's side of the Tahoe. He stands 5'10" tall and weighs a fit 185 pounds with short black hair and hazel eyes. He is wearing a blue t-shirt, faded blue jeans, black belt and tennis shoes. He has a pocket knife clipped in his right, front pocket, a shotgun shell holder belt around his waist with 10 shells in it and he is holding a 20 gauge pump shotgun in his hands. An attractive 21 year old Caucasian woman gets out of the back passenger's side. She stands just barely 5'1" tall and weighs a petite 100 pounds with long red hair and green eyes. She is wearing a purple tank top, faded blue jeans, black belt and tennis shoes. She has a brown, clip on single magazine holder on her left hip with a loaded 7 round magazine and a brown, clip on holster on her right hip. She is holding a Smith and Wesson 380 auto in her right hand.

The five strangers step in front of their vehicles and look around at the vehicles and campsite in front of them. As the five strangers take a step forward, Ken steps out from behind Mike's van.

Ken raises his shotgun, "Stop! That's far enough!"

The five strangers raise their weapons at Ken. At that moment, the rest of the group steps out from behind the vehicles with their weapons ready. The five strangers glance around and realize they are outnumbered and out gunned. The man who got out of the pickup truck takes one step forward.

The man raises his pistol at Ken, "Put down your weapons!"

Ken replies, "I don't think so! Put your weapons down!"

The man replies in a stern voice, "That's not going to happen!"

At that moment, Jody steps out from behind the Tahoe with his AR-15 pointed at the man.

Jody speaks, "You don't have much of a choice in the matter. You can put your weapons down and we can talk or we can shoot this out. The decision is yours and you have thirty seconds to decide."

The man looks back at Jody, then looks at the four others that are with him. Everyone waits to see what the strangers are going to do. Ken keeps his shotgun aimed in and his finger on the trigger. The man doing the talking looks at his four companions and nods his head. The five of them lay their weapons on the ground.

Jody hollers, "Lisa, Ashley, come pick up their weapons!"

Lisa and Ashley walk over to the group of strangers and pick up their weapons.

Jody walks up to the five strangers, "Okay. Come on into our camp and have a seat."

The five strangers walk towards the large tent while Jody follows them. The strangers get to the large tent and find a place to sit. Jody and the others are standing around the five strangers.

Jody looks at his brother, "You and Marissa resume watch."

Michael, Jody's brother, and Marissa head off to their watch location. Jody turns his attention back to the five strangers.

Jody questions, "So, what are your names?"

The man that did the talking replies, "I'm Greg."

The large 35 year old man is next, "I'm Allen." He motions to the 33 year old woman, "And this is my fiancée, Rachel."

The 25 year old man answers, "I'm Chad." He motions to the 21 year old woman, "And this is my girlfriend, Amber."

Jody nods, "My name is Jody."

Jody points to each member of the group and introduces them. The kids and Rochelle step out of the large tent and Jody introduces them.

Once Jody finishes introducing the group, he speaks up, "Okay everyone, let's all sit down and do some talking." He looks at the strangers, "Sorry to be so forceful, but you can't take any chances now a days."

Greg nods his head, "I know what you mean."

Everyone finds a seat and wonders what these strangers will be able to tell them.

CHAPTER 29

Jody is the last to sit down. Everyone is still quiet. The new people don't know quite what to make of Jody and the others, and Jody and the others don't really know what to make of the strangers.

Jody is the first to speak, "So, where are you all from?"

Greg replies, "I'm from Baxter Springs."

Allen replies next, "The four of us are from Joplin."

Greg questions, "What about all of you?"

Jody replies, "We are from all around, but we just all happened to be in Miami for the holiday weekend."

Shana looks at Greg, "How was it in Baxter?"

Greg shakes his head, "Not good at all. I was listening to my police radio, I'm a reserve police officer there, and things went bad fast. After the first twenty-four hours, I couldn't reach anyone." He pauses, "I stayed inside as long as I could, but when I saw more and more of those things, I decided it was time to go. This was the only direction open at the time and I figured maybe hide out at the lake until I could figure out what to do next."

Allen nods his head, "It was the same in Joplin. I mean, we were loaded up to go camping for the weekend when it all started. We stayed inside also, but those things were everywhere." He pauses, "We also decided to get out

234

while we could. We live just off 7th street and Black Cat Road area so we headed towards Kansas."

Jody questions, "How was Galena?"

Chad shakes his head, "Gone. Completely overrun. We barely made it thru."

Greg speaks up, "Anyway, I ran into them on the way here and we decided it would be better to team up."

Ken questions next, "So, where do you all plan on heading?"

Greg sighs, "I honestly don't know."

Rachel speaks up, "We were going to hide out here for a day or two and try to figure something out."

Jody nods, "Yeah, we planned the same thing. We got here yesterday and so far we've had no sign of those things."

Michael, Lindsey's husband, speaks up, "Hell, you're the first people we've seen since this all started."

Amber nods, "Same here. Other than running into Greg, you all are the only other people we've seen."

Mike looks at Jody, "What do you think?"

Everyone kind of gets a puzzled look by that question.

Jody sighs, "I'm okay with it, but its not just up to me. The group has to decide."

Janet looks at Jody, "What are you two talking about?"

Jody replies, "I'm okay with Greg and them staying here with us, but its not just my decision."

Greg speaks up, "There is definitely more safety in numbers."

Rachel nods, "Yeah, and if you all have a routine going already, we will be happy to pitch in."

Allen speaks up, "And we have our own supplies so we wouldn't need anything like that from you all."

Ken nods, "I'm good with it."

Mike speaks up, "Me too."

Jody glances at the others, "What do you all think?"

The rest of the group is quiet for a moment, but then each one looks at the other and starts nodding.

Jody nods, "Okay." He pauses, "Lisa, go ahead and give them their weapons back. Do you all have tents and sleeping bags?"

Allen replies, "Yeah, the four of us have sleeping bags and I have a four person tent."

Greg nods, "Yeah, I have a single person tent and sleeping bag."

Jody points to where Grace's tent use to be, "Allen, if the four of you want to set your tent up there, that will be good. Greg, just wherever you find a spot will work."

Lisa hands back all their weapons.

Greg questions, "I notice you all have a watch. How do you have it set up?"

Jody replies, "We have two person teams and each team stands two hours of watch."

Chad sighs, "Well, we'd be more than happy to pitch in on that."

Jody nods, "Okay. Just so happens we have an odd number right now." He pauses, "Allen, if you and Rachel want to partner and be team eight and Chad, you and Amber can be team nine."

Allen nods, "Works for me."

Chad replies, "Sounds good."

Jody looks at Greg, "Ken's partner left this morning. You can partner with him which is team one."

Greg nods, "Fine with me. It'll be nice to have even more people watching our back."

Jody looks at Ken, "You good with that?"

Ken nods, "No problem."

Jody stands up, "Well, with nine teams we can go to one hour shifts now. Everyone good with that?"

Everyone looks around and nods.

Greg stands up, "Well, we'll get set up."

Greg, Allen, Rachel, Chad and Amber head off to their vehicles. Jody glances at Ken and gives a quick, unnoticed motion with his head. Ken walks over to Jody.

Ken whispers, "What's up?"

Jody whispers back while making sure no one is watching them, "Keep your eye on them. I'm going to do the same."

Ken whispers back, "You read my mind."

As Greg and his small group get their things together, everyone else goes back to trying to find whatever they can to occupy their time. Jody returns to his tent to keep planning their route.

The rest of the day has passed slowly. Everyone has been doing whatever they can to pass the time. The kids have managed to keep Shadow and Lucky occupied while the adults have mainly been resting or talking with each other. Greg and his group have been keeping to themselves for the most part.

Jody has made his way out of his tent and over by the lake. Jody breathes in the air and clears his mind. Jody knows that tonight he must get everyone mentally prepared for the trip ahead.

Lindsey walks up to Jody, "How's it going?"

Jody takes in another breath of fresh air, "Good. Just enjoying the view."

Lindsey nods, "I know. This view makes you forget for a moment what is going on."

Jody nods, "Yes it does."

Lindsey looks at Jody, "You holding up okay? I know we've kind of put a lot of responsibility on you."

Jody looks at Lindsey, "I'm okay. Thanks for asking though." He pauses, "How about you?"

Lindsey sighs, "Its getting better. Still not sure how to break the news to Daniel that we're not going home."

Jody puts his hand on Lindsey's shoulder, "Give it time. You'll figure out how to tell him."

Lindsey smiles, "Thanks."

Jody smiles back, "No problem." He pauses and his eyes narrow, "Is that a hickey I see?"

Lindsey's eyes widen, "Oh my God! Is it that noticeable?"

Jody lightly chuckles, "Kind of, yeah. Hey, nothing wrong with having some closeness with the hubby."

Lindsey chuckles, "Yeah."

Jody glances around, "Well, if you want to let the others know to gather up, we'll get dinner out of the way and discuss our next move."

Lindsey nods, "Okay."

Lindsey and Jody share a hug, then Lindsey walks off to inform everyone. Jody looks back to the lake, closes his eyes and takes one more deep breath.

Everyone has finished eating and are gathered around the front of the large tent. The sun is getting lower in the partly cloudy sky. Lisa and Ashley are standing watch at the moment. Once Lucky and Shadow have been walked and taken care of, they are put back inside the large tent.

Jody looks at Zach and Tyler, "Hey boys, can you two take over watch again while we discuss the movements for tomorrow?"

Zach nods, "Sure."

Tyler smiles, "Yep."

Zach and Tyler head off to relieve Lisa and Ashley for the moment.

Greg questions, "You're going to have the kids stand watch?"

Jody smiles, "They are more than capable."

Lisa and Ashley walk up and find a seat.

Ken looks at Jody, "Okay little buddy, what do you got for us?"

Jody takes a breath, "First, we need to know if Greg and the others are wanting to travel with us."

Chad questions, "Are you all headed to a certain place?"

Mike nods, "Yeah, it's quite a long ways, but it'll be worth it once we get there."

Rachel questions, "Where is it?"

Ken replies, "It's called Fort Pulaski. It's on a small island just off the coast of Georgia."

Amber gets a surprised look, "Wow, that is a long ways."

Shana speaks up, "Yeah, but of all the options we thought of, it's the best one."

Jody speaks up again, "Before you decide, you should know that we've made up some rules for the group."

Janet chimes in, "First, anyone that gets infected is out of the group, no exceptions."

Ashley speaks up, "Second, anyone outside the group that is infected will not be allowed in."

Lisa goes next, "Third, if we encounter other survivors. As you have seen, we take a decisive stance on them. We can't trust just anyone. They can go away or they can join us after surrendering their weapons."

Michael, Lindsey's husband, speaks up, "Fourth, if anyone in the group tries to hurt another or becomes a threat to the group, they are out. No exceptions. They can leave on their own or be dealt with. Plus, they get none of the supplies or weapons, just their personal belongings."

Lindsey chimes in, "Finally, anyone can chose to leave on their own anytime they want. If they do, they take their share of the supplies and their weapons with them."

Mike speaks again, "Also, around here, Jody will call the shots. He is open to ideas, but ultimately we are looking to him to make the decisions."

Jody smiles at how everyone has seemed to step up, "If you want to travel with us and you're okay with all that, then we welcome you to the group."

It gets quiet for a minute.

Greg nods, "I'm good with it."

Allen looks at Rachel, "What do you think sweetheart?"

Rachel replies, "I think we should stay with them. It'll definitely be safer and if that's all they're asking, I'm okay with that."

Allen looks at Jody, "Okay, we're in."

Amber looks at Chad, "I think we should stay with them too."

Chad nods, "Me too." He looks at Jody, "Amber and I are in."

Jody nods, "Good. Welcome to the family."

Ken returns to the topic at hand, "So, what is in store for us tomorrow?"

Jody takes a deep breath, "First things first. How are we sitting on supplies dad?"

Mike replies, "We're okay. We could use some more if the situation presents itself."

Jody nods, "Okay, it probably will tomorrow." He pauses, "We will pack up at dawn and head out. We will skirt around the lake. I know that will take us through two small communities, Langley and Disney, but we have to think about fuel conservation too. I think we can get through those two places okay."

Codi questions, "And after that?"

Jody continues, "We will stay on Highway 28 until we reach Highway 20 East. We will take that highway all the way to the town of Jay." He pauses, "It runs thru the middle of town, but we will also pass a discount store. If we get the chance, we will stop and try to gather what supplies we can there."

Michael, Jody's brother, questions, "Stopping in a town? Kind of dangerous don't you think bro?"

Jody nods, "Yeah, but I have faith in all of you that we can pull it off. Especially with our new members." He pauses, "After we get thru Jay, we will continue on Highway 20 until we reach the east end of Lake Eucha State Park. We will pull just off the highway and camp there for the night." Jody pauses again, "I know that is not a long trip, but we are going to travel slow and I want to make sure we have plenty of sunlight to setup camp at the end of each day."

Ryan speaks up, "Good idea. We definitely don't want to be fumbling around in the dark."

Jody nods at Ryan, "Exactly." Jody looks around at everyone, "So, that's the plan. Everyone good with that?"

Everyone in the group looks around at each other. No one is too fond of the idea of going into towns, but they trust Jody's judgment and they all start nodding.

Jody sighs, "Good. So, let's get back to our watch rotation and whoever is on watch at sunrise, wake everyone up." He pauses, "Tomorrow is a big day so everyone get as much rest tonight as you can."

Jody stands up and starts off for his tent. Everyone else starts to move around also. Lisa and Ashley return to their watch.

CHAPTER 30

Michael, Jody's brother, and Marissa are standing watch now. Everyone else has pretty much retired to their tents. Codi and Ryan are laying down in their tent knowing that their watch will be starting soon. Ryan and Codi have their sleeping bags laying next to each other and they are laying on top of them.

Ryan looks at Codi, "How are you doing?"

Codi sighs, "I'm doing okay. Its still just sinking in about everything that has happened so far and what we are going to do." She pauses, "I have to admit, I'm scared."

Ryan whispers back, "Me too."

Codi slides over against Ryan, "Promise me something."

Ryan replies, "What's that?"

Codi whispers, "If I become infected, that you don't let me become one of those things."

Ryan places his hand on Codi's waist, "You don't have to worry about that happening."

Codi looks at Ryan, "Promise me."

Ryan nods slightly, "Okay, I promise."

Codi leans close and kisses Ryan.

Codi leans away, "How much time do we have?"

Ryan is quiet for a second, "About thirty minutes." He pauses, "Plenty of time."

Codi smiles and press herself against Ryan, "Oh yes."

Ryan and Codi start kissing more passionately and for a little while, they forget about the world outside.

Lindsey and Michael, her husband, are standing watch as the sun starts to break the horizon. It is a clear, warmer morning with a slight breeze. Lindsey looks over at the camp and doesn't see anyone else awake.

Lindsey looks at Michael, her husband, "I'm going to go wake everyone up."

Michael, Lindsey's husband, nods, "Okay."

Lindsey heads off to the campsite from the vehicles. Lindsey makes her way from tent to tent making sure everyone is awake. Once she is finished waking everyone, Lindsey returns to where Michael, her husband, is at.

Greg makes his way over to the campsite in front of the large tent and notices that everyone else is already there, but still in their sleeping attire. The kids start eating breakfast while the adults gather around to see how the morning is going to go.

Lisa looks at Jody, "So, how do you want to do things this morning?"

Jody stretches, "Well, once the kids are done eating, I want Zach and Tyler to take over watch for now. Dad and Codi can get Lucky and Shadow out and let them do their business." He pauses, "Then once everyone eats and gets changed, we'll pack everything up and get on the road."

Mike nods, "Sounds good to me."

The kids finish up eating, then Tyler and Zach go get changed and pack up their belongings. Zach puts on his black t-shirt, blue jeans, tennis shoes and desert digital boonie cover. Zach is wearing his knife and pistol. Tyler puts on his camouflage t-shirt, camouflage pants, tennis shoes and woodland digital boonie cover. Tyler is wearing his knife and carrying his single shot shotgun. Zach and Tyler relieve Lindsey and her husband on watch.

All the adults start having breakfast while Codi and Mike take care of Lucky and Shadow. Once the dogs have been walked and fed, Codi and Mike eat their breakfast. It doesn't take long before everyone is finished eating and they all head off to their tents to get changed and to start packing up their belongings.

In about twenty minutes, Ken is the first to return to the campsite in front of the large tent with his belongings. Ken is wearing a blue t-shirt, blue jeans, black belt, black boots and camouflage baseball cap. Ken is wearing his knife, pistol and spare magazines and carrying his shotgun. Shana is the next to arrive. Shana is wearing a white t-shirt, faded blue jeans, brown belt, tennis shoes and the black baseball cap she got from Jody. Shana is wearing her knife, pistol and spare magazine and carrying her shotgun and personal belongings.

Rochelle arrives next. Rochelle is wearing a blue top, blue jeans and tennis shoes. Rochelle is also wearing her knife and pistol and carrying her personal belongings. Mike is the next to arrive. Mike is wearing a blue and gray collared shirt, blue jeans, brown belt and tennis shoes. Mike is wearing his knife, pistol and spare magazines and carrying his shotgun and personal belongings.

Michael, Jody's brother, and Marissa walk up at the same time. Marissa is wearing a blue t-shirt, blue jeans, black belt, tennis shoes and black baseball cap she had gotten from Jody before. Marissa is wearing her knife, pistol and spare magazines and is carrying her shotgun and personal belongings. Michael, Jody's brother, is wearing an ACU digital camouflage t-shirt, blue jeans, brown belt, tennis shoes and a white baseball cap. Michael, Jody's brother, is wearing his knife, pistol and spare magazines and carrying his shotgun and personal belongings.

Lindsey, Daniel and Michael, Lindsey's husband, walk up next. Daniel is wearing a gray t-shirt, blue jeans and tennis shoes. Lindsey is wearing a gray t-shirt, faded blue jeans, tennis shoes and white baseball cap she had gotten from Jody before. Lindsey is wearing her knife, pistol and spare magazines and she is carrying her shotgun along with her and Daniel's personal belongings. Michael, Lindsey's husband, is wearing a blue t-shirt, blue jeans, tennis shoes and black baseball cap. Michael, Lindsey's husband, is wearing his knife, pistol and spare magazines and is carrying his shotgun and personal belongings.

Codi and Ryan walk up next. Codi is wearing a red t-shirt, faded blue jeans and tennis shoes. Codi is wearing her knife, pistol and spare magazines and is carrying her rifle and personal belongings. Ryan is wearing a black t-shirt, blue jeans, tennis shoes and blue baseball cap. Ryan is wearing his knife, pistol and spare magazines and is carrying his shotgun and personal belongings.

Ashley is the next to show up. Ashley is wearing a green tank top, faded blue jeans and tennis shoes. Ashley is wearing her knife, pistol and spare magazines and is carrying her shotgun and personal belongings. Lisa walks up next. Lisa is wearing an urban digital camouflage tank top, urban digital camouflage BDU pants, black riggers belt, black boots and an urban digital camouflage boonie cover. Lisa is wearing her knife, pistol and spare magazines and is carrying her shotgun and personal belongings.

Allen and Rachel walk up next. Allen is wearing a blue t-shirt, camouflage pants, brown belt, brown boots and navy blue baseball cap. Allen is wearing his hunting knife and rifle shell holder belt and is carrying his rifle and personal belongings. Rachel is wearing a camouflage tank top, camouflage pants, brown belt and tennis shoes. Rachel is wearing her pistol and spare magazines and is carrying her personal belongings.

Next to walk up is Chad and Amber. Chad is wearing a green t-shirt, black cargo pants, black belt and tennis shoes. Chad is wearing his knife and 10 shell shotgun shell holder and is carrying his shotgun and personal belongings. Amber is wearing a blue tank top, faded blue jeans, black belt and tennis shoes. Amber is wearing her pistol and spare magazines and carrying her personal belongings. Greg walks up next. Greg is wearing his black t-shirt, black tactical pants, black belt, black boots and black baseball cap. Greg is wearing his knife, pistol and spare magazines and is carrying his personal belongings.

Jody and Janet are the last to arrive. Janet is wearing a black and gray, thin strapped tank top, blue jean Capri pants and tennis shoes. Janet is wearing her knife, pistol and spare magazines. Janet is carrying her shotgun and personal belongings. Jody is wearing an ACU digital camouflage t-shirt, ACU digital camouflage BDU pants, tan riggers belt, brown combat boots and an ACU digital camouflage boonie cover. Jody is wearing his knife, pistol and spare magazines for his pistol and rifle. Jody is carrying his rifle and personal belongings.

Once everyone is back in front of the large tent, they set their things down and wait for what to do next. Jody looks around and sees that everyone is ready.

Jody speaks, "Let's get our personal things loaded up, then breakdown and load the tents. We'll put the large tent in Dad's van." He looks at Greg, "Since Ken's ride left and you two are partners now, can Ken ride with you?"

Greg nods, "No problem."

Jody nods back, "Good. We will convoy in the same order. Allen, you'll fall in line behind Lindsey's Trailblazer and Greg, you'll bring up the rear behind them."

Allen nods, "Okay."

Greg takes a breath, "Sounds good to me."

Jody smiles at everyone's efficiency in getting ready to go, "Okay, let's load up in our assigned vehicles, get the tents and get on the road. We have a full day ahead."

Shana questions, "What about Ty and Zach's things?"

Rochelle speaks up, "I'll load their things while they continue watch."

Jody nods, "Let's get to it."

It only takes a few minutes and everyone has their personal belongings loaded. Everyone, except Allen and Chad, leaves their shotguns and rifles in their vehicles as they go to breakdown the tents and get them loaded.

It takes about ten minutes with the help of everyone to breakdown the tents. As everyone is finishing getting the tents back into their carrying cases, Tyler comes running up to Jody and the others.

Tyler speaks out of breath, "They're coming down the trail."

Jody looks over towards the vehicles, "Who?"

Tyler takes another breath, "Zombies."

Jody hollers to everyone, "Get the tents and get to the vehicles, now!"

Jody runs for Janet's van as Janet grabs Jody's tent. Everyone who owns a tent grabs it and heads for their vehicle. Mike and Codi get Lucky and Shadow and take the dogs to the vehicles. Ken grabs the large tent and takes it over to Mike's van.

Jody opens the passenger's door of Janet's van and pulls out his AR-15. Jody looks over to the trail leading into the open area and sees four zombies staggering towards them.

Jody yells, "Everyone get in their vehicles!"

Jody takes aim at the group of zombies with his scoped AR-15. Jody squeezes the trigger and the shot rings out. Everyone stops for a moment when they hear the gunshot, knowing this has just gotten real. One zombie falls to the ground from the headshot. Jody takes aim again and fires. Another zombie falls to the ground. Jody takes aim at the third zombie and fires. The shot is true and the third zombie falls. As Jody takes aim at the last zombie, he hears a gunshot from someone else. Jody watches as the last zombie falls. Jody quickly looks around and sees Allen holding his rifle at his shoulder.

Jody nods to Allen, "Thanks." He glances around, "Okay everyone, let's get out of here."

Mike slides the van door shut after getting Shadow in the van, then he looks over to the tree line to the left of the campsite. Mike's eyes widen.

Mike points, "Look!"

Everyone looks to where Mike is pointing and sees about twenty zombies staggering out of the trees towards them.

Jody yells, "Let's go!"

Everyone gets in their vehicles and starts them up. Janet pulls away first, heading for the trail that leads back to the county road. Everyone falls in behind Janet in their assigned order. In a minute, the campsite and zombies are long gone.

CHAPTER 31

Janet continues to drive east on Highway 20 towards the town of Jay. The morning drive from the events at the lake has been relatively quiet. The sun is getting closer to the noon sky and Jody knows they are just a few miles from the town where they intend to gather supplies.

Jody looks at Janet, "Pull over and stop. We need to talk before we get into town."

Janet pulls the van to a stop on the shoulder of the empty highway. Everyone else in the convoy pulls over and stops, wondering what is going on. Jody gets out of the van followed by Janet, Ryan and Codi. Jody, Janet, Ryan and Codi walk back to Mike's van as everyone else gets out of their vehicles and walks over to Mike's van.

Jody looks at everyone, "I just wanted to cover a few things before we get into town. First, let's get the dogs out now so when we get to the store, they won't be restless. Also, we should go ahead and get something to eat." He pauses, "Once we get to the store, I want to break up into three groups. My dad, Shana, Rochelle and the kids will stay with the vehicles and keep watch outside."

Ken questions, "What are the other two teams going to do?"

Jody takes a breath, "One team will procure food and water, for both us and the dogs, and maps. The other team

249

will procure medicine, hygiene supplies, batteries and as many two way radios they can get their hands on." He pauses, "I want to make sure that we have enough radios that at least each team will have one, but if we can get enough for everyone, that would be best."

Greg questions, "How do you want to break up into teams?"

Jody sighs, "I've been thinking about that. Ken and Greg will lead one team. They will take Allen, Rachel, Chad, Amber, Marissa and my brother with them. That group will be responsible for the medicine and things." He pauses, "I will take Janet, Lisa, Ashley, Ryan, Codi, Lindsey and her husband with me to get the food, water and maps." He pauses again, "Everyone got that?"

Everyone looks around and nods, knowing what their job will be.

Jody speaks again, "One more thing before we eat and take care of the dogs. If we get split up, I want to make a plan for that."

Lisa questions, "What do you think we should do?"

Jody sighs, "I've been thinking on it, but does anyone have a suggestion?"

Mike speaks up, "How about we set a rally point like in the military if the unit gets split up?"

Jody nods, "That's a good idea."

Ken chimes in, "Well, we all know where we are going to camp for the night. Why not make that the rally point?"

Allen nods, "That's as good an idea as any."

Ashley questions, "What if a couple of you get there and no one else has made it yet?"

Lindsey speaks up, "I say we set a time frame. If you make it to the rally point, wait a set period of time to see if anyone else shows up."

Chad questions, "What if not everyone makes it there in the set time?"

Lisa speaks up, "Then whoever has made it will have the option of waiting longer or moving on."

Jody smiles at how everyone is stepping up and contributing, "That's what we'll do. The rally point is the east end of Lake Eucha Park on Highway 20. If you make it there, wait forty-eight hours if possible, then move on or wait longer at your discretion. If you move on, leave a message as to which way you went and where you plan on stopping next." He pauses, "That work for everyone?"

Everyone looks around and nods to each other.

Jody glances around, "Okay, let's get the dogs taken care of and eat, then get moving again."

Everyone breaks up and heads off to their vehicles as Mike and Codi get Lucky and Shadow out of the vehicles.

Janet drives the van slowly down the road towards the discount store which she can see up ahead on her left. Jody continues to glance around. Even though they have not seen anyone or anything so far since they entered town, Jody is staying ever vigil to make sure nothing comes up on them unexpectedly. Janet weaves around a couple of abandoned cars and slows down to turn into the parking lot.

Everyone in the group sees the seventeen vehicles in the parking lot and they all wonder the same thing. Where are the occupants of the vehicles at? Janet slowly heads towards the main entrance of the store.

Jody looks at Janet, "Pull all the way up to right in front of the doors."

Janet nods and continues to drive closer. Janet turns out of the isle and pulls up in front of the store, pulling forward enough so everyone else can park in behind her. Janet puts the van in park and turns it off. Jody gets out of the van as Janet sets the keys on the dashboard. Seeing that

Jody has all his weapons, everyone else gets out with all their weapons too. Jody walks over in front of the main doors and is quickly joined by everyone else.

Jody looks at Mike, "Okay dad, you, Shana, Rochelle and the three boys hang out here. Honk, fire off a shot or do whatever to get our attention if something happens." He pauses, "If you have to, all of you jump in your van and get out of here. Okay?"

Mike nods, "Okay."

Jody looks at Ken, "Let's get the teams in and out as fast as we can. Obviously if either of us run into trouble, we will be able to hear each other shoot or yell."

Ken nods, "Let's do this."

Jody starts for the front door of the store. Janet, Lisa, Ashley, Ryan, Codi, Lindsey and Michael, Lindsey's husband, follow Jody. Ken starts for the doors with Greg, Allen, Rachel, Chad, Amber, Marissa and Michael, Jody's brother, behind him.

Jody and his group walk into the store, glance around and spot the grocery section.

Jody whispers, "Ashley, Codi and Janet, grab baskets."

Ashley, Codi and Janet each grab a basket and follow Jody. Jody stays at the front while Lisa is at the back, keeping an eye out behind them.

Ken and his group walk into the store, glance around and spot the Pharmacy and hygiene section.

Ken whispers, "Rachel, Amber and Marissa, grab a basket."

Rachel, Amber and Marissa each grab a basket and follow Ken. Ken stays at the front while Greg is at the back, keeping an eye out so nothing will sneak up on them. The two groups quickly lose sight of each other as they head off to get their assigned supplies.

As Jody and his group pass by the registers, they see some road maps and plastic sacks. Jody motions to Lindsey and her husband and points over to the registers. Lindsey walks over to the road maps and grabs a handful of Oklahoma and Arkansas maps and places them in Ashley's basket. Michael, Lindsey's husband, grabs a bunch of sacks and also places them in Ashley's basket.

Jody starts walking again, keeping his AR-15 at the ready. Janet, Ashley and Codi try to keep the baskets as quiet as possible as they walk. Lisa continues to look back to make sure nothing comes up behind them. The walk seems like it takes an hour, but after a few minutes, the group finds the canned goods isle. The shelves are over half empty from being looted by others.

Jody whispers to the others, "Lisa will watch one end of the isle while I watch the other end. The rest of you load up as much as you can, then we'll head for the water."

Lisa walks to one end and Jody walks to the other end of the isle. Janet, Ashley, Ryan, Codi, Lindsey and Michael, Lindsey's husband, start loading up the sacks with canned goods. It doesn't take long and they have filled up Ashley's basket and half filled Codi's basket, but the shelves are now empty.

Jody glances back and sees that they are done loading the food. Jody motions for everyone to follow him. The group walks up behind Jody and Lisa walks up behind the others. Jody starts for the back of the grocery section to where the bottles of water will be.

Ken walks over to the pharmacy counter and looks around while everyone waits. Once he is sure it is safe, Ken motions for the others to join him. The rest of the group walks up to Ken.

Ken whispers, "Greg and I will stand watch. The rest of you load up sacks with antibiotics, cold and flu stuff and anything else that might be useful. After that, we will head over to the hygiene stuff and grab razors, soap, shampoo, scissors and battery operated trimmers."

Everyone nods and heads into the pharmacy area while Ken and Greg stand watch. It is eerily quiet in the store. It only takes a few minutes for the group to load up all the medicine they could find and place it in Amber's basket.

Once finished in the pharmacy, Ken leads the group over to the hygiene area where Ken and Greg again stand watch while the rest of the group gathers up the hygiene supplies. In a couple more minutes, the shelves are empty and Amber's basket is full. Ken motions for everyone to join him. Everyone walks over to Ken.

Ken whispers, "Okay, now let's head to the electronics section. Keep a close eye out cause we'll be in the back of the store which is a long way from the doors and the vehicles."

Ken starts off for the back of the store and everyone falls in line behind him like before.

Jody and the others reach the bottled water area and still they haven't seen or heard anything in the store yet.

Jody whispers to the others, "Just like before, Lisa and I will watch while you all load up the water."

Everyone nods and starts grabbing packages of bottled water while Jody and Lisa keep an eye out for any survivors or zombies. In only a couple minutes, the group has filled Codi's basket the rest of the way and half filled Janet's basket. Once they are done loading the water, the group walks over to Jody and Lisa.

Jody whispers, "Okay, good work everyone. Let's make our way to the pet section and then we'll be done."

Everyone nods. Jody starts walking towards where the pet section is and everyone falls in line behind him like before. As they begin to move, Ryan bumps into the end of the shelf and they hear something fall to the ground on the other side of the isle. The noise echoes thru the grocery section. Everyone stops for a second and looks around. Jody listens closely for a few seconds and once he is sure he doesn't hear anything, he continues on with everyone following him.

In what seems like an hour later, Ken and the others arrive in the electronics section of the store a few minutes after leaving the hygiene area. Ken wanders slowly until he finds the batteries and the two way radios.

Ken whispers to everyone, "Greg and I will keep watch again. Michael, Chad and Allen will load up the batteries while Rachel, Amber and Marissa will gather up the radios. Load everything in Rachel's basket. Marissa, we won't need your basket so just leave it here."

Everyone nods and heads off to their assigned tasks while Ken and Greg stand watch. Rachel, Amber and Marissa find enough of the same radios for everyone in the group to have one and they start back to the baskets. Michael, Jody's brother, Chad and Allen start loading sacks with batteries. As Chad is placing batteries in a sack, he drops a pack on the floor and it echoes thru the store.

Everyone stops when they hear the sound. Ken and Greg spin around quickly to see what the noise was. Chad reaches down and picks up the package of batteries and places them in the sack. In only a couple minutes, they have all the radios and batteries in Rachel's basket.

Ken whispers to everyone, "Okay, let's head back to the vehicles. Hopefully the other group will already be there."

Everyone nods and Ken starts the slow walk towards the front of the store. Everyone falls in behind Ken like before.

CHAPTER 32

Jody is watching one end of the isle and Lisa is watching the other end while Janet, Ashley, Ryan, Codi, Lindsey and her husband load up the dog food in Janet's basket. Jody looks back and sees that they are nearly done. Jody starts walking over to the group. Lisa sees Jody walking towards the group and she also starts walking towards them. Jody walks up to the group as Lindsey loads the last of the dog food.

Lisa is nearly to the group when she stops suddenly and points to the far end of the isle where Jody was at, "Look!"

Everyone turns and looks back at the end of the isle where Jody was at and they all see what Lisa is pointing at. Numerous zombies come staggering around the corner straight for them.

Jody yells, "Hurry, the other way!"

Janet, Codi and Ashley start pushing their baskets towards the other end of the isle when they suddenly stop.

Janet yells, "We're trapped!"

More zombies come around the end of the isle where Lisa was at.

Jody yells, "Lisa, Ryan and Michael, take us out that way! Aim for their heads! Lindsey and I will cover the rear!"

Lisa, Ryan and Michael, Lindsey's husband, step in front of the baskets, raise their shotguns and start firing. Jody and Lindsey take aim at the larger group of zombies coming from the rear and they start firing, Lindsey with her shotgun and Jody with his AR-15. The sound of the gunshots echo through the whole store.

Being so close, nearly every shot is on target and the zombies start falling to the floor at a rapid rate. Lisa, Ryan and Michael, Lindsey's husband, walk towards the group of zombies in front of them as they continue to fire. Janet, Codi and Ashley slowly push the baskets while following Lisa, Ryan and Michael, Lindsey's husband. Jody and Lindsey continue to shoot at the zombies behind the group.

Lisa empties her shotgun first. Lisa places her shotgun in Codi's basket, pulls out her pistol and continues to fire. Ryan and Michael, Lindsey's husband, both run out of shotgun shells so they, too, place their shotguns in Codi's basket, pull out their pistols and continue shooting. Lindsey empties her shotgun, places it in Janet's basket, then pulls out her pistol and starts firing again.

Finally, the last of the zombies in front of the group falls, but their bodies are blocking up the isle where the baskets can't get through. The group of zombies behind the group just keep coming around the corner.

Lisa yells, "The bodies are blocking the isle!"

Jody yells back, "Lisa, you cover Ryan and Michael while they pull enough bodies out of the way for the baskets to get through!"

Ryan and Michael, Lindsey's husband, holster their pistols. Lisa steps through the bodies of the fallen zombies which she figures to be about twenty, and steps out into the main isle. Lisa doesn't see any more zombies and motions to Ryan and Michael, Lindsey's husband.

Jody yells, "Janet, Codi, Ashley! Help us hold off this group while they clear the isle!"

Ashley and Janet grab their shotguns from their baskets while Codi grabs her rifle. The three of them line up next to Jody and Lindsey and start firing. The noise is deafening as at least thirty zombies have already come into the isle and there doesn't seem to be an end to them.

Ken and his group are halfway to the front doors when they hear the gunshots from the other group echo through the store. Ken and the others stop.

Greg speaks up, "Sounds like the others are in trouble."

Michael, Jody's brother, glances around, "We have to go help them."

Ken shakes his head, "No. We can't risk it. We have to get our supplies to the vehicles first."

Marissa looks at Ken, "We can't leave them!"

Ken stays calm, "Once we get the supplies to the vehicles, we'll come back for them. Now let's move!"

Ken starts walking again, with a little more urgency, and the rest of the group follows. Each one wondering if the others are okay.

Mike, Shana, Rochelle, Zach, Tyler and Daniel are waiting outside when they hear all the gunfire from Jody's group.

Shana looks at Mike, "They're in trouble!"

Mike glances around the parking lot to make sure nothing is coming towards them.

Once he is sure it's clear, Mike looks at the others, "Zach, Tyler, Daniel, get in the vehicles! Shana and

Rochelle, help me start up the vehicles. That way they will be running when the others get here."

Zach helps Daniel into his car seat while Tyler gets in Lisa's Jeep and starts it up. Tyler climbs into the backseat as Zach walks up and gets in the backseat of Lisa's Jeep. Shana, Mike and Rochelle start up the rest of the vehicles. Mike walks back over to the main doors. Shana and Rochelle walk up to Mike.

Mike looks at Rochelle, "Go ahead and get in your Jeep. If there are signs of trouble, Shana and I will grab Daniel and get in my van and you'll follow us. Okay?"

Rochelle nods, "Okay."

Rochelle heads off and gets in the driver's seat of Lisa's Jeep. Shana and Mike continue to watch the front doors and the parking lot.

Ryan and Michael, Lindsey's husband, continue to move the bodies of the zombies out of the way while Lisa stands watch. Jody, Lindsey, Ashley, Codi and Janet continue to shoot at the zombies coming from behind the group.

Michael, Lindsey's husband, yells "Okay, it's clear!"

Jody yells, "Back to your baskets! Lisa, lead us out of here!"

Ashley tosses her empty shotgun in her basket and starts pushing. Codi tosses her empty rifle in her basket and quickly follows Ashley. Janet tosses her empty shotgun in her basket and falls in behind Codi.

Lisa, Michael, Lindsey's husband, and Ryan lead the way with Ashley, Codi and Janet right behind them. Jody and Lindsey stay where they are at for the moment as Lindsey reloads her pistol and Jody reloads his AR-15.

Lindsey looks back and sees Janet, the last basket, turn the corner out of the isle.

Lindsey taps Jody, "They're clear!"

Jody nods, "Let's go!"

Jody and Lindsey turn and run as more zombies stagger around the corner and make their way through the other bodies on the floor. Jody and Lindsey get to the end of the isle and quickly look back. Jody and Lindsey see that the zombies are slowed by all the bodies on the floor and know that they have narrowly escaped. Jody and Lindsey quickly catch up to the others.

Mike and Shana wait patiently, yet anxiously for the others. Finally, Mike and Shana see movement coming towards the doors. The two of them ready their shotguns. After a couple of seconds, Mike and Shana lower their shotguns when they see Ken and his group approach the front doors.

Ken and his group hurry out the front doors of the store and they see Mike and Shana have the vehicles ready to go.

Ken yells, "Quick, load up the supplies!"

Ken makes his way over to Mike and Shana while the others push the baskets up to the vehicles.

Mike looks at Ken, "Did you see the others at all?"

Ken shakes his head, "No. We'll head back in after the supplies are loaded to see if we can find them."

Mike shakes his head, "No. We can't risk that."

Shana looks at Mike, "What? We can't leave them!"

Mike sighs, "We might have to. Losing half the group is one thing, but we can't risk losing the other half too." He pauses, "They'll have to make it out on their own."

The others have finished loading up the supplies and quickly rush over to where Mike, Ken and Shana are at.

Marissa speaks while catching her breath, "Supplies are loaded. Let's go."

Mike shakes his head, "No one is going back in."

Everyone looks at Mike in amazement at what he just said.

Michael, Jody's brother, replies, "We can't leave them."

Ken nods, "Mike is right. We can't risk everyone. They'll have to fight their way out. We have to stay ready to get out of here."

At that moment, the sound of the gunfire stops. Everyone outside the store starts looking at each other, thinking the same thing, are the others okay.

Mike looks at the others, "Everyone get ready by their vehicles. Either they are on their way out or whatever attacked them will be coming this way soon."

Everyone heads over to their vehicles and waits to see if it will be Jody and the others coming out the doors or something else.

Lisa, Ryan and Michael, Lindsey's husband, continue as fast as they can without losing everyone behind them. Finally, Lisa sees the front doors of the store. Lisa glances around and doesn't see any zombies. Lisa breathes a sigh of relief and she leads the group out the front doors to where the vehicles are parked.

Mike and the others see Lisa and the rest of the group come out of the store. Everyone starts towards Lisa and the others with smiles on their faces.

Jody yells, "Hurry! Get the supplies loaded and get your weapons! We have to get out of here, fast!"

Everyone can tell by Jody's voice that whatever it was they ran into and got away from, its still not safe. Everyone moves fast, grabbing whatever they can and tossing it in any vehicle where there is space for supplies.

Jody looks at Mike and Ken while catching his breath, "A huge group of zombies trapped us. We shot our way out, but there are more inside."

Lisa yells, "We're loaded up!"

Jody nods, "Okay! Everyone, make sure you have your guns and let's get out of here!"

Jody watches the front doors while everyone else loads up in their vehicles. Jody walks over to Janet's van and gets in the passenger's seat.

Jody looks at Janet who seems obviously shaken up, "Everything is okay. We're safe." Jody places his hand on Janet's shoulder, "Just calm yourself down, pull back out on the highway and let's get out of this town."

Janet swallows the lump in her throat and just feeling Jody's touch makes her feel better, "Okay."

Janet puts the van in drive and pulls away from the store. Everyone else falls in line behind Janet. A couple minutes after the convoy pulls off, nearly forty zombies stagger out the front doors of the store.

CHAPTER 33

Janet keeps the van at a steady 40 mph as the town of Jay is long behind them and the trees of Lake Eucha State Park have been on their right for many miles. Jody can tell that they are getting close to where they will camp for the night. The convoy has made good time, but with the events of today at the store, Jody feels that it would be best to go ahead and stop for the night so everyone can rest.

Jody sees the county road ahead that pretty much marks the end of the park on his map, "Hey babe, go about a mile pass this county road, then pull off. There should be a good place to camp off the highway."

Janet nods and replies, still a little shaken, "Okay."

Janet continues to drive down the highway, but slows down some when she passes the county road turn. Jody continues to look around, hoping he can spot what he is looking for. Codi is holding Lucky and petting him as she is trying to forget what happened earlier at the store. Ryan is just staring out the window. Janet's van, like all the other vehicles, has been quiet since leaving the store as each person deals with the events that happened at the store in their own mind.

Jody finally spots what he was hoping to see, "Pull off just ahead."

Janet slows the van down and brings it to a stop on the shoulder of the highway.

Janet glances around, "Why here?"

Jody smiles and points at a pond, "It might be cool water, but we can at least clean up."

Janet smiles, "That would be nice and given how hot it's been out, the water might be pretty warm."

Janet puts the van in park and shuts it off. Jody gets out of the van. Codi and Ryan get out of the van as Janet sets the keys on the dashboard, then gets out of the van.

Jody glances around, making sure he doesn't see any zombies around, while everyone else gets out of their vehicles and makes their way over to Jody, Janet, Ryan and Codi.

Ken questions, "What's up little buddy?"

Jody looks around some more, "I know we've got plenty of daylight left, but after today, I want to go ahead and stop."

Lisa nods, "Good idea."

Jody points at the pond, "Let's set up camp by the pond. Zach and Tyler will keep watch while we setup camp."

Everyone nods.

Jody continues, "Once camp is done, let's get the dogs taken care of and start our normal watch rotation. Also, anyone that wants to clean or wash up, can use the pond. I know it's not a hot shower, but it's better than nothing."

Mike chuckles slightly, "It sure is. Besides, keeping up our hygiene is more important than most people think."

Amber speaks up, "I don't care what kind of water it is, I can't wait to clean up and wash my clothes."

Jody smiles, "Alright then, Zach and Tyler take watch and let's get to it."

Zach and Tyler find a good place that allows them to see the highway and the campsite while everyone starts setting up the tents.

It only takes about thirty minutes and the camp is all set up. Everyone has their personal belongings in their tent that they will need for the overnight stay. Everyone meets back in front of the large tent which is in the middle of the four smaller tents and Greg's single person tent.

Jody glances around, "Okay, now that we got that done, let's get the dogs out and walked around and get cleaned up if anyone wants to."

Rachel questions, "How do you want to handle the washing up?"

Jody sighs and starts thinking.

Ken speaks up, "Greg and I have the first watch. Why don't all the women go first since none of them will be on watch? Then all the men can go once Lisa and Ashley take over watch from us."

Jody nods, "Great idea. Okay, ladies will have one hour to wash up and do whatever. No men will be over by the pond or be looking over there. If any of you ladies see anything, just yell. Then once they are done and Lisa and Ashley take over watch, the men will go. Sound good?"

Everyone looks around and nods at each other. All the women head off to get their towels, hygiene things and changes of clothes. The men all stay gathered around the front of the large tent. Once the women gather their things, they start making their way to the pond. As Ashley walks by the men on her way to the pond, she drops her shampoo bottle. Zach quickly picks it up and hands it back to Ashley.

Ashley smiles at Zach, "Thanks."

Zach smiles and kind of looks away, "Sure, anytime."

Ashley walks off towards the pond to join the rest of the women and Zach sits back down. Jody smiles as he realizes Zach has developed some kind of crush on Ashley.

Everyone is finished cleaning up and Lisa and Ashley are nearly at the end of their watch. Everyone except Lisa and Ashley have ate now as Michael, Jody's brother, and Marissa prepare to take over the watch. You can tell everyone feels better having cleaned up, but the events of the store are still weighing on their minds.

Michael, Jody's brother, and Marissa relieve Lisa and Ashley from watch. Lisa and Ashley walk over to the rest of the group in front of the large tent. Shadow and Lucky are laying on the ground in the middle of everyone. As Lisa and Ashley walk up, Jody is putting his folding shovel away. Lisa notices that Jody has dug a hole in the middle of the campsite.

Lisa and Ashley grab their can of soup for dinner and look for a place to sit. Zach slides over to make room and Ashley sits down next to Zach.

Ashley smiles, "Thanks."

Zach just smiles back. Shana looks at her son and shakes her head, knowing he likes Ashley. Lisa finds a spot next to Rochelle. Jody walks back up after putting his shovel away.

Ashley questions, "What's the hole for?"

Jody replies as he sits down next to Janet, "So we can build a fire tonight. Being down in the hole, it won't cast as much of a glow and give us away."

Lisa nods, "Smart thinking."

Ken smiles and replies, "It's amazing all the little things they teach you in survival training."

Mike smiles and nods, "Yes it is."

Lindsey questions, "So, what's tomorrow's plan?"

Jody sighs and replies, "Let me go grab the maps and I'll cover tomorrow's route with everyone."

Jody heads off to get the maps that they got from the store. Jody returns in a couple minutes with an Oklahoma and Arkansas map for each team. Jody hands a person from each team a map of each state.

Jody opens his Oklahoma map, "I'll tell Michael and Marissa later. Everyone open your Oklahoma map and locate where we are at now."

Jody waits while a person from each team opens their map and locates their current location. Once Jody is sure everyone is ready, he begins to lay out the course for tomorrow.

Jody speaks, "Tomorrow is going to just be a travel day. We will continue on Highway 20 East until we reach Arkansas, then we will take Highway 43 South towards Maysville." He pauses, "We will have to go far enough south until we can turn east and not have to go through the Fayetteville area."

Greg questions, "Where do you plan on stopping for tomorrow?"

Jody sighs, "We'll cross over a river just north of Siloam Springs. I think if we can reach there by dinner time, that is where we'll camp." He pauses, "We have one more problem."

Lindsey questions, "What's that?"

Jody replies, "We got food and water which is good, but we can always use more. However, we are going to have to start finding gas for the vehicles. We have four of the five gallon gas cans, but as you've noticed, we haven't passed too many cars on the highways."

Codi questions, "What do we do about that?"

Jody takes a drink of water, "Just inside the northern city limit of Siloam Springs is John Brown University. I think some of us should make a run there from the river when we camp and see if there are vehicles there that we can get gas from."

Ken speaks up, "If we camp at dinner time, you're talking about making a nighttime run into a populated area. Is that a good idea?"

Jody sighs, "It will be a little dangerous, but I think it will be safer than waiting until the next day. It's not that far from the river to the university so it should only take a couple hours or so. Plus, the cover of night will help us avoid other potential survivors if there are any."

Mike speaks up, "It's risky, but we can't afford to run out of gas and that is probably going to be our best chance right now."

Jody nods, "We will stop and gather what we can along the way, but I know it won't be enough. We can also gather some more supplies from the university kitchen."

Lisa nods, "You've gotten us this far. I trust your judgment on this."

Janet nods, "Me too."

Jody glances around, "Anyone else have anything on the plans?"

Everyone is quiet.

Jody stands up, "Okay, I'm going to let Michael and Marissa know. I would suggest everyone get as much rest as they can. Jody heads off to where Michael, his brother, and Marissa are standing watch while the others start going about their business.

Mike and Shana have taken over watch for Michael, Jody's brother, and Marissa. Everyone else is pretty much doing their own thing to pass the time. Jody is laying down in his tent that he shares with Janet, Mike and Shana. Janet walks into the tent and zips up the door.

Jody looks over at Janet, "Hey girl, how are you doing? I can tell what happened at the store has bothered you."

Janet steps over and lays down next to Jody, "Yeah. I was scared pretty bad."

Jody puts his arm around Janet, "Its okay to be scared."

Janet rolls over and looks at Jody, "You don't seem to be scared."

Jody smiles, "Well, I am. It's just that I keep it inside and let it drive me to accomplish what we need to accomplish." He pauses, "Being scared doesn't become a bad thing until you let it turn into panic. That's when people make mistakes or freeze up. That's when people die."

Janet sighs, "We could have died today."

Jody moves a little closer, "Yes, each day brings the possibility of dying." He pauses, "But I'm not going to let that happen to you."

Janet moves in towards Jody, "I love you."

Jody closes his eyes, "I love you too."

Just as Jody finishes his words, their lips meet. It's a good, passionate kiss. Jody and Janet continue kissing for a couple minutes, then start touching as well.

Jody leans back for a moment, "Do you want to?'

Janet knows what Jody is talking about, "Yes."

Jody starts to remove Janet's clothes and Janet removes Jody's clothes. For the next little while, they share their physical love for each other and forget about all the craziness that has been happening.

CHAPTER 34

Lisa and Ashley are back on watch as the stars like up the clear night sky. The temperature has dropped some, but it is still a comfortable night. The night is eerily quiet as everyone is now asleep or at least in their tents. A few faint sounds of wild animals is all Lisa and Ashley hear, but they stay ever ready in case someone or something comes out of the darkness.

Ashley whispers to Lisa, "Today, at the store, I was pretty scared."

Lisa nods and whispers back, "So was I."

Ashley looks at Lisa, "Really? You didn't seem like it."

Lisa smiles, "Well, it's because I've had training to help me keep control of my emotions during stressful times. The emotions are still there, I'm just able to overcome them because I revert back to my training." She pauses, "But, I was still scared and worried that we might not get out of there."

Ashley glances around, "I know and that was a store in a small town. I hate to think what it will be like when we are in or near a large town or city."

Lisa nods, "I'm sure Jody is going to do his best to avoid those places, but there is always the chance we will have to go into or near one for supplies."

Ashley nods, "Yeah, that's true."

Lisa looks at Ashley, "So, I think Zach has taken a liking to you."

Ashley smiles, "Yeah, I think so too. It's pretty cute actually. He's a teenage boy and it happens."

Lisa smiles, "It sure does. I think we all can remember what it was like as teenagers and getting a crush on someone."

Ashley nods and glances around, "Oh yes. The young love days."

Lisa and Ashley chuckle quietly as they continue to look around and pass the time with conversation.

Lindsey and Michael, her husband, are laying down in the tent they share with Lisa and Ashley. Neither of them have been able to sleep since Lisa and Ashley left to take over watch.

Lindsey whispers to her husband, "I don't know about you, but I was kind of scared today at the store." She pauses, "Not real bad since Jody, you and the others were there, but still scared."

Michael, Lindsey's husband, whispers back, "Yeah, I was too. Up until then it was just talk about zombies and stuff except for those four at the first campsite which we didn't have to deal with and the one in the gun shop. At the store though, it was real for the first time."

Lindsey nods, "Yeah, it wasn't at all like I thought it would be."

Michael, Lindsey's husband, looks at Lindsey, "I know what you mean." He pauses, "I'm actually proud of myself and everyone else though on how we all responded to the situation. No one really froze up or panicked."

Lindsey slightly smiles, "Yeah, I was pretty proud of that too. I wasn't sure how I'd react the first time we were faced with a lot of them because the one at the gun shop was by itself. It was a shock, but not real scary."

Michael, Lindsey's husband, sighs, "Yep. I actually feel better about the trip now seeing that everyone is able to fight against those things."

Lindsey nods and sighs, "Yeah, me too." She pauses, "Now all that worries me is what is going to happen if we run into other survivors that are not friendly."

Michael, Lindsey's husband, rolls over and slides his arm around Lindsey's waist, "Let's not worry about that right now." He gives a sly smile, "We have the tent to ourselves."

Lindsey rolls over, looks at Michael, her husband, and smiles her beautiful smile, "We sure do."

Lindsey and Michael, her husband, share a passionate kiss as they take their alone time to show their love for each other in a physical way.

Chad and Amber are on watch now as it is getting ever closer to sunrise.

Amber looks over at her boyfriend, "You know, I'm happy that we ran into this other group. They seem to be good people."

Chad nods, "Yeah, I feel better with having them around too. They seem to know what they're doing. Not to mention, just more safety in numbers."

Amber nods, "That's for sure. The way it's starting to look, we definitely are going to need their help and I know they are probably happy to have our help too."

Chad glances around, "Oh yeah, I'm sure they feel the same way we do. I have to admit, at first I was worried about them, but after that first day at the campsite, plus the fact they brought their dogs with them, I started feeling much better about them."

Amber smiles and nods, "I know. I didn't figure they'd be bad people since they actually were thoughtful enough to save their dogs too."

The sun starts to break across the horizon and light up the morning sky.

Chad sighs and looks around, "Well, we better start waking everyone up. I'll keep watch if you want to go start waking them up."

Amber smiles, "Okay."

Amber gives Chad a nice, loving kiss, then heads off to the campsite to start waking everyone for the new day.

Once everyone is awake, they wash up, get dressed for the day and get something to eat. After eating, Zach and Tyler take over watch. Everyone else gathers up their personal belongings and loads them in their vehicles. Shana grabs Zach and Tyler's things and loads them up. As everyone is breaking down the tents, Mike and Codi take Shadow and Lucky for a little walk around the camp area and the pond.

It doesn't take long and the tents are packed up in the vehicles as well. Jody and the others wait by the vehicles for Mike, Codi and the dogs. After getting their morning business done and sniffing the entire area, Mike puts Shadow in his van while Codi puts Lucky in Janet's van. Mike and Codi meet up with the rest of the group.

Jody looks around at everyone, "First, I want to say that everyone did a great job yesterday, especially at the store. It was a tough situation, but we got through it by working together." He pauses, "And just in case any of you were wondering, Mike and Ken made the right decision by not coming for us. We can't risk the entire group to save part of it. I would have done the same thing if I was in their place."

Everyone looks around at each other and nods. Jody smiles as Janet takes his hand.

Jody continues, "Okay. We have a nice trip ahead of us today. I want to get to our next campsite no later than dinner. I know it's not real far miles wise, but we are not going to drive any faster than usual. Today, we only stop for emergencies and for the opportunity to get gas for the vehicles." He pauses, "Have all the radios been tested and handed out?"

Ken nods, "Yep. Greg and I got that done."

Jody nods, "Good. Use the radios if anything comes up. Other than that, let's load up and get going."

Everyone nods and heads off to their vehicles. Janet starts up her van and pulls onto the highway. Everyone falls in behind Janet and the next part of the trip has begun.

It has been an uneventful drive the entire day as the sun has moved into the evening sky. Jody looks out the window of Janet's van and knows that they are getting close to their stopping point for the night. Jody has been thinking about the trip to John Brown University all day and how he wants to handle it. Jody is also happy that they managed to get some gas, but knows that they need much more. Jody is figuring on not only getting gas from vehicles still parked at the university, but grabbing some more supplies as well.

Janet glances around, wondering how much further the river is. Codi and Ryan continue looking around as well to see if they can spot any zombies in the area. Finally, Jody sees what he's been looking for.

Jody points ahead, "There's the river. Go across the bridge and pull off the highway. We will camp along the riverbank."

Janet nods, "Okay baby."

Jody smiles at Janet's response. Janet starts slowing down and everyone follows suit. Janet drives the van across the bridge and just far enough so everyone can make it across the bridge, then Janet pulls off on the side of the highway. Everyone else pulls off the highway. Janet puts her van in park and shuts off the engine. Jody gets out of the van with all his weapons. Ryan and Codi also get out with their weapons while Janet sets her keys on the dashboard, then gets out with her weapons. Everyone else in the convoy shuts off their vehicles and gets out with their weapons. Jody, Janet, Ryan and Codi look around while everyone makes their way over to them.

Ken looks at Jody, "Okay little buddy, how do you want to handle this?"

Jody looks around, "Zach and Tyler will take watch while we set up the campsite. After that, we'll get the dogs taken care of and eat dinner." He pauses, "Then we'll talk about the trip to John Brown University."

Mike looks at his son, "Do you still want to try and make the trip into town tonight?"

Jody looks at the sky and nods, "Yeah. I think we can get everything done and get into town before the sun sets, if we hurry."

Lisa speaks up, "Then let's stop talking and get to it."

Jody smiles and chuckles, "You heard the lady."

Everyone smiles and heads off to get their tents and personal things while Zach and Tyler take over watch.

It doesn't take long and the campsite is set up and the dogs have been taken care of. Everyone starts eating. Jody takes Zach and Tyler their dinner so they can eat while they keep watch. Jody returns to the group.

Greg looks at Jody, "So, how are we going to handle the trip?"

Jody replies, "Well, since you and Ken handled getting the gas during the trip today, I'll lead the group into the university." He pauses and looks at Janet, "Which means you'll have to go to, being my partner."

Janet nods and smiles, "That's okay."

Ken speaks up, "So, who are you going to take with you?"

Jody sighs, "I don't have anyone specific in mind. I think it's best if we just randomly pick."

Mike nods, "That works for me."

Chad questions, "How do you want to pick?"

Jody replies, "I'll pick a number between one and a hundred. I'll tell it to Janet and Rochelle. The three teams who go over or are not the closest, will join Janet and myself."

Lindsey nods, "Let's get to it."

Jody leans over and whispers to Janet and Rochelle, "The number is forty-one."

Janet and Rochelle nod.

Jody looks at Mike, "You and Shana pick first."

Mike and Shana whisper to each other, then Mike replies, "Thirty-three."

Jody smiles and looks at Marissa and his brother, "Okay, your turn."

Michael, Jody's brother, and Marissa whisper to each other, then Marissa replies, "Fifty-six."

Jody nods and looks at Lisa and Ashley, "Your turn ladies."

Lisa and Ashley whisper to each other, then Lisa replies, "Twenty-two."

Jody nods and looks at Lindsey and her husband, "Okay, your next."

Lindsey and Michael, her husband, whisper to each other, then Lindsey replies, "Sixty-nine."

Jody nods, then looks at Ryan and Codi, "Okay, let's hear your pick."

Ryan and Codi whisper to each other, then Codi replies, "Forty."

Jody nods, then looks at Allen and Rachel, "Your turn."

Allen and Rachel whisper to each other, then Allen speaks, "Forty-nine."

Jody nods and looks at Chad and Amber, "And now you two."

Chad and Amber whisper to each other, then Chad speaks, "Thirteen."

Jody nods and looks at Janet and Rochelle, "What was the number ladies?"

Janet and Rochelle speak at the same time, "Forty-one."

Jody sighs and speaks, "Three teams went over. That means, Allen and Rachel, My brother and Marissa and Lindsey and her husband will join Janet and I."

Marissa questions, "So, what's the plan?"

Jody replies, "We will take the highway south to Villa View Drive, then west on that road to Savannah Lane, then turn south. We will park at the end of that road and walk the rest of the way."

Allen questions, "What vehicles are we taking?"

Jody glances around, "Janet's van and your Tahoe. We can put more supplies in those and the full gas cans."

Michael, Jody's brother, questions, "When are we leaving?"

Jody looks around and notices everyone is finished with dinner, "We leave in ten minutes."

Lindsey nods, "Then let's get ready."

Jody, Janet, Allen, Rachel, Lindsey, Marissa and both Michaels get up and start getting their things ready to go.

CHAPTER 35

Jody looks out the window of the van while Janet drives south on the highway. Jody has his h-harness and cartridge belt gear sitting behind his seat. Jody has his spare magazines for his rifle and pistol on his gear now and his pistol is in the tactical drop holster on his gear. Lindsey and Michael, her husband, are riding in the backseat of the van. Allen follows Janet with his Tahoe. Rachel, Marissa and Michael, Jody's brother, are riding with Allen.

Michael, Lindsey's husband, questions, "How are we going to transport any supplies back to the vehicles?"

Jody continues to glance around, "We will grab duffle bags or backpacks at the college."

Janet nods as she slows the van down and prepares to make the first turn, "Good thinking."

Lindsey glances around, "So, are we going to get the gas and bring it back first or get gas and supplies at the same time."

Jody replies as Janet turns onto the first road, "We'll get the gas and get it back to the vehicles first, then look around for any supplies."

Michael, Lindsey's husband, looks at Jody's gear, "So, why are you bringing all that stuff?"

Jody sighs and smiles, "Because you never know when you might need it. I have water, food and other things that are very useful in case we end up not being able to make it back tonight."

Janet starts to slow down as she prepares to make the final turn, "Are you expecting that?"

Jody looks at Janet, "No, but this is the first time any part of the group has been this far from the campsite. It doesn't hurt to be prepared for the possibility that we might have to stay a night away from camp."

Lindsey nods, "That's a great idea. Being prepared and thinking of the unexpected is going to keep us out of a bad situation."

Jody nods, "Exactly."

Janet sees the end of the road as the sun starts to set, "There is the end of the road. I can see the university."

Jody nods, "Yeah, its not far from the end of the road. We'll park the vehicles there and proceed on foot."

Janet slows the van to a stop and puts it in park. Allen pulls his Tahoe to a stop behind Janet's van. Everyone gets out as Janet and Allen shut off their vehicles and place their keys on the dashboards of the vehicles. Everyone gathers around while Jody puts on his gear and grabs his rifle.

Jody speaks, "I'll take point. Lindsey, I want you to bring up the rear. Everyone else will carry the gas cans. When we get there, Lindsey and I will provide cover while all of you get the gas." He pauses, "We'll bring the gas back here and load it in Allen's Tahoe, then we'll head back for any supplies we can find."

Everyone nods and Lindsey questions, "What if we run into trouble?"

Jody replies, "If it's just a few, we fight them off and continue. If it's a lot, we get back to the vehicles and get out of here. Okay?"

Everyone nods again. Jody starts heading towards the university. Janet and the others fall in behind Jody and Lindsey takes up the very important position of rear security.

Ken and Greg are standing watch as the rest of the group that didn't go tries to pass the time doing whatever they can while they wait on Jody and the others to return. Rochelle, Zach, Tyler and Daniel are playing with Shadow and Lucky. Shadow is smiling big as he chases Daniel around because Daniel has Shadow's squeaker toy. When Shadow gets close, Daniel throws the toy to Tyler. Shadow runs over to Tyler and waits for Tyler to throw his toy so he can chase it. Lucky is making his way back and forth between Rochelle and Zach, getting petted by both of them.

Mike, Shana, Lisa, Ashley, Ryan and Codi are watching the kids play with the dogs. Chad and Amber are in their tent having some alone time. Mike and the others smile as they watch the kids getting the chance to be kids and play for the first time since this all began. Shadow is also enjoying the chance to play some.

Mike glances around, "Now, this is more like it."

Shana smiles, "I know. Its nice to see the boys get the chance to be boys." She pauses, "I'm still worried about the others though."

Lisa nods as she watches the kids, "Me too."

Ashley reaches down and pets Lucky as he makes his way over to her, "I know. I hate just sitting here waiting."

Codi smiles as she watches Lucky get familiar with the others, "Yeah, its just as stressful as being out there."

Ryan nods, "Ain't that the truth."

Ashley looks back up and sees Zach looking at her and Lucky. Zach looks away when Ashley looks at him. Everyone continues to watch and enjoy the moment while they wait for the others.

Jody slows down as they approach a parking lot behind the first building of the university. The sun has completely set, but Jody doesn't see any movement around the parking lot. It's a small parking lot, most likely faculty parking. Jody stops and takes a knee. Everyone stops behind Jody. Jody gazes at the parking lot, hoping to catch any movement. Jody doesn't see any movement, but he does see about fifteen cars. Jody turns and motions for everyone to join him. The rest of the group walks up to Jody.

Jody whispers, "Okay, I don't see any movement. Lindsey and I will block off the first row cars. Get the gas if you can get into those cars. Be careful, we can't afford to set off any alarms so look for older model cars."

Everyone nods. Jody heads off to the left of the first row of cars and Lindsey heads off to the right. Jody takes a knee and continues to look around. Lindsey does the same. The rest of the group moves in and they each find a car that they can siphon gas from. No one sets off a car alarm and in about ten minutes, all the gas cans are full. Jody looks back over his shoulder and sees the group gathering together. Jody heads over to them and so does Lindsey.

Jody whispers, "Okay, let's get these back to the vehicles and return for some supplies."

Jody starts off towards the vehicles. Everyone falls in behind him and Lindsey returns to her rear security position. Jody leads them to about fifty yards from the vehicles when he suddenly stops and takes a knee. Everyone else stops behind Jody. Each person is wondering what is going on, when they spot what caused Jody to stop. Everyone sees movement over by their vehicles. Jody motions with his hand for the group to stay put. Jody starts moving towards the vehicles. Jody continues to look around and doesn't spot any other movement. Not noticing any other movement, Jody slides his rifle to his side and pulls out his combat knife.

Jody slowly moves up towards the zombie, being extremely quit. Jody circles around behind the zombie and moves in to take care of the zombie so the others will be able to return to the vehicles. When Jody gets to within a couple feet of the zombie, he drives his combat knife into the back of the zombie's head. The zombie falls as Jody removes his knife. Jody wipes his knife off on the zombie's clothes, then puts his knife away.

Jody looks back over to the others and motions for them to come over to the vehicles. Lindsey leads the rest of the group over to the vehicles. Jody notices that Marissa is limping some as she approaches the vehicles. Jody and Lindsey stand guard as Allen opens the back of his Tahoe. Everyone sets their gas cans down and Allen loads them in the back of his vehicle. Once the gas cans are loaded, everyone heads over to Jody and Lindsey.

Jody looks at the others, "Okay, let's head back and see what we can find." He pauses and looks at Marissa, "How you doing?"

Marissa sighs, "Knees are hurting some, but I'll be okay."

Jody sighs, "Okay. Let's get moving."

Jody heads off for the university again. Everyone falls in behind him and Lindsey takes the rear security position.

Lisa and Ashley are standing watch now. The playing in the camp has stopped as Shadow, Daniel and Tyler are all worn out. Shadow is laying at Mike's feet while everyone is just sitting around waiting for the others to return. Lisa and Ashley walk around the outside of the campsite. At that moment, Shadow's head pops up and he lets out a low growl sound.

Mike looks at Shadow and whispers, "Shadow, quiet."

Mike starts looking around and so do the others. Ashley comes walking up from over by the vehicles.

Ashley looks at Mike and Ken, "We spotted movement on the bridge."

Ken and Mike follow Ashley back over to where Lisa is at as Rochelle moves over to keep an eye on Shadow. Lisa is kneeling by a tree, watching the bridge. Mike, Ken and Ashley walk up quietly and look over at the bridge. The four of them see two zombies staggering across the bridge.

Ken whispers to Lisa, "Any other movement?"

Lisa whispers back, "No, just those two."

Mike whispers, "We have to take them out."

Ken nods, "Yeah, but we can't risk gunfire. We'll have to take them out quietly."

Ashley questions, "What do you suggest?"

Ken glances around, "Ashley, you keep looking out. We'll head up there and take them out with our knives."

Ashley nods, "Okay."

Ken pulls out his knife and starts for the bridge. Lisa and Mike pull their knives and follow Ken. The two zombies spot Ken, Mike and Lisa and start staggering towards them at a fairly quick pace. Ken closes in on one of the zombies as Mike and Lisa close in on the other zombie. The zombies start making gasping and growling noises as they get closer to Ken, Mike and Lisa. Ken walks up to the zombie on the left and raises his knife. As the zombie reaches for Ken, Ken drives his knife forward into the zombie's left eye. The zombie falls as Ken removes his knife.

The other zombie turns it's attention to Mike as Mike and Lisa approach the zombie. Seeing that Mike has the zombie's attention, Lisa moves to the side of the zombie.

Mike knows what Lisa is doing and Mike moves to his right to draw the zombie's look away from Lisa. As the zombie staggers towards Mike, Lisa sneaks up and rams her knife into the back of the zombie's head. As Lisa removes her knife, the zombie falls.

Ken glances around, "Okay, let's get back before anymore come along."

Ken, Mike and Lisa hurry back over to Ashley.

Ashley questions, "Did you see anymore?"

Lisa shakes her head, "No, just those two."

Ken whispers, "Okay. Return to your regular watch. Mike and I are headed back to camp."

Ken and Mike walk off as Lisa and Ashley return to patrolling the perimeter of the campsite.

CHAPTER 36

Jody and the others have made it back to the first building of the campus. So far Jody and the others haven't seen anything, but the group is staying ever ready. They know that zombies can appear at any time. Jody slowly works his way to the corner of the building with everyone right behind him.

Jody slowly peeks around the corner of the building. Jody sees some other buildings of the campus and he can make out the open area in between all the buildings. The buildings are arranged in a square around the large open area in the middle. Jody continues to gaze at the area, hoping to spot any movement or see a building that might be the cafeteria.

Jody starts to take a step, then stops. Everyone wonders what is going on. Jody spots movement in the open area in the middle of the buildings, a lot of movement. Jody can tell that it is a large number of zombies. Jody glances at the buildings again and something catches his eye and Jody shakes his head like he couldn't believe if what he saw was real or not because it was a quick flash of light that looked like a flashlight beam. Jody steps back and looks at the others.

Janet questions, "What's out there?"

Jody sighs, "I see a lot of movement in the courtyard area. I think we can skirt around the building off to the right and avoid them seeing us." He pauses, "I also think I saw what looked like a flashlight beam in one of the buildings over that way too."

Michael, Jody's brother, replies, "There might be other survivors here."

Jody nods, "Quite possible. I want to check the building where I think I saw the light."

Marissa questions, "Is that a good idea? What if there are survivors and they aren't friendly?"

Jody glances around, "I'm willing to take the chance if it'll save us time on having to search every building for the cafeteria." He pauses, "What do you all think?"

Michael, Lindsey's husband, replies, "I agree. Wandering around in the dark with a lot of zombies around isn't the best thing to do."

The others nod.

Jody sighs and whispers, "Okay. Stay close to me and move as fast as you safely can. Lindsey, you've got rear security."

Lindsey nods, "No problem."

Jody turns back around and moves to the corner of the building again. Jody looks at the courtyard area again and notices the zombies are still just wandering the courtyard area. Jody looks over to the building where he plans on making his run to. It looks like a dorm building and is about fifty yards away. Jody gets into a low crouch and takes off at a fairly fast pace.

The rest of the group quickly follows. Everyone is doing okay with keeping up, but Marissa starts to slow down some and the limping gets worse. Allen, who is a big man, starts to slow down some too. Lindsey slows down so that she can keep Marissa and Allen in front of her.

Jody makes it to the building and looks back at the others. Janet is the next to arrive followed quickly by

Rachel, his brother and Lindsey's husband. Jody can see that Marissa and Allen are struggling some and knows that could become a problem if they have to get out of there quickly.

A few seconds later, Marissa, Allen and Lindsey make it to the others. Jody looks at Lindsey and nods, knowing she risked slowing down and being spotted just to make sure the others made it across okay. Lindsey nods back. Jody works his way down the back wall of the building, passing windows and a closed door. Jody reaches the end of the building and slowly looks around the corner at the courtyard area.

Jody continues to see the zombies wandering around, but can tell that they have not been spotted yet. Jody looks over at the next building and it is the building where he thinks he saw the light. Jody takes one more look at the courtyard, then makes a run for the next building. It is another fifty yard run. Jody makes it across quickly and looks back.

Janet, Rachel and both Michaels come running up just a few seconds later. Allen and Marissa are doing their best, but it is obvious they are having troubles. Lindsey stays with Allen and Marissa, continuing to look around in case they are spotted. Finally, Allen, Marissa and Lindsey make it across. Jody looks back around the corner at the courtyard. The zombies continue to stagger around, unaware of Jody and the others.

Jody looks back at the others and whispers, "Okay, let's see if there is a back door into this building."

Rachel whispers, "From the looks of this building, I think this might be the cafeteria."

Lindsey nods, "That's what I'm thinking too."

Jody sighs, "I think you two are right. Stick close."

Jody slowly starts his way down the back of the building. Jody thinks he makes out a doorway ahead and slows down to a very slow walk. When Jody gets about ten feet from the door, the door suddenly opens. Jody stops and brings his AR-15 up at the door. Everyone stops behind Jody. Jody takes a combat shooting stance and waits to see what comes through the door.

A female, looking to be in her mid-twenties and wearing a police officer uniform walks out of the door followed by a young man who looks to be the age of one of the students at the university. The woman and the young man are each carrying a duffle bag. The woman and young man stop when they see Jody and the others. The woman reaches down towards her pistol.

Jody whispers, "Don't or I'll shoot."

The woman moves her hand away from her pistol. Jody can make out the uniform she is wearing and Jody slowly lowers his rifle.

The woman glances around, then looks at Jody, "Who are you?"

Jody whispers, "Just some people passing through. The questions is, who are you?"

The woman whispers back, "I'm Officer Cook and this is Jason. We are holding up here with other survivors."

Jody glances around, then back at Officer Cook, "We are trying to find some supplies, but we need to take a break for a few minutes."

Officer Cook replies, "This is nearly the last of the food. Follow us, we will take you to somewhere safe."

Jason whispers, "Is it safe to trust them? Look at all the guns they have."

Officer Cook sighs, "They would've killed us already if they were hostile."

Jody whispers, "We mean you no harm as long as you don't mean us any."

Officer Cook nods, "Okay, this way."

Officer Cook and Jason start off for a building behind the one they are at now. Jody motions to the others to follow him and Jody starts out after Officer Cook and Jason.

Mike and Shana are standing watch now. The night is eerily quiet as they patrol the perimeter of the campsite. Mike and Shana know that if there were two zombies wandering the area and found them, there could be more.

Shana whispers to Mike, "I sure hope they get back soon. I'm really starting to worry about them."

Mike nods and whispers back, "I'm a little worried too, but I think they'll be okay. Jody has a good head on his shoulders. If it gets too dangerous, he won't risk it."

Shana glances around, "Yeah, Jody definitely has been amazing since this all began. Actually, everyone has done good so far."

Mike smiles, "Everyone has done a great job so far. I'm pleasantly surprised by that." He pauses, "But it sounds like you might still have feelings for Jody."

Shana smiles, "I love and care about him, but we have decided to just be friends and I think that is how I really feel anyways even though we had a relationship. Plus, I know he likes Janet." She pauses, "But strange as it sounds, Michael and I dated years ago and I really had feelings for him. Those feelings are coming back now."

Mike nods, "Yeah, I think Jody likes Janet too, but I know he still strongly cares about you and the boys." He pauses, "So, you're really feeling that way for my oldest boy now. I can understand that, you two were very much in love back then."

Shana smiles again, "Yes we were, but I'm not sure that I should say anything right now. I've got so much to worry about with the boys anyway."

Mike glances around, "Yeah, but those two boys have sure come a long way. They have stepped up and helped out a lot."

Shana nods, "I know, I'm pretty proud of them."

Mike and Shana continue to talk while they slowly patrol the perimeter of the campsite.

Officer Cook and Jason lead Jody and the others into one of the common areas of one of the dorm buildings. As they walk in, Officer Cook hands her duffle bag to Jason and he walks off. There are candles lighting up the large room and Jody can see at least twenty other people in the room. The rest of the group walks in and Officer Cook closes the door behind them. Jody now notices that Officer Cook is not a local police officer, but from Joplin, Missouri.

Jody looks at Officer Cook, "You're from Joplin?"

Officer Cook nods, "Yeah. I was at a store when everything went crazy. I grabbed some kids that were running away. I was on south Rangeline. This was the only direction I could go." She pauses and starts to slowly walk towards the far end of the room, "My brother lives in Fort Smith and told me to try and make it to him on the base there."

Jody motions to the others, "Get some rest for a minute."

Janet and the others find a seat.

Jody follows Officer Cook, "Looks like you didn't make it."

Officer Cook sighs, "We got this far, but it got too bad to travel any further. Especially since I had three kids with me. I got us to this campus and we've been waiting for our chance to move on. Only problem is, other than my pistol and shotgun, there are no other guns here."

Jody glances around and notices everyone watching him and the others, "How are you all doing on supplies?"

Officer Cook sighs, "We're running dangerously low." She stops and grabs a bottle of water, then starts walking again, "We can't afford to have you take any."

Jody nods, "We won't. We'll rest for a few minutes, then head back to our camp."

Officer Cook looks at Jody, "You're camping outside?"

Jody nods, "Yeah. We're heading east to a safe place or at least someplace we think will be safe."

Officer Cook stops, reaches down and hands the bottle of water to someone Jody can't see from where he is at, "Well, I wish you all luck."

Jody glances around again, "Same to all of you. You know you can't stay here much longer."

Officer Cook turns around, "I know."

Officer Cook starts to walk off and Jody sees who she handed the water to. Jody gets a shocked look on his face as he can't believe who he is looking at.

CHAPTER 37

Rochelle, Zach, Tyler, Daniel, Lucky and Shadow are all in the large tent. It is getting later in the night and they are trying to get some rest. Lucky and Shadow have passed out from all the attention and playing. Daniel is laying in his sleeping bag which is next to Rochelle and her sleeping bag.

Daniel looks at Rochelle, "Is my mom coming back soon?"

Rochelle rolls over and looks at Daniel, "I'm sure they'll be back real soon. Its just that it is dark outside so they can't go as fast."

Daniel gets a sad look, "I'm scared."

Rochelle gives a caring look, "Do you want to sleep with me until they get back?"

Daniel nods his head.

Rochelle smiles and holds her sleeping bag open, "Come on."

Daniel gets out of his sleeping bag and lays down next to Rochelle in her sleeping bag.

Rochelle whispers, "Its going to be okay. Just get some sleep and they'll be here when you wake up."

Daniel closes his eyes as he curls up next to Rochelle. Zach and Tyler both smile as they watch Rochelle become motherly with Daniel.

Tyler looks at Zach and whispers, "Hey."

Zach looks at Tyler, "What?"

Tyler smiles, "If you're scared, maybe Ashley will let you stay with her."

Zach smiles and rolls over, "Shut up."

Tyler chuckles and rolls over to try and get some rest.

Jody continues to stare in disbelief at the three kids sitting by the wall. Jody recognizes them immediately, they are Janet's kids.

Jody looks at Officer Cook, "Are these the kids you helped?"

Officer Cook nods, "Yes. Why?"

Jody replies while staring at the kids, "I know them."

Jody squats down and removes his boonie hat. The three kids recognize Jody once his hat is off. The first kid, Tyler, a 7 year old boy who stands around four and a half feet tall and has a thin build with short, blonde hair and blue eyes. Tyler is wearing khaki shorts, purple t-shirt and tennis shoes. The second kid, Angela, a 6 year old girl who stands around four feet tall and also has a trim build with long, blonde hair and blue eyes. Angela is wearing a pink dress with pink shorts underneath and pink cowboy boots. The third kid, Sean, is a 3 year old boy who is right around three feet tall and holds an average build for his age with short blonde hair and blue eyes. Sean is wearing a red t-shirt, blue jeans and tennis shoes.

Tyler, Angela and Sean get up quickly and start hugging Jody. They know Jody well and know he's a good friend of their mom. Jody starts hugging the kids back.

Jody looks at the kids, "Are you okay? We thought we lost you."

Angela replies, "We were so scared."

Tyler replies, "Do you know where our mom is?"

Jody leans back and smiles, "Hold on a second."

Jody stands back up and Sean holds his arms out, wanting Jody to hold him. Jody slides his rifle around to his back and picks Sean up. Jody still can't believe they found Janet's kids. Jody looks over to the door where Janet and the others are at.

Jody motions with his free arm, "Janet."

Janet barely hears Jody, but sees him motioning to her. Janet starts across the room, unable to make out the kids yet in the low light. About halfway across the room, Janet stops and she gets a complete look of shock on her face. Janet can see clearly now that the kids with Jody are her kids. Tyler, Angela and Sean look over and see their mom.

Tyler and Angela both yell and run for Janet, "Mom!"

Jody starts over towards Janet with Sean. Janet drops to her knees and sets her shotgun down as Tyler and Angela run into her arms. Janet squeezes Tyler and Angela tight as they hug their mom with all their strength.

Janet speaks as tears come to her eyes, "Oh my God, I thought I lost you."

Jody walks up and sets Sean down. Sean runs over and hugs Janet along with Tyler and Angela. Janet continues to hug her kids.

Officer Cook walks up, "What's going on?"

Jody smiles at Officer Cook, "I'll never be able to thank you enough. These are her kids. We thought they died with their dad." Jody looks at Janet, "This is Officer Cook. She rescued your kids and brought them here with her."

Janet looks up at Officer Cook and smiles, "Thank you so much."

Officer Cook smiles back, "It was my pleasure."

Knowing she is no longer needed, Officer Cook walks off to start working on distributing supplies.

Jody looks at Janet, "Take your time."

Jody walks off and heads back over to the rest of the group by the door. Everyone is smiling when Jody tells them about Janet's kids. As they sit and rest, Jody and the others notice a man walk over to Janet and her kids. Janet starts talking to the man as if she knows him.

After about ten minutes or so, Janet gets up and grabs her shotgun. The man she was talking to walks back off and over to the far end of the room. Janet, Tyler, Angela and Sean walk over to Jody and the others.

Jody looks at Janet, "Are you ready?"

Janet kind of looks at Jody, "Yeah."

Jody sighs and looks at the others, "Everyone ready to head back?"

Everyone nods.

Jody glances around, "I'm going to tell Officer Cook we're leaving. Same as before, I'll take point and Lindsey will take rear security."

Jody walks off to find Officer Cook as the others get ready to leave.

Ryan and Codi are standing watch now. The two of them are walking the perimeter of the camp, each wondering when the others will return or if they will return. Ryan and Codi haven't heard echoes of gunfire or anything so they hold hope that its just taking longer due to being night.

Ryan and Codi walk over by the vehicles on the shoulder of the highway when they hear what sounds like vehicles approaching.

Ryan looks at Codi, "Do you hear that?"

Codi nods, "Yes. Do you think its them?"

Ryan glances around, "Go warn the others. I'm going to hide by the trees and keep an eye out."

Codi looks at Ryan, "But…"

Ryan interrupts, "Just go."

Codi sighs, "Be careful."

Codi runs off towards the campsite. Ryan backs away from the highway over to the group of trees Lisa and the others used to watch the zombies on the bridge earlier.

The sound of the vehicles gets closer. Ryan wonders if its Jody and the others or if its other survivors. Ryan doesn't spot any headlights coming down the highway, but he can tell the vehicles are heading right towards them. Finally, Ryan makes out the shape of two vehicles on the highway driving towards him.

Codi comes running back up, "The others are getting ready."

Ryan points, "Over there."

Codi looks and sees the two vehicles. The vehicles are driving slow and as they get closer, they start to slow down.

Ryan whispers, "Looks like they are slowing down. It has to be them."

Codi whispers back, "I sure hope so."

Finally, the vehicles get close enough that Ryan and Codi can make out Janet's van and Allen's Tahoe. Both Ryan and Codi breath a sigh of relief and start walking towards the highway as the van and Tahoe park on the shoulder of the highway.

Jody, Lindsey and Michael, her husband, get out of the van as Allen, Rachel, Marissa and Michael, Jody's brother, get out of the Tahoe. Jody and the others walk over to Ryan and Codi.

Codi glances around, "Where's Janet?"

Jody smiles, "She's coming." He pauses, "We have a little surprise."

Janet gets out of her van followed by her kids. Ryan and Codi just stare as Janet and her kids walk up.

Ryan questions, "Who are they?"

Janet smiles big, "These are my kids. A Joplin police officer saved them and just happened to be here."

Codi can't believe it, "Oh my God."

Jody glances around, "Let's get back to the camp."

Jody and the others walk over to the campsite. Everyone else is awake and sitting in front of the large tent. Everyone breathes a sigh of relief when they see Ryan and Codi walk up with Jody and the others. Everyone gets a puzzled look when they see the kids with Janet. Daniel runs over to Lindsey and they embrace.

Ken looks at Jody, "Who are the kids?"

Jody sighs, smiles and points at each kid as he says their name, "Everyone, this is Tyler, Angela and Sean." He pauses, "These are Janet's kids."

Everyone just sits in stunned silence, not believing what they just heard and each one amazed at how they could cross paths with how the world has changed so much.

Ashley let's out a big smile and breaks the silence, "That's awesome!"

Jody and the others sit down as Ryan and Codi stand watch, but remain near the large tent so they can hear what is being said.

Mike questions, "How did it go?"

Jody takes a drink of water, "We got plenty of gas to help us, but no supplies."

Lindsey speaks up, "We ran into a bunch of survivors holding up at the university. They were nearly out of supplies so we decided that we shouldn't take any from them."

Lisa questions, "So, what do we do now?"

Jody glances around, "I'm sure you all are tired just like us. Let's stick to the watch rotation and get some sleep. We will discuss what to do next in the morning."

Janet looks at Jody, "The kids don't have sleeping bags or anything."

Jody nods, "You and Sean can use mine that we were sharing. I can use my poncho liner."

Shana speaks up, "The other two can use my sleeping bag. I can make do for the night without it."

Janet smiles, "Thanks."

Jody stands up, "Okay, whoever is on watch at sunrise, wake everyone up."

Jody starts to make his way off to his tent as everyone else gets ready to return to their tents. Ryan and Codi head back over to the perimeter of the camp.

Shana walks up to Jody, "Is there enough room under that poncho liner for two?"

Jody smiles, "Yep. You're more than welcome to share."

Shana follows Jody as Janet takes her kids over to their tent. Everyone else starts getting ready to go back to sleep.

CHAPTER 38

Lindsey and Michael, her husband, are standing watch now. The two of them slowly walk the perimeter of the campsite while everyone sleeps.

Lindsey whispers to her husband, "I can't believe we found so many survivors at the university."

Michael, Lindsey's husband, nods and whispers back, "I know." He pauses, "I don't think they have much of a chance though. They didn't seem to have any kind of plan or many weapons."

Lindsey nods and glances around, "Yeah, I'm thinking that too. Makes me glad we've got the group we have."

Michael, Lindsey's husband, sighs, "Me too." He pauses, "Its getting close to time for the next watch."

Lindsey looks at Michael, her husband, "I'm going to let Janet and Jody sleep because Janet just got her kids back and she needs to be there if they wake up." She pauses, "I'm going to wake up Allen and Rachel."

Michael, Lindsey's husband, nods, "Sounds good to me."

Lindsey and Michael, her husband, share a nice kiss, then Lindsey heads off to wake up Allen and Rachel.

Its nearly sunrise and Lisa and Ashley are on watch now. Ashley is going around waking everyone up as Lisa keeps watch at the perimeter of the campsite. Ashley finishes waking everyone up and returns to where Lisa is at.

In about fifteen minutes, everyone has gathered in front of the large tent except for Janet's kids. Jody and Shana are the last to walk up and sit down. Jody sits next to Janet and notices right away that she seems distant. Jody knows that Janet is still thinking about her kids.

Jody pulls out his two way radio, "Lisa, you and Ashley come on in so we can all talk."

Lisa replies, "Okay."

Once Lisa and Ashley walk up, Jody looks around and sees how tired everyone is.

Jody takes a drink of water, "I know you all are tired, just as I am. This is what I want to do today." He pauses, "We are going to stay here for the day. I have back road directions to the store in town. We need to send a group to get sleeping bags for my dad and Janet's kids, along with clothes for her kids."

Greg questions, "Is it safe to stay here another day?"

Jody nods, "I think we'll be okay." He looks at Mike, "Are we okay on supplies?"

Mike nods, "Yeah, we're good for now."

Jody glances around, "We need to rest and relax a day and get our energy back. If we push too hard, we'll start making mistakes as exhaustion sets in."

Ken questions, "When do you want to make the run to the store?"

Jody sighs, "After breakfast."

Ken glances around, "Well, I'll lead the team into town since you went last night. I'll take three of the four teams with me that didn't go last night."

Jody nods, "Sounds good. Janet, will you get the clothing sizes for the kids?"

Hearing her name, Janet comes out of her daze, "What's that?"

Jody looks at Janet, "Can you get the clothing sizes of the kids for Ken?"

Janet looks at Jody, then looks away, "That won't be necessary."

Jody gets a puzzled look, "Why not?"

Janet sighs and is unable to look at Jody, "I'm taking the kids and going back to the university."

Everyone is shocked by Janet's response.

Lindsey looks at Janet with surprise, "What?"

Rachel replies also shocked, "Why? That's crazy."

Janet can't even look at the others, "They're heading to Fort Sill, Oklahoma. One of them heard it was safe there."

Ashley can't believe it, "Even if its safe now, there is no way to survive there. We already discussed options like that."

Janet replies defensively, "He said it would be okay."

Jody looks at Janet with a puzzled look, "What? Who said that?"

Marissa speaks up, "It's obvious everyone. It's the guy she was talking to last night in the common room."

Michael, Lindsey's husband, speaks up, "Don't be crazy Janet. You just got your kids back. You need to think about keeping them safe."

Janet stands up, "I'm not going to discuss it. I've made up my mind and I can leave if I want to."

Janet walks off towards the tent where her kids are sleeping. Jody gets up and heads after Janet.

Jody walks up next to Janet, "Hey, what's going on? Why leave now? You have your kids and everything is okay."

Janet stops at the front of the tent, "I don't want to talk about it."

Jody can't believe what he is hearing, "What about us? Just going to walk off and that's it?"

Janet can't look at Jody, "I'm not discussing it. I've made up my mind and we are leaving as soon as I get the kids up." She pauses, "I want my share of the supplies."

Jody sighs, knowing what it is, "Its not that you're thinking it's a safer decision. It was the man you talked to, isn't it? Let me guess, he's one of the guys you were seeing after you split from your husband and before me." He pauses, "Or he's someone you've wanted to be with and now you have the chance to."

Janet remains quiet, then replies, "He said that my family is suppose to have went to Fort Sill the last time he heard from them."

Jody sighs and shakes his head, "But you don't know for sure." He pauses, "How do you even know if what he said is true."

Janet looks at Jody, "I have to think about my kids and my family."

Jody shakes his head again, "I can't believe you'd do this. Not just to me, but to the kids as well. What you have here is the best thing for you and the kids." He pauses, "Its a mistake. This man can't keep you safe and won't be there for you when things get bad."

Janet unzips the tent, not even looking at Jody.

Jody shakes his head, "I just can't believe this. Everything we've had, shared and talked about. Just to up and throw it away overnight."

Janet gets a sad tone, "I'm sorry Jody, I really am. I never meant to hurt you."

Janet steps inside the tent. Jody stands quietly and tries to remember that which he has always asked from others towards him and that is to respect his decisions.

Jody sighs, not wanting to leave the last thing he said be something hurtful or bad, "Well, I don't understand and not sure you're telling me everything, but its your choice and I have to respect that." He pauses, "I'll always love and care about you and the kids. Good luck, I really hope you all make it."

Jody turns and walks off. Janet starts waking her kids up to get ready to leave.

Jody is standing by the river as he hears Janet start up her van. Jody is doing everything he can to hold back his emotions. Jody thought that he had something special with Janet. As Janet drives away, Mike and Shadow walk up to Jody.

Mike looks at his son, "There is nothing you could have done differently. She, for whatever reason, made her decision."

Jody sniffles, holding back his emotions, "I just never thought that Janet would hurt me like this. I trusted her and loved her. Plus, all the things she said to me." He pauses, "How could she do it? Risk the kids and walk away from something so good?"

Mike sighs, "No one can answer that question son. You just have to come to terms with the fact that this happened for a reason."

Shadow sits down against Jody's leg, sensing something is wrong.

Jody looks down at Shadow, "They won't make it to Fort Sill."

Mike puts his hand on Jody's shoulder, "We all know that, but she has to live how she thinks is right, even when everyone else knows its not."

Mike walks off to leave his son alone. Jody squats down and starts to pet Shadow as he stares at the river and thinks about everything he had with Janet and what they could have had together, even in this crazy new world.

Nearly an hour has passed and Michael, Jody's brother, and Marissa are standing watch now. Everyone has been sitting around quietly since Janet left. Jody finally walks back over to the others who are sitting around in front of the large tent.

Jody looks at everyone and speaks, "Obviously we have some adjustments to make now." He pauses, "Zach and Ty, take over watch for a bit. Okay?"

Zach nods, "Okay."

Zach and Tyler grab their guns and head off to replace Marissa and Michael, Jody's brother, on watch. A few moments later, Michael, Jody's brother, and Marissa join the rest of the group.

Jody speaks with a depressed tone, "Okay. With Janet gone, I want to make a few adjustments now that I don't have a partner and one of our vehicles is gone."

Ken nods, "What did you have in mind?"

Jody glances around, "I want dad to come off the partner teams and focus solely on inventory, the kids and dogs."

Shana questions, "What about me?"

Jody looks at Shana, "You will partner with Ashley now and Lisa will partner with me." He pauses, "There is a reason to my madness so just trust me on this."

Codi looks at Jody, "What about the vehicle arrangements? Where will the three of us that were riding with Janet ride now?"

Mike speaks up, "The three of you can fit in my van for now. It'll be crowded, but we can all fit."

Jody nods, "That's what I was thinking. Until we can find a vehicle somewhere that has the keys in it that we can use."

Lisa knows it will be good to keep Jody's mind off Janet, "So, what is our next move? Where are we going?"

Jody glances around, "We will use the back roads and side streets to skirt around the city and get back on the highway headed south." He pauses, "I was told by one student who was coming in from Little Rock that the Interstate is somewhat cluttered with vehicles, but can be traveled on. So, we'll pick up the interstate just north of Fort Smith and head east."

Michael, Lindsey's husband, looks at Jody, "Are you sure you want to get on an interstate? Not much room to run with the vehicles if we get trapped."

Jody nods, "You're right. However, we don't have another option. Right now we need to get headed east and there are not many back highways to take from here."

Greg questions, "Where do you want to stop next?"

Jody takes a breath, "We'll stop on the interstate between Clarksville and Russellville by Lake Dardanelle."

At that moment, everyone hears what sounds like faint echoes of gunfire.

Rochelle stands up, "What's that?"

Chad looks around, "Sounds like gunshots."

Ken nods, "It is gunshots."

Lindsey looks at Jody, "I can't be certain, but it sounds like it could be coming from the direction of the university."

Jody stands up, "I'm almost certain it is."

Allen looks at Jody, "Should we go try and help them."

Jody shakes his head, "No, it's too late for that. There were too many zombies at the university already and the gunfire will certainly draw more. We have to pack up and get out of here, now."

Ashley looks at Jody, "What about Janet and the kids?"

Jody fights back his emotions, "She made her choice. As much as it hurts me to think about something happening to her and the kids and as much as I want to go help them, we can't risk the group for one person, just like before at the store in Jay." He pauses, "Come on, we have to get out of here before zombies start wandering into the area."

Everyone hurries off to get their things and break down the camp as quickly as possible while Zach and Tyler continue to stand guard.

CHAPTER 39

Its getting closer to noon as the convoy of vehicles, minus Janet's van, nears the Interstate turn off before Fort Smith. The sky is clear except for a few puffy, white clouds and a nice, warm breeze is blowing across the countryside. Lisa keeps a close eye on Mike's van. So far, the trip has been uneventful.

Shana looks around, "Its amazing that we haven't seen anyone else out traveling. The only time we've seen anyone has been when we were camping or at the university where they were holding up."

Lisa nods, "I know. I figured at some point we'd see other vehicles or people out here. Its like a ghost country instead of a ghost town."

Rochelle speaks up, "Maybe its good we haven't seen anyone else. I mean, remember what Jody said, they could try to hurt us."

Zach nods, "Yeah, I like that its just us. We're doing just fine on our own."

Shana keeps glancing around, "You two have a point there. I'd have to agree with you."

Lisa chimes in, "Me too. I'd rather keep the group we have and not worry about other survivors."

Lisa slows down as she sees the turn signal of Mike's van come on. Lisa turns onto the Interstate behind Mike's van and the rest of the convoy follows.

Shana sighs, "Well, let's see how traveling on an Interstate works out."

Lisa glances around, "I know. Its definitely the most risky thing we've done as far as traveling because there is no way off this road if we run into something."

It gets quiet again in the Jeep Liberty as the convoy starts heading east on the Interstate, then stops.

Lisa looks at Shana, "Wonder what's going on."

Jody gets out of Mike's van and walks over to a black 2000 Hyundai Elantra GLS. Jody looks in driver's window of the four door car as everyone else gets out of their vehicles except Daniel. Jody turns back to the group and smiles as they walk up to him.

Ken questions, "What's going on?"

Jody replies, "I'm going to take this car since we lost Janet's van. Doesn't appear to be blood or damage to it and the keys are in the ignition."

Ryan nods, "Cool. You want us to jump in with you?"

Jody shakes his head, "No. It will be an easier fit if Shana, Zach and Tyler join me in this car and Ryan and Codi, you move over to Lisa's vehicle."

Mike questions, "Do you want me to move back to third in the convoy?"

Jody nods, "Yep. We'll lead in this car and the rest of the order will be like before Janet left." He pauses, "Just grab weapons for now, we'll reorganize the gear and supplies when we make it to our stop."

Everyone nods and heads back to the vehicles. Ryan and Codi head over and get in Lisa's Jeep Liberty. Shana, Zach and Tyler walk back up to Jody.

Jody looks at Shana, "I'm going to have you drive so I can focus on the directions."

Shana nods, "Okay."

Shana gets in the driver's seat and starts the car up. It sounds like it is in good running shape. Jody gets in the passenger's seat as Zach and Tyler get in the back seat. Shana drives off slowly and the rest of the convoy falls in line behind the new lead car.

Its getting near dinner time as the convoy is about to their stopping point for the evening. Jody looks out the window and can see Lake Dardanelle still. Jody keeps glancing around, looking for the right spot to stop.

Jody looks over at Shana, "Up ahead, maybe a mile, go ahead and stop. The lake should be pretty close to the road."

Shana nods, "Okay."

Shana weaves around a couple of abandoned cars, then starts to slow down. Shana pulls off the road onto the shoulder of the highway. The rest of the vehicles pull in behind Jody's car. Jody, Shana, Zach and Tyler get out.

Shana turns and looks at her kids, "Keep an eye out while the rest of us discuss what to do."

Zach and Tyler stay by the car as the rest of the group, except Daniel, walks up to Shana and Jody.

Jody looks around, "This will be good for the night. Let's setup over by the water. Zach and Ty will take watch until we get camp set up."

Everyone nods.

Jody looks at the others, "Well, let's get to it so we can get the dogs out and everyone can eat."

Everyone heads off to start getting the tents and their personal gear. Zach and Tyler grab their weapons and start keeping watch.

The camp is completely set up and everyone has eaten their dinner. All the sleeping bags are set up in the newly assigned tent breakdown. Jody has loaned his sleeping bag to his dad while he uses his poncho and poncho liner to sleep with. Allen, Chad, Rachel and Amber still share a tent. Lindsey, her husband, Shana and Ashley now share a tent. Michael, Jody's brother, Marissa, Ryan and Codi still share a tent. Jody, Lisa, Ken and Greg now share a tent. Mike, Rochelle, the kids and dogs are in the large tent now.

Michael, Jody's brother, and Marissa are on watch now. Mike, Ken and Greg are watching Zach, Tyler and Daniel play with Shadow and Lucky in front of the large tent. Jody is in his tent making plans for the next day. Everyone else is either resting in their tents or sitting around in front of the large tent.

Shana walks into Jody's tent, "Hey Jo, what are you doing?"

Jody looks up from his map, "Going over the plans for tomorrow."

Shana walks over and sits next to Jody, "So, how far do you think we'll get tomorrow?"

Jody glances at the map, then at Shana, "I'm hoping tomorrow will be our last night in Arkansas."

Shana nods, "Wow, that'd be good."

Jody nods, "Yeah, but we're going to have to look at getting more supplies and gas soon."

Shana sighs, "Any ideas on that?"

Jody shakes his head, "Not yet, but we'll see how it goes tomorrow. We might just run into something that can help." He looks up at Shana, "How are you holding up?"

Shana shrugs, "Okay I guess." She pauses, "How are doing, with Janet leaving?"

Jody gives a weak smiles, "Okay, trying to keep my mind off it."

Shana nods, "I can understand that."

Jody looks at Shana closer, "Are you okay, really?"

Shana sighs, "I still miss Cory and wonder about him. I also wonder about Zach and Ty and if I can keep them safe." She pauses, "Plus, I'm getting feelings for your brother again."

Jody moves over and puts his arm around Shana, "Hey, Zach and Ty will be okay. None of us, especially me, will let anything happen to them. As for Cory, I know it's sad, but he made his choice and there is nothing you could have done about it." He pauses, "And I know you're getting feelings for Michael, I can see it by the way you've been acting around him. I think its cool."

Shana leans her head on Jody's shoulder, "Really? Don't say anything." She pauses, "Now, are you really okay?"

Jody sighs and hugs Shana tight, "Its hard to deal with knowing I trusted her and she betrayed that trust."

Shana hugs Jody tight, "I know and I'm sorry."

Jody and Shana hold each other for a few minutes.

Jody finally speaks, "Well, time to go talk to everyone about the plans. Do you want to go let everyone know and I'll be there in a few minutes."

Shana replies, "Okay."

Shana turns her head and gives Jody a brief kiss on the cheek. Jody smiles as Shana gets up and walks out of the tent.

Zach and Tyler have taken over watch for the moment while everyone has gathered in front of the large tent.

Everyone knows what this meeting is about. Jody walks up and sits down next to Lindsey and Lisa.

Ken looks at Jody, "So, what's the plan little buddy?"

Jody looks around at the group, "We are going to get off the Interstate before Little Rock and go north around the city of Conway. We will cut back south at the town of Beebe until we reach the Interstate again. We'll take the Interstate to Highway 63, then turn south towards Stuttgart. Our final stopping point will be where Highway 212 and 165 link up just west of the southern end of White River National Wildlife Refuge. There is a river there we can camp out at." He pauses and looks at Mike, "How are our supplies doing?"

Mike sighs, "We are doing okay, but if we can get some more, that would be good. We may have about four days worth left."

Lindsey questions, "Is there a town along the way that we could find more supplies in?"

Allen questions, "What about Conway?"

Jody shakes his head, "No, Conway is too big of a town."

Lisa speaks up, "What about Stuttgart?"

Jody nods his head, "That is where I'm thinking."

Greg questions, "What about getting more gas?"

Michael, Lindsey's husband, speaks up, "Why don't we check some of the abandoned vehicles along the way? There should be plenty of them on the Interstate."

Jody nods, "That's a good idea and the safest bet. If we can't find enough along the highway, we'll check in Stuttgart as well."

Michael, Jody's brother, speaks up, "So, we just rest for the night now?"

Jody nods, "Pretty much. I think whoever wants to get cleaned up, can do so. Otherwise, we just relax, keep the watch rotation going and get started again in the morning."

Ashley smiles, "Sounds good to me. I could use some washing up."

Jody smiles, "Well, women and kids first, then us guys last."

Jody stands up and starts for his tent. Everyone else starts getting up and getting ready to either go clean up or rest.

Ryan and Codi are standing watch now and most everyone else is sleeping. The two of them are walking the perimeter of the camp. The stars are shining bright and a light breeze is blowing. The night is serene and quiet. If it wasn't for the world being overran by zombies, it would be the perfect night.

Codi looks at Ryan, "This is such a beautiful night."

Ryan looks up at the sky, "Yes it is."

As the two of them look over by the lake, they see some movement.

Codi whispers, "Did you see that?"

Ryan nods and whispers back, "Yeah."

Ryan and Codi slowly start making their way towards the lake. The night is too dark and they can't make out what it is by the lake. As Ryan and Codi get closer, they see motion again, but they still can't make out what it is. Ryan and Codi keep slowly stepping towards the lake. Each step seems like an eternity. As they get closer, Ryan and Codi hold their breath, wondering if it is a zombie or not.

Codi takes a step and a stick breaks under her foot. Ryan and Codi freeze in place. Suddenly, they see movement and two glowing eyes looking at them from the lake. Ryan and Codi kneel down as they finally see what it was by the lake. Ryan and Codi see a deer turn and run off.

Ryan breathes out, "It was just a deer."

Codi smiles, "That was pretty intense."

Ryan stands back up, "It sure was."

Codi stands up, "Well, at least it wasn't a zombie."

Ryan smiles and turns back towards the camp. Ryan and Codi continue their patrol of the perimeter of the camp.

CHAPTER 40

Lisa and Jody are in their tent. Neither has fallen asleep since Ryan and Codi relieved them for watch. Ken and Greg are sound asleep. Lisa rolls over in her sleeping bag and sees Jody laying with his poncho and poncho liner wrapped around him.

Lisa whispers to Jody, "That can't be comfortable. It has no padding."

Jody whispers back, "It's okay, I've slept like this before when I was in the Marines."

Lisa whispers, "Well, if it gets too uncomfortable, I'll share with you. It's no big deal."

Jody smiles and whispers back, "Thanks girl."

Lisa questions, keeping her voice down, "Can I ask you something?"

Jody nods and whispers, "Of course."

Lisa whispers, "Why did you switch the teams around like you did?"

Jody replies in a whisper tone, "You are a quick study and you have some formal training in weapons and tactics, as well as you studied hand-to-hand from me." He pauses, "I wanted you with me to watch and learn my thought process on surviving and how I plan our moves with the group. In case something happens to me. Ken and I are really the only two trained in survival scenarios. I wanted a third in case one of us go down. You were my obvious choice."

Lisa replies in a soft tone, "Oh, that makes sense."

Jody nods and whispers again, "Of course, everyone has been picking up on some things. Plus, I know Lindsey is a quick learner and good at picking things up from observing. That's why I keep picking her team too."

Lisa nods, "You're always planning ahead." She pauses, "Now, how are you doing?"

Jody sighs, "Okay. It's still hard with what Janet did, but I'm trying to keep my mind off it and focused on the now."

Lisa whispers, "Well, I'm here for you if you ever need something."

Jody smiles, "Thanks Lisa. You've been such a great friend to me. It's hard to believe we've known each other for four years now." He pauses, "I know I don't say this to you much, but you know I love ya."

Lisa smiles, "Yeah, I know. Crazy that its been that long already and you've been a great friend to me. I love you too."

Jody smiles again, "We should try to get some sleep. It'll be light before we know it."

Lisa sighs, "Oh yes. Well, the offer stands anytime."

Jody continues to smile, "Thanks."

Jody and Lisa both try to get comfortable and get some rest before sunrise.

Its about mid-afternoon as the convoy is making its way through the town of Stuttgart. They have managed to find some gasoline along the way. Shana slows the car down as they get closer to the south end of town and they have yet to see a store. However, they have also not seen any zombies either.

Zach glances around, "Surely there is a store close to this road. We are nearly out of town."

Jody sighs, "We might have to skip trying to find supplies. I don't really want to go roaming around town looking for a store."

Tyler smiles and speaks excitedly, "Hey, there it is!"

Everyone looks off to their right and they see the store Tyler is talking about. Shana slows down and makes a right turn on the next road. The rest of the convoy follows Shana's car.

Shana questions, "How are we going to handle getting the supplies from the store?"

Zach chimes in, "Are we all going in or just some?"

Jody shakes his head, "No, just half the group will go. The rest will keep watch outside and get gasoline from any vehicles in the parking lot."

Shana slows the car down and turns into the parking lot. Shana drives up to the doors of the grocery entrance of the store and parks. The rest of the convoy pulls in behind Shana's car and parks. Shana turns the car off as Jody, Zach and Tyler get out. Shana gets out of the car and heads over to Jody, Zach and Tyler as the rest of the group walks up except for Daniel.

Ken glances around, "How do you want to play this?"

Jody glances around, "I'll take three groups with me inside. We'll get the maps and supplies. You and the others gather as much gasoline as you can from the cars in the parking lot. Zach and Ty can stand watch and Rochelle can watch Daniel and the dogs."

Greg questions, "Who's going with you?"

Jody sighs and is quiet for a moment, "I'll take Shana and Ashley, Lindsey and Michael, and Ryan and Codi."

Everyone nods.

Jody glances around, "Okay, let's get going so we can get to our campsite by dinner."

Everyone going into the store heads off to grab their weapons. The others grab their weapons and the gas cans as Zach and Tyler stands watch.

A large group of nearly 40 zombies are wandering down a back street in Stuttgart when they hear the sound of vehicles in the distance. The group of zombies stop and look around trying to figure out where the noise is coming from.

The group of zombies continue to look around, snarling as they listen to the sound of vehicles in the distance. One zombie turns and starts to slowly stagger towards the south of town in the direction of the store. The rest of the zombies start to follow the first zombie.

Jody and the others are slowly making their way through the grocery section of the store after they have collected the Mississippi and Alabama maps. Ashley and Shana are pushing baskets. Codi and Lindsey are loading the baskets with food while Lisa, Ryan, Jody and Michael, Lindsey's husband, are keeping a watch out for zombies. They get Ashley's basket completely filled with food, but it appears they have emptied the last of the shelves.

Ryan glances around, "What now?"

Lisa looks at Jody, "We should get more water."

Jody nods, "Yeah, definitely."

Jody starts towards the end of the isle when everyone hears a noise from behind them. Everyone stops and turns around. Lindsey, who is behind the group, brings her shotgun up and points it at the end of the isle. Lisa walks up next to Lindsey and aims her shotgun at the end of the isle as well. The sound gets closer, but it doesn't sound like a person walking. Everyone gets a puzzled look, trying to figure out what it is. The noise is more like nails on concrete.

Lisa whispers, "What is that?"

Lindsey whispers back, "I don't know. Sounds like an animal, like a dog or something."

At that moment, an average sized German Sheppard steps into the end of the isle. Lindsey and Lisa tighten their grip on their shotguns, but relax when they see it's a dog. The rest of the group let's out a collective sigh.

Ashley sighs, "Its just a dog."

Lindsey lowers her shotgun, bends over and holds her hand out, "Here boy."

The dog looks at Lindsey and the others closely, but doesn't move towards them. Lindsey slowly moves her hand some and calls to the dog again. Jody takes a step towards Lindsey and Lisa and the dog jumps back, very much afraid of the group of people. Jody stops when he sees the reaction of the dog. Jody spins around and brings his AR-15 up, expecting to see something behind him, but nothing is there.

Jody looks back at Lindsey, "He's afraid of us."

Lisa nods, "It looks that way."

Lindsey motions with her hand again, "Can you blame him. I'm sure he's spent as much time avoiding zombies as we have." She pauses, "We can't leave him here though."

Michael, Lindsey's husband, slowly takes a step forward. The German Sheppard runs off this time.

Lindsey calls to the dog, "Stop, wait."

Jody sighs, "It's no use. Its way to jumpy for us to even get close to it." He pauses, "I'm sorry Lindsey."

Lindsey sighs, "Yeah, your right. I hope he stays okay."

Codi speaks up, "Let's get to the water."

Jody nods, turns around and heads off down the aisle. The rest of the group follows as Lisa brings up the rear.

Ken and the others are wandering the parking lot, gathering whatever gasoline they can and putting it in their vehicles. Rochelle has Daniel at Mike's van watching Lucky and Shadow. Zach and Tyler continue to walk around the vehicles keeping an eye out.

Marissa finishes putting some gas in Lisa's Jeep Liberty and she looks at Michael, Jody's brother, "So, I've noticed Shana has been watching you closely as of late."

Michael, Jody's brother, glances around, "What?"

Marissa smiles, "You heard me."

Michael, Jody's brother, replies, "Yeah, I've been watching her too." He pauses, "You know, she and I use to be a couple many years ago."

Marissa replies, "Really? I didn't know that. I knew she and Jody were together not too long ago."

Michael, Jody's brother, nods, "Yeah. I was okay with that."

Marissa glances around, "Looks to me like she has discovered some old feelings for you."

Michael, Jody's brother, smiles, "Maybe so."

Marissa smiles, "What about you? How do you feel?"

Michael, Jody's brother, sighs and let's out a smile, "I think I'm getting those feelings too."

Suddenly, everyone hears Zach's voice, "Zombies!"

Marissa and Michael, Jody's brother, turn around and see the large group of zombies staggering into the far end of the parking lot.

Marissa's eyes widen, "Oh my God!"

Ken hollers to the rest of the group, "Everyone back to the vehicles!"

Everyone rushes back over to the vehicles.

Mike looks at Rochelle, "Get Daniel back in his seat."

Ken looks at Zach, "Go over to the doors and yell for Jody and the others."

Zach nods and runs off. Rochelle takes Daniel to the Trailblazer and gets him in his seat. Mike shuts the door to his van so Lucky and Shadow can't get out. After Rochelle gets Daniel in his seat, she hurries over to the rest of the group. Zach comes running back up to everyone. Everyone looks over and sees the group of zombies getting closer.

Ken speaks, "The others are not going to make it." He pauses, "Rochelle, start all the vehicles."

Greg questions, "What are we going to do?"

Amber questions, "Should we leave?"

Mike looks at the group of zombies, "I think we can hold them off, but if more come, then we might have to leave."

Rochelle heads off to start the vehicles.

Ken glances around, "Okay. Zach and Ty, keep a lookout for any other zombies. Everyone else, get with your partner and take cover by a vehicle. When I start shooting, pick a target and start shooting."

Everyone nods. Zach and Tyler head off to get a better view. Ken and the others take cover by the vehicles as the group of zombies gets closer.

Amber whispers to Chad, "Is this really happening?"

Chad whispers back, "Stay calm and it'll be okay."

At that moment, the sound of Ken's shotgun rings out. The sound is deafening and disturbs the silence that hangs over the town. One of the zombies falls to the ground. Ken fires again and another zombie falls as the rest of the zombies continue to close in. Suddenly, the rest of the group opens fire. The sound echoes across the town as zombies start to fall to the pavement.

Jody and the others are halfway to the door when they hear Zach's voice, "Hurry, zombies!"

Jody looks at the others, "Let's go."

Jody speeds up to a fast walk as everyone speeds up as well. As the group gets closer to the main doors, they hear gunshots ring out from outside, many gunshots.

Michael, Lindsey's husband, speaks, "It sounds like a war out there."

Jody speaks as they continue to the doors, "When we get outside, Ashley and Shana, take the baskets to my dad's van and start loading the supplies. Ryan and Codi, help them with that. Everyone else, start shooting zombies."

Everyone prepares themselves for what they will see outside as the main doors are just ahead. The echo of gunshots continue to ring out as Jody and the others exit the store and see what is going on.

Ken and the others continue to shoot as the group of zombies has been dwindled down to about ten now. The last ten zombies continue to close in on Ken and the others. The zombies are only twenty feet away now.

Shana, Ashley, Ryan and Codi head for Mike's van as Jody and the others rush over and start shooting at the final zombies. As Shana, Ashley, Ryan and Codi load the supplies in Mike's van, the last zombie falls a mere ten feet from Ken.

Ken looks over and sees Jody, "We need to get out of here. There could be more coming."

Ryan yells, "We're all loaded up!"

Jody looks around, "Everyone get loaded up and let's get out of here!"

Shana and Ashley push the baskets out of the way. Everyone quickly loads up in their vehicles. Shana pulls away from the store and everyone falls in line.

About two miles outside of Stuttgart, a man is finishing putting gas in a car. The man is wearing a prison inmate outfit. The man looks up when he hears the gunshots echo from the store in town. The man puts the gas can in the trunk of the car and walks over to the open driver's door.

The man reaches in and grabs a pistol from the driver's seat and turns around, "Sounds like we might have another group of survivors in the area."

The man looks at who he is talking to. It is a group of nine other men, all dressed in inmate outfits. Seven of them have pistols and two of them have shotguns.

The leader of the group, the man by the car, smiles an evil smile and speaks again, "Let's track them down and see what they might have to offer."

The ten men hurry up and get in their cars.

CHAPTER 41

It is nearly 4pm now as the convoy is nearing its destination for the day. A few clouds have moved in to make the sky overcast, lowering the temperature to a tolerable 84 degrees.

Jody looks over at Shana, "It should be coming up in the next mile or so."

Shana slows the car down. Zach spots the sign for the highway intersection ahead.

Zach speaks, "I think this is it."

Shana nods, "There is plenty of water around."

Jody glances around, "This will work just fine. Go ahead and pull off the highway just beyond the highway intersection."

Shana nods and continues on, swerving around an abandoned car. After another quarter of a mile, Shana pulls off on the shoulder of the highway and puts the car in park. Jody, Zach and Tyler get out of the car as Shana turns the car off. Shana gets out and walks over to Jody, Zach and Tyler as the rest of the group walks up, except for Daniel.

Jody glances around and points, "Let's set up camp over there. As before, Zach and Ty will take watch while we do that."

Ken chimes in, "Once we get camp set up, let's get the dogs taken care of and get some food. Then we can clean up."

Everyone nods and heads off to get the tents and their personal belongings while Zach and Tyler begin their watch.

Its been an hour since the group reached its destination. Camp is completely set up, Shadow and Lucky have been walked and fed and everyone else has eaten and are now gathered in front of the large tent. Ken and Greg have just started their watch.

Rochelle questions, "So, what now?

Jody looks around, "Well, I think we should get cleaned up for those that want to and just get some rest. It was quite an exciting day."

Zach speaks up, "I can take Daniel and Ty to get cleaned up if everyone else wants to get cleaned up."

Shana smiles at how her son has stepped up, "I think that should work. There is plenty of water around us so if we spread out, the boys can go on one side and the girls on the other." She pauses, "Sound good to you Jo?"

Jody nods, "Yeah, the boys and guys can go on the east side of camp and the girls and ladies on the west side of camp. That way we can all get cleaned up before it gets too late."

Mike speaks up, "I'll stay with the dogs until the others are done, then I'll get cleaned up."

Jody nods, "Sounds good. I want to get each group's map of Mississippi. I'm going to plot all our stop points on each map, just in case anyone gets separated."

Greg speaks up, "Good idea."

Jody gets up and goes around gathering up the maps.

Once Jody is done, he looks at the group, "Okay, let's get to it. I'll work on the maps and clean up with my dad when everyone else is done."

Jody heads off to his tent as everyone gets up and heads off to get their things together to clean up. Mike goes into the large tent where Lucky and Shadow are laying down.

The inmate leader from before is making his way through the woods towards the campsite where Jody and the others are. Four other inmates are following the leader. The inmate leader has his pistol ready. Three of the inmates with him have pistols and one has a shotgun. The inmate leader stops for a moment when he hears something not too far away.

The inmate leader looks at the other inmates, "Okay, we sneak up on them and take them by surprise. If they try to resist, start shooting."

The five inmates work their way towards the camp as they can hear the sound of people in water. The leader stops again when he sees what they have been hearing. The inmates watch closely as they see Zach standing on the bank of the lake and all the men and boys of the group in the water except for Mike and Jody back in camp and Greg and Ken who are still on watch.

The inmate leader whispers to the others, "I only see one with a gun. Let's charge them and if that kid tries to shoot at us, we kill him."

The four inmates nods at their leader. The inmate leader rushes out of the trees which are about fifty yards away from where Zach and the others are at.

Zach sees the five inmates running at them, "Survivors!"

Everyone hears Zach yell. Ken and Greg are walking towards the lake when they hear Zach and see the inmates. Ken and Greg start towards the five inmates.

Everyone in the water starts for the bank of the lake. The five inmates close in quickly, then the leader spots Ken and Greg running at them and realizes they made a tactical error.

The inmate leader yells, "Over there, start shooting!"

The four inmates turn their attention to Ken and Greg and open fire as they continue to follow the inmate leader towards the others that are coming out of the water. Ken and Greg return fire at the inmates.

Zach raises his pistol as the inmate leader gets closer. The inmate leader sees Zach and brings his pistol up. Michael, Lindsey's husband, rushes by and tackles Zach out of the way as the inmate leader fires at Zach. The bullet narrowly misses.

The women on the other side of camp are hurrying out of the water to try and get back to camp as Rochelle is watching out for them. Mike grabs his shotgun and starts out of the large tent. Jody grabs his AR-15 and heads for where the shooting is at.

The inmate with the shotgun aims in at Greg and fires. The shot finds its mark and Greg falls to the ground. Ken returns fire and the inmate with the shotgun is hit in his left knee and falls. Ken stops moving forward as the fire from the inmates is more than he can return.

The inmate leader spots Mike and Jody running towards them and realizes they have to retreat. The inmate leader decides he needs some insurance to make sure the strangers don't shoot at him while he retreats so he rushes over to the bank where he sees a young child laying on the ground, frozen with fear.

The inmate leader grabs Daniel and yells, "Let's get out of here!"

Ken turns his attention to the other three inmates and pulls out his pistol. Ken fires as the four inmates run for the trees, leaving their wounded comrade behind.

Mike spots Greg on the ground and starts for him. Jody runs as fast as he can to try and catch up to the other four inmates who now have Daniel. Jody holds his fire for fear of hitting Daniel. Jody starts to close the gap as the inmates reach the trees that they came from. The inmate leader looks back and sees Jody closing in with Ken not far behind him.

The inmate leader yells, "Stop or I'll kill the kid!" He pauses and turns to run off, "You'll be hearing from us!"

The inmate leader runs off after the other three inmates. Jody and Ken heed the warning and stop their pursuit. The inmates disappear into the woods. Jody and Ken turn back to see Mike kneeling over Greg and the other inmate laying on the ground holding his leg.

Jody speaks while breathing heavy, "Grab that guy over there. I'm going to check on Greg."

Ken heads over towards the wounded inmate as Jody makes his way over to Mike and Greg. Jody stops and looks down at Mike and Greg.

Mike looks up, "Don't bother, its too late."

Jody gets a very upset look on his face, "What?"

Mike sighs, "The shotgun blast hit him in the chest. There is no pulse and part of his chest is missing."

Jody looks away in disgust and sees the rest of the group heading towards them. Jody motions for them to go back to camp.

Jody looks back at his dad, "Leave him here for now. Let's help Ken get that wounded guy and let's see what we can find out about who attacked us."

Mike nods and stands up. Jody and Mike make their way over to Ken who is standing over the wounded inmate. Jody and Mike stop next to Ken and look down at the inmate who is still holding his leg where he was shot. The inmate gets a scared look on his face when he sees the three men standing over him.

Jody notices the uniform immediately, "He's a prison inmate."

Ken replies coldheartedly, "Want me to finish him?"

Mike sighs, "As much as I'd like that, we need him for now."

Jody nods, "Dad, head back to camp and get the others settled down. Ken and I will bring this piece of shit."

Mike heads off for camp as Jody and Ken each grab one of the inmate's arms.

The inmate leader, still carrying Daniel, and the other three inmates make it back to their vehicle. The inmate leader puts Daniel down and holds onto Daniel's shoulder. Daniel is still crying since being grabbed at the lake.

One of the inmate's looks at the leader, "What now?"

The inmate leader replies while catching his breath, "I want you three to take this kid back to our camp."

A second inmate questions, "What are you going to do?"

The inmate leader replies, "I'm going to make contact with them and tell them what we want in order for us to return this kid."

The third inmate speaks up, "What if they come after us? I saw at least seven men and there could be more."

The inmate leader speaks again, "They won't as long as we have this kid. Besides, they don't know how many of us there are."

The first inmate nods, "Okay. You want us to leave the car for you?"

The inmate leader replies, "No, take it. I'll walk back." He pauses, "If I don't make it back before midnight, kill the kid."

330

The three inmates look at each other, then back to the inmate leader and nod. The inmate leader turns and starts walking back towards the stranger's camp as the other three get in the car with Daniel and drive off for their camp.

CHAPTER 42

Jody walks back over to the rest of the group which is waiting around in front of the large tent. Everyone looks obviously shaken up by the incident. Ken is staying with the wounded inmate off behind the campsite where him and Jody moved the inmate to. Jody hears the others as he walks up.

Lindsey speaks frantically, "They took Daniel!"

Michael, Lindsey's husband, sighs, "It's my fault. I shouldn't have let him out of my sight for even a second."

Allen shakes his head, "It's not your fault. You saved Zach from being shot by that guy. You couldn't have done both."

Zach speaks in a depressed tone, "It's my fault. I had the chance to shoot him and didn't."

Jody speaks up, "It's nobody's fault."

Everyone stops and looks over at Jody.

Jody speaks again, "We can't anticipate every possible situation. We had a good defensive camp position and we had guards set up. These things happen and there was nothing we could've done about it."

Lindsey starts to shed some tears, "They took Daniel! They took my baby!"

Jody sighs and speaks in a disgusted tone, "I know and that pisses me off." He pauses, "But I don't think they're going to hurt him."

Lisa looks at Jody, "What makes you say that?"

Jody replies, "They were obviously coming for something, most likely supplies. My guess is, they'll make contact soon enough and bargain something from us for Daniel's return."

Michael, Lindsey's husband, replies, "What makes you think that. Maybe they plan on attacking us again instead."

Jody replies, "Because I know their type. They saw we're willing to fight back, but we have something that they want. Now they have something we want."

Ashley questions, "What do you mean, their type?"

Jody glances around, "Ken wounded one of them and he's watching him now. He's a prison inmate. No doubt the others are also."

Michael, Jody's brother, nods, "You're right bro. If they're inmates and they think they have the upper hand, they'll play the game to get what they want rather than risk confrontation."

Lindsey wipes away some tears, "Whatever they want, we have to give it to them."

Michael, Lindsey's husband, moves over and puts his arm around Lindsey to comfort her.

Jody nods, "Don't worry about that Lindsey. We'll get Daniel back."

Allen looks around and notices Greg is missing, "Hey. Where's Greg at?"

Mike speaks up, "He's dead. He was shot in the chest with a shotgun."

Everyone gets quiet.

Finally, Shana speaks up, "So, what now?"

Jody glances around again, "Right now we're going to deviate from the assigned teams. All they know is that there are us men here. I want everyone to stay in their tents." He looks at his brother, "I want you and dad to stay out here and keep a look out for anyone."

Lisa looks at Jody, "What are you going to do?"

Jody sighs, "Ken and I are going to talk to the wounded inmate and see what we can learn from him."

Rachel looks at Jody, "You're going to torture him?"

Jody shrugs, "If need be. That will depend on how much he cooperates." He pauses, "Okay everyone, let's get to it before they come back."

Jody turns and walks off to where Ken and the wounded inmate are at. Mike and Michael, Jody's brother, grab their weapons and take watch as everyone else heads off to the tents.

Ken is standing over the wounded inmate who is still holding his leg. Jody is standing back a few feet, looking at the inmate like he is waiting for something.

Jody shakes his head, "Don't feel like talking."

Jody looks at Ken and nods. Ken steps on the inmate's gunshot wound and presses down. The inmate screams out in pain. Ken grinds his boot on the wound for a few seconds, then pulls his foot away. The inmate grabs his leg as tears run down his face.

Jody questions again in a coldhearted tone, "How many of you are there?"

The inmate finally replies through his heavy breathing, "There are ten of us."

Jody nods, "And who is in charge?"

The inmate looks at Jody, but doesn't say anything. Jody looks at Ken and nods. Ken bends down with his knife in his hand. Ken grabs the inmate's left ear and cuts the top of the ear off with his knife. The inmate screams out in pain again and grabs his left ear. Ken raises back up.

Jody questions again, "Who's in charge?"

The inmate replies in obvious pain, "Jackson, the one who grabbed the kid. He's running the show."

Jody nods, "What was he in prison for?"

The inmate looks at Ken, then back to Jody, "First degree murder."

Jody glances around, "Are all the others inmates?"

The inmate replies, "Yes. Most in for violent crimes."

Jody nods and sighs, "What weapons do they have?"

The inmate swallows hard, but doesn't reply. Jody looks at Ken and nods again. Ken leans down and grabs the inmate's gunshot wound and squeezes. The inmate cries out in pain and reaches down to remove Ken's hand. As the inmate's right hand gets close, Ken let's go of the leg, grabs the inmate's right hand and pins it to the ground as he drives his knife through the inmate's hand. The inmate screams in pain once again.

Jody moves closer and squats down next to the inmate, "This will all stop if you answer my last two questions. What weapons do they have?"

The inmate takes a deep breath, "Two of us have shotguns, everyone else has just a pistol. That's why we've attacked other groups of survivors. We take their supplies and any weapons they might have."

Jody takes a deep breath, "Well, that raises an extra question. Is that all you've been looking for?"

The inmate shakes his head, "No. We've been trying to find women too."

Jody shakes his head, "I figured as much. How far is your camp?"

The inmate breaths rapidly through the pain, "Maybe about seven miles or so east."

Jody nods and smiles, "Thank you." He stands up and looks at Ken, "Finish it."

The inmate's eyes widen, "Hey, you said if I cooperated this would all stop. You lied to me."

Jody looks back at the inmate and replies coldheartedly, "The torture is stopping. However, you killed one of ours and we can't keep you around."

Jody turns and walks off.

The inmate yells, "You can't do this!"

Ken leans down with his knife in his hand. Jody continues to walk off. Everyone in the camp has heard the inmate's screams and they hear the inmate scream one more time, then there is silence.

The inmate leader, Jackson, is walking down the highway. Jackson has been walking for maybe half an hour or so when he sees the stranger's campsite up ahead and off to the side of the highway. Jackson continues to walk towards camp.

Mike and Michael, Jody's brother, spot Jackson on the highway and hurry over to Jody and Ken.

Mike looks at his son, "Someone is coming."

Jody nods, "Okay. You and Michael alert everyone to remain quiet, then hide. Ken, you stay with me."

Ken nods. Mike and Michael, Jody's brother, rush to each tent and alerts everyone to be quiet, then they hide behind the large tent. Jody and Ken wait for the person to arrive.

Jackson walks off the highway and sees Jody and Ken standing in the middle of the camp. Jackson slowly approaches the campsite, looking around to see if he can spot anyone else.

Jackson stops about fifty feet from the campsite, "Hello, can I come into your camp?!"

Jody motions with his hand, "Come on in."

Jackson walks up and stops about ten feet from Jody and Ken. Jackson looks around, but doesn't see or hear anyone else.

Jackson smiles, "Nice day, isn't it?"

Jody replies uncaringly, "Let's dispense with the pleasantries. Who are you and what do you want?"

Jackson nods, "Right to business, I like that. My name is Jackson and I'm here to discuss how you can get the kid back."

Jody replies, "Well, we want the kid back so what's it going to take?"

Jackson glances around, "Who all is here with you?"

Jody sighs, "That's none of your concern. You've seen all of us when you attacked us earlier."

Jackson nods and replies in a tone of I don't believe you, "Really? I didn't see the kid's mother."

Jody sighs again and gets a firmer tone, "What do you want for the kid?"

Jackson nods and smiles, "All business, I like that." He pauses, "Its simple, you bring all the food, water and guns you have."

Jody nods, "How did I guess that would be it?"

Jackson glances around and looks back at Jody, "And any women you have in camp." He pauses and gets a glaring look, "And I don't want to hear you say you don't have any women here. If you show up with no women, that kid is dead so you better find at least one."

Jody looks up at the sky and back at Jackson, "When do you want to do this? Its going to start getting dark real soon."

Jackson nods, "First thing in the morning. Take this highway east. You'll turn north on a county road about three miles down. Stay on that road for a couple miles, then turn east. About a mile down that road, you'll see our vehicles. Our camp is off to the north side of that road."

Jody nods, "We'll be there."

Jackson smiles, "Good."

Jackson turns and walks off back towards the highway. Jody and Ken watches Jackson leave. Jackson has a smile on his face like he has gotten the better of these strangers.

CHAPTER 43

Not long after Jackson leaves camp, everyone is back together in front of the large tent. Jody looks around at everyone and notices that the moral of the group is down with the loss of Greg and the kidnapping of Daniel.

Jody speaks to the group, "Okay, time to decide what to do."

Michael, Lindsey's husband, questions, "What did they ask for?"

Ken replies, "All of our food, water and guns."

Lisa shakes her head, "Of course."

Jody chimes in, "And any women we have."

Everyone looks at Jody in somewhat disbelief.

Ashley is puzzled, "What?"

Jody sighs, "They're prison inmates. No doubt they haven't had a woman in awhile so they want any women in our group. For obvious reasons."

Amber gets a disgusted look, "That's sick."

Ken speaks up, "There is no way we can give them what they want."

Michael, Lindsey's husband, speaks up, "If we don't, they'll kill Daniel."

Jody sighs, "And if we do, they'll come and kill all of us. Then have their way with you women."

Chad questions, "What makes you say that?"

Mike replies, "Because, if we give up all our weapons, we have no way to defend ourselves. They can just come right back and finish us off just to make sure we didn't hold out on them."

Jody notices Lindsey has kept her head down, "Hey Lindsey, what do you think? Its your son and your opinion matters more than ours."

Michael, Lindsey's husband, looks at Jody, "She's getting a migraine from all the stress."

Lindsey replies, "I want Daniel back, but I'm not going to tell all the women in the group to subject themselves to those people." She pauses, "Plus, they'll just come back after us like you all said."

Shana speaks up, "There has to be a way to get Daniel back and not risk all of us."

Michael, Jody's brother, nods at Shana, "Yeah, there has to be something we can do."

Shana looks over and smiles at Michael, Jody's brother, and he smiles back.

Marissa looks at Jody, "Surely you have an idea or plan Jody."

Everyone looks at Jody.

Jody glances around at the group, "I do, but its dangerous."

Codi speaks up, "Let's hear it."

Jody sighs, "I'll take dad's van with some food and water, along with some of the guns. Ken will hide out in the van. I'll take one female with me so they don't think something is up." He pauses, "When they think they have what they want and we have Daniel, we'll kill them."

Ryan speaks up, "That sounds very dangerous."

Allen questions, "Why not take more people?"

Jody shakes his head, "I'm not putting more than one female at risk and if we take too many guys, we can't hide them all. If they see any other guys other than me, they'll probably think something is up." He pauses, "There is nine of them. They have one shotgun and eight pistols."

Ken chimes in, "If we get the drop on them, we can take them out before they realize what's going on. Especially if we kill their leader."

Rachel questions, "Who would be the female that goes?"

Jody looks around, "Only one comes to mind that I know will help us out the best in this situation, but I won't make her go." He pauses, "Lisa. She has the training and I know she can shoot."

Everyone looks over at Lisa.

Lisa sees the looks on their faces and nods, "Of course I'll go."

Jody looks over at Lindsey, "I'd have you go Lindsey, but I need clear heads and don't need Daniel to get excited when he sees you." He pauses, "That's my plan, but I'm not going to risk Daniel unless you're okay with it."

Silence falls over the camp as everyone waits for Lindsey's answer.

Lindsey looks up and stares at Jody, "Promise me, because I know if you give me your word, you'll make it happen, promise me you'll bring Daniel back."

Jody stares at Lindsey with a completely serious look, "I promise, I'll bring him back."

Lindsey nods, "Okay. Do it."

Jody nods, "Alright, Ken, Lisa and I will leave at dawn. I'll take the shotguns and my rifle along with what is already in dad's van."

Everyone nods and Jody stands up.

Jody starts towards Mike's van, "Everyone bring the weapons I mentioned."

Jody opens the back of Mike's van. Jody grabs two cases of water and walks around to the side door. Lisa walks up and opens the side door while everyone places their shotguns in the back of the van. Jody sets the two cases of water inside the van. With the middle seats removed, there is plenty of room for Ken to hide between the front seats and the back bench seat. Lisa closes the side door and Jody closes the back door. Lisa and Jody walk back over to the group in front of the large tent.

Jody speaks, "Okay, we'll keep watch like usual. As soon as the sun rises, Ken, Lisa and I will leave." He pauses, "One more thing I want to do. I want Ashley and Shana to move in with Lisa and I. Ken and my dad will partner up and move in with Lindsey and Michael."

Mike speaks up, "I'll give you your sleeping bag back and I'll use Greg's sleeping bag."

Jody nods, "Okay." He pauses, "Let's get to it."

Everyone nods and heads off. Shana and Ashley take watch while everyone else gets settled in for the night.

Jody and Lisa are laying down in their tent while Ashley and Shana are on watch. Neither is finding sleep easy.

Lisa rolls over and looks at Jody who's back is to her, "Hey, you awake?"

Jody rolls over, "Yeah. I see you're not able to sleep either."

Lisa sighs, "Nope. I keep thinking about tomorrow."

Jody gazes at Lisa, "Me too."

Lisa looks away, "We could die tomorrow trying to get Daniel back."

Jody sighs, "It's possible, but I think we'll be okay."

Lisa looks back at Jody, "You're always positive, but this time the odds are against us."

Jody nods slightly, "Yeah, they are." He pauses, "But I have to stay positive. If I start thinking that we won't succeed, then we won't."

Lisa reaches her hand out and touches Jody's hand, "I have to admit, I'm scared about tomorrow."

Jody squeezes Lisa's hand, "That is completely understandable. I'm scared some too, but as long as we keep our heads, everything will be okay."

Lisa smiles, "Thanks. I just can't get it out of my mind that this could be our last night alive."

Jody gazes at Lisa, "That's not going to happen. All of us are coming back tomorrow." He pauses, "If it'll make you feel better, you can sleep with me tonight. I know I could use some calming of the nerves."

Lisa gets out of her sleeping bag and slides into Jody's sleeping bag.

Lisa lays on her right side, "Thanks." She pauses, "I thought this might feel weird, but it feels comfortable."

Jody lays behind Lisa and puts his arm around her, "I know. I thought the same thing, but I think its pretty comfortable myself."

Jody and Lisa close their eyes and find with the closeness that they are soon able to fall asleep.

As the sun starts to rise over the clear morning sky, Jody pulls away from the campsite in Mike's van. Lisa is sitting in the passenger's seat and Ken is sitting on the back bench seat. Jody starts slowly down the highway.

Lisa questions, "How are we going to handle this?"

Jody replies, "When we get there, I'll back the van up so the bench seat will block their view of Ken. You and I will get out. You open the side door and I'll open the back door. You and I will grab the two cases of water and place them on the ground behind the van, but we'll leave the side door open so Ken will be able to get out when the shooting starts."

Ken questions, "So, how do you want to deal with the inmates?"

Jody thinks for a minute, "I have no doubt that they'll be overly confident. I'll talk to the leader because I'm sure he'll expect us to just hand everything over. I'm going to talk him into sending Daniel to us the same time we send Lisa to them." He pauses, "If he agrees, I'll take the leader when Lisa and Daniel pass each other and Lisa, you take the inmate with the shotgun."

Lisa nods, "What if they don't agree?"

Jody takes a breath as he continues to drive, "I'll take the leader and you take the inmate that has Daniel. If the leader has Daniel, then you take the inmate with the shotgun."

Ken glances around, "I'll come out shooting as soon as I hear you fire." He pauses, "Take the one's directly in front of you, then work your way out to the sides. That way the one's with the easy, direct frontal shots won't have a chance and if they do get shots off, it'll be the inmates that are going to have to shoot at an angle."

Jody nods, "When the shooting starts, if Daniel is walking towards us, Lisa, you grab him and get him to the ground. If they keep Daniel and we have to shoot while they have him, I'm going for Daniel while the shooting is going on." He pauses, "I don't want Daniel catching a stray bullet from one of those idiots."

Lisa nods, "Sounds like we got everything covered."

Ken nods, "Yeah, except for one thing."

Lisa questions, "What's that?"

Jody smiles, "The part where we don't get killed."

Lisa looks at Jody, "Well, I don't know about you, but I plan on making it back. I didn't survive all those years working in the jail to let an inmate get me now."

Jody chuckles slightly, "Me either."

Ken smiles, "Well, we should be getting close. Let's just stay ready. They might try something when we first get there."

Jody continues to drive as the talking dies down.

Jackson is standing in a clearing about fifty feet from where their tents are at. Jackson is watching the trail that leads to their campsite from the road, waiting for the strangers to arrive. Jackson is holding his pistol in his right hand and his left hand is holding the back of Daniel's neck. A few feet to Jackson's right is the inmate with the shotgun.

Three inmates are spread out behind Jackson and the inmate with the shotgun. Two inmates are standing off to Jackson's right about twenty feet and the last two inmates are about twenty feet off to Jackson's left.

The inmate with the shotgun looks at Jackson, "So, how do you want to handle this?"

Jackson glances around, "We have the numbers and they don't know much about us. We show force and they'll give us what we want."

Another inmate questions, "What do you want us to do after we get the stuff?"

Jackson sighs, "We'll let him go with the kid, then we'll follow them to their camp and kill whoever is there."

A third inmate questions, "What about the women they bring?"

Jackson replies, "One of you will stay here and guard the women while we take care of them. No one touches the women until I have my pick." He pauses, "If there is only the kid's mother, she is mine before anyone else gets her. Is that understood?!"

Jackson looks around and the other inmates are nodding. None of them appear to want to cross Jackson.

Jackson looks down at Daniel, "I hope your mom is a good looking woman. It's been many years since I've been with a woman."

Daniel continues to cry as Jackson grips the back of his neck. Jackson looks back up to the trail and waits for the strangers to arrive.

CHAPTER 44

Jody drives the van down the county road that Jackson told him about and he sees a few vehicles ahead on his left. Jody passes the cars and sees the trail up ahead. Jody stops at the turn off to the trail and he sees Jackson standing at the far end of the trail in a clearing.

Jody pulls forward and backs the van up to the trail. Jody slowly backs the van down the trail towards the clearing where Jackson and the eight other inmates are waiting with Daniel. Ken gets down between the front seats and the bench seat so he can't be seen.

Jody backs the van up to the clearing and stops about ten yards from Jackson and Daniel. Jody puts the van in park and turns it off. Jody gets out of the driver's side. Jackson and the other inmates wait in anticipation to see what females have come.

Jackson notices Jody is wearing his pistol and spare magazines. Lisa gets out of the passenger's side. Jackson and the other inmates notice Lisa immediately and they all like what they see. Jackson also notices Lisa wearing her pistol and spare magazines.

Lisa opens up the side door as Jody opens the back door of the van. Lisa pulls out a case of water and walks around to the back of the van. Lisa sets the case of water down as Jody grabs the other case of water from the side door of the van. Jody gives a quick, unnoticed nod to Ken. Ken knows by the nod that Jody likes the set up of the inmates.

Jody walks around to the back of the van and sets the case of water on the ground. Jody and Lisa move off to their right so Jackson and the other inmates can see the food, water and guns in the back of the van. Jackson smiles at what he sees, thinking that these strangers have made a big mistake. Jackson returns his focus to Jody and Lisa. Jackson looks Lisa over and can't wait for his chance.

Jody speaks, "Okay. I did as you asked."

Jackson glances around, "Just one female is all."

Jody glances around at all the inmates, knowing they are distracted by Lisa's presence, "That's all we have in our group."

Jackson nods slightly, "Put down your guns and send her over. After that, my men will get the supplies. Then you and the boy can leave."

Jody shakes his head, "That's not going to happen."

Jackson speaks louder, "You don't have a say in this."

Jody replies louder, "I don't trust you and if I'm unarmed, I have no way of making sure you follow through on your word." He pauses, "Likewise, I'm sure you don't trust me."

Jackson holds tight to Daniel, "You're right about that."

Jody speaks up, "You send Daniel and I'll send her, at the same time. Once I have the kid and you have everything, I'll drop my pistol out the window as I drive off."

Jackson looks down, then back up, "I don't think so."

Jody and Lisa glance around at each of the inmates getting a mental picture of where everyone is at for when the time comes. Ken lies in wait, knowing that the time is about to come.

Jackson shakes his head, "Looks like we have a problem."

Jody pauses for a moment, then smiles, "My old First Lieutenant use to say, don't tell me problems, tell me solutions."

Jackson chuckles slightly, "And what is your solution?"

Just as Jackson finishes his question, Jody quickly draws his pistol and fires two shots at Jackson. Jackson is caught off guard and before he can raise his pistol, both shots hit him in the chest. Blood flies and Jackson falls to the ground on his back, letting go of Daniel.

Lisa reacts quickly and draws her pistol, aiming in on the inmate with the shotgun. All the inmates freeze in shock as they see Jackson fall. Lisa fires twice and both shots hit the inmate with the shotgun in the chest. The inmate drops his shotgun as he collapses to the ground in a pool of blood.

Jody starts moving towards Daniel as he aims in at another inmate. Ken hops out of the van with his shotgun ready, aims in at an inmate and fires. Ken's aim is true and one of the inmates is blown off his feet. Jody fires again while moving towards Daniel. Jody's first shot misses, but the next two find their mark. Jody's fourth shot also misses as the inmate falls to the ground.

Lisa moves her aim to another inmate and fires three quick shots. The first two hit the inmate, one in the chest and one in the neck as the third shot misses. The inmate falls to the ground. Ken moves his shotgun to another inmate. The four remaining inmates finally react and raise their pistols. Ken fires his shotgun and another inmate is blown off his feet.

Jody reaches Daniel when he sees an inmate to his right aiming at him. Jody spins Daniel away with his left arm and body as the inmate fires. Jody brings his pistol around and fires three shots. Two shots miss, but the third shot hits the inmate in the right shoulder. The inmate drops his pistol. The other three inmates start firing at Lisa and

Ken, but with their adrenaline going and the shock factor, the bullets miss. Lisa drops to a knee and steadies herself as she aims at another inmate.

Lisa fires three shots and her aim is true. Two of the shots hit the inmate in the chest and the third shot hits the inmate in the head. The inmate falls to the ground. Ken brings his shotgun around at another inmate. Ken fires and the inmate is blown off his feet from the powerful, well aimed shotgun blast.

Lisa looks over and sees the inmate Jody shot in the shoulder reaching down for his pistol. Lisa and Jody both aim and fire at the same time. Lisa's first shot hits the inmate in the stomach as her second shot misses. Jody's shot hits the inmate in the head. The inmate falls back to the ground.

The last inmate tries to steady himself as he aims towards Lisa, Jody and Daniel. Before the inmate can fire, Ken fires his shotgun and the inmate takes the full blast to the neck and face. The inmate wheels around and falls to the ground. Jody, Lisa and Ken look around and see all the inmates are down.

Jody stands up next to Daniel as Lisa and Ken make their way over to Jody. Jody holsters his pistol as Lisa and Ken walk up. Lisa holsters her pistol as well. Jody smiles at Ken and Lisa. Ken and Lisa nod at Jody.

Jody glances around, "Great job you two. It went just how I hoped it would."

Ken looks at Jody's left arm, "Did your hopes include getting shot?"

Lisa gets a panicked look, "You've been shot!?"

Jody looks at his left arm and sees a little blood just below the shoulder on the outside of the arm. Jody looks closely at his arm, then back to Lisa and Ken.

Jody smiles, "No, didn't plan that. The guy must have shot me when I grabbed Daniel and pulled him away."

Lisa looks at Jody's arm.

Lisa sounds concerned, "Are you okay?"

Jody nods, "Yeah, he barely grazed me. It kind of burns some, but I think the bleeding has already stopped."

Ken steps up and pats Jody on his right shoulder, "Well, don't take this the wrong way little buddy, but better you than me. Your younger and will heal faster. I'm too old to be getting shot."

Jody chuckles slightly, "Thanks man."

Lisa still has a concerned look, "I can't believe you two are joking about this."

Jody looks at Lisa and smiles at her concern for him, "Its okay Lisa. I'll be fine." He pauses, "I like that you're concerned about me though."

Lisa finally breaks a smile, "Well, you know ..."

Lisa doesn't finish her sentence because the three of them hear Jackson moan.

Jody looks at Lisa, "Get Daniel to the van and make sure he's okay."

Lisa questions, "Are we going to take their stuff?"

Jody shakes his head, "No, we need to get out of here. All that shooting could bring zombies this way."

Lisa nods, "Okay."

Lisa takes Daniel over to the van.

Jody looks at Ken, "Check the others. If any are alive, you know what to do."

Ken nods and walks off. Lisa puts the two cases of water back in the van and closes the back door. Lisa climbs in the van with Daniel and they sit on the bench seat in the back of the van. Jody steps over to Jackson and kneels next to him. Jackson looks at Jody, but doesn't manage to say anything. Jody pulls his pistol from his holster.

Jody smiles at Jackson, "Looks like I found the solution."

Jackson manages some words, "You can't do this."

Jody aims his pistol at Jackson's head, "I'm just fulfilling your sentence."

Jackson's eyes widen as Jody pulls the trigger. Jackson's body goes limp. Jody stands up and puts his pistol away.

Ken walks back up, "The others are dead."

Jody nods, "Good, let's get out of here."

Jody and Ken make their way to the van and get in. Jody looks in his rearview mirror and smiles as Daniel is hugging Lisa tight. Jody starts the van and pulls away.

Lindsey and Michael, her husband, are in their tent, waiting for Jody, Lisa and Ken to return, hopefully with Daniel. Lindsey has her eyes covered as Michael, her husband, tries to comfort her.

Lindsey sniffles, "I just don't know what I'll do without Daniel."

Michael, Lindsey's husband, runs his hand up and down Lindsey's back, "Daniel will be okay. They'll bring him back."

Lindsey leans over against her husband, "I don't even want to go on without Daniel. There's no reason to."

Michael, Lindsey's husband, puts his arm around Lindsey, "Sure there's a reason." He pauses, "But don't think like that. Daniel is going to be okay."

Lindsey sniffles again, but remains quiet.

Michael, Lindsey's husband, speaks softly, "You once said that you trusted Jody completely. He gave you his word that he'd bring Daniel back." He pauses, "Trust in him now. I know he won't let anything happen to Daniel without dying first."

Lindsey sniffles one more time and nestles against her husband. Michael, Lindsey's husband, just continues to hold his wife and do his best to console her.

CHAPTER 45

Allen and Rachel are on watch now. Everyone else is sitting around and waiting to see if Jody, Ken and Lisa return with Daniel. Lindsey is laying down in her tent as the migraine is nearly gone now. Shadow and Lucky are laying in front of the large tent watching everyone around them pass the time.

Suddenly, Shadow's ears perk up and he starts wagging his stub tail as he looks over towards the highway like he hears something. Everyone notices Shadow and they all look over towards the highway too. The talking dies down as everyone listens for what has Shadow's attention.

Codi whispers, "What do you think it is?"

Mike whispers back, "I think he hears the van. He would always get excited like that when he'd hear me pull up to the house."

Allen and Rachel start making their way back around from the west side of camp when they hear a vehicle coming down the highway. Allen and Rachel hurry over to the rest of the vehicles and hide behind Allen's Tahoe, getting ready just in case its not Jody and the others.

Allen raises up his rifle and looks through the scope. Rachel holds her breath, hoping its their people and not the inmates or other survivors. Allen finally breaks a smile as he sees Mike's van come into view.

Allen lowers his rifle, "Its them."

Rachel breaks a smile, "Thank goodness."

Allen looks at Rachel, "Go tell the others, I'll wait for them here."

Rachel nods, "Okay."

Rachel hurries off to let the rest of the group know. Allen watches as the van gets closer and closer. Allen's only hope now is that everyone is okay and that they were able to get Daniel back.

Jody pulls the van up and parks it by the other vehicles. Allen walks up as Jody and Ken get out of the van. Allen holds his breath as he sees the sliding door open. Lisa hops out, then turns around. Lisa picks Daniel up and helps him out of the van. Allen gets a big smile on his face as Lisa sets Daniel down.

Jody looks at Allen, "Hey man."

Allen nods his head, "Its good to see you all back."

Ken glances around, "Its good to be back."

Lisa takes Daniel's hand and they start walking towards camp with Jody, Ken and Allen close behind them. Lindsey is making her way out of her tent when she looks over and sees Lisa, Daniel, Jody, Ken and Allen walking towards camp. Lindsey's eyes widen as she can't believe what she is seeing.

Lindsey takes off running towards Daniel, "Daniel!"

Daniel looks over and sees his mom. Lisa smiles and let's go of Daniel's hand.

Daniel starts to run towards Lindsey, "Momma!"

Everyone watches as Lindsey and Daniel reach each other. Lindsey scoops Daniel up in her arms and hugs him tight. Daniel squeezes Lindsey as tightly as he can. Lisa, Jody, Ken and Allen make their way over to the rest of the group in front of the large tent. Shadow stands up and really starts wagging his stub tail in excitement.

Michael, Lindsey's husband, shakes Jody's hand, "Thank you so much."

Jody smiles, "My pleasure."

Michael, Lindsey's husband, greets Ken and Lisa in the same way as Shana walks over to Jody.

Shana gives Jody a hug, "Good to see you back."

Jody smiles, "Good to be back."

Jody and Shana step back as Mike walks over and gives his son a hug. Rochelle hurries over to Lisa and hugs her mom, happy to see her back. Mike greets Ken as Michael, Jody's brother, walks over and greets Jody and welcomes him back.

As the rest of the group welcomes back Jody, Ken and Lisa, Lindsey and Daniel start making their way over to the rest of the group in front of the large tent. Jody smiles as he watches Lindsey and Daniel walking towards them, hand in hand.

Lindsey let's go of Daniel's hand as she walks up. Michael, Lindsey's husband, gives Daniel a big hug. Lindsey continues over to Jody.

Lindsey gives Jody a big hug, "I can never thank you enough for bringing Daniel back."

Jody hugs Lindsey back, "You don't have to thank me, it was my pleasure."

Lindsey continues to hug Jody and smiles, "Thank you so much."

Jody just continues to hug Lindsey.

Shana looks over and notices Jody's left arm for the first time, "Jody, you're bleeding!"

Jody steps back from hugging Lindsey, "Yeah, I took a grazing shot."

Lindsey gets a worried look, "You were shot?"

Jody smiles, "It's nothing. The bleeding has already stopped."

Shana walks over to Jody, "We need to clean it up and get a bandage on it so it doesn't get infected."

Jody looks at Lindsey and smiles, "That's the nurse in her coming out."

Jody and Shana head off to get Jody's arm taken care of. Lindsey turns and walks over to Ken.

Lindsey gives Ken a hug, "Thank you so much."

Ken hugs Lindsey, "No problem."

Lindsey then steps over and gives Lisa a hug, "I can't thank you enough."

Lisa hugs Lindsey, "Your welcome."

Shadow makes a little whimper sound as if to say, where is my attention. Everyone looks over at Shadow and sees him staring at Lindsey, Lisa and Ken and wagging his stub tail.

Lisa kneels down, "Well, come here boy."

Shadow hurries over to get his attention from Lisa as everyone else has a good chuckle. Lindsey walks over and sits down next to Daniel and her husband. Lindsey takes Daniel in her arms again as everyone waits for Jody and Shana to return.

In about twenty minutes, Jody and Shana return to the campsite where everyone is waiting. The two of them notice the mood is much better than before. Shana sits down next to Michael, Jody's brother. Jody sits down next to Lisa.

Mike looks at Jody, "So, what do you want to do?"

Ryan questions, "Should we get packed up and on the road?"

Jody glances around, "No. I think its best if we stay here for the day and rest. We've all been emotionally drained over losing Greg and Daniel's kidnapping."

Lisa nudges Jody, "Rest sounds good to me."

Jody smiles, "Me too, that's why I said it."

Marissa looks at Jody, "So, is there any chance of the inmates coming back?"

Ken speaks up quickly, "Nope. They were taken care of."

Ashley smiles, "Good. They deserved it."

Jody looks over at Mike, "We good on supplies for now?"

Mike nods, "Yeah, food and water is okay. Gas is still a concern."

Chad speaks up, "It's getting harder and harder to find, even in abandoned vehicles."

Amber questions, "What do we do if we can't find anymore and run out?"

Jody sighs, "That's when we start walking and doing our best to keep our things and supplies with us."

Everyone gets quiet.

Lisa speaks up, "Let's worry about that, if and when the time comes."

Jody smiles at how Lisa took control of that topic.

Ken nods, "She's right. Let's stay focused on what we're doing now." He pauses, "So, everyone can retrieve their weapons from the van, then we'll continue the watch rotation like usual."

Everyone nods and gets up to get their weapons from Mike's van.

Jody and Lisa are on watch now. The day has been quiet since they returned this morning. Michael, Jody's brother, is over by the water cleaning his weapons. Shana sees him and walks over to check on him, not sure why he is by himself.

Shana walks up next to Michael, Jody's brother, "Hey, what's up?"

Michael, Jody's brother, looks up at Shana, "Not much, just cleaning my weapons and enjoying the quiet scenery."

Shana glances around, "Do you want me to leave you alone?"

Michael, Jody's brother, shrugs, "You can stay if you want."

Shana sits down next to Michael, Jody's brother, "I don't know about you, but I was worried this morning for Jody and the others."

Michael, Jody's brother, nods in agreement, "Me too." He pauses, "You still have feelings for Jody, don't you?"

Shana sighs, "Yeah, but not like that. I love him, but its pretty much just like the love for a good friend."

It gets quiet for a minute. Shana decides that its time to say something.

Shana takes a breath, "I do have those feelings for someone."

Michael, Jody's brother, sighs, "Really?"

Shana looks at Michael, Jody's brother, and smiles, "Yeah." She pauses, "You."

Michael, Jody's brother, looks at Shana and sees her smiling. Michael, Jody's brother, remembers how much they cared for each other, but its been so long ago, he figured that there was no chance of them ever being back together.

Shana stares at Michael, Jody's brother, "I realized now that any of us could be gone at any time and I needed to tell you how I feel."

Michael, Jody's brother, is still quiet as he just stares at Shana.

Shana speaks again, "Well, do you have anything to say?"

Michael, Jody's brother, finally breaks a smile, "I just can't believe it. I never figured that we'd have another chance."

Shana smiles ever bigger at a response she wasn't sure she'd hear.

Michael, Jody's brother, continues, "Ever since this all began, I started having feelings for you. I just thought that you still wanted to be with Jody."

Shana shakes her head slightly, "No. Jody and I talked about it and we decided that we're just great, close friends." She pauses, "And we talked about you."

Michael, Jody's brother, smiles, "Really? He was okay with this?"

Shana nods, "Of course he's okay with it. He actually knew it was coming before I said anything. He's pretty amazing."

Michael, Jody's brother, shakes his head and smiles again, "Yes he is."

Shana looks around, "So, what now?"

Michael, Jody's brother, glances around, "I'm going to finish cleaning my weapons."

Shana looks back at Michael, Jody's brother, and smiles, "That's not what I meant."

Michael, Jody's brother, smiles back, "I know." He pauses, "We'll just take things slow and one step at a time."

Shana nods and glances around, "Sounds good to me."

Shana leans over and gives Michael, Jody's brother, a kiss. It's a nice kiss. Shana and Michael, Jody's brother, separate when they hear someone walking near them. Shana and Michael, Jody's brother, look over and see Jody and Lisa, who are patrolling the camp, smiling at them.

Shana stands up, "I'm going to check on the boys. I'll talk to you later." She pauses, "Love you."

Michael, Jody's brother, smiles, "Love you too."

Shana heads off back to the camp as Michael, Jody's brother, finishes cleaning his weapons.

Lindsey, Daniel and Michael, her husband, are laying in their tent. Ken and Mike are out by the large tent with the rest of the group.

Daniel looks at Lindsey, "Momma?"

Lindsey looks at Daniel, "What is it Daniel?"

Daniel questions, "Are we going home?"

Lindsey gets quiet and looks at Michael, her husband. The two of them know that they must tell Daniel what is going on.

Lindsey pulls Daniel close to her, "No. We can't go home."

Daniel looks up at Lindsey, "Ever?"

Lindsey sighs, "Ever." She pauses, "There are bad things out there and bad people. We have to go someplace safe. Home isn't safe anymore."

Michael, Lindsey's husband, tries to help, "We are going to make a new home, with the others." He pauses, "I know it won't be like our old home, but we'll make it as fun as possible. How does that sound?"

Daniel sighs, "I guess that's okay. I miss grandma and grandpa."

Lindsey nods, "Me too." She pauses, "But we have all these new people who are like family. They'll be there to play with you and you can do things with them."

Michael, Lindsey's husband, chimes in, "And there is Lucky and Shadow."

Daniel gives a little smile, "I like Lucky and Shadow. They're fun."

Lindsey smiles, "I promise, we'll make it as fun as we can. Okay?"

Daniel leans into Lindsey, "Okay momma."

Lindsey looks at Michael, her husband, and smiles, hoping Daniel will be okay. Michael, Lindsey's husband, smiles back and nods, trying to reassure Lindsey that everything will be okay and that Daniel will adjust. Lindsey leans over and gives Michael, her husband, a brief, but nice kiss. Michael, Lindsey's husband, puts his hand on Daniel's shoulder as he kisses Lindsey.

CHAPTER 46

Michael, Jody's brother, and Marissa are on watch now and it is nearly sunrise. The two of them are walking the perimeter of the campsite keeping an eye out for zombies or other survivors. Neither one can believe how serene the dawn is. It is so quiet and the sky is so clear.

Michael, Jody's brother, and Marissa reach the east side of camp and stop. The two of them watch as the sun breaks the horizon.

Marissa takes a breath, "Look at that. Its amazing how something can be so beautiful in such an ugly world now."

Michael, Jody's brother, nods his head, "I know."

Michael, Jody's brother, and Marissa stare at the sunrise for a minute.

Marissa sighs, "Well, I guess I should wake the others up so we can get ready to go."

Michael, Jody's brother, glances around, "Yep, I'll keep watch."

Marissa starts to walk off and Michael, Jody's brother, watches her.

Michael, Jody's brother, notices Marissa is limping, "Knees still acting up?"

Marissa looks back, "I'll be okay." She pauses as she sees the worried look on his face, "Don't worry. If it gets too bad, I'll rest."

Michael, Jody's brother, smiles, "Okay."

Marissa heads off to wake everyone up as Michael, Jody's brother, continues to walk the perimeter of the camp.

Shana continues to drive down the highway as the convoy approaches Lake Village, Arkansas. Jody continues to look around at the surroundings, but doesn't see any zombies wandering around. Jody hopes that they won't have any problems making their way through Lake Village.

Shana glances at Jody, "So, after we pass through Lake Village, what then?"

Jody glances around, "We'll pick up Highway 82 and cross over into Mississippi."

Zach questions while looking around, "Where are we going to stop for the night?"

Jody glances in the mirror, "We're going to stop on Highway 1 by Lake Washington."

Shana slows down and weaves around an abandoned car on the highway. Jody was hoping to not have to go through another town so soon, but he couldn't find another way on the map.

Shana looks down at the gas gauge, "At least this car gets better gas mileage than your Explorer."

Tyler questions, "Will we have to walk sometime?"

Jody sighs, "If I had to guess, we will start losing vehicles before long."

Jody glances around and sees an intersection ahead and notices that it's a four way intersection. Jody remembers that he didn't see a road heading east off the highway at this intersection on the map.

Jody looks at Shana, "Slow down."

Shana slows the car down and glances at Jody, "What is it?"

Jody points ahead, "See that intersection. The left turn wasn't on the map, but it heads east. Let's take it and see if it leads us around Lake Village."

Shana questions, "What if its' just a dead end road? That'll waste some gas."

Jody sighs, "I know, but I'd rather chance it than have to go through another town again. We need a break from excitement for one day."

Zach glances around, "If it is a dead end, we can still double back and go through town and pick up some gas there if needed."

Shana looks in the rearview mirror and smiles at Zach, proud of how her son has grown so much since this all began.

Jody nods, "You're absolutely right Zach. That's good thinking."

Shana slows down even more as they approach the intersection. Jody sees the sign for the turn off and its marked as State Highway 257. Shana puts on the turn signal and turns left onto the new road. Everyone in the convoy follows, realizing this is not the way that was planned on their maps.

Ken is riding with Mike in his van now since Greg was killed. Shadow is sitting between the two front seats with his usual big smile on his face.

Ken is looking at his map, "I don't see this road on the map. This is not the way that Jody had planned."

Mike glances around, "I'm sure he has his reasons. He probably wants to avoid going through another town so soon."

Ken nods in agreement, "I don't blame him. We've got supplies for a few days and gas for one more day."

Mike reaches down and pets Shadow, "Well, let's just see where it goes."

The talking dies down as Mike continues to follow Lisa's Jeep Liberty.

Allen is keeping his Tahoe close to Lindsey's Trailblazer. The convoy has been on this new road for a few miles now. Chad, Amber, Allen and Rachel continue to look around, hoping that they'll run into a highway that's on their map.

Chad shakes his head, "I don't like this. I think we're lost."

Allen glances around, "Well, we started east and now we're headed south so we might run into the highway we're looking for."

Amber sighs, "I hope so. I don't want to be lost out here in the middle of nowhere."

Rachel looks out the window, "I know what you mean."

Allen starts to slow down as the rest of the convoy is slowing down in front of him. Chad, Amber and Rachel look around hoping to see the highway they are looking for. Allen sees Lindsey's left turn signal come on.

Chad finally sees the road sign, "Look, it's the Highway 82. Its our highway."

Amber smiles, "Thank you God."

Allen turns onto the highway and catches back up to the rest of the convoy. Everyone breathes easier as they are back on track.

Lisa is keeping a close eye on Jody's car in front of her. It has been awhile since they crossed into Mississippi and got on Highway 1. Lisa knows they must be getting close to their stopping point for the day. Codi, Ryan and Rochelle continue to look around. They see trees of the wildlife refuge off to their east.

Codi continues to glance around, "We should be getting close."

Ryan is looking at his map, "It should be just up ahead according to the map."

Lisa glances around, "We should be close, its getting on towards dinner time."

At that time, Lisa sees the brake lights on Jody's car come on as Shana starts slowing down some.

Rochelle looks off to her right, "I see water."

Codi and Ryan look to their right and see what has to be Lake Washington.

Lisa nods, "That's got to be it."

Lisa continues to slow down to keep a safe distance from Jody's car. Lisa watches as Shana pulls the car off on the shoulder of the highway. Lisa pulls off on the shoulder of the highway and stops behind Jody's car. The rest of the convoy pulls off the highway and stops.

Lisa shuts the Jeep off and gets out. Ryan, Codi and Rochelle get out and walk towards Jody, Shana, Zach and Tyler. Jody nods at Lisa as she walks up. Jody waits till everyone else gets there.

Jody looks around, "What do you think?"

Lisa glances around and points, "I think we should set up camp over there."

Ken looks around and nods, "That looks like a good place to me."

Jody smiles, "Then its settled. Zach and Tyler will take watch and the rest of us will setup camp."

Zach and Tyler head off to keep a look out and everyone else heads off to get their tents and stuff.

Its been a couple of hours since the group has set up camp. Everyone has eaten and gotten cleaned up. Shadow and Lucky have been fed and walked around. Jody has been in his tent looking over the map. After talking with his dad earlier about the supplies and gas situation, he knows what must be done.

Jody walks out of his tent and over in front of the large tent where everyone else is at. Shana and Ashley are nearing the end of their watch.

Jody looks over at Zach, "Why don't you and Tyler take over watch so the rest of us can talk."

Zach nods, "Okay."

Zach and Tyler head off to replace Shana and Ashley. Jody sits down next to Lisa and waits. In a couple minutes, Shana and Ashley walk up and sit down.

Jody takes a breath, "Okay, I talked with my dad earlier and our supplies are doing okay, but our gas situation is not looking good."

Ashley questions, "What are you thinking?"

Jody sighs, "We're not having much luck finding enough gas on the highway." He pauses, "We're going to have to go into town if we want to keep the vehicles running."

Amber looks at Jody, "What do you suggest?"

Jody looks around at everyone, "I'm saying that we need to go into the next big town and get gasoline, supplies if possible."

Allen questions, "What's the next town?"

Jody replies, "Yazoo City."

Marissa questions, "How big is Yazoo City?"

It gets quiet for a minute.

Mike finally speaks up, "I would say its about the same size as Miami."

Michael, Jody's brother, speaks up, "That's a pretty good sized town to be venturing into."

Michael, Lindsey's husband, looks around, "I know its dangerous, but we need gasoline."

Lindsey chimes in, "Absolutely. We have far too long to travel to take the chance of walking now."

Chad questions, "Where are we going to stop for the night?"

Jody pulls out his map, "I'd like to make it south of Canton on Highway 43 at Ross R Barnett Reservoir."

Lisa looks at the map, "I think we should be able to get there, barring any problems in Yazoo City."

Mike sighs and looks at the others, "Well, that sounds like the plan then. Make sure everyone marks in on their maps."

Ken glances around, "Well, let's get back to our watch rotation and head out first thing in the morning."

Shana gets up, "I think we have a little time left on our watch."

Michael, Jody's brother, speaks up, "Na, its so close to time, Marissa and I will go ahead and take over."

Shana looks at Michael, Jody's brother, "Thanks."

Michael, Jody's brother, and Marissa get up and head off to take over watch as everyone else goes on about their own way to pass the time until they go to sleep.

CHAPTER 47

The stars light up the clear night sky and the breeze carries the smell of the fresh water across the camp. Allen and Rachel are standing watch while everyone else is sleeping. The two of them have been relatively quiet for most of the watch.

Finally, Rachel looks at Allen, "I can't believe Greg is gone."

Allen nods his head slightly, "I know. I don't understand why other survivors would act that way. You'd think they'd want to work together since there are so many zombies and so few of us."

Rachel sighs, "I know. It would make more sense for everyone to band together like we did with the others." She pauses, "I think Jody did the right thing by killing them. They were too dangerous."

Allen nods and glances around, "Yeah, I think so too. Normally I wouldn't condone killing others, but what they did, they deserved it."

Rachel glances around, "Absolutely." She pauses, "I'm just worried that Greg won't be the last to die."

Allen looks at Rachel, "I'm almost certain others will, but try not to think about it."

Rachel looks at Allen, "I try, but I can't help it. I don't know what I'd do if I lost you."

Allen takes a breath, "If something was to happen to me, I'd want you to press on with the others and stay alive." He pauses, "I know how hurt you'll be, but I'd want you to go on."

Rachel nods and replies, "I'd want the same thing for you if something happens to me."

At that moment, Allen's watch beeps once alerting him that it is time for them to wake up the next team for watch.

Allen smiles, "Well, let's not try to think about it too much." He pauses, "Why don't you wake Chad and Amber while I keep watch."

Rachel smiles, "Okay."

Allen and Rachel share a nice kiss, then Rachel heads off to wake up Chad and Amber. Allen continues to walk the perimeter of the camp.

Its nearly sunrise and Ryan and Codi are on watch now. The summer breeze continues to blow across the water carrying the smell of the lake and fish across the camp. Ryan and Codi stop walking as they see the eastern sky start to change colors due to the impending sunrise.

Codi smiles, "Its so beautiful. Hard to believe something so beautiful in a world so ugly now."

Ryan nods, "I know."

Codi sighs, "I can't help but think about Greg being killed and how that could happen to any of us. Up until now, people left on their own."

Ryan sighs and glances around, "I know. I've been thinking about it too. How lucky we've been until now."

Codi nods and looks back at the sunrise, "I don't know what I'd do if I lost you."

Ryan looks at Codi, "I know it'd be hard, but I'd want you to try and go on."

Codi looks at Ryan, "I'd want you to do the same if something happens to me."

Ryan gives a slight smile, "Let's try not to think about it."

Codi smiles slightly and sighs, "Its hard not to because it will eventually happen. I'm sure we'll lose more people."

Ryan nods and replies, "I'm sure of it too, but let's do our best to remain positive about making it to our final destination, together."

Codi nods and squints as the sun breaks the horizon, "It seems so far away."

Ryan holds his hand up to cover his eyes, "It does, but we'll be there before we know it."

Codi looks back at Ryan, "Well, I better go wake everyone up so we can eat and get on the road."

Ryan looks at Codi, "Okay."

Ryan and Codi share a brief, but nice kiss. Codi heads off to the camp to wake everyone up and Ryan continues to patrol the perimeter of the campsite.

Shana continues to drive the Hyundai along the highway leading towards Yazoo City. Jody, Zach and Tyler are looking around, hoping to spot more abandoned cars that might help them in their quest for fuel.

Shana glances over at Jody, "So, are we going to stay on the highway or get off into town?"

Jody looks over at Shana, "We'll stay on the highway. This Highway 16 & 149 runs across the south of town so we should have a few gas stations and I'm hoping plenty of cars along the way."

Zach glances around, "I hope so cause I haven't seen too many cars yet and we're almost there."

Shana looks ahead and sees the town. Jody glances around and his hopes are fading some as Zach is right, they are nearly to town and they haven't passed hardly any cars at all.

Jody sighs, "If we don't spot anything, we'll continue on to Canton. Its closer to Jackson and the interstate so there might be more cars there."

Shana nods and starts to slow down as they near the city limits, "Okay." She pauses, "Boys, keep your eyes open."

Jody, Zach and Tyler continue to look around as the convoy enters the town.

Mike is keeping his van close to Lisa's Jeep as they have nearly crossed the town and haven't found a place to stop and check for gas yet.

Mike reaches down and pets Shadow, "Not looking good big boy."

Shadow just looks up at Mike, wondering what he is saying.

Ken shakes his head, "Yeah, doesn't look like we're going to have much luck here."

Suddenly, Lisa's brake lights come on and Mike starts to slow down. Both Mike and Ken look ahead and see a sign for a well known gas station chain.

Mike smiles, "They must see something they like if we're slowing down."

Ken sighs, "I hope so."

Mike continues to follow Lisa's Jeep as they near the gas station. It is a good sized gas station. Mike slows down even more as they near the gas station.

Shana pulls the car to a stop on the side of the road next to the gas station. Jody smiles as he sees about twenty cars either on the parking lot or road around the gas station and knows that they should be able to find enough gas to get them by. Shana puts the car in park and shuts it off as the rest of the convoy pulls up and stops. Jody, Shana, Zach and Tyler get out and look around as the rest of the group makes their way over to them.

Jody looks around, "Okay, let's have Zach and Tyler and Shana and Ashley keep watch. The rest of us will check the cars for gas."

Everyone nods. Zach, Tyler, Shana and Ashley spread out as the rest of the group grabs the gas cans and start checking cars for gasoline. Everyone is hoping they can find enough to get them by for a bit.

It is a slow process, but as the minutes pass away, the group continues to fill up the gas cans and take them over to their vehicles and pour them in. After nearly half an hour, the group has checked all except a few of cars on the road. Jody motions for everyone to join him by the vehicles.

Jody glances around, "We've scored big here. I think we've got almost a full tank in every vehicle now. We just have four cars here in the road to check."

Allen looks around, "Why don't Chad, Amber, Rachel and I check the gas station for food and water while you all finish with the cars?"

Ken glances around, "That's a good idea."

Jody looks around and isn't sure about it, but decides to take the chance, "Okay. While your two groups are inside, Codi and dad will let the dogs out while the rest of us check the cars. We'll keep the same four on watch."

Everyone nods. Shana, Ashley, Zach and Tyler spread back out as Mike gets Shadow out of the van and Codi gets Lucky out of Lisa's Jeep. Allen, Rachel, Chad and Amber head for the gas station store while the rest of the group heads for the cars in the road.

Allen, Rachel, Chad and Amber stop at the doors in the front of the store. Allen and Chad look through the glass doors and they don't see anything. Allen, Chad, Rachel and Amber slowly enter the store.

Jody and Lisa are at one car, Lindsey and Michael, her husband, are at another car, Michael, Jody's brother, and Marissa are checking out a car and Ryan and Ken are checking out a car. Mike and Codi have Shadow and Lucky out. The two dogs are sniffing everything they can and relieving themselves everywhere as they are checking out the new surroundings.

Allen, Chad, Rachel and Amber glance around after they step inside the store.

Allen whispers, "Rachel and I will head to the back and check on water. You two look around for some food."

Allen and Rachel slowly make their way towards the back of the store as Chad and Amber head off to their right to look for some food. Right away, Chad and Amber notice the shelves are picked pretty clean. Allen and Rachel reach the drink coolers in the back, but notice that they are pretty much empty except for a couple six packs of water. Allen glances around and spots the bathroom hallway leading into the back.

Allen whispers to Rachel, "I'm going to check the hallway there and see if I can find the door to the cooler. You grab those two things of water."

Rachel nods as Allen walks off. Rachel holsters her pistol and opens the glass door. Rachel bends down to grab the water and looks through the empty shelves into the cooler area. Rachel's eyes widen as she sees a body on the floor with a zombie eating on it.

Rachel looks up and notices Allen has already went down the hallway, "Allen!"

Allen grabs the handle of the door to the cooler and pulls it open when he hears Rachel's voice calling to him.

Allen turns his head back to the store and let's go of the door as it is nearly halfway open.

Suddenly, the cooler door bursts open as three zombies pour out of the cooler right on top of Allen. Allen's eyes widen as he is knocked back against the wall behind him. The three zombies are on Allen before he can raise his rifle up. One zombie leans in and Allen pushes the zombie with his left hand. Another zombie leans in and bites Allen on his left arm.

Allen screams, "Help!"

The third zombie leans in and sinks it's teeth into Allen's shoulder. The three zombies press into Allen and their weight causes Allen to fall to the floor as the three zombies grab at Allen and continue to bite him. The three zombies are taking bites of flesh out of Allen as Allen tries to struggle to get away. Finally, one zombie sinks it's teeth into Allen's neck and rips a huge chunk of flesh out. Blood starts pouring out of Allen's neck as his jugular vein has been ripped out.

Rachel, Chad and Amber run up to the hallway entrance and see the zombies on top of Allen.

Rachel screams again, "Allen, no!"

Chad raises his shotgun and fires. The blast echoes through the store as one of the zombie's head explodes. With the three of them fixated on Allen, they didn't notice the cooler door didn't shut all the way. Chad pumps his shotgun again when the cooler door bursts open and three more zombies come staggering out.

Chad, Amber and Rachel all freeze for a moment. Suddenly, Rachel feels a hand grab her from behind. Jody and Lisa, having heard all the noise, ran into the store to check out what was going on while the rest of the group got the dogs back in the vehicles and the gas cans put up.

Jody yells as he pulls on Rachel's arm, "Let's go, we got to get out of here!"

Lisa grabs Amber's arm and pulls her away, "Get to the vehicles, now!"

Lisa raises her shotgun up as Amber runs for the front doors. Lisa fires and drops one of the zombies that are staggering towards them.

Chad yells, "What about Allen?!"

Jody pushes Rachel towards the front door and grabs Chad, "It's too late! Run!"

Lisa pumps and fires her shotgun again and another zombie falls to the floor.

Then, Jody and the others hear Ken's voice, "Hurry! Zombies are coming down the road!"

Lisa takes off for the front doors and grabs Rachel along the way. Jody pushes Chad towards the front door. Amber runs out the front door and by Ken. Lisa and Rachel are the next to exit the store quickly followed by Jody and Chad. Ken sees the zombie staggering towards the front. Ken raises his shotgun and fires. The zombie's head explodes as Ken turns and makes his way towards the vehicles.

Jody yells as he sees the large group of zombies coming from their north, "Get in the vehicles and let's get out of here!"

Everyone dashes for their assigned vehicles. Chad, Amber and Rachel make their way over to Allen's Tahoe, then stop. Jody notices Chad, Amber and Rachel just standing outside the Tahoe.

Jody looks at Shana, "I'm going to get them in Allen's vehicle. Follow me with the car."

Shana nods, "Okay."

As everyone loads up, Jody runs over to Allen's Tahoe.

Jody yells, "You three, get in!"

Chad, Amber and Rachel finally start moving as Jody gets in the driver's seat of the Tahoe. Chad and Amber get in the back seat as Rachel gets in the passenger's seat. Jody grabs the keys off the dashboard and starts up the Tahoe. Jody puts the vehicle in drive and pulls away, passing the rest of the convoy.

As the Tahoe passes her, Shana pulls away from the store in the Hyundai and quickly catches up to the Tahoe Jody is now driving. The rest of the convoy pulls away and quickly catches up to Jody and Shana.

CHAPTER 48

Jody has been driving around the reservoir for a little bit now, looking to get on the eastern side of it and find a place to stop for the night. Rachel has been crying the whole trip since losing Allen in Yazoo City. Jody knows that in the hurried confusion of leaving the store, some of the others may not know that Allen didn't make it.

Jody sees a good spot ahead and starts slowing down. Jody glances around and feels that the area is a good place for camp. Jody pulls to a stop on the side of the highway, puts the Tahoe in park and shuts it off. Jody gets out, but Chad, Amber and Rachel stay in the vehicle.

The rest of the convoy pulls to a stop and everyone gets out. Everyone makes their way over to Jody.

Jody glances around, "We'll set up camp over by the water, then we'll get the dogs out and eat. After that, people can clean up if they want."

Marissa questions, "What happened back there?"

Lisa shakes her head, "They got attacked by zombies inside the store." She pauses, "Allen didn't make it."

Jody and Lisa notice the somewhat shocked looks on everyone's face at the news. Rachel, Chad and Amber finally make their way over to the rest of the group.

Marissa walks over and hugs Rachel, "I'm so sorry."

Rachel just hugs Marissa back, unable to say anything.

Chad speaks in a solemn tone, "So, what's the plan?"

Jody replies, "We'll camp here tonight, get an inventory and see about tomorrow."

Ken looks at Zach and Tyler, "You boys want to take watch and the rest of us will get started on setting up camp."

Tyler nods, "Sure thing."

Everyone starts moving back to their vehicles to get the tents and their things except for Rachel.

Jody looks at Marissa, "Why don't you stay with Rachel. The rest of us can take care of camp."

Marissa nods. Everyone heads off to get camp set up while Zach and Tyler stand watch. Marissa waits with Rachel by the vehicles, trying her best to console her.

Its been a couple of hours since the camp has been set up. Shadow and Lucky have walked around and marked their new territory and everyone has finished eating. Shana and Ashley are on watch now and the camp has been pretty quiet.

Jody is laying in his tent looking over the map, planning their next stop. Lisa walks in and sits down on her sleeping bag.

Lisa lays her shotgun down, "So, how's it looking for our next stop?"

Jody replies while looking at the map, "Still trying to figure it out. We can make it to the Alabama state line, but there doesn't seem to be any places with water around."

Lisa moves over next to Jody and looks at the map. Jody sits up by Lisa and the two of them hold the map in their laps.

Lisa speaks while looking at the map, "Looks like we have a couple of options. We can drop south and take the interstate or we can take these smaller highways to the north, then east."

Jody nods, "Yeah, those are the two routes I've been looking at so far. If we get on the interstate, we can make it farther cause we can travel a little faster. However, we have to pass by a larger town, Meridian." He pauses, "If we go the other way, we won't make it as far, but we don't have any larger towns to deal with."

Lisa leans against Jody's right arm to get a closer look at the map, "I'm thinking the interstate would be better right now because we can travel farther. With gas getting more scarce, we need to get more miles out of the day." She pauses, "Even if it means a little more danger."

Jody looks at Lisa and smiles, "That's exactly what I've been thinking. Its nice to hear that you feel the same way." He pauses, "Even though its more dangerous. Especially since what happened today."

Lisa sighs, "Yeah, that was a bad deal. I feel so sorry for Rachel."

Jody nods slightly, "Me too." He pauses, "How are you doing?"

Lisa looks at Jody, "I'm okay. It was hard at first knowing how much I lost, but I'm slowly moving on." She pauses, "How about you?"

Jody gives a slight smile, "I'm the same. The hurt isn't as bad because I know everything happens for a reason."

Lisa smiles, "Yeah, it does." She pauses, "So, we take the interstate. Where do we stop next?"

Jody looks back at the map, "I'm thinking that if we don't have any problems, we can get off the interstate in Alabama on Highway 80 and stop at the river between Bellamy and Demopolis."

Lisa looks closely at the map, "Yeah, I think we could make that." She pauses, "Why don't I go get the others gathered up. I think it will help ease their minds if they know we have the next travel plans made. People tend to rest easier when they have a known plan."

Jody nods, "Good thinking. I'll be out there in a few minutes."

Lisa slides the map off her lap, then turns and gives Jody a hug.

Jody smiles and hugs Lisa back, "What's this for?"

Lisa smiles as she hugs Jody, "Just in case. Like we've seen, you never know when something will happen."

Jody squeezes Lisa, "You're right about that."

Jody and Lisa stop hugging and smile at each other. Lisa gets up, grabs her shotgun and heads off to get everyone gathered up. Jody smiles as he watches Lisa walk off.

Its been about five minutes and everyone is gathered around the front of the large tent. Zach and Tyler have taken over watch while the group has their meeting. Each team has their map out, except for Rachel. Shadow is laying at Mike's feet and Codi is holding Lucky in her lap. Jody walks up and sits down next to Lisa.

Jody sighs, "Okay. I know today has been rough beyond what words can describe, but I wanted to share with you what Lisa and I came up with for the next part of the trip."

Lisa speaks up, "We know the route we chose is a little more dangerous, but we feel its important to get more miles out of each day given that gas is getting harder to find without going into a big city."

Ken nods, "Which we want to avoid if possible."

Jody nods, "Exactly." He pauses, "If you look at your maps, we will go south from here to the interstate, then we'll take the interstate east all the way to Alabama."

Lisa chimes in, "You'll notice that takes us near a larger town, but it's going to be faster."

Michael, Lindsey's husband, questions, "What about Meridian?"

Jody replies, "If the interstate is clear, we won't even slow down. If the interstate is blocked, we'll get off on one of the north or south highways, then find a back highway into Alabama."

Lisa looks around, "Sound good to everyone?"

Everyone nods as they mark their maps.

Shana questions, "Where are we going to stop?"

Lisa replies, "If we don't run into any problems, we'll get off the interstate in Alabama and get on Highway 80. We'll stop at the river between Bellamy and Demopolis."

Mike looks up, "That's a good little ways."

Ryan questions, "What if we do have problems?"

Jody replies, "Then we'll go as far as we can before we start to lose the sun. We'll camp wherever we have to then."

Everyone nods again as they mark their maps.

Lindsey questions, "Is anything within the group going to change given what happened today?"

It gets quiet in the camp.

Jody finally breaks the silence, "No. I just want Rachel to hang out with Rochelle for now and help with Daniel and the dogs. We'll keep everything else the same." He pauses, "We're down to seven teams, but we'll keep the watches at an hour still. Okay?"

Everyone nods in agreement.

Jody glances around, "What happened today could not be avoided. Allen was a good man and did a lot to help this group. I know his loss is sad, but let's try to remember the good things about him."

Rachel sniffles as everyone else is quiet for a moment.

Ken speaks up, "Okay. Let's get back to the watch rotation. If there is anyone left that wants to clean up, do so. Other than that, let's try to get some rest."

Marissa and Michael, Jody's brother, get up and start heading off to get ready for their watch. Everyone else breaks up and goes their separate ways. Mike and Codi take Lucky and Shadow back into the large tent with Daniel.

Its early morning and everyone is finding sleep hard to come by. Mike and Ken are on watch now as the stars light up the early morning sky. Lindsey and Michael, her husband, are laying in their tent unable to fall asleep since Mike and Ken left for watch.

Lindsey rolls over and looks at Michael, her husband, "Can't sleep either?"

Michael, Lindsey's husband, sighs, "Nope. Just been thinking about today and how that could happen to any of us."

Lindsey sighs and nods, "Me too." She pauses, "I couldn't imagine losing you or Daniel. It was bad enough when he was kidnapped, but knowing that zombies had gotten either of you, I don't think I could take it."

Michael, Lindsey's husband, slides closer to Lindsey, "Me either. If something were to happen to you or Daniel, I don't think I could handle it." He pauses, "I would want you to try and go on if something did happen to me though."

Lindsey sighs, "I'd want you to do the same if something happens to me." She pauses, "The most important thing is being there for Daniel and keeping him safe."

Michael, Lindsey's husband, nods, "Totally. I'm not going to let anything happen to him again like I did before. I should have never let him out of my reach."

Lindsey slides over next to Michael, her husband, "You saved Zach's life by risking your own. There was nothing more you could do. It wasn't your fault. Besides, it all worked out."

Michael, Lindsey's husband, reaches over and places his arm around Lindsey, "Yeah."

Lindsey and Michael, her husband, lean close and kiss each other. After what has happened, they can't help but feel a stronger connection knowing that something could happen to either one of them at any time. Lindsey and Michael, her husband, continue to passionately kiss and they decide to share their love for each other as they get lost in the moment.

CHAPTER 49

Its nearly sunrise and Jody and Lisa are on watch now. Jody, like always while on watch, is wearing his H-harness gear and his full ACU digital camouflage uniform. Lisa has on her urban digital camouflage clothing. The two of them are walking the perimeter of the camp. The sun starts to rise as it lights up the eastern horizon.

Jody looks at Lisa, "I'm betting the others didn't get much sleep, like we didn't."

Lisa nods, "I'd guess that too."

Jody sighs, "I'm thinking we should stay here another day and rest. If we travel today and run into problems, we don't want everyone exhausted."

Lisa nods slightly, "I think that's a good idea. As long as we have the supplies for it."

Jody glances around, "I talked to dad last night and we're sitting okay on supplies."

Lisa looks around and replies, "Then I think staying here for the day is a good move."

Jody looks back at Lisa, "Why don't you go around and let everyone know. I'll keep watch until you get back."

Lisa smiles, "Okay."

Lisa heads off to inform everyone in camp of the plan to rest for the day while Jody continues to walk the perimeter of the camp.

It has been a restful day for the group. The mostly clear skies and mid 80's temperature has made it a nice day to rest. Most everyone has just laid around all morning and early afternoon. As it has drawn closer to evening time, most everyone decided to change into their swimming attire and head down to the water to swim around some and clean up. Rachel has stayed in camp. Chad and Amber just finished their watch and have stayed in camp as Mike and Ken have taken over watch now. Shadow and Lucky are also down by the water, enjoying themselves. Everyone is doing their best to forget what has happened and just clear their heads.

About ten minutes into Mike and Ken's watch, Jody looks up at the sky and notices it is starting to get near evening time. Which means it's going to be time to eat soon.

Jody looks at the others, "We'll probably be eating in an hour or so. I'm going to go ahead and go get dried off and changed. I must say though, this was nice."

Lindsey smiles, "It sure was." She looks at Daniel, "Did you have fun today?"

Daniel smiles, "Yeah!"

Lisa glances around, "I think I'm going to go get dried off and changed too."

Lindsey nods and looks at Michael, her husband, "I'm going to go ahead and go also. It'll take me longer to get Daniel dried off and changed, then myself."

Michael, Lindsey's husband, smiles, "I'll join you."

Lindsey takes Daniel's hand and they start out of the water. Right behind them is Michael, Lindsey's husband, Jody and Lisa. The others have stayed in the water for now.

Shadow is laying in the water along the bank. Shadow loves water and his smile is as big as it can get. Shana and

Michael, Jody's brother, are swimming around together and talking. Tyler is playing around near Shadow and Lucky. Ashley, Ryan and Codi are talking while splashing around in the water. Zach is watching Ashley most of the time, but trying not to show it so everyone won't notice. Marissa makes her way up to the bank and sits next to Shadow and starts petting him.

Mike and Ken make their way over by the water while walking around keeping watch.

Mike smiles, "It's nice to see everyone able to relax and have some fun."

Ken nods, "I know. This was definitely needed."

Mike turns around to start walking back towards the road, "I don't know about Rachel, Chad and Amber though."

Ken walks next to Mike, "I think Chad and Amber will be okay. They'll be sad, but okay. Rachel, I don't know about. We'll have to keep an eye on her for sure."

Mike nods, "Yeah, we will."

Mike and Ken continue to walk while the others play around in the water except for Rachel, Chad and Amber who are already in camp and Jody, Lisa, Lindsey, Michael, Lindsey's husband, and Daniel who headed back to their tents to dry off and change.

Its been a couple of hours now and everyone has gotten out of the water, dried off and changed for the night. The dogs have been walked and fed and everyone in the group has eaten. Michael, Jody's brother, and Marissa are on watch now.

The rest of the group is sitting around in front of the large tent, except for Rachel. Rachel is laying down in her tent. Shadow and Lucky are sitting in front of Tyler like they are waiting for him to do something. Tyler pulls a dog toy from behind his back.

Shadow and Lucky both stand up in anticipation. Tyler fakes like he is going to throw the toy and both Shadow and Lucky move slightly in reaction. Everyone watches the two dogs with smiles. Tyler finally tosses the toy across to Daniel. Shadow and Lucky both break for the toy.

Daniel picks the toy up quickly as Shadow and Lucky come running at him. Shadow has a hard time stopping and bumps into Daniel. Daniel falls to his butt and tosses the dog toy back across the way to Zach this time. Shadow and Lucky turn and run after the toy again.

Daniel lays to his back in a dramatic way and calls to Lindsey in his dramatic voice, "Momma, momma! Shadow got me!"

Lindsey smiles at her son, "He sure did."

Everyone has a good laugh over Daniel's reaction. Michael, Jody's brother, and Marissa hear everyone from the camp and smile.

Marissa glances around, "It's good to see everyone relaxing and getting their minds off what happened."

Michael, Jody's brother, replies, "Yeah. Spending the extra day here was a good idea." He pauses, "Everyone needed the chance to relax and clear their heads."

Marissa looks over at Michael, Jody's brother, "So, how are things with you and Shana progressing?"

Michael, Jody's brother, smiles, "Good. We finally told each other how we felt after Greg was killed." He pauses, "And we kissed."

Marissa smiles, "Oh really. Cool."

Michael, Jody's brother, glances around and continues to smile, "Yeah, it was nice. I'm just happy to have her back in my life."

Marissa nods, "She's a lucky lady to have you."

Michael, Jody's brother, glances over at Marissa, "Thanks." He pauses, "She's pretty wonderful herself."

Marissa glances around, "She seems to be."

Michael, Jody's brother, and Marissa continue to walk the perimeter of the camp and talk while everyone else continues to watch Shadow and Lucky wear themselves out playing.

Its been a long, but uneventful drive towards Alabama. Everyone was worried when they reached Meridian that there might be trouble, but they made it through without any problems. The convoy is nearing the Alabama state line. Jody is back in the car with Shana, Zach and Tyler while Chad is driving Allen's Tahoe now with Amber and Rachel riding with him.

Lisa keeps her eyes on the road and the back of Shana's car. Ryan, Codi and Rochelle are looking around to make sure they don't see anything like zombies or other survivors.

Rochelle sighs, "I can't wait to get to the campsite for tonight. This has been a long, slow day."

Lisa smiles at her daughter, "Yeah, which I'm kind of glad. We needed another uneventful day."

Codi chimes in, "You can say that again."

Ryan continues to look around, "You know, we've probably traveled at least halfway to Fort Pulaski, if not more than halfway."

Lisa nods while watching the road, "Oh yeah, I'd say at least halfway. We've done pretty good given what we've had to go through and how we've had to adapt to a world full of zombies and dangerous people."

Ryan nods in agreement, "We sure have. I mean, to make it this far and only lose two people so far other than the people that left on their own. I'd say we've been lucky so far."

Lucky looks up at Ryan, thinking Ryan was talking to him.

Codi smiles at Lucky's reaction, "Yeah, its been luck along with us knowing what to do and everyone pitching in to do their part." She pauses, "But even two is too many."

Rochelle nods in agreement, "It sure is."

Lisa sighs, "Yeah, but reality is that we'll probably lose more before this is over and we make it to Fort Pulaski." She pauses, "I don't want to see it happen, but the odds are definitely against us."

It gets quiet in Lisa's Jeep as everyone thinks about what Lisa said. None of them want to think about it, but they each know that they will probably lose more people on the trip before they reach their destination.

The sun is getting lower in the evening sky as the convoy has crossed into Alabama, gotten off the interstate and passed the town of Bellamy. Shana glances around as she drives the car along the highway, knowing that they are getting close to their stopping point for the night. Jody, Zach and Tyler are keeping a watch out for zombies and other survivors, but also for the river which is where they plan on camping for the night.

Jody looks over at Shana, "You might start slowing down, I'm sure it's coming up real soon."

Shana starts to slow down.

Zach glances around, "We made pretty good time."

Shana glances in the rearview mirror, "Remember son, we're in the eastern time zone now so it's actually 5pm."

Zach nods, "Oh yeah."

Tyler speaks up, "I think I see the river."

Jody looks ahead and spots a bridge, "It sure is, good eyes Ty." He pauses, "We'll stop on the far side of the river."

Shana nods, "Okay."

Shana slows the car down as they near the bridge. Jody, Zach and Tyler continue to look around, but they don't see anything. Shana drives across the bridge and once she is sure she is far enough for everyone to make it across the bridge, Shana pulls over on the side of the highway. Shana puts the car in park and shuts it off. The rest of the convoy pulls in behind Shana's car as Jody, Shana, Zach and Tyler get out.

The rest of the group gets out of their vehicles and makes their way over to Jody, Shana, Zach and Tyler.

Jody glances around, "This is a good spot. We got some trees around for cover and a good open area by the river."

Ken glances around, "Well, let's get to it so we can get the dogs taken care of and eat after we get camp set up."

Zach and Tyler already know what to do and head off to stand watch while everyone else heads off to get their things and set up camp.

CHAPTER 50

Its been a couple hours since camp was set up. Everyone has finished eating and the dogs have been fed and walked. Shana and Ashley are on watch now. The evening air has cooled some and the wind has picked up a bit, the signs that a storm is coming.

Lisa and Jody make their way from their tent where they have been planning the next day of travel and they walk over to where the rest of the group is waiting in front of the large tent.

Jody and Lisa sit down and glance around. Zach and Tyler have already taken over watch and Ashley and Shana are back in camp. The wind is making it a little more difficult for everyone to hold onto their maps.

Ken speaks, "I think we got a storm catching up to us."

Lindsey nods, "Most definitely."

Jody glances around, "Well, maybe it will hold off until we are gone in the morning."

Ashley smiles, "That would be nice."

Lisa speaks up, "Okay, we've got the travel plans for tomorrow. We'll go over them quick so everyone can get their maps put away in case it starts raining."

Jody speaks up, "Okay, our stopping point for tomorrow will be right around Tuskegee. They have a small national forest there so I'm sure we'll be able to find some water."

Lisa chimes in, "We'll stay on Highway 80 the whole way. That will take us right through part of Montgomery, but we have to chance it cause the more we try to go out and around places, the more gas we'll use."

Ken nods, "Well, that'll give us a chance to stop for more gas if we don't run into problems. It's best if we stay on top of the gas situation and not wait until we're nearly out."

Mike nods, "Absolutely. It would be a tough trip for us on foot, but even more so if we keep the dogs with us because they won't be able to go as fast or far as us."

Codi speaks up, "And I'm not leaving Lucky behind anywhere."

Jody smiles, "I don't blame you. I would never leave Shadow either."

Everyone smiles as they mark down the travel plans on their maps.

Jody questions, "How are everyone's radios? Any batteries need replaced?"

Everyone looks around and kind of motions that they are okay.

Lisa speaks up, "Good. Make sure you have your radio on your person at all times. You never know when we might get split up."

Amber sighs, "I don't even like the thought of that."

Marissa smiles, "Me either."

Ken nods, "I don't as well, but it's a possibility that we have to stay prepared for."

Shana questions, "So, are we sticking to the original plan if that does happen? Use the next stopping point to meet up at and wait as long as possible?"

Jody nods, "I think we should keep to that plan unless someone has come up with a better idea."

Ryan speaks up, "We have the radios now. We could use them to find each other and perhaps meet up sooner."

Michael, Lindsey's husband, nods, "That would work as long as you're in range. These things don't transmit much more than maybe five miles."

Michael, Jody's brother, chimes in, "Why don't we stick to the regular plan. If your able to reach someone on the radio, then meet up with them if you can."

Chad nods, "That sounds good to me."

Rochelle speaks up, "We just have to make sure that someone is always with Daniel because he doesn't have a radio." She pauses, "I'll do my best to stay with him, but if something happens to me, someone else needs to watch for him."

Jody nods, "Absolutely. Daniel will be taken care of as well as Zach and Tyler."

A big gust of wind kicks up and nearly rips the maps out of everyone's hands.

Ken looks around, "Okay, let's get the maps put away and get back to our watch rotation. Try to get some rest tonight because we are driving across the whole state tomorrow."

Everyone folds up their maps and gets up to head their separate ways for the night.

Jody and Lisa are on watch now as it is nearly sunrise. Jody is wearing his ACU digital camouflage uniform and H-Harness gear except now he has his poncho on as well since the rain has arrived. Lisa is wearing her urban digital camouflage uniform and a poncho as well. It is nearly sunrise, but with the dark clouds and rain falling, it's hard to tell as the visibility is very poor.

Jody looks at Lisa, "Let's wake everyone up so they can get ready. It's going to take a little longer with the rain."

Lisa nods and heads off to camp as Jody continues to walk the perimeter of the camp. Lisa returns in a few minutes.

Lisa smiles, "They're all up and moving."

Jody smiles back, "And none too happy about the rain I'm sure."

Lisa chuckles, "Probably not."

Jody glances around and he can't see much, "Why don't you go ahead and load up your personal belongings, then I'll do mine when you're done."

Lisa nods, "Okay."

Lisa heads off to her tent. Lisa already has her stuff packed since she knew she was going to be on watch when it was time to leave. Lisa steps into the tent and sees Shana and Ashley slowly getting ready. Lisa grabs her things, including her sleeping bag, and runs off to her Jeep. Lisa loads up her belongings, then goes to find Jody.

Lisa walks up to Jody, "Okay, your turn."

Jody nods and heads off to the tent.

Jody stops by the doorway into the tent, "Ladies, it's me."

Ashley replies, "Come on in, it's okay. We haven't started changing yet."

Jody steps into the tent, "Wonderful weather we're having."

Shana smiles, "Oh yeah, it's great."

Ashley chuckles as Jody picks up his stuff, including his sleeping bag, and heads off for his dad's van which is where he's kept his things since all that fits in the car is Shana, Zach and Tyler's things. Once Jody is done, he returns to standing watch with Lisa.

Shana and Ashley are in their tent getting ready. Shana puts on her gray t-shirt, faded blue jeans, tennis shoes and baseball cap. Shana also puts on her gray pullover hoodie.

Ashley puts on her black tank top over her white tank top, pair of faded blue jeans and her tennis shoes. Ashley also puts on her yellow, zip up hooded jacket.

Shana and Ashley pack up the rest of their things as they listen to the rain on the tent.

Shana looks at Ashley, "Ready?"

Ashley smiles and shakes her head, "No, but let's go."

Shana and Ashley leave their shotguns in the tent as they head off to load up their personal belongings and sleeping bags.

Rochelle, Zach, Tyler and Daniel are getting ready in the large tent as Shadow and Lucky are waiting patiently for their chance to go outside. Rochelle puts on her black top, blue jeans and tennis shoes. Rochelle also puts on her blue, zip up jacket.

Zach changes into his red t-shirt, blue jeans, tennis shoes and puts on his boonie hat. Zach also puts on his black and gray, skull zip up hooded jacket. Tyler changes into his camouflage t-shirt, camouflage pants, tennis shoes and puts on his boonie hat. Tyler also puts on his camouflage, zip up jacket.

Once she is done, Rochelle helps Daniel get changed. Daniel puts on his blue shirt, blue jeans and tennis shoes. Daniel also puts on his blue, zip up jacket.

Once Rochelle, Zach, Tyler and Daniel are changed, they pack up their personal belongings. Tyler leaves his shotgun in the tent along with the dogs as they head off to the vehicles to load their things and sleeping bags. Rochelle carries Daniel's things and loads them up, then has Daniel follow her over to load up her things as Zach and Tyler head off to put their stuff in the car.

Chad, Rachel and Amber are getting ready as they listen to the rain falling on their tent. Rachel, who still seems really depressed, changes into her orange and white stripped tank top, brown cargo pants and tennis shoes. Rachel also puts on her pink, zip up hooded jacket.

Amber changes into her black t-shirt, faded blue jeans and tennis shoes. Amber also puts on her teal, zip up jacket. Chad gets dressed in his green t-shirt, faded blue jeans and tennis shoes. Chad also puts on his blue, zip up jacket.

Chad, Amber and Rachel gather up their belongings and sleeping bags. Chad leaves his shotgun in the tent as the three of them hurry off to load their things in the Tahoe.

Ken, Mike, Lindsey and Michael, Lindsey's husband, are in their tent getting ready. Being a smaller tent, there is not nearly as much room to work around in. Ken and Mike make sure that their backs are turned as Lindsey gets changed.

Lindsey changes into her light and dark pink checkered tank top, faded blue jeans, tennis shoes and baseball cap. Lindsey also puts on her gray, zip up hooded jacket. Michael, Lindsey's husband, gets dressed in his black t-shirt, blue jeans, tennis shoes and baseball cap. Michael also puts on his black, zip up hooded jacket.

Mike changes into his gray USMC collared shirt, blue jeans, tennis shoes and baseball cap. Mike also puts on his maroon and gray, zip up hooded jacket. Ken gets dressed in his blue t-shirt, blues jeans, black boots and baseball cap. Ken also puts on his camouflage jacket.

The four of them gather up their personal belongings. As Mike is packing, he looks at his wife's urn that is laying in his bag. Once the four of them is packed, they leave their shotguns and head off to their vehicles to load up their things and sleeping bags.

Ryan, Codi, Marissa and Michael, Jody's brother, are getting ready in their tent. It too is a smaller tent which makes in a little more difficult for the four of them. Ryan and Michael, Jody's brother, make sure their backs are turned when Codi and Marissa get changed.

Ryan changes into his black t-shirt, blue jeans, tennis shoes and his baseball cap. Ryan also puts on his black, pullover hoodie. Codi gets dressed in her gray t-shirt, blue jeans and tennis shoes. Codi also puts on her gray, pullover hoodie.

Marissa changes into her black t-shirt, faded black jeans, tennis shoes and baseball cap. Marissa also puts on her brown, blue and white, zip up hooded jacket. Michael, Jody's brother, gets dressed in his ACU digital camouflage t-shirt, faded blue jeans, tennis shoes and baseball cap. Michael, Jody's brother, also puts on his green USMC pullover hoodie.

The four of them gather up their personal belongings. Codi leaves her rifle and the other three leave their shotguns as they head off to load up their stuff and sleeping bags in their vehicles.

As Codi, Ryan, Marissa and Michael, Jody's brother, finish loading up their belongings, they notice everyone else is also loading up their things too.

Ryan glances around, "I can hardly see anything in this weather."

Michael, Jody's brother, replies, "I know. Maybe it will get better when the sun is completely up."

Marissa smiles, "I hope so."

The four of them start heading back to camp with everyone else.

CHAPTER 51

The group has made it back over to the tents. The sunrise has brought a little light to the area, but the dark clouds and rain still make the visibility poor. Zach and Tyler have taken over watch as the rest of the group is preparing to take the tents down so they can pack them up.

The group starts on the four smaller tents first while Shadow and Lucky wait inside the large tent. The group gets the tents about halfway broken down when Tyler runs up to Jody.

Tyler speaks out of breath, "Zombies, lots of them. Across the river."

Jody puts the tent down and starts making his way over to the river where Zach is still waiting. Everyone can tell that something is wrong when they see Tyler and Jody walk off. The rest of the group except for Chad, Amber and Rachel walk over to where Jody, Zach and Tyler are at by the river.

Jody and the others look across the river and can make out a large group of zombies through the rain. With the little sunlight and rainfall, they can't tell how many zombies, but they are guessing around a hundred. The zombies seem to want to get to the group of survivors, but are puzzled about how to get around the river.

Jody glances around at everyone, "Back to the tents, we have to hurry and get loaded up and get out of here."

With nearly everyone focused on the river, no one was watching the trees on the side of the river where camp was at or up by the road where the cars are parked.

Jody looks at Zach and Tyler, "Get over by camp, but keep an eye this way, okay boys?"

Zach and Tyler nod at Jody. Jody and the others turn to start back over to camp.

The group hears Amber's voice screaming, "Zombies!"

Jody and the others are surprised by the scream and run back towards camp. When they arrive, the group sees a huge group of zombies coming out of the trees from the east and a large group of zombies coming from by the highway. All together, there is nearly three hundred zombies or more.

Jody yells, "Forget the tents! Get the dogs, get to the cars and get out of here as fast as you can!"

Jody turns his attention to the zombies coming from by the road and the cars. Jody brings his AR-15 up from under his poncho, takes aim and fires. A zombie falls to the ground.

Codi and Mike run for the large tent where Lucky and Shadow are at. The zombies are closing in on the group as everyone else besides Mike and Codi start shooting. Chad, Rachel and Amber realize they are in a bad spot and they start to slowly make their way towards the Tahoe.

Michael, Jody's brother, runs over to Shana, "Quick, let's go!" He looks at Zach and Tyler, "Boys, follow us!"

Michael, Jody's brother, and Shana start heading towards the vehicles and shooting as they walk. Zach and Tyler are close behind them also shooting.

Rochelle has Daniel next to her as Lindsey and Michael, Lindsey's husband, come running up. Michael, Lindsey's husband, drops his empty shotgun and picks up

Daniel. Michael, Lindsey's husband, draws his pistol and starts for the vehicles with Rochelle and Lindsey right behind him.

Lindsey hears a scream and looks off to her right. Chad is laying on the ground with two zombies on top of him and Amber is trapped by zombies near where Chad is at. Lindsey starts to head towards Amber to try and help her. Michael, Lindsey's husband, Rochelle and Daniel don't realize Lindsey is no longer with them.

Mike tosses his empty shotgun on the ground and gets Shadow out of the tent. Mike hooks Shadow's leash on as Shadow is looking around and growling at all the zombies. Mike draws his pistol and turns towards the vehicles. A zombie is nearly on top of him. Mike raises his pistol and fires quickly. The shot is true as the zombie falls at Mike's feet. Mike pulls on the leash and starts making his way towards the vehicles with Shadow.

Codi is right behind Mike at the large tent. Codi fires her last shot from her rifle, then drops it on the ground. Codi picks up Lucky and draws her pistol. Codi looks around trying to spot Ryan, but the zombies are everywhere and she can't see him. Codi fires at a zombie and starts to make her way towards the vehicles.

Jody and Lisa start moving towards the vehicles and firing at any zombie they can see. As one zombie falls, two more seem to appear in its place. Jody looks around and spots Rachel trapped by the back of the large tent and starts back over to help her. Lisa is so focused on the zombies, she doesn't see Jody leave.

Ashley runs up next to Lisa and fires at a zombie with her last shotgun shell. Ashley drops her shotgun and draws her pistol. Lisa fires her last shot from her shotgun. Lisa quickly switches the shotgun to her right hand and draws her pistol with her left hand. Lisa and Ashley continue to fire as they make their way towards the vehicles.

Ken and Marissa have stuck to each other's side and have been slowly making their way towards the vehicles. The zombies seem to be everywhere and the hundred yards to the vehicles seems like a mile. Marissa catches something out of the corner of her eye and turns to her right. Marissa screams out in pain as she turns because her leg was stuck and didn't turn. A loud snap and pop sounds out from Marissa's right knee.

Marissa falls to the ground and drops her shotgun. Marissa grabs her knee as a zombie closes in. Marissa sees the zombie and tries to focus, but the pain is excruciating. As the zombie gets to a few feet away, Ken turns and fires his last shotgun shell and blows the zombie's head clean off.

Ken steps over and helps Marissa to her feet, "Come on, we got to get out of here!"

Marissa wraps her left arm around Ken and draws her pistol. Ken switches his shotgun to his left hand and draws his pistol with his right hand. Ken and Marissa slowly make their way towards the vehicles.

Michael, Jody's brother, Shana, Zach and Tyler have quickly made their way by the main portion of the zombies and they are nearing the vehicles. Zach and Tyler both fire their last shots. Shana and Michael, Jody's brother, both fire their last shots from their shotguns. Zach reloads as Shana hands her shotgun to Tyler to carry.

A zombie closes in quickly on Shana as she tries to draw her pistol. Suddenly, the butt of a shotgun comes across and smashes into the side of the zombie's head, knocking the zombie away. Seeing her chance, Shana gets her pistol out and fires at the zombie, killing it.

Seeing a clear shot to the vehicles, Michael, Jody's brother, Shana, Zach and Tyler make a run for it. The four of them make it to the Hyundai. Zach and Tyler quickly get in the backseat. Michael, Jody's brother, climbs in the passenger's seat and Shana gets in the driver's seat. The four of them quickly shut the doors and lock them as a zombie hits the passenger's side of the car.

Michael, Jody's brother, yells, "Get us out of here!"

Shana glances around as she starts the car, "What about the others?!"

Michael, Jody's brother, looks at the zombie that is desperately trying to get in the car, "We can't wait, there are too many! Go!"

Shana puts the car in gear and speeds away to the east.

Michael, Lindsey's husband, Rochelle and Daniel have been navigating their way through the horde of zombies towards the vehicles. Michael, Lindsey's husband, is doing his best to shoot the zombies while carrying Daniel.

Mike has made his way around most of the zombies with Shadow. Mike knows he is nearly out of ammo that he has on him for his pistol. Mike shoots two more zombies and notices his pistol is empty. However, Mike sees a clear shot to his van.

Mike pulls on the leash, "Come on big boy! Let's get the stick!"

Mike starts speeding up. Shadow, having heard his favorite word which describes his favorite toy, starts running after Mike. A zombie steps over to try and cut them off, but Mike shoves the zombie hard without slowing down and the zombie falls to the ground. Mike and Shadow finally reach his van. Mike gets Shadow in the van, then climbs in the driver's seat. Mike doesn't see any zombies too close so he starts the van up, but waits.

Lisa and Ashley have made their way through the mass of zombies, firing as much as they can and reloading as quickly as possible. Both ladies know they are running short on ammunition, but they can see the vehicles ahead of them and very few zombies now stand in their way. Lisa fires a couple more times and notices her pistol is empty. Ashley turns and sees a zombie closing in towards Lisa. Lisa is reloading with her last magazine as Ashley fires at the zombie. The shot is true and the zombie falls to the ground.

Lisa and Ashley start moving again. The two of them realize that they have made it through and around most of the zombies and have a shot to get to the vehicles. Lisa and Ashley go for broke and sprint for the vehicles as some zombies spot them, turn and start heading after them.

Mike lowers his window as he sees Lisa and Ashley getting closer, "Over here!"

Lisa and Ashley see Mike in his van and turn towards the van. Lisa and Ashley finally make it to the van. Lisa climbs in the passenger's seat as Ashley gets in the back with Shadow. Mike raises his window and notices about ten zombies headed towards them.

Mike glances at Lisa, "We're not going to be able to wait."

Lisa sighs, "Go, we'll try to link up with them later."

Mike puts the van in drive and speeds away as the zombies continue towards where they were parked.

As more of the group is making its way towards the vehicles, more zombies are turning and heading towards the vehicles as well.

Lindsey reaches Amber and fires at a zombie, killing it just before it grabs Amber. Lindsey pumps her shotgun, but notices it is empty. Lindsey switches her shotgun to her left hand and draws her pistol with her right hand.

Lindsey looks at Amber, "Let's go! Watch our back!"

Lindsey and Amber turn towards the vehicles and see a wall of zombies in their way. Lindsey starts firing at the zombies and so does Amber. Lindsey starts moving to her left when she hears a scream behind her. Lindsey spins around and sees that a zombie has come up behind them, grabbed Amber and has bitten her on the shoulder.

The zombie tackles Amber to the ground and bites her again. Lindsey steps over and shoots the zombie in the head, killing it. Amber is bleeding profusely from her shoulder and neck. Lindsey knows that its too late to save Amber. Lindsey looks around and doesn't spot any of the others. Lindsey starts to worry, but keeps it under control and starts trying to find her way to the vehicles and away from the zombies.

Jody runs up to Rachel and fires his rifle at a zombie that is nearly on top of her. The zombie falls dead to the ground.

Jody looks at Rachel, "Are you okay?"

Rachel shakes her head, "No."

Jody looks down and sees that Rachel has been bitten on her left forearm.

Rachel looks at Jody, "Go. Leave me here. I'll try to draw them away."

Jody nods at Rachel. Rachel starts towards the river as Jody turns back towards the direction of the vehicles. Jody looks around, trying to spot anyone else from the group which he now realizes he has been separated from.

Michael, Lindsey's husband, Rochelle and Daniel have made their way to the Trailblazer and they notice two vehicles already missing. Michael, Lindsey's husband, sets Daniel down and looks around. Rochelle helps Daniel into his car seat.

Michael, Lindsey's husband, finally notices that Lindsey is no longer with them and he also sees a good sized group of zombies getting closer to their location.

Michael, Lindsey's husband, looks at Rochelle, "Did you see what happened to Lindsey?!"

Rochelle shakes her head as she climbs in next to Daniel, "No!"

Michael, Lindsey's husband, catches motion out of the corner of his eye and spins to his left, bringing his pistol up.

Ryan holds his hands up while running up to the Trailblazer, "Wait!"

Michael, Lindsey's husband, lowers his pistol, "Have you seen any of the others?!"

Ryan shakes his head, "No! I got separated from Codi when she went after Lucky!"

Ryan and Michael, Lindsey's husband, looks around and sees the zombies closing in on them.

Rochelle yells from inside the Trailblazer, "We have to get out of here!"

Ryan hurries over and gets in the passenger's seat. Michael, Lindsey's husband, is hesitant about leaving.

Ryan yells, "I know you don't want to leave without knowing what happened to her, neither do I, but we have to get out of here before those zombies get here!"

Michael, Lindsey's husband, reluctantly climbs into the driver's seat and closes the door as the zombies are a mere hundred feet away. Michael, Lindsey's husband, starts up the Trailblazer and looks in the rearview mirror. Seeing Daniel and knowing he must keep him safe, Michael, Lindsey's husband, puts the Trailblazer in gear and speeds away as the zombies nearly reach them.

Ken and Marissa have continued to battle their way towards the vehicles as they hear the third vehicle speed away. Ken fires his last shot from his pistol and starts to reload. Ken spots a zombie closing in on them when suddenly the zombie is hit in the head by a bullet and falls to the ground. Ken looks over his shoulder and sees Codi, carrying Lucky, running up to him and Marissa.

Codi smiles, "Am I glad to finally see someone else!"

Ken nods and glances around, "I think we're nearly in the clear!"

Ken finishes reloading as Marissa and Codi shoot a couple more zombies. Seeing their chance, Ken, Marissa and Codi start speeding up as fast as they can with Marissa being hurt. Ken fires two more times and the last two zombies between them and the vehicles fall.

Ken, Marissa and Codi stop at Lisa's Jeep, noticing which three vehicles are missing, but also noticing the zombies that have made their way back over near the vehicles as they were chasing the others who have already left.

Ken yells, "Get in!"

Marissa hops and hobbles her way around to the passenger's side and gets in as Ken gets in the driver's seat. Codi opens the back door and sets Lucky in the backseat, then climbs in next to him.

Ken starts up the Jeep as a zombie crashes into the back of the vehicle, beating on the back window, trying to get in. Ken puts the Jeep in drive and speeds away.

Lindsey hears the fourth vehicle speed off and wonders if she is now alone. Lindsey fires and kills another zombie, but notices her pistol is empty again. Lindsey starts to reload with her last magazine, knowing she doesn't have enough ammo to keep herself alive if she is alone. As she reloads, Lindsey sees a zombie closing in and reaching out for her.

Lindsey realizes she isn't going to be able to react in time when she suddenly sees the zombie's head snap back and the zombie falls at her feet. Lindsey is shocked, yet happy as she knows now that she is not alone.

Jody runs up to Lindsey, "You okay?!"

Lindsey nods, "Yes!" She pauses, "I thought everyone was gone!"

Jody glances around, "So did I until I spotted you!" He pauses, "We're not going to be able to make it to the vehicles, there are too many. That's why I started this way and saw you!"

Jody fires his AR-15 once more and kills another zombie, but he notices his rifle is empty. Jody switches his rifle over to his left hand and draws his pistol with his right hand.

Lindsey glances around, "What now?!"

Jody points with his pistol, "This way! We'll skirt down the river and try to lose them using the trees and water as a barrier!"

Jody and Lindsey each fire again and two more zombies fall. Lindsey looks in the direction Jody was talking about and she doesn't see any zombies except for a group of them which looks like they are eating something on the ground by the river.

Jody and Lindsey start running and they quickly start to put some distance between them and the zombies which continue to stagger after them as quickly as they can.

CHAPTER 52

Shana continues to drive the car east along Highway 80 through the pouring rain. The road visibility is not very good and with the other abandoned cars on the highway, Shana can't go as fast as she'd like. Shana, Michael, Jody's brother, Zach and Tyler are each wondering the same thing, did anyone else make it.

Shana sees a turn off ahead, but isn't really sure if the highway they want to stay on goes straight or if they have to turn. As they get closer, Michael, Jody's brother, sees a couple of zombies in the middle of the highway just beyond the turnoff.

Michael, Jody's brother, looks at Shana, "We can't risk hitting them and damaging the car so turn right at the intersection."

Shana nods and starts slowing down. The two zombies see the car and start staggering towards it. Shana quickly turns onto the new road and speeds up. The zombies are quickly lost in the rearview mirror.

Shana glances around, "We need to find out where we're at before we get too lost."

Zach and Tyler continue to look around and Zach spots a highway sign.

Zach speaks up, "Look, there's a highway sign."

Shana slows the car down some so they can read the sign as they pass by it.

Tyler speaks out loud as they drive passed the sign, "Highway 28 south."

Michael, Jody's brother, glances around, "Okay, I think we're safe for now. Let's pull over, get one of the maps out and figure out what to do next to get back heading east."

Shana nods, "Sounds good to me."

Shana slows the car down and pulls over onto the edge of the highway. Shana puts the car in park, but leaves it running.

Mike continues to drive his van away from the campsite. Lisa and Ashley keep a watch out for more zombies since they got turned around on the highway because some zombies were blocking their way when they first pulled away from the campsite. The three of them each wonder the same thing though, who else escaped.

Mike glances around through the rain, "We're headed in the wrong direction. We need to find a way back east."

Lisa continues to look around, "Maybe we can find another highway around here going north or south that will lead to another one headed back east."

Ashley spots a turnoff up ahead, "Look, I think there's another highway coming up."

Mike starts to slow the van down. Shadow is sitting in between Mike and Lisa. Shadow is staring at the windshield wipers because he loves to chase them back and forth across the windshield.

Lisa spots the highway sign, "Its Highway 28 north." She pauses, "That's as good as any to start with."

Mike nods, "I'm all for it."

Mike slows the van some more and turns onto the new highway.

Ashley glances around, "We should probably stop and look at a map if we have one. That way we won't get too lost if we take a wrong turn somewhere."

Lisa nods, "Good idea."

Mike glances around again, "I don't see any zombies so this is as good a place as any."

Mike starts to slow the van back down and pulls over onto the edge of the highway. Mike puts the van in park, but leaves it running.

Michael, Lindsey's husband, continues to drive the Trailblazer east on Highway 80 away from the campsite. Ryan and Rochelle keep looking around trying their best to see if they can spot anything through the pouring rain. Each one of them is wondering, who else escaped the campsite.

Ryan sees an intersection ahead, "Look, an intersection. Let's see which way the highway goes."

Michael, Lindsey's husband, starts slowing down the Trailblazer. As they approach the intersection, Rochelle is the first to spot the highway sign.

Rochelle speaks up, "It says Highway 80 east is straight and Highway 28 south is right."

Ryan looks over at Michael, Lindsey's husband, and questions, "Which way do you think we should go?"

Michael, Lindsey's husband, starts to slow down the Trailblazer as they approach the intersection. The three of them look off to the right down Highway 28 and they see a couple of zombies staggering south along the highway.

Michael, Lindsey's husband, replies, "I say we avoid those things and keep going straight for now."

Ryan nods, "Sounds good to me."

Michael, Lindsey's husband, starts to speed back up. Ryan and Rochelle continue to look around. They travel a little farther on the highway when they see a problem up ahead on the highway.

Ryan sighs, "Looks like the highway is blocked."

Michael, Lindsey's husband, starts to slow down the Trailblazer again.

Rochelle questions, "Should we try going off the highway and around them?"

Michael, Lindsey's husband, glances around, "No, that's too risky. We might get stuck in the mud or grass."

Ryan spots a small road coming up to their right, "Hey, look over there. I think it's a road."

Rochelle sees what Ryan is talking about, "It sure is."

Michael, Lindsey's husband, slows the Trailblazer down some more as they pass a sign that shows the name of the road. It is County Highway 57 south. Michael, Lindsey's husband, turns right onto the small back highway and speeds up some.

Ryan glances around, "Why don't we pull over and look at a map if we have one. Find out where we're at so we don't get lost."

Rochelle nods, "I like that idea."

Michael, Lindsey's husband, slows the Trailblazer down and stops on the edge of the county highway, but leaves the vehicle running.

Ken continues to drive the Jeep along Highway 80 east. Marissa is doing her best to deal with the pain of her right knee. Marissa knows that the injury is bad. Codi continues to look around to see if she can spot any zombies. The three of them each wonder the same thing, who all made it out of the camp alive. Lucky continues to sit next to Codi, wondering what's going on.

Ken speaks as he focuses on the road, "There were three vehicles already gone when we left. Maybe we can catch up to them."

Codi glances around, "That sure would be nice."

Marissa continues to hold her knee, "I think I hurt it bad."

Ken glances at Marissa, "Just hang in there. We're safe for now. I promise, no marathons."

Marissa manages a smile.

Codi points up ahead, "Look, another highway."

Ken slows the Jeep down so they can see what the highway signs read.

As they get closer, Codi reads the sign out loud, "Highway 80 east is straight and Highway 28 south is right."

Ken nods, "We keep going straight then."

Ken speeds the Jeep back up as Codi continues to keep an eye out and Marissa does her best to contain the pain in her right knee. Not too much farther down the highway and Ken and Codi see a problem up ahead.

Ken sighs, "Looks like the highway is blocked."

Codi gets a frustrated look, then spots a highway sign, "Look, County Highway 57 south is coming up. We could go that way and find another way around."

Ken sighs and shakes his head, "I don't like the idea of getting off the main highway right now. I know its risky, but I'm going to go off the road and around those cars."

Marissa sighs through the pain, "I hope we don't get stuck. There is no way I can walk."

Ken slows down as he approaches the abandoned cars blocking the highway. Ken starts to weave over to his left as he figures that is the safest side from what he sees. Ken drives the Jeep off the highway onto the ground next to the highway. The Jeep swerves and fishtails a second as the tires spin, but Ken holds the Jeep steady enough and it continues to move forward.

Once he clears the five abandoned cars, Ken starts to bring the Jeep back up to the highway. The tires start to spin again and the Jeep starts slowing down due to losing traction. Ken let's off the gas for a moment and when he feels the tires regain traction, he steps on the gas again. The Jeep lunges forward and then starts to lose traction again. However, the forward momentum is enough and Ken pulls the Jeep back up onto the highway. Ken starts to speed up again.

Codi sighs, "That was a bit scary."

Marissa agrees, "I thought we were stuck for sure."

Ken smiles, "Just got to have faith."

Ken and Codi continue to glance around as they continue on down Highway 80 east.

Jody and Lindsey have continued to run south along the riverbank, putting as much distance between them and the zombies as possible. Jody and Lindsey finally slow up to a walk.

Lindsey looks around trying to catch her breath, "How far do you think we've gone?"

Jody replies trying to catch his breath, "I'd say two or three miles at least, maybe more."

Lindsey shakes her head, "I don't know how much longer I can keep this up."

Jody takes a deep breath, "Me either. We're going to tire out, they won't."

Lindsey continues to catch her breath, "Any ideas?"

Jody looks around some more, "We have a big head start on them. If we can find a place to hide out for awhile, they will lose track of us. Then we can figure out what to do after that."

Lindsey nods as she is finally catching her breath, "Sounds good to me."

Jody nods and smiles, "Now we just have to find a place to hold up in."

Jody and Lindsey look around some more and Lindsey thinks she sees something in the distance off to their left.

Lindsey points, "Over there, is that a barn or house?"

Jody looks off to where Lindsey is pointing and sees some kind of building through the pouring rain.

Jody nods, "I think so, let's go check it out." He pauses, "Good eyes girl."

Lindsey smiles and the two of them start jogging towards the building. As they get closer, Lindsey and Jody can make out the building now and it's a nice, big barn. As Jody and Lindsey get even closer, they notice that the barn appears to be in good shape.

Jody and Lindsey stop at the barbwire fence that is about fifty yards from the barn. Jody helps Lindsey through the fence, then Lindsey helps Jody through. Jody and Lindsey cautiously approach the barn. Lindsey and Jody have their pistols ready, just in case they run into zombies or survivors.

Lindsey and Jody reach the barn doors and they have yet to see or hear anything. Jody holsters his pistol and leans his rifle against the wall of the barn. Lindsey covers Jody as Jody opens the barn door enough for them to squeeze through.

Jody grabs his rifle and draws his pistol again. Jody steps inside the barn with Lindsey right behind him. Jody and Lindsey look around, but don't see anything and they don't hear anything. Most of all, Lindsey and Jody doesn't smell anything.

Jody holsters his pistol and closes the door behind them. Jody latches the doors shut. Jody draws his pistol again. Lindsey and Jody walk around the entire barn. They don't see anything to indicate zombies were present or other survivors. As they pass by each door and window, Jody locks them so no one else can get inside the barn.

Lindsey glances around, "Well, its empty and we got it all locked up. What now?"

Jody looks around and spots a ladder leading up to the loft, "I say we climb up in the loft and if its clear, we pull the ladder up and just wait for awhile."

Lindsey nods, "Sounds good to me."

Jody walks over to the ladder and starts to climb up it. Once Jody makes it up to the loft, Lindsey climbs up the ladder. Jody and Lindsey make sure the loft is clear, then pull the ladder up and lay it next to the edge of the loft.

Jody and Lindsey walk over by the loft doors and sit down. Jody pulls out one of his canteens from his belt and hands it to Lindsey.

CHAPTER 53

Michael, Jody's brother, and Shana are stopped and looking at one of the maps while Zach and Tyler are still keeping an eye out for zombies. Shana and Michael, Jody's brother, are trying to figure out where they are at and how to get back to the main highway without backtracking.

Michael, Jody's brother, points at the map, "We are right here."

Shana nods as the rain continues to pour down, "Looks like if we keep going south we will run into County Highway 57 and we can take that back north to Highway 80."

Michael, Jody's brother, sighs, "That's still fairly close. I'd like to put more distance between us and the horde before we turn back north." He pauses, "What if we continue south to County Highway 19. It looks like it runs north, straight into Demopolis and back to Highway 80."

Shana looks over the map and nods, "That sounds like a good idea."

Zach questions, "Do either of you have your radio on you?"

Shana reaches down and unclips the radio from her waist, "Yep."

Zach glances around, "Maybe we can reach the others if they made it."

Shana sighs, "Its worth a shot."

Michael, Jody's brother, shakes his head, "In this weather, it won't transmit very far or well."

Shana clicks the button and speaks into the radio, "This is Shana, is anyone out there?"

Shana releases the button and the four of them wait. After a minute, Shana tries again and the four of them wait again for any response.

After another minute, Michael, Jody's brother, shakes his head, "We're going to have to wait till the storm passes." He looks at Shana, "Let's just continue on for now with our plan."

Shana nods and clips the radio back to her waist. Shana puts the car in drive and starts to slowly drive south on Highway 28.

Mike, Lisa and Ashley are sitting in the van looking around to make sure no zombies are in the area. Its still hard to see well with the heavy storm pouring rain on them. Mike pulls out his map and the three of them start looking it over.

Mike speaks, "I know its dangerous, but we've got to get circled back around."

Lisa glances over the map, "If we don't just turn around and head back and we take a more roundabout way, then maybe the zombies will have wandered off by the time we pass back by."

Ashley nods, "I like that idea."

Mike points at the map, "We are here. If we go north a bit further, we will reach County Highway 23."

Lisa nods, "Look at this. We should pass a turn off for Larkin Road here soon. If we go north to County Road 23 and take it east, it intersects with Larkin Road also."

Ashley chimes in, "I see what you're saying. Go north to 23, then bring Larkin Road back down to the highway we're on, then back to Highway 80 and back pass our old campsite."

Lisa nods, "Yep. By then the zombies may have wandered off where we can drive on by and get back on track."

Mike nods, "I think it's a good plan." He pauses, "Does either of you have a radio on you that you can use while I drive?"

Lisa nods, "I do."

Mike sighs, "I know it's a long shot, especially in this weather, but give it a try and see if we can reach anyone."

Lisa pulls the radio out and clicks the button, "This is Lisa, is there anyone out there who can hear me. Please respond."

Mike, Ashley and Lisa sit quietly for a minute. Shadow is just looking at them, wondering what is going on. Lisa tries again and the three of them wait.

After another minute, Lisa shakes her head, "I don't think so."

Ashley let's out a dejected sigh, "I hope the others made it."

Mike nods as he hands the map to Lisa, "Me too."

Mike puts the van in drive and slowly starts driving north.

Michael, Lindsey's husband, and Ryan are looking over one of their maps while Rochelle is trying to keep Daniel occupied after what has happened.

Ryan points at the map, "We're here right now. We need to find a way to get back around to Highway 80 beyond the road block."

Michael, Lindsey's husband, speaks while looking over the map, "Looks like if we keep going south we will run into County Highway 21 and we can take that northeast to County Highway 19." He pauses, "Looks like County Highway 19 runs right into Highway 80 at Demopolis."

Ryan nods, "It sure looks that way. I like the sound of that plan."

Rochelle questions, "I don't suppose either of you have your radio on you?"

Michael, Lindsey's husband, shakes his head, "I don't. It's in my belongings in the back."

Ryan nods, "I've got mine."

Michael, Lindsey's husband, glances around, "It won't transmit very well in this weather, but its worth a shot."

Ryan pulls the radio out and clicks the button, "This is Ryan, is there anyone out there who can hear me?"

It gets quiet for a minute.

Daniel looks at Michael, Lindsey's husband, "Where's mom?"

Michael, Lindsey's husband, looks back at Daniel, "I'm not sure Daniel, but I'm sure she is okay."

Ryan tries the radio again, but they get no response.

Rochelle sighs, "I don't like not knowing."

Ryan shakes his head, "Me either."

Michael, Lindsey's husband, glances around, "Well, let's just keep going and we'll keep trying every so often to reach someone on the radio."

Michael, Lindsey's husband, puts the Trailblazer back in drive and starts driving slowly south.

Ken continues to drive east on Highway 80 as the vehicle with him, Marissa, Codi and Lucky are nearing the town of Demopolis. Ken starts to slow the Jeep down as they get closer to town.

Ken glances around through the pouring rain, "I'm thinking we should keep going straight on this highway. This is a smaller town so we shouldn't have a problem getting through it quickly."

Codi nods, "Yeah, I think so too."

Marissa has finally gotten to where the pain is bearable, but she knows her knee is done, "As long as we don't have to walk or run."

Ken slows up a little more as they pass the city limit sign. Ken pulls his radio from his belt.

Codi looks at Ken, "Do you think it will work in this weather?"

Ken shakes his head, "No, but its worth a try." He clicks the button, "This is Ken, anyone out there hear me? Respond, over."

It gets quiet in the Jeep except for the sound of the rain. Ken tries again with the radio as they slowly make their way through town. Codi and Marissa are keeping a close eye out for any zombies or survivors.

Ken puts his radio up, "Storm is too heavy right now." He pauses as he looks in the rearview mirror, "Good news is that I can see clearer skies behind us. Maybe the storm will pass in the next hour or so."

Codi smiles her cute smile, "I hope so. It'd be nice for at least one thing to go our way right now."

Marissa nods, "Amen."

Ken continues to drive the Jeep through town while Codi and Marissa keep a look out. They don't encounter anything and soon find themselves leaving the east side of town and continuing east on Highway 80.

Jody and Lindsey are still sitting in the loft of the barn, listening to the rain falling outside. Jody has removed his poncho and hung it up to dry.

Jody starts to remove his boots, "I don't suppose you have your radio on you? My batteries are low in mine."

Lindsey smiles her beautiful smile, "Actually, I do." She pauses, "Do you think it'll work in this weather?"

Jody sets his boots off to the side and removes his socks, "Not really, but its worth a try."

Lindsey pulls her radio out and clicks the button, "This is Lindsey, is there anyone out there who can hear me?"

It gets quiet in the barn except for the rain falling on the roof. Lindsey tries again, but after another minute of silence, she puts the radio away.

Jody sighs, "Well, it was a long shot."

Lindsey nods, "I wonder if any of the others made it."

Jody takes a sip of water from his other canteen, "I know I heard one vehicle drive off, maybe two. I'm not sure after that."

Lindsey nods, "I heard a couple of vehicles too." She pauses, "Did you see anyone not make it?"

Jody nods and sighs, "Yeah, Rachel didn't make it."

Lindsey sighs, "Neither did Chad or Amber."

Jody stretches, "So, that's three that we know of."

Lindsey nods slightly, "Yeah."

Jody slides his gear around and starts digging into his buttpack, "You really should get out of those wet clothes and hang them up so they can dry off."

Lindsey sighs, "That would be nice, but I don't have anything to change into."

Jody pulls out a small package with something silver looking in it, "You can cover up with this. Its an emergency sleeping bag."

Jody tosses it over to Lindsey.

Lindsey picks up the emergency sleeping bag, "Awesome."

Lindsey takes her jacket, shoes and socks off without thinking about it. Jody turns around and faces away from Lindsey as she removes her shirt.

Lindsey smiles at Jody, "Sorry, I didn't even think about that. You're such a gentleman though."

Jody smiles, "Well, you know I love you like a sister, but still, I don't need to watch you undress."

Lindsey continues to remove her clothes, "Aw, thanks. You know I love you like a bro."

Jody nods, "Thank you."

Lindsey gets all her clothes off and hangs them up to dry. Lindsey opens the package and pulls out the emergency sleeping bag. Lindsey climbs into the emergency sleeping bag and sits back down.

Lindsey glances around, "Ok, you can turn back around."

Jody turns back around and sits down. Jody smiles at Lindsey.

Lindsey takes a sip of water, "So, how long should we wait do you think?"

Jody shrugs, "Not really sure. At least till the rain quits and our stuff is dry." He pauses, "I say maybe this afternoon. That will give plenty of time for the zombies to hopefully wander off so we can return to the camp and get one of the vehicles."

Lindsey nods, "Yeah, definitely want to give plenty of time for that." She pauses, "You know, we might end up having to stay the night here."

Jody smiles, "Maybe so. At least its been warm at night so we won't have to worry about getting cold." He pauses, "But, we'll cross that bridge when we get there."

Lindsey nods, "You're right about that." She pauses, "My main concern is that we have no food."

Jody smiles, "Not exactly."

Lindsey looks at Jody, "What?"

Jody continues to smile, "I have three days of survival food rations in my buttpack. They aren't the most tasty things, but they will keep you alive."

Lindsey chuckles some, "I don't care how they taste, if its edible, I'm good with it."

Jody chuckles at Lindsey. The two of them lay back and try to relax some as they listen to the rain fall and wonder if any of the others made it out okay.

CHAPTER 54

Shana continues to drive the car south on Highway 28. The rain is still coming down, but not as heavy as before as Shana and the others can see the sky clearing off to the west.

Michael, Jody's brother, continues to look around, "We should be getting close to the turnoff for County Highway 19."

Zach, who now has the radio from Shana, clicks the button on the radio, "This is Zach, anyone out there?"

As everyone waits for a response, Tyler points up ahead, "I think I see a turn."

Michael, Jody's brother, looks back ahead and nods, "I think you're right Tyler."

Shana starts slowing the car down as they get closer to what they hope is County Highway 19. Its been a slow drive in the heavy rain, but Shana knows they can speed up some as the rain is letting up.

Michael, Jody's brother, spots the highway sign, "Yep, its our turnoff."

Shana slows down even more as she prepares to make the turn. Michael, Jody's brother, Zach and Tyler continue to look around for zombies and other survivors. Shana turns the car onto County Highway 19 heading north towards Demopolis.

Shana glances around, "Well, before long we should be back on Highway 80 and headed back east."

Michael, Jody's brother, nods, "And maybe even running into some of the others."

Zach sighs, "That would be nice."

It gets quiet in the car again as Shana continues to drive slowly north towards Demopolis.

Mike turns his van onto County Highway 23 east as the rain starts to lighten up. Lisa and Ashley continue to look around to make sure there are no zombies in the area.

Mike glances around, "We should reach Larkin Road pretty soon."

Lisa nods, "Yeah, it should be coming up quickly."

Ashley continues to glance around, "I hope if it's a dirt road, it won't be too muddy to drive on."

Mike nods slightly, "I guess we'll see when we get there."

Lisa pulls out her radio again and clicks the button, "This is Lisa, is there anyone out there who can hear me?"

Mike and Ashley get quiet as all three of them hope to hear a response from someone. However, the radio remains silent.

Ashley looks over and pets Shadow, "Well, maybe we'll reach someone once we get back to Highway 80."

Lisa nods as she puts the radio away, "Yeah, maybe so."

Mike starts to slow down, "I think I see a road coming up."

Lisa and Ashley look up ahead and see what Mike is talking about. Mike slows the van to a stop at the turnoff as the three of them look for a road sign.

Lisa spots the sign, "Yep, this is it."

Mike turns the van onto Larkin Road. Its a back road so Mike doesn't speed up very much as they start to head back south.

Michael, Lindsey's husband, continues to drive the Trailblazer along County Highway 57 as he is looking for the turnoff to County Highway 21. Ryan continues to keep a watch out for zombies while Rochelle tries to keep Daniel calm and his mind off his mom.

Michael, Lindsey's husband, glances around, "We should be getting close to the turnoff."

Ryan pulls out his radio, "Yeah, it should be coming up anytime now." Ryan clicks the button on the radio, "This is Ryan, is there anyone out there who can hear me?"

It gets quiet in the Trailblazer as everyone hopes to hear a voice over the radio. After a minute of silence, they know its no use.

Rochelle looks up and out the windshield, "I think I see the turn coming up."

Michael, Lindsey's husband, looks back ahead and since the rain has let up some, he sees the road ahead more clearly.

Michael, Lindsey's husband, nods, "I think that's it."

Michael, Lindsey's husband, starts slowing down as they near the upcoming turnoff. Ryan looks around for zombies as he clips the radio back to his belt. Michael, Lindsey's husband, slows the Trailblazer even more as the turnoff is getting closer.

Ryan spots the road signs, "Hey, this is it."

Michael, Lindsey's husband, slows the Trailblazer to a near stop, then turns the Trailblazer onto County Highway 21 east.

Ryan nods, "Well, now we just keep going until we reach County Highway 19."

Rochelle sighs, "Maybe by then we'll be able to reach someone on the radio."

Michael, Lindsey's husband, nods slightly, "Well, if we don't, then we'll just continue on to the next stop."

It gets quiet again in the Trailblazer as Michael, Lindsey's husband, focuses on the new road ahead.

Ken continues to drive Lisa's Jeep Liberty along Highway 80 east, heading towards Montgomery. Codi is in the backseat, petting on Lucky and trying to keep her mind off what might have happened to Ryan. Marissa is sitting with her eyes closed, trying not to think about the pain in her right knee.

Ken speaks up, getting the others attention, "Looks like we're about to get to Uniontown."

Marissa opens her eyes and Codi looks up.

Marissa questions, "Is it very big?"

Ken replies, sure of himself, "No, I don't think so."

Codi glances around, "Should we go around it or through it?"

Ken is quiet for a second, then answers, "I think we'll be okay going through it. Its smaller than Demopolis."

Marissa nods, "Sounds good to me."

Ken glances around, "Try your radio Marissa, see if you can reach anyone."

Ken starts to slow down the Jeep as Marissa pulls out her radio. Codi keeps looking around for zombies as they enter the small town.

Marissa presses the button on the radio, "This is Marissa, can anyone hear me?"

Ken, Codi and Marissa get quiet as they hope to hear a response from someone. After a minute of silence, Marissa tries again. After another minute of silence, the three of them lose hope of contacting someone.

Marissa puts her radio away, "Well, nothing."

Ken continues glancing around as they are nearly through the small town, "Well, we'll just continue on for now." He pauses, "However, we're going to have to think about what we're going to do about Montgomery when we get there."

Codi questions, "What do you mean?"

Ken replies, "It's a big city and with there only being three of us, I think its too risky to go through town. If we run into trouble, we won't be able to do much about it."

Marissa speaks up, "Yeah, probably best if we go around it."

Codi pulls out the map, "I'll start looking at options."

Ken nods as he drives the Jeep out of Uniontown and they continue eastward on Highway 80.

Jody and Lindsey have just been relaxing in the loft of the barn. Jody has been checking outside every so often to see if any zombies are wandering around. Jody quietly moves back over to his resting spot after checking outside while Lindsey continues to lay inside the emergency sleeping bag.

Lindsey looks at Jody, "See anything?"

Jody shakes his head as he sits down, "Nothing yet."

Lindsey sighs, "Well, sounds like the rain is letting up some."

Jody nods, "Yeah, it is. Which is good for us. We might not have to wait all day."

Lindsey smiles, "That would be nice, but either way is good to me." She pauses, "It'd be nice to see some zombies wander by us and keep going south."

Jody nods, "Yeah, that's what I'd like to see too. I know some of them followed us out of the campsite." He pauses, "You doing okay?"

Lindsey shifts around to get more comfortable, "For the most part. Obviously I'm worried about what has happened to Daniel and Michael."

Jody sighs and tries to be reassuring, "I'm sure they made it out okay. Michael seemed very adamant about keeping Daniel safe."

Lindsey sighs, "Yeah, I'm sure Michael would rather die before letting something happen to Daniel." She pauses, "What about you?"

Jody replies, trying not to sound to sad or upset, "I'm okay. Even though my dad and brother have made it this far, I'm a realist and I know that I might eventually lose one of them."

Lindsey tries to lift Jody's spirits by being supportive, "Well, I hope not. Your brother is a good guy and your dad is awesome."

Jody smiles at Lindsey, "Thanks." He pauses, "You know, if you want to get some rest, I can wake you in a couple hours."

Lindsey smiles back at Jody, "Thanks. Probably should get a short nap, just in case." She pauses, "Once I get up, I'll let you get a nap in."

Jody nods, "Sounds good to me."

Lindsey tries to get as comfortable as she can. Lindsey closes her eyes and tries to get some rest as Jody sits and waits, keeping his ears open for any noise outside the barn.

As the different smaller groups wonder what has happened to the others, the horde of zombies that attacked their campsite has started wandering off in different directions. Most of the zombies have headed south as they were following Jody and Lindsey before losing sight of them. The rest of the zombies have started wandering off towards the east and west of the campsite.

Even with all the zombies the group killed at the campsite while escaping, at least a hundred zombies have made their way south in the direction where Jody and Lindsey ran off to and nearly fifty have went east of the campsite while about fifty more went west of the campsite.

The zombies continue to stagger their way through the woods and near the highway, looking for anything living that they can eat.

CHAPTER 55

Michael, Jody's brother, Zach and Tyler continue to look around for zombies as Shana focuses on the road. The rain has let up to a light drizzle now and the sun is starting to break through the clouds. Shana starts to slow the car down as they near the town of Demopolis.

Shana glances around as they pass the city limit sign, "Well, I hope we don't run into any problems trying to get back on Highway 80."

Michael, Jody's brother, continues to look around, "I doubt we will. This town isn't very big and we'll be through it in no time."

Zach sighs, "Good, cause I don't think the four of us could handle another incident like the campsite by ourselves."

Michael, Jody's brother, nods, "Yeah, if we run into something like that without the others around to help, I think we're in trouble."

Tyler looks around and spots a sign ahead, "I think I see the turn for the highway."

Shana looks up the road and starts to slow down.

Michael, Jody's brother, also looks ahead and spots the sign Tyler mentioned, "Yep, this is it."

Shana slows the car down some more, then turns right onto Highway 80 east. Shana speeds back up now that they are back on a major highway and the road conditions are much better.

Shana smiles, "We should be out of town in no time and headed on down the highway towards our stopping point for the day."

Michael, Jody's brother, glances around, "Hopefully when we get there, others will be waiting for us or catch up to us there." He pauses, "I'm not sure how far the four of us are going to make it on our own."

Zach speaks up, "I think we'll do okay."

Tyler nods, "Me too."

Michael, Jody's brother, and Shana both smile at Zach and Tyler's confidence. The talking dies down as they leave Demopolis and continue east on Highway 80.

Lisa and Ashley continue to keep a watch out for zombies as Mike carefully drives the van down the back road. The rain is a drizzle now and the sun is starting to break through the clouds.

Mike starts to slow the van down, "I think we're about back to Highway 28."

Lisa and Ashley look up ahead and see the road coming to an end at what looks like a highway.

Lisa nods, "I think you're right."

Ashley sighs, "Hopefully we gave enough time for the zombies to wander off."

Mike slows the van down and turns left onto Highway 28, "We'll be finding out before too long."

Mike speeds the van back up as Lisa and Ashley look around for zombies.

Lisa continues glancing around, "I'm more worried that by going out of the way and having to double back that we won't reach our assigned stopping point before dark."

She pauses, "We'll have to decide then if we stop for the night or risk traveling during the night."

Ashley starts petting Shadow who is just looking for attention, "I don't even want to think about getting stuck out in the middle of nowhere at night."

Mike smiles, "Oh no, we'll stop and find someplace safe before it gets dark."

Mike concentrates on the highway as Lisa looks around and Ashley is giving Shadow his attention. It doesn't take them long before they spot another highway up ahead.

Mike points, "I think we're about back to Highway 80."

Lisa looks ahead and sees the upcoming highway, "Yep, that should be it."

Mike starts to slow the van down as they pass the highway signs which confirm what they thought. As the highway quickly approaches, Mike slows the van even more, then turns left onto Highway 80 east.

Mike starts to press down on the accelerator, "Well, we'll find out soon enough if the road by the campsite is clear."

Lisa smiles, "Yeah, we definitely need luck on our side."

The talking dies down as Mike, Lisa and Ashley all get a little apprehensive about passing by the old campsite where the horde of zombies attacked them and might still be waiting.

Ryan and Rochelle continue to look around for zombies as Daniel has fallen asleep now. Michael, Lindsey's husband, knows that they must be getting close to the next turnoff. The rain is just a drizzle now as the sun is attempting to break through the clouds.

Ryan smiles, "I think I see the turnoff ahead."

Michael, Lindsey's husband, starts to slow the Trailblazer down as they near a set of highway signs.

Rochelle smiles when she sees the highway sign, "Yep, its County Highway 19 coming up."

Michael, Lindsey's husband, slows the Trailblazer down some more and turns left onto County Highway 19 headed for Demopolis.

Ryan starts looking around again, "I hope we don't have trouble in this town."

Rochelle nods in agreement as they near the city limit sign, "I know what you mean."

Michael, Lindsey's husband, stays optimistic, "It's a smaller town. I think we'll be okay."

Michael, Lindsey's husband, glances around as they cross into the town of Demopolis. Ryan and Rochelle are keeping a close watch out for any zombies and for Highway 80. They drive pass some smaller buildings as they head into town.

Michael, Lindsey's husband, starts to slow the Trailblazer down, "I think we're coming up to our turn."

Ryan looks up ahead and spots the highway signs, "Yep, you're right."

Michael, Lindsey's husband, slows the Trailblazer down and turns right onto Highway 80 east, then speeds back up.

Ryan lets out a sigh, "Well, we're back on track."

Rochelle smiles, "Good. Now if we could just find some of the others."

Michael, Lindsey's husband, nods in agreement, "That would be nice indeed."

The talking stops as they leave Demopolis and continue eastward, not realizing they are now following two of the other groups.

Ken continues to focus on the road as the rain has let up to a drizzle and the sun is starting to break through the clouds. Marissa is keeping an eye out for zombies while Codi has been going over their options on the map. Ken sees a highway sign showing that they are nearing the town of Selma, which is a bit bigger of a town.

Ken glances in the rearview mirror, "Any luck."

Codi nods, "I think I have something that will work." She pauses, "Highway 80 takes us right through Montgomery and there is no southern way around on other highways without going well out of the way."

Marissa questions, "Is there a northern way around?"

Codi smiles, "Yep and it's not too much out of the way. Just beyond this town coming up, we will take Highway 14. That will take us just north of Montgomery." She pauses, "We can take it all the way to a small town called Notasulga, then turn south on Highway 81 and that will take us right to Tuskegee."

Ken smiles as they near the town of Selma, "That sounds good to me."

Marissa smiles as well, "Me too. Good work Codi."

Codi sets the map to the side and sees Lucky staring at her. Codi starts to pet Lucky as they near the city limits of Selma.

Ken glances around, "Looks like we're going to pass through the north side of town."

Marissa sighs, "As long as the road is clear and we don't run into any problems, I'll be happy."

Codi smiles, "Me too."

Ken slows the Jeep down some as they pass the city limit sign and start into the town of Selma. It is about the same size as Miami, but so far, they haven't seen any signs of zombies. They continue on and pass a shopping center, then start into more of the town.

Codi continues to look around, "I don't see anything."

Marissa chimes in, "Me either."

Ken slows the Jeep down a little more so he can navigate safely around the abandoned vehicles. In just a few minutes, Ken, Marissa and Codi realize that they are getting near the east edge of town when they pass another shopping center.

Ken glances around, "That wasn't too bad. Keep an eye out for our turnoff."

Codi and Marissa continue to look around as they pass Range Street. Codi spots some highway signs ahead.

Codi points, "This might be it coming up."

Ken starts to slow the Jeep down as they near the highway signs.

Marissa smiles, "This is it. Looks like we stay straight to get on Highway 14."

Ken nods and drives the Jeep onto Highway 14 east as they exit the town of Selma and continue on.

Lindsey has managed to fall asleep as the rain has almost completely let up now and the sun is starting to break through the clouds. Jody quietly gets up from his resting spot and makes his way over to the loft door. Jody peeks out the cracks between the wooden boards that make up the loft door. Jody sees a few zombies emerge from the trees over near the river where him and Lindsey were at before they spotted the barn.

The zombies seem to be just wandering aimlessly as they don't appear to be after Jody and Lindsey anymore. Jody sighs as he hopes they put enough distance between them and the zombies that the zombies won't be able to follow them over to the barn. Jody continues to watch as the zombies continue south along the river and don't turn towards the barn.

Jody smiles to himself as he realizes that they were able to get far enough ahead that the zombies lost sight, smell and sound of him and Lindsey. The few zombies continue on pass the farm and barn as Jody sees a few more zombies emerge from the woods.

Jody looks back over at Lindsey and decides not to wake her yet. Jody figures he'll let Lindsey sleep unless the zombies turn towards the barn. Jody looks back out the loft door and continues to watch the zombies wander by.

CHAPTER 56

The rain has completely stopped now as Ken continues to drive the Jeep along Highway 14 east as they are approaching another small town named Autaugaville. Marissa and Codi continue to keep a look out for zombies or survivors, but they haven't spotted any yet.

Marissa looks ahead, "Looks like were nearly to another town."

Ken glances around, "Yeah, but it doesn't look very big though."

Codi chimes in as she pets Lucky for a minute, "We shouldn't have a problem with it. It's got to be smaller than the other towns we've passed thru already."

Ken slows down the Jeep some as they approach the city limits of the little town. The three of them notice immediately that this is definitely smaller than the others. Ken keeps his eyes on the road so he doesn't miss if the highway changes as Marissa and Codi maintain a watchful eye.

Codi speaks while glancing at the map, "This should be the last town until we reach the area north of Montgomery."

Ken nods slightly, "We'll have to stay on our toes once we get there. It's a big city and zombies could've wandered anywhere from it."

It gets quiet in the Jeep again as they exit the town and continue along Highway 14 east.

Shana continues to drive the car along Highway 80 east as they have passed through Uniontown and are halfway to Selma. Michael, Jody's brother, Zach and Tyler are still watching out for zombies and other survivors.

Michael, Jody's brother, finally speaks, "So, we need to decide what we're going to do."

Shana replies while keeping her eyes on the road, "What do you mean?"

Michael, Jody's brother, continues to glance around, "Highway 80 runs right thru Montgomery. I'm not too sure that's a good idea given its only the four of us. I think we should find a way around."

Zach nods, "I agree. It's too dangerous."

Shana sighs, "Okay. Get the map out and find us a way around it, but hurry cause we're getting closer and I'm going to be able to speed up some now that the rain has stopped."

Michael, Jody's brother, pulls out the map and starts looking it over while Zach and Tyler continue to keep watching for zombies.

Michael, Lindsey's husband, shuts the windshield wipers off on the Trailblazer as the rain has stopped. Ryan and Rochelle continue looking around while Daniel is still asleep.

Ryan spots a highway sign, "Looks like we're nearly to Unionville."

Michael, Lindsey's husband, nods, "Yeah, but it's a small town. We shouldn't have any problems with it." He pauses, "What worries me is Montgomery."

Rochelle looks at Michael, Lindsey's husband, "What do you mean?"

Michael, Lindsey's husband, replies, "Highway 80 runs right thru Montgomery and it's a bigger city. We might want to see if we could go around it."

Ryan nods in agreement, "I think that's a good idea. With it just being us, it's too dangerous to risk going thru a large city."

Michael, Lindsey's husband, slows the Trailblazer down as they near the city limits of Uniontown, "Ryan, why don't you check out the map and see what you can find while Rochelle continues to keep a look out."

Ryan reaches for the map, "Okay."

Ryan pulls the map out and starts going over options as they enter Uniontown. Michael, Lindsey's husband, slows the Trailblazer a little more as Rochelle looks around to see if she can spot any zombies or survivors.

Ryan goes over the map carefully as it doesn't take long for them to reach the other side of Uniontown. Michael, Lindsey's husband, speeds back up as they exit the town and continue along Highway 80 east.

Shadow appears a little dejected as Mike turns the windshield wipers off on the van since the rain has stopped. Lisa and Ashley continue looking around as they know they are about to pass their old campsite.

Mike glances around, "Okay, it's just ahead so let's stay sharp in case we run into problems."

Lisa and Ashley look around while Mike focuses on the road. Lisa and Ashley both look south as they cross the river where they were camped next to. They see the tents in the distance and they also spot about ten zombies still in the campsite along with the many zombies laying around that were killed during the escape. From best they can tell, it looks like the zombies are eating on something. Lisa glances around some more as Ashley keeps her eyes on the campsite.

Mike questions, "Anything?"

Ashley sighs, "A few zombies, but not much."

Lisa shakes her head, "It looks like they were eating on something."

Mike sighs as they pass the campsite and head on down the highway, "That would mean at least one person didn't make it."

It gets quiet in the van as each one of them thinks about the rest of the group that they've grown so attached to and who might not have made it.

After a short time, Mike spots a problem ahead, "Hey, it looks like the road is blocked."

Lisa and Ashley look ahead and see what Mike is talking about. Mike starts to slow the van down.

Ashley questions, "Looks like there is another road heading south, maybe we should go that way."

Lisa sighs, "I don't like the idea of getting off the main highway, but we might have too."

Mike slows the van down more and stops. Lisa, Ashley and Mike look around and ponder their options. After a minute, Mike spots something.

Mike points at the grass on the left of the highway, "Look over there. Those tire tracks are fairly fresh. It could be some of the others made it."

Lisa and Ashley spot the tire tracks that Mike is talking about. The two of them smile as it raises their hopes some.

Lisa nods, "Well, if whoever that was made it around, I say we try it. There are no zombies around."

Ashley smiles and nods, "I say, go for it."

Mike puts the van in drive and starts around the abandoned cars. The ground is still in fairly rough condition from the rain. The van digs through the grass and the tires spin some, but the van keeps going. Mike uses his many years of experience and keeps the van from getting stuck. After a few short moments of worry, Mike pulls the van back onto the highway.

Ashley gets excited as they hit the pavement and start moving again, "Yes!"

Mike smiles and reaches down to rub Shadow's head, "We made it big boy. It was probably your extra weight that held the van down enough."

Shadow looks up at Mike with his usual big smile and look of wonder at what Mike is saying. Lisa and Ashley get a good chuckle.

Mike spots a sign for Demopolis, "Looks like we're nearly to town."

Ashley questions, "Should we go around or thru it."

Lisa replies, "Its not that big of a town so I say we go thru it."

Mike nods, "Yeah, I agree."

Mike slows the van down as they start to near Demopolis. Ashley and Lisa continue to look around for zombies as Mike keeps one hand on the steering wheel and the other petting Shadow. Mike slows the van down a little more as they pass the city limit sign.

Lisa and Ashley keep a close eye on the side roads so no zombies or other survivors catch them by surprise. Lisa and Ashley are also keeping an eye out in case they spot one of the other vehicles from their group. Mike carefully navigates his way around the abandoned cars as they make their way thru the town.

Lisa and Ashley breath a little easier as they see the east end of town coming up. Mike starts to speed up some as he dodges a couple more abandoned cars. Before Mike, Lisa and Ashley know it, they are leaving Demopolis and continuing along Highway 80 east.

Lindsey has taken over watch in the barn while Jody is trying to get a short nap in. Lindsey feels a little more rested than before, but still wonders about what happened to the others. Lindsey checks her clothes and smiles as they appear to be getting more dry. Jody shifts around as he tries to get more comfortable in his sleep.

Lindsey quietly makes her way over to the loft door. Lindsey peeks through the cracks in the door and notices that the rain has completely stopped now. Lindsey spots a few zombies over by the river, but none of them appear to be heading towards the barn. The zombies look to be continuing to wander south. Lindsey also notices that as soon as a few zombies wander off, a few more wander out of the trees from the direction of their old campsite.

Lindsey sighs as she makes her way back over to her resting place. Lindsey gets back inside the emergency sleeping bag and sits back down. Lindsey wonders how many zombies followed them from the campsite and if her and Jody are going to end up having to sleep in the barn.

The large group of about a hundred zombies that followed Lindsey and Jody south out of the campsite has started to string out amongst the trees as they have wandered south. For the most part, the zombies are now in smaller groups and some are even wandering alone. The zombies continue to stagger their way south, looking for the two living creatures they were chasing from the campsite.

The zombies continue to sniff at the air and stagger along through the trees. Only a small number of them have passed the barn where Lindsey and Jody are holding up as nearly seventy five of them are still wandering amongst the trees between the barn and the old campsite.

CHAPTER 57

Ken continues to drive the Jeep along Highway 14 east as Codi and Marissa keep looking around for zombies or other survivors. Codi pulls out the map to make sure of the direction they are going.

Marissa speaks up, "Looks like an intersection coming up."

Codi speaks while looking at the map, "We'll stay on this road until it splits off north towards Prattville. Otherwise we'll end up on County Road 4 west."

Ken slows the Jeep down as they get closer to the upcoming intersection. As they get closer, Ken, Marissa and Codi realize something odd.

Marissa glances around, "Looks like the north and south turnoffs are blocked off by vehicles."

Ken nods in a agreement, "Yeah, but it looks like the vehicles were purposely arranged like that."

Ken slows the Jeep down to almost a stop.

Codi sees the signs for the north and south roads, "That's County Road 47 and 27. We keep going straight anyway."

Ken starts to slowly speed up, "I don't like how those vehicles are arranged though. It's like someone doesn't want you to turn there."

Marissa nods and glances around, "I know."

447

The three of them continue on for a short distance, then they see another road heading off to the south.

Codi glances at the map, "This road coming up is County Road 29 south. We'll pass the north turnoff of it soon."

As Ken drives the Jeep slowly pass the turnoff, the three of them see that it looks intentionally blocked off with cars too. Ken starts to speed back up when the three of them see the turnoff for County Road 29 north. Ken slows down again, wondering if it will be blocked too.

As they drive by the turnoff, Ken shakes his head, "This is weird. I don't like it at all."

Codi glances at the map, "We should be coming up to where our road splits off and heads towards Prattville."

Marissa sighs, "Let's hope it's clear."

Ken speeds the Jeep up, but it's not long before they see the signs for the turnoff ahead. Ken starts to slow the Jeep back down. Ken, Marissa and Codi hold their breath as they hope the highway they need is clear.

As they get closer, Ken can see that there is going to be a problem. Ken slows the Jeep to a crawl as they get nearly to the turnoff they need. Codi and Marissa each let out a dejected sigh as they see the road they need is also blocked off. Ken pulls the Jeep to a stop and puts it in park.

Ken glances around, "This is crazy. Someone has intentionally blocked these roads." He pauses, "I'm going to check to see if we can drive around the cars. Marissa, keep an eye out and Codi, check the map for alternative routes."

Codi and Marissa nod as Ken gets out of the Jeep. Ken slowly makes his way over towards the abandoned cars blocking the road. Marissa keeps a watchful eye from the Jeep while Codi looks over the map.

Ken keeps his hand on his pistol as he glances around while walking towards the cars. Ken looks back over his shoulder towards the Jeep as he thought he heard something. When he looks back towards the barricade, something in the first car catches his eye. Ken sees what looks like a small sign attached to the driver's seat. Ken slowly and carefully walks closer to the car to get a better look. As Ken approaches the car, he can make out that there is a sign attached to the seat.

Ken walks up next to the driver's window and looks in at the sign. Ken almost can't believe what he's reading. Ken glances around and notices that there is no way around the barricade of vehicles, but the note has him intrigued. Ken makes his way back over to the Jeep and gets in.

Codi speaks up, "I found another route around."

Marissa and Codi notice that Ken is quiet and has a different look on his face.

Marissa questions, "What is it Ken?"

Ken looks at Codi and Marissa, "I saw a sign left in the first vehicle."

Marissa looks a little shocked, "Really? What did it say?"

Ken sighs, "It said that they blocked the roads so that people might find one of the notes at each intersection." He pauses, "They have setup a safe haven for survivors at Maxwell Air Force Base."

Codi looks back at the map to see if she can spot the base.

Marissa can't believe what Ken said, "Wow, that's crazy."

Ken nods, "Yeah. It said continue straight until you reach Highway 31 and 6 south, then take Washington Ferry Road over to the base. Someone will be waiting at the gate."

Codi nods and looks up from the map, "Yeah, its not that far from here." She pauses, "What do you two think?"

Marissa sighs, "Its worth checking out. If it's a safe place, we can get some rest and maybe get supplies."

449

Ken glances around, "I'm not too big on trusting others with it being just the three of us, but right now, we could use the break. Besides, with all the northern roads blocked, we need some time to find another way around."

Codi sighs, "Yeah, it could be dangerous, but being stuck out here on our own isn't the best option either."

Ken nods, "I think we should check it out."

Marissa nods in agreement, "Me too."

Codi glances around, "Okay, let's do it."

Ken puts the Jeep back in drive and slowly starts to drive off. Each one of them wonders what they'll find at the Air Force Base.

Shana continues to drive the car east as she notices they are nearly to the town of Selma. Zach and Tyler are keeping a close watch out for zombies while Michael, Jody's brother, keeps looking over the map.

Shana questions, "Found anything yet?"

Michael, Jody's brother, nods, "Yeah, it looks like the shortest way around Montgomery will be to take Highway 14 east. It goes around north of Montgomery and all the way to a town called Notasulga, from there we go straight south to Tuskegee."

Shana nods, "Sounds like a good plan to me."

Zach speaks up, "Hopefully when we get there, some of the others will be there."

Tyler sighs, "Yeah, I miss them."

Shana nods as she starts to slow the car down because they are nearing the city limits of Selma, "Me too Ty."

Michael, Jody's brother, glances around as they cross into the city of Selma, "I'm sure some of the others made it out of there."

Michael, Jody's brother, folds up the map.

Shana questions as she navigates through the streets and around abandoned cars, "So, where do we pick up Highway 14 at?"

Michael, Jody's brother, glances around, "It should be just on the other side of town."

Zach and Tyler continue to look around for zombies and survivors. Michael, Jody's brother, puts the map up and starts looking around also. Shana slows the car a bit more as she makes her way around a few more abandoned cars.

Zach speaks up, "Looks like we're getting close to the edge of town."

Shana nods, "It would appear that way. Keep your eyes open for the highway signs."

As they pass the last couple of buildings and start towards the east edge of town, Michael, Jody's brother, sees what they are looking for, "Up ahead. It's the highway turnoff."

Shana starts to speed back up some.

Tyler speaks up, "Looks like we go straight mom."

Shana nods, "It sure does."

Shana speeds up some more as she drives the car onto Highway 14 east. Now that they are back on the open highway, Shana speeds back up to their normal travel speed. The talking quiets down as each one of them wonders if they will eventually link up with others from their group.

As Shana stays focused on the road, Michael, Jody's brother, Zach and Tyler keep looking out for zombies. None of them realize how much time has passed since they left Selma until they see a sign for another town called, Autaugaville.

Shana looks at Michael, Jody's brother, "Is this a very big town coming up?"

Michael, Jody's brother, glances around, "No. According to the map, it should be really small."

Shana nods, "Good."

Shana slows the car down some as they get closer to the town. Now that they are nearly to the town, Shana can see that it is definitely smaller. Shana slows the car a bit more as they pass the city limit sign of Autaugaville. Michael, Jody's brother, Zach and Tyler glance around and realize that with a town this small, they probably won't see any zombies.

It doesn't take long for Shana to navigate around the few abandoned cars in the road and they soon see the east edge of town. Shana starts to speed back up as they exit the town and continue east on Highway 14.

Michael, Lindsey's husband, continues to drive the Trailblazer east on Highway 80 as they are nearing the town of Selma. Rochelle is looking around for zombies and other survivors while Ryan is looking over the map for options to get around Montgomery.

Michael, Lindsey's husband, glances over at Ryan, "Any luck yet? We're getting close to another town."

Ryan nods, "I think I got something for us. It looks like going north around the city will be easier and less out of the way."

Rochelle speaks up while glancing around, "That'll save on gas and time. I like the sound of both."

Ryan looks up, "We should run into Highway 14 on the other side of this town coming up. We can take that highway around Montgomery and all the way to a town called, Notasulga. From there, we can go straight south to Tuskegee."

Michael, Lindsey's husband, nods as he starts to slow the Trailblazer down, "That sounds good to me."

Rochelle nods in agreement as they pass the city limit sign for Selma, "Me too."

Michael, Lindsey's husband, slows the Trailblazer down some more as he navigates around a couple of abandoned cars.

Ryan folds up the map, "Once we get thru here, we should pass thru one more small town before we reach the way around Montgomery."

Michael, Lindsey's husband, nods as he weaves around a couple more cars. Rochelle can tell that they are getting close to the east edge of town by how everything is starting to space back out again. Daniel starts to wake up so Rochelle turns her attention to him.

Ryan sees the east edge of town and a couple of highway signs, "This might be it coming up."

Michael, Lindsey's husband, slows down a little more and spots what they are looking for, "Yep, Highway 14 east goes straight."

Michael, Lindsey's husband, moves the Trailblazer over and gets on Highway 14 east. Ryan continues to glance around while they head out of the town eastward on their new highway.

CHAPTER 58

Mike continues to pet Shadow as he keeps his eyes on the highway. Lisa and Ashley keep looking around to see if they can spot any zombies or survivors. Before long, the three of them spot a highway sign that shows they are getting close to a place called Uniontown.

Ashley questions, "I wonder how big of a town this is that we're coming up to?"

Mike glances around while petting Shadow, "I'm betting it's pretty small."

Lisa nods, "Yeah, I don't think we'll have a problem with it."

Mike starts to slow the van down as they are getting closer to town, "I don't think we're going to have too many problems until we reach Montgomery."

Ashley looks at Mike, "What are you saying?"

Mike replies as they get closer to Uniontown, "Highway 80 takes us right thru Montgomery and it's a bigger city. I'm not sure if that's going to be the best thing to do."

Lisa glances around as they start into Uniontown, "I'm thinking we should find a way around Montgomery."

Mike nods in agreement as he slows the van some more, "Me too."

Ashley glances around for zombies, "If that's what you two think, I'm all for it."

Lisa pulls out the map and unfolds it, "Ashley, keep an eye out for zombies and stuff. I'm going to see what I can find as far as a way around Montgomery."

Ashley continues to look around as they are nearly thru Uniontown, "Okay."

Mike sees the east edge of town coming up, "Well, we're about out of this town."

Lisa starts looking over the map while Ashley keeps a watchful eye out. Shadow decides to lay down as Mike starts to speed the van back up. Mike glances around at the open highway as they leave Uniontown and continue east on Highway 80.

Lindsey checks her clothes again and smiles as they are dry. Lindsey quietly makes her way over to the loft door of the barn. Lindsey looks out the cracks in the loft door and sees more zombies slowly wandering south over by the river. Lindsey can tell by the sun it is nearly noon, maybe even a little after. Lindsey figures its about time to wake Jody up.

Lindsey quietly makes her way over to where Jody is napping. Lindsey remembers what Jody said about waking him up so Lindsey uses her foot to tap Jody on the bottom of his foot. Jody's eyes snap open and he looks up at Lindsey.

Lindsey smiles at Jody, "Its around noon."

Jody gives a slight nod and smiles back, "Okay."

Lindsey makes her way back over to her resting spot as Jody sits up. Lindsey climbs inside the emergency sleeping bag and sits back down.

Jody takes a sip of water, "So, how's it been while I was napping?"

Lindsey also takes a sip of water, "Small groups of zombies wandering south over by the river. None of them have come this way though."

Jody nods as he checks his boots and socks, "Well, its time to make a decision. We can stay here until tomorrow or try to make our way back to the campsite. Either way, we're not making it to Tuskegee by tonight."

Lindsey sighs, "So, even if we make it back to the campsite and get a vehicle, we're going to be staying the night on the road somewhere or driving thru the night."

Jody nods, "Yep."

Jody puts his socks back on, then his boots.

Lindsey sighs, "What do you think?"

Jody is tying his boots, "I'm thinking we try and get back. It's been half a day so whatever amount followed us has probably strung out enough that we can weave our way back without being seen." He pauses, "If we're lucky."

Lindsey nods, "I'm thinking we should try it too. The longer we stay in here, the more risk we run of being spotted somehow and getting trapped in here."

Jody grabs his gear and starts digging in his buttpack, "Well, let's eat a few rations then get started on the way back."

Lindsey nods and stands up, "Sounds good to me."

Lindsey steps out of the emergency sleeping bag. Lindsey sets the emergency sleeping bag over next to Jody while Jody pulls out his survival rations and opens them. While Jody breaks apart the survival food bars and puts the rest of them back, Lindsey puts her pants and shirt back on.

Jody folds up the emergency sleeping bag as Lindsey puts on her socks and shoes. Jody puts the emergency sleeping bag and remainder of the survival rations back in his buttpack. Jody grabs the rations for Lindsey and walks over to her.

Jody hands Lindsey her rations, "Here you go. Enjoy."

Lindsey smiles, "Thanks."

Jody heads back over to his spot and sits down. Lindsey takes a bite and gets a look on her face as she wasn't expecting the rations to taste like that.

Jody smiles at Lindsey as he picks up his rations, "Not the tastiest things in the world, but they'll keep you alive."

Lindsey finishes the first bite, "Right!"

Jody chuckles quietly as him and Lindsey continue to eat their rations and prepare mentally for the trip back to the campsite.

Ken continues to follow the military HUMVEE along the road inside Maxwell AFB. Ken, Codi and Marissa couldn't believe it when they ran into the four armed air force personnel at the gate and two more arrived to show them the way to where they are living at on base. Ken focuses on the HUMVEE as Codi and Marissa continue to look around.

The three of them follow the HUMVEE out of what appears to be the training areas and into the main area of the base as it would appear to them. Ken starts to slow down as the HUMVEE in front of them does. They are approaching some buildings that would appear to be housing barracks and some tents spread around.

The section is surrounded by razor wire and Ken can see a makeshift entry gate ahead. The two armed air force personnel at the gate opens the gate and waves the HUMVEE and Jeep through. Ken follows the HUMVEE as it heads for a building that looks like it might be some offices.

The HUMVEE pulls up and parks in front of the building. Ken pulls the jeep in beside the HUMVEE, puts the Jeep in park and turns it off.

Ken looks at Codi and Marissa, "I know they took our weapons for now, but keep on your guard. Just in case something appears wrong."

Codi and Marissa nod.

Codi questions, "What about Lucky?"

Ken opens his door, "I've cracked the windows so he can stay in the Jeep for now."

Ken gets out and walks around to the passenger's door. Codi gets out and joins Ken. The two air force personnel from the HUMVEE walk over to the Jeep. One is a Staff Sergeant and one is a Tech Sergeant. Both of them are carrying pistols on their right hips.

Ken looks at the two men, "She injured her knee. She's not able to walk."

The Staff Sergeant pulls out a handheld radio, "We need a wheelchair over to the intake building."

Marissa speaks from inside the car with the passenger's door open, "Thanks."

Ken looks around, "So, what have you done here?"

The Tech Sergeant replies, "When it all started, we managed to secure this part of the base. Being that it was a holiday weekend, we got lucky that many of the personnel were gone." He pauses, "We set up a perimeter around these few buildings and sent patrols out to clear out the rest of the base inside the fence line."

The Staff Sergeant continues, "We cleared the base out, but at a cost. We have enough personnel to keep this area secure and keep patrols running and guards at the base gates."

A woman arrives with a wheelchair. Ken helps Marissa out of the Jeep and into the wheelchair.

The Tech Sergeant turns, "Follow us. We'll take you to the Colonel. He's in charge of this place."

Ken and Codi follow the Tech Sergeant and Staff Sergeant while the lady pushes Marissa along in the wheelchair. Two armed air force personnel which appear to be guarding the building, open the doors as the Tech Sergeant and others walk up.

The Tech Sergeant leads everyone into an office area inside the building. Sitting at the desk is an African-American man looking to be in his late fifties. The man stands up when the Tech Sergeant and others walk up.

The Tech Sergeant salutes the man, "Sir, we found these three coming up to the back gate."

The Colonel returns the salute, "Thank you." He looks over at Ken, "What's your name?"

Ken replies, "Ken." He points to Codi, "This is Codi and Marissa is the one in the wheelchair."

The Colonel looks over at Marissa, "What happened?"

Marissa replies, "I've got bad knees and while trying to get away from some zombies, I blew my right knee out."

The Colonel shakes his head, "Sorry to hear about that." He pauses, "This is how it works here. We are willing to offer you a place to live and provide security as long as you don't cause problems and you pitch in and help with whatever we ask."

Ken glances around, "I'm not sure if we'll be staying or not. We have to talk that over."

The Colonel nods, "That's fine. If you decide that you want to leave, we'll return your weapons to you and escort you to the gate." He pauses, "However, all new arrivals must have guards with them until we are certain you're not a threat to anyone here. Also, all new arrivals must be checked out by our medical staff before you can enter the housing area or chow hall."

Ken nods, "We'd be okay with that."

Codi speaks up, "I have a dog in the car."

The Colonel looks at Codi, "As long as the dog is not aggressive and stays on a leash, you can keep it with you.

Make sure your dog uses the designated areas for using the bathroom."

Codi nods, "I will."

The Colonel smiles, "Well then, I'll have the Staff Sergeant get everything set up for the three of you. I've got some more things to take care of."

Marissa smiles, "Thanks."

The Colonel looks at the Staff Sergeant, "Carry on."

The Staff Sergeant salutes, "Yes sir." He looks at Ken, "This way."

The Staff Sergeant walks off. Ken and Codi follow while the lady pushes Marissa along with them. Two armed air force personnel who were standing in the corner of the room also follow them.

CHAPTER 53

Shana continues to drive the car along Highway 14 east as Michael, Jody's brother, Zach and Tyler continue to keep a watch out for zombies. Shana sees an intersecting road coming up and she starts to slow the car down. Michael, Jody's brother, glances around and sees the road signs.

Michael, Jody's brother, motions, "Looks like County Road 47 north and County Road 27 south. That means we're getting closer."

As they get closer, Zach speaks up, "It looks like the roads are blocked off by cars."

Shana slows down even more and all four of them notice that the county roads are blocked by cars like Zach had mentioned.

Shana gets a puzzled look, "That's weird. Those cars don't look like normal abandoned cars. It looks more like they were put there to block the roads."

Michael, Jody's brother, nods, "They sure do. If so, that means there might be other survivors around. Let's keep our eyes open."

Shana speeds back up and before long, they see more highway signs.

Michael, Jody's brother, motions, "We're coming up to the airport road and another county road south."

Shana starts to slow down the car. As they near the intersections for the roads, the four of them notice the same thing as before.

Zach shakes his head, "These roads look blocked too."

Tyler speaks up, "I hope our road isn't blocked."

Michael, Jody's brother, and Shana look at each other and give a look of, we hope so also. Shana speeds the car back up and soon they see a county road headed north. Shana slows the car again.

Michael, Jody's brother, sighs, "This one is blocked too. I'm really not liking this."

Shana glances around and speeds the car back up, "Me either."

The four of them continue on and finally see the road sign they were looking for.

Shana smiles, "Looks like we'll be branching off to the left off this highway."

Shana starts to slow the car down as they get closer to their turnoff. Shana's heart sinks though as she can see the highway up ahead and it appears to her that it is blocked off. Michael, Jody's brother, Zach and Tyler are keeping a close eye out for zombies and other survivors.

As they near the highway exchange, Shana pulls the car to a stop and puts it in park. The four of them can see that the direction they need to go is blocked off.

Zach speaks up, "Maybe we can get around the cars or move them out of the way."

Michael, Jody's brother, looks at Shana, "You three stay here. I'm going to check it out and see. If not, we'll find another way around."

Michael, Jody's brother, gets out of the car and slowly starts to make his way over to the cars blocking the highway that they need. Michael, Jody's brother, keeps glancing back over his shoulder to make sure nothing is behind him. Shana, Zach and Tyler keep an eye out from the car.

Michael, Jody's brother, cautiously walks up towards the first car. Michael, Jody's brother, notices right away as he approaches the car that moving it won't be an option since the car's tires are flat. Michael, Jody's brother, sighs as he glances around, hoping to see a way to get around the roadblock. While glancing around, Michael, Jody's brother, notices something in the car on the driver's seat. Michael, Jody's brother, wonders what it is and slowly approaches the car.

Michael, Jody's brother, gets a puzzled look as he gets to the driver's window and notices the note fixed to the driver's seat. Michael, Jody's brother, reads over the note and can't believe what it says. Michael, Jody's brother, makes his way back over to his car and gets back in.

Shana looks at Michael, Jody's brother, and notices the look on his face, "What is it?"

Michael, Jody's brother, blinks a couple of times and looks at Shana, "There was a note on the driver's seat of that car."

Zach speaks up, "What did it say?"

Michael, Jody's brother, pulls out the map, "It said that they blocked off the roads and left a note at each intersection. That there is a safe haven at Maxwell Air Force Base and gave the directions to get there."

Tyler smiles, "A safe place. Maybe the others are there."

Shana gets a little more excited, "Could be."

Michael, Jody's brother, looks at the map, "The base isn't that far." He pauses, "What do you think?"

Zach replies quickly, "Its worth checking out isn't it? I mean, we might find the others there or we could at least get some rest. Maybe some supplies."

Shana nods and smiles at Zach's comment, "I'd have to agree. It's worth checking into." She pauses, "Only one problem."

Tyler looks at Shana, "What's that mom?"

Michael, Jody's brother, sighs, "What if the survivors there are not friendly?"

It gets quiet in the car for a minute.

Shana finally speaks, "Well, I think we need to take the chance, especially if it could link us back up with some of the others."

Michael, Jody's brother, nods, "I'm thinking the same thing. Let's go check it out, but let's also stay cautious just in case we need to get out of there."

Shana nods and puts the car back in drive. Michael, Jody's brother, Zach and Tyler go back to looking out for zombies while Shana speeds the car up and starts to head for Maxwell Air Force Base.

Jody and Lindsey have made their way out of the barn and back into the trees heading north towards their old campsite. Jody and Lindsey are moving slowly, making sure they don't stumble into a bad situation as they know the woods are probably full of zombies that chased them south.

Jody stops every ten feet or so and listens around. Lindsey is following behind Jody a few feet and she is keeping a watch behind them to make sure nothing sneaks up on them. Jody takes a few steps, then stops and looks around.

Jody whispers to Lindsey, "I think I hear something."

Lindsey listens closely and she nods at Jody. Lindsey points in the direction where she thinks the noise is coming from. Jody is carrying his AR-15 in his left hand and Lindsey is carrying her shotgun in her left hand. Neither of them have their pistols drawn or their knives.

Jody whispers again, "If we can avoid them, we will. If there is only a few or less, we'll use our knives. If there is a bunch, we'll have to use our pistols."

Lindsey nods and whispers back, "Okay."

Jody slowly starts moving to his right and Lindsey stays with him. Jody is doing his best to circle away from the noise without giving up too much ground in heading towards their old campsite. Jody and Lindsey stop again and listen. The two of them hear the noise coming towards them again.

Jody whispers, "I think it's too late. It must have either spotted us, heard us or smelled us."

Lindsey whispers back, "What now?"

Jody whispers in return, "Let's see what it is."

Jody and Lindsey wait where they are at. Finally, a zombie comes into view about twenty yards in front of them. Jody glances around and doesn't see any other zombies.

Jody sets his rifle down and pulls out his knife, "Keep a look out."

Lindsey nods as Jody walks straight for the zombie. As the zombie gets closer, Jody raises his knife. The zombie reaches for Jody and snarls. Jody drives his knife straight forward into the zombie's head. The zombie's arms fall to it's side. Jody removes his knife and the zombie falls to the ground. Jody wipes his knife off and puts it away. Jody makes his way back over to Lindsey.

Jody picks up his rifle, "Okay, let's keep going."

Jody and Lindsey start slowly making their way north again.

Michael, Lindsey's husband, stays focused on the road while Ryan and Rochelle keep a watch out for zombies and other survivors.

Ryan sees a highway sign, "Looks like we're getting close to Autaugaville."

Rochelle questions, "Is it a very big town?"

Michael, Lindsey's husband, glances around, "I'm guessing not cause I don't really see much in the distance."

Daniel has been up from his nap for a bit and looks at Michael, Lindsey's husband, "What about mom?"

Michael, Lindsey's husband, looks at Daniel in the mirror, "Still nothing yet Daniel, but we're going to keep looking, okay."

Daniel sounds sad, "Okay."

The Trailblazer passes a cemetery as they get closer to town. Michael, Lindsey's husband, starts to slow down the Trailblazer. Ryan and Rochelle look around and notice that it is a very small town they are coming up to.

Ryan speaks up, "We get through this town and it shouldn't be too much longer until we start heading around Montgomery."

Michael, Lindsey's husband, slows the Trailblazer some more as they enter the small town of Autaugaville. Michael, Lindsey's husband, navigates around a couple of cars in the road and before long, notices that they are about across the town.

Michael, Lindsey's husband, starts to speed the Trailblazer back up as they leave the town, "Well, that was easy enough."

Ryan and Rochelle continue to keep a look out while Michael, Lindsey's husband, stays focused on the road.

Jody and Lindsey continue to slowly make their way north thru the woods back to their old campsite. So far, Jody and Lindsey have managed to avoid a couple of groups of zombies. However, it is taking Jody and Lindsey quite a bit of time to slowly make their way through the woods. Jody stops again and looks around.

Lindsey whispers to Jody, "How far do you think we've gone?"

Jody glances around and whispers back, "If I had to guess, about a mile and a half or so."

Lindsey quickly looks to her right, thinking she heard something. Jody starts to move and Lindsey taps him on the shoulder. Jody immediately stops in place and listens. Jody hears what must have caught Lindsey's attention.

Lindsey taps Jody's shoulder, points and whispers, "Over there."

Jody looks in the direction Lindsey is pointing. Jody sees the three zombies that Lindsey spotted. Jody and Lindsey watch as the zombies aimlessly stagger around the woods, but appear to be heading on an intersecting course with them.

Lindsey whispers, "What do you want to do?"

Jody whispers back, "We could make it pass them if we move quickly, but I'm more about slow and safe right now." He pauses, "Let's get rid of them."

Lindsey whispers back, "Okay."

Jody and Lindsey draw their knives out and start to slowly make their way towards the zombies. As they start to close in, the zombies see Jody and Lindsey. The three zombies turn and start walking as quickly as they can towards Jody and Lindsey.

Jody whispers, "When I say so, split to the right."

Jody and Lindsey continue to close in on the zombies.

Once they are about ten yards from the zombies, Jody speaks to Lindsey, "Now."

Lindsey starts to move off to the right and Jody starts to move off to the left. One zombie turns towards Lindsey and the other two turn towards Jody.

Lindsey moves fast and puts about fifteen yards between herself and Jody. The zombie closes in on her in a quick staggering walk. Lindsey finally stops and allows the zombie to get closer. As the zombie approaches Lindsey, it raises its arms and starts to snarl. Lindsey quickly raises her knife. As the zombie gets close enough, it attempts to grab Lindsey. Lindsey hops to her left as the hands of the zombie barely miss grabbing her. Lindsey drives her knife into the zombie's head. As Lindsey removes her knife, the zombie falls to the ground. Lindsey glances around and starts for where Jody is at.

Jody continues to move quickly to his left as the two zombies close in on him. As the two zombies get closer, Jody raises his knife up. The two zombies raise their arms and begin to snarl as they get closer to Jody. Jody moves quickly as the zombies get within reaching distance. Jody sidesteps quickly to his right and jabs the closest zombie with his rifle that is in his left hand. The second zombie steps closer and reaches for Jody. Jody kicks the second zombie in the stomach with his right foot, pushing the zombie backwards.

Jody sees his chance and quickly brings his rifle down and knife up, ramming it into the first zombie's head. Jody quickly withdraws his knife and the first zombie falls to the ground, but the second zombie is closing back in, reaching and snarling at Jody. Jody steps to his left as the hands of the zombie barely miss him. Jody drives his knife forward into the zombies head.

Jody pulls his knife out and the second zombie falls to the ground. Jody hears the shuffle of feet and snarling from behind him. Jody looks over his shoulder and sees another zombie nearly on top of him that he wasn't able to hear in all the commotion.

As the zombie's hands are nearly about to grab Jody and it's head starts to lean towards him, Lindsey's hand comes flying in from the side and her knife drives into the zombie's head. The zombie's arms fall to it's side and Jody steps back as Lindsey pulls her knife out of the zombie's head. The zombie falls to the ground at Jody's feet.

Jody looks at Lindsey with a smile and whispers, "Thank you."

Lindsey smiles and whispers back, "No problem bro."

Jody and Lindsey wipe off their knives and put them away. Jody and Lindsey start slowly moving north again towards their old campsite.

CHAPTER 60

Lisa is keeping an eye out for zombies and looking over the map while Mike continues to drive the van along Highway 80 east. Ashley is giving Shadow some attention while looking up every so often to see where they are at. Mike sees a highway sign about the upcoming town of Selma.

Mike looks at Lisa, "Any luck on a way around Montgomery?"

Lisa nods and replies, "Yeah, I think I've got one. If we take Highway 14 east it will take us around the north side of Montgomery and it's a much shorter diversion around the city than the southern route. Plus, we can take Highway 14 all the way to a town called Notasulga. From there, we can take Highway 81 straight south to Tuskegee."

Ashley looks up at Lisa, "I like the sound of that."

Mike nods and glances around, "Me too. So, where do we pick up Highway 14 east at?"

Lisa looks up and sees that they are getting closer to the town of Selma, "We should pick it up on the east side of this town."

Mike replies, "Sounds good to me. I say we go that way then."

Lisa folds the map back up, "Once we pass thru Selma, there is one more small town and then we'll skirt north of Montgomery."

Ashley returns her attention to Shadow as he paws at her. Lisa starts to look around to see if she can spot any zombies or other survivors. As they start to get closer to the west end of Selma, Mike starts to slow the van down. Mike sees the city limits sign and slows down some more.

Mike glances around, "Okay, keep your eyes open for zombies and survivors. Also, let's not miss where the highway branches off for us."

Ashley looks up from giving Shadow attention so she can help keep an eye out. Lisa continues to look around, but notices that the town appears to be vacant. Mike slows down to a safer speed as he maneuvers around a couple of abandoned vehicles.

The van passes a shopping center and starts into more of a residential part of town. Mike keeps the van at a safe speed as they pass a couple of side streets. Lisa and Ashley continue to look around, but they don't see any signs of life or zombies. Mike weaves his way around a couple of more abandoned cars as they make their way across town.

Lisa can tell that they are getting closer to the east edge of town as they leave the more residential area and pass another shopping center. Mike glances around to make sure they haven't passed their highway turnoff.

Ashley speaks up, "There it is. Up ahead."

Lisa and Mike look up the road and see the sign Ashley is talking about.

Mike nods, "Yep, that's our turn."

Lisa smiles as they get closer, "Looks like we stay straight in order to get on Highway 14 east."

Mike nods and moves the van over into the left lane. Mike starts to speed back up as they pass the highway exchange for Highway 14 and Highway 80. They exit the

471

east side of the town and Mike speeds back up to their regular highway speed.

Jody and Lindsey have continued to make their way north towards their old campsite. Jody figures that they must be getting close. Jody stops and listens.

Lindsey whispers, "How close do you think we are?"

Jody glances around, "We should be close."

Jody starts walking again and Lindsey stays right with him, looking behind them every so often to make sure no zombies walk up on them. Jody and Lindsey continue slowly north as the sun has moved into the mid-afternoon sky. Jody stops again and this time he kneels down on one knee.

Lindsey whispers, "What's that noise?"

Jody and Lindsey continue to listen. The two of them hear the sound of what appears to be animals eating. Jody looks at Lindsey and shakes his head.

Lindsey has a puzzled look and whispers, "It sounds like something eating something else."

Jody glances around and whispers, "Yeah, but I don't think its an animal." He pauses, "Let's go, but very slowly."

Jody and Lindsey start moving again towards the noise. As Jody and Lindsey slowly and cautiously move towards the sound, the woods start to thin out into less and less trees. Jody moves slowly from one tree to the next as they move forward. Finally, Jody and Lindsey see what they've been looking for. Jody and Lindsey stop next to a tree.

Jody whispers, "It's the campsite."

Lindsey nods and whispers, "And plenty of zombies."

Jody and Lindsey see three groups of zombies that are still on top of the bodies of Chad, Amber and Rachel. Jody and Lindsey look around at how they can get to the last two vehicles.

Lindsey whispers, "So, what do you think?"

Jody glances around and whispers back, "I think if we skirt along the edge of the campsite, sticking to the trees, we can make it up to the highway and get away in one of the vehicles before they can spot us."

Lindsey nods and whispers back, "Sounds good to me."

Jody and Lindsey slowly start to make their way around the campsite. Jody is glancing around to make sure there are no zombies in their way while Lindsey is keeping an eye on the zombies in the campsite. As they walk slowly, Jody stops as he sees a bunch of tree branches and twigs on the ground. Lindsey stops behind Jody, keeping an eye on the zombies in the campsite.

Jody whispers, "We can't walk this way. We'll make too much noise."

Lindsey taps Jody on the shoulder and whispers, "It doesn't matter now."

Jody looks back over his shoulder and sees what Lindsey is talking about. A couple of the zombies have spotted Jody and Lindsey. Once the two zombies start towards Jody and Lindsey, the rest of the zombies spot them and start towards them as well.

Jody glances around, "Run for the vehicles."

Jody and Lindsey take off running as the zombies start staggering as fast as they can towards them. Jody and Lindsey see the highway and the last two vehicles that are left, Mike's truck and Allen's Tahoe.

Jody yells while running, "Head for the truck!"

Jody and Lindsey have a good head start, but the group of zombies continue after them. It doesn't take long for Jody and Lindsey to cover the open ground to the vehicles.

Jody runs around to the driver's side of the truck as Lindsey runs up to the passenger's side.

Lindsey opens the door and looks back, "They're getting closer."

Jody gets in behind the steering wheel and shuts the driver's door. Jody grabs the keys off the dashboard as Lindsey climbs in the passenger's side and shuts the door. Jody puts the key in the ignition and starts the truck. The zombies have closed to within ten yards of the truck. Jody puts the truck in drive and speeds away to the east on Highway 80.

Lindsey looks back at the zombies as they continue after the truck, "We made it!"

Jody smiles and breathes a sigh of relief, "Yes we did." He pauses, "Great work today girl. I couldn't have done it without you."

Lindsey looks at Jody and smiles, "Thanks. I know I couldn't have made it without you."

Jody and Lindsey look back at the highway as they put the group of zombies way behind them. Now all Jody and Lindsey are thinking about is since four vehicles were missing, who all made it and if they can catch up to them.

Ken and Codi are standing in an open grass area designated for pets that is near the office building where they met the Colonel. Marissa is still in the hospital building getting her knee looked at by the doctor.

Ken looks around at the different people walking around and the different air force personnel, "I was hoping we'd run into some of the others here."

Codi sighs, "I know. I was hoping so too."

Ken and Codi look over towards the road as they hear a couple of vehicles driving towards them. Codi and Ken watch as the HUMVEE that led them in comes driving towards them, but they can't see the vehicle behind the HUMVEE. Ken and Codi walk over closer to the road as the HUMVEE drives by. Neither Ken nor Codi can believe what they see behind the HUMVEE.

Shana continues to follow the HUMVEE along the road as Michael, Jody's brother, Zach and Tyler keep looking around. The four of them can't believe what they are seeing.

Shana glances around, "This place is amazing."

Michael, Jody's brother, nods as he looks around, "I know what you mean. Let's just stay on guard, just in case. Especially since they took our weapons."

Shana continues to follow the HUMVEE as it approaches the office building where the Colonel's office is at. Ken looks at Codi is disbelief.

Codi smiles, "I wonder who it is."

Ken smiles as well, "Let's go find out."

Ken and Codi start walking towards the office building as the HUMVEE and the car with Shana and the others drive on. The HUMVEE pulls into the parking lot in front of the office building and Shana pulls in behind the HUMVEE. The HUMVEE pulls into a parking spot in front of the building, next to Lisa's Jeep that Ken was driving.

Michael, Jody's brother, spots the Jeep, "Look! I swear that's Lisa's Jeep."

Shana smiles, "I think you're right."

Shana pulls the car into a parking spot next to the HUMVEE. Shana, Zach, Tyler and Michael, Jody's brother, get out of the car and follows the Staff Sergeant and Tech Sergeant into the building. Ken and Codi walk up to the parking lot of the office building with their two armed guards. Ken and Codi walk across the parking lot to where the Jeep and car are parked. Ken and Codi anxiously wait to see who it was in the car.

After a few minutes, the door to the office building opens up and the Staff Sergeant walks out followed by Shana, Michael, Jody's brother, Zach and Tyler. The four of them are followed by two armed guards. Ken and Codi smile when they see the four of them.

Ken motions with his hand, "Hey, over here!"

Michael, Jody's brother, spots Ken, "Hey!"

Ken, Codi and Lucky start walking towards Shana and the others. Shana, Zach and Tyler are excited to finally see someone else from the group.

As Ken and Codi get close, the Staff Sergeant holds up his hand, "Come no closer. They have to be checked out before they can interact with anyone else here."

Ken and Codi stop. Lucky is standing next to Codi. Lucky is all excited when he sees Zach and Tyler, two of his play friends.

Ken speaks to Michael, Jody's brother, "We'll be waiting for you outside the medical building."

Michael, Jody's brother, nods, "Okay. See you soon."

The Staff Sergeant leads Shana and the others away towards the medical building.

Codi picks up Lucky, "I can't believe we found some of the others."

Ken watches Shana and the others walk off, "Me either. Let's go tell Marissa, then wait for them."

Codi nods, "Okay."

Ken and Codi head off for the medical building to find Marissa and share the good news.

CHAPTER 61

Jody continues to drive the truck east on Highway 80 as they are getting closer to the town of Demopolis. Lindsey looks up in the sky and can tell its getting near dinner time. Jody slows the truck down some as he sees a highway sign coming up. Lindsey is looking at the map that was in the truck.

Jody speaks while glancing around, "Looks like County Highway 57 south coming up."

Lindsey looks up from the map, "Yeah, not long after this intersection we should get to Demopolis."

Jody slows the truck down some more as they get closer to the turnoff. Lindsey lowers the map and her heart sinks a bit as she sees the highway is blocked ahead. Jody also sees that the road is blocked and slows the truck down some more.

As they get up to the abandoned cars blocking the road, Jody pulls the truck to a stop, "Well, what do you think? We're already way behind anyone who may have survived if they are heading for Tuskegee."

Lindsey looks around, then back at the map, "There is a way around, but it'll take us a bit more time." She pauses and looks up, "I say we try to make it around the vehicles."

Jody glances up at the sky and nods, "Me too. Its getting later and saving time is going to be important."

Jody and Lindsey look around to try and spot the best way around the abandoned cars.

Lindsey smiles and points to the left side of the highway, "Look over there. Those tire tracks, they seem fairly fresh. Maybe it was some of the others. If they can make it around, surely we can."

Jody looks over to where Lindsey is pointing, "You're right and with half the day of sun drying the ground some, we shouldn't have a problem."

Jody slowly drives the truck over to the left side of the highway. Jody pushes down on the accelerator and takes the truck off the highway onto the ground. The ground is still somewhat soft from the rain, but the tires of the truck keep their traction. Jody is careful not to press down too hard on the accelerator so the tires won't spin.

In just a long minute, Jody drives the truck back up onto the highway on the opposite side of the abandoned cars. Jody glances around and starts to speed back up. Lindsey looks back at the map.

Jody smiles, "That wasn't so bad."

Lindsey smiles and replies, "Nope. Looks like we should be good about not having to go around Demopolis. It doesn't appear to be very big."

Jody continues to glance around while he drives the truck on towards Demopolis. Lindsey looks up from the map in time to see that they are nearly to the city limits of the town. Jody starts to slow the truck down some as they pass the city limit sign of Demopolis.

Lindsey looks around and notices right away that they appear to be on the southern edge of the city. Jody slows the truck down a little more to weave around a few abandoned cars. Lindsey stays very alert for zombies and signs of other survivors.

Before long, Jody and Lindsey see the east edge of town coming up. Jody maneuvers around a couple more abandoned cars, then speeds back up as they exit the town of Demopolis.

Mike continues to drive the van along Highway 14 east as they are getting closer to the town of Autaugaville. Lisa and Ashley keep looking around for zombies and any signs of other survivors. Shadow is sitting between Mike and Lisa, just staring and smiling at Mike. Finally, Shadow paws at Mike's seat.

Mike looks over at Shadow, then back to the road, "I know big boy, you're probably getting hungry and needing to get out of the van."

Lisa reaches over and pets Shadow, "Let's get thru this town and down the road a little ways, then we can make a brief pit stop."

Ashley nods, "I like the sound of that. I need to get out too."

Mike smiles and starts to slow the van down some as they near the little town. Mike glances around and can tell that this town they are nearly to is small and shouldn't be a problem. Lisa and Ashley continue to keep a watch out. Mike slows the van even more as they cross the city limits into the town.

Lisa and Ashley can tell that it is a small town and they should be thru it in no time at all. Mike weaves his way around one abandoned vehicle and before long, the three of them see the east side of town. Mike starts to speed back up as they exit the little town of Autaugaville and continue on east.

Being dinner time now, Ken, Codi, Shana, Michael, Jody's brother, Zach and Tyler are in the chow hall building on the base. Marissa is still in the hospital and Lucky is back in the pen area where the pets are kept. The six of them are just happy to see someone else from the group and happy to get a decent meal.

Ken shakes his head, "I still can't believe we were able to find each other."

Michael, Jody's brother, questions, "Do you know if anyone else made it?"

Codi sighs, "No, but there were three other vehicles gone when we left the campsite. So, if you four are in one of them, who knows who might be in the other two."

Shana nods and glances around, "Yeah, we were the first vehicle to leave the campsite. Crazy that you all beat us here."

Ken nods and takes a drink of water, "Well, we just stayed on the highway and decided to try to go north around Montgomery."

Zach speaks up after taking a bite of food, "We did take a different route around some vehicles on the highway."

Codi nods, "That must be why we got ahead of you cause we went around those vehicles."

Michael, Jody's brother, looks at Ken, "So, how's Marissa doing?"

Ken shakes his head, "Not good. Her right knee is totally shot. The doctor said that there is no way she'll be able to put any weight on it for awhile."

At that time, the doors to the chow hall open up. Ken and the others look over to the doors. None of them can believe their eyes.

The Staff Sergeant is standing at the chow hall doors with Michael, Lindsey's husband, Ryan, Rochelle and Daniel behind him. The Staff Sergeant points to the food line, then turns and walks off.

Rochelle takes Daniel's hand and they follow Ryan and Michael, Lindsey's husband, over to the food line. Once they get their food, Michael, Lindsey's husband, starts looking around for a place to sit.

Ken stands up and waves, "Over here!"

Michael, Lindsey's husband, Ryan and Rochelle can't believe their eyes as they spot Ken waving to them. They get excited at seeing someone else from the group as they walk towards the table where Ken and the others are at. Once they get to the table, Michael, Lindsey's husband, Ryan, Rochelle and Daniel can't believe who all is there.

Ken smiles at them, "Have a seat."

Codi stands up in excitement to see that Ryan is okay. Ryan sets his tray down next to Codi and they embrace.

Codi squeezes Ryan tight, "Oh my God, I'm so happy to see you. I was so worried."

Ryan hugs his wife close, "Me too. I started to think that I'd never see you again."

Ryan and Codi share a kiss as Michael, Lindsey's husband, Rochelle and Daniel sit down. Ryan and Codi finally stop hugging each other and sit down at the table. Everyone at the table is smiling and happy to see others from the group made it.

Michael, Lindsey's husband, questions, "So, is there anyone else here besides us?"

Ken replies, "Marissa is in the hospital. She hurt her right knee really bad."

Daniel looks around, "Is my mom here?"

Codi looks over at Daniel, "I'm sorry Daniel, but we haven't seen her."

Rochelle questions, "So, do you know of anyone who didn't make it?"

Ken shakes his head, "No. I know there were three other cars gone from the campsite when Marissa, Codi and I got away." Ken motions to Shana with his head, "They

481

were in one and you guys were in another. That means there is still one more vehicle out there that we know of."

Michael, Jody's brother, speaks up, "But we're still missing my dad, Lisa, Ashley, Jody, Lindsey, Chad, Amber and Rachel. Not to mention Shadow. That's a lot for one vehicle so hopefully after you guys left, others made it out too."

Ken nods, "Well, let's try not to think about that right now. Let's just get some food in our bellies and enjoy the fact that we were able to find each other."

Everyone at the table nods. Michael, Lindsey's husband, and Daniel are still somewhat sad that they don't know what happened to Lindsey. Rochelle is also still saddened by not knowing what has happened to Lisa. Codi and Ryan are holding hands while they eat, full of joy to have found each other. The group continues to talk and share their stories of escape from the campsite and the trip that brought them all to the air force base.

Jody continues to drive the truck east as the sun is getting lower in the sky behind them. Lindsey continues to look around as they are nearly to the town of Uniontown. Jody and Lindsey both know that it will be dark soon and they'll have to make a decision as to continuing on or finding a place to sleep for the night.

Jody starts to slow the truck down as they enter the city limits of Uniontown. Jody and Lindsey both can tell that this is a smaller town and shouldn't be trouble.

Lindsey glances around, "So, what do you want to do about tonight?"

Jody sighs as he makes his way around an abandoned car, "I'm still not sure yet. I say we stop just a ways down the highway after we get thru this town, get a bite to eat and look at our options."

Lindsey nods while glancing around, "Sounds good to me." She pauses, "Looks like we might have an hour, maybe two of daylight left."

Jody nods in agreement as he starts to speed the truck back up, "I'd say you're right."

Lindsey continues to look around as they leave the town and start back out on the highway, "I want to get there as soon as possible, but traveling at night and thru a large city is pretty dangerous."

Jody sighs, "Yep, it sure is. Look over the map for possible alternate routes around Montgomery and possible stopping places for us if we decide to not drive thru the night."

Lindsey pulls out the map, "Okay."

Lindsey starts looking over the map as Jody focuses on the highway ahead of them.

CHAPTER 62

Ken and the others walk out of the chow hall building. All of them are still talking and smiling, not only about having found each other, but from having a nice, cooked meal.

Michael, Jody's brother, glances around, "Hey, let's go check on Marissa. I'm sure she'd be happy to see who all has made it."

Rochelle nods, "That's a good idea."

Ken and the others start walking towards the medical building. All of them still can't believe how well the air force base is set up and defended.

Michael, Lindsey's husband, speaks while walking, "So, have they given you all a place to sleep for the night?"

Ken nods, "They assigned Codi and I to temporary tent two."

Shana looks at Ken, "Really? We got assigned to that tent also."

Ryan smiles, "So did we."

Zach sounds excited, "Sweet! We get to stay together."

Ken and the others near the medical building and they can't believe their eyes as they see the Staff Sergeant walk out of the medical building doors with Mike, Lisa and Ashley behind him.

Rochelle gets a huge smile on her face, "Mom!"

Mike, Lisa and Ashley spot Ken and the others. Lisa smiles as she sees Rochelle running towards her. Lisa and Rochelle embrace as Ken and the others walk up to Mike and Ashley.

Ken holds out his hand to Mike, "Good to see you."

Mike shakes Ken's hand, "Its good to see all of you."

Michael, Jody's brother, steps up and gives Mike a hug, "Good to see you dad."

Mike hugs his oldest son, "I'm so happy you made it."

Everyone starts to greet each other. It is all smiles as most of the group has found their way back together.

Ashley questions, "Does anyone know about Jody, Lindsey, Marissa, Chad, Amber and Rachel?"

Ken sighs, "Well, when we left the campsite, three other vehicles were already gone." He pauses, "Now that you three are here, that's all of the vehicles that were gone so all we can hope for is that they got out after we did."

Codi chimes in, "Marissa is in the hospital. We're going to see her." She pauses, "What about Shadow?"

Mike smiles, "He's over in the pet pen enjoying his dinner and making new friends."

Lisa nods, "Well, we ate dinner before we got here so if you're going to go see Marissa, then we can join you."

Rochelle questions, "So, where are you three staying tonight?"

Mike replies, "We were assigned to temp tent two."

Tyler smiles, "That's where all of us are staying."

Ashley smiles her beautiful smile, "Awesome!"

Ryan looks around, "Well, shall we get going to visit with Marissa some before we have to go to our tent for the night."

Everyone nods and starts for the doors of the medical building as the Staff Sergeant walks off. The air force guards follow the group into the medical building. Everyone is smiling and talking as they head for Marissa's room.

Jody and Lindsey have stopped at the intersection of Highway 80 and County Road 45. The two of them have already finished eating and are now looking over the map that they have spread out on the hood of the truck. Jody and Lindsey are still staying aware of their surroundings so no zombies sneak up on them.

Lindsey looks over the map, "I'm thinking that time is more important than a safer, more out of the way route. No telling how far behind the others we might be."

Jody glances over the map, "I have to agree. I say we take the most direct route and try to get to Tuskegee as fast as possible, even if it means going thru a city."

Lindsey points at the map, "I'd say that the best thing to do is just stay on Highway 80. It looks like it cuts across the southern part of the city, then links up with the interstate for a short distance."

Jody nods at what Lindsey is saying, "Yeah, then it branches off again a little ways east of Montgomery and takes us straight to Tuskegee." He pauses, "So, that is the plan. Just stay on Highway 80 all the way to Tuskegee."

Lindsey looks up from the map and glances around, "Its getting darker. The sun will be completely set before we reach Montgomery." She pauses, "What do you want to do, drive thru the night or find a place to sleep?"

Jody sighs and glances up at the sky, "It might be dangerous to drive at night, especially thru a city or town, but I think we should. If we drive straight thru, we should make it to Tuskegee somewhere around 3am or so." He pauses, "If others are there, that's great. If not, we can get some rest there and see if anyone else shows up when it gets to be daytime."

Lindsey nods while glancing around some more, "I think you're right. As dangerous as it is, we can't afford to risk falling any further behind if the others got away and didn't get slowed down." She pauses, "Plus, it looks like once we get thru Montgomery, all we have is a little town called Shorter, then its clear to Tuskegee."

Jody nods slightly, "Yeah, then we get thru Tuskegee and find a place in the forest along the highway to stop. Most likely there'll be a river or lake and that's where the others will have stopped if they made it that far."

Lindsey sighs and looks up at the sky, "Well, let's get to it before we burn the last of our daylight."

Jody smiles, "Yep."

Lindsey folds up the map. Jody and Lindsey get back in the truck. Jody starts up the truck, puts it in drive and starts out towards the town of Selma. The sun continues to get lower towards the horizon as they near the town of Selma.

Jody starts to slow the truck some as they near the city limits. Lindsey keeps a close eye out for zombies and other survivors while Jody keeps a close eye out for the road signs. Jody slows the truck even more as they enter the town of Selma. Jody weaves around a couple of abandoned cars as they pass a shopping center. Lindsey continues to glance around as they enter a more residential area.

Lindsey points, "Looks like our turn is coming up."

Jody sees the sign where the highway turns right up ahead. Jody slows down to nearly a stop as he makes the turn. Jody quickly weaves left to avoid an abandoned car that was just around the turn that they couldn't see from the other road.

Jody speeds up some as they continue thru residential areas of the town. Lindsey keeps looking around for any signs of zombies or other survivors, but she is unable to spot signs of either. Jody weaves around a couple more abandoned cars as they make their way thru the city.

As they continue on, Jody and Lindsey both wonder when they are going to reach the city limits and start back out on the open highway. After a few more blocks of residential areas, Jody and Lindsey see a large river ahead. The truck crosses over the river and Jody and Lindsey notice that they are leaving the more populated area and start to get more away from the actual town.

Jody glances around, "I think we're almost out of town."

Lindsey nods as she looks around, "I think your right."

Jody speeds up some and they drive thru a small residential area and see a sign for an airport. They continue on and pass thru another small residential section, then Jody and Lindsey notice that they seem to be back on the open highway.

Lindsey smiles, "I think that's it."

Jody nods and starts to speed the truck back up, "I believe you're right."

Jody and Lindsey continue on east as the sun is nearly set in the western horizon.

Ken and the others have been visiting with Marissa for a short time. It has been mostly smiles and an upbeat mood while they have all talked about the escape from the campsite and the trip that has brought them all back together.

Michael, Lindsey's husband, and Daniel are still somewhat sad since they have not found Lindsey or know what has happened to her. Everyone wonders if Jody, Lindsey, Chad, Amber and Rachel made it okay and if so, where are they.

Mike finally brings up the big question, "So, what do you all think? They have offered to let us stay here."

Lisa is the first to speak, "It's a nice place they've built and they seem to be doing well, but I've been thinking about it some and I'm not sure if staying is the best thing right now."

Michael, Lindsey's husband, nods, "I know. Plus, with the others still possibly out there somewhere or maybe they've made it to Tuskegee and they're waiting on us, I'm not sure we should abandon the plans we made just yet."

Marissa looks around at the others, "Well, I can tell you that after the doctor saw me and checked my knee, it's going to be hard for me to travel." She pauses, "They said that I won't be able to put any pressure on my knee for quite some time and maybe not ever be able to use it unless I get surgery done."

Michael, Jody's brother, nods slightly at Marissa, "That does complicate things a lot. If we knew it was a safe trip the rest of the way, then we could just have you rest and use crutches to get around on."

Ken chimes in, "But if we run into more trouble, especially like we did at the campsite or with any other survivors again, you might not be able to get away again."

Lisa speaks up, "Well, we don't have to figure it out at this moment. None of us are going anywhere at least until tomorrow." She pauses, "And it's time for us to have to get to the tent before curfew."

Marissa smiles, "You all go ahead and go. I'll see you in the morning after breakfast."

Everyone says goodnight to Marissa. Ken and the others make their way out of the room as Marissa does her best to get comfortable. While the others head for their tent, Marissa can't help but think about her options and what looks like the decision she is going to have to make.

The sun has completely set as Jody and Lindsey are nearing the city of Montgomery. The two of them hope that they will be able to make it thru the city without running into a problem, but they also know that the chances are good that they'll see zombies in a city the size of Montgomery.

Jody does his best to stay focused on the road as Lindsey is doing her best to keep an eye out for zombies and other survivors. Being nighttime now, their ability to see has been greatly hindered since there are no man made lights left to light up the night. The moon and stars provide a little bit of light, but not much.

Jody has slowed down some since it is more dangerous for them while driving in the dark. Jody has kept the headlights on while out on the open highway, but he's not sure he wants to keep them on while driving thru the city.

Lindsey points to a sign ahead, "Look, there's a sign for the airport. We should be getting to the Interstate 65 exchange soon which we'll take north for a short ways before getting back off on Highway 80 and 8 again."

Jody glances around, "Once we reach the Interstate, I'm going to turn the headlights off. I know we'll have to drive pretty slow, but I don't want to broadcast to the possible hundreds or thousands of zombies that dinner is served."

Lindsey nods as Jody slows the truck down some, "Right! I like the way you think."

Jody looks over and smiles at Lindsey, "Once we're thru the city, I'll turn the headlights back on and we should be okay for awhile. I'll turn them off again before we reach Tuskegee so nothing can spot us and possibly find us."

Lindsey glances around, "Sounds good to me."

Jody spots a road sign ahead, "Well, this looks like our turn coming up."

Jody slows the truck down and shuts off the headlights as they reach the exchange for the interstate. Numerous cars have been abandoned on the ramp for the interstate. Jody slows the truck nearly to a stop. As Jody slowly and cautiously maneuvers the truck around the abandoned cars, Lindsey does her best to keep an eye out for any motion in the dark.

Jody finally gets the truck around the abandoned cars and onto the interstate. Lindsey smiles as Jody speeds the truck back up some. Jody keeps the truck at a steady, slow speed so he'll have time to react if anything is in their way. Jody and Lindsey notice one thing right away as they cross over a small river, most of the abandoned cars are on the other side of the interstate as people were trying to get out of the city. Jody weaves his way around a couple of abandoned vehicles as Lindsey strains to see anything in the dark.

Before long, Lindsey sees the highway sign they are looking for, "Looks like our turn is coming up. This is going to take us into the very southern part of the city."

Jody nods, "Let's stay sharp."

Jody slows the truck down some and weaves around another abandoned vehicle. Lindsey continues her watching for zombies as Jody slowly pulls the truck onto the exit ramp which is clear of vehicles. Jody glances around as he pulls the truck onto the highway. Jody speeds the truck back up to a safe speed.

Lindsey looks around, but doesn't see any signs of movement in the darkness. It doesn't take long on the new highway and Jody and Lindsey see the outlines of buildings off to their left which appears to be a shopping center. Lindsey keeps an eye on the shopping center as Jody weaves the truck around an abandoned semi.

Not long after the shopping center is behind them, Jody and Lindsey notice that they are headed more into the city now. Jody focuses hard on the road as Lindsey stays ever vigilant on her watch. As they continue along the highway thru the southern part of the city, Jody and Lindsey are surprised that they haven't seen anything yet.

Lindsey sighs, "I figured we'd seen something by now."

Jody nods slightly, "Me too."

Jody slows some as they pass a highway exchange where Jody has to avoid a few more abandoned vehicles. Jody speeds back up, but before long he has to slow back down as they approach another highway exit. Lindsey looks off to the south and her eyes widen as she spots what appears to be another shopping center type place in the distance.

Lindsey points, "I see movement over there. Can't really make out what it is, but definitely a lot of movement."

Jody stays focused on the road, "As long as it stays over there, I'll be happy."

Lindsey smiles at Jody's response, "Me too."

Jody speeds back up and other than some abandoned vehicles, the drive is a fairly nice one for a ways. Lindsey remains focused on trying to spot anything in the dark. Jody slows the truck again as they pass another highway exchange by what appears to be a hospital on their left. Jody slowly makes his way around some abandoned vehicles and speeds back up.

Jody and Lindsey are starting to feel good about the trip thru the city, like they might actually make it without a hitch. Before long, they pass another shopping center area and highway exchange. As they continue on, Jody and Lindsey are unaware of the zombies that have heard the truck in the night and have started moving towards the sound.

Jody starts to slow the truck again as another shopping center area appears on their left and they approach another highway exchange. Lindsey is glancing around in the dark, then her head stops as she spots something that she doesn't like.

Lindsey's eyes widen, "Oh my God!"

Jody replies to Lindsey's expression while he stays focused on the road, "What is it?"

Lindsey looks over at Jody, "Zombies, hundreds and maybe a thousand just off the highway! Get us out of here!"

Jody glances over to the right and even in the darkness, he can see the wave of zombies heading their way just twenty feet or so from the highway.

Jody turns on the headlights, "Screw it, they know we're here now!"

Jody presses down on the accelerator and races away from the massive horde of zombies. Jody weaves around a couple of cars, then sees a few zombies in the road ahead of them as they pass the exchange for Troy Highway and the highway they're on bends to the north.

Jody sighs, "Zombies!"

Lindsey, who was looking back behind them, looks forward and quickly spots a way out, "It's clear on the right shoulder."

Jody quickly weaves the truck to the right, just missing the first zombie and narrowly missing an abandoned car which would have ended their trip. Jody flies around the three zombies and races away into the night, leaving the horde of zombies behind them. Jody and Lindsey breathe a sigh of relief, but wonder if they'll see anymore zombies before they get out of the city.

CHAPTER 63

Ken and the others are back at the tent they were assigned to stay in for the night. It is getting fairly late, but none of them have fallen asleep yet except for Daniel. Each of them has been thinking about whether to stay at the air force base or continue on with their original plan.

Rochelle whispers to Lisa, "So mom, what do you think? Should we stay here or go on tomorrow?"

Lisa glances around at the others, "This place appears to be very safe and secure for now and I certainly would understand staying. If not permanently, at least for a time." She pauses, "However, for me its like the other options we talked about. It is still able to be surrounded with no way of escape. Plus, Jody, Lindsey and the others are still possibly out there and I can't abandon them."

Mike looks at Lisa, "So, you've decided to move on."

Lisa nods her head, "Yeah, in the morning after breakfast." She looks at Rochelle, "I want you to come with me, but you're an adult now and you have to make up your mind for yourself."

Rochelle sighs, "It feels so safe here, but if you're not staying mom, then I'm not either."

Lisa nods, "Okay."

Codi speaks up, "This could be our chance at a stable life and there are so many people here that it feels safe."

494

Ryan looks at Codi, "Are you saying you want to stay?"

Codi looks over at Ryan, "It's an idea, but I'm not one hundred percent certain." She pauses, "Jody and the others are still out there and if we didn't continue on, I'd feel like we abandoned them."

Ken speaks up, "As safe as it seems here, I'm still convinced that the original plan is the best choice. Plus, if any of the others made it out of the campsite, they could be waiting at Tuskegee for us." He pauses, "I agree with Lisa. I'm leaving tomorrow too."

Michael, Jody's brother, looks at Shana, "What do you think?"

Shana glances at Zach and Tyler, "I owe it to the boys to make the best decision for our safety, but I also think we owe it to Jody to at least see if they made it to Tuskegee. He's done so much for us that I wouldn't feel right to not at least go that far."

Zach looks at Shana, "Mom, I know you want what's best for Ty and me, but I don't want to stay here. I think the best choice is to continue on to Fort Pulaski."

Tyler speaks up, "Me too."

Shana smiles at her boys, "Well then, I guess that means that the three of us are leaving in the morning too."

Michael, Jody's brother, nods, "Well, if you three are going, so am I. Besides, there is no way I'm staying here without trying to find my brother."

Mike speaks up, "Absolutely. This place may seem safe for now, but looking at the long term, Fort Pulaski is the way to go." He pauses, "And I'm not going to sit here either while my son could be out there needing help."

Codi looks over at Ashley, "What about you Ashley?"

Ashley sighs, "I'm not sure right now. Part of me wants to stay because of the safe feeling I have right now, but then another part of me thinks that its best to move on before it might be too late."

Michael, Lindsey's husband, finally speaks up, "Well, I know I have to think about the safety of Daniel, but there is no way I'm staying here. If Lindsey is out there and made it away from the old campsite, I'm going to do my best to find her." He pauses, "So, Daniel and I are leaving in the morning with the others."

Ryan looks over at Codi, "I know this is a big decision and maybe we should sleep on it."

Codi nods, "Yeah, I think you're right."

Ashley decides to speak up, "I'm going. Hearing all of you just makes me feel like it's the better option right now. We don't know what's out there, but we do know that there are large groups of zombies and maybe some ten times larger than what we've seen so far. I think trying to get to the island is best."

Mike looks around, "Well, Codi and Ryan are right. We should try to get some rest since we're planning on getting back out on the road tomorrow."

Everyone nods at each other. Everyone heads off to their cot and do their best to try and get some sleep.

Jody and Lindsey are continuing east on Highway 80 as they have managed to leave the city of Montgomery far behind them. Both of them feel lucky to have made it thru the city without too many problems, but seeing that massive group of zombies also tells them that any large city or surrounding area is not going to be safe.

Jody focuses on the highway as Lindsey looks around to see if there is any movement in the dark. Both of them know that they should be getting close to Tuskegee since they went thru the tiny town of Shorter an hour ago.

Lindsey spots a highway sign, "Looks like a few miles to Tuskegee."

Jody sighs, "Yeah, I'm sure ready to get there."

Lindsey nods in agreement, "Me too. This has been a long day since we first escaped the campsite."

Jody glances around as they near the city limits of their last town to pass thru for the night, "This highway runs right thru the middle of town so I'm shutting the headlights off again."

Lindsey nods again as she looks around in the dark, "Okay."

Jody turns the headlights off and slows the truck down as they pass the city limit sign of Tuskegee. Jody steers the truck around a couple of abandoned vehicles and Lindsey spots what appears to be a school on the right side of the highway. Jody and Lindsey continue on slowly and start into a more residential area of town.

Lindsey keeps a constant look out for any kind of motion in the dark, but figures this town will be about the same as Selma was since it appears to be smaller. The drive is slow and cautious, but they leave the residential area and enter a more open area of town like someplace a park and few houses would be.

Lindsey stares into the darkness around the highway, but so far hasn't seen anything moving. Jody stays focused on the highway as he has had to maneuver around a few vehicles in the road. In no time at all, the truck starts back into a more residential and business section of town. Jody weaves the truck around an abandoned semi as Lindsey spots a couple of fast food places.

After a few blocks, Jody and Lindsey notice that they must be in the old downtown area of Tuskegee. The truck passes thru it quickly and starts back into another residential area. Lindsey still hasn't spotted any movement in the dark and that makes her feel somewhat comfortable, but also makes her a little nervous because she knows there had to be zombies in this town and she wonders where they have wandered off to. Jody weaves around another abandoned car as they as they spot a large lake off to their right.

Lindsey points, "Look, the lake. That means we should be getting to the forest anytime now."

Jody smiles and nods, "Yep."

Jody continues slowly and cautiously still as they leave the residential area and enter a forest area.

Lindsey looks puzzled, "I didn't see a city limit sign showing we left the town."

Jody focuses on the road as in the forest, it is extremely dark, "I don't think we have yet."

Jody was right as they quickly exit the small forest section and they see another small lake off on their left as they also pass a few houses, but nothing close to an actual neighborhood. Before long, Jody and Lindsey spot the city limit sign and they know that Tuskegee is now behind them. In just a short distance, the truck enters the forest again.

Jody weaves around another vehicle, "We should reach a river before long. I'm just going to keep going slow and leave the headlights off now that our eyes are adjusted to the night."

Lindsey nods, "Sounds good to me."

Jody continues on slowly and Lindsey sees a road coming up. They pass the road and continue on. Before long, Jody and Lindsey spot a small bridge ahead.

Lindsey smiles, "I think this could be it."

Jody slows down even more and the trees open up a little as they near the river. Jody creeps the truck forward and across the bridge. Once across the bridge, Jody pulls the truck off to the right side of the highway.

Jody looks at Lindsey as he puts the truck in park, "I think this will do."

Lindsey nods, "Me too." She pauses, "What now?"

Jody shuts off the truck, "Let's walk a small perimeter around the area just to make sure nothing is here. Maybe just a couple hundred feet, maybe a hundred yards. I don't want to get much further from the truck than that."

Lindsey smiles, "Me either."

Jody and Lindsey get out of the truck. Jody leaves his empty rifle in the truck and Lindsey leaves her empty shotgun in the truck. The two of them take a slow walk along the bank of the river for a short ways, then cut thru the tress in a semicircle until they get back to the highway. Jody and Lindsey cross the highway and do the same thing on the other side.

Once they get back to the highway, Jody nods, "Good enough for me."

Lindsey questions as they walk back to the truck, "What do you want to do about getting some rest?"

Jody glances around, "Well, my brother and Marissa's sleeping bags are in the truck. However, I don't want to sleep out in the open and the cab of the truck is actually too small for one person, let alone both of us."

Lindsey walks around to the back of the truck, "Well, there is a lid on the bed of the truck. Why don't we climb inside and pull the lid down. We can prop it open slightly so there is air and we can sleep in there." She pauses, "Nothing passing by will ever be able to spot us and we can keep the keys on us so no one can access the truck."

Jody walks up by Lindsey, "That's a good idea. Good thinking."

Jody raises the lid that covers the bed of the truck. Lindsey retrieves their weapons from the cab and locks the doors of the truck. Jody climbs in and shifts the things around in the bed of the truck to make room for the two sleeping bags. Jody pushes the supplies and personal belonging of his brother and Marissa as far to the side as possible. Jody sets his gear off to the side as well. Lindsey keeps watch as Jody lays out the two sleeping bags.

Jody whispers to Lindsey, "It's going to be a tight fit. Not much room but enough as long as neither one of us is the type that moves a lot in our sleep."

Lindsey smiles and quietly chuckles, "I guess we'll find out."

Lindsey hands the AR-15 and shotgun to Jody. Jody sets them off to the side as Lindsey climbs into the bed of the truck. Lindsey notices what Jody was saying about the space.

Lindsey smiles, "Wow, it is a tight fit. Guess it's a good thing we don't mind being around each other."

Jody smiles and chuckles to himself, "Yeah, good thing."

Lindsey wiggles her way into one sleeping bag. Jody lowers the lid, but props it slightly open, then Jody wiggles his way into the other sleeping bag.

Lindsey whispers to Jody as she finds a place in her sleeping bag to set her pistol, "How do you want to do this?"

Jody sighs, "I know it's dangerous, but I've set my watch alarm and we're only going to have about four hours of rest before sunrise so let's both go to sleep. I'm going to chance that there are no survivors out and about and if there are zombies in the area, I'm certain they won't spot us inside here."

Lindsey whispers, "Okay."

Jody whispers back, "Besides, I'm a super light sleeper and usually any little noise wakes me up."

Lindsey rolls onto her side, "That's good."

Jody smiles as he gets comfortable, "No so much before, but definitely a good thing since all this started."

Jody and Lindsey both get as comfortable as they can and do their best to get some sleep. Each one wonders what the rest of the night holds and if they'll find any of the others from the group.

CHAPTER 64

While Jody and Lindsey are drifting off to sleep in the forest outside of Tuskegee, Codi wakes up in the tent that her and the others were assigned to. Codi sits up in her cot and holds her stomach as if she is feeling sick. Codi swings her legs around and sits, doubled over on the edge of her cot like she might puke.

After a couple of minutes, Codi reaches over and gently shakes Ryan, "Babe, wake up."

Ryan's eyes pop open when he hears Codi's voice and feels her hand touch him. Like everyone else, Ryan has become more of a light sleeper since the zombie apocalypse began.

Ryan looks at Codi and whispers, "What's wrong?"

Codi has a look of discomfort on her face, "I'm not sure. I'm feeling sick again and have some stomach pain." She pauses, "It's like before, but worse this time."

Ryan sits up on the edge of his cot, "Maybe we need to get you over to the medical building and have you checked out. We've kept it hidden from the others, but we need to find out what's going on with you."

Codi nods and whispers, "Okay."

Ryan and Codi quietly get dressed and make their way over to the doorway of the tent. Four air force personnel are standing guard outside the tent. Ryan explains what is going on to them. One of the air force guards radios in that they will be taking Ryan and Codi over to the medical building.

Once they get the clearance, two of the air force personnel escort Ryan and Codi over to the medical building while everyone else sleeps.

The forest outside of Tuskegee is quiet and calm as the sun begins to rise. The new day is slightly overcast, but the warm breeze keeps the temperature at a comfortable level. Jody and Lindsey have managed to get some rest in the cramped quarters of the back of the truck. Not long after the sun has broken the eastern horizon, Jody's watch alarm starts beeping.

Jody's eyes pop open and he reaches down and shuts the alarm off. Jody allows his eyes to focus and he listens to see if he can hear anything that might be outside of the truck. Once he's sure there is nothing around, Jody reaches over and gently shakes Lindsey to wake her up.

Jody whispers, "Hey girl, time to wake up."

Lindsey quickly wakes up when she feels Jody's hand touch her shoulder.

Lindsey glances around, "I had the weirdest dream that I was in a coffin."

Jody smiles and whispers back, "Kind of feels like we are, doesn't it?"

Lindsey smiles and chuckles lightly, "Right."

Jody reaches up and gently pushes the lid of the truck bed up. Jody puts on his glasses, grabs his pistol and sits up, looking around to see if there are any zombies in the general area. Once he is certain it is okay, Jody wiggles out of the sleeping bag. Jody puts his boots back on as he slept in the rest of his clothes. Jody climbs out of the back of the truck with his pistol.

Lindsey wiggles out of her sleeping bag and puts her shoes back on as she slept in the rest of her clothes. Lindsey grabs her pistol and climbs out of the back of the truck. Lindsey looks around as her eyes focus to the daylight.

Lindsey speaks while looking around, "I guess none of the others made it here. If they did, they've already moved on."

Jody nods as he glances around, "Its only been a day since we escaped the campsite. They may have gotten held up somewhere. I think we should wait for awhile and see if any of them show up."

Lindsey nods and looks at Jody, "So, what do you want to do to pass the time?"

Jody looks over at Lindsey, "Well, there are a hand full of shotgun shells in their things. You can load your shotgun. After that, I think we should eat, then look over the map and plan out the rest of the trip to Fort Pulaski."

Lindsey glances around again, "Sounds good to me."

Jody heads around to the cab of the truck to get the map out while Lindsey grabs her shotgun and the shotgun shells. Lindsey loads her shotgun as Jody pulls the map of Alabama and the map of Georgia out. Lindsey grabs some food and a couple bottles of water. Lindsey and Jody start to eat as they wait and hope that some of the others show up.

When Ken and the others woke up, they realized right away that Ryan and Codi were missing. Ken went over and talked to the guards at the front of the tent and found out that Ryan and Codi went over to the hospital a few hours earlier.

Ken and the others have gone over to the medical building to find Ryan and Codi. As Ken and the others walk into the waiting area, they see Ryan and Codi walking out of the back and into the waiting area.

Ken looks at Ryan and Codi, "Everything okay?"

Ryan nods, "Yeah, Codi wasn't feeling good so we came over here to have her checked out."

Mike looks around and nods, "Well, since we're here why don't we check on Marissa and let her know what we've decided before we go eat and get our things to leave."

Lisa nods, "Sounds good to me."

Ken and the others head off to Marissa's room. Everyone walks into Marissa's room as Marissa is finishing her breakfast. Marissa smiles as she sees everyone walk into the room.

Marissa looks at everyone, "Good morning. How are you all doing?"

Michael, Jody's brother, smiles, "We're doing good. The question is, how are you doing?"

Marissa shrugs, "The same. The pain is constant and the doctor has talked about needing to do surgery to fix my knee, then rehabbing it for awhile."

Ken looks at Marissa, "Well, we talked things over last night and we've decided to leave after breakfast. We know it's safe here for now, but we know some of the others could be out there and we think Fort Pulaski is still the best decision."

Marissa nods and lets out a slight smile, "I figured that much." She pauses, "I thought about it a lot too last night before sleeping. As much as I want to go, I think its best if I stay here for now. With my knee the way it is, I wouldn't be able to keep up if we ran into trouble."

Lisa nods slightly, "Well, we certainly understand. You've got to think of your wellbeing first and this place is safe enough for now."

Mike chimes in, "Besides, you can always try to get to Fort Pulaski later after your knee is better."

Marissa nods, "That's what I was thinking."

Ashley looks caringly at Marissa, "We're sure going to miss you though."

Marissa smiles at Ashley, "I'm going to miss you all too. Especially not knowing what happened to Jody, Lindsey, Chad, Amber and Rachel."

Codi speaks up, "Well, you won't be alone cause Ryan, Lucky and I will be here with you."

Everyone looks over at Codi, kind of shocked by what she just said.

Ryan looks at the others, "We've decided to stay here." He pauses, "I guess we can tell you all now. Codi has been getting a little sick off and on. We had an idea of what it might have been and it was confirmed this morning, Codi is pregnant."

Everyone in the group is taken by surprise by the news, but after a couple seconds, it is all smiles.

Ashley walks over and gives Codi a big hug, "Congratulations!"

Codi smiles and hugs Ashley back, "Thanks."

Ashley steps back, "How far along?"

Codi sighs, "Already a month is what they think."

Rochelle smiles, "Well, in a bad world now, that is some good news."

Ryan nods and smiles, "We figured it'd be best if we stayed here until after the birth. They have better medical facilities here and it'll be safer for Codi." He pauses, "We also figured that once the baby is born and ready to travel, we can try to make it to Fort Pulaski with Marissa."

Ken motions with his hand, "Hey, no explanation needed. Trust me, we all understand and feel you're making the best decision."

Lisa nods and speaks up, "Definitely. Its much safer for you two to stay here and have the baby rather than risking it out there and trying to have the baby at Fort Pulaski where there is only us and no medical facilities of any kind."

Codi smiles, "I'm glad you all understand. If you do find the others, let them know that we're thinking of them too and wish them the best."

Michael, Lindsey's husband, speaks up, "I hate to be the rain on the parade, but we really need to get going before it gets too late."

Shana nods in agreement, "He's right. We've got to get some breakfast, then get our things and get on the road to Tuskegee."

Everyone looks back at Marissa.

Marissa lets out a smile, "Goodbye everyone."

Everyone gives Marissa a hug goodbye, then Ken and the others make their way out of the medical building and head for the chow hall.

Jody and Lindsey have finished eating and have the maps spread out on the hood of the truck. The two of them have been going over the different options for the rest of the trip to Fort Pulaski. One thing they both know is that in order to get to Fort Pulaski, they are going to have to go thru at least part of Savannah.

Lindsey runs her finger along the map, "I think that this route is the best for the next day's trip."

Jody nods, "I think you're right. We can just stay on Highway 80 and 8, skirt around the north of Columbus and continue on until we reach Highway 96 in Georgia. We just stay on Highway 96 and stop at the river between Reynolds and Fort Valley. We can stay there for the night."

Lindsey looks up at Jody, "There is one thing we also need to think about."

Jody looks at Lindsey, "What's that?"

Lindsey sighs, "It might just be the two of us from here on out. We're going to need more supplies and gas. Also, when are we going to move on."

Jody nods, "Yeah. I figure we'll wait here for a day and if nobody is here by the morning, we'll leave." He pauses, "I figure we can find gas in some abandoned cars along the way in Columbus or the other smaller towns. We can also raid any stores that we might pass along the highway. I really wouldn't want to get too far off the trail if its just the two of us."

Lindsey glances around, "I hear you there." She pauses, "Well, I think we might want to walk the perimeter again, just to be on the safe side."

Jody glances around, "Good idea." He pauses, "Looks like we're going to get to know each other's life story and everything about each other cause we've got an entire day of time to pass."

Lindsey smiles and chuckles, "Right! Lots of stories today."

Jody folds up the maps and puts them in the cab of the truck. Lindsey grabs her shotgun as she is already wearing her pistol. Jody is wearing his gear and has just his pistol since his rifle is out of ammo. Jody and Lindsey start to walk slowly along the bank of the river and talk as they check around for zombies or other survivors.

CHAPTER 65

Ken and the others are standing on the parking lot in front of the building where they met the Colonel. Ken and the others have finished breakfast and have all their things packed and waiting by the vehicles. All of them are waiting on the Staff Sergeant to have their weapons brought to them. Mike has already loaded Shadow up in the van.

Ken looks at Ryan and Codi, "Are you sure you don't want us to leave a vehicle for you?"

Ryan shakes his head, "We're sure, besides, you'll need them to keep enough supplies on hand."

Codi chimes in, "Plus, we can get a vehicle to use from around here before we leave."

Ashley glances around, "So, how do we want to divide up who's riding in what vehicle?"

Lisa speaks up, "Well, Rochelle and I will take my Jeep for now. Why don't you ride with Michael and Daniel in the Trailblazer for now. Shana, Michael and the boys can take the Hyundai." She pauses, "Ken and Mike can take the van with Shadow. Does that sound good to everyone?"

Michael, Jody's brother, nods, "Sounds good to me."

Everyone else nods in agreement.

Zach questions, "What about partners now?"

Ken sees the Staff Sergeant and a couple of air force personnel approaching with their weapons, "We'll worry about setting those up once we stop for the night at the forest outside of Tuskegee."

The Staff Sergeant looks at Ken and the others, "Here are your weapons back. I wish we could give you ammo or supplies, but we have to keep everything we have."

Mike replies, "That's okay. We have enough supplies in our vehicles to get us by for now. Thanks for the gasoline though, it really helps."

The Staff Sergeant nods, "Our pleasure. We wish you'd stay, but we understand why you're leaving. Remember, you're always welcome back here if you need a place to stay."

Michael, Lindsey's husband, nods, "Thanks."

Everyone except for Ryan and Codi retrieve their weapons from the two air force personnel.

The Staff Sergeant glances around, "So, you all know how to get to where you're going?"

Ken nods, "Yeah, we planned out our route while waiting on the guns."

The Staff Sergeant nods, "Well, just follow the HUMVEE to the gate. Good Luck, I hope you all make it to wherever you're going."

Shana smiles, "Thanks."

The Staff Sergeant walks off and the two air force personnel head over and get in the HUMVEE.

Codi looks at everyone, "Well, let's keep this to as few of tears as we can."

Ashley steps over and hugs Codi as tears enter her eyes, "I'm going to miss your face."

Codi hugs Ashley as she gets tears in her eyes, "I'm going to miss you girly."

Its hugs all around as everyone says goodbye to Ryan and Codi. Codi also goes over to the van and says goodbye to Shadow. Once all the hugs and goodbyes are done, Ken and the others load up in their assigned vehicles. The HUMVEE pulls away. The van pulls away first, then the Jeep followed by the Trailblazer and the Hyundai is last. Codi and Ryan wave goodbye as the vehicles pull away and they watch the people that they had become so close to, as close as family since this all began, drive away. Ryan and Codi can only hope that they all make it to Fort Pulaski and that they might one day see them again.

Jody and Lindsey have the sleeping bags laid out on the top of the lid covering the bed of the truck. Jody and Lindsey are sitting on the sleeping bags, having just finished lunch as the sun is in the noon sky.

Jody is just staring off, "So, that's what I did in the Marine Corps."

Lindsey can't believe what she just heard and knows that it must have taken a lot of trust from Jody to tell her.

Lindsey takes Jody's hand, "I can understand why you have trouble sleeping sometimes."

Jody looks at Lindsey, "Thanks for listening."

Lindsey smiles, "Of course."

Jody decides to change the subject, "I still think its awesome how you and Michael ended up together now. After knowing each other, then each having your own life and somehow ending up back together. That sure is something."

Lindsey nods and keeps smiling, "Yeah, its just meant to be for us. He's the love of my life." She pauses and gets a sadder look, "I really hope him and Daniel are safe."

Jody squeezes Lindsey's hand, "I'm sure they are."

Lindsey looks at Jody and her smile returns, "Thanks."

Jody returns the smile, "Anytime." He pauses, "I don't know about you, but I'm kind of tired."

Lindsey glances around, "Yeah, me too. Those four hours were not a whole lot of rest."

Jody glances around, "Why don't you get a nap in and I'll keep watch. I'll wake you up in three hours and we'll switch."

Lindsey nods slightly, "Sounds good to me."

Lindsey and Jody let go of each other's hand. Lindsey slides down onto the sleeping bag. Lindsey's shotgun is sitting on the roof of the truck cab just above their heads so either one of them can get to it. Lindsey lays on her side facing away from Jody.

Lindsey speaks, "Thanks for everything you've done."

Jody smiles and puts his hand on Lindsey's shoulder, "Its my pleasure, but don't sell yourself short. You've done more than pull your share of everything, even saving my life back there with the zombies."

Lindsey rolls over and is now facing Jody.

Lindsey smiles as she takes Jody's hand, "Well, just returning the favor."

Jody smiles at Lindsey. Lindsey closes her eyes as Jody sits next to her and continues to glance around, keeping an eye on the area around them. In a couple minutes, Lindsey is able to fall asleep.

Its just a little after noon as Ken and the others continue on towards their destination. The convoy made it back north to Highway 14 and since then, they have made it quite a ways east. The convoy has recently passed thru a small town called Tallassee and are on their way to Notasulga.

Mike is keeping his eyes on the highway and one hand on Shadow as Ken is looking over the map. Ken nods at the progress that they've made in the first half of the day.

Ken looks up at the road, "We've made some good time. We should reach Notasulga in a couple of hours. From there we'll head south and should reach Tuskegee just after dinner time."

Mike nods as he stays focused on the highway, "We should probably stop sometime after we turn south and get something to eat before we reach Tuskegee." He pauses, "Plus, I know Shadow will need to get out and do his thing."

Ken looks down at Shadow and smiles, "We can most certainly do that."

Shadow looks up at Ken and has his usual, big smile on his face. Ken reaches down and pets Shadow as Mike continues to focus on the road ahead.

A little over an hour has passed and Lisa is continuing to stay focused on the back of Mike's van. Lisa is pleased with the time they have made and knows that they are getting closer to the town of Notasulga. Rochelle continues to look around and keeps an eye out for zombies.

Rochelle questions, "So, do you think we'll make it to Tuskegee before it gets dark?"

Lisa keeps her eyes on the road, "Definitely. We've been making good time." She pauses, "We'll probably stop sometime after we turn south and get some food and take a break."

Rochelle looks at Lisa, "I really hope the others are already there waiting for us. I miss them, especially Jody and Lindsey."

Lisa nods slightly as her expression changes to one of concern, "Me too. I miss Jody and Lindsey as well."

Rochelle goes back to glancing around, "I don't know what we would've done if this happened and we didn't have Jody around at the start. We probably wouldn't have made it." She pauses, "He's a great guy."

Lisa can't help but let out a little smile, "Yes he is. I feel lucky that we were there with him and the others when this all happened."

Rochelle nods slightly, "Yeah, very lucky."

The talking dies down as Lisa and Rochelle each think about Jody, Lindsey, Chad, Amber and Rachel. Lisa and Rochelle each hope that they are alive and that they'll meet up with them at Tuskegee.

Another hour has passed as Michael, Lindsey's husband, keeps a close eye on the back of Lisa's Jeep. Ashley has been keeping an eye out for zombies while Daniel has fallen asleep in his car seat.

Ashley continues to look around, "We should be getting close to Notasulga."

At that time, Michael, Lindsey's husband, sees the brake lights of the Jeep come on. Michael, Lindsey's husband, starts to slow the Trailblazer down as they pass a road sign that shows they are close to Notasulga.

Michael, Lindsey's husband, smiles, "Yep, I'd say we're close."

Michael, Lindsey's husband, slows the Trailblazer down some more as they enter the town of Notasulga. Its an extremely small town. Ashley keeps a look out for Highway 81 south which is the highway they need. In a very short time after entering the town, Michael, Lindsey's husband, sees the turn signal of the Jeep come on. Michael, Lindsey's husband, slows the Trailblazer down and turns onto Highway 81 south behind Lisa's Jeep.

Ashley smiles, "Well, that was easy enough."

Michael, Lindsey's husband, nods, "It helps when the town is this small."

Ashley chuckles some, "It sure does."

Michael, Lindsey's husband, stays close to the Jeep as it doesn't take them long before they leave the town of Notasulga behind them.

Ashley glances around again, "You know, I really hope Jody, Lindsey and the others have already made it there."

Michael, Lindsey's husband, nods slightly, "Me too."

The talking dies down some as Michael, Lindsey's husband, does his best to stay focused on the road and not think about if Lindsey is alive or dead. Ashley continues to look around, hoping that when they get to their stopping point for the night, the others will already be there.

Its been a couple of hours since the convoy turned south. Shana is keeping an eye on the back of the Trailblazer as Michael, Jody's brother, Zach and Tyler are keeping an eye out for zombies. Shana is pleased with the time they have made, but knows that it is close to dinner time and that they are getting close to Tuskegee.

Shana sighs as she stays focused on the road, "I wonder if we'll stop before Tuskegee."

Zach continues to glance around, "I hope so, I could use a break."

Michael, Jody's brother, smiles, "Me too."

Tyler stares out his window, "I hope Jody and the others are there waiting for us. I really miss them."

Shana looks in the mirror at Tyler, "Me too."

Michael, Jody's brother, looks out his window, "If anyone could have made it out of there, it would be Jody and I'm sure he'd do everything he could to get the others out too."

Zach nods, "Yeah, he's pretty good and seems to know a lot."

Shana smiles, "Well, he's had the right training, that's for sure."

Michael, Jody's brother, smiles again, "He sure has."

At that time, Shana sees the brake lights of the Trailblazer come on. Shana starts to slow the car down.

Zach looks ahead, "I wonder what's going on."

Michael, Jody's brother, glances around, "I'm sure they've just decided to stop and take a break."

Shana pulls the car to a stop behind the Trailblazer and the other two vehicles. Shana puts the car in park and shuts it off. Shana, Zach, Tyler and Michael, Jody's brother, gets out of the car and heads over to the rest of the group.

CHAPTER 66

Lindsey has been sitting on the lid of the truck bed quietly for awhile since her and Jody switched over from her napping to him napping. Lindsey looks up at the sky, then picks up Jody's watch that he let her use to keep track of the time. Lindsey knows she can't reach Jody's foot to tap it to wake him up, but she remembers part of their conversation when Jody mentioned that if someone he trusts is near him while he's sleeping then he's okay and isn't jumpy.

Lindsey reaches over and gently places her hand on Jody's shoulder as she whispers, "Hey, it's time to wake up."

Jody's eyes open up, but he doesn't make any sudden movements. Jody looks up at Lindsey and smiles.

Lindsey smiles back, "I'm glad you didn't get all jumpy and crazy waking up."

Jody stretches and sits up, "Na, I think I'm to the point that I trust being asleep around you." He smiles at Lindsey, "So, you ready to eat and walk the perimeter?"

Lindsey smiles back, "Sure am."

Lindsey gets down from the lid of the truck bed. Jody hands Lindsey her shotgun, then he gets down. Jody puts on his gear as Lindsey gets some food and two bottles of water out.

516

Lindsey sets the food and water on the hood of the truck, "It's going to get dark in a few hours."

Jody nods and glances around, "Yeah. I'm hoping if anyone shows that it'll be before then." He pauses, "If not, we'll sleep tonight like we did early this morning and we'll leave tomorrow after breakfast."

Lindsey nods, "Okay."

Jody and Lindsey start eating and as they eat, they both hope that some of the others find them before they decide to leave in the morning.

Ken and the others have finished eating and Mike has walked Shadow around and has gotten him loaded back up in the van. Everyone meets over by the van as Ken is holding his map.

Ken speaks to the group while looking at the map, "We should be about an hour from Tuskegee. There appears to be a road that we can take that will allow us to skirt the east edge of town and link us up with Highway 80. From there we'll head east into the forest."

Ashley questions, "How far do you want to go into the forest before stopping for the night?"

Lisa glances around, "Well, we'll either go until we reach the east edge, then stop or we'll stop sooner if we run into the others that might have made it there." She pauses, "There should be at least one river we'll cross so that's the best chance of finding them if they made it."

Michael, Lindsey's husband, questions, "How long do we plan on waiting if no one is there?"

Mike sighs, "Ken and I talked about that and we think that we can rest for the night and we have enough supplies that we can go ahead and stay another day before moving on. That's of course if we don't run into any problems."

Michael, Jody's brother, speaks up, "Sounds good. We should get loaded up and get moving. We're going to be running out of daylight in a couple of hours."

Shana chimes in, "And we definitely want to make it to a stopping point before dark."

Ken folds up the map, "You two are right. Let's get going."

Everyone heads back off to their vehicles. Once loaded up, Mike pulls the van away. Lisa falls in behind him with her Jeep as Michael, Lindsey's husband, pulls in behind the Jeep with the Trailblazer. Shana pulls in behind the Trailblazer with the Hyundai and the convoy continues on towards its destination for tonight.

Lindsey and Jody have made it halfway around the perimeter that they have laid out around the truck. The two of them have continued to tell stories about themselves.

Lindsey talks while walking, "You know what I really miss, my babies. All my pit bulls."

Jody nods slightly, "I bet you do. Its hard to lose doggies, especially when you've grown so attached to them that they are just like any other close family member."

Lindsey smiles as she recalls her dogs, "I can remember so clearly that when Michael and I would lay down, they would just have to be there. A couple of them would get up in bed with us." She pauses and chuckles, "I would practically be squashed and would almost always end up with a paw in my face at some point."

Jody lets out a good chuckle, "That's too funny! Its amazing how they just work their way in." He pauses, "Shadow did that all the time to me. He'd actually beat me to the bed and lay across the bed so all I'd have is a little bit of space on the edge of the bed. He'd stay there for awhile, then he'd hop down and lay next to the bed."

Lindsey smiles and chuckles, "That's funny." She pauses, "I'm glad Shadow has been with us. I don't know what my life would be like without any dogs in it."

Jody nods and glances around, "Right. I know what you mean. Who knows, we ran into that dog in the store awhile back. We might find more before we get to Fort Pulaski."

Lindsey smiles and glances around, "That'd be awesome if we did." She pauses, "You know what?"

Jody looks at Lindsey, "What's that?"

Lindsey looks at Jody, "Since you write books, we should find some notebooks so you can write our story about everything that has happened since this all began." She pauses, "You may never get the chance to get it published, but if society does manage to recover, it'd be a great record of things that happened."

Jody nods, "That's a really good idea girl. Next time we stop for supplies we'll have to see if we can find some notebooks or paper." He pauses, "You'll have to help me too."

Lindsey smiles, "Sure thing."

Jody and Lindsey continue to talk while they walk the rest of the perimeter. Both of them hope that before long, some of the others arrive.

Mike stays focused on the road as the convoy is nearly to Tuskegee. Shadow is sitting between Mike and Ken with his usual smile, waiting for his attention. Ken keeps looking around for zombies and for the turn off that they need in order to skirt around Tuskegee.

Ken speaks, "It should be close."

Mike nods as he keeps his eyes on the road, "Yeah, we're nearly to Tuskegee."

Ken reaches down and pets Shadow, "I've tried not to show too much emotion, but I really hope the others made it out and we manage to meet back up with them."

Mike nods slightly, "I know what you mean. I really hate not knowing what happened to them."

Ken nods, then sees a road coming up, "I think this might be it cause we are about to the city limits."

Mike starts to slow the van down as they near the upcoming road.

Ken smiles as they get closer, "Yep, this is it."

Mike slows the van some more and turns onto the new road. Ken continues to pet Shadow and look around as Mike speeds the van back up. The rest of the convoy makes the turn and catches back up to the vehicle in front of them.

Lindsey and Jody have been back at the truck for a little while. Both of them notice that the sun is getting lower in the sky and they know it'll be dark soon.

Lindsey sighs, "I'm betting we have about an hour of daylight left."

Jody glances up at the sky, then looks at his watch, "Yep, about that."

Lindsey glances around and lets out a depressed sigh, "I was really hoping we'd find some of the others today."

Jody puts his hand on Lindsey's shoulder, "There's still time."

At that moment, Jody and Lindsey both look back west along the highway as they swear they hear something that sounds like vehicles coming towards them. Jody and Lindsey each wonder if it is some vehicles and if its their people or someone else.

Lindsey looks at Jody, "Do you hear that?"

Jody nods, "Oh yes."

Lindsey looks back at the road as the sound gets louder, "I wonder if it's any of them."

Jody glances around, "We can't take the chance and stay here in the open. Let's head over to those trees until we can see who it is. I've got the keys so they can't take the truck."

Lindsey grabs her shotgun as she is already wearing her pistol and Jody grabs his rifle even though its empty and he is already wearing his gear with his pistol. Jody and Lindsey run over to the trees which are only about fifteen yards from the truck. The noise is getting louder and Jody and Lindsey can definitely make out the sound of multiple vehicles now.

Ken continues to look around as Mike stays focused on the road. They haven't been in the forest very long, but with the trees all around, its already getting darker even though the sun hasn't set yet. Ken looks out the window to his right.

Mike suddenly says something in excitement, "Look! I see a vehicle up ahead on the far side of that bridge and I swear it looks like my truck!"

Ken looks back ahead and sees what Mike is talking about, "It sure does. Let's stop and check it out."

Mike starts slowing the van down as they near the bridge and the closer they get, the more Ken and Mike are sure it's their truck. Mike takes the van slowly across the bridge and stops in the road beside the truck. The rest of the convoy stops.

Jody and Lindsey can see the vehicles now from their hiding place in the trees and knows that it's the vehicles from their group. The two of them stay hidden though until they see who it is that gets out of the vehicles.

Ken and Mike get out of the van. Lisa and Rochelle get out of the Jeep as Michael, Lindsey's husband, Ashley and Daniel get out of the Trailblazer. Shana, Zach, Tyler and Michael, Jody's brother, get out of the Hyundai. Everyone walks over by the truck.

Mike looks at the others, "This is definitely my truck."

Michael, Jody's brother, glances around, "Yeah, but I wonder who drove it here and where they are."

At that time, Jody and Lindsey step out from their hiding spot behind the trees.

Jody hollers to Ken and the others, "Man, are you all a sight for sore eyes!"

Ken and the others look over to the trees and they see Jody and Lindsey walking towards them. Everyone has a huge smile on their face.

Daniel sees Lindsey, "Momma!"

Daniel takes off running towards Lindsey. Lindsey has a huge smile as she runs towards Daniel. Lindsey drops her shotgun as Daniel jumps into her arms.

Lindsey squeezes Daniel tight, "I've missed you so much! I was so worried about you!" Lindsey gets tears in her eyes, "I love you so much Daniel!"

Daniel hugs Lindsey as tight as he can, "I love you momma!"

Jody stops next to Lindsey and Daniel and picks up Lindsey's shotgun. Ken and the others quickly make their way over to Jody, Lindsey and Daniel. Lindsey stands up, still holding onto Daniel.

Jody smiles as the others walk up, "Its good to see all of you."

Lisa doesn't stop as she gets closer and she wraps her arms around Jody, "It's so good to see you."

Jody does his best to hug Lisa back while he is holding his rifle and Lindsey's shotgun. Michael, Lindsey's husband, steps up to Lindsey and Daniel and takes them in his arms.

Michael, Lindsey's husband, gets tears in his eyes, "I thought I lost you. I love you so much."

Lindsey smiles as she melts into her husband's arms, "I thought I lost you too." She sniffles, "I love you."

Lisa steps back and Mike gives Jody a hug, then Michael, Jody's brother, steps up and hugs Jody.

Ashley looks at Jody, "My turn."

Jody hands his rifle and Lindsey's shotgun to his brother as Ashley steps up and wraps her arms around Jody.

Ashley squeezes Jody tight, "I'm so happy to see you again. I've missed you so much."

Jody hugs Ashley, "I've missed you too."

Ashley steps back and looks over at Lindsey who is still holding Daniel and still in her husband's arms.

Ashley smiles, "Okay, make some room cause its my turn."

Lindsey smiles as Michael, Lindsey's husband, steps back. Ashley steps over and gives Lindsey a huge hug.

Lindsey smiles as she wraps her free arm around Ashley, "It's so good to see you."

Ashley smiles, "It's good to see you too. I thought we'd never see the two of you again."

Shana, who is now hugging Jody, smiles, "I thought the same thing."

Jody hugs Shana back, "We were beginning to wonder if we were going to be stuck on our own."

Mike glances around, "Well, as happy as this reunion is, let's get the vehicles out of the middle of the highway and get things ready for tonight. Plus, I'm sure Shadow is ready to see the two of you again."

Jody looks at his dad, then at Lindsey, "Sounds good to us."

Mike, Lisa, Shana and Michael, Lindsey's husband, head over to move the vehicles while everyone else waits.

CHAPTER 67

The vehicles have been moved off the highway and Jody and Lindsey have showed everyone else the perimeter they have been walking around the truck. Now the group is back over at the vehicles as the sun is nearly set in the west.

Lindsey looks at Jody, "How do we want to handle tonight?"

Jody glances around at everyone, "Well, first we need to establish teams again. As far as sleeping, we have no tents, but it's nice outside so we can sleep in just the sleeping bags unless the weather gets bad again."

Ken looks at Jody, "How do you want the teams set up?"

Jody sighs as he knows they are missing people, "Well, they'll be the same for the most part. Lisa and I, Lindsey and her husband, Shana and my brother and you and my dad." He pauses, "Since that is only four teams, I'm going to make another team, Zach and Ashley."

Shana looks at Jody, "What?"

Jody sighs, "We need as many teams as we can get and Zach is old enough and has more than proven himself capable. That'll allow us to do two hour shifts and get enough rest at the same time." He pauses, "Rochelle, Tyler and Daniel will continue to stay together and help with Shadow."

Lindsey looks at Ken, "So, do you all know what happened to Ryan, Codi and Marissa?"

Ken nods, "Yeah, they made it out of the camp. Marissa hurt her knee really bad. We all ended up linking back up at Maxwell Air Force Base where they had set up a safe haven. It was really nice."

Mike picks up the story, "We decided that we needed to continue on in case others made it out and headed here. Marissa decided to stay because of her knee and she couldn't walk. Ryan and Codi decided to stay because they found out Codi is pregnant." He pauses, "They wanted us to make sure that if we found anyone else that we let you know that they're praying for you."

Lindsey smiles, "I'm glad to hear they're okay."

Ashley looks at Lindsey, "You only asked about them. Do you know about Chad, Amber and Rachel?"

Lindsey looks at Jody.

Jody speaks up, "They didn't make it out of the campsite. Lindsey went to help Amber as soon as Chad was taken and I went to help Rachel. Once Amber and Rachel were killed, I found Lindsey and we escaped on foot."

Lindsey nods, "We held up in a barn for most of the day, then made our way back to the campsite. We got the truck and headed here. We got here early this morning and have been waiting to see if anyone else would show up."

Michael, Lindsey's husband, brings up the next topic, "So, we know no one else is coming. When are we going to continue on?"

Jody glances around at everyone, "I say, first thing in the morning, after we eat. If that sounds good to everyone."

Everyone looks around and nods.

Lisa speaks up, "Well, we should probably get things set up for the night before the sun completely sets and get our watch rotation started."

Tyler speaks up, "What about Shadow?"

Jody sighs, "Since we don't have a tent for him to stay in, he'll have to stay in the van for the night. Whoever is on watch will check in on him each time they are by the vehicles. Okay?"

Everyone nods again.

Jody continues, "Well, let's get to it."

Everyone heads off and grabs their sleeping bags. The group sets up the sleeping bags in the clearing just off to the side of the highway near the vehicles. Lisa gets her last 20 shotgun shells and reloads her shotgun. Jody gets the last of his rifle ammo which gives him close to one full magazine. The others in the group reload their weapons, but they all know that their ammunition supply is running low. Jody and Lisa begin their watch as everyone else tries to get comfortable.

It is nearing the end of Michael, Lindsey's husband, and Lindsey's watch. Jody and Lisa fell asleep not long after they were relieved. Michael, Lindsey's husband, and Lindsey stop by the vehicles.

Michael, Lindsey's husband, looks at Lindsey, "I still can't believe that we found each other. I was trying to hold it together for Daniel, but I was hurting so bad inside thinking I'd lost you."

Lindsey smiles at her husband, "I know. I stayed as focused as I could on what Jody and I had to do to get away, but I was crushed inside thinking about you and Daniel."

Michael, Lindsey's husband, looks away, "So, you and Jody were trapped in a barn, then when you got here the two of you slept in the bed of the truck for a few hours." He pauses, "How'd you all pass the time and wait out the zombies?"

Lindsey can tell her husband is a bit bothered, "Well, in the barn we just dried out our clothes, talked a little and each took a nap while the other kept watch. After we got here and rested, we pretty much learned each other's life story while waiting to see if anyone else would show up." She pauses, "We learned about as much as we could about each other I think."

Michael, Lindsey's husband, remains quiet.

Lindsey moves closer to her husband, "And you've got nothing to worry about. Besides from him being a total gentleman and the fact most of my talk was about you and Daniel, we pretty much came to the conclusion that we see each other as brother and sister cause we have so much in common." She pauses, "You're the love of my life and you'll never be without me. I'm yours, always have been and always will be."

Michael, Lindsey's husband, looks at Lindsey, "So, nothing there?"

Lindsey smiles, "Nope. He doesn't see me in that way and I don't look at him like that. I love him like a brother and he loves me like a sister." She gets more stern, "You're it for me, period. You're just going to have to accept that you're stuck with me."

Michael, Lindsey's husband, smiles, "Thank you."

Lindsey returns the smile, "You'll never have to worry about me and my love for you."

Lindsey and Michael, her husband, share a nice kiss, a kiss neither of them wants to end. Finally, the two of them step back and continue on to finish the rest of their watch.

Michael, Jody's brother, and Shana are on watch now as Lindsey and Michael, her husband, are now asleep with

Daniel next to them. Michael, Jody's brother, and Shana stop by the river near the bridge.

Michael, Jody's brother, speaks while looking around, "I hate that Chad, Amber and Rachel didn't make it, but I'm so happy we found Jody and Lindsey."

Shana smiles, "Me too. I was really worried that we'd never see any of them again. As much as I wanted to stay where it was safe, we definitely made the right decision in continuing on."

Michael, Jody's brother, nods, "We sure did." He pauses and looks at Shana, "All this recently also made me realize how much I really care for you. I couldn't imagine being without you or the boys."

Shana looks at Michael, Jody's brother, "I'm not much for sharing my emotions, but I too took a long look at that." She pauses, "There is no way I could be without you in my life. I know we were apart for so long, but those feelings I think were always there."

Michael, Jody's brother, looks away, "Yeah, after the second time we tried and ended up falling apart, I just never could see myself with anyone else and I pretty much gave up on trying."

Shana sighs, "I know, it hurt so much that time and I fell in with anyone who'd convince me that they were there for me." She pauses, "But you were still there on my mind. When Jody and I tried, it was good, but still not the same as it was when I was with you." She pauses again, "I want to be with you and even though the world as we knew it is gone, I'm feeling better since I'm getting to be with you."

Shana looks away from Michael, Jody's brother.

Michael, Jody's brother, looks back at Shana, "I know. I didn't have much of a life and other than losing people I care about, I'm almost happy that this happened cause it brought us back together." He pauses, "I know that sounds crazy, but I can't help but feel that way."

Shana looks back at Michael, Jody's brother, "No reason to think that or feel that way. Everything happens for a reason and we're together now, that's all that matters because we can't change anything that has happened."

Michael, Jody's brother, smiles and steps close to Shana, "I'm so happy you're here with me. I love you."

Shana smiles back, "I love you too."

Michael, Jody's brother, and Shana share a nice kiss before continuing on with their watch.

Ashley and Zach have taken over watch now as Michael, Jody's brother, and Shana are fast asleep. Ashley and Zach have been walking quietly for about an hour of their watch. The two of them are walking through the trees around the small campsite.

Zach speaks while they walk, "It feels so weird actually being on a team and taking watch like everyone else."

Ashley smiles, "Well, you have more than proven you're capable of the responsibility." She pauses, "I just can't believe we actually found Jody and Lindsey."

Zach nods, "I know. I kept hoping we would, but I really didn't think we'd ever see them again." He pauses, "I'm feeling good about the rest of the trip. I think we're going to make it okay."

Ashley looks at Zach, "Me too. I've always been a positive person and tried to stay that way through all this, but I was really starting to have my doubts." She pauses, "I just hope we don't lose anyone else."

Zach nods, "Me too. I don't want to lose anyone else either." He pauses and looks at Ashley, "I'm going to do everything I can to keep you all safe."

Ashley looks at Zach and smiles, "Thank you. That's so sweet."

Zach smiles, but looks away from Ashley as he still seems to have developed a crush on her. Ashley chuckles to herself at Zach's reaction as she knows he likes her.

Zach changes the subject, "So, where are you from?"

Ashley smiles at how Zach is trying to play things off, "Well, before this all happened I was living in Neosho."

Ashley and Zach continue to talk and get to know more about each other as they pass their time on their watch.

Ken and Mike are on watch now as Ashley and Zach are back in camp and asleep. Mike and Ken stop by the van to check in on Shadow. Shadow is stretched out sleeping in the van.

Mike smiles as he sees Shadow, "Things are so simple for him. He doesn't even know what has happened, he just knows he's having fun on a trip."

Ken nods, "I know. I wish things were that simple for us."

Mike looks at Ken, "I know, right." He pauses, "I hate that we lost more people, but I'm happy that we found Jody and Lindsey."

Ken sighs and glances around, "Me too. I don't like losing anyone, but both of them are valuable to the group. It would've been a big loss if we didn't have them."

Mike nods, "Yeah, for sure. It's crazy that we've made it this far and that we only got one state left to cross before we reach Fort Pulaski."

Ken nods, "Yeah, but this is going to get even more dangerous. We have to get across Georgia, then make our way thru Savannah and if we get thru all that, we have to make sure the island is clear which has a coast guard station on it." He pauses, "It's going to be a great place to hold up and make a living, but it's going to be a lot of work making sure it's safe."

Mike glances around, "You're right about that. Also, chances are that we'll still lose someone before all is said and done."

Ken looks around, "Yeah, a good chance of that."

Mike and Ken start walking again as they continue on with their watch.

CHAPTER 68

The sun has risen over the camp and everyone is awake now. It is another nice, warm and clear skied morning. The group has loaded their sleeping bags up and Mike has walked Shadow. Everyone is eating now as Shadow is doing his best to look pitiful so maybe someone will give him a bite to eat even though he's already had his dog food.

Lisa questions while eating, "So, what's the plan for travel today?"

Lindsey replies after taking a drink of water, "Jody and I planned out a route which should still be good for all of us."

Ken looks at Jody, "What is it?"

Jody glances at everyone, "We'll just stay on Highway 80 and 8, skirt around the north of Columbus and continue on until we reach Highway 96 in Georgia. We'll just stay on Highway 96 and stop at the river between Reynolds and Fort Valley. We'll camp there for the night."

Mike nods, "Sounds good."

Shana questions, "What about supplies and gas?"

Lindsey replies, "We'll stop somewhere along the way and pick up more supplies. As far as gas, we'll keep doing what we did before, just hit up abandoned cars along the way."

532

Michael, Lindsey's husband, looks at Jody, "How do you want to break down the vehicles and who rides where?"

Jody takes a drink of water, "I thought about that last night. I'll take the lead in the truck with Ashley. Lisa and Rochelle will follow me in the Jeep. Dad, Ken and Shadow will be third in the van. You, Lindsey and Daniel will be fourth in the Trailblazer and Shana, Zach, Tyler and my brother will bring up the rear in the Hyundai." He pauses, "That sound good to everyone?"

Everyone looks around at each other and nods.

Jody continues, "When we're done eating, everyone move your things over to your vehicle, then we'll get moving."

Michael, Jody's brother, questions, "What about Marissa's things?"

Jody finishes his bite of food and places the last piece down for Shadow, "We'll keep it in the truck for now."

Shadow hurries over to the food with his stub tail wagging. Jody pets Shadow as he devours the small bite of food. Everyone else finishes up eating and treating Shadow to small pieces of food, then they start getting ready to leave.

The drive has been uneventful as the convoy has nearly made its way all the way around Columbus. Everyone has been keeping an eye out for a possible place to stop and get some supplies. Jody keeps an eye on the road as Ashley is looking around for zombies and hopefully a store. Jody knows that they are getting close to leaving the Columbus area and he was hoping to find a store along the route.

Ashley finally spots something, "Look, coming up at our turn to head away from town. It's a discount store. We should be able to get into it easily and its just off the intersection so it's not out of the way."

Jody nods, "Works for me."

Jody slows the truck down some as he looks for the exit. The rest of the convoy slows down behind him. Jody weaves around a couple of abandoned cars, then spots the exit. Jody slowly drives the truck off the main highway and onto the side road that leads to the store. The store is about a quarter mile from the highway.

The convoy slowly weaves its way around the clogged up road and they pull into the parking lot. It's just a regular store and not a super store, but they know they might be able to find some stuff to help them. Jody pulls the truck up in front of the main doors. Jody puts the truck in park and turns it off. Jody places the keys on the dashboard as the rest of the convoy stops behind him.

Jody and Ashley get out of the truck and look around. Jody and Ashley are soon joined by the rest of the group as Shadow waits in the van. Everyone is glancing around because they know being this close to the main part of town, there could be plenty of zombies around.

Jody looks at the others, "I know this place doesn't have a grocery section, but we can find some food and check on getting some tents."

Ken questions, "Who's going and who's staying?"

Jody thinks for a second, "Myself and Lisa will go in with Lindsey and Michael and Ashley and Zach. The rest of you wait here. It shouldn't take us long."

Zach gets a smile on his face as he knows this is his first chance to go on a mission for the group.

Jody looks at Ashley, "Once we get inside, you and Zach each grab a basket."

Ashley nods, "Okay."

Jody, Lisa, Lindsey, Michael, Lindsey's husband, Ashley and Zach grab their weapons and head for the store as the others wait outside and keep watch.

Jody and Lisa are walking in front with Ashley and Zach behind them with carts as Lindsey and Michael, her husband, are bringing up the rear. It didn't take them long to find what water and food was left and they have that stuff in Zach's cart.

Lisa looks at Jody, "What now?"

Jody glances around, "Let's see if there are any tents in the outdoor section, then we'll stop at the hygiene stuff on the way out."

Lisa nods and whispers, "Okay."

Jody and Lisa start walking towards the back corner of the store where the outdoor section is at. The sound of the baskets echo through the empty store. Everyone of them is straining to hear anything and they keep glancing around to make sure no zombies walk up on them.

It is a slow walk and seems like it takes an hour even though it only takes a few minutes. Jody and Lisa cover each other as they check around each isle until they spot the isle they are looking for. Jody and Lisa start down the aisle with the others close behind them.

Jody checks the shelves while Lisa keeps watch at one end of the isle and Lindsey and Michael, her husband, are watching the other end of the isle. Jody smiles as he sees what he's looking for. Jody finds two smaller, four person tents and one larger tent. Jody loads the first tent in Ashley's basket when everyone hears something coming towards them.

Jody looks over to Lisa, "See anything?"

Lisa shakes her head, "Nope."

Lindsey looks at Jody, "We've got a zombie coming our way. Just one."

Jody nods and grabs the second tent, "Take care of it."

Lindsey nods, "Okay."

Michael, Lindsey's husband, changes his pistol over to his left hand and pulls out the jungle primitive knife from his hip. The zombie staggers quickly towards Michael, Lindsey's husband, and Lindsey. Michael, Lindsey's husband, waits for the zombie to get closer, then steps towards the zombie and swings the large knife at the zombie's head. Michael, Lindsey's husband, buries the knife deep in the zombie's head. The zombie's arms fall to its side. The zombie falls to the floor as Michael, Lindsey's husband, removes the knife.

Jody loads the last tent in Ashley's cart as Michael, Lindsey's husband, wipes the blade off and puts his knife up. Jody motions to Lisa and Jody, Lisa, Ashley and Zach walk over to Lindsey and Michael, her husband.

Jody smiles and nods, "Good work, let's get the hygiene stuff and get out of here."

Jody and Lisa start for the hygiene section while everyone else follows like before.

Mike, Ken, Michael, Jody's brother, and Shana are keeping watch while Rochelle, Tyler and Daniel are waiting in the vehicles. Shadow is sitting in the passenger's seat of the van, wanting to see what is going on.

Ken glances around, "I hope they hurry up. I don't like being stopped this close to a city."

Mike nods in agreement, "I know, me either. If there were that many zombies that found us out in the country, I'd hate to see how many are walking around in a city."

Michael, Jody's brother, sighs, "I don't even want to think about it."

Shana lets out a smile, "Me either."

Mike looks over at Shadow and he notices that Shadow's head is fixed off to his left.

Mike whispers, "Hey, Shadow sees or hears something."

Ken, Shana and Michael, Jody's brother, look over at Shadow and notices that he is fixed on something. Ken motions with his hand for the others to follow him. Ken makes his way to the back of the van and slowly peeks around to see if he can spot anything. Ken's eyes get wide as he spots about twenty zombies walking along the road. Ken notices that the zombies don't seem to know that they are there.

Shana whispers, "See anything?"

Ken nods and whispers back, "About twenty zombies in the road, but they appear to not have noticed us."

Michael, Jody's brother, whispers, "That's good. Let's keep it that way."

About that time, Jody and the others come out of the store and start towards the vehicles. Ken, Mike, Shana and Michael, Jody's brother, spin around and see Jody and the others. Ken and Mike start motioning with their hands for Jody and the others to stop and be quiet while Shana and Michael, Jody's brother, are pointing at the zombies out on the road. Jody and the others spot the zombies and stop immediately.

Jody whispers, "Nobody move."

Everyone in the group stands as still as they can, hoping that the zombies won't spot them.

Jody whispers again, "Be ready to move fast if we get spotted. Ashley, take your basket to the truck and Zach, take your basket to the van."

Ken quietly moves back over so he can keep an eye on the group of zombies. Ken sighs as the zombies are nearly out of sight. Everyone in the group breathes a sigh of relief, but too soon as the last zombie looks over at the store and spots Jody and the others just outside of the front door of the store.

Jody speaks, "Move, we're spotted."

Jody and Lisa run for the vehicles as Ashley pushes her basket over to the truck and Zach pushes his basket over to the van. Lindsey and Michael, Lindsey's husband, hurry over to the van. The zombie turns and starts towards Jody and the others. The rest of the group of zombies turn around and start back towards the store.

Jody looks over and sees the zombies, "Load fast and let's go!"

Jody and Ashley toss the tents in the back of the van as Mike, Ken, Lindsey and Michael, Lindsey's husband, unload Zach's basket into the back of the van. Ashley shoves her basket out of the way and Jody and Ashley get in the truck. Zach pushes his basket away and runs for the car.

The rest of the group gets in their vehicles as the group of zombies start onto the parking lot. All the vehicles fire up and Jody puts the truck in drive. Jody presses down on the accelerator and speeds away. The rest of the convoy speeds away, leaving the group of zombies slowly chasing after them.

CHAPTER 69

The convoy has made it out of the Columbus metropolitan area and has been out on the open highway for awhile. It is late morning now as the highway is mostly clear of vehicles, allowing the convoy to keep a good pace.

Jody speaks to Ashley while keeping his eyes on the road, "We should be getting close to where we'll be picking up Highway 96."

Ashley continues to look around, "I would think so."

Jody starts to slow the truck down.

Ashley looks over at Jody, "See something?"

Jody has a somewhat puzzled look, "I think we're coming up to a small town or community."

Ashley looks at the highway ahead and sees what Jody is talking about, "It sure does look like it."

Jody slows down the truck some more as him and Ashley finally see a road sign.

Ashley reads the sign out loud, "Geneva? I don't remember seeing that on the map."

Jody glances around, "I don't think its big enough to make it on the map."

Ashley starts looking around as they enter the very small community. Jody keeps focused on the highway, not wanting to miss their turn onto the new highway.

Ashley points, "There, Highway 96. Looks like we just stay straight."

Jody nods, "Yep."

Jody weaves the truck around an abandoned car and pulls onto Highway 96 as Highway 80 heads off to the north. The rest of the convoy follows the truck.

Lisa stays focused on the back of the truck as the convoy has moved on from the small community of Geneva. Rochelle continues to look around for any signs of zombies and other survivors. Rochelle sees a road sign coming up.

Rochelle looks at Lisa, "Looks like we're nearing Junction City."

Lisa glances over at Rochelle, "I don't think its anything to worry about."

Rochelle sighs, "I'm so ready to get to Fort Pulaski. We're getting so close, I'm actually getting excited."

Lisa smiles at her daughter's reaction, "Me too, but we still have plenty of dangerous areas to go thru so we need to stay focused on that."

Lisa sees the brake lights of the truck come on and she starts to slow the Jeep down. Lisa follows the truck and it appears that they are going to be going around the southern edge of Junction City.

Lisa glances around, "Looks like the highway goes around the town."

Rochelle smiles as she looks around, "Good. I'm ready to avoid towns and cities."

Lisa nods, "Me too."

Lisa weaves around an abandoned semi as she continues to stay close to the truck in front of her that is leading the convoy. It doesn't take long and the convoy is putting Junction City behind them.

Lisa smiles, "That was easy enough."

Rochelle nods as she continues to look around. The convoy heads back onto the open highway.

Mike is staying focused on Lisa's Jeep in front of the van while he is petting Shadow. Ken is continuing to keep an eye out for zombies and other survivors. Shadow is just sitting between Mike and Ken, enjoying the attention he is getting. Mike and Ken both know that they should be stopping anytime for lunch since it is after the noon hour now.

Mike glances around, "I wonder where Jody plans on stopping."

Ken keeps looking around, "I'm sure it'll be anytime now. He knows that everyone needs a break and Shadow is going to need to get out of the van."

Mike nods, "We're making good time though. We'll make it to our stopping point probably before dinner."

Ken nods as he looks around and sees a large lake coming up on the right side of the highway, "Yeah, but we should still stop for the night where we plan. No need to push it and end up in a bad place or situation."

Mike continues to pet Shadow while he stays focused on the road, "Most definitely. As close as we're getting, playing it safe is of the utmost importance."

Ken looks around as they pass the large lake, "Oh yeah. No sense in taking chances now. We got lucky enough to escape the campsite that got overrun and to find everyone again."

Mike glances around, "You can say that again."

Mike sees the brake lights of the Jeep come on and he starts to slow the van down, "This must be it because I don't see anything around."

Ken continues to glance around, "Yeah, I think its break time."

Mike continues to slow the van down and he eventually pulls to a stop behind Lisa's jeep. Mike and Ken get out, leaving Shadow in the van for now as they go to meet up with the rest of the group.

The group took an extra long break since they have been making good time which Shadow didn't mind as he got to check out plenty of new locations. The convoy has been back on the highway as the day enters the early afternoon time.

Michael, Lindsey's husband, is keeping a close eye on the van in front of the Trailblazer. Lindsey is looking around for any signs of zombies or other survivors while Daniel has drifted off to sleep.

Lindsey spots a road sign, "Looks like we're getting close to Butler." She pauses, "It's a little bit bigger town than the last couple we've passed thru."

Michael, Lindsey's husband, glances around, "Maybe we won't have to go thru the town."

Lindsey smiles, "That would be nice. I think I've had enough excitement for awhile."

Michael, Lindsey's husband, chuckles, "Me too."

The two of them see the town of Butler getting closer. Michael, Lindsey's husband, starts to slow the Trailblazer down as he sees the brake lights of the van come on.

Michael, Lindsey's husband, sighs, "Well, let's see how this goes."

The convoy passes a small forest on the left side of the highway and continues on. Lindsey continues to glance around while Michael, Lindsey's husband, stays focused on the road. Before they know it, they pass an intersection and the highway starts to veer off to the south.

Lindsey glances around and smiles, "I think the highway is going to go around the town."

The convoy continues on and it becomes obvious to Lindsey and Michael, her husband, that they are not going to have to go thru the town of Butler.

Michael, Lindsey's husband, let's out a sigh of relief, "Nice. We get to avoid going thru the town. Maybe our luck is changing for the better."

Lindsey chuckles at her husband, "I don't know, I'd say we've been pretty lucky so far. Just to survive our camp being overrun and finding everyone again."

Michael, Lindsey's husband, looks at his wife, "You're right about that."

Michael, Lindsey's husband, returns his eyes to the road as Lindsey continues to look around. Before long, the convoy is around the town of Butler and back on the open highway.

As the sun enters the mid-afternoon sky, Shana keeps her eyes focused on the Trailblazer in front of her. Michael, Jody's brother, Zach and Tyler keep a watch out for zombies and other survivors.

Michael, Jody's brother, keeps glancing around, "We should be getting close to Reynolds."

Zach nods, "And that's the last town we'll have to deal with today."

Tyler smiles, "I'm ready to stop and camp for the night. I'm getting tired of being in the car."

Shana smiles at Tyler's words, "Me too."

Zach sighs, "Before long, we won't be in the cars at all. We'll be at Fort Pulaski."

Michael, Jody's brother, nods, "Yep, probably a couple more days before we get there. Given we don't run into anymore problems."

Shana starts to slow the car down, "As happy as I am to think about Fort Pulaski, I'm not going to get excited until we're actually there. We've already seen how fast things can go bad."

Michael, Jody's brother, looks at Shana, "Ain't that the truth."

Tyler points, "I think we're almost to the town."

Michael, Jody's brother, looks back ahead and he sees the town getting real close. Shana slows the car down some more as the convoy is slowing down in front of her.

Zach looks around, "I don't think we're going around this town."

Shana sighs, "Nope. It looks like we're going thru this one."

Shana slows the car a little more as the convoy enters the town of Reynolds. The four of them can tell that the town is not very big and that they should be thru it in no time. Shana veers around an abandoned car in the highway and stays close to the Trailblazer in front of her.

As the convoy continues on, Zach sees a store off to the right of the highway. The town appears deserted like all the others they've seen in the past. Before long and a few more blocks, Tyler spots a bed and breakfast on the left side of the highway.

Shana weaves around an abandoned pickup truck as the convoy starts to speed back up. A few more blocks and the convoy is leaving the town of Reynolds behind them.

Shana smiles, "That was easy enough."

Zach nods, "I can go for easy."

Michael, Jody's brother, chuckles, "Well, next stop will be to camp for the night."

Tyler lets out a dramatically sarcastic sigh, "I'm so ready."

Everyone in the car shares a nice little laugh at Tyler's response as the convoy heads back onto the open highway.

CHAPTER 70

Its getting closer to dinner time as the convoy has made its way down the highway from Reynolds towards the stopping point for the night. Ashley continues to look around for zombies and other survivors as Jody keeps an eye on the road and keeps a look out for the river. After a couple more miles, Jody spots the river they are stopping at for the night.

Jody smiles, "There's the river."

Ashley looks up ahead and sees the bridge, "Awesome. I'm ready to stop for the night and get out of the truck."

Jody nods and chuckles slightly, "Me too."

Jody drives the truck slowly across the bridge and pulls over on the side of the highway far enough from the bridge so the rest of the vehicles in the convoy can pull in behind him. Everyone gets out of their vehicles and meets over by the van.

Jody glances around at the small, open area next to the highway and the river, "This spot will work for the night."

Lisa looks around, "One team should walk a perimeter while the rest of the group sets up the tents."

Jody nods, "Good idea. Since we're the first team, we'll take care of that while the tents are being set up." Jody looks at Ken, "You want to oversee that."

Ken nods, "Sure thing."

Jody walks over to the truck and puts his gear on that has his pistol and he grabs his AR-15. Lisa, already wearing her pistol, grabs her shotgun from the Jeep Liberty. Jody and Lisa head off to check out the area while the rest of the group sets up camp.

Jody and Lisa have started their actual watch now. Shadow has been fed and walked. The rest of the group is eating their dinner right now. The sun is starting to get lower in the sky, but there is still an hour or so of daylight left. Jody and Lisa make their way over to the campsite.

Mike looks over at Jody, "So, we have the teams set up. How do you want to break down the tents?"

Jody continues to glance around, "Myself, Lisa, Lindsey and her husband will take one of the four person tents. You, Ken, Shana and my brother will take the other four person tent. Everyone else, including Shadow, will go in the large tent." He pauses, "Sound good to everyone?"

Everyone looks around and nods at each other.

Jody glances around some more, "When Lisa and I finish our watch, we'll get our map and plan the route for tomorrow. Once we have it planned out, we'll get everyone together and let you all know what the plan is."

Everyone nods again. Jody and Lisa return to their walking of the perimeter. The rest of the group continues to eat.

Ashley finishes a drink of water, "I know we're getting close and I have to admit, I'm getting kind of excited."

Zach smiles and nods as he finishes a bite of food, "Me too. We might have a couple days left, three at the most before we get there."

Mike nods as he finishes his last bite of food, "Yeah, but we're going to have to find a place to stock up on supplies. A lot of supplies so that once we get there, we can spend some time making sure the island is safe and fortified before needing to gather more supplies."

Shana looks at Mike after taking a drink of water, "How many days of food and water do we have left?"

Mike thinks for a second, "I'd say, at our current numbers, five. Enough to get there, but not much after that."

Ken finishes his last bite of food, "Remember everyone, we still have at least one major populated area to get thru, Savannah. Not to mention any others before we get there." He pauses, "Its okay to get a little excited, but let's not think too much about the end and make the mistake of overlooking something along the way."

Lindsey nods as she finishes her dinner and takes a drink of water, "Ken's right. Its easy to lose focus thinking about how close we're getting and if we lose focus, that's when something bad can happen."

Michael, Jody's brother, nods as he finishes his dinner and gives his last bite to Shadow, "Yeah, cause trying to get thru Savannah worries me. That's a pretty good sized city and no real way to go around it."

Michael, Lindsey's husband, nods in agreement as he finishes his last bite, "What really worries me too is that there is a Coast Guard Station on the island. We're going to have to clear it and the entire island before we can rest and settle in."

Ken nods, "Not to mention, we have to figure out a way to destroy the bridge leading to the island or block it off somehow." He pauses, "There is still a lot of work to be done."

The campsite gets quiet as everyone thinks about what all still lies ahead of them before they can finally relax at Fort Pulaski.

Lindsey and Michael, her husband, are on watch now. Jody and Lisa have eaten their dinner and are now in their tent looking over the map of Georgia, planning the next day's trip.

Jody sighs as he sits next to Lisa and the two of them are looking at the map, "It looks like you're right. We don't really have a way around the Warner Robins area. We'll just have to stay on Highway 96 and risk going thru the southern section of that metro area."

Lisa nods, "So, how far do you think we'll make it?"

Jody continues to look over the map, "Well, once we get thru the Warner Robins area, its not long until we reach Interstate 16. That's what we're going to take all the way to Savannah. So, we should be able to make some good time."

Lisa looks over the map, "It looks like there is a good river we can stop at just south of Dublin."

Jody nods at Lisa's suggestion, "That looks like a good spot to me. Plus, it puts us not far from Savannah so we can stop just outside of Savannah the following day and rest before trying to make it thru the city and get to the island."

Lisa sighs, "I wish we had a city map of Savannah. That'd help a ton."

Jody nods and sighs, "It sure would. Maybe we'll find one somewhere. If not, we know its Highway 80 that runs to Tybee Island and runs into the bridge that leads over to the island that Fort Pulaski is on."

Lisa nods, "Well, we'll figure it out when we get there I guess."

Jody looks at Lisa and smiles, "Yep, we will. I guess we should go tell the others the plan for tomorrow."

Lisa starts folding up the map, "Yep."

Jody stands up and Lisa follows him out of the tent.

549

Ken and Mike are on watch now. Everyone else has turned in for the night. Ken and Mike are walking the perimeter of the campsite.

Mike whispers while looking around, "From listening to the plan earlier, it sounds like we'll stop tomorrow, then be stopping once more outside of Savannah."

Ken nods and whispers back, "Yeah, then we'll have to figure out how we're going to get thru Savannah to get to Fort Pulaski."

Mike nods, "Yeah, it'd be nice if we had a map of the city."

Ken smiles, "It sure would be." He pauses, "Maybe we'll find one along the way."

Mike sighs, "Well, once we get thru Warner Robins tomorrow, that's the last metro type area until Savannah. I'm happy about that."

Ken glances around, "Me too. Plus, we can probably find some gas for the vehicles there or on the interstate which will supply us all the way to Fort Pulaski."

Mike looks around some, "You know, I didn't want to show it much earlier, but I'm kind of excited that we're this close to the destination."

Ken smiles and nods, "Yeah, I wasn't going to show it either, but I'm getting a little excited about it myself."

Mike smiles and looks around, "Maybe we won't lose anyone else now."

Ken nods and looks around, "That'd be nice."

Mike and Ken continue to talk while they walk the perimeter of the campsite.

Its morning time now and everyone is awake. The group has finished their breakfast and Mike is walking Shadow before they get a start on the day. Ashley and Zach are on watch now.

Jody looks at the others, "While Mike takes care of Shadow and Ashley and Zach are keeping watch, the rest of us will pack up our things and load them up. I'll load up Ashley's things in the truck and Shana, you load Zach's things in the car. Ken, you load up my dad's things in the van." He pauses, "After that, we'll break the tents down and load them up, then get on the road."

Everyone nods and Ashley and Zach resume their watch as Mike takes Shadow over by the river. Jody grabs his and Ashley's belongings and heads for the truck. Shana grabs her and Zach's things and heads for the Hyundai. Ken grabs his and Mike's belongings and heads for the van. Everyone else grabs their belongings and heads for their vehicle.

Ashley looks around, "Well, we should be on the road in about half an hour."

Zach nods, "Yeah, as much as I'm not wanting another long day in the car, I'm ready to get going cause it puts us one day closer to Fort Pulaski."

Ashley smiles and nods, "I know what you mean. I just hope we don't run into any trouble."

Zach looks at Ashley, "We shouldn't have any trouble with Fort Valley."

Ashley nods, "Yeah, but then there is Warner Robins and its more of a city than a small town."

Zach looks around and sees that they are breaking down the tents now, "I know, but if we can get thru there without a problem. We should be good all the way to Savannah."

Ashley smiles her beautiful smile, "I like the sound of that."

The group finishes loading up the tents and Mike gets Shadow into the van. The group meets up at the van.

Jody looks at the others, "Okay, just like yesterday. Keep your eyes out for anything and your two way radios ready in case something comes up."

Everyone nods and heads off to their vehicles.

CHAPTER 71

The convoy has barely made it down the highway about three miles when Jody sees something in the road up ahead. Ashley also spots what Jody sees.

Ashley gets a puzzled look, "What do you think that is?"

Jody pulls the truck to a stop half a mile from what they are looking at, "It looks like something blocking the road. Almost like those orange barrels they use for construction."

Ken's voice comes over Ashley's two way radio, "What's going on up there?"

Ashley replies over the radio, "There is something blocking the highway about half a mile ahead."

Jody looks at Ashley, "Let them know to stay here and we'll check out the roadblock. If everything is okay, we'll clear the roadblock and they can catch up to us." He pauses, "If something is wrong, I'll take off my boonie cover and put it back on."

Ashley relays the message to everyone in the other vehicles. Jody slowly starts driving the truck forward while the rest of the convoy pulls off to the side of the highway. Everyone gets out of the vehicles and Ken grabs a pair of binoculars from his gear that he brought from the house in Oklahoma.

Jody speaks to Ashley while glancing around, "Keep a close eye out. This could be done intentionally. When we get out, I'm going to leave my rifle in the truck."

Ashley nods while looking around, "Okay."

Jody slowly pulls the truck closer to the blockade. Jody and Ashley see about ten orange barrels strung across the highway, blocking any chance of them driving around the roadblock. The barrels are blocking the highway, just before an intersection with a road running off to the north and south. On the southwest corner of the intersection, is a small church with a small house behind it.

Jody pulls the truck to a stop at the orange barrels. Jody and Ashley look around for a minute. Once they are sure that they don't see anything, Jody and Ashley get out of the truck.

Jody looks at Ashley, "Keep a look out. I'm going to move some of the barrels."

Ashley nods, "Okay."

Ashley steps over in front of the truck as Jody walks over to the barrels. Jody grabs the first barrel when he hears the doors of the church open. Ashley and Jody both look over at the church. Ashley and Jody see twelve people walk out of the church, seven men and five women. One man is dressed like a minister and the other six men are carrying weapons, four shotguns and two handguns. The five women are carrying blunt weapons that have blood on them and three of them also have knives.

Jody looks at the people closely. The minister is carrying a bible in his hand, but no weapons. Jody is getting a bad feeling about the group of people. Jody removes his boonie cover, wipes his forehead and puts his boonie cover back on. Ken sees Jody's signal.

Ken looks at the others, "Okay. Mike, Lindsey, Shana and both Michaels, come with me. Everyone else wait here. We're going to sneak down towards them using the trees on the south side of the road."

Mike, Shana, Lindsey, Michael, Jody's brother, and Michael, Lindsey's husband, all grab their weapons.

Jody slowly walks over to Ashley who is still looking at the group that came out of the church. The group that came out of the church is slowly making their way towards Jody and Ashley, led by the minister.

Jody nods as they get closer, "Hello."

The minister smiles, "Hello to you." He pauses, "I must say, we were not expecting to see anyone around here."

Jody is not getting a good vibe, "We're just passing thru. We're heading to Warner Robins to check on some family we lost touch with when this all started."

The minister smiles, "Son, you two shouldn't be out traveling with the end of the world upon us. Its far too dangerous."

Ashley starts to get an uneasy feeling too due to the way the group of people are staring at them, "We know, we've lost some people along the way."

The minister smiles, "That's because you haven't repented your sins and you're being punished. We've kept the evil away by giving what is necessary to the Lord."

Jody can tell that things are about to get bad so he steps over in front of Ashley, "We each face salvation in our own way. All we want is to get to our family."

The minister continues to smile and shakes his head, "I'm afraid that's not going to happen my son."

At that time, the six men raise their weapons and point them at Jody and Ashley.

Jody holds up his hands, "Whoa, wait a minute. There's no need for violence. We're all in this together."

The minister chuckles slightly, "No my son, we are not in this with you because we are the righteous and because we give to the Lord what he commands of us during these times." He pauses, "The blood of sinners."

Ashley whispers to Jody, "What now?"

Jody whispers back without moving his lips, "No sudden movements. Follow my lead."

The minister glances at the men and women who are right behind him, "We'll start with the blood of the woman. That will buy us more time from the Lord and keep the evil away."

Jody shakes his head, "You're crazy if you think that's going to happen."

The minister looks at Jody with a sinister grin, "What makes you think you can stop us?"

The six men and five women start to walk towards Jody and Ashley. However, staying squarely focused on Jody and Ashley, the minister and his people have not seen what Jody has out of the corner of his eye.

Jody continues to hold up his hands, "Let us go and no one will get hurt."

The minister chuckles again, "Get them."

As the six men and five women start walking towards Jody and Ashley, Ken yells from off to the groups left, "Don't move and drop your weapons, now!"

The minister and the men and women turn to their left and see Ken and the others with their weapons ready.

Jody seizes the moment and whispers to Ashley, "Hide behind the truck, this is going to get bad."

Ashley slips behind the truck.

The minister gets a very upset look on his face, "Kill all the sinners!"

The men and women turn towards Ken and the others. Jody takes the opportunity and draws his pistol. Jody aims and fires at the minister, but one of the women unknowingly steps in the way and Jody's bullet kills the woman. The minister looks back at Jody as Ken and the others open fire and so do the men from the church group.

Ken's shot kills one of the men, Lindsey's shot kills one of the women and Lisa's shot wounds one of the men. The rest of the shots from both sides miss.

The minister screams as he starts to run for the church, "You will all burn in hell!"

Jody tries to take aim at the minister, but he can't get a clear shot. The remaining men from the church group fire again, but they are all off the mark. Ken and the others, from all their experience, take their time and aim.

Mike pulls the trigger first and his shot is true as his shot strikes the minister in the side of the head. The minister collapses to the ground in a pool of blood. Ken's shot wounds one man and Lisa's shot kills a woman. Michael, Jody's brother, wounds a woman and Michael, Lindsey's husband, wounds one of the men.

The church group looks over and sees the minister laying dead at the steps of the church. The wounded men and women make their way over to the minister, then look back at Ken and the others. The men and women from the church drop their weapons, grab the minister's body and start to make their way into the church.

Jody can see that the fight is over, "Ashley, help me move some of these barrels so we can get out of here." He looks over at Ken, "Get back to your vehicles and let's get out of here!"

Ken nods and turns to the others, "Let's go!"

Ken and the others jog quickly for their vehicles which are only a half mile away. Ashley and Jody quickly move the barrels blocking half of the highway. As Jody and Ashley finish moving the last barrel, Ken and the others reach their vehicles and get loaded up. Lisa starts up the Jeep and pulls away with the rest of the convoy falling in behind her.

Jody and Ashley get in the truck and wait for the convoy to catch up to them. Once the convoy reaches Jody and Ashley who are waiting in the truck, Jody starts driving off down the highway away from the church and the fanatics that they just had to deal with. The rest of the convoy follows the truck as they head on towards Fort Valley.

Michael, Lindsey's husband, slows the Trailblazer down as the convoy crosses into the town of Fort Valley. It's a little bit bigger town than the last few that they've been thru.

Michael, Lindsey's husband, shakes his head as he weaves around an abandoned car, "I can't believe those people. That's having too much belief in your faith and your religious leader."

Lindsey sighs as she looks around at the passing houses and buildings, "Those people were fanatics. True faithful followers and believers would've been open and caring towards us. Not trying to sacrifice someone and kill us."

Michael, Lindsey's husband, keeps his eyes on the road as the convoy has made its way about halfway thru the town, "You're right about that. It's bad enough that we have to deal with a world overran by zombies, but twice now we've had to deal with other people trying to kill us." He pauses, "I'm so ready to get to Fort Pulaski where it'll be just our group and we decide who comes around."

Lindsey nods as the convoy turns south and passes a hotel, "I know what you mean. Its going to be nice to have our own place where we can make a home and keep people away."

Michael, Lindsey's husband, weaves around another abandoned car as Lindsey spots a couple of zombies off to their right. The zombies are slowly staggering towards the convoy, but the zombies are moving much too slow and the convoy is soon gone.

Michael, Lindsey's husband, follows the van in front of him closely as they turn left and start heading back to the east. The convoy passes thru a couple more residential areas where they spot a few more zombies and have to maneuver their way around some abandoned vehicles. Before long though, the convoy is heading out of Fort Valley and on towards Warner Robins.

Michael, Lindsey's husband, smiles, "That's one more town out of the way."

Lindsey smiles at her husband as she continues to look around.

CHAPTER 72

The convoy continues east as the sun is getting closer to the mid morning sky. The convoy is nearing the southern edge of Warner Robins. Everyone knows that this will be their last metro type area, but they also know that this might be their last chance to get more gasoline for the vehicles.

Jody slows the truck down as they cross into the southern section of Warner Robins. The convoy weaves around an abandoned semi and abandoned car as they pass thru some residential areas. Ashley looks around and spots a couple of zombies off to the south.

Ashley speaks to Jody, "There are a couple of zombies over there."

Jody keeps his eyes on the road, "That's okay. As long as it's not a large group of them, we'll be okay." He pauses, "I'm hoping we run into a group of vehicles so we can get some gas."

Ashley nods and continues to look around. Jody weaves around another abandoned semi as they pass thru another residential area with a few businesses mixed in. Ashley keeps looking around as they are nearly halfway across Warner Robins. Jody can tell that they are getting into more of a business district and he hopes that will bring more cars.

The convoy maneuvers around an abandoned car and a couple of bodies in the road. Finally, Jody sees a few fast food places up ahead and he also sees what he was hoping to find. A half mile up the road is a bunch of abandoned vehicles, at least thirty or so.

Jody glances at Ashley, "Looks like we hit the jackpot on gas if there is some in those vehicles ahead."

Ashley looks up the road and smiles, "I hope there's a way thru all of them and the road isn't completely blocked."

Jody smiles and nods, "Good point."

Jody slows the truck down as they near all the abandoned vehicles. As they get closer, Jody can't see a clear path so he slows the truck down some more and as they get up close to the abandoned vehicles, Jody stops the truck and puts it in park.

Ashley looks at Jody, "What's wrong?"

Jody sighs, "I can't see a clear path from here so I want to get out and look. That way we don't get started into all the vehicles only to find out that there is no way thru."

Ashley nods and smiles, "Good idea."

The rest of the convoy is stopped behind the truck. Jody and Ashley get out of the truck. This time, Jody grabs his rifle as he is already wearing his pistol. Everyone in the group sees Jody and Ashley get out of the truck so they get out of their vehicles and make their way up to Jody and Ashley.

Ken looks at Jody, "What's up little buddy?"

Jody looks around, "This is as good a chance as any to get some gas. Lisa and I am going to scout a path thru the vehicles on foot. Ken, you, my dad, my brother, Shana, Lindsey and her husband work on getting some gas from these vehicles. Ashley and Zach will keep a look out." He pauses, "Roe, you, Tyler and Daniel can get Shadow out while we do our things."

Everyone nods.

Jody speaks again, "Everyone be careful."

Lisa retrieves her shotgun from the Jeep, then joins Jody by the truck. Ken and the others retrieve the gas cans while Zach and Ashley move to a good location near the convoy so they can keep watch. Roe, Tyler and Daniel head over to the van and get Shadow out so he can do his business.

Jody and Lisa start slowly into the maze of abandoned vehicles. Jody is in front as Lisa is a couple steps behind him. Once they get pass the first few vehicles, Ken and the others move up and start checking the vehicles for gas.

Lisa whispers to Jody as they slowly move forward, "This is going to be a good quarter to half mile of weaving thru these vehicles."

Jody nods and whispers back, "I'm just glad that so far there seems to be a path we can drive thru."

As Jody and Lisa continue on, Ken and the others start working on getting gasoline. Lindsey and Michael, her husband, stop at a mid-sized car. Lindsey makes sure there are no zombies in the car, then she opens the door and pulls the handle to pop open the gas tank cover. Michael, Lindsey's husband, takes the gas cap off and starts to siphon the gas as Lindsey keeps a look out.

Michael, Jody's brother, and Shana walk up to a pickup truck. Michael, Jody's brother, checks the cab and bed of the truck. Once he's sure it's okay, Michael, Jody's brother, motions to Shana. Shana walks over as Michael, Jody's brother, removes the gas cap. Shana starts to siphon the gas as Michael, Jody's brother, keeps watch.

Ken and Mike walk up to a van that is near a moving truck. Ken spots Jody and Lisa up the road, then returns his focus to the van. Ken walks around the van as Mike waits. Once Ken is sure everything is okay, he motions to Mike. Mike walks up and removes the gas cap. Ken keeps watch while Mike siphons the gas.

Rochelle, Tyler and Daniel are walking Shadow around their vehicles. Shadow is enjoying his chance to sniff the new area and mark his territory. Ashley and Zach continue to look around to make sure no zombies walk up on them.

Jody and Lisa continue to find a path thru the vehicles until they get near the end. Jody and Lisa both stop as they realize that they are going to have to move a car out of the way in order for them to be able to drive thru the abandoned vehicles.

Lisa whispers as she looks around, "We're going to have to move that car. Once we do, we'll be good to drive thru, very slowly, but able to drive thru."

Jody nods and glances around, "Yep."

Jody slowly approaches the car and looks it over closely. Jody notices there are no bodies in the car. Lisa walks up next to Jody.

Jody whispers, "Okay, you put it in neutral and steer. I'll push."

Lisa nods and opens the door. Lisa lays her shotgun in the front seat, then puts the car in neutral. Jody lays his rifle on the trunk and starts to push. Lisa and Jody start to slowly move the car off to the side of the road.

Lindsey and Michael, her husband, get back to their vehicles and pour the gas they siphoned into the Trailblazer. About that time, Shana and Michael, Jody's brother, walk up with their gas can. Shana puts the gas they siphoned into the van's gas tank as Rochelle, Tyler and Daniel walk up with Shadow.

Mike and Ken are finishing up getting the gas out of the van. Mike puts the cap on the gas can as Ken looks over at the moving truck like he heard something.

Mike looks at Ken, "What is it?"

Ken gets a puzzled look, "I'm not sure, just thought I heard something."

At that time, Ken and Mike hears Zach's voice, "Zombies!"

Mike and Ken look back at their vehicles where everyone else is at except for them and Lisa and Jody. Ken and Mike see a large group of zombies coming down the highway from the direction where they already drove thru.

Mike's eyes widen, "Let's get out of here." Mike looks back over at Ken, "Look out!"

A zombie has walked up behind Ken from over by the moving truck and neither of them saw it until it is too late. Ken starts to turn around when he feels the zombie's hands grab him and he hears the zombie's snarl. Before Ken can jerk away, the zombie sinks it's teeth into Ken's left shoulder and takes a chunk of flesh out of Ken's shoulder.

Ken screams in pain as he finally jerks away from the zombie. The zombie steps towards Ken again, but Ken raises his pistol and fires. The zombie's head explodes and the zombie falls to the pavement. The blood starts to pour out of Ken's shoulder.

Mike looks at Ken, "No!"

Ken motions to Mike, "Let's get to the vehicles before those others get here."

Mike and Ken start for their vehicles. Hearing the yell from Zach and the scream from Ken, Jody and Lisa turn around after getting the car out of the way and they both see the large group of zombies. Jody and Lisa run for the vehicles as fast as they can.

Rochelle and Tyler get Shadow back into the van and shut the door. Lindsey grabs Daniel and rushes back over to the Trailblazer. Lindsey gets Daniel back in his seat and shuts the door. Mike and Ken come up to the rest of the group by the vehicles. Ashley and Zach hurry over to the others as they all see Jody and Lisa are nearly back.

Ken reaches into the van and grabs his shotgun and the rest of his shotgun shells. Jody and Lisa finally get back to the vehicles as the group of zombies are about two hundred yards away.

Jody speaks to the others, "We got a way thru. It'll be a very slow drive, but we can make it so let's get loaded up."

Ken speaks thru the pain as the blood continues to pour from his shoulder, "Those things will catch up to us as slow as we'll have to go. I'll hold them off while you guys get out of here."

Lisa, not knowing Ken was bitten, replies, "What?"

Ken turns so that the rest of the group can see his shoulder, "One of them got me back there. This is the end of the road for me." He swallows and continues, "There's no time, you all get out of here."

Ashley looks at Ken, "You can't stay here. They'll kill you."

Ken replies through the pain, "Remember the rules. Anyone infected is out of the group." He pauses as he sees the zombies getting closer, "Go now, get out of here!"

Jody nods at Ken, "Everyone get loaded up."

Mike puts the gas can in the back of the van as everyone, except Jody, heads off to their vehicles. The group sits and waits for Jody.

Jody holds out his hand to Ken, "Go easy man. Thanks for everything you've done and what you're about to do for us. We couldn't have made it this far without you. Sorry it had to end this way brother."

Ken shakes Jody's hand, "Me too." He pauses, "You get them to Fort Pulaski for me."

Jody nods, "You got it bro."

Ken turns to face the zombies, "They don't know the fight they're in for."

Jody rushes over to the truck and starts it up. Jody starts to drive the truck slowly into the maze of abandoned vehicles and the rest of the convoy follows. Everyone waves at Ken as they pass by.

Ken turns to face the zombies as they are less than twenty-five yards away and he knows that he needs to slow them down to give the convoy a chance to get away. Ken raises his shotgun and starts firing. Zombies start falling as they continue to stagger towards Ken. Ken empties his shotgun, then quickly reloads it with the last five shells.

Ken looks up at the zombies closing in on him, "Come get some of this."

Ken fires his shotgun and his shots are true as five more zombies fall. Ken drops his shotgun and pulls out his pistol. Ken knows he has twenty shots. Ken starts to fire as fast as he can while maintaining accuracy. Zombies start to fall. Ken ejects his empty magazine and reloads with another seven round magazine.

The zombies are only fifteen yards away now and Ken can hear them snarling. Ken fires his next seven shots rapidly and more zombies fall. Ken quickly reloads with his last seven shot magazine. Ken looks over his shoulder and sees that the convoy is about halfway thru the abandoned vehicles. Ken knows that by killing the lead zombies and forcing the others to walk around the bodies, he has bought enough time for the convoy to get away.

Ken turns back to the zombies, "Let's finish this."

Ken raises his pistol as the zombies are just fifteen feet away. Ken fires quickly and five more zombies fall to the pavement. Ken guesses that there are about ten zombies left and he knows what he's going to have to do. Ken fires his sixth shot and kills one more zombie. Ken takes a deep breath as he turns the pistol on himself and places it under his chin.

Ken smiles as the zombies are nearly on him. With nothing left to say or do, Ken pulls the trigger and kills himself. The remaining zombies stop at Ken's body as the convoy pulls out of the abandoned car maze and speeds off.

CHAPTER 73

The convoy has reached Interstate 16 as the sun has reached the partly cloudy noon sky. Everyone is still in shock over losing Ken. Ashley has remained quiet and has been able to fight back the tears even though she is sad over the loss. Jody has also been quiet, not feeling good over the loss of his friend and trying to stay focused on the rest of the trip.

Ashley finally breaks the silence in the truck, "I just can't believe he's gone. If anyone would have made it, I figured Ken would."

Jody nods slightly, "Yeah, me too. Its just another reminder of how this new world is and that any of us could be gone at any time."

Ashley sighs as she stares out the window, "I felt so bad for leaving him behind."

Jody places his right hand on Ashley's shoulder, "Its what he wanted. Ken wanted his death to make a difference for the group and it did. He bought us time to get thru the maze of vehicles without the zombies being able to catch up to us."

Ashley nods slightly as she sniffles, "Yeah, you're right." She pauses, "I still figured that I'd be killed long before him with all his skills and training."

Jody sighs, "It was just his time and one of those freak things that happen. There is nothing any of us could have done about it." He pauses and decides to change the subject, "I think it's about time to stop for a lunch break. I'm sure everyone could use a break."

Ashley nods as she continues to stare out the window, "Yeah, probably so."

Jody starts to slow the truck down.

The group has finished eating lunch and Mike has gotten Shadow back in the van after his walk. The group meets up by the van to discuss a few things.

Jody looks at the group, "I know you all are probably just as shocked and sad as I am over the loss of Ken. None of us would've expected him to not make it. We'll each mourn in our own way." He pauses, "But we also need to learn the lesson, that at any time, any of us can be killed, no matter what training we've had, what skills we possess or how smart and safe we are. We need to keep our heads about us and do everything we can to ensure the rest of the group makes it to Fort Pulaski."

The group is quiet for a minute.

Mike finally speaks up, "Losing Ken is a great loss and I for one will miss him, but we can't be so saddened by his loss that we lose focus on what we're doing. The goal still remains, we have to make it to Fort Pulaski."

Everyone in the group still has a downtrodden look, but Mike's words make sense as they all start to nod slowly.

Lisa looks at Jody, "Okay, so what now?"

Jody takes a breath, "We'll stay in the vehicle order that we're in right now and everyone will stay in the vehicles that they're currently in."

Lindsey nods and looks around at the group, "What about the teams and the tent assignments?"

Jody sighs and glances at everyone, "My dad will no longer be in a team. That'll leave us with just four teams, so the shifts will be two hours long." He pauses, "As for the tent assignments, my dad will move over to the large tent and Zach and Ashley will move over to the smaller tent with Shana and my brother."

Everyone nods.

Michael, Jody's brother, looks at Jody, "So, the plan still the same for the rest of today?"

Jody nods, "Yeah. We'll continue on the interstate until we reach the river south of Dublin, then we'll stop and set up camp for the night."

Michael, Lindsey's husband, looks around, "Well, we should probably get moving before we lose too much more time."

Jody glances around, "Yep. Let's get loaded up and get on the road."

Everyone heads off to their assigned vehicles. Jody pulls the truck away and the rest of the convoy follows.

The sun is starting into the mid-afternoon sky as the convoy is passing south of the town of Dudley as they are getting nearer to their stopping point for the night. Michael, Lindsey's husband, is keeping his eyes on the back of the van as Lindsey is looking around for any signs of zombies and other survivors.

Michael, Lindsey's husband, sighs, "You know what honey, I can't believe how much our group has dwindled since we first left the house."

Lindsey nods as she continues to look around, "I know, me either. We found Greg and them, and now all of them are gone as well. I sometimes wonder if the others that left the group awhile back are still okay."

Michael, Lindsey's husband, nods, "I wonder that too. Seeing now how dangerous it has been and that even someone like Ken who has all the skill in the world can be killed, we definitely have done the right thing by sticking with the group." He pauses, "I seriously doubt we'd ever made it on our own."

Lindsey nods in agreement, "Right. Sticking with the group was definitely the right move, even with having lost as many as we have." She pauses, "You know what I'm kind of worried about though?"

Michael, Lindsey's husband, glances over at Lindsey, "What's that?"

Lindsey sighs and looks at her husband, "I'm worried that when we get to Fort Pulaski, other people will have already gotten there and they won't be friendly."

Michael, Lindsey's husband, nods as he looks back at the road, "I've actually thought about that too. Maybe when we stop for the night we should bring it up to the others and see what Jody has to say about that possibility."

Lindsey nods as she looks back out the window, "Yeah, we probably should."

Michael, Lindsey's husband, continues to focus on the highway as Lindsey continues her watch for zombies and other survivors.

As the sun reaches the evening sky, the convoy has pulled off on the side of the interstate next to a river just south of the town of Dublin. Everyone gets out of their vehicles and meets up at the van.

Jody looks around, "This clearing will make a good spot to set up the tents for the night." He pauses, "My dad and Tyler will keep a look out while Roe watches Daniel. The rest of us will set up the tents and get our personal things, then we'll start the watch rotation while they get their personal things. Sound good?"

Everyone nods. Mike and Tyler move off to a spot to keep watch while Rochelle is waiting with Daniel. Jody and the rest of the group grab the tents and head over to the opening near the highway and the river. Jody, Lisa, Ashley and Zach work on setting up the large tent. Shana and Michael, Jody's brother, work on setting up one of the smaller tents while Lindsey and Michael, her husband, work on setting up the other smaller tent.

It doesn't take long for all the tents to be set up. Jody and the others head back to the vehicles to get their personal belongings. Jody stops to talk to Mike while the others grab their things.

Jody looks at Mike, "After you get your things, I want you to inventory the food and water. Also, check the amount of gas in each vehicle. I know the truck is starting to run low."

Mike nods, "Okay."

Jody carries his things over to the tent that he is sharing with Lisa, Lindsey and her husband. Jody puts his things up, then him and Lisa take over watch. Mike and Tyler grab their things and head over to the large tent. Rochelle grabs her things and Daniel's things and takes them over to the large tent with Daniel walking right behind her.

Mike looks at everyone that is standing around the new campsite, "Jody has me doing something right now so I need Roe and Tyler to take care of Shadow. Everyone else can get something to eat."

Rochelle and Tyler nod and start heading for the van. Mike heads off to the vehicles as Jody and Lisa walk the perimeter of the camp. The rest of the group grabs some food and water and starts eating dinner.

An hour has passed and everyone has finished eating except for Jody and Lisa who are still on watch. Mike has also finished all the inventorying of items and gas. Rochelle and Tyler walked Shadow around the area and now Shadow is laying in front of the large tent with the rest of the group sitting around. Jody and Lisa make their way over to the others.

Jody looks around at everyone, "Okay, from now on when we get together to talk, whoever is on watch will come in long enough for the discussion, then head back to watch."

Everyone nods.

Jody looks at Mike, "How are we looking as far as food and water?"

Mike replies, "We have four days worth left and that's it."

Shana looks at Mike, "I saw you looking in each vehicle. What was that for?"

Mike looks over at Shana, "I was checking how much gas each vehicle had left."

Jody speaks up, "How are we looking on gas?"

Mike sighs, "Not as good. The truck is going to make it maybe to Savannah, but no further if I had to guess. The Jeep Liberty is doing okay, but not too much better than the truck. The van is sitting okay for now and so is the Trailblazer. The Hyundai is doing just fine." He pauses, "We still have the gas can that I filled up. I never got to use it back there."

Michael, Jody's brother, speaks up, "We can put it in the truck."

Jody shakes his head, "I want to hold off on that for now. Once I get off watch, Lisa and I are going to go over a few things for tomorrow's trip and what our options are going to be once we get to Savannah." He pauses, "Once we get ready to talk about those things, I'll have everyone come into the camp. Okay?"

Everyone nods.

Michael, Lindsey's husband, speaks up, "Lindsey and I both thought about something on the way here. What if there are already people at Fort Pulaski?"

Lisa looks at Jody, "That's a good question."

Jody sighs, "Yes it is. I'll have to think about it and its something we can discuss when we get back together. Good thinking Michael." He pauses, "Okay, let's get back to it."

Jody and Lisa head off to finish their watch while everyone else tries to make themselves comfortable and pass the time.

CHAPTER 74

Lindsey and Michael, her husband, are nearing the end of their watch as Jody and Lisa have been planning out the next day's trip and the possible options for when they reach Savannah. Jody and Lisa walk out to the others in front of the large tent.

Jody speaks into his two way radio, "Lindsey, you two come on in so we can talk."

Lindsey's voice comes back over the two way radio, "Okay."

In a minute, Lindsey and Michael, her husband, walk up to the rest of the group which is sitting around a small fire in front of the large tent. Shadow is laying at Mike's feet. Lindsey and Michael, her husband, sit down.

Jody looks around at everyone, "Well, it looks like tomorrow is going to be our last open road day. We're only about 120 miles from Savannah."

Jody notices that his words bring a smile to everyone's face, knowing that they are close.

Lisa speaks up, "We are going to stay on the interstate tomorrow. We have no specific stopping point. What we're going to do is look for a place as we get closer to Savannah." She pauses, "We're also going to stop along the way if there are any travel plazas to see if we can find a map of Savannah."

Lindsey looks at Jody, "What are we going to do about getting thru Savannah?"

Jody sighs, "What we do know is that Highway 80 is what'll take us to the island where Fort Pulaski is at. However, it also runs thru Savannah. We'll have to take that way if we can't find a city map."

Ashley questions, "It was mentioned earlier, what are we going to do if we get to Fort Pulaski and there are already people there. Any ideas?"

Jody sighs and glances around, "I want us all to discuss that. I think the first thing, it's going to depend on if the people there are friendly or not." He pauses, "If there are people there and they are friendly, what do you all think?"

Shana speaks up, "I think if they are friendly, we still need to be careful and it'll also depend on how many of them there are. I mean, it's a tough call."

Rochelle speaks up to everyone's surprise, "I'm just going to have a hard time trusting anyone outside of our group. No matter if they're friendly or not."

Michael, Jody's brother, nods, "It is going to be a tough call."

Mike speaks up, "If they are friendly, we should work out a deal with them. Maybe split the fort in half to start with or maybe we camp outside the fort until we know for sure they can be trusted."

Michael, Lindsey's husband, nods and speaks up, "Those are both good ideas. I agree, it all depends on how many people there are. I think that is true for if they're not friendly also."

Zach decides to speak up, "We've come too far and lost too much to not have our place in the end. Unless there are too many people there for us to handle, I say we stay there or take it from them."

Jody looks at Zach, "That's risky, but I understand what you're saying and why you feel like that."

Lisa glances around at everyone, "Well, we have another day to think about it. Whatever we decide, we all need to agree on it because if we choose to fight, it'll put us all in danger."

Mike nods in agreement, "A lot of danger. I'm not wanting to have to move on and look elsewhere, but its an option we also have to look at."

Jody nods and glances around at everyone, "Well, we can think on it some more, but for now, let's just get some rest and get ready for tomorrow."

Everyone nods. Lindsey and Michael, her husband, head off to finish the last of their watch. Mike takes Shadow for one more walk before turning in for the night. Everyone else heads off to their tents.

Ashley and Zach are on watch now and everyone else is asleep. The two of them are walking the perimeter of the camp.

Ashley looks at Zach while they walk, "I was surprised to hear what you had to say earlier."

Zach looks at Ashley, "I hope you don't think less of me for what I said. It's just, we've come a long way and we've lost so much that I can't imagine not making a home at Fort Pulaski. Besides, we don't have any other place to go."

Ashley nods as they continue to walk, "That's true. We don't have any other place to go." She pauses, "And I don't think any less of you for saying what you said."

Zach smiles, "Thanks. I think I surprised everyone just by speaking up."

Ashley smiles and chuckles slightly, "Yeah, you've come a long way since this all began. It's almost like you went from the kids table to the grown up table at the holidays."

Zach chuckles, "It kind of feels that way."

Ashley glances around, "Well, you've done good and I feel safe with you being my teammate."

Zach looks at Ashley again, "Thank you." He pauses, "You know, I was worried at first about if I was going to be able to help in this new world and I was also worried about if you and the other ladies would be able to help. I was sure wrong about that. I feel very confident in everyone now."

Ashley smiles, "Thanks. I have to admit, I wasn't sure how I was going to do the first time we ran into some zombies, but I surprised myself." She pauses, "Now, I'm confident that our group will make it the rest of the way and be okay."

Zach nods and looks around, "Me too."

Ashley and Zach continue to walk around the perimeter of the camp while everyone else sleeps.

Its morning time now, just about time for the sun to rise. Michael, Jody's brother, and Shana are on watch now. The two of them are walking the perimeter of the camp as they wait for the time to wake everyone up.

Shana looks at Michael, Jody's brother, "You know, I can't believe what Zach said last night about taking the fort by force if need be."

Michael, Jody's brother, nods and looks at Shana, "I know, I was pretty shocked myself. It almost worries me that people in our group are becoming bloodthirsty."

Shana nods, "I know. I'm hoping it doesn't get to that. I mean, until now we've only had to kill other people in defending ourselves."

Michael, Jody's brother, sighs, "Yeah. I think it's going to be okay. I don't think it's going to go that far. In fact, I think that we're not going to run into anyone at the fort."

Shana looks at Michael, Jody's brother, with a somewhat surprised look, "Really? What makes you say that?"

Michael, Jody's brother, shrugs, "Just a feeling. Unless people were already there or on the island, I don't think they'd head there since it's not someplace you'd first think of." He pauses, "Who knows, maybe I'm just thinking positive."

Shana smiles, "Well, nothing wrong with that."

The sun breaks the eastern horizon, shedding light across the campsite.

Shana glances around, "Well, I guess it's time to wake everyone up."

Michael, Jody's brother, steps close to Shana, "I'll keep watch if you want to wake everyone up."

Shana stares lovingly at Michael, Jody's brother, "Okay."

Shana and Michael, Jody's brother, share a nice kiss, then Shana heads off to wake up the rest of the group.

The convoy has been making its way along the interstate for a little ways as the sun continues to rise in the morning sky. Everyone figures that they'll make it to their next stopping point by noon.

Lindsey is looking out the window of the Trailblazer, "Looks like we're going to passing a town called Metter in a couple of miles."

Michael, Lindsey's husband, keeps his eyes on the road, "Yeah, maybe we'll pass a place to check for food and water as well as a map of Savannah."

Lindsey smiles, "That would be nice."

Michael, Lindsey's husband, starts to slow the Trailblazer down as the van in front of him is slowing down. The convoy continues to slow down as they get closer to the turnoff for the town of Metter.

Michael, Lindsey's husband, glances around, "I wonder why we're slowing down."

Lindsey keeps looking around, "I don't know. They must have seen something."

The convoy keeps slowing down until they are at a complete stop. Lindsey sees Jody and Ashley getting out of the truck.

Lindsey looks at Daniel, "What here, we'll be right back. Okay?"

Daniel looks at Lindsey, "Okay mom."

Lindsey and Michael, her husband, get out of the Trailblazer and meet up with the rest of the group by the van.

Lisa looks at Jody, "What's going on?"

Jody glances around, "I spotted a small travel store up at the exit ahead. I want to check it out for some water, food and possibly a map that we can use."

Mike steps over and sees the place Jody is talking about, "So, are we all going?"

Jody shakes his head slightly, "No. Just two teams will go, everyone else will stay here. It shouldn't take us long."

Ashley looks at Jody, "So, who's going?"

Jody looks around at everyone, "Well, myself and Lisa are going."

Jody gets quiet for a minute while he thinks.

Lindsey speaks up, "Michael and I will go with you."

Michael, Lindsey's husband, nods, "Yeah, we'll go with you two."

Jody nods, "Thanks." He pauses, "We'll take the Hyundai."

Everyone nods.

Jody looks at the others, "If anything goes wrong, the rest of you get out of here."

Mike nods, "Okay."

Jody, Lisa, Lindsey and Michael, her husband, head off to grab their weapons while everyone else waits.

CHAPTER 75

Jody slowly drives the Hyundai up towards the travel store at the end of the off ramp. Lisa, Lindsey and Michael, Lindsey's husband, are looking around to keep their eyes out for any zombies or other survivors. One thing that the four of them notice is that there are no cars around the area.

Jody pulls the car up to the front of the store and puts it in park. Jody turns the car off and sets the keys on the dashboard.

Jody glances around, "Let's be careful and get in and out as quick as we can. Grab only things in sight."

Lisa, Lindsey and Michael, Lindsey's husband, nod as the four of them get out of the car. Jody and Lisa slowly make their way towards the front doors as Lindsey and Michael, her husband, keep a look out. Jody and Lisa stop at the front doors and look inside through the glass. When they are sure they don't see anything, Jody and Lisa quickly enter the store.

Lindsey and Michael, her husband, move up to the front doors. Jody and Lisa look around and see the shelves are pretty empty. Lindsey and Michael, her husband, slip inside the store.

Jody looks at Lindsey, "You and Michael want to look for food and a map, Lisa and I will check for water."

Lindsey nods, "Okay."

Jody and Lisa start to slowly make their way towards the back of the store while Lindsey and Michael, her husband, make their way over to the food isle.

Jody and Lisa slowly approach the refrigerators in the back where the drinks use to be kept. Jody and Lisa keep their eyes moving around just in case there are any zombies hiding in the store. The two of them remember what happened to Allen and they are not letting down their guard.

Lindsey and Michael, her husband, look over the food shelves and notice that all the food is pretty much gone. All that is left is some beef jerky. Michael, Lindsey's husband, grabs the two boxes of beef jerky that is left.

Lindsey looks at her husband, "Let's check on a map."

Michael, Lindsey's husband, nods, "Okay."

Lindsey and Michael, her husband, make their way towards the rack of maps. Lindsey sees a spiral notebook and package of ink pens on the shelf next to the rack of maps.

Jody and Lisa make it to the refrigerators and notice that they are pretty much empty. Jody sees two six packs of bottled water and some half gallons of milk.

Lisa sighs, "Not much to choose from."

Jody nods and glances around, "Yeah, no kidding. I'll grab the water, but I'm sure the milk has spoiled since there has been no power for awhile."

Lisa looks around, "Okay."

Jody slides his rifle around to his back, opens the glass door and grabs the two six packs of water. Jody shuts the door and looks around. Jody sees Lindsey and Michael, her husband, over by the front doors.

Jody motions with his head, "Looks like they're ready."

Lisa looks over and sees Lindsey and Michael, her husband, waiting by the doors. Jody and Lisa slowly make their way towards the doors. Jody and Lisa walk up to Lindsey and Michael, Lindsey's husband.

Jody looks at Lindsey, "I hope you two did better than we did."

Michael, Lindsey's husband, shakes his head, "We got two boxes of beef jerky."

Lisa sighs, "Great, we got two six packs of water."

Lindsey smiles and brings her left hand around from behind her back, "We did find this."

Jody and Lisa look at Lindsey's hand and they see a spiral notebook, a package of ink pens and most of all, a city map of Savannah.

Jody smiles, "Awesome. Good job you two." He glances around, "Let's get out of here."

Jody, Lisa, Lindsey and Michael, Lindsey's husband, make their way out of the store and towards their car when they hear something from over by the side of the store. Lisa whirls around and brings her shotgun up. Jody, Lindsey and Michael, Lindsey's husband, all turn and look over by the edge of the store.

The four of them hold their breath when they finally see what was making the noise. A pit bull, looking to be around maybe a year old, comes around the corner of the building. It's a beautiful looking dog and appears to be underfed.

Lindsey's eyes brighten up as she sees the pit bull. The pit bull sees the four humans and stops, unsure what to make of the humans in front of it. Lindsey opens the car door and sets the map, pens, spiral notebook and her shotgun in the car. Lisa keeps her shotgun aimed in at the pit bull in case it becomes aggressive.

Lindsey turns around and takes a couple steps towards the pit bull. The pit bull cowards away.

Lindsey squats down and holds out her hand, "Here girl."

The pit bull looks at Lindsey closely, not sure what to make of her.

Lindsey slowly moves her hand again, "Here girl, its okay. Here girl."

Lisa speaks while keeping her shotgun ready, "It might be too scared."

The pit bull continues to look at Lindsey, then the pit bull lays it's ears back and starts to wag it's tail. Lindsey smiles at the pit-bull's reaction.

Lindsey coaxes the pit bull again, "Well, come here girl. It's okay."

The pit bull starts panting and smiling as it makes it's way over towards Lindsey. The pit bull stops at Lindsey's hand and sniffs Lindsey's hand. After a few seconds, the pit bull licks Lindsey's hand.

Lindsey reaches up and starts to pet the pit bull, "Awe, you're such a pretty girl."

Jody, Lisa and Michael, Lindsey's husband, smile at Lindsey and the pit bull.

Lisa lowers her shotgun, "Seems friendly enough."

Lindsey nods, "She is just trying to survive like us." Lindsey looks over at Jody, "We can't leave her here. She's already underfed and no doubt if any zombies find her, she won't make it."

Michael, Lindsey's husband, glances around, "Is it a good idea to take in another dog? I mean, we already have one and not sure how Shadow will react." He pauses, "I wouldn't want to leave her either, but we have to think about that."

Jody is quiet for a moment.

Lindsey pleads with Jody, "It just wouldn't be right to leave her. She's obviously friendly."

Lisa, Lindsey and Michael, Lindsey's husband, look at Jody to see what he's going to decide.

Jody sighs, then smiles and looks at Lisa, "Let's go back in the store and see if we can find more dog food and treats." He pauses, "Lindsey, you and Michael wait here and get her in the car."

Lindsey smiles at Jody, "Thank you."

Jody smiles and nods at Lindsey. Jody sets the water on the hood of the car. Jody and Lisa start to make their way back to the store as Lindsey and Michael, her husband, put the water and beef jerky in the car. As Lisa and Jody enter the store, Lindsey and Michael, her husband, work on getting the pit bull into the car.

Mike and the others are still waiting on Jody, Lisa, Lindsey and Michael, Lindsey's husband, to get back from the store. Michael, Jody's brother, has Shadow out of the van and walking around with his harness and leash on. Everyone is feeling okay since they haven't heard any gunshots coming from the store, but the longer Jody and the others are gone, the more they start to worry.

Finally, Mike and the others see the Hyundai start back down the off ramp towards where the rest of the convoy is waiting. Everyone starts making their way over to the van as Jody drives the car up, turns it around and pulls the car in at the back of the convoy.

Jody, Lisa, Lindsey and Michael, Lindsey's husband, get out of the car. Mike and the others start towards the car.

Shana questions, "Any luck?"

Jody nods, "Some. We only found a little water and some beef jerky, but we did find a map of Savannah."

Ashley smiles, "Awesome!"

Lindsey smiles, "We found something else too."

Rochelle looks at Lindsey, "What?"

Lindsey opens the back passenger's car door and reaches inside and grabs the leash that Jody got from the store. Lindsey steps back and the pit bull jumps out of the car. The pit bull has a huge smile on its face and is wagging its tail.

Lindsey looks around at everyone, "We couldn't leave her there."

Michael, Lindsey's husband, nods, "We grabbed more dog food and treats too."

Michael, Jody's brother, holds onto Shadow's leash tightly just in case Shadow tries to charge the pit bull. Shadow sees the pit bull and the pit bull sees Shadow.

Mike looks at Jody, "This could be a problem."

Jody nods, "Yeah, that's why we're going to find out now. If it is, then we'll have to leave the pit bull behind. We already talked about that possibility."

Shadow is standing and staring at the pit bull. Shadow starts to wag his stub tail and whimper as if he wants to go over to the pit bull. The pit bull is still smiling and wagging it's tail.

Jody looks at Lindsey and his brother, "Okay, slowly let them get close to each other."

Lindsey starts to walk the pit bull towards Shadow and Michael, Jody's brother, starts to let Shadow slowly walk towards the pit bull. The pit bull continues to wag it's tail and Shadow continues to wag his stub tail as they get closer to each other.

The two dogs get close enough to each other that they start to sniff each other. Everyone in the group looks on with anticipation, hoping the two dogs will get along. Shadow and the pit bull continue to sniff each other, but neither one of them growls or starts to get aggressive.

Mike smiles, "Looks like it might be okay."

Lindsey nods and smiles, "I think its going to be."

Shadow and the pit bull stop sniffing each other and the two dogs sit down next to each other.

Jody sighs and smiles, "Good." He looks around, "We should get going. For now though, let's keep Shadow in the van and Lindsey, can you have the pit bull ride with you in the Trailblazer?"

Lindsey nods, "Sure." She reaches down and pets the pit bull, "We need to get her a name too."

Shana smiles, "Well, shall we get going?"

Jody nods, "Yep, let's get going."

Everyone heads off to their vehicles.

CHAPTER 76

The convoy has continued on its way towards Savannah as the sun is just about to the noon sky. Jody continues to focus on the highway and the road he is looking for as Ashley is looking around to see if she can spot any zombies or other survivors. Jody knows that they are getting close to Savannah and they will need to stop for the rest of the day so they can plan their trip thru Savannah.

Jody catches sight of a small river up ahead and a larger body of water off on the right side of the interstate. Jody starts to slow the truck down and the rest of the convoy starts to slow down behind the truck.

Jody glances over at Ashley, "See that river and lake up ahead? We're going to stop there for the rest of the day and night. I don't want to risk getting any closer to Savannah."

Ashley nods and picks up her two way radio, "Hey everyone, we're going to be stopping just up the highway."

Jody slows the truck down even more as they cross over the river. Jody sees a building off beyond the lake that reminds him of something. As the convoy gets up to the lake, Jody pulls the truck off on the shoulder of the interstate and stops. The rest of the convoy pulls to a stop behind the truck.

Jody and Ashley get out of the truck. Everyone else in the group gets out of their vehicles except for Daniel. The pit bull sits and waits in the Trailblazer and Shadow waits in the van. The group gathers by the truck.

Jody looks around, "We'll camp over by the lake for the rest of today and tonight. I want us to get plenty of rest and have plenty of time to plan for how we're going to get thru Savannah and to Fort Pulaski tomorrow."

Lisa glances around and sees the building that Jody had noticed earlier, "We might consider checking out that building. It looks like a jail."

The rest of the group looks over and sees the building Lisa is talking about.

Michael, Jody's brother, nods, "If it is, that means a sheriff's office might be close also and we might find some weapons or ammo."

Jody nods and looks at the group, "That's something we can think about after we get camp set up." He pauses, "Dad and Tyler will keep a look out while we set up camp. Once we get the tents set up and our stuff over to the camp, we'll let the dogs out and start the watch rotation."

Mike nods, "Sounds good."

Mike and Tyler wait by the edge of the interstate while Jody, Lisa, Lindsey, Michael, Lindsey's husband, Ashley, Zach, Shana and Michael, Jody's brother, start to get the tents from the vehicles.

The camp is completely set up and the dogs have been walked. Jody and Lisa are on watch as everyone else is eating lunch. Shadow is laying at Mike's feet trying to look really sad in hopes of getting a bite of food. The pit bull is sitting next to Lindsey, seeming to have taken a real liking to her.

Ashley finishes a bite of food, "I can't believe we're this close. I mean, tomorrow we go thru Savannah and reach Fort Pulaski."

Rochelle nods as she takes a drink of water, "I know. It's really hard to believe that we've made it this far."

Mike sighs and holds down his last bite for Shadow, "I know, but we've got to be more focused now than ever before. This is by far the largest portion of a city we'll have had to go thru. We won't be able to avoid it like the other places we've been."

Michael, Lindsey's husband, nods, "And a city this size, there are probably thousands of zombies wandering around."

Lindsey reaches over and pets the pit bull, "Well, not only do we have to make it thru the city, but we have to do so in a way as to not draw attention to ourselves so we don't have a bunch of zombies following us to Fort Pulaski."

Zach speaks up after finishing his last bite of food, "I'm sure Jody will come up with a good plan. He's done really good so far."

Shana nods, "He sure has." She pauses, "But everyone has done a good job. We wouldn't have made it this far if not for each of us."

Michael, Jody's brother, nods in agreement, "You're right about that and tomorrow we're going to have to work together perfectly if we want to make it to Fort Pulaski in one piece."

Daniel starts petting the pit bull.

Tyler looks over at the pit bull, "So, do you have a name for her yet?"

Lindsey smiles, "Yep, we decided on Anastasia." She pauses, "Ana or Stasia for short. Its what Daniel liked the most."

Mike smiles at Daniel, "Well, she seems like a very good dog, very nice and friendly."

Daniel smiles, "Yeah, she's great."

Everyone smiles at Daniel.

Michael, Lindsey's husband, looks at his watch, "Well, we better get a short nap or just rest a bit cause our shift starts in an hour."

Lindsey nods, "Yeah, I think stretching out the legs and back will be a good thing before watch. Being cramped up in the vehicles for so long sure stiffens you up."

Everyone nods and chuckles because they all know what Lindsey is talking about. Lindsey and Michael, her husband, get up and head off to their tent while the others remain in front of the large tent.

Lindsey and Michael, her husband, are on watch now. Jody and Lisa have finished eating and are in their tent looking over the city map of Savannah. The two of them are trying to plan their best route to get thru Savannah and to Fort Pulaski.

Jody sighs and shakes his head, "Well, it looks like we have a choice. We can either take the most direct route which leads us thru the heart of the city or we can take a more roundabout approach."

Lisa nods as she looks at the map, "Yeah, the more direct route will save time and gas, but definitely put us in more danger of running into zombies or survivors. If we go around, it'll take more time and gas, but will probably be the safer route cause we go thru less of the populated part of the city." She pauses, "It's a tough call."

Jody looks at Lisa, "Well, I should probably tell you something about my idea."

Lisa looks at Jody, "What is it?"

Jody sighs, "I'm figuring on only taking three vehicles thru the city. That way we can consolidate the gas and we won't be making as much noise."

Lisa gets a surprised look, "Really? Not all of us will fit in three vehicles with the gear and supplies."

Jody nods, "I know. Eight of us will walk with the vehicles. If we do run into problems, we can pile in wherever there is room and get out of there in the vehicles or we can all escape on foot if needed."

Lisa sighs, "That's pretty risky. I mean, walking thru the city when there are potentially thousands of zombies everywhere."

Jody sighs, "I know, but if we're on foot, we have a better view of everything, plus we won't have to drive up to a corner in order to see what's around it. We can walk up to each intersection and scout the way without making noise."

Lisa nods slightly, "I see your point there. The quieter we are the less chance we have of drawing zombies to us." She pauses, "But in doing that, which direction do we want to take. I mean, walking is definitely going to take longer, but I'd rather take longer than walk thru the heart of the city."

Jody looks back at the map, "I'm with you on that one. I know it'll be an all day process if we walk, but I would definitely want to avoid the heart of the city being on foot."

Lisa looks back at the map, "Okay, so we're going to take the more roundabout way. What vehicles are going and who is going to drive them?"

Jody is quiet for a second, "We'll take the van, Trailblazer and the Hyundai. I figure my dad and Shadow will be in the van. Rochelle, Daniel and Anastasia will be in the Trailblazer and Tyler can drive the car."

Lisa looks at Jody again, "Tyler driving the car?"

Jody looks at Lisa and smiles, "It won't be hard to show him and he's big enough to handle it. We'll put the car in the middle of the other two also."

Lisa sighs and nods, "Okay. So we have the vehicles in place. What about those of us on foot?"

Jody looks back at the map, "First, we won't start walking from here. We'll take all the vehicles to a stopping point, gabbing gas along the way if possible." He pauses, "But when we start walking, I want us to be in the point position ahead of the vehicles. We'll have Ashley and Zach second, by the first vehicle. Shana and my brother will be third by the last vehicle and Lindsey and her husband will be rear security behind the vehicles."

Lisa looks back at the map, "That sounds good. Besides, we can use hand signals to communicate along with our two way radios if needed." She pauses, "What do you think? Have the van first, the car second and the Trailblazer last?"

Jody nods as he continues to look over the map, "Yeah, that sounds like a good order to have them in." He pauses, "Now all we need to do is come up with a feasible route to take."

Lisa continues to look over the map, "From what I can see, it looks like the best route to take is going to be around thru the southern part of the city pretty near to this Hunter Army Airfield."

Jody nods at Lisa's suggestion, "Yeah, I think your right about that. It looks like we'll be able to take this Chatham Parkway all the way down until it runs into Veterans Parkway, then we can take that around to Wm F Lynes Parkway."

Lisa nods, "And we can stay on that as it turns into West Derenne Ave and we can stay on that all the way to Skidaway Road which looks like the farthest road to the east we can go before having to turn back north."

Jody and Lisa are running over the map with their fingers, following the path they've plotted out and their hands touch. Jody and Lisa stop, look at each other for a moment and smile before moving their hands back.

Jody looks back at the map, "You've got it so far. Once we turn north, we'll stay on Skidaway Road until we reach East Victory Drive which is Highway 80, then we'll stay on Highway 80 all the way to Fort Pulaski Road."

Lisa nods as she looks back at the map, "That should be easy enough to remember. Not too many twists and turns in there."

Jody nods while looking at the map, "Yeah. If anything comes up, we'll just have to adjust on the fly."

Lisa smiles and looks over at Jody, "We've been pretty good at that so far."

Jody looks up at Lisa, "We sure have."

Jody and Lisa stare at each other for a moment.

Jody smiles, "Well, we should probably get the others together and let them know about the plan."

Lisa returns the smile, "Why don't we stretch out and relax until Lindsey and her husband finish their watch. We could use the break."

Jody is quiet again, then nods as he continues to stare and smile at Lisa, "You're right. We could use some relaxation."

Lisa pulls the map out of the way. Jody and Lisa move over and lay down on their sleeping bags next to each other.

CHAPTER 77

Shana and Michael, Jody's brother, have taken over watch now. Jody and Lisa are with everyone else sitting in front of the large tent. Lisa is holding the city map of Savannah.

Jody picks up his two way radio, "Shana, why don't you two come in so we can talk about tomorrow."

Shana's voice comes back over the radio, "Okay."

In just a minute, Shana and Michael, Jody's brother, walk up and sit down with the rest of the group. Shadow and Anastasia are laying in the middle of everyone, basking in the sun and getting them a nap.

Jody looks at the group, "Okay, Lisa and I have come up with the plan for crossing Savannah. First, I want to share with you the parts of the plan that helped us come up with the route we're going to take."

Mike looks at Jody, "Like what?"

Jody glances around, "First, after we go a little ways tomorrow, we are going to consolidate down to three vehicles."

Ashley looks at Jody with puzzlement, "Will everyone be able to fit in three vehicles with our gear and supplies?"

Lisa shakes her head, "We don't plan on everyone riding all the way thru town."

Everyone gets a surprised look by what Lisa said.

Jody continues, "We discussed it and we think its best if we walk thru the city like we would on a military patrol in hostile territory." He pauses, "That way there'd be less noise and the point team will be able to scout ahead without having to drive up on every turn."

Lindsey glances around at everyone and nods, "That makes sense. I mean, last thing we want is to make a lot of noise and we sure don't want to drive up to an intersection only to find out there are hundreds or thousands of zombies around the corner."

Mike nods in agreement, "It sounds dangerous, but I have to say that the reasoning makes sense to me too. What vehicles are we going to go down to?"

Lisa picks up the explanation, "We are going to take the van, Trailblazer and the Hyundai."

Zach questions, "Are all the teams going to walk?"

Jody nods his head, "Yes. We'll have the van in the front, followed by the Hyundai and the Trailblazer will be last." He pauses, "The point team will be ahead of the convoy, the second team will be by the van, the third team will be by the Trailblazer and the last team will be rear security behind the convoy."

Michael, Lindsey's husband, looks at Jody, "So, who will be in what vehicle?"

Lisa speaks up, "Mike will be in the van with Shadow. Rochelle, Daniel and Anastasia will be in the Trailblazer and Tyler will be in the Hyundai."

Shana gets a surprised look, "Tyler in the Hyundai by himself? That means he'll have to be driving."

Tyler gets a smile on his face.

Jody nods, "That's right. I think he's big enough to handle that."

Shana sighs, "I don't know."

Tyler speaks up, "Mom, I can handle it."

Jody smiles and nods, "He can. I'm going to take him out after we talk and go over how to handle the car."

Michael, Jody's brother, questions, "What if we run into problems and have to escape quickly?"

Jody sighs and continues, "The front two teams will jump in the van, the third team will get in the car and the last team will get in the Trailblazer. Pack in however you can and we'll drive off." He pauses, "If that's an option. We might have to escape on foot in which case, we abandon the vehicles and escape on foot."

Rochelle looks at everyone, "That sounds very dangerous."

Lisa nods, "It'll be dangerous. We managed to avoid Montgomery for the most part, but we have no real way to avoid Savannah." She pauses, "We decided on this plan which also means that we'll be taking a more roundabout way to Fort Pulaski to avoid going thru the heart of the city."

Ashley speaks up, "Now that I like the sound of."

Jody sighs and glances around, "Now, this is the basic plan. We may have to adapt on the fly if things come up like blocked roads, finding stuff that might be useful and other things."

Lindsey glances at everyone, "So, what order will the teams be in around the convoy?"

Lisa replies, "Jody and I will be in the front, running point. Ashley and Zach will be second by the van. Shana and Michael will be third by the Trailblazer and Lindsey and Michael will be rear security. One team member will be on one side of the convoy and the second will be on the other side of the convoy." She pauses, "Basically, we'll have the convoy surrounded."

Mike nods, "Three hundred and sixty degree coverage. Good idea." He pauses, "You're planning this like a real military operation, aren't you?"

Jody nods and smiles, "You better believe it. We can't afford not to with what were facing."

Michael, Jody's brother, speaks up, "So, what about the jail that we're close to? Do we want to check it out for stuff?"

Lisa looks at Jody, then answers, "No. We decided its better not to risk using ammo and possibly there being too many zombies inside and we have to get out of here." She pauses, "The plan is to just rest for the remainder of the day and night so we'll be fresh for tomorrow."

Shana nods, "Sounds like we've pretty much got everything covered. So, what's the route we plan on taking tomorrow?"

Jody looks at Lisa, "Okay, let's get the map and let them know the route we're taking."

Lisa pulls the map up into her lap. Jody and Lisa go over the route for the next day while the rest of the group listens intently.

Ashley and Zach are on watch now. Jody is off teaching Tyler how to drive the Hyundai while Lisa is sitting with Rochelle and Mike in front of the large tent along with Shadow. Lindsey, Michael, her husband, Daniel and Anastasia are in the tent Lindsey and her husband share with Jody and Lisa. Shana and Michael, Jody's brother, are in the tent they share with Ashley and Zach.

Shana is laying next to Michael, Jody's brother, "I'm still surprised that they want Tyler to drive a car tomorrow."

Michael, Jody's brother, nods, "I was pretty surprised too, but this is the last push to Fort Pulaski and in order for us to make it, everyone is going to have to come out of their comfort zone and pitch in to make it happen."

Shana nods, "You're right. I just hope that we don't run into problems and have to abandon the plan. I especially don't want it to go so wrong that we all get split up again." She pauses, "Getting split up out in the country is one thing, getting split up in a big city is totally different."

Michael, Jody's brother, sighs, "Ain't that the truth. I don't even want to think about that happening."

Shana sighs, "I don't want to think about it either, but I can't help it. If we have to get away in the vehicles, it's going to be just us and Tyler in the car."

Michael, Jody's brother, looks at Shana, "Let's just do our best to stay positive. That's not going to happen. We're going to make it thru, all of us and we're going to get to Fort Pulaski and start a new life. A safe life."

Shana looks at Michael, Jody's brother, and smiles, "Yeah, you're right. Thanks for trying to make me feel better about it."

Michael, Jody's brother, smiles, "No problem." He pauses, "Do you feel better?"

Shana returns the smile, "Some." She pauses, "But I really need to get to thinking about something else."

Michael, Jody's brother, continues to smile, "Well, I can think of something."

Shana stares lovingly at Michael, Jody's brother, "Oh really, like what?"

Michael, Jody's brother, stares into Shana's eyes, "I could tell you or I could show you."

Shana gives Michael, Jody's brother, a devilish grin, "Show me."

Michael, Jody's brother, moves closer to Shana and the two of them kiss. The kissing soon turns into kissing more passionately and soon the touching follows. The kissing and touching continues for a few minutes.

Michael, Jody's brother, whispers thru the kissing, "Do you want to?"

Shana whispers back thru the kissing, "Yes."

Michael, Jody's brother, and Shana continue the kissing and touching, then before long, the two of them show their physical love for each other, losing themselves in the moment.

Jody is sitting in the passenger's seat of the Hyundai and Tyler is sitting in the driver's seat. Jody has the driver's seat and steering wheel adjusted so Tyler can see out the front of the car and reach the pedals.

Jody is smiling, "Okay, I think you're going to be ready for tomorrow, but let's go down and back one more time."

Tyler smiles, "Okay."

Tyler keeps his foot on the brake as he puts the car in drive. Tyler slowly pushes down on the accelerator and the car starts to move forward. Tyler remembers what Jody said about steady pressure until he reaches the right speed, then just hold the pedal in place. Tyler looks down and sees he is at the right speed so he holds the car steady.

After reaching the turnaround point, Tyler applies the brake and turns the car halfway around. Tyler puts the car in reverse and let's it slowly back up on it's own as he steers. Once far enough back, Tyler stops the car and puts it back in drive. Tyler pushes down on the accelerator again and completes the turnaround, then starts back to where the other vehicles are parked.

Once they reach the other vehicles, Tyler turns the car around again and pulls it to a stop at the back of the convoy. Tyler puts the car in park and turns it off.

Jody looks at Tyler and smiles, "Great job big man."

Tyler smiles back, "That was fun." His expression changes to more of a worried look, "Jody?"

Jody replies knowing something is bothering Tyler, "What is it bud?"

Tyler replies, "I'm scared about tomorrow."

Jody knows he has to say something to help get Tyler's mind off what bad could happen.

Jody looks around and whispers to Tyler, "Want to know a secret?"

Tyler nods slightly, "Yeah."

Jody whispers again, "I'm scared too."

Tyler's eyes get big in disbelief, "You are?"

Jody nods and whispers, "Yep, but we can't let the others know that. Okay? Just our secret."

Tyler smiles as he feels better hearing that Jody is scared too, "Okay."

Jody smiles at Tyler, "Well, let's get back to camp."

Tyler puts the keys on the dashboard. Jody and Tyler get out of the car and head for the camp.

CHAPTER 78

The rest of the day went by without incident as everyone mainly spent their time laying around, visiting or playing with the dogs when they were not on watch. Night has now fallen over the camp and the stars light up the clear sky. A soft breeze blows across the camp carrying the smell of the lake and trees through the air. Jody and Lisa are on watch now. Mike, Rochelle, Tyler, Daniel, Shadow and Anastasia are all in the large tent sleeping. Shana, Michael, Jody's brother, Ashley and Zach are in their tent getting some sleep.

Lindsey and Michael, her husband, are in their tent that they share with Jody and Lisa. Neither has fallen asleep yet, knowing that they have about an hour until their turn for watch.

Lindsey rolls over and sees that Michael, her husband, is also awake, "Can't sleep either?"

Michael, Lindsey's husband, looks at Lindsey, "Nope. Thinking about tomorrow."

Lindsey sighs, "Me too. It's going to be a long and dangerous day. We're so close and I can't help but think about someone in the group not making it." She pauses, "I mean, we've pretty much become a small family. Mike is pretty much like dad to us all and the others are brothers and sisters and a couple of nephews."

Michael, Lindsey's husband, nods slightly, "That's pretty much how I see them too. I mean, we've lost so much yet I still think of how lucky we are to be a part of this, family more or less."

Lindsey smiles, "I'm glad you see it that way too. Of course I still miss all those we've lost or don't know what happened to, but I also feel lucky that we have the group that we have. Everyone has pulled together so much and everyone is just there for each other. It's pretty amazing."

Michael, Lindsey's husband, smiles, "It really is."

Lindsey loses her smile, "That's why tomorrow worries and scares me so much. I don't want to lose anyone else, especially you or Daniel."

Michael, Lindsey's husband, tries to comfort Lindsey even though he too feels the same way, "That's not going to happen. I don't want to lose anyone either, especially you or Daniel, but I think we're all going to be okay tomorrow."

Lindsey reaches over and takes her husband's hand, "Thanks honey."

Michael, Lindsey's husband, slides over next to Lindsey, "Anytime sweetheart."

Lindsey glances around, "You know, we have about an hour before its time for our watch."

Michael, Lindsey's husband, stares into Lindsey's eyes, "Really? What did you have in mind?"

Lindsey stares into her husband's eyes and gives him a devilish grin, "I think you know."

Michael, Lindsey's husband, moves closer to Lindsey and they share a nice, passionate kiss. The two of them continue to kiss until the moment gets to be too much and they share their physical love for each other.

Jody and Lisa are walking the perimeter of the camp during their watch. The two of them are enjoying the clear night and each one is thinking about the next day and the trip across Savannah. Both of them are also thinking about how nice it will be to reach Fort Pulaski.

Jody looks at Lisa, "I've been thinking some about tomorrow."

Lisa looks back at Jody, "Really? What about?"

Jody talks while walking, "About our weapon situation. A couple of the others lost their shotguns and Zach never had one."

Lisa nods, "True. What did you have in mind?"

Jody glances around, "Well, we have the baseball bats still and of course, we each have a knife." He pauses, "Since the two of us will be at point and have the most possibility of running into trouble, we'll keep our weapons."

Lisa nods and smiles, "That's true. So, what are you wanting to do with the others?"

Jody is quiet for a second, "I figure that I'll have my brother give Ashley his shotgun. That'll give her a shotgun and pistol, then Zach can take the aluminum bat so he'll have that and his pistol."

Lisa glances around, "Yeah, that's a good idea."

Jody continues, "I figure Shana will keep her shotgun and pistol and my brother will have his pistol and he can take one of the wooden bats." He pauses, "Lindsey can keep her shotgun and pistol and her husband has just a pistol right now so we can give him the other wooden bat."

Lisa nods at Jody's idea, "That sounds pretty good to me."

Jody sighs, "To be honest, I hope we stumble across a gun store or something. We're almost out of shotgun shells, everyone's pistol ammo and my rifle ammo."

Lisa looks at Jody, "Yeah, that would be nice. I mean, just making it across Savannah is going to be great, but it would be even better if we had more weapons, ammo and supplies when we get to Fort Pulaski. That way we don't have to go out right after getting there and search for stuff."

Jody nods, "That's what I'm hoping for." He pauses, "Well, we'll just keep our fingers crossed."

Lisa smiles, "All of them and toes too."

Jody looks at Lisa, smiles and chuckles slightly.

Jody puts his hand on Lisa's shoulder, "You got that right."

Jody and Lisa continue to walk the perimeter of the camp.

Shana and Michael, Jody's brother, are on watch now as its early morning and the stars and moon are still shining bright in the night sky. Ashley and Zach are in the tent they share with Michael, Jody's brother, and Shana. The two of them woke up when Shana and Michael, Jody's brother, went off for their watch.

Ashley rolls over and looks at Zach, "You asleep."

Zach rolls over and faces Ashley, "Nope."

Ashley sighs, "I wasn't sleeping that good before, but I can't get back to sleep now at all." She pauses, "I'm worried about tomorrow and the trip thru Savannah."

Zach nods slightly, "Me too. The idea of walking thru the city is pretty scary."

Ashley nods slightly in return, "It sure is scary. I mean, I've gone on supply runs before, but this is so much different. We're going to walk thru a city with potentially thousands of zombies around."

Zach sighs, "I know. This really is the first time I'm going to be actually involved in the possible contact with the zombies and not just standing watch or waiting in the vehicles." He pauses, "I just hope I do okay."

Ashley smiles, "I'm sure you'll do fine. I felt the same way when this all first started, but I surprised myself and I'm sure you're stronger than I am."

Zach smiles at Ashley who he has grown to really like, "Thanks. I just don't want to let everyone down because they're really trusting me." He pauses, "I just want us all to make it to Fort Pulaski."

Ashley nods slightly, "Me too." She pauses, "I can't imagine the thought of losing anyone else. I mean, its like we're all one big family."

Zach nods slightly at Ashley's words, "That's how I feel too."

Ashley shifts around a little, "Well, we should probably try to doze off some more before it's our turn on watch."

Zach stares at Ashley, "Yeah, you're right." He pauses because he is unsure if he should say what is on his mind next, "I know nothing will happen between us, but would you mind if maybe we cuddled together. It's just, well ..."

Ashley smiles and interrupts before Zach says anymore, "I'd like that. I could use that feeling of comfort right now too. I just wasn't sure how to say it."

Zach smiles as Ashley moves over next to him.

Zach puts his arm around Ashley, "Thanks."

Ashley smiles and closes her eyes, "Thank you."

Zach and Ashley do their best to get their mind off the trip and get some more rest before their watch.

Michael, Jody's brother, and Shana are walking the perimeter of the camp. The clear night is so quiet to the two of them that they feel like their footsteps are echoing for miles.

Michael, Jody's brother, whispers to Shana as they walk, "It's such a beautiful night. Well, early morning that is."

Shana looks up at the clear sky, "It sure is." She pauses, "I just hope tomorrow all of us are enjoying this kind of night at Fort Pulaski."

Michael, Jody's brother, nods in agreement, "Yeah, me too. I'm ready to put this trip behind us and start fresh."

Shana glances around, "So am I. Its just, I'm worried about the trip thru Savannah still. I can't seem to get it off my mind. Especially with Tyler having to drive the car."

Michael, Jody's brother, smiles, "I know. That was a surprise, but from what Jody said earlier, Tyler did a good job practicing."

Shana sighs, "Yeah, he's a quick learner. I just don't want anything to go wrong and I definitely don't want us to lose anyone else." She pauses, "I mean, we're just a big family now."

Michael, Jody's brother, looks at Shana, "Oh yes, I think everyone of us sees it like that. We've become family to each other. That's really the only way we've managed to make it this far and not be killed or have our group fall apart."

Shana nods, "Yeah, everyone looks out for each other. Especially when we all got separated. The first thing we all thought about was finding each other and getting the group back together." She pauses, "And somehow we did."

Michael, Jody's brother, sighs, "Yeah, we got pretty lucky to get the group back together after that."

Shana nods and looks around, "Now we just need the same kind of luck for tomorrow."

Michael, Jody's brother, glances around, "Yes we do."

Michael, Jody's brother, and Shana get quiet again as they continue to walk. Each of them thinking about the trip thru Savannah and the possibility of losing more of the group.

CHAPTER 79

Its morning and the group is awake and getting their things together for the big day. It is a good day to travel as the sky is dotted with small clouds and the temperature is holding in the upper 70's. Once everyone has their things together, Jody hollers to the rest of the group to meet with him in front of the large tent. The group gets together in front of the large tent.

Lindsey looks at Jody, "So, what's up?"

Jody looks around at everyone, "I want to go ahead and load everything up in the van, Trailblazer and Hyundai. That way we won't have to do it once we stop later."

Mike nods, "Good idea. Keep the stop time to a minimum."

Lisa speaks up, "We're also going to make a change with the current weapon situation since some of you only have a pistol and knife now."

Shana looks at Lisa, "What's the change?"

Lisa looks at Michael, Jody's brother, "We want you to give your shotgun to Ashley. We're going to break out the baseball bats now. Both Michaels will take a wooden bat and Zach will take the aluminum bat."

Everyone nods and Michael, Jody's brother, steps over and hands his shotgun and the remainder of his spare shells to Ashley.

Michael, Lindsey's husband, looks at Jody, "I'm taking it that since we're using the bats now that we're not going to use guns unless absolutely necessary."

Jody nods, "Yes. Use bats and knives if possible. Use guns only as a last resort and in dire need. We want to keep the noise level down as much as possible. Any gunfire will echo for quite a ways in the city the way it is now."

Lisa nods and chimes in, "And we don't want to draw more zombies if we can avoid it."

Ashley questions, "If we're walking, how are we going to communicate?"

Jody glances around at everyone, "We'll use hand signals whenever possible and the two way radios if need be. After we get loaded up, I'll go over the signals we'll actually use. It won't be many."

Lisa speaks up, "We'll stick to the plan unless something goes wrong or if an opportunity arises that we can't pass up."

Michael, Jody's brother, looks at Jody, "We should probably get going unless we have more to talk about."

Jody shakes his head slightly, "Nope, that's all for now. Let's get everything loaded in the three vehicles, grab the bats and cover the signals. Oh, and let the dogs walk around before we leave."

Everyone nods, grabs their personal belongings and heads for the vehicles.

The convoy has just turned south on Chatham Parkway as the morning sun brightens up the clear sky. A few clouds dot the sky and are being blown along by a soft, warm breeze. Jody accelerates the truck up to a safe speed as Chatham Parkway is clear of vehicles. The rest of the convoy stays close to the vehicle in front of them.

Before long the convoy passes by a couple of side roads and an animal clinic. Ashley looks around while Jody continues to focus on the road. Lisa keeps the Jeep close to the truck. Rochelle is looking around for zombies. Mike keeps the van close to the Jeep. Shadow is sitting in the passenger's seat staring at the windshield wipers, hoping that they'll move.

Michael, Lindsey's husband, is keeping the Trailblazer close to the van. Lindsey is in the passenger's seat looking around for zombies. Daniel is in his seat and Anastasia is sitting next to Daniel, looking out the window. Shana keeps the Hyundai close to the Trailblazer. Michael, Jody's brother, is looking around for zombies as well as Zach and Tyler.

The convoy continues south on Chatham Parkway and they pass a few more buildings and a couple more side roads. So far the drive has been uneventful which none of the members of the group minds. Jody swerves the truck around an abandoned truck, then swerves again around an abandoned car.

Ashley looks at Jody, "Looks like we're coming up to a major road or highway."

Jody nods, "Yep."

Jody slows the truck some just in case they are approaching Veterans Parkway. As they get closer, Ashley and Jody see the name of the road and its Ogeechee Road. Jody speeds the truck back up as he swerves to miss another abandoned car. The rest of the convoy keeps pace. Again, the driver's stay focused on the road while the others keep watch for zombies and other survivors.

Jody weaves around a couple more abandoned cars and everyone in the convoy has noticed the same thing, there is more abandoned traffic which could mean more chances of zombies. The convoy passes two small lakes, then another side road as everyone in the group sees another highway ahead.

Jody starts to slow the truck, "I hope this is it."

Ashley nods, "Me too."

Jody slows the truck down as they approach the highway. The convoy gets closer to the highway and everyone in the group sees the sign, "Veterans Parkway". Jody slows the truck even more as he exits off Chatham Parkway. Jody weaves the truck around an abandoned semi, then pulls the truck onto Veterans Parkway heading east. The rest of the convoy makes the exit and catches up to the truck.

Jody speeds the truck back up to a safe speed as he weaves around a couple more abandoned cars. The convoy makes its way around the abandoned cars and keeps pace with the truck. The convoy heads thru a sharp curve and passes between two small lakes. As the convoy comes out of the curve and veers around another abandoned semi, they pass a side road. Once the convoy passes Garrard Ave, they see a highway exchange up ahead. Lisa starts to slow the Jeep down as the truck in front of her slows down.

Lisa sighs, "I think this should be where we run into the next parkway."

Rochelle continues to look around, "Well, so far everything has gone okay."

A little further and Lisa and Rochelle see the sign for Wm F Lynes Parkway. Lisa keeps the Jeep close to the truck as the convoy weaves around a string of abandoned cars and everyone in the group knows that they are getting closer to the more populated area of the city. The convoy keeps to the right of the highway as they exit off Veterans Parkway and merge onto Wm F Lynes Parkway.

The convoy maneuvers around more abandoned vehicles as they speed back up some. Each person in the group is feeling good about the trip so far, but they know that it is going to get worse and harder. Just as soon as the convoy gets on Wm F Lynes Parkway, they pass another connecting parkway. The convoy slows down some as the highway they are on is becoming more and more cluttered with abandoned vehicles.

Michael, Lindsey's husband, keeps the Trailblazer close to the van, "Well, looks like we're getting more into the populated area."

Lindsey nods while glancing around, "Yeah, I just hope that the highway stays clear enough for us to drive on and we all don't end up walking."

Michael, Lindsey's husband, nods in agreement, "Me too."

The convoy continues east on Wm F Lynes Parkway as they pass by a small lake and everyone can see Hunter Army Airfield off to their south. The convoy soon passes over some railroad tracks as they find themselves running parallel with Perimeter Road. Jody slows the truck some as he maneuvers around more abandoned vehicles. Ashley and Jody both see a residential area coming up on the north side of the highway.

Jody slows the truck a little more, "Well, looks like we're getting closer to the stopping point."

Ashley sighs, "Yeah, we'll be walking soon enough."

Shana slows the car some as the rest of the convoy slows down in front of her. Michael, Jody's brother, looks over and sees the residential area. Michael, Jody's brother, also sees something else.

Michael, Jody's brother, points off to the residential area, "Look."

Shana, Zach and Tyler look off to where Michael, Jody's brother, is pointing and they see a small group of zombies, eight in all, wandering around aimlessly.

Shana looks back at the road, "Just as long as they stay over there and leave us alone, I'll be okay with it."

Zach nods, "Yeah, me too."

The convoy continues on and they start to pass the residential area. The convoy weaves around more abandoned vehicles and keeps heading east. Everyone in the group knows that they are getting close to the stopping point. Jody glances around as he spots a couple of zombies off to the north in the residential area, but doesn't pay them too much mind.

The convoy slowly makes its way east and continues to maneuver around abandoned vehicles. Before long, Jody and Ashley see a major road and intersection coming up.

Jody glances around, "If this is West Derenne Ave coming up, then it'll be time for us to stop."

Ashley nods, "I'm guessing it is since we're getting into more of the city."

Jody starts to slow the truck down some more as the convoy nears the upcoming intersection. Finally, Jody and Ashley see the road sign and the intersection is where the road changes into West Derenne Ave. Jody slows the truck even more as Ashley continues to look around.

Jody glances around as they are nearly to the intersection, "See any zombies?"

Ashley shakes her head as she continues to look around, "Nope."

As the convoy gets to the intersection where Wm F Lynes Parkway changes into West Derenne Ave, Jody pulls the truck to a stop on the side of the road. The rest of the convoy pulls in behind the truck and stops. Jody shuts the truck off, grabs his h-harness gear, which has his pistol and knife on it, grabs his rifle and gets out of the truck. Ashley grabs her shotgun and gets out of the truck.

The rest of the group sees Jody and Ashley get out of the truck and everyone gets out of their vehicles. The dogs remain in the vehicles. Everyone has on their knives and pistols. Lisa also has her shotgun, Zach also has the aluminum baseball bat, Shana also has her shotgun, Michael, Jody's brother, also has a wooden baseball bat and Michael, Lindsey's husband, also has a wooden baseball bat.

Mike looks at Jody, "So, I'm guessing its time to consolidate and begin the patrol."

Jody nods while glancing around, "Yep. Just like we planned."

Lindsey questions, "Should we let the dogs out before we get started? It could be awhile before we stop again for them."

Jody looks back at Lindsey, "Good idea." He pauses, "Okay, we'll all keep a look out while Lindsey and my dad let the dogs out. Soon as they're done, we'll get on our way."

Everyone nods as Mike heads off to get Shadow and Lindsey heads off to get Anastasia.

CHAPTER 80

The group has been patrolling for a short distance now. Jody and Lisa are in front of the three vehicles by about ten yards. Jody is about five feet from one side of the road and Lisa is about five feet from the other side of the road. Mike has the van just idling along behind Jody and Lisa as Shadow is sitting in the passenger's seat, still waiting for the windshield wipers to come on.

In the gap between the van and the Hyundai, Ashley and Zach are in their position. Ashley is on the same side of the road as Jody and Zach is on the same side as Lisa. Tyler has both hands on the steering wheel as he just lets the car idle along and he is keeping pace with the van.

In the gap between the Hyundai and the Trailblazer is Michael, Jody's brother, and Shana. Michael, Jody's brother, is on the same side of the road as Ashley and Shana is on the same side of the road as Zach. Rochelle is keeping the Trailblazer at a steady distance from the Hyundai. Daniel is in his seat and he is petting Anastasia who is sitting next to Daniel.

About ten yards behind the Trailblazer is Michael, Lindsey's husband, and Lindsey. Lindsey is on the same side of the road as Jody and Michael, Lindsey's husband, is on the same side of the road as Lisa. So far, the patrol hasn't seen anything, but they know that their luck can't hold out forever.

614

The patrol passes Abercorn Street and the road that they are on changes into East Derenne Avenue. The patrol is approaching the next intersection. Jody and Lisa speed walk ahead to the corners of the intersection. Jody checks to the north and Lisa checks to the south as the rest of the patrol slows down.

Once Jody and Lisa are sure the side roads are clear, they motion for the rest of the patrol to keep moving. The patrol starts moving forward again as they get their distance behind Jody and Lisa. The patrol moves slowly along and they start to come to the next intersection. Jody and Lisa move forward like before and the patrol stops.

This time after checking north, Jody looks over to Lisa. Lisa motions that she sees something. Jody moves forward just enough to see what Lisa is talking about. Jody sees the three zombies staggering towards the road they are on. Jody motions for the patrol to stay where they're at. Jody quickly crosses over to where Lisa is at.

Lisa whispers to Jody, "What do you want to do?"

Jody glances around, "They're almost to the corner. Let's dispatch them, then we'll move on."

Lisa nods, "Okay."

Jody and Lisa pull out their knives. Jody and Lisa are hiding by the building on the corner, waiting for the zombies to come around the corner. In a few seconds which seems like forever, the three zombies stagger pass the edge of the building. Jody and Lisa lunge out and they each drive their knives into a zombie's head. Jody and Lisa remove their knives as the two zombies fall. The last zombie turns towards Jody and Lisa and reaches for them as it starts to growl and chomp it's teeth.

Jody quickly brings his knife around and drives it into the zombie's head. The zombie falls to the ground as Jody removes his knife. Jody and Lisa wipe their knives off and put them away. Lisa checks the side road again and she is certain it is clear. Jody returns to his side of the road. Once

Jody and Lisa are certain everything is clear, they motion for the convoy to start moving again as the two of them start walking.

The patrol has made it a ways without any other incidents so far. Each person in the group is wondering when and where they'll run into the next group of zombies. None of them believe that they'll make it all the way thru the city without a major encounter or a problem. The patrol is coming up to a major intersection. Jody and Lisa move ahead and realize that the road they're coming up to is a larger road than the others before.

The patrol stops and waits for Jody and Lisa. While Jody and Lisa are checking out the side street, Lindsey and Michael, her husband, hear something behind them. Lindsey and Michael, her husband, turn around and see two zombies staggering up behind them. Lindsey and Michael, her husband, start slowly moving towards the two zombies.

Lindsey draws her knife as Michael, Lindsey's husband, readies his wooden bat. As the zombie closes in on Lindsey, it reaches for her and starts to snarl and chomp it's teeth. Lindsey waits for the moment, then when the zombie is close enough, she drives her knife into the zombie's head. The zombie falls as Lindsey removes her knife.

Michael, Lindsey's husband, waits for the zombie to get closer. The zombie raises it's arms and reaches for Michael, Lindsey's husband. As the zombie staggers closer, Michael, Lindsey's husband, swings the wooden bat, striking the zombie in the head with a loud thud. Michael, Lindsey's husband, swings the bat again. This time the blow knocks the zombie to the ground. Michael,

Lindsey's husband, steps over the zombie and delivers numerous blows to the zombie's head and the zombie stops moving. Michael, Lindsey's husband, steps away and he and Lindsey return to their place in the patrol.

Jody and Lisa watch as Lindsey and Michael, her husband, kill the zombies. Once the zombies are finished, Jody motions for the patrol to start moving again. Jody and Lisa start walking and the patrol starts moving. The patrol takes it's time and they pass a couple more intersections. Jody and Lisa handle the intersections as they did all the others.

Once the patrol passes the last intersection, Jody and Lisa see something up ahead. The two of them see a river and a large road coming up on the far side of the river. Jody and Lisa continue walking towards the river ahead. It only takes a few minutes for the patrol to reach the river. As the patrol is crossing over the river, they see the sign for the road up ahead, but more importantly, Jody and Lisa see something much better.

As the patrol gets closer to Harry S Truman Parkway, Jody and Lisa see what looks like some military vehicles up ahead. Jody looks at Lisa as Lisa looks at Jody. The two of them smile at each other and Jody calls the patrol to a stop with his hand signal. Jody makes his way over to Lisa.

Lisa whispers to Jody, "Do you see that? It looks like military vehicles."

Jody nods and whispers back, "Yeah, that's exactly what it is." He pauses, "I think we should stop and check it out. Maybe there are things we can use there."

Lisa nods as she glances around, "Sounds good to me."

Jody looks back and motions for the patrol to start moving again.

Jody and Lisa slowly approach Harry S Truman
Parkway and as they've gotten closer, they can see more
clearly now. The military convoy they saw consists of two
armored HUMVEE vehicles with mounted 50 caliber
machine guns, one transport HUMVEE and one seven ton
truck. Numerous civilian vehicles are spread out along the
parkway, but there is enough of an opening to still drive
thru. Also strung out along the parkway around the convoy
are numerous bodies of the soldiers who were a part of the
convoy.

Once the patrol reaches Harry S Truman Parkway,
Jody motions for the patrol to stop. The patrol stops about a
hundred feet from the front of the military vehicles. Jody
turns around and gives the hand signal for the group to
meet up in the middle of the patrol next to the Hyundai.
Each person that is walking starts towards the Hyundai.
Mike puts the van in park, shuts it off and gets out. Tyler
puts the Hyundai in park, shuts it off and gets out. Rochelle
puts the Trailblazer in park, shuts it off and her and Daniel
get out.

Once the group is together, Jody looks at each of them,
"I want to check out this military convoy and see if there is
anything there we can use."

Michael, Jody's brother, questions, "How do you want
to go about doing that?"

Jody replies, "You and Shana check out the transport
HUMVEE and see if there's anything in it. Lisa and I will
check out the seven ton truck. Lindsey, you, your husband,
Ashley and Zach will check the bodies of the soldiers.
Grab any rifles, pistols and spare ammo that they have and
start bringing them over by the seven ton truck."

Mike nods and glances around, "What about the rest
of us?"

Jody looks around, "You, Roe, Tyler and Daniel will
wait by the seven ton and make a note of everything that is
brought over."

Lindsey looks at Jody, "Sounds like you might want to take the truck."

Jody nods, "If possible and someone can drive it, we'll be able to load everything in it and then some."

Michael, Lindsey's husband, questions, "What about the armored HUMVEES? Do we want to take them?"

Jody shakes his head, "No, they don't have much room. Just check them for weapons." He pauses, "Okay, let's do this. Everyone be careful."

The group starts over to the military vehicles, staying aware of their surroundings because they know with all the abandoned vehicles, zombies could be lurking anywhere. Mike, Tyler, Rochelle and Daniel stop at the front of the seven ton truck. Jody and Lisa make their way towards the back of the truck as Michael, Jody's brother, and Shana branch off to head over to the transport HUMVEE. Lindsey and Michael, her husband, head for one armored HUMVEE while Zach and Ashley head for the other.

Jody and Lisa reach the back of the seven ton truck. Lisa stands watch as Jody climbs up on the back of the truck. Jody pulls out his pistol as he prepares to move the flap covering the back of the truck. Jody slowly pulls the flap open enough where he can see inside and he can't believe his eyes.

Lisa looks up at Jody, "What's in there?"

Jody looks down at Lisa, "Food. Lots of food."

Jody climbs into the back of the seven ton truck and puts his pistol away. Jody sees numerous boxes of MREs and he starts to count them. Lisa waits patiently and keeps looking around while waiting for Jody to come back out of the truck.

Michael, Jody's brother, and Shana slowly approach the transport HUMVEE. Shana takes up a position on the left side and Michael, Jody's brother, takes up position on the right side. The two of them look at each other as they grab the back flap which is blocking their view of what is in the back of the HUMVEE. Michael, Jody's brother, and Shana nod to each other, then pull the flap open on each side so they can see in the back of the HUMVEE. Michael, Jody's brother, and Shana can't believe their eyes.

Michael, Jody's brother, climbs up into the crowded back of the HUMVEE. Michael, Jody's brother, immediately sees two cases marked as fragmentation grenades and one case marked as smoke grenades. Michael, Jody's brother, also quickly spots four AT4 rocket launchers. However, it is the rest of the boxes that has Michael, Jody's brother, the happiest. Michael, Jody's brother, starts counting the cases of 5.56 ammo and 9mm ammo.

Lindsey and Michael, her husband, has checked one armored HUMVEE and found nothing, but they found a couple of bodies on the ground, each with an M4 rifle, M9 Beretta pistol, six loaded magazines for the rifle and three loaded magazines for the pistol. Lindsey and Michael, her husband, grab the weapons and extra magazines and start back for the seven ton truck.

Ashley and Zach also had no luck with the armored HUMVEE that they checked out, but they too found a couple of bodies with the same weapons and spare magazines. Ashley and Zach grab the weapons and spare magazines and start for the seven ton truck.

Jody climbs down from the back of the truck and him and Lisa start towards where Mike is at. Jody and Lisa walk up to Mike, Rochelle, Tyler and Daniel. Jody glances around and sees the rest of the group making their way over to them. Michael, Jody's brother, and Shana walk up next. Michael, Lindsey's husband, and Lindsey walk up and put down the weapons and spare magazines they found. Zach and Ashley walk up last and put down the weapons and spare magazines they also found.

Jody looks at the others, "Good work."

Mike questions, "Was there anything in the truck and the transport HUMVEE?"

Jody nods, "There are a hundred boxes of MREs in the back of the truck."

Everyone smiles at the thought of that much food.

Lisa smiles, "They may not be the best tasting things, but that'll give us a nice supply of food to go with what we already have."

Michael, Jody's brother, smiles and nods, "I'll raise your food with weapons." He pauses as everyone looks over at him, "There are two cases of frag grenades, one case of smoke grenades, four rocket launchers and I counted ten thousand rounds of 9mm ammo, ten thousand rounds of 5.56 ammo and five thousand rounds of 5.56 belt ammo."

Lindsey gets a big smile, "That's awesome!"

Michael, Lindsey's husband, nods, "Yeah it is. We spotted other bodies too that we can get weapons off of if you want us too."

Everyone gets quiet as they look at Jody.

Jody glances around and nods, "Okay, you four keep grabbing weapons and ammo. My brother, Shana, Lisa and I will move the stuff from the HUMVEE over to the seven ton truck. Dad, you, Rochelle, Tyler and Daniel stay here and keep whatever they bring over sorted out."

Everyone nods at their assignments. Jody, Lisa, Shana and Michael, Jody's brother, head off for the HUMVEE. Zach, Ashley, Lindsey and Michael, Lindsey's husband, head off to find more bodies. While Jody and the others work vigorously to get everything moved over to the seven ton, Lindsey and her small group find more weapons and spare magazines and take them back to Mike, then start looking again. However, with everything going on, none of them see what is lurking and making its way towards Mike, Rochelle, Tyler and Daniel.

It takes a little time, but Lindsey and the others finish finding all the extra weapons and magazines so they head over to the back of the seven ton to see if they can help Jody and the others with anything. Jody climbs down from the back of the seven ton as Lindsey and her small group walk up to help load the last few cases of ammo.

Mike, Rochelle, Tyler and Daniel are waiting by the front of the seven ton truck where Lindsey and her small group have set down a nice bunch of weapons and spare magazines.

Mike looks at Rochelle and Tyler, "Okay, let's sort the weapons into separate groups and the spare magazines into separate groups, then get a recount of everything."

Mike, Rochelle and Tyler start sorting everything while Daniel waits behind them about twenty feet. As Jody and the others are at the back of the truck and Mike, Rochelle and Tyler are at the front of the truck finishing up what they are doing, they all hear Daniel.

Daniel cries out, "No!"

Mike spins around quickly and sees two zombies closing in on Daniel. Mike quickly draws his knife and rushes over towards Daniel and the zombies. The zombies are nearly to Daniel when out of nowhere, Mike reaches over with his left hand and grabs the shoulder of one zombie, stopping it from getting any closer to Daniel and at the same time he drives his knife into the head of the other zombie.

As Mike pulls his knife out, the zombie falls to the ground. The other zombie turns quickly on Mike and bites at Mike's left arm. Mike quickly brings his knife around and drives it into the zombie's head as the zombie's head lays against Mike's left arm. Mike pulls his knife out and the zombie falls to the ground. Mike glances at his arm, then wipes the knife off and puts it away as Jody and the rest of the group come running up. Daniel runs over to Lindsey and hugs onto her.

Lisa questions, "Everyone okay?"

Mike nods, "Yeah, two zombies snuck up on us somehow, but we got them."

Ashley shakes her head, "It's amazing how those things can just pop up out of nowhere like those cheesy scary movies."

Lindsey smiles, "Right!"

Jody glances around, "So no one got hurt?"

Mike shakes his head, "Nope."

Jody nods, "Okay then, how'd we do on weapons and spare magazines?"

Rochelle looks at Jody, "We have ten M4 rifles, ten M9 pistols and four SAW guns. We have sixty M4 magazines, thirty M9 magazines and twelve drums for the SAW guns."

Ashley looks at Rochelle, "What is a SAW gun?"

Jody looks at Ashley and smiles, "Its a nice weapon. It is a fully automatic weapon, pretty much like a machine gun."

Ashley nods, "Cool."

Jody looks around, "Before we get moving again, we're going to change up our weapons."

Michael, Jody's brother, questions, "What do you want to do?"

Jody replies, "I want us to all carry the same type of weapon and ammo, except for a couple exceptions. I want Tyler to take Lisa's shotgun and Shana's LC9 pistol. Rochelle will take Lindsey's shotgun and Ashley's LC9 pistol. I'll keep my AR-15 and pistol since they're the same ammo as the M4 and M9."

Lisa looks at Jody, "What about the rest of us?"

Jody glances around, "If you don't have a 9mm pistol, swap your pistol out with one of the M9 pistols and grab a couple extra magazines. Also, everyone grab an M4 rifle and a couple spare magazines as well. We'll put the swapped out weapons in the pile and load the rest in the back of the seven ton."

Lindsey nods, "Okay. So obviously we're taking the seven ton. What are we going to do with the other vehicles?"

Jody sighs, "First, can anyone drive the seven ton?"

It gets quiet for a minute.

Michael, Lindsey's husband, speaks up, "I'm sure I can. Well, I'll sure give it a try."

Jody smiles, "Good. So this is what we'll do. The van will stay in the lead with my dad and Shadow. The seven ton will be next and Tyler will ride shotgun in it. The Trailblazer will be last with Rochelle, Daniel and Anastasia." He pauses, "I'll walk point, Ashley and Zach will be second still and Shana and my brother will be third. Lisa will take rear security."

Lindsey realizes Jody didn't mention her name, "What about me?"

Jody looks at Lindsey and smiles, "I've got a special place and job for you. I'm going to have you on top of the seven ton with your weapons, but also one of the SAW guns. That'll give you more of a bird's eye view so you can alert us of things that we can't see by being at ground level."

Lindsey smiles at Jody, "Sounds good to me."

Jody looks around at everyone, "Okay, let's get the weapons swapped out and the remaining weapons loaded up so we can get out of here."

Everyone starts moving. Mike flexes his left arm a second as he waits his turn to swap out his pistol and get a rifle.

CHAPTER 81

The patrol has been walking for awhile again. Jody is about ten yards in front of the van which Mike is driving as Shadow sits in the passenger's seat. Ashley and Zach are in the gap between the van and the seven ton truck. Ashley is on the left side of the road and Zach is on the right side of the road. Michael, Lindsey's husband, has the seven ton truck about five yards behind the van. Tyler is riding shotgun and keeping a look out for zombies.

Lindsey is sitting on top of the canopy covering the back of the seven ton truck. Lindsey has her M4 rifle and the SAW gun sitting next to her. Lindsey is using her lookout position to see all the way around the patrol. Michael, Jody's brother, and Shana are at the gap between the seven ton truck and the Trailblazer. Michael, Jody's brother, is on the same side of the road as Ashley and Shana is on the same side of the road as Zach.

Rochelle is keeping the Trailblazer about five yards behind the seven ton truck. Daniel is sitting in his seat and Anastasia is laying in the seat next to Daniel. Lisa is walking about ten yards behind the Trailblazer. The patrol has made its way for awhile since picking up the military stuff and the sun is now crossing into the noon sky.

Jody sees a road coming up ahead. Jody motions for the patrol to stop. The vehicles stop and so does everyone else walking. Lindsey picks up the binoculars she borrowed from Jody and looks around. Jody waits and continues to glance around, looking back at Lindsey every so often.

Lindsey scans the area, then looks over at Jody. Jody looks up at Lindsey. Lindsey gives Jody a thumbs up. Jody nods and slowly makes his way over to the corner of the cross street. Jody looks up at the street sign and sees it is Skidaway Road, the street where they make their next turn. Jody checks to road to the north and to the south. Once Jody is sure he doesn't see anything, he motions for the patrol to start moving again.

Jody starts to slowly walk around the corner and north on Skidaway Road. The rest of the patrol slowly makes its way around the corner and the three vehicles weave around a couple of abandoned vehicles in the road. Before long, the patrol is heading north on Skidaway Road.

Jody keeps glancing around as he slowly walks north along the road. Lindsey keeps scanning the area with the binoculars. The patrol passes a couple of side roads without incident. The patrol slowly pushes forward and before anyone can see it, a zombie comes out of an alley on the east side of the road near the middle of the patrol.

Zach spots the lone zombie as it staggers towards the patrol. Zach sees his chance and pulls out his knife. Shana also sees the zombie and pulls out her knife. Zach and Shana both start towards the zombie. The zombie turns towards Shana. Zach seizes the opportunity and closes in quickly behind the zombie. As the zombie gets closer to Shana, Zach comes up from behind the zombie and rams his knife into the back of the zombie's head. The zombie stops moving and falls to the ground when Zach removes his knife.

Zach wipes his knife off and looks at Shana. Shana smiles at Zach, then the two of them return to their place in the patrol. The patrol passes one more side road and everyone sees off to their right what looks like a university. The patrol continues north on Skidaway Road.

In a short time, the patrol has passed the university and Delesseps Avenue. Everyone is still feeling good about not having ran into any large groups of zombies. Jody leads the patrol thru a couple of small intersections and the vehicles are having to constantly weave around abandoned vehicles, but so far the road has remained clear enough for the convoy to get thru.

Before long, the patrol starts to close in on more of a main road running off to the west from Skidaway Road. Lindsey is keeping a constant watch from atop the seven ton truck as Jody focuses on the road ahead and Lisa looks behind the patrol every few steps to make sure nothing sneaks up on them.

Jody slows the patrol down as they near the larger side road. Lindsey looks down at Jody and gives a thumbs up. Jody makes his way to the intersection and looks down East 52nd Street. Once he is sure all is clear, Jody motions for the patrol to start moving again. The patrol passes East 52nd Street and continues north. The patrol passes another side street on the east and three more on the west side of the road they're on.

After passing the last side street to the west, the area opens up for a little ways. Lindsey looks thru the binoculars and sees a city square up ahead to the west side of the road and it has some shops and a movie cinema. Lindsey also sees something that she doesn't like. Lindsey spots about twenty zombies wandering around one of the parking lots.

Lindsey picks up the two way radio, "Jody."

Jody replies over the two way radio, "What is it Lindsey?"

Lindsey continues to look thru the binoculars as she speaks into the radio, "Up ahead on the left in that town square shopping area. I see about twenty zombies wandering around."

Jody replies, "Have they given any signs of having seen or heard us?"

Lindsey replies while keeping constant watch of the zombies, "Doesn't seem like it."

Jody replies, "Okay. Keep your eyes on them and let me know. I believe just beyond that square is our next turn."

Lindsey replies, "Okay."

Lindsey sets down the radio and keeps a constant watch on the group of zombies. Jody puts his radio up and returns his focus to the road ahead. Everyone else heard Lindsey's transmission and start to wonder if now is the time a large group a zombies will find them.

The patrol passes a couple of side streets as they get closer to the square. Lindsey maintains a vigilant watch on the zombies and so far, the zombies are unaware of the group moving thru the area. Jody looks over at the square as the patrol starts to pass by it. Jody hopes that the zombies don't see them and they can get by without drawing attention to themselves.

In a few tense minutes which seems like hours, the patrol passes the square and everyone breathes a sigh of relief. Jody sees a sign for the next road ahead and it is the road they are looking for, East Victory Drive which is also Highway 80. Everyone in the group sees the road sign before long and they all start to get a good feeling knowing that this is the last turn they'll make until they reach the bridge leading over to the island Fort Pulaski is on.

Lindsey comes over the two way radio again, "It looks like the zombies must have heard us. They're slowly starting to stagger their way in this general direction."

Jody comes back over the radio, "Okay. Keep watching them and let me know if they start to close in. We're nearly to our last turn. We'll try not to slow down as much if it's possible."

Lindsey replies, "Okay."

Jody stops the patrol a little shy of East Victory Drive. Jody quickly scouts out the new road they plan to travel on and he is sure it is clear. Jody motions for the patrol to start moving again. Jody leads the patrol around the corner and onto East Victory Drive. Lindsey maintains a watch on the group of zombies behind them. As far as Lindsey can tell, the zombies are not completely sure of their location so it appears the patrol is pulling away from them.

Once on the new road, the van, seven ton truck and Trailblazer slowly work their way around numerous abandoned vehicles. One thing everyone has noticed and kind of finds ironic is that the name of the road that leads to their final destination is named "victory".

The patrol has gone a little ways on East Victory Drive and so far hasn't encountered any problems. Lindsey has continued to watch the group of zombies that were behind them, but that group of zombies have appeared to fall far enough behind that they no longer appear to be a threat. The patrol has passed a few more side streets without incident or seeing anything.

Lindsey picks up the two way radio, "Jody."

Jody comes back over the radio, "What is it?"

Lindsey replies with a cheerful tone, "We've lost the group of zombies that were behind us."

Jody replies with an equally cheerful tone, "That's good news. Okay, return to your normal watch now."

Lindsey replies, "Okay."

Everyone heard the good news and for a moment, the group feels a little better. The patrol continues on into the afternoon as they pass a couple more side roads, then Jody and Lindsey both spot a curve in the highway ahead. Lindsey uses the binoculars to scan the area as Jody keeps the patrol slowly moving forward. Jody looks back at Lindsey and she gives him the thumbs up.

Jody leads the patrol into the curve where the van, seven ton truck and Trailblazer have to maneuver their way around more abandoned vehicles. One thing everyone has noticed also is that even though there are abandoned vehicles, there are not as many as before. Once thru the curve, the patrol passes by an abandoned fire department.

Lindsey picks up her radio, "Jody."

Jody comes back over the radio, "What do you see?"

Lindsey replies, "There's a bridge up ahead."

Jody replies, "Can you see if the bridge is blocked or anything is moving?"

Lindsey replies, "I don't see anything moving, but we might have a couple cars next to each other that we won't be able to get around."

Jody replies back, "Okay. Keep a watch on the far side of the bridge."

Jody continues to lead the patrol towards the bridge, thinking of what he wants to do if the bridge is blocked. The patrol continues on and in a short time, they reach the bridge. Lindsey maintains a watch on the far side of the bridge with the binoculars while Jody slowly leads the patrol out onto the bridge. The tension amongst everyone in the group goes up because they know that if they run into problems on a bridge, they have no chance to evade and have to either push forward or retreat. Everyone also knows how easy it can be to get boxed in on a long bridge.

The patrol continues forward and the vehicles have managed to make their way so far, but that soon becomes a slight problem. Jody sees the spot Lindsey mentioned and what she said is true, two cars are positioned enough to block the road. Jody calls the patrol to a stop. Jody looks back and points at Ashley and Zach to come up to him. Ashley and Zach head up to meet with Jody.

Jody looks at Ashley and Zach when they walk up, "Okay. We have to move one of the cars so our vehicles can make it thru. Ashley, you'll steer the car while Zach and I push."

Ashley nods, "Okay."

Jody, Ashley and Zach move up slowly towards the smaller car on the left. Jody walks ahead of Ashley and Zach and approaches the car with his rifle ready. Jody quickly checks the car and finds it to be empty. Ashley walks up to the driver's side and opens the door. Ashley gets inside and puts the car in neutral. Jody and Zach begin to push on the back of the car. Jody and Zach slowly start to get the car moving forward.

Lindsey continues to watch the far side of the bridge while Jody and Zach push the car. Ashley steers the car over to the side of the bridge. The rest of the group sits in stressful anticipation. None of them like being stuck in the open like this.

Finally, Jody, Zach and Ashley get the car moved out of the way. Jody, Ashley and Zach make their way back to the patrol. Ashley and Zach return to their positions.

Jody grabs his radio, "Lindsey, is it still clear on the far end of the bridge?"

Lindsey comes back over the radio, "Yes. We're clear."

Jody replies, "Okay."

Jody puts the radio away and motions for the patrol to start moving again.

CHAPTER 82

The patrol has put the bridge well behind them and passed a small residential area. The group can tell that for the most part, the majority of the city is behind them now. Jody leads the patrol across some open land for a little ways. Lindsey is using the binoculars to look ahead of the patrol.

Lindsey picks up her radio, "Jody."

Jody comes back over the radio, "What is it Lindsey?"

Lindsey replies, "The highway is going to split up ahead and we have to stay straight. Also looks like we're coming up on another residential area."

Jody responds, "Okay. Keep me posted."

Lindsey returns to scanning the area with the binoculars as Jody leads the patrol on towards the east. Ashley and Zach are keeping pace with their spot in the patrol and keeping their eyes moving so no zombies come out of nowhere like they did before. Shana and Michael, Jody's brother, is staying equally vigilant looking for zombies. Lisa continues to look behind the patrol every few steps, knowing that zombies could sneak up on them at any moment. However, they all feel good about Lindsey being in her vantage point and spotting a lot of things for them.

Jody leads the patrol to where the highway splits and the van, seven ton truck and Trailblazer have to weave around a couple of abandoned cars. Before long, the patrol enters the next residential area. Jody takes his time to make sure each side street is clear before moving the patrol ahead. The patrol soon passes a church and just as soon as the patrol passes the church, a zombie comes staggering out from behind the church towards the back of the patrol. Lisa takes another step, then looks back and she sees the zombie. The zombie is moving at a fairly fast stagger and is closing in on the patrol.

Lisa grabs her two way radio, "I got one behind us."

Jody, hearing the transmission from Lisa, calls the patrol to a stop. Lindsey turns around on top of the seven ton and sees the zombie closing in on Lisa. Lisa pulls out her knife and starts towards the zombie. As the zombie gets closer, it raises its arms and starts to growl and chomp it's teeth. Lisa waits for the zombie and once the zombie is close enough, Lisa lunges forward and drives the knife into the zombie's head. Lisa pulls her knife out and the zombie falls to the ground. Lisa wipes her knife off and puts it away.

Lisa grabs her radio, "Okay, it's clear."

Jody motions for the patrol to start moving again. Lisa returns to her spot about ten yards behind the Trailblazer and Lindsey returns to scanning the area. The patrol passes another side street.

Lindsey picks up her radio, "Jody."

Jody responds, "Go ahead."

Lindsey replies, "Looks like this highway merges with another highway up ahead. From what I can see, its all clear."

Jody smiles and replies, "Okay."

The patrol continues on and passes one more side street, then Jody sees the interchange Lindsey mentioned. Jody leads the patrol up onto the ramp leading to the highway that is merging with the highway they are on. The van, seven ton truck and Trailblazer once again have to dodge a couple of abandoned vehicles.

The patrol continues on and for the most part they don't see anything around other than a few abandoned cars and some empty residential areas. Jody looks at his watch and sees that they are only an hour and a half from their usual stop time for dinner. After the patrol passes another neighborhood, everyone sees the land open up again around them.

Lindsey picks up her radio, "Jody, we got a bridge coming up. It looks clear."

Jody replies, "Okay. Keep an eye on the far side like last time."

Jody leads the patrol towards the bridge and everyone starts to get apprehensive again, not wanting to run into any problems on the bridge. The patrol reaches the bridge and Jody slowly starts to lead them across. Lindsey is fixed on the far side of the bridge, but sees nothing moving.

The bridge is not as long as the last one and soon the patrol is across it. Everyone in the group breathes a sigh of relief as they know they are one bridge closer to their final destination. The patrol quickly starts into a residential area, however, most of the streets don't run up to the highway. As the patrol continues cautiously on, Jody spots a church up ahead on the left and a produce store up ahead on the right.

Jody stops the patrol before the intersection where the church and produce store are at. Jody checks both directions out and he is sure it is clear.

Just as Jody is ready to signal the patrol to start moving again, Lindsey's voice comes over the radio, "Jody, stop! We have a problem."

Jody replies, "What is it?"

Lindsey responds, "You need to come look at this."

Jody motions for Ashley and Zach to move up to the front of the patrol. As Ashley and Zach move up, Shana and Michael, Jody's brother, move up to the halfway spot of the patrol. Jody makes his way back towards the seven ton truck to see what Lindsey is talking about.

After about ten minutes on top of the seven ton truck, Jody and Lindsey climb down to the street. Jody motions for the group to join him by the seven ton. Mike puts the van in park and gets out. Michael, Lindsey's husband, puts the seven ton in park and him and Tyler get out. Rochelle puts the Trailblazer in park and she gets out while Daniel stays in the vehicle. The group meets up with Jody and Lindsey.

Lisa questions, "What's going on?"

Jody sighs, "About a mile up the road is a miniature golf course. There's a large group of zombies there also, many of them blocking the road."

Michael, Lindsey's husband, questions, "Is there a way around?"

Jody shakes his head, "No. There's a side road right next to the highway, but it's also blocked."

Mike questions, "How many zombies?"

Lindsey speaks up, "We guessed right around a hundred."

Ashley glances around at the others, "What are we going to do?"

Jody looks at Lindsey, then at the others, "We're not going back because, honestly, we have nowhere to go back to and we can't go around. That leaves only one choice." He pauses, "We go thru them."

Rochelle looks at Jody, "And how do we do that?"

Jody glances at everyone, "We're going to drive up on them and stop a couple blocks shy. Those in the vehicles will stay in the vehicles. Those of us walking will get on a line in front of the van. Lindsey will stay on top of the seven ton." He pauses, "Lindsey will open fire with the SAW gun and the rest of us will use our rifles."

Lindsey nods, "With that much firepower we should be able to kill them all before they can get to us."

Shana poses the next question, "That's going to cause a lot of noise. What about that?"

Jody sighs, "This is our last populated area before we reach Fort Pulaski according to the map. Once we finish killing the zombies, we'll all get in the vehicles and ride the rest of the way."

Michael, Jody's brother, looks at Jody, "How do we want to do that?"

Lindsey glances around at everyone, "Jody will get in the van. Ashley, Zach, Shana and Michael will get in the back of the seven ton and Lisa will get in the Trailblazer."

Lisa nods, "Sounds like a good plan to me." She pauses, "We should probably get moving if we're going to make this happen."

Jody looks at everyone, "Everyone good with that?"

Everyone looks at each other and nods.

Jody smiles, "Good. Let's get back to our positions and once we stop, everyone walking move up to the front."

Everyone nods again and heads off to their spots and vehicles.

Jody slowly walks the patrol up closer to the large group of zombies. Once the patrol is about three blocks away, the zombies see them. Jody motions for the patrol to stop. Once the patrol stops, Ashley, Zach, Shana, Michael,

Jody's brother, and Lisa rush up to the front of the patrol next to Jody and spread out. The zombies start to stagger their way towards the group.

Jody holds up his left hand, "Open fire as soon as you hear Lindsey fire!"

Jody quickly lowers his left hand. Lindsey is aimed in at the front of the large group of zombies and she pulls the trigger, letting off a five round burst from the SAW gun. The SAW gun echoes across the land as the bullets rip into the zombies and two of them fall. Jody, Lisa, Ashley, Zach, Shana and Michael, Jody's brother, all open fire on the horde of zombies staggering their way.

Bullets fill the air and four more zombies fall. The SAW gun comes to life again as Lindsey fires off five round bursts as fast as she can. Jody and the others are taking as well aimed shots as they can. Zombies are falling all over the place and it quickly becomes like a shooting gallery. The noise from the weapons is deafening as more and more zombies fall.

The horde of zombies close to within two blocks, but have been considerable reduced in number. Lindsey sprays the horde of zombies with burst after burst and it becomes obvious that the zombies are not going to make it thru the wall of lead coming at them from Jody and the others. By the time the zombies get to a block away, there is only a dozen of them left.

The shooting continues as the remaining zombies advance into the hail of gunfire, but with almost as quickly as it started, the last zombie falls and the shooting stops. Jody looks at the others standing in front of the van with him and they all start nodding to each other. Jody looks back at Lindsey and sees that she is already scouting ahead with the binoculars.

Jody and the others reload their rifles, then Jody looks back up at Lindsey. Lindsey gives Jody the thumbs up.

Jody yells to the others standing around him, "Okay, let's load up and get out of here!"

Jody heads over and gets in the van as Shadow moves out of the passenger's seat. Ashley, Zach, Shana and Michael, Jody's brother, rush to the seven ton truck and climb up in the back. Lisa hurries to the Trailblazer and gets in the passenger's seat.

Mike starts to pull the van away and the seven ton truck and Trailblazer follow. The small convoy does its best to avoid some of the bodies and those it can't avoid, they drive over them. Before long, the convoy puts the horde of zombie bodies behind them.

CHAPTER 83

The convoy has made it thru the zombie bodies and across the bridge. The land around Highway 80 opens up and there are no more residential areas or buildings of any kind. The convoy drives thru a hard right curve and everyone can see water on their left and land beyond the water. Everyone in the group, except for the four in the back of the seven ton truck, starts to get excited as they know they are about to Fort Pulaski.

The convoy weaves around a couple of abandoned cars and continues on. Jody ponders what to do first when they reach the bridge to Fort Pulaski. The convoy keeps going southeast and before long, a bridge comes into view on the left. The convoy maneuvers around a few more cars and closes in on the bridge.

Jody looks at Mike, "As soon as we get across the bridge, go ahead and stop."

Mike nods, "Okay."

Mike slows the van down as they close in on the bridge. No one can see Fort Pulaski yet, but they know it is not far from the bridge. Mike slows the van even more as he weaves around a couple of abandoned vehicles. Mike and Jody see the sign at the bridge and it says, "Fort Pulaski Road".

Mike slows the van and turns onto the bridge. Mike speeds back up as the other two vehicles turn onto the bridge. Lindsey maintains a watch from atop the seven ton and she doesn't see anything moving around on the far side of the bridge. Mike weaves around a couple more abandoned vehicles on the bridge, then the convoy drives off the bridge and Mike pulls the van over and to a stop. The two other vehicles pull to a stop behind the van.

Jody gets out of the van. Mike puts the van in park and gets out. Everyone else in the group, including Daniel, gets out of the vehicles and walks over to Jody and Mike.

Lisa looks at Jody, "What's up?"

Jody glances around at everyone, "I wanted to take care of this now so we don't have to come back to the bridge later." He pauses, "How do you want to handle the bridge? Do you want to use these abandoned vehicles, jam them together and block the bridge or do you want to collapse part of the bridge by using the rocket launchers?"

Everyone gets quiet for a minute.

Ashley speaks up, "If we blow the bridge up, then there'll be no way the zombies can get across to us."

Lindsey nods, "True, but that also land locks us on the island. We'd have to find a boat in order to get back to the mainland if we needed to."

Shana nods at Lindsey's suggestion, "I think you're right. If we block the bridge, we can always unblock it later if needed. If we blow the bridge up, we have no other option than a boat."

Michael, Lindsey's husband, speaks up, "The safest bet is to blow it up. That way, we leave no doubt that the zombies are not able to reach us."

Mike glances at everyone, "If we jam the vehicles in tight, zombies won't be able to get thru."

Jody nods, "Also, we're still going to maintain a watch at Fort Pulaski so someone will always be keeping an eye out."

Lisa glances around, "I go for blocking it right now and leaving our options open. We can blow it up later if we decide that we'll be better off doing that, but I'd hold off on that until we know the fort and island is clear."

Jody looks at everyone, "So, shall we vote on it? All those in favor of blowing up the bridge, raise your hand."

Everyone looks around at each other, then Ashley, Rochelle, Zach and Michael, Lindsey's husband, raise their hand.

Jody nods, "That's four. Those who want to block the bridge, raise your hand."

Jody raises up his hand. Lisa, Lindsey, Shana, Michael, Jody's brother, Tyler and Mike raise their hand.

Jody looks around at everyone, "That's seven. Okay, we block the bridge."

Michael, Jody's brother, questions, "Are we going to do that now?"

Jody nods, "Yep. There are enough vehicles on the bridge and on the highway that we can go ahead and block the bridge." He pauses, "Mike, Rochelle, Tyler and Daniel will wait here. The rest of you, grab your weapons and follow me."

Mike, Rochelle, Tyler and Daniel stay where they're at as everyone else heads off to grab their rifles.

It has taken some time, but Jody and the others finally return to the vehicles.

Mike looks at Jody, "Everything good?"

Jody nods, "Yep. We got those cars jammed together pretty good."

Michael, Jody's brother, nods, "Yeah, no way a zombie is getting thru there."

Lisa looks up and notices how late its getting, "We should probably get to Fort Pulaski so we can check it out and secure it before the sun sets."

Jody nods, "Okay. Everyone load up."

Everyone nods and heads back off to their vehicles. Mike pulls the van away and the other two vehicles follow. It is a short drive thru some woods and the convoy soon finds themselves pulling into a parking lot just to the west of Fort Pulaski. Mike sees that they can drive no further and he parks the van in a space closest to the walkway leading to Fort Pulaski. The seven ton truck and Trailblazer pull in and park next to the van. Everyone gets out with all their weapons and meets Mike and Jody by the van. Anastasia and Shadow remain in the vehicles.

The group looks at Fort Pulaski and surrounding area. There is an open patch of land in front of the fort in a triangle shape that has a moat around it. The walkway leads around the south side of the land and they see the bridge that leads across the moat. The group is facing the main wall which faces to the east. The walls of Fort Pulaski are two stories high and eleven feet thick and made of brick. The north and south walls run straight back and are a little less than half the length of the main, front wall. There are two walls angled off the side walls that are a little over half the length of the main wall and they come together in the back of the fort across from the main entrance.

There is a seven foot deep moat that runs around the entire fort and the moat is between thirty-two and forty-eight feet wide. The only entrance, which is in the middle of the main wall, is a drawbridge entrance. The top of the walls are flat with a small wall lining it so people can walk around the top of the walls. A flagpole sits on top of the main wall right over the main entrance. The inside of the fort is an open grass area with a couple of trees near the main wall. On the outside of the fort and behind it is mostly open land with some trees and surrounding the rest of the fort is mainly trees on the north and south sides.

All along the walls inside the fort are archways. The main wall is lined with living quarters, and kitchen area. Along the north and south walls it is mainly open where cannons use to sit. The angled northeast and southeast walls are where the prisoners use to be kept.

Jody looks at the others, "This is it."

The rest of the group smiles as they quickly realize that once they get inside the fort and raise the drawbridge, it is going to be an almost impenetrable place for them to live in.

Jody glances around, "Let's take it slow and we're all going inside."

Mike looks at Jody, "You don't want to leave anyone out here with the vehicles."

Jody shakes his head, "Nope. Once we make sure its clear inside, we'll put a watch up above the main entrance while the rest of us bring the personal belongings and supplies in." He pauses, "We'll unload the weapons and ammo tomorrow when the sun comes back out."

Everyone nods and follows Jody and Lisa along the walkway. The group is staying ready in case they run across any survivors or zombies. Jody and the others make it to the first bridge that leads across the triangle moat. The group crosses the bridge and starts towards the main entrance to the fort.

Jody and Lisa have the rest of the group wait at the drawbridge and the two of them cross over the drawbridge first and step inside the fort. Once Jody and Lisa are sure everything is clear, Jody motions for the rest of the group to come into the fort. The rest of the group crosses the drawbridge and steps inside the fort with Jody and Lisa. Everyone gets a good look at the inside of the fort and they are even more happy than before.

Jody speaks to the group, "Dad, Rochelle, Tyler and Daniel will wait here. Zach and Ashley will go up to the upper embattlements and make sure they are clear. Lindsey, you and your husband take the south and southeast wall. Shana, you and my brother take the north and northeast wall. Lisa and I will clear the main wall."

Everyone nods and they split up. The group is certain that the fort is empty because they can see most of it from the entrance and figured if there were zombies, they'd been seen by now.

Lindsey and Michael, her husband, head over to the south and start clearing the open areas and prisoner cell areas. Shana and Michael, Jody's brother, head off to the north and start doing the same thing. Ashley and Zach make their way up to the upper embattlements and start walking around the top of the fort. Jody and Lisa head to the southwest corner and start clearing the rooms along the main wall.

It doesn't take long before the group has checked the entire inside of the fort. The sun is getting really low in the sky now as the group meets back up at the main entrance.

Jody looks at the others, "Everything good?"

Lindsey nods, "Our side is clear."

Shana nods also, "So is our side."

Zach speaks up, "The upper level is also clear."

Jody nods and smiles, "Then it looks like the fort is ours."

It was a long trip and they lost so much along the way, but everyone smiles at what Jody just said.

Mike looks at Jody, "So, what now?"

Jody replies, "You, Rochelle, Tyler and Daniel head up to the embattlement above the entrance. The rest of us will grab the tents, personal belongings, some food and water. Once we get that inside, we'll bring the dogs in and set up for the night. Once set up, we'll raise the drawbridge and make plans while we eat."

Everyone nods at Jody's instructions. Jody, Lisa, Ashley, Zach, Shana, Michael, Jody's brother, Lindsey and Michael, Lindsey's husband, head back off for the parking lot. Mike, Rochelle, Tyler and Daniel make their way up to the embattlement over the main entrance. Mike makes sure no one is watching as he flexes his left arm some more.

The drawbridge has been raised and the group has set up their camp for the night by the two trees near the main wall and entrance. Everyone has eaten and Shadow and Anastasia have been allowed to roam around and explore. As the sun is getting lower in the sky, the group is back together around their fire in front of the large tent.

Ashley is all smiles, "I still can't believe its finally over. We made it here."

Shana nods in agreement, "I know. I have to admit, there were times I wasn't sure we'd make it."

Lisa sighs, "I had my doubts at times too."

Michael, Jody's brother, takes a hold of Shana's hand, "Yeah, but we did make it. We've lost so much, but we actually made it here."

Michael, Lindsey's husband, smiles, "In the beginning, I really had my doubts traveling this far. After seeing this place, it was worth the trip."

Lindsey takes her husband's hand and places her other arm around Daniel, "Yeah. Now we can start over again with a feeling of peace and safety."

Zach speaks up, "And it's all because of Jody. He got us thru everything and led us here."

Jody smiles and shakes his head, "Thanks, but I didn't do it alone. When we first started, I stepped up and took charge, but the more we traveled, the more everyone stepped up and participated. I couldn't have done it alone and I'm happy that I had all of you with me."

Rochelle smiles, "True. I know I've grown a lot thru all this."

Mike has remained quiet so far, but finally speaks up, "It was definitely a group effort, but even more so, a family effort." He pauses, "I see all of you as my family. My sons and daughters, and my grandkids."

Ashley smiles at Mike, "Awe, thank you. I think I speak for everyone that we all look to you like a father figure and share that same family feeling."

Everyone nods.

Jody speaks up, "It's not quite over yet though. Tomorrow we'll clear the rest of the island, starting with the Coast Guard Station."

Lisa looks at Jody, "How do you want to handle tomorrow?"

Jody glances at everyone, "Ashley and Zach will stay here and stand guard. The other six of us will head out just after dawn. Dad, Rochelle, Tyler and Daniel will take care of the dogs and look around at what we can use around here as storage and living space."

Lindsey nods, "Sounds good."

Mike feels that he's been quiet long enough, "I'm sorry, but I'm afraid I won't be able to help."

Everyone looks at Mike in shock and puzzlement.

Shana questions, "What are you saying?"

Mike does his best to smile, "The journey is over for me. I didn't say anything sooner because I was going to make sure I saw all of you make it here." He pauses and holds out his left arm, "One of the zombies got me back there when they tried to attack Daniel at the military convoy."

Everyone looks over and sees a bite mark on the inside of Mike's left forearm.

Ashley shakes her head, "No. It can't be."

Jody remains quiet as he knows what must happen and he doesn't want it to. Mike has always been his hero and he can't stand to lose him. Michael, Jody's brother, starts to get tears in his eyes, knowing that he is going to lose his dad.

Mike looks at everyone, "It's too late. I can already feel the fever and my body is really starting to ache. It won't be long."

Tyler starts to get tears in his eyes, "There has to be something we can do."

Mike looks around and smiles at everyone, "Its time for me to go. I'm just happy I got to be here when you all made it and I'm so very proud of everyone." He looks at Jody, "You and Michael come with me, okay."

Mike stands up. Jody fights back his emotions as he stands up. Michael, Jody's brother, stands up as tears start to roll down his face.

Mike looks at the group, "I love you all."

One by one, the group walks over, hugs Mike and says their goodbyes. None of them can believe that they made it here and now they are going to lose Mike who has been their rock, voice of reason and father figure. Everyone starts to shed tears. Once Mike says his goodbyes, he goes over to Shadow.

Mike leans down and pets Shadow, "Well, big boy. I'm leaving it up to you to look after everyone now."

Shadow smiles his big smile at Mike, his daddy.

Mike turns to his two sons, "Let's go."

Mike, Jody and Michael, Jody's brother, walk away from the camp and over to one of the far storage areas on the other side of the fort.

Mike looks at his sons, "It has to be this way. I'll become one of those things and I don't want that."

Michael, Jody's brother, nods and replies through the tears, "Okay."

Jody stands there quietly and for the first time in many years, tears come to Jody's eyes.

Mike smiles, "I've always been so proud of the two of you. I wish I could be there with you both for many more years, but its not meant to be." He pauses, "Its time for me to be with your mother."

Jody finally manages a word, "Yeah."

Mike sighs, "In my suitcase is your mom's urn. I'd like you to bury us together."

Jody and Michael, his brother, both nod.

Mike smiles at his sons, "I love you both."

Michael, Jody's brother, hugs Mike, "I love you dad."

After a long hug, Michael, Jody's brother, steps back.

Jody steps over, hugs his dad and whispers, "I love you dad."

Mike hugs Jody and whispers, "Look after them all, okay?"

Jody nods slightly and whispers back, "Yes sir."

Jody steps back next to his brother. Mike pulls out his pistol and gets down on his knees.

The group sits quietly by the campfire and waits. It is eerily quiet now as no one knows what to say to each other. None of them can believe that they'll never see Mike again. Everyone is crying, then suddenly a shot rings out.

EPILOGUE

Its just before dawn and Lisa is going around the camp waking everyone up. Jody is up on the embattlements on the east side of the fort. Everyone slowly gets up and dressed, then they meet with Lisa in front of the large tent.

Shana questions, "Is everything okay?"

Lisa looks at everyone, "Yeah. Jody just wanted everyone to come up to the embattlement on the east side of the fort."

Zach questions, "What for?"

Lisa shrugs, "I don't know. He didn't say." She pauses, "He said you don't need to bring your weapons unless you want to."

Michael, Jody's brother, sighs, "Well, let's go see what's going on."

Lisa leads the others across the fort. Shadow and Anastasia decide to get up and walk around. Lisa and the others climb up to the embattlements and they see Jody standing where the two angled walls meet. Lisa and the others make their way over to where Jody is standing.

Michael, Lindsey's husband, looks at Jody, "What's going on?"

Jody continues to look off to the east as the sun is just below the horizon, "My dad use to say that no matter how bad things get or what might have happened, tomorrow is a new day and life goes on, it must go on."

Everyone looks at Jody in puzzlement.

Jody continues, "We've come a long way in a much different world than the one we use to know. We've lost people we love and given up our earthly belongings. We've each faced fear and we've also felt happiness. We've all grown as human beings and we've become such a close knit group, just like a family."

Everyone remains quiet for the time being.

Lisa nods her head, "You're right about all of that."

Jody looks at the group that he has grown so close to, "Come over here and join me."

Jody turns to face the eastern horizon again. Lisa steps up on Jody's right. Rochelle steps up on Lisa's right. Lindsey steps up on Jody's left and Daniel is standing in front of Lindsey. Michael, Lindsey's husband, steps up on Lindsey's left. To the left of Michael, Lindsey's husband, is Shana and Michael, Jody's brother, is on Shana's left. Tyler is standing in front of Shana. To the left of Michael, Jody's brother, is Ashley and Zach is on Ashley's left.

Jody doesn't say anything, but he puts his left hand on Lindsey's shoulder and takes Lisa's left hand with his right hand. Lisa puts her right arm around Rochelle. Lindsey places her right hand on Daniel's shoulder. Michael, Lindsey's husband, takes Lindsey's left hand with his right hand and places his left hand on Shana's right shoulder. Shana puts her right hand on Tyler's shoulder. Michael, Jody's brother, takes Shana's left hand with his right hand and he takes Ashley's right hand with his left hand. Ashley takes Zach's right hand with her left hand.

The group just stands together, looking out at the eastern horizon as the sun starts to rise and the light breaks thru the nighttime darkness. It is a beautiful sunrise, perhaps the most beautiful sunrise any of them have ever seen before. It is such a serene moment with the breeze lightly blowing across them. Everyone is quiet, taking in the moment and it doesn't take them very long to realize why Jody wanted all of them to join him.

Lindsey finally speaks, "It's so beautiful."

Jody smiles and nods, "Tomorrow has now become today and for us, there is a new beginning and a new tomorrow to look forward to." He pauses, "For us, life goes on."

Everyone ponders on what Jody has said as they watch the magnificent sunrise.

THE END